SOMEBODY
STOP HER

SOMEBODY STOP HER

Vitaly S. Alexius

Podium

Podium

SOMEBODY
STOP HER

PART ONE

CHAPTER ONE

The Dastardly Neighbor

D ad, I think our neighbors are supervillains."

"Oh, son, everybody is a villain in their own way. Some people don't recycle. It miffs your mother quite a bit, you know."

"But Daaad, I'm serious. They dress weird, they live in a church, and there's a really creepy old car standing in the driveway!"

"Son, that's the 1888 Saint Mary's Cathedral and a 1925 Rolls-Royce Phantom. Eccentricity and preservation of landmark buildings and cars isn't villainy."

"Whatever. Look, Dad, the cathedral is making deep rumbling sounds all day and night!"

"Probably just the air conditioner."

"Look, I'm going to find evidence and prove it to you."

"Good luck, son."

Martin grew tired of hearing his father's deep, overtly cheerful tone and stomped into the kitchen. He could see Saint Mary's Cathedral from his kitchen windows, its gargoyles and dark parapets looming over his family's new quaint two-story home. Ever since his family had moved into the small town of Saint Mary, next door to the town's historic Gothic cathedral, Martin had been haunted by increasing suspicions. At night he had seen eerie silver lights flashing behind the stained glass windows and heard a low rumble coming from down deep. The cathedral *had* to be a supervillain's secret base.

However, like his dad said, he needed evidence of criminality to prove anything. For this purpose alone, Martin had gotten up at six AM today. He couldn't sleep in, terrified that the supervillains next door were plotting nefarious deeds against humanity. He had to act fast, before they decided to blow up the moon or something. Somebody had to stop them, and regrettably this job had fallen to Martin, as his father refused to budge his heroic butt off the couch without government authorization.

"Yo, pipsqueak." Martin's sister descended from the stairwell, interrupting his frantic kitchen-pacing. Her orange curly hair gracefully swayed on its own as if an invisible fan was present in the kitchen. Golden eyes settled on Martin. "You're up early for once. Excited for your new school? I wouldn't be. Everything in this tiny town sucks balls. There're three haircut parlors and zero movie theaters. Honestly, Mom's lucky that she is stuck on her disaster-prevention overtime thing—she doesn't have to deal with Boringville central!"

"Morning, Ember," Martin sighed.

Ember snapped her fingers, and a flickering off-color refraction shaped like her turned off the kitchen lights. Martin suddenly felt as if he had never pressed the light switch on this morning. It was an extremely unnerving feeling. As their mom, the national prognosticator, was barely showing up at home these days due to some future emergency, his sister was becoming progressively more overbearing.

"Don't waste electricity," she said. "It ain't free, you know. Dad is too nice to properly manage your inexperienced butt. As always, the task to elevate chaff to potential falls to me."

"I'm not chaff," Martin gritted out, glaring at his big sister. "You know your power is really screwing with my head. Why do you keep using it on me?"

"Deal with it, boyo. I'm training you to oppose supervillains in the future, see? Nobody else in this family is nice enough to do that for you."

A refraction of her flickered in front of him, stabbing a fork into the table in between his fingers. Martin flinched backwards, unable to escape the annoying feeling that the fork had always been there.

"Too slow." She shook her head. "If I was a villain, you'd be fork-skewered already." Another refraction of her pulled the fork from the table's surface, leaving it pristine.

Ember had already gotten her hero license at nineteen and was constantly bugging Martin with her power all while poking fun at his inadequacies. Martin chose not to tell her about his neighbor-related suspicions, feeling far too irritated with her. Almost any recent interaction with his sister inevitably led to a sibling fight in which he'd get severely walloped and made fun of. Sadly, it was impossible to win a fight against someone who could make ghostly copies that changed the outcome of events in a five-meter radius.

"All right," Ember said, glancing at a wall clock. "I got state-watch duties, unlike some baby sloths who still haven't awakened to their power. Toodles, nerdlet."

As his tiresome sister departed from the kitchen, Martin got back to the most concerning issue at hand—relentlessly observing the cathedral next door.

Now, how can I acquire evidence of our neighbor's misdeeds? he wondered. He badly needed to gain access into the building next door, needed to find a weak link in the defense perimeter . . .

Martin saw a girl with platinum blonde hair, who looked approximately his age, climbing up a rope ladder on the great oak in his neighbor's yard. Yes! This was his chance. He shoved the recorder pen, which he had wisely borrowed from his dad's office, into his pocket and quickly headed out into his own backyard. The two yards were separated by a stone fence capped with timeworn gothic motif metal bars. He made sure to make a lot of noise, rustling through a pile of leaves as he rushed across the yard. Soon enough, he was beneath the great oak that grew partway onto his family's yard. The noises that he made were noticed.

"Heya! You must be the new neighbor!" The silver-blue-eyed, silver-haired girl waved from the tree. "I'm Alexa! But you can call me by my supervillain name—Cassiopeia Terror Nova!"

Well, that was easy, Martin thought, making sure that the pen was still recording. It was *too* easy, in fact.

"Don't judge me, it's a work in progress, okay?" The girl noticed his silence and waved an arm.

Now that Martin was right beneath the oak, he noticed that the ladder led to the most absurd looking tree house, sitting between massive oak branches. It was made entirely out of random street and traffic signs, nailed atop each other in a jumble of colors and letters. The roof of the makeshift, lopsided structure was made out of an enormous bent highway exit sign.

"Exit 7b, Dimmsdale Avenue. Saint Mary Township." He read the words on the sign aloud.

"Gimme a minute to do some patching. I think a meteorite hit one of the walls," Alexa said, hastily climbing onto a huge branch. Martin watched her pull out a pink nail gun from a black-and-pink backpack and proceed to nail a stop sign to one of the walls of the tree house. He reached a dawning realization that all of the signs were in fact clearly taken from the town and surrounding areas.

"Impressive, ain't it? My Fortress of Solitude, made entirely out of stolen signs." Alexa grinned, shamelessly confessing to her crimes and climbing down to Martin's level. "I mean, it's nowhere as cool as my dad's fission reactor room in the catacombs beneath the cathedral, but like I'm still working on it, you know. I even made a small nuclear reactor. It doesn't work yet, but like . . . Hey, why do I feel like I am the only one talking?"

Bingo! Martin thought, grinning madly. *Ha ha ha, I got them!* There was no way now that his dad wouldn't believe him!

"Ah, I see your wide smile of doubtless adoration! You are so flabbergasted by my amazing fortress of wicked deeds that you have forgotten how to speak."

Alexa jumped off the rope ladder, heading to the fence. She shoved an arm through the gap in the bars, offering a handshake which Martin failed to reciprocate. "Do you want to be my minion? I could show you my maleficent up-tree abode."

Martin blinked at the girl. Was she serious? He already had enough evidence to put her and her family away for good.

"Look, I do appreciate the strong and silent minion type, but you've got a long way to go towards throwing my enemies off skyscrapers and cliffsides with those tiny kitten arms. Exercise is important, you dig?"

Martin turned and started to run.

"I didn't say to exercise right now! God! Why is it so hard to find intelligent minions these days?!" Alexa lamented from behind him.

All he had to do now was play the pen recording to his father and—

Something crashed into Martin, sending him flying. He landed onto one of his mom's decorative yard rocks with a crunch.

"I'm going to name you Mittens, on account of your catlike skittishness," Alexa declared. "First minion Mittens, please don't run unless I tell you otherwise. A proper chain of command must be followed if we're to commit crimes of any serious complexity."

Martin noticed that a black pendant with the number 8 on it was swinging from the girl's neck. A fractal-like eight-pointed star glimmered beneath the number.

"My name's Martin, damn it!" Martin groaned from beneath her.

"Unimportant. Minion name supersedes civilian name."

"Please get off me."

"Are you going to run some more without my authorization?"

"No."

"Oookay, then." Alexa rolled off Martin, who sat up, feeling for his precious pen full of evidence. The pen was no longer in one piece. Shards of it filled his pocket and littered the ground. In hindsight, running in plain sight of a villain was a stupid decision.

"How the heck did you get over the fence?" Martin groaned, rubbing his new bruises.

"Jump boots. Made them myself!" Alexa pointed at her sneakers. The shoes looked as if someone had duct-taped a series of layered springs to them. "They're inspired by the fantastic nineteenth-century villain Spring-Heeled Jack, the Terror of London, my great-great-great-grandfather. Jack used to pounce on unsuspecting British citizens and deprive them of their sanity and jewelry. He also had a swanky steampunk flintlock that shot fireballs. Do you want to see my pocket raygun, Mittens?"

Before Martin could produce an answer, Alexa produced a device from her backpack. It looked like an old pink hair dryer with a series of additional bits taped to it.

"Behold my deadly raygun!" She shook the hair dryer in front of his face.

Martin sighed. Either this teenage supervillain was smarter than she initially seemed or . . .

No, scratch that. She stole traffic signs. Nobody who stole traffic signs could be wise.

"Look, I'd love to admire your lovely raygun," Martin said, lying through his teeth, "but I have to get ready for school."

"Ah, yes. School. I suppose I should also pay a visit to the local educational institution. Mind-numbing though it may be, I do need to find more minions my age. Daddums is really up my nerves about my lackluster social skills, but honestly it's hard to connect with people when you've got my schedule." Alexa ran a hand through her silver hair. "I'll see you on the bus, Mittens."

Martin watched the girl rush towards the fence in a series of increasingly terrifying jumps, eventually making a big leap over the gothic spikes. The boots actually worked! She was anything but ordinary. He had been right all along—his neighbors were genuine supervillains, no doubt about it. He needed to get a new recording pen. Luckily, his dad had plenty of them just lying around, as he was an undercover agent of Super Central Authority.

Armed with a new recording pen, Martin sat on the bus, waiting for Alexa to emerge from the church. She did not. The school bus doors closed with a whoosh, dashing his hopes to catch the dastardly neighbor in another confession. He watched the bus pass by a series of perfectly ordinary, colorful suburban homes, Saint Mary's Cathedral growing distant.

His eyes inevitably drifted to the blue sky, towards the Superstate space elevator. The Titanomachy space station megastructure was visible to the naked eye—a series of colossal white rings that were circling the entire planet, rippling ever so slightly, warped by the atmospheric refraction of the stratosphere. Up there was the future. His destiny—full of heroism, hope, love, and adoration.

Ember, being a super, was allowed on the space elevator. Martin wasn't. He sighed, wistfully dreaming of a day when he too would awaken and become a hero just like his parents, defending humanity against those who sought to threaten—

"*Thunk!*" A loud thump on the roof above him made Martin twitch in surprise.

Alexa's upside-down face looked at him from the bus window.

"Open the window, minion!" she mouthed at him, knocking on the glass. She was now wearing a very dirty, oversized orange safety jacket and a construction worker's hard hat that was loosely dangling from her head.

Martin promptly stood up and pulled the window down. The teenage supervillain slid into the school bus with a nonchalant expression, as if boarding moving school buses via the roof was the most mundane thing to do. Other kids stared at her with their mouths wide open. She was making an impression on them already. This displeased Martin—after all, this girl was his nemesis, a villain. He saw himself as the just hero, destined to stop her before she could trick impressionable kids into thinking that villainy was cool.

"Do you not know how to use doors? Why are you late?" he pressed as Alexa flopped down into the seat next to him.

"Forgot to breakfast. You know how it goes, Mittens." She pulled a fistful of bacon out of her safety jacket's pocket.

"Martin," Martin corrected. He wasn't going to be called Mittens by the other students!

"Uh-huh. Want some pocket bacon?" She offered him her very greasy meal.

"No thanks. I already ate." Martin blanched. "Seriously, though, stop calling me Mittens. It's not cool."

"Hrm. You know what? You're right. It's too long of a name for emergencies. If this bus explodes, I'm going to call you M. Got it? You're eh-M during an emergency situation." Alexa ponderously chewed on her bacon bouquet.

"Why would this bus explode?" Martin glared at her. "Is it because you set a bomb on it or something?"

"Don't be a dum-dum," Alexa replied. "Do I look like someone who could jeopardize her own safety *and* the safety of her potential minions? Look at my vest—does it not make you feel safe?"

Martin looked at the grimy construction worker getup that fit her quite poorly. "Did you steal that vest and hard hat from a construction site?"

"Um, yeah?" Alexa nodded.

"Why?" Martin inquired, raising an eyebrow.

"Plus-ten in safety, duh. One can never be too safe when attending public institutions!" Alexa twirled in her bright orange safety jacket, tipping her hard hat at him. "M'laddie."

The other kids roared with laughter of approval. She was definitely giving them some much needed Monday morning entertainment. Unacceptable! Martin wasn't going to have her be the cool example to follow. Villainy wasn't cool.

"I don't think it's cool to steal road signs!" he loudly announced. "What if we get into a traffic accident because you dismantled all of the traffic signs in town?"

"All right, we're going back to 'Mittens' because your kitten-like cluelessness is showing. Let me educate you. Smart villains don't commit crimes in their own backyard. That's a rookie mistake—this is why you're the minion brawn and I'm the brains in charge. Undoubtedly, if you were left to your own devices, you'd commit half-assed crimes right in this bus. Well, not under my watch, Mister! We're committing whole-ass crimes!"

"I'm not committing *any* crimes, damn it!" Martin declared angrily. "I literally saw the sign say 'Saint Mary Township' on your tree house! You can't just take a highway exit sign and get away with it!"

"Starting to sound a little heroic there, Mittens." Alexa raised an eyebrow, stuffing the remainder of the oil-dripping bacon into her mouth and wiping her hands on the safety jacket.

"My name is Martin. You can't take stop signs. Somebody ought to stop *you*!" Martin pressed on, looming over her. He was in too deep now to back away, stepping into the boots of his dad without meaning to do so.

"I think you need to be taught a lesson in respect, before we proceed any further." The villainous girl pulled out her duct tape pink hair dryer contraption and pointed it at his head.

"You . . ." Martin froze halfway into another sentence. Did the raygun actually work, like the shoes?

"What's your name?" Alexa said.

"Huh?"

"Say your name!" She pressed the barrel of the hair dryer to his temple.

"Mart—"

"*Wrong answer!*" The villain put her finger on the trigger.

"My name is Mittens," Martin croaked.

"Louder!" the girl demanded, silver hair fluttering beneath the yellow hard hat. Martin noticed that the hard hat had a large bullet hole in it, the fiberglass warped inward.

"Mittens. I'm Mittens," he said, his voice breaking.

"Much too quiet. I had such high hopes for you. Oh, well." She shrugged. The expression in her eyes grew colder, more distant, uncaring. It was the face of a villain about to execute a bystander who was simply in the way.

"*My name is Mittens!*" Martin yelled, sweating profusely.

"That's right." Alexa smiled mischievously. "Now let me conclude this demonstration of our power dynamic."

She pressed the trigger. Martin yelped, expecting his head to be vaporized, but only felt a very mild brain freeze envelop his mind. Alexa shoved the hair dryer back into her pink "Dora the Terraformer" backpack.

"Ow, what the heck?" he muttered, rubbing his temple, mildly annoyed.

"Witness the devastating power of my death ray!" Alexa cackled from her seat.

"I'm not dead." Martin muttered.

"Not physically, no. But socially, you're absolutely toast." She grinned.

Martin glanced around the bus at the other students. She was right. He could see his social status rapidly sinking while Alexa's flew to new heights. He could see his doom expressed in the giggles of their future classmates. He would forever be known as Mittens now.

She had won, beaten him in whatever fiendish game this was. He'd thought that school would be his getaway from his sister's bothersome ways, but alas, here too he was accosted by a girl who was actively involved in vexing him. At least Alexa was a self-professed villain, someone that he was allowed—no, *had*—to take down for her crimes. The very superhero principles embedded deep in his heart demanded it!

Alexa turned to the window, using its fogged up surface as a board to draw some kind of a complex schematic. It was undoubtedly a design idea for a deadly superweapon which she would use to hold the world hostage when she was older. Martin, unable to comprehend her technical diagram, slumped back into his seat, feeling like a hero utterly defeated by a worthy opponent.

Was being annoying a crime? No. Stealing signs was, however. That was her weak point. That was how he inevitably would get her, Martin assured himself. He swore to get his revenge, waiting for a chance to strike.

As the bus made a turn on another street, the rays of light refracting through the diagram drawn on the window made a distinctive pattern of light and shadow on the seat in front of him. The shadows cast from incomprehensible mathematical formulas, gibberish letters, and old scratches left on the bus seat years ago somehow converged together into a single phrase:

[I'm so sorry. *They* are watching me.]

Martin blinked, and as the bus drove forward, the message vanished as if it had never existed to begin with.

CHAPTER TWO

The Authority Parable

W hy so grum, crumbum?" Alexa smiled, readjusting her oversized helmet.

"Congrats, you've successfully bullied me into having a dumb nickname," Martin grumbled, emerging out of the bus and taking the first step towards his new school. "Also, what was that text on the seat?"

"What text on the seat?" Alexa made an innocent "I don't know what you're talking about" face.

Martin squinted at her suspiciously. Was the supervillain girl messing with him somehow?

"What's your next move, genius?" he asked.

"Thank you for acknowledging my brilliance." The white-haired girl nodded. "What grade is this supposed to be anyway?"

"Eight." Martin said. "How do you not know this?"

"Like Sherlock Holmes once said—it is of the highest importance not to have useless facts elbowing out the useful ones. I do not clutter my brain with unnecessary things. That's what minions are for. See, you're my Dr. Watson."

"My purpose is to be your Watson?" Martin sighed.

"Indeed. You're the intellectually inferior patsy that serves as a kindly foil to my cunning ingenuity."

"Hey! I'm smart." Martin tried to defend himself. "I won several spelling bees and mathematics competitions!"

"I very much doubt that your current bee-mongering and number-counting are of any value to the brutal realities of the universe. Do you know how to make homemade explosive devices from household chemicals? Do you know how to fix a dislocated joint? Do you know how to jumpstart an ice cream truck? Do you know how to fire a—"

"Why would I need to know these things?" Martin interrupted. "I'm only fourteen, and they don't teach those sorts of things in school."

"Then I really don't see much educational value in attending this school," she said with a face of mild disappointment.

"Wait . . . have you not gone to school before?" Martin asked. "Is that even legal?"

"You're really asking a supervillain's daughter whether something they've done is legal?"

"Point taken." Martin nodded.

"See. You're already fitting nicely into your Watson shoes." Alexa grinned.

"How did you even exist before I came into the picture?" he muttered, feeling somehow deeply bothered by the Watson label.

"Don't think of yourself as so special. I've had other minions before. It's just that they've all . . . umm . . . been forcefully retired," Alexa explained, making Martin frown. "Such are the dire hardships of being a supervillain. Surviving by the barest margins while minions tragically perish in battle for a greater cause."

"How come you're so open about the supervillain biz anyway?" he pressed.

"Answer me this riddle, Mr. Mittens—who has better chances of winning a fistfight if both are of equal power parameters: a hero who is wearing a hundred clear plastic bags on their face, or a villain who isn't?"

"Um. I guess the one without the bags. Is that the answer you're expecting?" Martin looked at her.

"Laws are chains that bind people into limited options. True power lies in absolute freedom. I'm a descendant of a long line of supervillains, of truly free men like Spring-Heeled Jack. Unlike you, Mittens, I wield the accumulated power of centuries of freedom. Deceptions such as secret identities are pointless because I'm not afraid of people bound by laws."

"Hrm." Martin made a noise of noncommitment, unconvinced by her argument.

"Take the bags off your face, Mittens! Become free." She bopped him on the nose as they stepped into the stairwell leading into the building.

"How?" Martin asked, ignoring the boop.

"Say the instructors at this school are terribly lame and uncaring. What are you going to do, sit there like a patsy or walk out?"

"Skipping school is bad," Martin answered. There would be no way in hell he would skip school! That was a dark path leading to supervillainy.

He stopped and pointed at the sky. Alexa's eyes followed his motion towards the man-made stars overhead, the lights of space station Titanomachy.

"Do you know what that is?" Martin asked. "The Superstate is the future, in which there is no world hunger, no poverty, no suffering. The tech developed by the Super Central Authority is changing the world! The SCA is improving countless lives, healing, protecting, and saving people!"

"Why haven't they cured world hunger then?" Alexa scoffed. "All they're doing up there is hoarding all the good tech, while the rest of us toil like peasants in the dirt down on the ground."

"What? No! It's villains like your father that prevent the Superstate from aiding humanity!" Martin declared. "How can you not understand that law and order is what keeps society moving forward!"

Something beeped on Alexa. She sighed, stopping to readjust herself. For some reason, she spun her head back and forth as if to note something.

"Pff . . . society," Alexa finally said darkly. "One needs only to take a step forward enough and all of your society disappears, replaced by nightmarish horrors beyond human comprehension . . ." She flickered ever so slightly.

"What?" Martin stared at the villainess.

"What?" She blinked back at him. "Um. Sorry, was I saying something? I totally forgot."

"Nightmarish horrors? Hello?" Martin waved a hand, offering her to continue. He was hoping she would confess to her nightmarish crimes. His new pen was recording everything.

Alexa rubbed a scratched-up bracelet made of black hexagons, microchips, and duct tape on her wrist, thinking about something. Martin blinked. He could have sworn that this bracelet wasn't there before. Maybe it was hidden under her sleeve or something.

"Never mind that. You ain't ready for the truth," she said, booping him on the nose again and bouncing off on her jump shoes into the school building.

Martin, having been thoroughly bamboozled, walked into the school after Alexa.

"Good morning, children!"

"Good morning, Miss Wickers!" the students responded back.

"We have two new students joining us today. Martin Kilborne from—"

"Kitten Mittens!" Alexa loudly said over the voice of the homeroom teacher, making everyone giggle. Martin tried to elbow her but ended up falling sideways, smacking into the floor as Alexa somehow smoothly took advantage of his motion to tip him over.

"Whoopsie. Didn't mean to do that," Alexa whispered to Martin. "My defense reflexes kicked in, sorry."

Miss Wickers frowned at the interruption. "Martin Kilborne, who moved to our town from upstate," she repeated. "And Alexa Terranova, who's been priorly homeschooled."

"Cassiopeia Terror Nova reporting for Earth Defense Academy!" Alexa announced, stepping on Martin's chest as he tried to get up. "And I prefer the term death-schooled!"

The class broke out in uneven, stifled laughter.

Miss Wickers turned just in time to see Martin get back up with Alexa grinning widely, like an innocent angel.

"Hrm. It says here in your record that you're a brunette," Miss Wickers muttered. Martin glanced at the papers on the homeroom teacher's desk. There was indeed a picture of Alexa with dark brown hair there.

"Kids and their hair highlights." The teacher looked at the girl before her with a sigh.

"Wowza, is that a genuine transparency-limited overhead projector?" Alexa asked, sarcastically judging the classroom equipment. "This antiquated tech leaves much to be desired."

"Does your dad work in construction, Alexa?" Miss Wickers said, looking at Alexa's outfit. "I understand that you're undoubtedly wanting to show off your heritage, but please dress properly next time."

"My dad works in world domination! Also, you think there's going to be a next time?" Alexa made a sour face. "Time loops suck ass. I'd rather not get stuck in one again."

"Stop being a disruption," Martin hissed at her.

"Make me." She stuck her tongue out at him.

"Right. Take a seat, please," Miss Wickers said tentatively, ignoring Alexa's proclamations, directing the pair towards two empty seats at the front.

"I'm ready to be educated, instructor-sama. Inject me with terrestrial knowledge brain-parasites!" Alexa saluted as Miss Wickers got back to the teacher's desk.

"Ms. Terranova," Miss Wickers pressed her authority, "please don't speak without raising your hand first."

"Acknowledged!" the teenage supervillain yelled, one hand raised in the air, the other still saluting the teacher.

"No," the teacher said. "Raise your hand, then I will call your name. Only then can you ask a question. Also, you don't need to salute me."

Alexa snapped her hand up, ending the salute.

"Yes, Ms. Terranova?"

"Procedure understood. When do I get my central authority brain parasite?" She grinned.

"You do not get a brain parasite here," Miss Wickers explained with a sigh. "Only the best public education courtesy of myself and other teachers at Saint Mary Middle School."

Alexa turned to Martin. "Get a load of this one. No brain parasite, she says!"

"Please don't speak to other students while class is in session. You may socialize in between classes and also during lunch break."

Alexa squinted at Miss Wickers.

"You don't need to wear your backpack now, sweetie."

Alexa still had her pink backpack on. "I always wear it," she said. "I'm not taking it off. My umm . . . uhh . . . asthma inhaler is inside. I could die of spontaneous suffocation at any moment, you know."

"Okay, fine." The teacher turned to the board, trying to ignore Alexa's villainous ways. "Let's start with some math problems."

Martin knew that Alexa was lying about the backpack. You'd have to be an idiot not to notice that obviously made-up explanation. The teacher should have forced the dastardly villain to remove her bag and confiscated it, locked it up! Who knew what kind of other unwholesome weapons she held therein? The brain-freeze-inducing raygun was probably just the tip of the iceberg.

He watched as Alexa grew more impatient with every minute, fingers rapidly tapping on the desk. He was waiting for her to snap and was rewarded with the sight of Alexa pulling out her hair dryer raygun from her backpack.

"Who does she think she is, bossing me around?" the girl muttered. "I'm supposed to learn linear math now? Ppfff."

"Why do you call it a raygun anyway? It's more of a freeze ray, if anything," Martin whispered, in an attempt to prevent Alexa from giving the teacher an icy migraine.

Alexa turned towards him, as expected. "It's a raygun because I called it that."

"Freeeeze-gun," Martin said.

"Are you criticizing my gun naming convention?"

"What if I am?" Martin smiled.

"Sounds like someone is asking for another death-raying on the noggin." Alexa pointed the raygun at Martin.

"*Freeze*-gunning," he pressed on.

Alexa pressed the trigger and Martin received a solid dose of brain freeze, right before Miss Wickers yanked the raygun out of Alexa's hands.

"Erk!" Alexa yelped.

"Please don't play around during class. I'll return your hair dryer at the end of the day." Miss Wickers walked off with the raygun.

Alexa angrily glared at Martin. He smiled, rubbing his aching head, enjoying this small teacher-assisted victory.

"You're going to regret this mutiny, Mittens," Alexa hissed bitterly.

"You're going to get detention if you keep going," Martin pointed out calmly.

"Big freaking deal," Alexa shot back. "As if I would care about that."

"They'll report you to the . . . principal."

"Big whoop. I can always blow up his office and walk away, not looking at the explosion."

"How?"

"Probably with a series of complex plots, using social hacking." She smiled mischievously.

"If you do that, you're going to juvie, 'cause blowing up offices is a serious crime, not to mention your sign stealing record!" Martin paused. "What the hell is social hacking?"

"Social hacking," Alexa explained, "is the blood of supervillainy, the manipulation of outcomes of social behaviors through cleverly orchestrated actions. In fact, I've already socially hacked you, your sister, your father . . . and a bunch of other simpletons who don't know any better. And I will keep doing it, until the Superstate is destroyed."

"What?!" Martin gasped.

"You know, you're so easy to hack because you're such a sheltered child of a hero." Alexa yawned. "But your sister isn't any better. She thinks that she's the brightest lightbulb in the universe, and yet she's just as dim as the rest of the heroes."

"You . . . you can't do that! That's *evil*!" he declared.

Alexa's bracelet beeped and she suddenly grabbed Martin's hand. Martin looked at her in mild annoyance. What was she trying to accomplish by holding his hand like that? Where was she going with this? He felt his heartbeat intensifying. Was she really socially hacking him right now?!

"Why are you holding my hand?" he finally asked.

"You'll see . . . in three, two, one," Alexa counted down.

The world suddenly grew very, very dark.

"Huh?!" Martin asked. It was pitch black. "Did you cut the power, just so you could mess with me?" he ground out. "Are you planning to escape from school while the power is out?"

"Look outside, M," Alexa said, her voice vibrating ever so slightly with nervous tension.

Martin turned his head and looked out the window, expecting to see maybe a cloud blocking out the sun. There was no sun at all there. The sky was pitch black, the ground gray and foggy. He turned his head back to the classroom, feeling unease. He shivered as he suddenly started to feel very cold, as if the temperature had suddenly dropped twenty degrees.

"I wanted to be nice to you, M, but you've left me no choice," Alexa said. The classroom behind her was extremely dim. It was as if all lights and colors had been drained from the world.

Martin blinked, waiting for his eyes to adjust to the sudden, inexplicable lack of light.

"What . . . what did you do?" he stammered out, turning his head. The classroom was now empty, seemingly devoid of other students and Miss Wickers.

"What didn't I do?" Alexa wiggled her eyebrows. Her eyes shone like pools of mercury as she smiled in the darkness.

The more his eyes got used to the murky twilight, the more he did not like what he saw. It was the same classroom, sure, but it looked wrong, unkempt, forsaken . . . abandoned.

He felt the surface of his desk in the darkness. It was scratched up, decayed, the wooden parts rotten and covered a deep layer of dust.

"Do you notice a distinctive lack of bacterium maybe?" Alexa asked. "No? Perhaps something bigger? What was it that the Lorax said? 'I speak for the . . .'"

The trees! The trees outside were gone! Martin felt panic rising in his chest.

Alexa smiled, stood up, and started to walk away.

"What the freaking hell?!" Martin yelled. "Come back here! What have you done?!" His foot stepped on something, and that something cracked beneath his boots. His eyes had finally adjusted to the darkness. He bent down and saw a grinning skull and then an entire dusty skeleton covered in tattered clothing. It was dressed like Miss Wickers. Martin gasped in shock.

Alexa got to the board. "Class is in session!" She picked up a paper from a table, and it immediately came apart under her touch, fluttering down as ashes and dust. "Let's see . . . who's in attendance today?"

Martin stood over the ancient corpse of Miss Wickers, heaving. A dull ache entered into his chest. His heart raced and he trembled, feeling colder and colder. He was experiencing something that he'd never had before—a panic attack. His breath came out as a small cloud, the moisture freezing in the chilly air.

"What is happening?!" He looked up at Alexa. "Where are we?"

The girl looked back at Martin, tapping her chin. "More like, *when* are we."

"Okay, fine! *When* are we?!" Martin squealed, feeling as though his heart was about to pounce out of his chest. He saw skeletons of other students littering the classroom, white bones protruding out of decayed clothing. He saw dark ruins of the town of Saint Mary out of the broken windows.

"Ah, yes. Martin . . . Kilborne, from upstate," Alexa said. "Welcome to Saint Mary Middle School, class of 2424."

"Alexa . . ." Martin whispered.

"You may speak only if you raise your hand, sweetie." The villainous girl perfectly emulated Miss Wickers's tone. She jumped onto the teacher's desk, which precariously groaned under her. She merrily swung her legs back and forth.

"Please . . . please . . . I don't know what you did," Martin choked, his eyes filling with tears. "Please, I won't . . ." Martin wasn't sure what exactly he wasn't going to do. The more he saw, the more terrified he became. This was a world devoid of life, of warmth, of people, of trees.

He saw something move out of the corner of his eye in the distance. He turned his head. A tall, incredibly long, impossible thing moved in the fog, enormous limbs slowly traversing over the city. Lightning flashed in the sky, starkly highlighting a colossal, misshapen figure. The thing was framed by a gargantuan supercell storm spinning overhead and far behind it.

"Christ! . . . What in God's name is that?" he whispered, feeling overwhelmed with dread.

"Raise your hand if you have a question," Alexa said.

Martin raised his hand, shaking like a leaf in the wind. All resistance had been drained out of him. He'd never been so terrified in his entire life.

"What is that?" he repeated, pinned in place by the sight of the cyclopean aberration.

"That's a skinwalker. His name is Mr. Noodles. Any other questions?"

Martin tried to formulate another question and found himself unable to speak, staring at the humongous monstrosity in the fog. He flapped his mouth like a fish for a while, hyperventilating.

"Tick tock, Mr. Kilborne. Time waits for no man." Alexa pointed to the broken clock on the wall frozen at exactly 9:17.

"What happened here?" He finally birthed a question, as barely audible words emerged out of his mouth.

"The future happened, my dear student."

"I don't understand," Martin stammered.

"Honestly," Alexa said, "I don't either. I've been looking for answers, but I simply haven't found enough information to formulate a hypothesis. Maybe the Large Hadron Collider made a black hole instead of the sun. Maybe a supervillain made all of the nukes in the world detonate at the same time. Maybe it was aliens? Or maybe a wizard did it . . ."

"A wizard?"

"It's as good a guess as any," Alexa sighed. "The skinwalkers don't like me very much—that's all I know for sure."

Martin stared at the supervillain girl in absolute stupefaction.

"I know that you blame people like me for being wrong, Martin. You want to declare me a monster. You're undoubtedly collecting evidence against me, trying to bring me down. You're free to do so. But understand something—the traffic signs in my tree house, I stole them from *this* city!"

Alexa jumped off the teacher's desk and walked towards the deeply perturbed boy.

"I take things from four hundred years in the future, Martin. There are no laws here against dismantling highway signs. Except for the occasional skinwalker—but they don't really believe in human rules. I take the signs as mementos of my victories against these buggers." Alexa pointed out of the window at the long-limbed eldritch thing.

Martin looked at Alexa. Bitter, frigid wind howled through the exposed, shattered building, ashes floating up and away. The monstrosity in the window drew nearer. Martin saw that it had hundreds of eyes that glowed silver under the pitch-black storm. The thing wore an enormous, dreadful cloak made up of randomly stitched patchwork of blood-stained human skins.

"You're going to help me retrieve my raygun from Miss Wickers," Alexa told him. "Because if you don't—one of those things will undoubtedly skin me alive. Do we understand each other, Martin?"

Martin nodded rapidly.

"That's the spirit."

Alexa's bracelet beeped. She sat down on her chair, grabbed Martin's hand, and guided him back to his seat. Colors returned to the world with a flash.

Martin saw the classroom as it was. As it should have been! Everything was back. The students, the teacher, trees, the sun, and the blue sky. Martin wrapped his head in his hands and started to whimper softly into his sleeve. He wanted to be a hero, to save the world, but his entire life he had been sheltered, protected by his parents. Faced with real death for the first time in his life, he snapped like a small twig.

"There, there," Alexa said, patting his head softly. "The future sucks ass, I know. I was raised by it, had to learn to survive in that awful darkness."

Martin choked, lifting his head and staring at her through tear-streaked eyes. She was looking back at him without fear. She was raised there? What did that even mean?

"Now, distract the teacher, please, so I can get my raygun. Without it, next time, I might not get so lucky."

"Next time? You're going back there?" Martin whispered.

"I don't control the future jumps," she answered far too calmly.

If she simply fell into the future, then it meant that she wasn't a villain—she was a victim. Martin was raised with the mindset of a hero—he knew that he had to help this girl now, no matter what.

"Ms. Terranova, turn around!" Miss Wickers said sharply. "Mr. Kilborne, pay attention! Please stop chatting during class! I can hear you whispering all the way over here."

"Shhhh . . . shut up!" Martin stood up, wiping his tears. If Alexa wasn't afraid, then he too should be strong. He faced his teacher head-on. "You don't know anything!!!"

"Excuse me?" Miss Wickers blinked.

"You and . . . everyone here! You're *all going to die*!" Martin shouted.

"Quality distraction," Alexa mouthed, giving Martin a thumbs-up.

"Now, sweetie, why would we all be dead?" the teacher asked, walking up to Martin.

"I don't know!" Martin answered. "I only know that in four hundred years, the city is in ruins, and skinwalkers are—"

Alexa quietly got up and slid towards the teacher's desk, trying to open the drawer. Martin saw her struggle with it, realizing in a panic that the teacher must have locked up the raygun.

"Look, Mr. Kilborne," Miss Wickers said sternly. "I don't know what this tomfoolery is, but you two are disrupting my classroom." She followed Martin's eyes and saw Alexa trying to lockpick her desk. "I see. Both of you—go to the vice principal, now!"

"Make me," Alexa muttered, twisting a pin in the drawer's lock.

The teacher grabbed the girl by her backpack, pulling her away from the desk.

"Mr. Canard! I've got a rowdy student here!" Miss Wickers yelled into the hallway as Alexa struggled against the bigger teacher, desperately trying to get to the desk drawer.

"She needs her raygun!" Martin pleaded. "Please!"

"Mr. Kilborne!" the homeroom teacher said. "With your perfect attendance record and prior grades, I honestly expected better of you!"

"You don't understand! I'm trying to protect her!" Martin repeated hopelessly.

"Yes, I see that Ms. Terranova is a terrible influence on you. I will be reporting this to your parents." She stared at Martin, and he shrunk back under the pressure of an experienced educator.

"Raygun rights are guaranteed to me by the Superstate constitution!" Alexa declared.

"Young lady, you are not an accredited superhero of age," Miss Wickers pointed out, undeterred.

"I'm just well preserved! This is clearly Supervillain discrimination!"

"One extra-rowdy student and one class clown!" Miss Wickers yelled into the hallway, one eyebrow twitching. "Will you hurry it up!"

A bald, extremely tall and bulky man wearing a tank top and Adidas workout pants emerged from the hallway, panting. Martin presumed that this was a gym teacher. Miss

Wickers handed Alexa off to Mr. Canard, who grabbed her by the construction vest and yanked her out of the classroom. Martin followed.

"I should have worked harder on my doctorate," Miss Wickers whispered under her breath, tiredly rubbing her face. "Eighth graders are the worst."

"Let go of me, you sweaty ruffian!" Alexa growled, unsuccessfully trying to kick the gym teacher.

"I'm sorry!" Martin followed them, whining like a puppy, not knowing what to do.

"Mittens!" Alexa shouted at Martin. "Save me from this smelly oversized brute before he throws me into the brig! Getting locked up is a big no-no! I'm allergic to confinement!"

Martin, for this part, assessed his possibility of defeating the gym teacher and found it wanting. There was no way that he could stop an adult three times his weight.

"Frig, Mittens, you're as useless as a pet rock!" the villainess hollered, unsuccessfully pelting the gym teacher with her skinny fists. "Why did I take you under my wing? This educational experience was a terrible mistake!"

CHAPTER THREE

The Detention of Doom

There will be serious repercussions for your unacceptable behavior!" Mr. Canard shoved Martin and Alexa into a small room.

"Take a bath, you savage!" the girl growled.

"No backpacks," the gym teacher declared, roughly pulling the pink backpack off Alexa.

"Hey!" she yelped. "Give that back, my supplies and funds are—" A metal door slammed in her face.

"Wait here while I get the vice principal," the gym teacher said from behind the door. He turned a key, locking the annoyed girl villain and the incredibly distraught boy hero in the waiting room. The room featured a single metal bench that faced the vice principal's office, separated from it by another door and a large glass panel reinforced with a thin metal mesh.

"Welp. I'm extra ticked now." Alexa rubbed her face where it had been impacted by the metal door. "This is fine . . . I just need to . . . Uhhh . . ."

"I don't understand," Martin spoke up. "How did you take me to 2424? You have a power that throws you randomly into the future?!"

Alexa lifted her weird bracelet to Martin's eyes. "It's part of a time machine system. Built by my father."

"What?! Why would anyone in their right mind repeatedly send their daughter into the future? Why not send a drone or something?!" Martin gasped at Alexa. "Does he not know what's out there?!"

"I think that when I was young and foolish . . . I must have acted out, disobeyed him, and so he erased my memory, strapped this bracelet to my wrist, and sent me four hundred years forward, into that city of death. He cast me there . . . all alone, to grow up, to learn how to fight. He likely wanted to teach me how to be a cunning, fearless, perfect villain. That was his education, see?"

"You think? What? I don't . . ."

"I woke up with this damn bracelet on me in this damn town outside of Saint Mary's Cathedral when I was eleven, okay? Okay!" Alexa hissed. "I don't remember much from before then."

Martin raised his eyes at the girl, feeling beyond sorry for her, beginning to understand her with dawning horror. He looked at the scratches all over her bracelet. Alexa followed his gaze.

"I can't get the bracelet off me. Believe me, I tried—it's made of some sort of indestructible bullshit. I don't know how to make it stop. I was only able to add a twenty-five-second warning timer to it. See?" She tapped at the flimsy-looking duct-taped extra bits sitting atop the shiny, slightly transparent black hexagons. Blue lights twinkled within the dark depths of the bracelet.

"But that's so . . ." Martin whispered.

"Evil? Nefarious? He's a supervillain. Were you expecting butterflies and sunshine? Father says hard times create strong men. He says experiencing the year 2424 in person . . . builds character." Alexa shuddered ever so slightly.

". . . mad," Martin finished. "No sane person would do something so cruel and pointless!"

"No. When I was ready, I understood that I was entrusted to change the future. Father can't rely on anyone else for this monumental task. Nobody else is worthy. He told me, 'Alexa, you need to help me figure out how to prevent the end of everything.'" She sighed. "I think . . . I kind of suck at it, though. I haven't gotten very far, and now I'm set way back due to the lack of the raygun and backpack."

"Your raygun gives me a mild migraine! What use is it in there?!" Martin started to pace back and forth in worry and frustration.

"Well . . . what's a mild migraine for you is actually quite painful for skinwalkers," Alexa explained. "Sometimes tech doesn't work the same out there as it does here. Some stuff is kinda really whack in 2424. That's why I suspect a wizard. Magical apocalypse, sounds cool, right?"

"I see," Martin sighed, feeling quite distraught.

"Yeppers, you screwed me big time. No raygun for Alexa! No nail gun, no sonic screwdriver or anything! Like, gee, thanks a whole bunch." She glared at him.

"Look, I said I'm sorry."

"Apologies ain't gonna stop skinwalkers, pal."

"Look, I'll figure something out." Martin wrung his hands.

"Yep. I'm locked in a very small room with none of my equipment, depending upon an idiot with no plan. Fantastic." Her wrist beeped.

"Here we go again," she sighed. "Welp, toodles."

Martin grabbed her hand.

"What are you doing, you infernal moron?"

"I'm holding your hand."

"I can see that. Why?"

"I'm coming with you."

"Look, I took you there the first time because I wanted to teach you a lesson. You were way obsessed with the whole town signs thing. I showed you that you were wrong. Now we are done." She tried to push his hand away. Martin refused to budge. He would not abandon a girl to be slaughtered by monsters.

"Seriously! Let go! I don't think you're gonna survive another trip, especially when I ain't got my backpack full of things to keep the skinwalkers away!"

Martin persistently clung to her hand. Alexa closed her eyes in resignation. The world rapidly darkened. Martin blinked. He couldn't see anything. The room was pitch black.

"Friggin idiot boy." Alexa clicked something on her helmet. A flickering light appeared atop her hard hat, cutting through the darkness. Disturbed ashes floated in the beam. Martin gulped. "You can let go of my hand now."

"Oh . . . right." Martin awkwardly released Alexa's hand.

"Righty-o. Please, aid me." The villainess jumped off the metal bench, grabbing and shaking it back and forth.

"What are you doing?"

"Breaking this bench, obviously."

"Why?"

"So we can break that reinforced window. Are you always this slow?"

"Can't we just quietly hide in this room?"

"No. They can smell humans, and doors don't hold them back for very long. Conclusion—hiding is bad. Running is good. Running really fast is better. Jumping in irregular patterns in a wide open space is optimal. Why do you think I wear jump shoes all the time? You think they're a fashion statement? Lift the damn bench, minion!"

Martin grabbed at the bench, and the ancient long-rusted metal groaned under their combined pull.

"I'm a hero, not a minion," he said, bending the bench back and forth with her.

"Really? You . . . a hero? Pfff, ha ha ha ha! Yeah, right. What's your power?"

"Some heroes don't manifest their power till they're . . . twenty," Martin muttered. It was when his dad had gotten his power. He'd been a late bloomer, and Martin expected the same.

"Right, then. Come back in six years. Now wiggle this bench! Wiggle it like your life depends on it, which it freaking does!" Alexa hissed.

A horrid noise came from the hallway, sounding like a hundred violins scraping against one another.

"Crap!" Alexa hissed louder. "One of them is onto us! Wiggle that bench, M! Put your whole back into it!" Martin pushed and pulled. A boom resounded outside of the metal door as something large smashed into it, the metal bending inward with a screech, drywall and tiles raining from the ceiling.

"Freaking hell! Hurry!" the villainess yelped.

Martin was sweating bullets. He shoved the bench with his entire being, putting all of himself into it, and it finally snapped off from its base, nearly dropping on their feet. Martin heaved the bench upwards, aiming for the glass window. A dark claw came through the metal door, long fingers rapidly growing in length, striking through open air with a sound akin to that of rapid gunfire. One of the claws shot across Alexa's thigh, slicing deep into it.

"Arsshhhiittt!" she hissed.

Martin slammed the bench into the window and its frame cracked, the reinforced glass crashing into the darkness of the vice principal's office, ancient dust billowing everywhere. The skinwalker's fingers began to retreat back into themselves, readying for another shot. Martin noticed them and froze like a deer in the headlights, unable to move.

Alexa's fight-or-flight reaction was far better—she jumped forward, then back again with an impressive twist, bounced off the wall, and grabbed Martin by his shirt as she flew upward. The shoes flung both of them through the broken window and into the vice principal's office beyond it.

Alexa rolled out of her landing, having let go of Martin and limped towards the outside leading window, looking out at the decrepit ruins of Saint Mary. It was a long way down. At least three floors.

"What now?" Martin groaned, getting off the dust-covered floor.

Alexa grabbed at a very raggedy curtain, ripping it from the pole. "Synthetic cloth. Takes hundreds of years to decompose. Even longer without microorganisms."

"Why is this relevant?" Martin whimpered, twitching every time the skinwalker slammed itself against the door. He heard fingers punching through metal as if it were made of paper.

"I chatter when I'm stressed, okay? Get off my back!" Alexa hissed, her leg bleeding heavily. Martin watched her rapidly tie two curtains to each other, attaching the end to a metal shelf next to the window.

"You're pretty good with knots, huh?" he said, walking towards the window and looking down.

"I've done this before." She flung the curtain out of the window. "Shoot. It's a few meters short. Whate—"

A porcupine-like sphere made entirely from oily black hands rolled into the room. Alexa shoved Martin out of the window just as the hand-sphere detonated with finger-spikes expanding all over the office, cutting through everything in sight. Martin grabbed at the curtain, sliding down.

He watched in horror as the obsidian finger-spikes retreated through Alexa's body. The bleeding girl pitched forward and fell from the window. There was a smile on her face as she passed over him, smashing into the ground below, the light of her helmet flickering and winking out.

"No!" Martin slid down the curtain, dropping a few meters down to the ground. His feet gave out as he landed. He didn't care for the pain in his joints, adrenaline pumping through his body. He crawled towards the bleeding girl.

"Alex . . . Alex . . . I'm sorry. Please, be alive," he whispered, grabbing at her. His hands came back covered in blood. She didn't answer.

"No no no!" Martin shook the girl. "Wake up, you have to wake up! Please! *Wake up!*"

An impossible, dark monstrosity emerged from the window above him, a hundred hands gripping the window frame. It wailed ominously, its cry piercing the omnipresent twilight. Hundreds of other skinwalkers across the city responded, joining, adding to the abominable song of inhuman shrieking and howling.

Alexa's bracelet beeped.

Martin desperately tried to feel for a heartbeat. She didn't have one. She wasn't breathing. Her eyes were open, unblinking, transfixed into the murky sky, staring past him, cracks of burst capillaries sinking into the lifeless void of her pupils. Something snapped inside Martin as he finally realized that the girl in his arms was dead. He knew then that he would never hear her voice again, never be told another dumb joke, never be called Mittens again. He clung to her rapidly cooling body, weeping as thousands of abominations all around him sang an alien symphony of despair.

He was suddenly bathed in blinding, brilliant light. He was on the ground outside, lying on unbelievably green grass and holding Alexa. Her heart was beating. She was alive! It was a miracle!

"Well, that freaking hurt something awful," she groaned.

"But . . . you . . . died. I watched you die!" Martin sputtered. He hugged her, crying. "You're alive! I can't believe it! *You're okay!*"

"Yeah, no thanks to you," she groaned beneath him. "I got you out of the building, but totes got porcupined. A little slow, Alexa. Should have been faster. Getting old. Getting sloppy. Okay, you can get off me now, Mittens."

"How? How are you alive?!" Martin cried, feeling that his throat was starting to get sore from constant shouting.

"Even if I get grievously injured or die out there . . . here I am fine. Daddums wouldn't want me dead, you see. I'm his biggest project. Sadly, I only partially understand how his tech works. The whole setup is really high-end villain stuff, built by a whole consortium of brainy supers and run by a very smart computer system. Time travel is mostly whack non-Euclidean math. I'm no good at that transtemporal algebra biz." The girl shrugged it all off, as if constant time travelling and dying horribly weren't a big deal.

"Huh?" Martin wiped his eyes.

"The temporal-jump bracelet is likely tied to the reactor beneath the cathedral and the triangulation antennas that Father buried in this city. As long as they remain intact, I won't get flung into empty space or become smeared across infinity, what with all this silly flapping back and forth between the future and the present."

Martin wasn't listening. He stared at her silver hair up close in the sunlight. It was silver all the way down to her roots. He remembered hearing it in a song once—a car accident made a kid's hair turn white due to stress.

"Your hair . . . it's not bleached at all, is it?" he whispered.

"Yeah." Alexa smiled sadly. "Got blessed with Marie Antoinette syndrome, courtesy of Skinwalker Inc. hair parlor."

Another realization struck a blow into his conscience, cracking it wide open. Humanity was dust and bones. There was only one living person in the future—Alexa.

"I saw no survivors in 2424, only bones," he muttered. "The giant skinwalker. He was wearing loads of fresh skins. How?"

"Yeah. Those used to belong to me," she confessed with a sigh. "Mr. Noodles is quite the collector."

As Martin gazed into her tired, pale, silver eyes, he understood something rather dreadful. Those silver eyes of hers looked much older than she initially seemed. Hers were the eyes of someone endlessly killed for God knew how many extra years, forced to grow up alone in that distant future.

Behind those mercurial eyes he saw an ocean of pain, purpose, and . . . persistence. She was utterly determined to keep pushing forward to save the world—all by herself. She didn't care how many times she died, but it did wear her out, carve her from within, breaking her bit by bit. Her wisecracking attitude was just a facade, a wall hiding a deep well of unbearable sorrow, of a girl haunted by responsibility, a mission far too great for someone so young.

Martin hugged her tighter, crying.

"I'm sorry! I'm so sorry! I didn't know! *I didn't know!*" He wept, unable to imagine the incomprehensible level of torture she's likely endured.

"Hey. It's alright, dawg," Alexa said. "Honestly, it's no biggie. Mr. Handsphere only made like twenty new holes in my lungs. I bet it just wanted to bless me with some speed holes for improved breathing, see? Plus ten in air intake." She inhaled deeply.

"Christ, you're incorrigible." Martin smiled. "What are you doing? I was trying to make you feel better, but you're always somehow one-upping me in the feel better department."

"And why wouldn't I? Just look at all this beautiful sunshine!" Alexa pointed out, shoving Martin off her. "You learn to appreciate it much more after the spooky roller coaster of getting stabbed in the heart and falling three floors down."

For a few minutes Martin quietly sat on the grass, looking at the green trees as they whispered and swayed in the summer breeze, enjoying the warmth of sun rays breaking through occasional white clouds.

He smiled at Alexa and for the first time thought of her not as a villain or a victim, but as a friend. As someone whom he finally understood.

"You!" Mr. Canard roared. "How did you get outside?! Delinquents! Trying to skip school on *my* watch?!" He was holding a sandwich, likely trying to enjoy early lunch or late breakfast in the schoolyard.

"Run?" Alexa inquired.

"Run," Martin confirmed.

They took off, with Mr. Canard chasing after them, flailing his sandwich like a deadly weapon, lettuce and pepperoni slices flying in the wind behind him.

"Wait up!" Martin panted, watching the girl accelerate away on her jump shoes, leaping over obstructions with trained ease. This skill didn't come to her naturally, he knew now—she wasn't a super with incredible agility. She must have had years of practice escaping from monsters in those raggedy-looking shoes of hers.

"BRB!" she shouted, vanishing behind a fence. Mr. Canard reached Martin with the ease of his long, well-trained legs. He opened a hand, ready to grab him, when Alexa came down from the sky like a flying meteor.

"Sheeshah! Pocket sand!" she yelled, swinging a fistful of sand into Mr. Canard's face. The blinded teacher tried to grab at her, but she was already bouncing away.

"Ha ha! I always wanted to do that! Too bad pocket sand doesn't work on skinwalkers." She laughed rambunctiously. "Come on, landlubber! Use those pasty legs!"

Mr. Canard tried to follow the voice of the rapidly bouncing girl and tripped on a concrete ledge, falling on his face.

"Avast! The muscleman is down!" She spun in the air, skirt fluttering, her safety vest glittering in the brilliant sunshine like a thousand orange stars. Martin stared at the twirling girl with his mouth open. Where a less persistent person would already have broken under the strain, she simply bent a bit under pressure, snapping back with great vigor like a steel spring.

She bounced beside him. "Pocket sand ain't no bear mace. Run, Mittens. We have escaping to do!"

Martin took off running. He knew he was skipping school, avoiding authority, and he didn't give a damn at this point. For the first time in his life, he felt free, liberated from responsibilities that his parents, sister, and teachers constantly burdened him with. Alexa's death in the world of tomorrow had broken something within him. He too now had a purpose greater than learning basic facts. He was her minion and he would assist her in any way possible, to prevent the horrific future from coming to pass. He wanted to stand along with Alexa, to face death, and to spit in its face.

He ran after the death-defying, leaping girl, and he smiled wider than ever before. He breathed, basked in the sunshine, the wind tugging at his clothes. She was right. The world in the now was much more vivid, felt much more awesome, after he had survived the horrors of 2424 by the barest of margins. He was finally, truly alive.

The metaphorical bags on his face had been ripped away by a most dastardly supervillain next door.

CHAPTER FOUR

The Villainous Shopping Experience

Delinquents! Stop!" the gym teacher roared, his muscles rippling and glistening with sweat as he trudged after the pair of escapees, emerging into the sunlit street. Martin's heart sank into his shoes. This man was persistent, a Terminator whose primary mission was apparently hunting down class-skipping students.

"Heck. I think he might be a retired super." Alexa squinted at the enraged teacher.

"How do you figure?" Martin asked, panting.

"Pocket sand didn't even slow him down! Do you think I should nail his feet to the floor? Would that work?"

"Please don't nail people's feet to the floor." Martin said dryly.

"You're right, Mittens," Alexa responded. I don't have my nail gun. Can't nail someone's feet to the floor without my trusty pink nail gun! By the way, you owe me a new nail gun, considering how it's your fault the school confiscated mine."

She pointed to the Home Hardware sign in the distance, continuing to speak breathlessly. "You better have a credit card on you, 'cause all of my cash stacks and diamonds are in my backpack."

Martin did have a credit card on him for buying lunch from town, given to him by his dad. He would be in deep trouble if he used it for buying hardware tools, if his dad were to look at the account balance. Alas, it seemed that he had no other choices presented to him, as Alexa had already turned in the direction of the shopping mall.

Martin's brain caught up to her last sentence. "Diamonds?"

"Skinwalkers don't care for shiny things made for human dating rituals. Jewelry is pretty easy to grab from broken storefront windows in 2424."

Of course her backpack was full of diamonds! Martin ground his teeth. If the vice principal or some teacher were to go through her bag, they would be very surprised indeed. Nail gun, stacks of cash, and diamond-encrusted jewelry! God knew what else was in there! Likely more than enough evidence to get her arrested for questioning. She would die horribly if she was flung into the future in handcuffs!

"Why don't you keep your diamonds at home, damn it!" Martin panted.

"A girl's gotta be ready for shopping anytime, you know. I also have plentiful shinies in my uptree fortress with the rest of my worldly possessions."

"Tree house? Don't you live in the church?"

"Naw. Daddums doesn't allow me inside the cathedral, on account I might steal some of his tools and damage the bracelet in a dumbass attempt to remove it, or screw with his precious time machine setup and get myself smeared across space-time." Alexa laughed, matching Martin's exhausted pace with mild bouncing. She was barely breaking a sweat.

"That's . . . awful," he panted. "Not being able to go inside your own house."

"Technically, it's not a house. It's a laboratory inside a cathedral. Daddums doesn't believe in living rooms, bedrooms, or kitchens. It's all work, work, and even more work, always surrounded by super interns and robots and brain jars. Honestly, he doesn't even have time to talk to me with that schedule of his."

"Stop!" The gym teacher was inexorably getting closer.

"Does someone actually stop when you yell that?" Alexa turned towards the teacher, bouncing backwards and pulling off her orange vest.

The muscular man merely glared, looking extremely irate. If he had eye lasers, Alexa would already be a pile of ashes. He tried to grab at her, but she leapt over him, wrapping her safety vest over his face, pulling him backwards with all of her weight. Somehow the teacher didn't even budge or fall over. He merely made a grunt as she hung off him by the vest.

"Hecking mountain troll! How do you manage to drive a car? Did you have to cut a hole in the roof?" She grinned, rapidly tying the vest with a complex knot over his head. She leapt off the teacher's back before he could grab her.

"I should have invested in a minion with more stamina." Alexa bounced back to where Martin was panting.

"I want jump shoes, too," Martin whined.

"Yeah, I don't think so. There ain't no way you'd manage such highly advanced recoil tech, bud. You'd probably break your neck as soon as you put them on."

The gym teacher roared, trying to remove the constricting vest from his face.

"That's right, elephantine mobster! We are going to the arcade, and there's nothing you can do about it! You won't stop us from playing duck murder and digital hopscotch!" Alexa yelled at him.

"Duck murder?" Martin whispered, as Alexa quietly pulled him into the Home Hardware shop.

"I don't know what it is you kids enjoy." She shrugged. "I'm too preoccupied for such frivolous pursuits. Having frequent business meetings with Skinwalker and Co. is a real time buster."

Martin made a promise to himself to take Alexa to the arcade someday. Her childhood had clearly been stolen from her by the future, and it was breaking his heart.

He watched as she grabbed a shopping cart, driving through the aisles, acquiring a variety of tools and random chemical containers with focused determination.

Martin muttered about the credit card bill, seeing the pile of purchases grow.

"I'll pay you back with some diamonds," Alexa cheerfully promised, which didn't make Martin feel any better.

"Look, I'm not happy about this either. They only have nail guns in blue," she grumbled, waving a blue nail gun at his face.

"It's a hardware store; they have paint," Martin deadpanned.

Alexa raised an eyebrow. "Did you just make a joke?"

"Is that not allowed?" he replied.

"Well, well, well. I see that I'm finally rubbing off on you." She winked.

Martin sighed deeply as Alexa swiped his card through the machine upon checkout. When Martin saw the total, he nearly had a heart attack. Power tools were expensive! His dad was going to throw a fit. Martin only got himself a bottle of water, gulping it greedily.

Alexa, uncaring for his inner struggle, rolled the cart out into the parking lot and proceeded to pour various chemicals into smaller bottles. She then stuffed bits of twisted toilet paper into the top.

"Are you making . . . some sort of grenades out of household chemicals in a parking lot?" he asked, watching Alexa strap several belts to herself. She worked quickly, with impressive precision, using shower curtain rings and metal wires to attach bottles and power tools to the belts.

"Yeppers. Could get sent to the future anyyyytime now. Gotta be ready. Dying is kinda incredibly painful, you know." She shoved the rest of her power tools into a new black electrician's backpack and glanced at him. "Right, sorry, you wouldn't know what that's like."

Martin looked at the girl villain. She looked like an adorable little Rambo.

She bounced up and down and side to side, getting used to the weight, readjusting and tightening the belts. Shoppers emerging from Home Hardware were giving her looks of mild amusement. They probably assumed she was a cosplayer of some sort.

She grabbed the water bottle from Martin's hands, finishing it. "Ah, yes. Hydration. Totally forgot about human necessities. I think it's time to refuel!"

Alexa shoved the empty glass bottle into the backpack and bounced towards the nearest fast food restaurant.

The McHeroes restaurant welcomed Martin with vibrant screens and posters featuring the latest top-tier heroes and meal options named after them. He watched as Alexa swiftly ordered enough burgers to feed a family of ten with his credit card.

"Come on, are you trying to max it out?" he demanded in annoyance, watching her press on all of the available burger buttons.

"Nah, just planning ahead," Alexa responded, handing Martin his card along with the receipt.

"How am I gonna explain this to my dad?" Martin whined, looking at the absurdly long receipt roll.

"You are a growing boy. Increased nutrition intake is important." Alexa wiggled her eyebrows and dragged Martin to a booth. She inserted a number tag dispensed by the digital cashier onto a slit in the table. A "RESERVED" sign flashed over the booth. As they sat down, the table came to life, its surface lighting up with an embedded screen. Martin looked at the moving picture of the world's mightiest hero Nonpareil on the screen with resignation. Nonpareil winked at Martin with one of his beady metal eyes embedded within his body. He was a very helpful shiny metal staple.

"I wonder what his weakness is." Alexa tapped the hero's grinning staple-face as he flew through the sky, punching through clouds with a sonic boom.

"He doesn't have one. His staple-body is indestructible," Martin said.

"I bet it's something really mundane like guns or water," she mused, making a gun shape with her fingers.

"You aren't listening to me at all, are you?"

"No, but someone else is." Alexa pointed at something.

Martin lifted his head. Alexa's finger gun was aimed at a teenage girl with long deep-blue hair who wore the gray cloak of an Equalizer. She was looking at the semi-transparent holo-menu.

"Who equalizes the Equalizers?!" Alexa yelled across the restaurant.

Green eyes focused on Martin and Alexa through the holographic screen.

"Eh?" Martin asked.

"The Equalizers think that they can make me join their dumb cult, so they sent a rep!" Alexa said. "Little do they know I'll be the one asking her to join me as a minion numero dos."

"Are you sure? What if she's just here having lunch or something?" Martin whispered. He knew that the Equalizers were one of the most formidable Earth-based, super-lead organizations that refused to join the Superstate on principle.

Alexa's massive order had arrived—packaged, smoking burgers raining from a delivery chute onto a container space within the table. Alexa unwrapped a burger and started to eat ravenously, intently staring at the gray-cloaked, blue-haired Equalizer. Martin pulled a burger from the burger pile for himself, chewing it slowly and ponderously.

Are the Equalizers really after Alexa? he wondered. *If so, why? What do they know that I don't?*

After filling up, the teenage villain proceeded to shove the rest of the burgers into her pockets.

"Now I'm ready for future adventures," she commented on her food hoarding. Pockets bulging with burgers, Alexa bounced towards the Equalizer's table. Martin got up with a sigh. It was as if she was actively looking for trouble.

"What's your mission?" The teenage villain arrived at her quarry.

The Equalizer raised her eyes at Alexa. "I exist to bring Equality to all," she spoke with a calm, nearly expressionless voice.

"Drop the spiel, babes. What's your personal goal?" Alexa asked.

"I serve to uplift all of humanity . . ."

"Look, doll," Alexa interrupted the Equalizer. "Don't do the robot voice thing. It's creepy as hell, and it ain't gonna convince me to join you. Speak from the heart, and I will consider Equality."

"You will consider Equality?" The girl's eyes opened a bit wider, the monotone voice gaining the smallest twinge of excitement. Martin nearly face-palmed. Alexa didn't look as if she was considering equality at all. She was grinning widely.

"Only if you offer me your heart and soul. I find myself low on adequately educated minions," Alexa said cheerfully.

Martin yearned to defend himself and resisted by the barest of margins. He was learning. Arguing with Alexa only made things worse.

"My heart belongs to Equality." The Equalizer's tone returned to an unenthusiastic drone as she made the equals sign with her fingers above the silver Enforcer pin that was glittering over her heart.

Martin gulped upon seeing the pin. This wasn't a low-ranking Equalizer. The girl was a genuine Enforcer! He'd seen videos of Enforcers executing supervillains in plain sight without remorse. These people were dangerous! The Equalizer Order often found ways to skirt around laws.

"I am Cassiopeia Terror Nova, as you have undoubtedly read in your *borger* menu!" Alexa declared.

Martin wasn't sure why her name would be on the McHeroes menu, but he kept quiet, feeling rather shy around authority. The Equalizer looked no older than Alexa, but her gray Enforcer cloak projected an aura of formidable power.

"I am Verse 24:19: 'No cottages shall burn upon the distant shores of Yore,'" she said.

"That's a mouthful! I'm gonna call you . . . No-Cottages . . . No, that's still too long and weird. Wait . . . got it! Cottie!" Alexa proclaimed.

"I am Verse 24:19," Cottie insisted, not knowing that in Martin's mind she was already doomed to be forevermore tagged as Cottie.

Once Alexa labeled someone, it stuck, and if they resisted, the villainess only managed to hammer it in harder with her social hacking bullshit. Seeing Alexa chatter away at the Equalizer from the outsider's perspective was giving Martin an understanding of how she operated.

"Minion name supersedes cult-assigned one, Cottie." Alexa plowed ahead like a freight train with no brakes.

"The Equalizers are not a cult. We are a highly respectable Order of . . ."

"Why follow unattainable equality when you can follow an adorable budding supervillain instead? Wink wink, nudge nudge." Alexa pointed at herself. "See, in my organization you can be minion number two, not whatever random ass verse number you are."

The Enforcer didn't seem convinced by Alexa's vocalized nudging and winking.

Alexa's bracelet beeped. She looked down at it with a small frown. "Welp, toodles. You can spy on me later in school, stalker-sama!"

She waved a hand at Cottie, turned, and slid into an empty booth, away from prying eyes, settling beneath the noisy flashing panel-screen of Knight Chalice. The world's third most powerful hero was busy signing plastic swords amidst a crowd of adoring fans who were cosplaying as medieval knights at what looked like a Renaissance fair. Martin followed after Alexa into the depths of the booth and grabbed her hand.

"You need to stop," Alexa said sternly. "You are going to die. I don't want to make a tiny gravestone with the name Mittens on it in 2424."

"But . . . you die all the time, and you are clearly fine."

Alexa rubbed her head. "Look at yourself, idiot. You are bruised, scratched up, and covered in questionable grime from the twenty-fifth century. The jump bracelet treats you like any other object I'm carrying. It will not reset your body if you die."

Martin persistently clung to Alexa.

The world around them rapidly darkened.

"Why are you doing this, Martin?" Alexa asked, looking at him from the decayed seat in the dark ruins of the mall complex. The McHeroes screens were twisted and shattered, and most of the dining hall roof now lay all over the floor in an unwholesome arrangement of jaggedy steel shards and faded panels.

"I am your minion, no?" Martin said after a bit of looking around in concern. "As such, my purpose is to protect you."

Alexa sighed. "Well, I walked myself right into that one, I suppose. Still, how about you learn to protect me from gym teachers first? Your presence in the future is extremely detrimental to your health. You will not survive forceful SpongeBob cosplay, like I have!"

"But . . ."

"No buts! Are you not listening?! I've been through this before, moron! I lost Zeke and Ike . . . Tommy, Klondike, and Miri!!!" Alexa's eyes glittered with wet sparkles. "The skinwalkers take no prisoners! They do not listen to reason! If you keep coming back here, your skin will be worn by Mr. Noodles as another reminder of my failure!"

"Oh." Martin blinked. That's what she meant earlier. Alexa did say she'd had minions before him.

"Why do you think I wasted time making a curtain rope? It was to save your posterior from Mr. Handsphere! If I was alone I could have just leapt out of the window, trusting my jump shoes to handle the landing!"

"Oh." Martin gulped. She was a villain, but she had saved him! Alexa just kept on hammering against his conscience as if she was intent to utterly dismantle it. Her actions were blending the distinction between hero and villain in Martin's mind. It was as if she was neither.

"White knight dummy, on an errand of self destruction." She sniffed, wiping tear sparks from her face. "I don't need you to die here, without purpose."

"I won't die without purpose. I'm here to help you!" Martin pressed his case. Now that he'd thought about it, it would probably be a smart idea to contact his dad, confess everything, and ask for help. Not that he could do that right now, from four hundred years in the future.

Alexa shoved the blue nail gun into his hands. "If you see a skinwalker, and you can't run away, aim for the eyes. Follow me!"

"Where are we going?" Martin asked, trailing her out of the ruined restaurant.

"Back to school. To get my raygun. It's my best weapon out here. This hodgepodge crap will only briefly annoy them." She pointed at her belt full of chemical cocktails and power tools, and stepped into the murky open air through an enormous jaggedy hole in the dining hall's wall.

The parking lot was occupied by numerous car ruins. Martin looked inside of one, shuddering as he noticed blackened skeletal shapes within. Dark, gloomy cloud formations slowly spun overhead, an entire ocean of broiling sky highlighted by occasional flashes of lightning. Transfixed by the constantly shifting, vast supercell storm above him, Martin forgot how to breathe.

An enormous spider with far too many elbows emerged from one of the burned down shops, shoving aside broken car remnants with an ear-piercing screech.

Alexa spun a lighter in her hands, igniting one of the bottles.

"Lighten up, Mr. Spoody!" She chucked the sparkling bottle into the spider's face, and it detonated with a blinding flash. The spider hollered, pawing the flames from its face.

"After me, M!" Alexa snapped a glow stick tied to her belt, bouncing off into the mist. Martin ran, following the tiny, rapidly moving orange light. His feet were hurting from the earlier fall. He tripped over some random debris, and the light vanished.

Martin clung to his nail gun, hissing in pain. The spider skinwalker was howling somewhere nearby, legs smashing through something.

Everything looked the same—gray foggy twilight engulfing the world. Martin didn't know which way Alexa had gone. Stricken with rising panic, he had to admit to himself that he was indeed an absolute idiot. For all of his earlier posturing and heroic declarations, unlike Alexa, he had no experience with this insane alien world.

Thumps of something enormous resounded nearby. Martin ran in a random direction, gasping for breath, his heart hammering in his chest. A flaming skinwalker spider skittered in front of him, screeching madly. Its legs stretched out towards Martin, aiming to crush him like a tiny bug. Martin lifted the nail gun, firing. It did absolutely nothing to stop the spider's advance as nails thunked into its abominable dark shell without result. The spider's finger-claws pincered Martin's leg, twisting it with a snap. He screamed.

An enormous something came down from the sky. It was a gigantic limb. It plucked the burning spider into the air, and a few other colossal limbs rushed towards the brilliant chemical fire. The convergence of limbs extinguished the flames with a supersonic boom, crushing the spider into liquid paste.

Martin squealed indignantly as he was wholly drenched in liquefied remnants of the spider skinwalker.

"Hollysheet. Well, that never happened before." Alexa landed next to Martin. "You look just like one of . . ."

Martin coughed, trying to get the foul black fluid out of his mouth. Alexa looked up and suddenly flung herself forward, slamming into Martin. He whimpered as both of them rolled through the horrid puddle, splashing the shiny black goo all around. Alexa's hand covered his mouth, silencing him, as they both ended up cowering under an island of rusted metal that was once a truck, both of their bodies covered in spider remnants.

A gigantic, grotesque face came down from the sky, searching for its prey. It was dotted with pale silver eyes that glowed ever so slightly from within. The shawl of human skins slid on the ground close to the two teens who clung to each other, trying to stay still and silent.

The head turned, and Martin looked right into a gigantic, pale, shimmering eye that peered right back at him. Martin trembled, expecting to be smashed into human paste. The eye looked right at him—no, past him! It couldn't see them at all beneath the black, thick gunk. Perhaps the titanic skinwalker thought of them as one of its kind.

The head lifted, vanishing in the somber sky, and the thumps of gigantic legs began to move away.

"I can't . . . believe it. It didn't see us," Martin whispered. Alexa simply nodded, holding a finger to her mouth, telling him to stay silent. She looked like a horror movie victim or perhaps a monster, covered in black glistening gore head to toe. She scooped a bunch of the black gunk off the ground, filling up her empty water bottle. The pair of humans slowly rose and started to walk towards the ruins of their school. Martin was forced to lean on Alexa as one of his legs refused to function. He hoped that it wasn't broken, but it was hurting worse with every step.

"I'm nominating you to explain why we look like this to the teachers," Alexa whispered to Martin as they limped on three and a half legs into the decrepit shell of Saint Mary Middle School. "'Cause I'm way too exhausted from supporting your broken minion ass to make earth-shattering jokes."

CHAPTER FIVE

Theft and Arson

Two teens covered in black gore flickered into the front of Miss Wickers's classroom just as she was handing out quizzes. As the teacher's back was turned, she did not see them suddenly appear into existence out of nothing, but the other students did, and they collectively made noises of befuddlement.

Alexa made a shushing noise at them, putting a finger to her lips. She placed one of her smaller-sized chemical grenade bottles atop the teacher's desk, dramatically spun her lighter in the air, and ignited the wick, while she quietly dragged Martin out of the classroom.

The students just stared, their mouths open.

Just as Alexa closed the door and Miss Wickers turned around to see what the students were gaping at, the teacher's desk detonated in a fiery explosion.

"Fire! *Fiiiire!*" the teacher shrieked in shock and surprise, rushing to grab a fire extinguisher. Her eyebrows were nearly gone, and a chunk of wood sliced a line across her cheek. The students clamored. Never had they seen such blatant disregard for authority and direct destruction of school property.

As the smoke from the burning desk reached the fire sprinkler system, an alarm sounded and the sprinklers activated. Whatever horrid chemical concoction Alexa had created, it was utterly immune to water. The desk fire hissed, sputtering, and blossomed even higher, acrid smoke blooming.

"Evacuate!" soaked Miss Wickers yelled, spraying foam from the fire extinguisher all over her desk. The chemical fire refused to surrender, the desk smoldering like an active volcano. The teacher began to coordinate students out of the classroom.

Alexa pulled Martin into a janitor's closet.

"What?" he muttered, wincing in pain as she started to scrape the black sludge off herself and him, sloshing it into one of her bag compartments, her headlamp occasionally blinding him.

"This blood is a precious resource that allows us to successfully integrate ourselves into skinwalker society. Also, it might be radioactive or something. Best not to keep it on your face all day."

"No, that's not what I'm talking about. Why did you set the teacher's desk on fire? Was that really necessary? What if she saw us? What if she'd been standing closer to her desk? Couldn't you wait until—"

"Ain't nobody got time for that," Alexa declared as she scraped skinwalker guts from his sneakers. "There's asking *what if* while standing around like a mushroom-covered log, and then there's jumping into the action."

"You do jump around a lot," Martin sighed.

"Hrm. I declare your leg out of place." She observed his injured foot. "Let me fix that for ya. Hang onto a broom or something."

"Out of what? . . . *eeeeeeerrk!*" Martin yelped as Alexa swiftly pulled and twisted his foot back into its socket.

"There. I've un-dislocated it. You're welcome." She grinned.

"Thanks." Martin nodded, feeling too hurt and tired to complain further. He felt as if this day had gone on for far too long already. As the fire alarm continued its wail and the entire school population evacuated outside, Alexa emerged from the closet with Martin in tow. He was thankfully able to walk on his own now, albeit slowly.

Martin glanced at the clock on the hallway wall. It was 11:32. It didn't feel like eleven in the morning. Wanting to know the real time, he wiped black gunk off his wristwatch. It was showing that it was 5:49 PM. They had spent the last several hours slowly making their way from the mall across the ruined city, freezing in place every time a monstrous thing came near. Had it not been for the crushed skinwalker residue, they'd already be dead many times over. It was no wonder he felt so drained, both emotionally and physically. His body had experienced far more hours than the day normally contained! He looked at Alexa—the poor girl must have had one screwed-up sleep schedule. Wait . . . how did she sleep at all?

Alexa, uncaring for Martin's looks of pity, produced a large hammer from her backpack and barged into the smoke-filled classroom. Awash with sputtering sprinklers, she swiftly swung the hammer at the desk drawer's lock, smashing it open. Martin watched as she freed her precious pink raygun from its desk prison, merrily cuddling it to her chest in the sprinkler rain without a care in the world.

"Mommy's back, my precious death ray," she muttered, nuzzling her raygun. "See? Don't be scared. I won't abandon you ever again!"

The duo emerged from the school, right into the waiting arms of Mr. Canard, who had been standing guard at the back door.

"Where were you?" he growled, dragging the pair of students down the stairs and onto the grass.

"In school, obviously. Being a studious drone." Alexa smiled. "Can I have my backpack back? I have important things in there that I must . . ."

"No." The gym teacher lowered himself to her eye level. "I've looked inside your backpack."

Martin gulped.

"Hey, you can't rummage in backpacks. That's private property," Alexa said.

"Why are you so filthy?" Mr. Canard asked, finally paying attention to how the kids looked.

Alexa looked at Martin, likely expecting that he'd come up with a reasonable explanation. Martin did not. He completely forgot to think of one, ignoring her request entirely.

"Uhhh . . . we were trying to escape from the fire, and the sprinkler water was very dirty," Martin said unconvincingly, after a few seconds of awkward silence.

"The fire?" The gym teacher squinted at Martin. "This school had zero cases of spontaneous desk fires before you two showed up. Z-e-r-o."

"You can't prove anything," Alexa said.

"Something very fishy is going on with you two. First you somehow fled from the vice principal's office and then the mall, and now I find you two soaked and covered in God knows what."

"Okay, okay, you got me," Alexa sighed. It's supervillain business. Put us down, you giraffopotamus."

At the word "supervillain," Mr. Canard lowered the two kids back to the ground. "I do not like the sound of that. Are you children involved in something dangerous?"

"Extremely dangerous is an understatement." Alexa nodded, yawning.

Mr. Canard looked at her, expecting further explanation. She didn't provide any. Instead, Alexa took off her backpack, placed it down on the grass beneath a willow tree, laid her head atop it, and closed her eyes.

"What?" Mr. Canard looked mildly confused.

"Please let her rest." Martin shuffled in one spot. "I don't know how long she's been awake today."

"Explain," the gym teacher quietly said.

"She's a hostage in a local supervillain's sinister plot," Martin began, "and she is forced to teleport into a very dangerous place at random. I . . . I've been trying to help her."

Martin glanced at Alexa. She began to snore quietly. She must have been utterly exhausted to pass out that quickly right on the lawn. "Please, return her backpack. The stuff in it isn't stolen."

"I should report this to the SCA," Mr. Canard said.

"You don't have to." Martin shook his head. "I'll deal with it. I'm in contact with Super Central Authority already."

"And why would I believe an eighth grader who just lied to me two minutes ago?" The gym teacher raised an eyebrow.

Martin took the recording pen out of his pocket. This one had miraculously managed to survive all of his misadventures with Alexa. He showed the base of the pen to Mr. Canard. He put his finger over the logo, and it recognized his fingerprint, projecting the SCA logo and a holographic menu into the air.

Mr. Canard simply nodded.

"It's a recording device and a communicator," Martin said. "Call base!"

The pen buzzed in response. The face of Ember came on, in her full gold and red armor regalia as the hero Resonance. She was inside a Superstate cruiser, clouds flashing behind the window.

"Martin? Shouldn't you be in class right now? Why are you calling on this line?" Ember squinted her eyes at him, not noticing Mr. Canard who stood off to the side.

"We've had a fire alarm go off, so now everyone's outside for a bit. Sorry, just wanted to tell Da . . . uhhh . . . Agent Sparrow something, but I see that this line forwards to you. I'll talk to you later!" Martin quickly stuttered, hanging up. His plan to confess everything to his dad had been foiled by his sister, who as Martin had guessed had been put in charge of answering the calls made by the SCA pens. He had no desire to confess anything to her, as she would likely jump to conclusions and do something rash like arrest Alexa.

"Right." The gym teacher relaxed, smiling. "I believe you now. I recognize the SCA tech keyed to you, because I'm a retired hero." He showed Martin a watch on his wrist and put his thumb on it, and the SCA logo shimmered into existence above it.

Martin sneaked another glance at sleeping Alexa, impressed with her powers of deduction.

"Look, if you need any help, kid, come straight to me. No more running away, okay? I'm one of the good guys, see?" The teacher tapped the watch again, and the holographic logo vanished.

Martin tiredly nodded. He was feeling exhausted and didn't know whom else to turn to. Mr. Canard walked towards Alexa. Martin was about to confess everything to the gym teacher, but when he turned, he suddenly saw the gray cloak of the Equalizer. The blue-haired Enforcer was standing perfectly still, staring right at them from behind a flower-covered bush, her face devoid of any expression, cloak swaying ever so slightly in the breeze. Martin gulped, all remnants of bravery draining out of him. She *was* observing them! Alexa was right! When did she get here? What was she planning to do? Why the hell did Alexa tell the Enforcer to find them at school?!

Paying no attention to Martin's dread over the Equalizer observer, the gym teacher gently picked up Alexa along with her backpack without waking her.

"Um?" Martin looked up at him.

"I'm not going to let a child sleep on the ground. I'll take her to my portable office. She can sleep on the couch there. Follow."

Mr. Canard took off in the direction of the portables.

Martin followed the retired super without further questions, glancing back at the Equalizer. He was feeling somewhat euphoric that there was finally a responsible adult helping them. Finally his school troubles were over!

He didn't notice that a black claw had unzipped her backpack from the inside, a small hand-shaped spider with far too many knuckles slowly emerging from within.

"Four hundred years of adventures . . . zzzz." Alexa muttered in her sleep, twitching. "Alexa and Martin dot com. Farmin fyturrr tatoes. Why won't the shkinwalkers just let me grow tasty taters?" She turned, the blanket provided by Mr. Canard slipping off the couch.

Martin picked up the blanket and covered her with it once again. He briefly smiled at her sleep muttering. He was extremely worried that her bracelet would beep and she would be flung into the future asleep and entirely defenseless.

He realized that ever since he'd become Alexa's friend, he'd been on edge—being rapidly flung from one disaster situation to another would do that to a person.

"You sure know how to turn someone's life upside down," he whispered at the sleeping girl.

Instead of the orderly, calm life in which his parents had provided and cared for his well-being, he was now cast adrift in the turbulent river of Alexa, not knowing whether he would be bashed against the rocks or spun about, feeling as though he was about to drown at any given moment.

He peered at his wristwatch, feeling tired and bored. It was a bit too stuffy and warm inside the portable office. Mr. Canard was taking a rather long time to return with Alexa's pink backpack for some reason. Martin sat next to Alexa on the couch and closed his eyes, and soon he too was asleep.

"Good tomorrow!" Alexa cheerfully announced into Martin's ear, waking him. She was wearing Mr. Canard's blanket like a cape and grinning wildly.

"Wuzsat?" he mumbled, rubbing sleep out of his face.

"This doesn't look like the lovely park I've decided to rest in." She rubbed her chin thoughtfully. "Let me guess, the gym teacher took pity on me and relocated me?"

Martin nodded.

"How lovely! One fewer enemy for us to destroy."

"Why do we need to destroy enemies?" Martin stretched.

"Treat everyone as a threat and you'll survive longer, my good minion." Alexa suddenly swung her hammer at Mr. Canard's desk, smashing it open.

"What the hell are you doing?" Martin blanched. "You can't just demolish another teacher's desk like that, especially since he was nice enough to let us stay in his office!"

"Haven't you learned anything, kitten? There's always a reason for all of my actions." Alexa threw drawers open one by one and dug through Mr. Canard's possessions.

"What reason could there possibly be for this?" Martin got off the couch. Just when he thought he understood Alexa, she threw another wrench into everything. Destroying their homeroom teacher's desk to get the raygun at least made some semblance of sense.

"Time, Mr. Mittens. Note the local time, please." Alexa nodded to the clock on the wall, returning to her rummaging.

"What does that have to do with anything?" Martin angrily said. "You know, Mr. Canard is actually pretty cool, a retired hero . . ."

His eyes drifted to the clock on the wall. It was 8:02 PM. Martin's face grew pale. His dad was going to murder him. Not physically, of course, but—

"Exactly. He left us in this office, to sleep for eight hours. Also, when I woke up, I noticed that my backpack was much lighter."

"Huh?"

"The compartment that contained skinwalker blood is empty," Alexa said darkly, her figure lit by a flickering halogen light overhead. "And then there's this. Observe."

Alexa pulled the bottle of skinwalker residue from her bag. The liquid inside had congealed into the shape of an angry, albeit very squished, spider. Finger-legs with too many joints angrily tapped against the bottle from within, and glowing blue eyes angrily observed the pair of teenagers.

Martin squeaked, jumping backwards upon seeing the bottled aberration.

"Yeah, we got us a smol spiderbro," Alexa shook the bottle. "There's also a bigger one out and about. I was tired and careless. I didn't know that they could reconstitute out of goop like that. We brought skinwalkers to the present, minion."

"We have to tell the SCA about this!" Martin yelped, pulling out his pen, the little holographic screen turning on as he shakily brushed his index finger against its base. The menu came up with about a hundred missed calls. Drats! The buzzer was off.

"Dial base!" he yelled at the pen. He didn't give a damn that he was outing himself and his family to a supervillain's daughter. There was a horrid monster loose in the present. A monster from the future that he'd helped bring here, like a fool!

Alexa grabbed the pen out of his hands. "No."

"Give it back!" Martin whined, unable to stop the far more agile Alexa.

"Martin? Where the hell . . ." His dad's voice echoed from the pen, an image of him and Ember flashing in the air, just as Alexa snapped it in half. The screen winked out with a flicker of static.

"What is wrong with you?!" Martin yelled, desperately grabbing at the pen shards on the floor. "Why?!"

"This is my mistake! I have to deal with it myself," Alexa answered.

Martin glared at her from the floor, not understanding.

"Do you think the SCA are a bunch of clueless middle-schoolers like yourself? Do you think they don't know anything about the future, Mittens? Your mother is a global prognosticator, is she not?" Alexa loomed over the boy who was still clutching at the pieces of his pen. "Do you really think they don't know anything about my unfortunate situation?"

"What?!" Martin angrily rose from the floor. He didn't like that Alexa somehow already knew about his mother's disaster-prevention job at the SCA. The girl villain was making far too much sense—his mom should have already been aware of the future, as she operated the biggest probability calculator server up on Titanomachy. Did his parents already know about the future and didn't deem it relevant to let Martin know? If so, they probably just didn't want to make him worry—after all, it was their job to prevent disasters, not Martin's.

"The true villains are the people in positions of authority. People bound by agreements, secrets, and laws. The sky-eyes of Titanomachy are always watching the ground. The Big Brother Superstate observes all and acts only in its own interests! It would do you some good to learn that," Alexa declared, hammering her point in.

"The supers of the SCA are good people!" Martin protested. "My parents are heroes! Their job is saving people . . ."

"Oh, really?" Alexa sneered. "Do you think it's a coincidence that you're my neighbor, Mittens? Ask yourself—why would a family of upstate city-dwelling supers suddenly move to a small town?"

"Um." He pondered her suggestion. Had his family intentionally moved to Saint Mary to spy on the Terranovas?

"Now that I've outed you as the little pawn of the SCA—do you really think that it was a coincidence that I asked you to be my minion?"

Martin gaped.

"Keep your friends close and your enemies closer."

"But you . . . but I . . ." Martin blinked. His worldview was sliding sideways, an avalanche of conclusions burying Martin within it. All along, Martin had thought that he was the one trying to catch Alexa, when in fact it was—

"You . . . you knew everything. You set me up." Martin stammered, "You're . . ."

"A supervillain?" Alexa clapped her hands. "Congratulations, you've solved the greatest mystery of all! It only took you all day! Oh, you look so adorable when you're surprised. Of course, I knew about your superhero family from the beginning. Remember I told you about social hacking? I got the SCA database password from a very clueless super who thought that I was his human resources manager on the phone. Even the most secure database on the planet has a weakness in the dumbest employee that uses it."

Martin simply stood there, feeling tricked, betrayed. He'd presumed that his friendship with Alexa was genuine, but now—

"Sorry. I'm a bit cranky due to the whole releasing a skinwalker biz," she said, returning to her desk, rummaging.

Martin gulped, putting aside his inner struggle about the nature of their friendship.

"Here we go!" The teenage villain announced, finding what she was looking for. She pulled out a wallet from the damaged desk.

"Why?" Martin asked, exasperated.

"I need to know where Mr. Canard lives," Alexa said as if that explained anything, pulling out a driver's license from within.

Martin's mind struggled with her answer, still trying to process being awake at eight PM. Did she want to rob the teacher or something? He could find no reasonable explanation for her actions.

"Want a pocket burger for breakfast?" Alexa unzipped one of her pockets, offering Martin a somewhat pancaked meal.

The face of Nonpareil printed atop the tinfoil burger wrapper was very smushed, and the staple-shaped super looked like he was very disappointed with the young hero.

CHAPTER SIX

The Guest from the Future

Chewing on a very stale McHeroes burger, Martin walked behind Alexa. On one hand, he needed to get home right away; on the other, Alexa was getting into some sort of deep trouble once again. Contrary to her confession of knowing everything and keeping enemies close, he felt that leaving her alone was not a decision he could live with. Now that he was fully awake, he understood why she didn't trust authority—after all, her biggest authority figure in her life, her dad, had thrown her into the death-grinder of humanity's dark future.

"So, um, no future jumps while I slept?" he asked tentatively.

"Nah," Alexa said, swallowing a tomato slice. "It's nice enough to give me a break when I'm passed out, plus a random length of time after, for breakfast. Daddums wouldn't want me to fight monsters on an empty stomach."

"Well, that's nice. Where are we going?"

"To the school bus, of course!" she declared.

"School buses don't run at eight PM. Also, they don't park at the school."

"Well, that's a big inconvenience. I require transit. We are on a tight deadline."

"A deadline for?"

"I'm operating on a hunch."

"A hunch being?" Martin inquired as Alexa scoped out potential methods of transit.

"Missing skinwalker, missing teacher. I think the two are related. Aha!" She spied an ice cream truck parked in the fenced-off lot behind the school and headed towards it.

"I thought you don't steal things from town," Martin muttered in disapproval, watching her lockpick the truck door with a hairpin that she pulled out of her hair.

"This is an emergency, M. The teacher's apartment ain't close, and every minute counts. We've already wasted precious hours sleeping!" Alexa, having defeated the door lock, jumped into the truck.

Martin stood outside the truck contemplating whether he was doing the right thing. Was he abetting car theft? How would she even . . .

The truck came to life, headlights igniting. Ice cream truck music filled the air with repeating twinkles. The truck's window rolled down, and Alexa's grinning face emerged from within. She was eating a striped popsicle. Right. He'd completely forgotten that she was boasting about her car jump-starting skills earlier.

"Get in. We're going skinwalker baby hunting!" she said between bites.

Martin sighed, walked around the truck, and climbed into the side seat.

"Lead the way, spiderbro-GPS!" Alexa placed the bottled skinwalker into the space under the windshield. The black spider-thing glared at her from within, silver eyes flashing as it angrily tapped against the glass.

"How intelligent are these things?" Martin asked nervously.

"I dunno. It's a very small bit of the big thing, and the big things mostly murder me, which doesn't say a whole lot about skinwalker high society or cultural institutions. Want an ice cream?" Alexa offered.

Martin shook his head.

"Come on, it's a strawberry." Alexa wiggled an ice cream package in front of his face.

"No! I'm not adding ice cream theft to potential charges of carjacking!" he ground out, tempted by the strawberry wrapper art.

"It's nice to know where you draw the line," she giggled, dropping the ice cream into his lap.

Martin stared at the chilly popsicle in his lap. If he took it back to the freezer, his finger-prints would be all over it as evidence. He was trapped. Alexa grinned from her seat at him, pressing on the gas.

The song of the ice cream truck wafted through the quiet evening streets of Saint Mary as the sun was setting, painting the world in orange tints. The girl supervillain recklessly drove the truck forward, not even slowing down at stop signs.

"Come on, stop signs exist for a reason!" Martin shouted, obsessed about traffic safety.

"Other drivers can afford to stop. We can't!" Alexa pointed out.

"What if someone hits us?!" Martin twitched as she blew through another stop sign.

"Eh, this truck is far heavier than the average car, we'll just plow right through them."

"I don't want to plow through anyone, damn it! Would you at least turn off the music?"

"No time to search for the off button," she shot back, clearly enjoying this far too much. "Besides, a stolen ice cream truck wouldn't be playing music. It'd be suspicious without it, if anything, you dig?"

Martin gave up, chewing his strawberry popsicle in resignation, wondering how he'd gotten to where he was. It all started out so simple. Making friends with a villain was his first mistake, he supposed. He only hoped that if they were caught his dad would—

His family's car passed by the ice cream truck, heading in the opposite direction, his dad's worried face visible through the windshield. Ember sat on the seat next to their dad. Time slowed down as Martin froze, exposed by the vibrant sunset rays, his popsicle dripping. Ember was looking quite bored—but she was undoubtedly using her power of bending probabilities to find him. Her arm was up in the air, an accusing finger pointing straight at Martin. Their dad saw him.

"Martin?! *Martin!*" he yelled, pushing on the brakes. Alexa pressed harder on the gas, the ice cream truck rushing straight through a red light.

"No no no no no." Martin sank into the seat. He was deeply regretting opening the ice cream.

"You'll never catch us, coppers!" Alexa yelled, adding to his internal anguish.

Martin thumped his head against the back of the seat.

Alexa drove on, laughing wildly and praising her own "incredibly amazing evasion skills" and how Martin was "forever blessed by this highly educational experience in getaway driving." Martin looked at the back mirror. He didn't know how, but she'd managed to elude his dad in the bulky ice cream truck. Perhaps it was her skinwalker-trained reaction skills or blatant disregard for traffic laws, or perhaps it was because his dad didn't have a siren on top of his car like a proper policeman. Either way, Martin's heart was running a million miles a minute as he spent the entirety of the drive thinking of reasonable excuses to explain the situation to his dad.

"Here we are. You may shower me in praises and tips for my fantastic taxi prowess." Alexa parked the truck in front of the 1024 Grimmins Drive apartment complex.

Martin glared at her, nervously chewing his popsicle stick.

"You're welcome for that refreshing ice cream, by the way," she said, disembarking from the vehicle. "Oh don't look at me like that, M. You're going to need the sugar soon, I reckon."

She chucked the blue nail gun at him. "Be ready for anything."

He wasn't even sure when she'd managed to pick the gun up from the skinwalker puddle. It wasn't that well wiped, he noted, as it was still a bit splattered with dry black streaks.

The lobby entrance of the Grimmins Drive complex, secured by a password entry, did not delay Alexa for long. She dialed random apartment numbers cheerfully yelling "Delivery!" until an old lady was nice or perhaps clueless enough to unlock the door.

Martin observed Alexa in the elevator. She looked visibly nervous and impatient. It was understandable—a skinwalker in the present would make her vulnerable; she wasn't death-proof here.

"Look," he started off, "I think we should let the authorities handle this. We're just two teenagers—"

"I think you should shush. I know what I'm doing, M. I've been dealing with skinwalkers longer than anyone here." She agitatedly stared daggers at the blinking light of the floor numbers, pulling out her sledgehammer and swinging it dangerously. Martin saw her take up position, compressing her body like a taut spring, ready to pounce.

The elevator doors dinged open and Alexa flew out, bouncing across the hallway with increasing speed. Flying through the air she smashed the sledgehammer against door number 1006. The wood cracked, the door opening. Alexa rolled into the apartment, lighter already in hand and a chemical bomb in another. Martin arrived several seconds later, to find her standing still in a completely empty, dark apartment.

"Well? Now what?" He looked at her. She was panting with visible irritation.

"Too late," she growled, reattaching the sledgehammer to her belt. "I'm too friggin late. Argh!"

"Please, we can let the SCA—"

"No. No. *No!* I friggin got this, darn it!" She snapped back at him, searching through the apartment.

"*Aha!*" She picked up a paper from the coffee table, flapping it in front of Martin's face.

"What?" He blanched.

"It's a banking notice! Don't you see? He must have gone to the bank! Hurry!" She bounced out of the apartment into the hallway.

"Wait! Alexa, please!" Martin rushed after the girl, increasingly stressed that he wasn't being listened to.

His arguments in the elevator and in the car while they drove to the bank were seemingly falling on deaf ears. Alexa was determined to catch the skinwalker herself.

"Alexa! Listen! Why would he be in the bank?!" he yelled, as ice cream truck tires squealed in front of the Superstate Bank, nearly crashing into the closed, one-story building.

The girl villain wasn't listening. She bounced up and down and up again, jumping onto the hood of the truck and then onto its roof. Martin watched as she took a run from the truck's roof, leaping onto the roof of the bank building. Surely, she wasn't planning to break into a—

"Just give me a minute! There's a nice poorly secured vent up here!" Alexa yelled from the roof. She was indeed planning to break into a bank. Martin began to sweat as he heard her smashing through something on the roof with her sledgehammer. He heard her panting grow distant as she descended into the vent. He couldn't believe it. This wasn't happening. He wasn't being an accessory to a spontaneous bank robbery!

He looked through the thick glass doors of the bank building and noticed that one of the vents was wiggling. With a loud crack, the vent door swung open and Alexa jumped down, bouncing towards Martin. She unlocked the door from the inside.

"Alexa! What are you doing?!" he yelled. "There're cameras everywhere! You can't do this!"

The teenage villain pulled Martin into the bank, closing the door shut behind them.

"He's here. I know he's here. The vault. The vault, M! The safest place in town! He's gotta be in the vault!" she ranted, turning away from Martin. This was now or never. She'd clearly gone insane. Martin pointed his blue nail gun down, aiming at her blanket cape. He had no choice but to stop her, before the crazy girl got both of them sent to juvie. He pressed the trigger, and Alexa fell on her face as her cape became trapped to the floor with a single nail shot.

"Frghhh?!" she yelled as he pushed her down, covering her with the cape and nailing her to the floor.

"This is for your own good!" Martin yelled.

"What are you doing, M?" The girl struggled to move as more nails went into her cape, binding her to the floor.

"We are not breaking into the vault! You are not robbing a bank!" Martin continued to secure the villain. He knew that he was doing the right thing. Nobody could die a thousand times and stay sane. She'd been driven mad by the skinwalkers. Martin had to stop her, had to call his dad for help.

"Mutiny! This is mutiny!" she hissed.

"I'm saving you from a life of crime," Martin reassured her, making sure that she wasn't getting away. His hands were shaking from the rush of adrenaline.

The locks on the vault door began to spin. Martin lifted his eyes to it in surprise. What was happening?

The enormous steel door of the vault swung open. Mr. Canard stood inside it, an alien structure of white bone pulsating with black organelles behind him. The ordinarily white scleras of his eyes were pitch black, while his pupils were silver and glowed with a pale blue light from within. Martin gasped. The gym teacher looked bloated, pregnant. He took a step forward, limbs flapping unnaturally as if he was just a puppet held up by invisible strings. His mouth snapped open with a crack, jaws sliding far wider than should have been possible. Black glistening spiders with far too many joints began to pour from the teacher's mouth. Martin screamed.

"What's happening? What are we yelling about?" Alexa muttered from beneath her blanket prison.

CHAPTER SEVEN

The Gold Rush

Martin regretted everything. He regretted nailing Alexa to the floor. He regretted not defending his pen from her grabby hands. He was struggling between regretting not listening to Alexa about the skinwalker in the bank vault and not heading straight to his dad when he had the chance. There were a lot of regrets to be had as spider after spider emerged from the mouth of the gym teacher.

Having been emptied of his spider children, Mr. Canard made a noise akin to that of several rubber balloons rubbing against each other. The noise formed into words that didn't quite sound like they were produced by a human mouth. It was as if some incomprehensibly alien being was trying to replicate separate letters from a very crappy vinyl recording using a hundred mouths to speak at once. Martin realized that the sound wasn't coming from Mr. Canard alone. It was coming from the hijacked gym teacher and also emanating from the numerous hand spiders on the floor.

"A L O v E L Y o n E w h O C o M e S S t R a I g H t t O U s!" Mr. Canard and the spiders hissed out in unison.

"What?" Martin uttered.

"This is a robbery! Everybody on the floor, now!!!" Alexa screamed from beneath the blanket.

A deafening siren resounded within the bank, and blast shields rolled down, blocking out all of the windows, doors, and teller booths. Bright lights flashed in the ceiling, blinding Martin. The spiders and Mr. Canard froze, confused by the sudden light and noise of shields slamming into the ground.

A voice spoke from the speakers as the siren quieted down. "This is the automated Superstate banking security system. These shields have been designed with supers in mind. Any attempt to escape will be met with increasing force. Surrender now."

The blinding lights dimmed, and the wall and ceiling panels of the bank's interior lit up with psychedelic swirling patterns. Thumping tones poured from the speakers. Martin stared at the swirling colorful walls, feeling a sudden loss of will and emergence of inexplicable . . . deep serenity.

"Remain calm," the speakers spoke. Everything is fine. Put down your weapons. Do not resist."

Martin lowered his nail gun. The friendly voice was right. There was no need to fight anyone. No need to resist. Just mere moments ago he was terrified out of his wits by Mr. Canard's spider-filled innards, but now Martin felt nothing but inner peace. Some deep, buried part of his mind screamed at him that this overwhelming calmness was a lie, a trick of some sort, but the swirling colorful patterns and the repeating thumps drowned it out. Martin started to sway along with the beat of the music, watching the spiders and Mr. Canard join in. He felt a deep bond of serenity with the dancing skinwalkers; even their spidery appearance no longer terrified him.

He wasn't sure how long he'd been entranced by the fractal beauty of the wall patterns, swaying back and forth. Time lost all meaning; only the dance of serenity mattered now.

"Nice to know that the hypno-pacifier works on skinwalkers," Alexa muttered from underneath the blanket. Martin distantly wondered how she could still speak. Perhaps the thick blanket acted as a barrier against the sea of calmness projected by the hypnotizing screens.

Alexa's bracelet beeped. She started to whisper out countdown numbers, shuffling underneath the blanket.

Martin watched as many grenade bottles flew out from beneath the blanket cloak, leaving a trail of sparks. The bottles rolled beneath Mr. Canard's feet, heading for the vault. Somehow in that instance, Martin broke out of the calm reverie with a single action. He calmly hugged Alexa with all of his being.

The bottles detonated with brilliant flashes, turning the vault into a self-contained furnace. The wall of fire devoured the alien bone-sphere and Mr. Canard, heading towards the two kids, vaporizing everything in its path.

The world darkened.

"Well?" Alexa asked, turning on her headlamp and shining it right into Martin's face as if she was interrogating him.

"You were right. He was in the vault." Martin exhaled, feeling deprived of inner peace and trying to cover his eyes from the bright light.

"I'm almost always right, you know. Except when I'm not." She smiled, standing up. The blanket-piercing nails easily emerged from the rotting, scorched floor. "Thanks for ruining my fashionable blanket-cape, by the way." She glanced at Martin.

"I'm sorry," Martin sighed. He was feeling bad for Mr. Canard. "How did you know about the automated security system?"

"Do you have amnesia or something? Because you keep forgetting that I'm a supervillain. Such info is important to know when you're planning to rob banks," she drawled. "While you learned useless bee facts at school, I've been studying the town's defenses and weaknesses. See, you have to blink at exactly the right frequency to defeat the hypno-pacifier. Also, having a thick blanket helps."

"Wait. You got this blanket just so you could rob a bank?"

"Gotta think twenty steps ahead of the curve if you want to survive, M."

"Right. Ummm . . . Did we make this future happen?"

"Hmmm?"

"This bank building looks like it was burned down ages ago, and the shields are down," Martin pointed out. "We brought skinwalkers into the past. Mr. Canard was infected with them. They can puppeteer supers, like some sort of an infection."

"I suppose we might have accelerated the process a little and helped obliterate this financial institution. Congratulations, you've helped contribute to the future!"

"I didn't want to make it worse, darn it!"

"I don't see how you can make the end of the world worse. Don't look so concerned. Seriously, what's another burned down building?" Alexa shrugged, prancing merrily into the ruins of the open vault. Martin watched as she started to smash various deposit boxes open, shoving well-preserved valuables into her bag. "Well, don't just stand there! Get your butt over here and help me loot the place. I'll open the boxes, you go through them."

Martin went over to the deposit boxes, helping Alexa rifle through them. The cash had all turned to dust, but gemstones and gold remained behind. Contrary to everything he believed in, he—a hero—was indeed robbing a bank. It was a surreal experience, to say the least.

A part of the bank floor had rotted away—a dark gaping hole was visible in the floor. Alexa pointed at the hole. "If you hear my wrist beep, drop whatever you're doing and follow me into this hole. It likely heads to the sewers. Wouldn't want to appear back here in the moment of the explosion."

Martin nodded. "How did you know that Mr. Canard would come here?" he asked, shoving jewelry into her bag.

"The bank papers."

"Seems a little far-fetched."

"All right, I knew it . . . because this sort of stuff happened to me before. Once a skin-walker gets into someone, they use the body's energy to make more and they prefer the nearest safe spots like this bank to grow their nests. Maybe they're attracted to all the metal, who knows."

"Um. How did he get into the vault?"

"He probably came into the bank, climbed up a wall, and stayed very still until the employees locked down the building. People rarely look up. You'd be surprised how inattentive office workers are. I've broken into plenty of buildings myself this way."

She emptied the tools from her backpack, attaching them all to her belts to make room for valuables.

"You've seen the skinwalkers get into someone before?" Martin asked.

"Yeah," Alexa sighed. "Poor Tommy."

"Sorry to ask, but you brought . . . other kids here?"

"Do I look like an idiot? How would teenagers help me with anything out here?"

"I'm a . . ."

"You are my ever-so-clueless M," Alexa interrupted. "And you were being an annoying nemesis. I only brought you here as a moral lesson, damn it! I wanted to show you that the world isn't as black and white as you think! That some people don't choose to do what you label as evil but are instead thrust into such roles due to events around them."

"There's always a better choice!" Martin said. "The Superstate exists thanks to hero collaboration. Combined powers, teams of heroes can do so much more! If it wasn't kids, then . . . ?"

"Since we might be here a while and this is the only place in town covered with super-designed blast shields, I think that I have the time to tell you about my former minions. Do you want to know how I robbed Fort Knox?"

"Fort Knox?" Martin gaped at her.

"Yeah."

"Okay." Martin nodded, and as the two of them continued to slowly empty out the deposit boxes into her backpack, Alexa began her tale.

I was nearly thirteen then. I'd managed to steal a lot of gold and gemstones from broken storefronts. I'd even thought that I was ready for minions, ready to take on the world of tomorrow with my own team. After much searching on the darknet, I found a reasonably priced, talented team of low-end supers—mercenaries willing to work for cash as villain minions. They weren't the best and only had about nine positive reviews on the online listing, but it was a team I could afford to hire. I paid them in stolen jewelry, via a darknet villain broker firm. That's how these things are done—the more you know.

I even had the perfect plan—I was going to raid the ruins of Fort Knox so that I could return to the present with tons of gold and hire even more mercenary minions. Enough of them to bring down all of the skinwalkers in the future. I was young and foolish then, and the villainous mercenary team saw right through me when they arrived in Saint Mary on their personal hovercraft.

"Little girl? Our leader is going to be a kid?" Thomas the tank said, looking at me like I was but an ant. He was a huge man, wearing about twenty machine guns on his back.

"My daddums is the one in charge, obviously," I lied. "He's funded this operation and is relaying commands via a microchip in my head, like a proper villain. He wouldn't want to go into the danger zone himself. The place where we are going has loads of lovely, giant monsters that will eat your face if you blink at them wrong. I might look young, but Dad trusts me to manage this mission. Therefore, I am in charge, so please pay me proper respect as my minions."

"Tommy, lay off the girl." Miri the healer responded. "She's listed as the team leader, therefore we must obey her. My apologies for Thomas—he can be quite brutish at times."

"No biggie," I said, smiling. "Now, Mr. Klondike, I understand you have the ability to freeze anything small in time, arresting all power within an object for a few days, as listed on your résumé?"

"That is indeed the case," Klondike answered. He was a frail-looking, ratty, skinny, balding man.

"Good. You're the primary reason I've chosen this team. Once we are flashed to the parallel world, you must freeze my bracelet in time, so it can't randomly transport us back until we secure the gold."

Klondike nodded. I had obscured the fact that this was the future from the broker and this team, as it wasn't smart to share that sort of info with people I didn't trust yet.

"Undoubtedly you've already read my short brief of the mission," I began.

Everyone except for Thomas nodded. He clearly found himself above reading briefs. Or maybe he couldn't read due to his superpower. Whatever.

"We are going to a parallel dimension, labelled as world 2424. Our mission is to liberate as much gold as possible from parallel Fort Knox. The only thing you have to fear there are giant monsters. There are no armies or heroes protecting the gold, as all humans appear to have perished in some unknown disaster."

I looked at the short blond man wearing glasses and the silver-haired old man with a very long gun.

"Zeke, I understand that your power allows you to hold about eleven tons of stuff in a pocket dimension, minus the hovercraft? We'll have a need for your hovercraft there, as a lot of the roads in world 2424 are impassable. Ike, there will be a lot of monsters trying to murder us. Keep them off us with that big gun, okay? If they get too close for comfort, Thomas, you deal with them. Everybody got it? Good. We'll fly as close to Fort Knox as possible before the bracelet activates."

The minion team made various noises of confirmation, and we all boarded the hovercraft, heading towards Kentucky. The first five hours of our journey passed by quickly, and when my bracelet beeped, I told the mercenaries to vanish the hovercraft away and hang onto me. We flashed onto the dark ruins of a superhighway.

"Welcome to world 2424," I said. "Try to avoid the wildlife. They bite. Get that hovercraft back out. We're going to need it to move fast."

The ruins of Louisville welcomed us with distant, empty windows of skyscraper ruins, the tallest buildings tipped onto each other. I told Zeke to avoid the city as that's where the monsters usually congregated, although they could roam anywhere. The skinwalkers were attracted by the light and noise of the hovercraft. They came for us in droves, screeching horrendously, but we were able to dodge them due to Ike's marvelous sniping skills.

Thankfully, Louisville lacked gargantuan things that were also quick, and soon enough we were at the gates of Fort Knox. I was going to order Thomas to detonate the doors into the facility with plastic explosives, but there was no need for such—the doors were conveniently left wide open. This should have been a warning, but I was greedy. The gold was within my reach, and so I ordered everyone to disembark and descend into the facility.

Deep within the bowels of the fort, we found our mountain of gold, all 150 million ounces of it, or two hundred trillion dollars if I could exchange it all for money without crashing the gold price. It was untouched, just sitting there, waiting for us as the automated defense systems were long dead and in ruin. Alas, I was limited only to ten tons, but I could come back here again and again with my team, I figured.

Zeke touched my head and my body froze in time, unable to move, unable to know what was going on.

When I unfroze, everyone except for Thomas was gone. A long, black, oily, endlessly long centipede was slowly entering into his right eye as he wept. He was lying in a giant puddle of blood, all of his bones broken and twisted, open lacerations bleeding all over. He was still alive thanks to his power, albeit too broken to flee. He looked at me with his one functional eye.

"I'm sorry. I'm so sorry," he wept. "We wanted the gold. We didn't tell you that Zeke could store much more . . ."

He heaved a great sigh, shuddering from the horrid pain of his injuries.

"The monsters, they came from all around as we were busy obsessing over the gold. There were too many for us to handle. They shredded . . . took my friends. This thing, burrowing inside me now. I can hear its thoughts. It wants to use my power to grow more of its kind, here in the safety of this bunker. Please kill me. Please, little girl. I don't want to turn into one of them!"

Thomas desperately looked at a C-4 bomb with his remaining eye. I grabbed it off the floor, setting the timer to detonate in five minutes. I did not have the time to take any of the gold. Now that I was no longer a statue frozen in time, the skinwalkers of all shapes and sizes came for me—hundreds of them. They poured from the white meshwork bone spheres located between the piles of gold like ants from a hive. My jump shoes saved me long enough to make it out of the doorway of the fort and into the hovercraft. Thousands of them poured from the maw of the fort, a black wave of monstrosities all out to get me. I drove the hovercraft out of the broken, long-rusted perimeter fence, and then a colossal limb came from the sky, smashing me and the machine in a single swat. I flashed into the present and went to a security guard, telling them that I got lost while looking for a bathroom.

"Damn." Martin looked at Alexa.

"Yeah," she said with a small sniff. "Never trust hired minions. Daddums is right. Never trust anyone."

"You can trust me." Martin offered a hand.

"You literally nailed me to the floor, like an hour ago."

"I just wanted to help you," he muttered, rubbing his head. "It won't happen again."

"Well, at least you have that going for you. You betrayed me because you're nice, a hero at heart." She tried to lift the bag with a groan. "I think that's about as much gold that I can lift safely. This backpack better not rip."

She dragged and shoved the backpack into the dark hole, hearing it roll and clang against broken concrete until it reached a wall. The bank-robbing villain winked at Martin and jumped down into the hole. Martin descended after her, sliding down a pile of rubble that she lit with her headlamp. Inside the sewer, Alexa tried to lift the bag and failed.

"Let me carry it," Martin offered.

"Yeah, I don't think so."

"Come on," Martin whined. "Let me make it up to you."

"Fine." Alexa picked up the backpack with a groan and shoved it at him. "Here you go. Drop it if you hear monsters coming and run. Minion life is more precious than a bunch of gold."

Martin nodded, putting the backpack on. Gold was a lot heavier than he thought, adding to the heavy feeling of betraying both Alexa and his conscience as a hero. Even if the owners of this stuff were long dead, he felt greatly ashamed taking their things.

CHAPTER EIGHT

Ill-Gotten Gains

The tunnel ended in a collapsed section, halting their journey. Martin finally relaxed, realizing that no skinwalkers would come at them from this direction or from the shielded bank.

"Pocket burger?" Alexa offered, sitting down on the pile of rubble.

"Um. Are you sure that those are still good?" He inquisitively looked at the tinfoil-wrapped offering.

"Probably?" She shrugged, unwrapping the incredibly crushed meal and biting into it. "More for me."

Martin was feeling hungry, but he wasn't hungry enough to enjoy that sort of meal.

"I see you're waiting to see if I die from this burger. Your decision is wise." Alexa winked at him. "I bet you're thinking, if she doesn't die, I can totally eat these after we flash back to the present!"

He looked at her dumbfounded. "I wasn't! Honestly! Why would . . ."

Alexa looked at him for a bit and then started to giggle. "You're far too easy to bamboozle. I don't even have to pretend to be Rep Agatha with you."

"What? Rep Agatha?" Martin frowned.

The pair sat somewhat awkwardly on a pile of rocks until Alexa's bracelet beeped and flashed them into the present.

"Never mind my fake civilian identity as a corporate middle manager! Woo! The path is clear. Mush, minion, mush!" Alexa directed Martin forward.

"Why do I feel like I've been set up to carry this?"

"Don't think too hard or you might blow a—"

A horrid boom resounded from behind them. The two teenagers turned, listening as concrete rocks rained down the distant tunnel.

"I think I know who made that hole," Alexa gulped.

"Who?"

"Delinqueeeeenttsssss!" Mr. Canard's voice resonated through the tunnel, sounding like a mix between the teacher's prior yelling and a skinwalker's unnatural screeching. "You'll paaaaay for deesssstroying my lovelyeeeeeeee hiveeeeeee!!"

On the one hand, Martin was relieved that Mr. Canard was alive; on the other, he was still clearly being possessed by a skinwalker.

"Welp. He's got immunity to explosions, can see through walls, and also can punch really hard. We're boned," Alexa commented.

Martin's face paled as he realized exactly what kind of a threat they were really facing.

"After me! Hop on the ladder, minion, and rise like the wind!" she whisper-yelled, already climbing up a ladder leading out of the sewers.

He climbed after her, panting and struggling not to slip from the rickety metal ladder, weighted down with the incredibly heavy gold-filled bag. The bag groaned at the seams, threatening to split open at any moment. Alexa shoved the manhole cover up and aside with a loud clang, emerging from the manhole into the late summer evening. Martin followed after her, nearly falling over.

"Deeelinquentssssssssssss!" Mr. Canard's voice vibrated from the tunnel depths as he drew near.

Alexa accelerated forward with the power of her shoes, leaping towards the ice cream truck, flying straight into the front seat. Merry music twinkles filled the air, the van's headlights blinding Martin as he pulled himself out of the manhole. The ice cream truck's engine roared in no way that an ice cream truck should, tires squealing as it rushed towards him. The vehicle turned sideways, right before it smashed into Martin, an open door presenting itself to him with Alexa's hand reaching out from within.

"In! In! In!" she yelled, silver hair swaying. "Freaking hurry! He's almost . . ."

Mr. Canard's bald head emerged from the manhole. It turned 180 degrees, like an owl's head would, the spine and muscles twisting at an angle impossible for a human. The gym teacher no longer had lips or eyebrows, looking more like a well-baked zombie. Alexa pulled Martin into the car, pressing on the gas.

"There you are," the backwards-rotated head in the manhole said casually, starting to sound more human. Muscular arms snapped upwards, pulling the gym teacher out of the sewer. His body was covered in hideous burns, muscles and bones exposed and pulsating, clothes shredded and blackened by the flames.

Martin stared at the infected teacher through the "objects may be closer than they appear" side mirror. Mr. Canard's head faced them as his body rotated towards the departing truck. Legs snapped into a runner's position.

Alexa pushed the ice cream truck to its top speed, but the gym teacher was rapidly gaining, muscular legs flashing back and forth, grime and blood flying off him as his body slowly repaired itself. Martin snapped his seat belt on, terrified of them crashing into something.

"Damn tank super," Alexa growled. Mr. Canard vanished from the mirror. In a few moments, he appeared on the side of the truck. The truck's door next to Alexa ripped off its hinges, flying away into the street, bouncing up and down the road, and raining sparks.

"Got you now!" the teacher roared, climbing into the truck.

Alexa pointed her pink raygun at the super, but he instantly moved out of the way, avoiding whatever invisible ray it was projecting. His large, extremely blistered arm slapped the raygun out of her hand, the hair dryer bouncing off the seat and flying out into the street.

"Go to timeout, delinquent." He smiled with a grotesque grin, grabbing Alexa by her shirt's collar.

The vehicle spun out of control as Mr. Canard pulled Alexa from the wheel. It rolled over the sidewalk, wheels flying over a small concrete barrier towards a kids' playground.

Martin watched in terror as the infected teacher flung his friend right out of the truck without regard for her safety. Alexa's yelp of surprise was interrupted as she was slammed into a concrete pole, sliding down like a limp ragdoll. The ice cream truck finished its journey by colliding into a swing set with a resounding crash of bending metal.

Martin and the teacher were both flung forward. Martin nearly smacked into the front panel, but was held back by the seat belt. The teacher, on the other hand, flew straight into the front window. As he scrambled backwards, getting momentarily tangled up in the folded, shatterproof glass, Martin lifted the nail gun from his belt and fired it at Mr. Canard's hand.

"This is going on your personal record!" Mr. Canard said indignantly, trying to grab at Martin. The fingers of his free hand missed Martin's clothes by a few millimeters as Martin backed away, bumping into the loot bag. The teenager flung the gold-filled backpack right at the gym teacher, trapping him with its weight for a few seconds.

The small skinwalker spider in the glass bottle observed Martin's struggle with curious eyes.

Martin threw open his door, jumping out of the truck. He knew that he had no way to outrun the super, and yet he still ran. The front of the truck looked severely mangled up, but the swing had somehow suffered no damage. The merry twinkle music from the damaged speaker slowed down to an eerie, deep, hiccupping reverb.

Martin glanced down. "This playground was funded and built by the Superstate" was printed in bold letters upon a golden plaque at the swing's base. The little hero turned deeper into the playground, knowing that this place was likely his only chance.

The gym teacher's feet thumped behind him.

"Foolish child," Mr. Canard hissed from behind Martin. "You might have torched my spawn, but my other shard shall wear your flesh." Several nails were protruding from his hand. He held a glass bottle in his other hand, filled with the second skinwalker they had brought from the future.

Martin ran up a metal stairwell, then jumped down a slide. Mr. Canard followed. The slide propelled Martin into an enclosed steel tube with a whoosh. He emerged on the other side and scrambled away on the gravel. The gym teacher followed Martin into the tube headfirst, sliding down. His massive body became stuck halfway in it, at the bend. He roared, unable to move forward or back, fist smashing against the metal with no result.

Martin let out a held breath. His plan had worked. This playground was made by the Superstate and was likely made of the same stuff that was used to build Titanomachy—it was far, far sturdier than what was necessary for a kids' playground, rustproof and made to last for a thousand years. There was no way for the skinwalker-piloted teacher to—

Mr. Canard flung the bottle at Martin. It detonated against a concrete barrier beside him. Martin spun, getting ready to run. A black spider, liberated from its confinement, jumped onto his pants. Acting without thinking, Martin tried to smack it away with the nail gun still held in his hand. The spider was faster, and Martin managed only to hit himself in the crotch with the full weight of the nail gun. He stumbled forward from the pain, collapsing onto the ground with a squeak. The spider skittered towards his face. Martin screamed as dozens of slick, multi-jointed fingers grabbed at his mouth, pulling his teeth apart.

The little monster clawed itself into him, and Martin fainted from the pain and shock.

CHAPTER NINE

The Checklist

Meeting a concrete pole with my head wasn't part of the plan. Or was it? Plans are hard, is what I'm saying.

Not every plan goes according to plan.

I tried to return to consciousness. It was difficult. Quirky colors of all sorts swam in my eyes. I focused my thoughts on the plan.

1. Find Martin Kilborne and make him your minion [√]
2. Die horribly while saving him [√]
3. Meet your Equalizer overseer [√]
4. Bring a skinwalker from the future and deliver it to Mr. Canard [√]
5. Steal Martin's Superstate pen and use it to call his sister while he's asleep [√]
6. Convince Ember Kilborne that I'm tech Agatha Myriamm and that I am running a maintenance test on the Tartarus System Sim [√]
7. Break the pen to hide the evidence [√]
8. Find infected Mr. Canard and make sure he's okay [√]
9. Try not to get injured in the present [x]
10. Make sure that Martin becomes infected with a skinwalker [?]

Eight out of ten today, not bad at all! Wearing a hard hat was a smart decision.

Martin slowly rose, blinking and wiping blood from his mouth. Finally, he had an acceptable body. Being in the bottle was annoying.

"How are you such a blundersome dolt?" Martin the Skinwalker walked towards the trapped Mr. Canard the Skinwalker, speaking with a slight hiss.

"This host is hard to control. It resists. Are you going to help me or . . . ?"

"No. Shed some weight and get out on your own. My parents are looking for me."

"Okay?"

"While you were busy propagating, I was learning, listening. Don't build a hive in such an obvious place next time."

Martin's hand pointed at the distant bank, which was now surrounded by flashing sirens of police cars. His dad's gray sedan was rolling towards them.

"This world is full of hosts and some of them carry the radiant spark of omniscience," Martin said. "They will grind you into dust with this power. Integrate into their society first, pretend to be your host, blend in, find their weaknesses, and strike only much later upon select targets that no one will miss. Do something about your eyes, too. They are far too noticeable—human eyes do not glow in the dark. Infect her when you can grow more shards."

Martin pointed his fingers at the passed-out Alexa.

Mr. Canard nodded, silver eyes shimmering from the darkness of the tube slide.

"Good." Martin turned away from the teacher and started walking towards his dad's car.

Alexa yelped into full consciousness as an armored glove harshly slapped across her face. She felt cold metal weight on her hands and saw a pair of oversized Superstate handcuffs locking them in place. It was a bit of an overkill. She didn't have any physical powers.

"Wake up, bitch," an icy voice demanded.

Alexa raised her eyes to the speaker. It was Hero Resonance, adorned in gold and red. Alexa knew exactly who it was underneath the golden mask. She'd done her research on the Kilbornes when she hacked into the SCA database.

Martin's sister Ember scowled at her, golden eyes flaring at the teenage supervillain. The hero held a steel bat with the SCA logo glittering on it.

A transparent refraction of her swung the bat at Alexa's arm, breaking it with a crack of splitting bone. Alexa yelled from the pain. She couldn't even move away in time or try to reduce the impact, too dizzy and hurt from her recent concussion.

Another refraction of the hero flashed into existence, bat slamming into Alexa's other arm. The handcuffed girl screamed, thrashing, tears forming in her eyes.

"I'm going to shatter every single bone in your body, over and over until your mind breaks from the agony. I had to erase all of the videos from the bank and make sure none of his prints were on that ice cream truck so that shit wouldn't be on Martin's record! I don't know how you've managed to involve my gullible idiot brother in your crimes, but it ends here. I'm going to enjoy making you into a vegetable." Ember seethed, bending down towards Alexa, seemingly uncaring for revealing herself.

She stepped back, and numerous copies of the hero flickered into existence all around Alexa. Off-color, transparent bats swung up into the air as Resonance prepared to strike the villain down from every possible angle.

Alexa blearily struggled in the handcuffs, expecting nothing but pain—

"Put down the bat, and undo the damage done to the girl, Hero Resonance," an emotionless voice ordered from somewhere nearby.

"What?" Ember's head snapped towards the newcomer.

The Equalizer stood six meters away from Ember, holding a long black railgun in her hands.

"Took you long enough," Alexa groaned, looking up at Cottie through tear-streaked eyes.

The Enforcer ignored Alexa's comment. "I said, undo the damage on her. Now, please. I will not ask a third time."

"You dare interrupt official Superstate business, Equalizer?" Ember barked.

"This doesn't look like the official business of simply arresting a villain. You look like you're about to murder her with all of these projections of yours. I have a micro-cam on my person. Give it up; you've already lost."

"No! Screw off! This monster's existence is a threat to my family!" Numerous flickering, off-color copies turned towards the Equalizer as Ember stepped towards the girl in the gray cloak.

The black railgun in the Enforcer's hand lit up as she put her finger on the trigger, and colors drained away from the world in a bubble all around her—the grass, bushes, and playground equipment turning gray. Cottie took a step forward, her robe billowing. As the grayscale circle emanating from the railgun reached the hero, it drained the color from her golden uniform and red hair. In that instant, every single copy of Ember popped out of existence. The hero's ordinarily floating hair fell down to her shoulders, and her cape sagged.

"What?! You . . . you can't! How?!" Ember yelped, eyes wide with panic. Her superpower had never failed her before.

"Resonance, I'd like you to meet my nullifier—Eva." The Enforcer nodded at her gun. "She's an electromagnetic vector accelerator, also known as the Song of the Void, one of the few weapons capable of shutting down superpowers."

"But . . ."

"I will not hesitate to take another step forward and shoot you in the leg if you refuse cooperation."

"Why would an Equalizer defend a vile supervillain like her?! Do you know what she's done? Who she's hurt?!"

"She is of great value to the Order." The emotionless voice of Cottie spoke calmly. "You will cooperate with the Paladin of Equality or suffer the consequences."

"Fffff . . . fine!" Ember angrily ground out. Cottie took a step back, releasing Ember from the nullification field. Two of the hero's copies flashed into being, rewinding the bat motion over the bleeding girl. Alexa's broken arms mended themselves as if they were never shattered, the pain persisting only in her memory.

"Thanks!" She smiled tiredly, lifting her handcuffed hands into the air.

Cottie let go of the trigger. The railgun went off with a bang of a supersonic rail cutting across the handcuffs, cleaving them in twain.

"Hey! Jeez, at least warn a person before you fire that thing." Alexa rubbed the flash out of her eyes.

"This isn't over, Equalizer. I will catch and break her sooner or later—you can't protect her forever! I will be reporting this matter to the Superstate. I'll have Equality declared a villain for this!" Ember growled, golden cape fluttering behind her theatrically as she turned, walking away.

Alexa stuck her tongue out at the hero's retreating form. Cottie approached her.

"You are acting very foolish for a daughter of a super-genius."

"Don't judge me! I'm a work in progress."

"Read this." Cottie slid the railgun back into her cloak and dropped a book into Alexa's lap.

Alexa read the title, looking at the quirkily illustrated girl on the front cover. "*How to Survive Middle School*." She looked back at Cottie, raising an eyebrow. "Really?"

"Yes. Really. I've been observing you. You're failing at being a middle-school student. Her eminence Equality personally sent me to supervise your integration into humanity."

"I don't need to bloody integrate into bloody humanity! I do what I want. I don't need no emotion-deprived Equalizers teaching me how to be a better human. Also, your super pope is dumb!"

"Today, you pissed off the wrong hero and nearly died for it," Cottie noted.

"All part of my genius, multistep, master plan," Alexa said. "Arghhh, friggin hell, my arms still feel like they're broken and also not really." She rubbed her recently unshattered parts, wincing from phantom pain.

The Equalizer sat on her knees next to the villainess. Emotionless emerald-green eyes looked at very tired silver ones.

"You cannot fight the entire world by yourself, little schemer." Cottie reached out and hugged Alexa.

"Wha . . . ? I'm as tall as you!" the girl villain protested.

"We all sacrifice ourselves for a greater cause."

"Do you even know what my cause is?"

"I'm willing to find out," Cottie said. "You are alone, just like I was once. So very, very alone."

"I am not!" Alexa shook her head, her face betraying her with a sour expression.

"I've been investigating, observing you. No caring parents, no relatives, no guardians, no friends . . . with the exception of that poor boy you've recently bullied into being your minion."

"I did not!" Alexa protested weakly.

"Are you sure your father is still alive? Nobody has seen him in a decade. When was the last time you talked to Dr. Terranova in person?"

"Uh. Daddums is definitely alive! He's just very busy with . . . uhh . . . global domination plans!" Alexa said, feeling her defenses crack under the relentless attack of the Equalizer.

"I do not believe that anyone has ever given you a hug."

"I've totally had hugs before . . . uhh . . ." Alexa whispered, more tears sparkling in her eyes.

"Shush and hug me back," Cottie told her, and Alexa did, sobbing into Cottie's gray cloak.

Cottie smiled ever so slightly as Alexa slowly relaxed.

"Hey. That's illegal. You can't show emotion, Miss Spock," Alexa sniffed.

"I've also never known my family," Cottie spoke calmly. "Equality saves orphans all around the world. I'm one of her children. My goal is to save you, to help you be more human."

"Oh. I guess we have something in common then," Alexa said, hugging Cottie back harder. "Hey, um, you haven't seen Martin by any chance, have you?"

CHAPTER TEN

The Puppeteer

Martin was moving amidst the ruins of the fallen, upon hundreds of limbs. He was not wandering aimlessly—no, he had a purpose. He stalked the flavor of prey with endless determination. He saw it—a small, fragile, pale creature with only four limbs and two eyes. A find most delightful. Small it was, but still fun to play with, to break. He advanced towards it, moving across the ancient broken things. He reached out for it, trapping it, enjoying its panicked flailing, and then something struck his face with a blinding flash. He was suddenly, inexplicably both the prey and the hunter. His face burned, melted off, raining down, droplets turning into a thousand shards of his consciousness which scurried away as a thousand small black spiders.

Martin awoke from the terrible dream, unable to scream. He realized that he could not move, could not speak. With increasing dread, he remembered that he was now trapped in a body that was no longer his own, a marionette driven by a sinister, alien intelligence. A fiendish thing from four hundred years in the future was living inside his head, controlling his every move.

Odd letters suddenly flickered, shimmered in his eyes, blocking a part of his vision:

> Terraforge GLM integration in progress. Please wait.

[What?] Martin thought.

> Terraforge GLM status: Integration 48 percent complete.

[What? What's going to happen when this thing completes?] he thought in panic.

[We'll be able to breed new seeds,] came a reply from his own head that sounded like his own voice, but a bit colder.

Martin watched as his own body got up on its own accord. It stood up and walked away from the bed, not folding the bedsheets.

[No! You have to fold those!] Martin protested mentally.

[Why?] the monster in his brain asked curiously. [Will your parents notice this irregularity?]

[No,] Martin thought. [Wait. Shit. I should trick . . .]

[I can hear your every thought. Nothing hides from me. You cannot trick me. You cannot lie to me. Your body belongs to me now. Weak though it may be, it is now mine to propagate with.]

[Crap. He knows what I'm thinking. Hey! I'm not weak!] Martin thought.

[You are. If you invested the time you usually spend folding your bedsheets into training your body, your meaty shell would already be stronger. Your mind is a disorganized mess, and your muscles leave much to be desired.]

[Great. I'm being lectured by a hideous spider from the future.]

[Quite interesting that.]

[Crap.]

[Yes. I am well aware that the one you call Alexa brought me here. I am connected to your brain meat. I am using its processing power to understand you and everything around it, including myself. This girl you label as a villain and a friend . . . Ah, you think that I can use her to bring more of my kind here? That does sound swell.]

[Hey! Don't you dare! Damn it, why did I think about that?!]

[You care for this human. Interesting.]

[Hey!]

[You greatly enjoy spending time with her. It will be easy to emulate this fascinating behavioral pattern to use her.]

[Uh. Um.]

[I can see your thoughts and draw conclusions from them. Nothing hides from me. Your attempts not to think about her are foolish.]

Martin would turn red, were he still in control of his body. But he wasn't. He was just a thought, a background personality. He watched as the skinwalker stretched his legs and arms, watched as his body exercised relentlessly on its own accord with a variety of squats, pushups, jumping jacks, lunges, and things he could not even name. He felt the tension of his muscles straining to their limits.

[See? You are weak and stiff. Easily broken. Not like my other shard in the one you call Mr. Canard. A strong human. Too strong . . . perhaps. It would explain why he is acting so foolish, lacking control, finesse.]

[I, uh . . .]

[Your mind is as weak as your body. Simple, easily understood. This weakness is a boon for me. Ah, I see. Your friend Alexa called me Spiderbro. It is an acceptable title, if a little odd. I did not have a human-applied label before. You are a curious thing.]

Martin's body finished exercising and took a refreshing shower. The skinwalker looked into the mirror, and Martin saw that his own eyes were taking on a silver tint.

[Ah, yes,] Spiderbro observed. [I took the liberty of improving your vision, but not too much. We wouldn't want to be noticed too soon, after all.]

Martin got dressed and proceeded downstairs. The wall clock hanging above the antique piano in the living room showed that it was seven in the morning.

"Good morning, Martin." His dad put down the newspaper. "I believe we have a lot of things to talk about."

Martin inwardly cringed. He'd been expecting this talk, fearing it, forgetting for a second that his body no longer belonged to him.

"I gave you a break yesterday, letting you off to sleep early, considering how we came home so late." His dad's round spectacles glinted on his face.

"He doesn't deserve no goddamned breaks! He broke into the bank with a villain! He was in a stolen car with her! He . . ." A shrill voice resounded, listing Martin's various crimes.

Martin's eyes shifted to the second person occupying the living room—his sister. Unlike his dad, who simply looked very disappointed, she looked extremely irate, golden eyes aflame with a thirst for Martin's takedown.

"I know," his dad said with a sigh. "I reviewed your report on the matter."

"I don't care that you know! You need to do something! Ground him till he's twenty! Put a Superstate criminal tracker on his leg! Take his credit card away! No more allowance! He should be in school or home! No more talking to that girl villain!"

"Ember, please stop yelling. You were yelling about this last night, and you're yelling the exact same thing this morning. You don't need to repeat yourself. I understand what you think must be done. I want to know why Martin did those things."

[I did it because I wanted to catch the villain next door. I'm sorry, Dad. I made a mistake . . . please forgive me,] Martin thought.

[We definitely won't be saying that,] Spiderbro thought.

"I told you that our neighbors are supervillains, Dad," Spiderbro said in Martin's voice. "Alexa, the girl from the cathedral next door, gave me a letter. It was from her father. He knew that you're all heroes. It said there is a death ray on the moon pointing at our house!" Martin's body sniffed dramatically. "And if I refused to comply . . . all of you would die. I don't know why he made his daughter steal the ice cream truck to break into the bank. We didn't take anything from there, I swear. Alexa has this bracelet on her that randomly teleports her around town. I don't know why. Like his daughter, I am a hostage, not a collaborator. Please understand. We were likely just a distraction from some other fiendish plan of his!"

Spiderbro spoke calmly, staring straight at the two Kilbornes. The skinwalker had no fear of Ember. It felt no worry, no guilt. The alien intelligence wasn't pressured or stressed by the authority of Martin's father—it thought of him only as prey labelled as Daniel Kilborne. Spiderbro made a far better liar than Martin ever hoped to be.

"A death ray? On the freaking moon?!" Ember yelled. "Do you really think the SCA prognosticators and observers would miss that? Are you a freaking imbecile?! God, why is my brother such an idiot?!"

"I see," his dad sighed, silencing Ember with a wave of his hand. "I'm sorry, Martin. I should have told you. The SCA relocated us here so that I could investigate Dr. Terranova's odd local project. Alas, it seems that he found out about us and sent us a message through you not to interfere with his work."

Martin's head nodded in agreement.

"You should still ground him for being an idiot! He assisted in—"

"Ember, enough."

"No! I'm—"

"Ember! Go to your room or outside. I'm tired of your interruptions. We've already contained the situation. I'm this town's SCA rep, therefore I will decide how to deal with local villain activity. Nothing of value was taken, and the SCA insurance will cover the damage to the bank and the ice cream truck. You erased the bank tapes. The local police will be told that this is an SCA matter. It doesn't need to go any further. Now, let me talk to Martin without your constant yelling."

Ember glared at their father, stood up huffing, and left. Martin's body turned to his dad. "Thanks, Dad. Em's always jumping to conclusions," his mouth spoke.

Daniel put his hand on Martin's shoulder. "She's got your mother's . . . rambunctious personality. It's my fault, Martin. I didn't expect for you to get involved. Dr. Terranova is skirting a very thin line. Using children in supervillain plans is frowned upon by both villains and heroes. I will get to the bottom of whatever he is doing sooner or later. This is why Ember and I are here. She's right. There's no way we'd miss a death ray on the moon. It would have to be gigantic to reach all the way down to the planet. You got tricked . . . by a letter. Villains lie, you ought to remember that."

"I'm sorry," Martin's body answered. "I won't commit any more crimes, I promise."

"See that you don't." Dad ruffled his hair. "Go have breakfast and off to school you go, kiddo. Don't cause any more trouble, okay? No more skipping class."

Spiderbro nodded to his dad and proceeded into the kitchen.

[Dad! *Dad!!!* There's a monster inside me! A lying spider from the future! It's planning to . . .] Martin screamed, but these words didn't go further than his thoughts.

[You don't even know what I'm planning,] Spiderbro interrupted Martin's inner screaming.

[You're planning to infect all of humanity with your kind!]

[Maybe I am, maybe I am not. I'm feeling . . . rather off balance now that I'm here. I do wish to propagate, but that seems ill-advised with all of these supers around.]

[That makes me feel soooo much better!]

[An infallible plan of action requires greater understanding of this world. I am but a tiny, rearranged shard of my prior self, currently operating on the extremely inadequate knowledge of a fourteen-year-old human child.]

[I'm not inadequately educated, damn it!] Martin defended himself.

[That's not what Alexa said.]

[Hey! Why are you bringing her into this?!]

[It's not my fault that you can't stop thinking about her.]

[Arghhhh!] Martin yelled mentally.

[I understand your frustrations. You wish to propagate, too? Alas, such an option is ill-advised now. Wait until I am fully integrated, then we can proceed with far greater efficiency. Propagation takes patience and intelligence. We must very thoroughly study our target first so as not to fail.]

[What? That's not . . . I . . .] Martin sputtered.

CHAPTER ELEVEN

The Paladin

I woke up in my unassailable tree fortress, my head and back throbbing. I touched my head, recalling the painful collision with a concrete pole preformed on me by Mr. Canard infected with a skinwalker.

"Well, it's a good thing I stole that lovely Super-manufactured helmet from the future," I mumbled drowsily. "Wait, where's my helmet?"

"I took it off to let you rest," Cottie said.

I yawned. The Paladin of Equality was sitting in front of me in a lotus pose, humming as she polished her railgun with a gray cloth.

"Morningghh, Cotes," I groaned.

"You know that's not good for you," she remarked.

"Hmm?"

"Using Benadryl to force yourself to sleep."

"I only do it occasionally, when I need a quick nap or after a nasty bump on the head." I shrugged as I brushed white hair out of my face. "Did I invite you into my up-tree fortress? Last night's a bit fuzzy."

"You did. I carried you most of the way."

"You might just outdo Mittens. Maybe I should make you my top minion!" I praised her. "Numero uno!"

"I'm not your minion. I am an Emissary of Equality," she insisted.

"Why not both?" I teased. Cottie ignored me, engrossed in polishing her railgun.

"Say, that's a nice railgun." I walked up to her. "What's her name?"

"Eva," Cottie replied, looking at me wearily.

"Oh, right," I muttered. "The Song of the Void! You introduced her to Ember yesterday."

The Equalizer nodded.

"Hi, Eva, I'm Alexa." I leaned towards the gun. "You and I are going to save the multiverse. Okay? Okay! Your master can come aboard the train with no brakes to nowhere and everywhere too! She's nice if a bit dry, like an old cracker left in the sun too long, but I'm certain that she'll shape up in no time at all."

"Eva does not speak," Cottie pointed out.

"Everything speaks. Everything everywhere is alive." I shook my head. "You're just bad at listening."

"I am perfectly good at listening," Cottie said defensively. "The gun does not speak."

"Alas, Mittens remains my numero uno by virtue of being more entertaining," I sighed.

"I am not here to entertain you," the Equalizer said.

"Why are you here, then?"

"To monitor you," she replied.

"Boooring," I rolled my eyes at her. "Why don't we adjust that 'monitor me' to 'help me save the world'?"

The Equalizer arched an eyebrow at me.

"What? I'm not allowed to save the world? Does saving the world go against the principles of your girl-pope now?" I asked.

"How will you save the world?" Cottie asked.

"By obliterating the Superstate," I said waving my arm at the Titanomachy megastructure visible through a rooftop window directly above us.

"That sounds incredibly villainous," she said.

"Oh, I'll do it without killing anyone important." I smiled. "Only one person will have to die."

"Who?"

"Me," I replied with a soft smile.

"You will die to stop the Superstate?"

"Yeppers." I nodded. "I'll die extra horrifically. Everyone on the planet will see it . . . and then the Superstate will fall. Everyone will be equalized, just like you people always wanted, see?"

"Why do you wish to destroy the Superstate?" the Equalizer inquired.

"Because they're secretly super duper evil," I said.

"Are they really?" Silver-green eyes examined me. "In which way are they evil?"

"If you're trying to play the role of my licensed psychiatrist, know that I'm very complicated," I said. "I . . . I'll tell you everything, in time, Cotes. After I die, promise. Not right now, though. Right now I have to play the role of a scary supervillain. They're listening, watching, monitoring me."

Cottie stared at me like I was mad. I wasn't mad. I had a plan. It had many steps. My little stairwell to the great ring in the sky, to a better tomorrow. To save everyone on Earth. She would understand. Everyone would understand it after I show them the truth of Tartarus. After I showed them the gods. After I revealed the truth behind everything . . . pull back the curtain.

I got up, stretching and downing a few Advils and coffee pills with water. Checking my reflection in a slightly damaged gold-plated mirror, a fatigued silver-haired girl looked back, forehead streaked with dried blood.

"You've got some very expensive stuff here," Cottie observed, glancing at a slightly charred Rembrandt.

"Why thank you, Cottie! Too bad Mittens is missing out on praising my excellent interior design skills," I smiled, twirling across a wall of priceless art. "Eh, whatever, we had a nice girls' only sleepover party!"

"There was no party. You passed out after rambling incoherently."

"Your brutal honesty is very pointy. Try being less square" I sighed, stepping into a very shoddily constructed camping style shower.

"I'm not a square."

"You are sooooo square." I pulled off my bloodstained clothes. "Don't you worry, my equalness-worshipping pal, I'm sure I can wear down those jagged edges with some elbow grease and a whole lot of—"

The shower blasted me with a spray of icy water.

"Eeeeeeeeerk! Damn it, I should really invest in a water heater!" I yelped, shivering from the icy spray.

Verse 24:19—"Cottie" was not her real name—didn't make out what exactly Terranova was going to use to wear down her jagged edges, as the rest of the villainess's speech was interrupted by Alexa's noisy squeal. She looked at the damaged, priceless art strewn all around the tree house in wonder. Subject Alexa Terranova was a mystery wrapped in an enigma. Did she somehow rob museums, secretly replacing the art there with copies, or were these some sort of elaborate copies? If so, why did they look so aged and worn?

She recalled the sacred words of Eminence Equality, the prophetess of the Equalizer Order, which were burned into her mind.

"Twenty-Four Nineteen. You are my most talented and dedicated Enforcer. I know that you will not fail me. I thus entrust the Song of the Void, and the most important mission of all, into your capable hands. This I have foreseen. Alexandra Terranova is the key with the power to reshape the world, and soon all villains and heroes will desire to wield her. The storm of all-devouring darkness comes, and she stands in its eye. Save her life, befriend her, aid her, make sure she remains human as long as possible. When the time comes, when she finally picks a side—be it hero or villain—end her life."

The Enforcer looked at the cheerful silver-haired girl who emerged from the shower. She had to become Alexa's friend, to protect and teach her to be human, only to kill her in the end. It was a heavy, terrible burden. The face of Verse 24:19 did not show the inner turmoil she felt. The equality of the world had a price, and that price was the life of just one girl.

"You know, the way you're cradling that big gun of yours and staring into my soul with those chilling emerald eyes is veeeeery suspicious." Alexa advanced towards Verse 24:19, wrapped up in a pink towel.

The Equalizer flinched back ever so slightly.

"Oh, I know!" The villainess grinned. "You undoubtedly also want a refreshing cold shower! Go ahead, there's plenty of rainwater in the tank!"

CHAPTER TWELVE

The Power of Loops

Verse 24:19 emerged from the shower in her gray cloak to discover Alexa applying pink Dora the Terraformer–themed Band-Aids to her various scratches. Many Band-Aids were already decorating the girl, far more than what was necessary. Even the gaping bullet hole in her construction helmet was now covered up with a whimsical arrangement of bandages.

"Want a Band-Aid?" she offered, rattling a box of Band-Aids in the direction of the Equalizer.

"No."

"Too bad. They would add some much needed color to that boring ass gray cloak of yours. I think you guys are doing equality wrong. See, if I was the Equalizer pope, I'd give your cloaks a psychedelic rainbow pattern with some fractals or something. All the pretty colors and shapes of the fractal machinery of the universe sorta idea! Stylish and fun!"

"Well, it's a good thing you're not her Eminence Equality, because I have no desire to look like a clown." The Equalizer calmly readjusted her railgun beneath the cloak, small water spheres rolling off the fluid-impervious surface.

"Wait. Did you shower in your cloak . . . with your gun? Who showers fully dressed?"

"The safety of this shower leaves much to be desired."

"Well, excuuuse me. I'm a supervillain, not a plumber!" Alexa threw up her arms.

"Also, the floor here is sloped at a 4.7-degree angle." Verse 24:19 tapped her steel reinforced boot on the uneven, warped floor. She noted that it was made from metal suitcases. She bent down to examine the suitcases, looking through the glass panels.

"Supervillain, not a carpenter!" Alexa yelled from what looked like a very shoddily made kitchen that featured a microwave and a freezer. She was digging bacon out of the freezer and shoving it into the microwave. "And before you criticize my cooking skills—supervillain, not a chef!"

The Equalizer had no intention of criticizing Alexa further. She looked at the floor and the walls of the tree house in deep concentration, the tiniest micro-expressions of bewilderment breaking through her normally calm face.

"Sup, dawg?" Alexa slammed the microwave door shut. The plate full of bacon started to spin behind her, highlighting her head with a yellow glow.

"Are these what I think they are?" Verse 24:19 looked at Alexa.

"Yeppers. Super-designed hydrogen bombs. One hundred megatons each, or two Tsar Bombas per suitcase."

"But . . . this is impossible. They're exactly the same bomb suitcase! This is hundreds of bombs with the exact same ID number!"

"Yeppers."

The Equalizer's neutral facade shattered, her face growing pale as she realized the implications of what the floor and the walls and the ceiling were lined with. "How many bombs is this?! How much uranium is in your walls?!"

"To be precise, there are exactly 444 hydrogen bombs in the walls, serial number 9838201." Alexa picked up a detonator with wires leading into the wall.

"Now, Cottie . . ."

"My name is Verse Twenty-Four Nineteen!"

"Wrong. Your name is Cottie, or I flip this switch and we'll have a lovely nuclear winter in very short order."

The Equalizer blinked. "You would vaporize millions of people just so I would respond to you as Cottie?!"

Alexa nodded.

"You know what? Fine! Call me whatever you want! I don't care!" Cottie said. "Why? Why would you do this?!" She pointed at the bombs.

"Safeties?" Alexa shrugged as if having the walls of her tree house lined with suitcase nukes was a very mundane thing to do.

"Safeties? What is wrong with you?!" Cottie advanced onto Alexa, her eye twitching.

"Ah, so I can make you angry," the teenage supervillain grinned. "Projecting hearty emotions at someone is the first step towards a healthy relationship, you know. Or minionship, in your case. See, my goal is to make you more human. Break yourself outta that boring square Equalizer box! Spread your wings and fly, my pretty butterfly!"

Cottie froze, reestablishing her neutral facial expression. "I don't understand," she finally stated.

"You're an Enforcer. I'm a villain. It's a bit of an oddball companionship, don't you find? Enforcers are known to kill supervillains, often without provocation, and then the evidence comes out that these villains were planning things that threatened the balance of global stability. It stands to reason that your Order has a super prognosticator. You prevent super-caused disasters before they happen," Alexa said.

Cottie started to sweat. Alexa knew! She had somehow deduced *everything*! She was even making references to dying for her cause!

"Do you know of the 'The rice and chessboard problem,' Cottie?" Alexa pulled out her bacon plate from the microwave, putting it onto an Egyptian-style golden table.

"What does that have to do with anything?" the Equalizer asked, staring at the coffee table that looked as if it had come straight from the tomb of the Tutankhamun museum exhibition.

"It's an exponential curve parable in which the inventor of chess tricked the king into giving him an absurd amount of rice. He asked the king to fill each chess square with twice the number of rice starting at only one grain. Basically, if the number of grains of rice doubles on every successive square of a chessboard, the sum of grains on all sixty-four squares is over eighteen quintillion. People underestimate the power of numbers. Okay?"

"My dear minion numero dos, the things you see around my tree house are genuine items of rarity and great value that I brought back from the future. I go there a lot, as you can see."

Alexa pointed at one of the paintings on her wall behind her. "That's the *Wanderer above the Sea of Fog* painted in 1818. The original, not a copy. A quintessential masterpiece of French Romanticism. I stole it from the future because it reminds me of my own personal struggle against . . . various elements."

Cottie looked at the painting of the Wanderer that depicted a man looking over misty mountain peaks. Alexa turned around, matching the posture of the man in the artwork.

"When I was younger, I simply took valuable items from the future, like this painting. Eventually, I realized something else—a new world is created with every jump. I don't know what happens to the old one. Maybe it just keeps going. Maybe it is destroyed. The point is that the future changes with every action of mine and every new jump takes me to a *new* future."

Alexa turned back to Cottie.

"Imagine if you could jump into the future several times a day. Now imagine that you could bring any item back, say . . . like a grain of rice. Now imagine that you buried this grain of rice somewhere safe, then jumped into the future again and dug it out, then came back to the present. You'd have twice the rice. Then four times. Then sixteen. Rinse and repeat. Over and over. An exponential curve. Now imagine that the object in question isn't a grain of rice. It's a super-designed hydrogen bomb in a small suitcase."

Alexa pointed at the floor covered in hydrogen bomb cases.

"With only sixty-four trips, I can produce eighteen quintillion bombs. Obviously, I don't have that many bombs, as I'm limited by carrying capacity and other . . . things, but you get my mathematical point, yes?"

Cottie looked at Alexa, eyes wide. "By Equality!" Her hands started to tremble ever so slightly as she completely lost control of her feelings.

"Enforcers exist to *equalize* villains and heroes who go too far. I can bet you're just waiting to shoot me with that gun for my future crimes against humanity or whatever. Well, if you do that, all of these synchronized bombs, including ones I've buried all over this yard, all around town, and all over the country, will all go off at the same time. You'll never find them all, and you'll never disarm them all, because there are too many. I have been jumping into the future and making copies of this bomb since I was twelve. *Big bada boom*." Alexa made an imaginary nuclear explosion with her hands.

She grabbed a bacon piece and let Cottie process her words some more, then walked up to the Equalizer, looking right into her emerald eyes. "No matter what I do in the future, no matter what I am planning to do—you can't kill me, Enforcer. If I die, these bombs will go off and the world will burn. It's the ultimate dead man's switch. Checkmate." Alexa booped Cottie in the nose.

Cottie's mouth became dry as she flopped it open and closed like a fish, her eye twitching ever so slightly. The teachings of Eminence Equality did not prepare her for this sort of mindblowing insanity.

Alexa offered Cottie a hand. "So, you might as well protect me for all of eternity with that big shiny gun of yours! Friends?"

The Equalizer returned the handshake, her palm sweaty. She had greatly underestimated the teenage supervillain during her initial analysis and was now paying the price.

No amount of cold showers or meditating would cure the terrifying dilemma Alexa had planted into her rapidly beating heart.

CHAPTER THIRTEEN

A Nutritious Breakfast

Spiderbro sat within the warm confines of Martin's head, who in turn stepped into the warm confines of the school bus, which would take them both to school. Martin did not expect to learn anything of value in school that could solve his brain spider problem. Martin did not want to go to school. Spiderbro, on the other hand, wanted to attend school very much. It was expecting to learn things about humanity to integrate better into the local environment, so that it could someday find a nice, safe place to breed and multiply.

Martin relentlessly tried to fight off, to resist the alien presence that was now in charge of his body, but it was no use. Every one of his attempts had been easily thrown off. It was akin to trying to catch ocean waves with bare hands. The young hero desperately wanted to hide away from the looks of other students who saw and greeted him as Alexa's minion.

Spiderbro fearlessly drove Martin's body forward.

"Look who decided to show up today," someone declared loudly. "Mittens! Thought they suspended him for setting the school on fire."

Martin's body stopped mid stride, turning. His eyes locked onto a muscular teenager in the front row who made the comment to a blonde girl sitting beside him.

[I see. This human subtype is labelled as a "jock."] Spiderbro had caught and dissected Martin's thought. [Hanging out with a "cheerleader" subtype as is their standard behavioral pattern.]

"Ah, you're the kid whose entire life revolves around proving your superiority to everyone else," Martin's mouth said, a hand pointing at the seat the bigger teenager was occupying.

"Say what?" The jock twitched.

"I merely wanted to point out that you are a pompous, staunch laddie who sadly lacks self-awareness due to insufficient mental capacity," Spiderbro added.

"What?!" the jock said, standing up, looming over the far smaller Martin. "I think that you belong in the back of the bus, along with that . . . pyromaniac weirdo. I think that someone needs to—"

Martin's body moved with impossible precision. His leg struck the jock's shin, and the muscular teenager yelled in surprise, bending over. Martin's arms guided the bigger body into the empty space between the seats, kicking him forward as the bus moved. The jock whimpered, hitting the floor face-first. Martin sat in the vacated seat next to the blonde cheerleader.

[What the frig are you doing, you dumb alien spider?!] Martin screamed inside his head. [Don't you want to blend in?!]

[Blending in does not work by hiding,] Spiderbro answered inside Martin's head. [I am establishing dominance to build trust. Something you failed to do. Once I am on top of the student food chain, along with my other shard as the top teacher, we shall rule this place of human learning.]

"I'll murder you!" the jock hissed from the floor. "Don't think you'll get away with this, Mittens!"

"Please don't fight on the bus," the bus driver said resolutely. "Don't make me get up. You, take a seat *now*!" The jock stood up, slowly limping to the back of the bus.

"You are welcome to challenge me again after class, bud," Spiderbro commented with Martin's lips, smiling at the retreating jock.

"What the . . ." The driver pressed on the brakes, and the bus lurched to a sudden stop. Martin's eyes looked ahead at the two people standing in the middle of the road. It was Alexa and that Equalizer girl . . . Cottie. The villain had too many bandages on for reasonability and was bouncing up and down excitedly, with her hands behind her. The Equalizer stood perfectly still, gray cloak fluttering in the wind, silver pin glittering on her chest. She looked determined as if she were a western novel sheriff waiting for the antagonist to emerge to have a shoot-out at noon.

The bus doors opened, and the pair of girls entered the bus.

"Hey, Alexa!" Martin's mouth began to speak.

Alexa's left arm emerged from behind her. She was holding a bowl of what appeared to be Froot Loops.

"Would you like some lööps, brother?" she asked.

"Hrm. Are you offering me your nutritious breakfast again?" Spiderbro made Martin's eyes focus on the bowl.

"Whoopsie!" Alexa slipped on the rubber floor mat, the bowl of Froot Loops tipping over, hundreds of colorful, small, ring-shaped cereal pieces raining down, bouncing, and scattering all over the floor of the bus. Martin's new, improved eyes tried to focus on all of them, to catch all of the motion—

Alexa's right hand emerged from her back, revealing her pink hair dryer contraption. Spiderbro, distracted by the Froot Loop waterfall, reacted far too late to the threat of the raygun. The villainess pressed the trigger.

The skinwalker-enhanced eyes could see a horrible ray shimmering from the barrel, flickering with a new, freakish color Martin could not name. His body tried to leap away, to get out of the path of the beam, but failed to do so in time. There was only so much space in the bus for the skinwalker to escape to.

The normally mildly annoying pocket ray gunfire struck Martin in the head, and the skinwalker inside his head screamed. Martin fell to the floor, twitching and frothing at the mouth. Alexa, still holding the trigger of the raygun, advanced towards the slain, shaking boy.

"Thought you'd be in Mittens, my little friend," she said, bending down.

"Is that boy having a seizure?!" The bus driver stood up.

"Remain in your place, citizen." Cottie put her hand on the bus driver's arm, her other hand resting on her railgun, visible beneath her gray cloak. "This is Enforcer business."

The driver gulped, sitting back down, forced into obedience by the calm voice of the Equalizer, staring with worry at her glittering Enforcer pin.

"Martin. This is your only chance!" Alexa said, leaning down to the twitching boy. "You will soon lose yourself forever to the skinwalker if you do not reassert control now! Awaken. Restrain, wield the spider in your head. Do it for me. Do it for the world! Be more!"

Martin's mind was aflame with agony. He could feel what the skinwalker felt. The little spider in his head was burning up, dying. Martin tried to take control of his own body but was in too much pain. He saw nothing but sparks in his eyes, felt nothing but the fire in his head. Alexa let go of the trigger. Martin stopped flailing on the floor. His eyes filled with dread and stared at the villainess.

"You're hurting me, Alexa! Please stop! Please!!!" Spiderbro whimpered, black-and-red tears dripping from Martin's eyes. Martin knew, felt it then—the little skinwalker was terrified of dying, not wanting to lose even more of itself to oblivion, not wanting to let go of its new human body and the intelligence and understanding it had granted.

Alexa pressed on the trigger once again, flooding both the skinwalker shard and the boy with pain. "Wake up, goddamn it! Ignite the power in your head!"

She pressed the raygun trigger on and off, drowning and releasing them from the ocean of suffering.

"Hrm. He's bleeding pretty badly. Are you sure you should keep this up?" Cottie stepped in, the slightest bit of concern in her eyes.

The burning sensation of the skinwalker intensified in Martin's head, and he coughed out black sludge along with copious amounts of his own blood. The little spider lost even more parts of itself, fried by the raygun.

"Make her stop! Please! We're both going to die!" the skinwalker wailed. "I can't hold myself together!" Martin suddenly understood that it had done severe damage to his body by burrowing from his mouth to get into his brain and then fixed it all, repaired it with its own flesh. That flesh was now melting away, coming apart, and killing them both with internal bleeding.

Alexa pressed her face against Martin's head, clicking the trigger in very quick intervals. Martin felt as if he were being dragged into the dark abyss by the river of agony.

"It's my fault. Everything is my fault," Alexa whispered into Martin's ear. "I planned all of this. A thousand little events, a thousand people pushed in just the right way, all to lead everything to this pivotal moment. I filed hundreds of anonymous reports to the SCA that my father was concocting villainous deeds. I got into the SCA database, pulling and pushing the bureaucratic machinery of the Superstate into action. I arranged, made sure that Daniel Kilborne would get this mission. That you, his son—the child of a prognosticator and a mental manipulator, someone utterly clueless and nice, someone who is still not awake to their power, could come here to this town, could become my friend, could trust me! I did all of this just so you could get infected with a tiny, weak skinwalker shard from the future!"

The feelings of confusion, betrayal, and anger overpowered the pain.

Martin wanted to scream at Alexa. He should have known better. He should have expected this! He suddenly saw the skinwalker spider in his head as a burning, sparkling, weblike shape, overlaid atop another, far wider, dim fractal web. He reached out towards it with all of his being, desiring, wishing, needing to do something!

The feelings of rage and Alexa's betrayal pushed him forward, making him desperately grab at the dying skinwalker with his entire mind and soul.

The fractal network around the skinwalker ignited in a radiant splendor of impossible colors, tendrils twisting, entwining, cocooning the little burning, dying life into itself. Martin's eyes flashed from within with a multitude of colors as his nails gripped into the floor mat. Alexa had released the raygun trigger in that instant.

A foreboding message flashed in Martin's vision woven from a million sparks, the letters swimming in and out of view.

Terraforge GLM status: Integration 98.74 percent complete.
System Error: Terraforge GLM system control lost
due to unknown interference.
Please consult the manufacturer for further details.

"What in the hell is wrong with you?! Why have you done this to me?!" both Martin and Spiderbro cried out in unison, grabbing at Alexa. She was giggling, no, laughing with the wild abandon of a supervillain as Martin shook her in impotent rage.

"I win," she finally pronounced with a wide grin.

CHAPTER FOURTEEN

The Trust Square

Martin released Alexa from his clutches, lost in his thoughts, tired of shaking her. She had been far more villainous than he had expected. Just how far back did her plan stretch?

"Is spilling cereal all over my bus part of the Equalizer business?" the bus driver inquired, looking at Cottie. "I'm kind of on a schedule here."

"The loops are an essential part of our business! Thank you for your participation. We'll be off now!" Alexa bowed to the bus driver.

"Yes," Cottie answered him with a slight nod. "You may depart now."

"Depart to where?" Martin blearily asked from the floor.

"That depends. How are you doing, number one?"

"Well, I just lost a whole bucket of blood. That's probably not healthy," Martin sighed, wiping his face with his sleeve.

"You'll be fine!"

"I don't feel like I'm fine. Seriously, what did you do?"

"Remember when you couldn't break a metal bench with your bare hands that one time?"

"Okay?"

"Well, you still can't." She grinned.

"What?"

"But you're a genuine hero now! Yay!" Alexa clapped.

"*What?!*" Martin looked at the villainess with wide open eyes.

She smiled even wider, helping Martin stand up. Then she looked at an extremely confused blonde that was occupying the other front row seat. "Out."

The cheerleader looked back at Alexa with a mildly challenging look.

"Go join your boyfriend in the back. And do be quick about it, unless you want to be raygunned too," the villainess said, twirling her pink raygun and nodding at Martin. "My patient zero needs the front row seat."

The blonde stared at Martin's pale blood-splattered face for a few seconds. Then she rushed out of her seat into the back of the bus, quickly moving past the trio. It was clear that she did not want to be raygunned.

Alexa guided Martin towards the window seat and sat beside him, swinging her legs. The boy looked at her with a look of confusion and irritation.

"Why, thank you, Alexa, for making me a hero *six* years ahead of schedule!" Alexa announced with a deep, fake voice.

"This isn't how it's supposed to be!" Martin shuddered. "There's supposed to be training at the Hero Academy for two years and graduation with a diploma listing my specialty skills from Grand Dean Otter! I don't even know what my power is!"

He couldn't believe that she had somehow managed to awaken him by nearly killing him right on the floor of the school bus, of all places! He felt weak from the blood loss, twisted up in some unnatural way. This was not how he was picturing his awakening. What had happened to him somehow felt very wrong, forced, dirty.

Maybe it was just the brain spider thing. No, it was definitely the brain spider thing!

"Well, whoop-de-doo. Aren't we spoiled with fancy pants luxuries? I simply graduated you the villain way, made you claw your way out of near-death into your power. You're welcome! You can still probably go hang out with Dean Otter, don't worry so much."

Martin turned, quietly staring out of the window onto the passing streets of Saint Mary, having put his aching head against the cool glass. He knew that the skinwalker was moving its tendrils inside of him, expeditiously trying to reassemble itself and repair the damage to his insides.

It was freaky as hell and frankly weirded him out.

"Look. There's a spider in my brain doing . . . stuff. I can feel, see what it's doing. It's not a fun thing to know. People aren't supposed to know what's going on inside them with this much graphic detail, damn it!"

"Hang on . . . I know what'll cheer you up." Alexa took off her new backpack.

Martin noted that the logo on it was silver-blue and featured the hero Knight Chalice. She dug into it, pulled out a notepad, ripped out a page, scribbled something on it, and slid it to Martin. He glanced at the lined piece of paper that was now lying on his lap.

Genuine Hero Academia Deathschool diploma! Superpower: control of one brain spider from 2424. ~ Dean Cassiopeia Terror Nova.

Martin rubbed his head in resignation.

Alexa yawned and glanced at Cottie, who was simply standing in the middle of the row next to their seats, swaying ever so slightly with every turn and stop of the school bus.

"Sit," Alexa stood up and pointed at the seat next to Martin, addressing Cottie. The Equalizer sat down next to Martin without an argument.

She had no idea what had just transpired between the boy and the villainess, but she would undoubtedly get to the bottom of it—

Alexa sat on Cottie's lap.

"You do know that there are other seats on this bus?" Cottie said, feeling somewhat awkward.

"I wouldn't want to leave Mittens unsupervised at this pivotal moment. Number one already threw *two* whole mutinies. That's twice more mutinies than necessary."

"Look, I can just stand—"

"Nopers. Am plenty comfortable where I am now." Alexa stretched atop Cottie. She took off her construction helmet, put it on Martin's head, and nuzzled into Cottie's armored chest.

Martin turned his now helmeted head away from the window to discover Alexa using Cottie as a couch. His image of The Equalizer Enforcers as the unbendable, dedicated killers of supers cracked. He'd never seen anyone so blatantly disregard the authority of an Equalizer and get away with it.

The sight he was presented with was far too absurd, like a robber that chose to nap atop a police car.

"How are you doing that?" he whispered at Alexa.

"Doing what now?"

"Uhrm. Sitting on her."

"I can sit on whomever, whenever I want to. It's a free country. Also, she's my minion. Being a minion implies being used in all sorts of ways."

Martin turned back towards the window to hide his reddening face.

[Stop that! Focus on the important things, human! Demand answers!] Spiderbro mentally hissed at Martin.

Alexa yawned again, stretching halfway onto Martin. "Gosh, I'm beat. Learn my lesson, don't try to take down concrete poles with your head."

Martin looked down at her bandage-covered face. "Uh. Sorry that happened. I wasn't fast enough."

[Why are you apologizing?] Spiderbro pressed. [Why are you like this? She planned everything, she set you and me up! Did you forget this already?]

"There're letters," Martin said.

"What kind of letters?" Alexa asked.

"I see weird letters in my eyes now," he confessed.

"What do these letters say?" The supervillain girl tilted her head.

"'Terraforge GLM status: Integration 99.92 percent complete. System Error: Terraforge GLM system control lost due to unknown interference. Please consult the manufacturer for further detail,'" Martin read.

"Ah, that." Alexa yawned. "Don't worry about it."

"Do you know what it means?" Martin demanded. "Surely you must! What's Terraforge? What's a GLM?"

"Well, don't quote me on this," Alexa muttered. "Terraforge is what skinwalkers are, I think. GLM stands for Gigaplex or Gargantuan Language Model. It's the thing that makes the text, sort of like an interface that talks. Happy?"

Martin blinked as he processed her words.

Alexa yawned wider. "Cottie, I'ma have a brief nap. You're in charge. Make sure number one doesn't start any more mutinies."

"Umm. What happens if you flash into the future now with us on the bus? Are we going to get flung into the future at forty miles an hour? Is this bus going to get flung into the future with us? What about all the other kids and the driver? How does it determine where you and the things you touch end and the bus begins?"

Alexa didn't answer any of his questions, as she was now quietly snoring atop him and the Equalizer.

Cottie turned towards Martin, observing him with her big emerald eyes.

"Hi. I'm Martin," he said to her stiffly.

"You aren't part of the prophecy," she finally commented.

"Ehhhh. Does this mean I'm not important?"

"It means you weren't mentioned by Eminence Equality, but you are theoretically valuable because Alexa seems to have involved you in her plans."

"Why are you here? Are you trying to make her join your order?" Martin felt mildly offended at being only *theoretically valuable*. "Convincing Alexa of anything is beyond useless."

"I'm not here to necessarily recruit her to our order," Cottie shook her head.

"Hrm. You seem to be much too agreeable. I've seen a video of one of your . . . Enforcers in action. You guys don't let anyone boss you around. Both heroes and villains know not to mess with the Equalizers. Why are you letting her sleep on your lap?"

"I'm here to aid her plan while making sure she remains human," Cottie replied.

"So, you know what her plan is?" Martin pointed at the snoring Alexa.

"No."

"Seriously?! What does she have on you? I don't believe for a second that you'd cooperate with her shenanigans so willingly." Martin nodded at Alexa's slightly drooling face. "Why do you let her call you Cottie? Is she plotting something dangerous? Did she blackmail you somehow?"

"Alexa buried an incredibly vast number of hydrogen bombs around the country," Cottie answered with her usual calmness.

"What?" Martin blanched. "How? When?"

"She used time travel to replicate a suitcase nuke . . ." Cottie proceeded to explain the concept to Martin in the same way Alexa had explained it to her, albeit in a far less dramatic fashion.

"But that's . . . so insane! Oh my God!" Martin whispered, looking out through the window of the bus at the peaceful city of Saint Mary.

He imagined nukes going off all around town, vaporizing buildings, trees, cars, people. It was the ultimate judgment day. Even if just one of them went off accidentally or was found and dug up by a random dumb criminal, it could spell disaster!

[Humans are so very gullible, especially you, my unfortunate host,] the skinwalker muttered in his head.

[Eh? What?] Martin thought back, distracted from imagining Armageddon.

[Think, human child. If the future really changed the way Alexa described it to the Equalizer, then how come the skinwalker she labelled as Mr. Noodles was wearing so many human skins? Where did these skins come from if not from the dead bodies of Alexa? Why did she make you rob a bank yesterday when she could have easily acquired infinite gold this way? Infinite anything really!]

Martin froze, his mouth snapping shut.

[Your parents can see the future, can they not? Would the Superstate, the eyes of Titanomachy, not notice Alexa burying hundreds of hydrogen bombs around town? Would they allow her to even bury a single one in Saint Mary? Think!]

Was the sneaky spider in his head right? There was no way that his dad and the SCA prognosticators would miss millions of bombs buried around town. It was all just a clever trick, a ruse set up entirely for this Equalizer's sake. That's how she got Cottie to obey her! A beautifully orchestrated lie!

[That's right. The whole time-travel concept she sold you is a lie,] Spiderbro added. [While I can't remember much of my former skinwalker self, I can examine your memories.

Your actions here do not impact the place where I came from, 2424 is not the future of your world. She is most likely jumping to a parallel dimension—another Earth, one that exists four hundred years ahead in time.]

[But what about the hole in the bank floor made by Mr. Canard?] Martin thought back.

[Just a coincidence. Do you really think that the supers would fail to repair their own bank? Besides, a lot of things in 2424 are damaged by fire and feature holes. What happened in the world where I came from cannot be stopped, cannot be prevented. The skinwalkers are a new life, part of the new biosphere. They will not vanish just because somebody flushes a toilet in your world in some sort of an amusing butterfly effect scenario.]

[Damn it!] Martin inwardly groaned, looking at the silver-haired sleeping girl.

He'd been duped again and again by Alexa. She'd been messing with him since the beginning all for one purpose—to get him infected with a skinwalker!

[See! You cannot trust her. She is a most fiendish villain,] Spiderbro concluded his thesis.

Martin looked at his own pale reflection in the glass window. His eyes were still tinted the tiniest bit silver.

[You'd rather have me trust an insidious alien spider that murders or enslaves people to make more of itself? Really?]

The skinwalker in his head grew silent at that.

Either it had nothing to say to that, or it had decided to take a nap because it was exhausted from repairing his insides. Did head spiders take naps?

Martin glanced at the Equalizer. He would not reveal his head spider's deductions to her. He had no reason to open up to her or to trust her. Cottie would have to figure out Alexa's bullshit on her own.

CHAPTER FIFTEEN

Mothra

Martin walked to school dragging his feet, burdened with dark questions and even darker thoughts. How much of the skinwalker's personality had now been overlaid over his own brain? How much of his brain had already been destroyed or rearranged by the thrashings of the little spider? How much had the forced power awakening in the moment of near-death screwed with him, messed up his mind?

Alexa merrily bounced to his right, seemingly looking at nothing in particular. She appeared like nothing but an airhead for the world. Martin knew better now. She was a devious ensnarer that had involved him in her vast, dangerous weblike plot that stretched an unknown number of years back and four hundred years forward in time.

Cottie walked stoically on his left, her multilayered carbon fiber steel boots kicking up small clouds of dust with every step. Her gray Equalizer cloak billowed behind her, armor joints clicking with every step, appearing for all eyes like a knight from some long-forgotten kingdom, now long lost in time. Her emotionless face terrified Martin to no end. He expected the Paladin of Equality to detect the evil lurking inside his brain, to turn to the side and to break his neck, to end him for no reason at all.

Thankfully, Alexa's infinite bomb threat was keeping the Equalizer under her control, but how long would that last?

Other students had given them a wide berth, whispering things behind their backs in hushed tones. Everyone was terrified of the presence of the Equalizer Enforcer, even more so after Alexa had declared Cottie as her "personal minion number two blessed by Pope Equality herself."

"Why so glu—" Alexa began.

"You know why, goddamn it!" Martin snapped.

"Oh, psh. You've evolved, it's time to toughen up, Mittens! Stick out your chest, because it's ready for a shiny Superstate access pin for being a goodly boy who turned into a hero today!"

Martin glared at the supervillain. He did not feel like a hero. He had done nothing heroic to gain his power.

"Congratulations, my man! You can now go up the pretty space elevator and look down upon the peasants who toil on the dirty ground with their sticks and stones, from your very own orbital ring estate, feeling all mighty and superior! What splendidness! Such serendipity! Your parents and big *admiral* sister will be so proud!" Alexa theatrically wrung her hands.

"You don't know how my family would react to this! So stop it!" Martin hissed.

"You know, I expected you to be a lot more excited for the opportunity that I've graciously blessed you with."

"What opportunity? What?!"

"The opportunity to be more! You've already grown so much in the past few days, compared to say . . . where you were two years ago." Alexa pulled out a picture from one of her vest pockets, brandishing it into Martin's face. He saw himself, looking around twelve years old, walking to school alone across the exocrine sidewalk of New New York Citadel District 9415.

"What the frig? Where did you get this?" Martin grabbed the photo out of Alexa's hands. Upon closer examination, the photograph looked severely scratched and worn out. It was printed on some kind of reinforced fiber-plastic, one that had been through a lot.

"The internet!" Alexa declared with a smile.

Martin glared. "I don't believe you for one second."

"Okay, you got me. I paid a detective to take it. You were one of many children on my list," she said.

"Why do you have a list of children?!" Martin shook the photo, and noticed that it said *Prospective #42* on the back.

"I'm Secret Santa. I send them presents!" Alexa innocently blinked her silver eyelashes at Martin.

"No. No, you're not, damn it! Quit screwing around! This is all part of your plan to infect people with skinwalkers, isn't it!"

"Okkie. I confess. One person," Alexa corrected. "You! I found this lovely photo in the desolate ruins of 2424 and thought that you were absolutely adorkable minion material."

"Yeah, right! What about the other forty-one?" Martin growled. "Well?!"

"What, my list can't start at forty-two? It's obviously a *Hitchhiker's Guide to the Galaxy* reference! You should read it! It's a whimsical space opera, guaranteed to entertain even a mild-mannered bee counter like yourself." Alexa grabbed the photo from Martin's hand, shoving it back into her pocket.

Martin glared at her, anger boiling over within him. His eye twitched.

"You . . . you can't do this to people! You're a manipulative fiend! You've tricked me, lied to me! I keep thinking that you're my friend, but you . . . you've been stalking me for years!"

"Not stalking. Investigating. Looking for the perfect . . ." Alexa smiled softly.

"Perfect *what*? Test subject?! A fucking patsy to give brain spiders to?!"

"What?" Alexa tilted her head to the side. "I thought you wanted to be a hero. Seriously, look at where you were two years ago versus where you are now, surrounded by two adorable femmes."

Alexa proudly pointed her hand at herself and then at Cottie. "Everyone is jelly of you now! Don't you hear the whispers and speculations on the nature of our relationship triangle?"

Martin sputtered. Then his anger returned.

"Becoming a hero is a very complex science, you stupid asshat! It takes years at the Hero Academy with instructor aid, observation, hero training, apprenticeship, and a very specific diet! You can't just hodgepodge it with a fucking near-death experience!!! Why would you do this?!!!"

Martin's screaming had reached the highest crescendo. He suddenly noticed that the Equalizer girl was looking at him, and his accusatory screechy tone broke down into a quiet mumble. She scared the bejesus out of him.

He remembered watching a very fuzzy video of an Equality Enforcer in action when he was only eight. The young knight in a gray cloak simply walked up to a super and shot them in the head. It was brutal, quick, and disturbing on all levels. No long-winded speeches, no epic fights. It took only a few seconds. Bang, and the hero was dead. The super's power didn't even work against an Equalizer!

Martin shivered, looking away from Cottie.

Alexa grabbed his face, turned it towards herself and stared into his eyes. "Look. Focus. There's a reason why I do all the things I do, Martin! The world ends very soon, if maybe it slipped your mind! Everyone will die if I fail! You, me, this town, every city on the planet will burn to ashes! We are *doomed*! *Doomed!*"

Martin let out some of his rage. "Why can't you just be straight with me? Why do you have to lie, manipulate me all the time?"

Alexa pointed up at the sky, not saying anything. The ring of Titanomachy glinted overhead, a myriad of lights twinkling between clouds.

"I don't understand," he said.

"You will, in time. All will be revealed in time," Alexa said with a sigh.

"Alexa desires to destroy the Superstate," Cottie commented with a nonchalant voice.

Martin choked.

"Why did you wake my power so early? What if there are horrible side effects?" Martin whined.

"Look, it worked for me. I didn't need no Superstate-designed drugs to be awesome sauce. I'm clearly fine."

"You are not fine! How are you fine?" Martin hissed.

"Cottie, gimme a hug, number one is being mean." Alexa pranced over to Cottie, burying herself into her cloak. The Equalizer stared at Martin expressionlessly. He wasn't sure if she was judging him. Martin expected the Equalizer to strike him, and he drew inward in fear, expecting awful things.

Cottie's arms wrapped around the girl villain. Martin sputtered. He'd never seen an Equalizer hug anyone before. Enforcers didn't hug villains or heroes; they shot them in the head. This simply didn't happen!

Where has the world gone wrong? he wondered. *How has Alexa managed to break the universe?*

A silver-blue eye peered out at him from Cottie's cloak. "Psstt. Come'ere. We can hang out under this invisibility cloak and steal the philosopher's stone from Dumb-ley-dore and cure cancer with it!"

Martin blanched. He definitely did not want to hide under the Enforcer's cloak and pretend to be some kind of rational Harry Potter.

Cottie rolled her eyes at Alexa's antics. Then she yipped, twitching ever so slightly.

"Sorry, wrong button!" Alexa yelled from beneath the cloak. "Seriously dawg, where's the invisibility mode on this thing?"

Martin's facade of anger cracked. He started to giggle nervously, unable to contain himself. He worried that the Equalizer was going to murder him for this disrespect, yet he could not stop himself. The whole situation was beyond absurd.

"Welcome to the fellowship of the lööps!" Alexa announced. "Villain, hero, Equalizer, and an angry smol spider from the future, all tied together with itty bitty strings of fate. Our adventure party is now in full order, and the real fun can begin!" She flapped Cottie's cloak like a pair of wings. "We're just missing the admiral. She'll join us soon, though! Soooooooooooooon!"

Martin blinked as the supervillain girl cackled from beneath the Enforcer's cloak. Who was Alexa talking about? Who was this "admiral?"

"Wait, can you turn into Mothra? Where's the lever for your pretty butterfly wings?" Alexa demanded.

CHAPTER SIXTEEN

Lunch on the Lakeshore

You don't listen to her, do you human child?] the skinwalker in Martin's head whispered.

[Huh?] Martin thought to the spider from the future.

["Your parents and big *admiral* sister will be so proud,"] the skinwalker replied, copying Alexa's voice.

[Ember isn't an admiral,] Martin replied. [She's just a young hero. Alexa's probably lying again, messing with me!]

[Possibly,] Spiderbro replied and fell silent.

Martin looked at his slightly scratched-up mechanical wristwatch. It was lunchtime. He couldn't believe it. Nothing had exploded. Nobody around him had gotten stabbed or died horribly for an entire half of the school day. Alexa had acted like a perfectly normal schoolgirl and not like an insane super-genius, hellbent on terrorizing the population of Saint Mary.

She went to class, answered questions from the teachers, made occasional jokes at Cottie's expense, and didn't harass him one bit. It was a miracle!

Martin expected her to snap at any moment and to start causing trouble, but alas, he was again and again stupefied with her perfectly mundane behavior. It was in fact so normal and ordinary without her hexagonal bracelet making a sound that he began to suspect that he was now in some sort of pleasant parallel universe where things didn't go horribly wrong with every hour.

The skinwalker spider in his head remained silent, observing the world through his eyes and enjoying the learning experience. A group of older kids, part of the friend group of the jock that Spiderbro had managed to piss off on the bus, gave them a wide berth, spooked by the imposing presence of Cottie.

The only thing that was bothering Martin was the fact that there was still another skinwalker somewhere nearby.

"Are we going to do something about Mr. Canard?" he asked Alexa.

"What's wrong with Mr. Canard?" The villainess tilted her head.

"He's infected with a skinwalker shard," Martin pointed out.

"I've called the SCA." Alexa shrugged. "Let the authorities deal with it."

Martin blinked, feeling stumped. This did not seem like her prior behavior of doing everything herself.

Martin was tired of slipping up on banana peels left and right. He thought hard about what he would do if he encountered the skinwalker himself, preparing himself mentally. The fact that the spider in his own head was now under his control was Martin's advantage.

The trio had descended down to the lakeshore park behind the school and now sat underneath a great willow tree facing the pebble beach.

Alexa studiously started to read the *How to Survive Middle School* book, resting her head against Cottie's lap. The Equalizer was sitting in a lotus pose, looking as serene as ever. Martin stared at their relaxed postures for a few minutes, and was about to suggest they head out to grab lunch from town, when an orange delivery drone descended from the sky bearing a large pizza box.

"Dig in, friends!" Alexa announced, swiping a credit card at the drone.

She had a credit card!

Martin expected alarms to go off on the drone, screaming about credit card theft, but no such thing occurred. The only criminal thing that had transpired was the fact that the pizza had pineapples on it along with miscellaneous meats. He chose not to complain, looking at the sparkling reflections of the orbital megastructure ring of Titanomachy upon the sky-blue water of Lake Eerie.

Alexa's figure was backlit by dancing sun puddles reflected from the lake's surface, her silver hair gently swaying in the wind as she enjoyed a slice of pizza.

Had she lied to him about the whole manipulation of SCA business to save him from the skinwalker's control? The more Martin thought about it, the more sense it made.

There was no way that a fourteen-year-old girl, no matter how clever, could manipulate the Superstate or decide which mission his father was given. The SCA had entire divisions of prognosticators at its disposal, including his mom.

The future seers could not be deceived or misled; thousands of super-geniuses constantly labored under the prognosticators setting up new security measures on Titanomachy against intrusions, be they physical or digital.

As soon as somebody planned attacking the Superstate, the SCA would come down on them like a ton of bricks. The orbital megastructure was indestructible, impregnable, a world unto itself, filled with countless heroes who were far more experienced and older than the little villainess who liked pineapples on her pizza.

Alexa noticed Martin staring at her and threw him a thumbs-up, as if confirming his theories.

Both her father and the villain minion team had manipulated and used her. Martin felt that she would not betray her first friend in a similar manner, that beneath the deception, she was someone that he could—

[Wowza. This is a lot of human feelings to process,] his brain resident commented.

[Don't make me mute you,] Martin thought back, annoyed that the little spider was spying on his personal thoughts.

[Okay, boss host, you do you.]

[That's right!] Martin pondered. [I'm . . .]

[I have noticed an irregularity. It could be nothing, or it could be something potentially dangerous to us both.]

[What sort of an irregularity? Are you talking about Alexa's unreasonably calm behavior?]

[No. There was a new student present in class. The teacher did not introduce her to the rest of the class like you, Alexa, or Cottie.]

[A new student? Why is this odd? Maybe she was sick yesterday or something?]

[You do not understand. She was also in class yesterday, but at the same time, she wasn't. You have two memories present in your mind. One memory shows an empty seat, the other a girl sitting there. I've been busy looking over your recent memories, so it's exactly the kind of a thing that would normally escape your attention, but I am a diligent analyzer. Someone is screwing with your memory.]

Martin gulped. [Oh. That's not good.]

"Hmm. There are fruits on here," Cottie commented, observing her pizza slice.

"You got something against the taste of pineapples on pizza, equality-chan? Do they violate the 117th commandment of her Divine Preeminence? 'Thou shall not flavor thine cheesy bread with tingly fruits'?" Alexa teased the Enforcer.

"No. This is an acceptable flavor. I've just never had, um, pizza before."

"Oh, my poor, sheltered child! My heart weeps for you. Growing up under rocks! Avoiding smiles! Climbing glaciers all day long. Carrying water buckets uphill both ways! Don't you worry, you and I are going to experience all the fun things the world can offer, from quad bikes to finding out how many licks it takes to get to the bottom of a lollipop!"

Cottie did not look like she was interested in lollipops, Martin noted, returning to his worries about yet another mysterious stranger who was now stalking them.

CHAPTER SEVENTEEN

How Do You Do, Fellow Kids?

After a nice pizza picnic at the beach, the trio went back to school. Martin lost the girls when he went to use the bathroom. His way back to the classroom was partially barricaded by a chatty group of students.

As he circled the group, he noticed a tall red-haired girl standing there. As Martin glanced at her, he realized that she looked awfully familiar and yet different. He tried to look past the inexplicably youthful features, past the darker hair and darker eyes, and found himself face to face with his worst fear—his sister.

"Ember?" he uttered.

"Ehm?" The girl turned, blinking and speaking with a fake accent. "My name is Dixie. You must be mistaken."

[This is definitely your sister,] Spiderbro confirmed Martin's suspicion. [Why is she here? Is she not too old for this educational experience?]

A barely perceptible refraction of Ember squinted angrily at Martin. He could only see the angry, ghostly resonance of his sister because his skinwalker eyes were far sharper than those of a human. It was definitely Ember!

"Why are you here, Ember?" Martin asked sternly.

The girl turned back to the crowd, resuming her chatter, throwing in a few jokes about dumb boys who can't tell people apart.

"Shut it, pipsqueak. I'm on a mission!" A barely visible ghost of Ember appeared in front of Martin's face, turning him around towards the row of lockers. The refraction directed his hand as if he was the one opening the locker.

"What mission? What the shit?" Martin hissed back. "You're nineteen! You can't just pretend to be in eighth grade."

"I'll do whatever it takes to protect my clueless brother and the rest of this town from supervillains," Ember's ghost replied. "There seems to be a lot of bullshit going on here, far too much for my liking."

"I don't need your protection. Ow! Stop that!" Martin protested as the ghostly ripple pulled him into the locker.

The refraction of Ember became far more visible, flickering with a menacing glow made up from offset colors, a green-and-blue ghost in the darkness of the locker, holding Martin down.

"This is hero business, Martin. Do you understand? Don't be going around calling me Ember. It'll be an inconvenience to organize another fake identity!"

Martin groaned. He'd expected to face an alien monster piloting a teacher in school or perhaps some stranger-type super looking into Alexa's shenanigans, not his irritating sister.

Just when things were looking up, somebody had to inject herself into the picture and ruin everything!

"Why do you have to be in *our* class, of all places?" he whispered at her angrily, feeling that anyone looking his way would likely assume that he was talking to himself in the depths of a locker, like some kind of a crazy person.

"Have to keep an eye out for my little defenseless bro. There's something very sketchy going on in this school, and I'm getting to the bottom of it as the local SCA agent. I'm actually quite impressed that you recognized me. Guess all those times I interacted with you via my avatars is finally paying off."

Martin said nothing about his brain spider giving him the necessary tips to recognize her. He chose to focus on Ember's looks instead. "You look weird. Not just the hair. You look like you're four years younger! What did you do to yourself?"

"Had my friends from the Academy magnify, shift, and add to my power to erase a few years from my body. 'Twas painful, but I'll live. I'll wind myself back to nineteen once the mission's done."

Martin stared at the glowing refraction of de-aged Ember. His sister was mental. There was no other description for it.

"You're watching . . . Alexa?" he guessed.

"Yes, I am." Ember nodded.

"Officially? You've got the full paperwork for this mission this fast?" Martin demanded. "Who in their right mind would approve of you pretending to be a fourteen-year-old student?! What's Alexa even guilty of?"

"Nothing yet," Ember replied. "She is talking a lot about taking down the Superstate, according to the Titanomachy observer analytics."

"Talking isn't a crime!" Martin declared. "There's no way a fourteen-year-old girl can take down Titanomachy!"

"Obviously she can't take down Titanomachy. This is . . . an unofficial mission." Ember shrugged. "At best, she'll take down your reputation. I filed my presence in this area under general inquiry . . ."

"You . . . you can't do that!" Martin accused.

"Can and will," Ember replied. "I'm pretty high up the SCA ladder. It pays to have friends in high places. Someday you'll understand. Someday . . . after you get your power and graduate from the Academy, I'll make you into the greatest hero of all."

Martin squinted at his sister, barely believing her words.

"You're messing with people, mentally," he accused her. "Why not transfer in like a normal student or even come in as a hero officer? Why do you have to shove yourself in as a memory of someone who's always been there?"

"What? This is perfectly standard procedure for a covert op. Superstate agents constantly inject themselves into human organizations. When you graduate from the Hero Academy, you too will become a Superstate employee—a predictor or an agent. Our family leans towards mind control and information gathering pretty heavily, you know."

Martin knew. He knew that far too well now. Except all of his mind control power was now permanently focused on a single skinwalker spider residing in his head, thanks to Alexa. He would not be a prognosticator like his mom, or an agent like his dad and his sister.

"Anyways. I'm gonna head to class. Don't blow my cover. I'm Dixie." The avatar of Ember smirked at Martin, fading away.

"Was that aurora borealis, localized to a single locker?" Alexa's voice resounded from beside Martin, making him twitch and bump his head against the metal shelf. Too preoccupied with being annoyed at his sister, he'd failed to notice Alexa's arrival in front of the locker.

"Ow. Damn it." Martin emerged from the locker while rubbing his head. "No. It's much worse than a locker-based weather phenomenon. It's my sister."

"Ah, yes. She's probably planning to murder me." Alexa nodded, looking far too cheerful for such a dark conversational note.

"What?!"

"Don't look so concerned. I'm a tough cookie. Also, I have Cottie now. I ain't scared of no wardens."

"Wardens?"

"That's the slang for SCA agents, yo. We're all prisoners of the gods from up above, don't you know? It ain't about protecting people. It's all about keeping the sheep in line with the doctrine of the all-seeing eye in the sky."

Martin chose not to argue with all of the *wrongness* in her statement. "Look, just be careful around her, okay? I don't want you getting hurt."

"Big whoop. Getting hurt is part of the game, Mittens! Accept the pain as a lesson, in order to avoid it next time. Accept the fear head-on and learn to defeat it. You won't cook that perfect pancake number one thousand without getting a little burned in the process. I had to get skewered only about 3,024 times before I made all of my lovely anti-skinwalker devices."

"Give me the fucking raygun," Martin growled.

"Eh?"

"If my sister is going to be a big headache, I'll give her one, too."

"All right, don't break it. And don't shoot Mr. Canard, please." Alexa unclipped the hair dryer raygun from her belt and chucked it at Martin. He caught it, nearly fumbling and dropping it.

"Why not?" Martin asked.

"Because I already told the SCA about him," she explained. "He'll be dealt with soon enough, don't worry."

Was that Alexa's plan for preventing the future apocalypse? If the SCA learned about skinwalkers, they could figure out a way to stop them, Martin thought.

[An interesting strategy,] Spiderbro commented. [Considering that you're now technically a skinwalker.]

[Oh.] Martin shuddered. Maybe the SCA could figure out how to fix him, after they fixed Mr. Canard.

"Um. Does this thing run out of charge or something? I'm planning to use it quite a bit." He waved the gun at Alexa.

"Nah, be my guest. There's a uranium battery in it. That's about two thousand years worth of zappery," she replied with a wink.

"Good." Martin nodded, heading towards the classroom.

[Steady my hand. We're hunting Ember,] Martin thought to his little brain spider.

[You got it, boss,] Spiderbro replied.

CHAPTER EIGHTEEN

Anger Management

Ember slumped her head onto the desk, rubbing her temples. She had a headache that would not go away. She wasn't sure if this was because she couldn't think of the most effective way to crush the damned little villain or because she'd failed to protect her dumbass brother from her vile influence. She was usually very good at destroying things. Breaking people with her power was easy.

If it weren't for that damn Equalizer and her nullification gun, she would already be done with this job!

Ember didn't understand why her reports about Equalizer interference were swallowed up without any sort of response to action. The Equalizer organization was clearly run by a monster who was training orphans to become living weapons. There was no question about it from looking at Verse 24:19's emotionless face. It was an unacceptable, horrid thing to do to a child, and it bothered Ember to no end that her superiors refused to do anything about it.

She had even submitted the perfect plan to destroy their cult. She could do it all alone, fly her cruiser straight into the heart of the Equalizer compound at full speed, crash into the building, and murder their leader. The Equalizers were just humans who were misled by a supervillain. There was literally no difference between Eminence Equality and any other supervillain who had human minions! With the leader dead, their organization would undoubtedly fall apart in a few days. Ember yearned to do something with her entire heart, desired to punish, to end injustice and suffering. The Equalizers stood in her way, and she would remove their poor misguided pawn one way or another.

Alas, Admiral Kolchi also refused to do anything about the Equalizers. It didn't matter, though, in the end. Kolchi was an idiot, and had made a fatal mistake in refusing to integrate GLMs into Titanomachy systems. Ember had taken full advantage of this. If her long-term plan paid off, someday she would gain full control of Titanomachy. Someday she would become the SCA admiral herself, stand above all, and rain hellfire on the Equalizer compound from the sky, obliterating the disgusting supervillain organization from the face of the Earth.

The chilling migraine let go and intensified once again. Maybe this endless headache was a side effect of the partial de-aging. Her face was itching like crazy, too, as if a million microscopic ants were crawling within it.

The things she did to protect her family, to protect and educate her careless brother!

Just another thirty minutes. Just another thirty goddamned minutes of this kindergarten. Arghhhhh!

Ember formed an avatar behind the classroom wall inside the janitor's closet, shoved the bucket and broom aside, and proceeded to kick the wall again and again in agitation, leaving small dents in the bricks.

The young SCA agent had no doubts that the questionable behavior of the retired super Mr. Canard was entirely because of Alexa Terranova.

Ember only saw a few minutes of the video footage from the cameras at the bank, of the two kids getting inside the building, before she scoured the hard drive data out of existence with an electromagnet that was built into her supersuit. The fourteen-year-old criminal was clearly destroying Martin's chances of being a hero with idiotic petty crimes.

Alexa Terranova was the lowest of the low. *What kind of a moron steals an ice cream truck to get into a bank just to set it on fire, of all things?*

Ember glared at Alexa with passionate hatred. She didn't believe Martin's "villain's letter" story one bit. Dr. Terranova had not been seen in public for many years now.

Hero Resonance wasn't an idiot. She'd dug deep into the matter this morning through her Academy friends and via whatever SCA databases she could access, trying to find anything of value. There was nothing at all to uncover, nothing on the doc who lived in the church. Someone had paid the bills, but it wasn't a person, just an automatic system sending money to another automatic system.

Villains didn't just up and disappear like a fart in the wind from the scanners of Titanomachy or from the reports of the Superstate prognosticators. If the prognosticators and Superstate systems could see no future or present activity for him, it meant only one thing—the doc was dead.

Everything had to be Alexa's fault! The blasted villain had to be stopped, broken, eliminated *now*!

Ember suspected that the little supervillain had accidentally killed her father four years ago and covered it up by locking up the cathedral somehow. The bones of the doctor were likely inside, waiting to be found. Ember had stalked the premises, tried to use her power to break a window, to open up the doors, but it was as if the building's outside was impervious to her attack. It was as if the inside didn't even exist to her super sense that normally allowed her avatars to get through anything. It was beyond irritating.

Villain tech be damned!

Ember could take the headache no longer. She raised her hand and asked the teacher for a bathroom break, whatever her name was . . . Fickers? Ickers?

She rushed into the bathroom, scratching at her face and splashing water on it.

The headache slowly subsided.

Ember suddenly deduced that the migraine was likely caused by Alexa—either a power or some infernal gadget on her person.

Why couldn't her brother see what kind of a *fiend* he was dealing with? All of Ember's training and motivation to push her little brother into the path of a great hero was turning out for naught. There was only one conclusion to it, one explanation—*the little idiot is in love with a bad girl.*

A refraction of Ember swung its ghostly fists against the mirror and the mirror shattered, detonating into a thousand pieces, shards of glass raining all around the bathroom. Ember scowled at the myriad of broken, twisted reflections of herself raining around her. Another pale ghost came into being, smashing its head against the sink, the ceramic shattering from the impact. Other avatars kicked at cubicle walls, smashed toilets. Everything in a five-meter radius became a zone where nothing of value remained intact as Ember let out her rage.

The agitated hero stepped away from the mirror, and the motions of her ghosts flickered in reverse, destruction all around rewinding the damage, cracks sealing themselves, shards flying back into place.

Her avatars didn't feel much. Destroying things and putting them back together always brought her joy, but this time all of the joy had been hampered by her utter inability to destroy one goddamned fourteen-year-old girl.

Biology teacher Tamara Kells made no noise from her distant bathroom stall, blinking in confusion as the sole witness to the inexplicable bathroom ruination and restoration which she witnessed through the small gap in the stall's wall. She swore to take it easier on drinking in the mornings.

Martin smiled, sliding Alexa's raygun into his backpack. He'd managed to chase his annoying sister away with a migraine.

[Great success!]

[She will likely return,] Spiderbro commented.

[Then she will enjoy more migraines,] Martin said mentally.

[You hate your human sibling this much, huh?]

[Yes,] Martin thought. [Ember made my entire life hell! She's five years older than me, and she's tried to control me, push me around, and boss me as long as I've known her!]

> Terraforge GLM Integration complete.
> LV 1 Tools available:
> Production of Terraforge carrier seeds.

A message suddenly flashed in his right eye.

[Carrier seeds? Meaning what?] Martin thought.

[Meaning we can grow new skinwalker shards,] Spiderbro replied. [You're pretty weak and thin, so you could probably grow one shard in your stomach and infect . . . one other human with it.]

Martin blanched. [*What?!* I'm not growing spiders in my stomach!]

[You do not wish to propagate?]

[Ew!] he shot back. [Obviously not! I'm not bloody infecting anyone!]

[Your human mind is very confusing,] Spiderbro mulled. [You don't want Alexa to be killed by your sister's hand?]

[What? No!] Martin sputtered mentally as he glanced at the white-haired supervillain. [Why would I want Alexa dead?]

[She lied to you and betrayed you,] Spiderbro explained. [She manipulated you into getting me into your head, almost killed us both with that raygun, and ruined your chances of ever getting a "proper power" as a hero. She committed several crimes attracting SCA attention to you.]

[I . . . er.] Martin's thoughts careened sideways.

[You could infect her,] Spiderbro suggested. [Control her.]

[No!]

[Why not?]

[. . .]

[You . . . like her?] Spiderbro asked. [Is that really a sufficient reason to endure her present company?]

[I . . . I don't want her hurt or mentally controlled,] Martin thought. [She's a victim of her supervillain father! I can save her!]

[Ah, I see,] Spiderbro mulled. [You wish to *gradually turn her into a hero*, to rescue her, to prove to yourself that *you're* a hero?]

[Yes, damn it!] Martin mentally barked, muting Spiderbro in annoyance.

Why was he arguing with a skinwalker shard . . . er, terraformer seed, anyway? He was in full control of the creature's thoughts now! His superpower was that he . . . *controlled skinwalkers.*

Something clicked in his mind.

Was this part of Alexa's plan, too? Him being able to mentally control skinwalkers? If the Terraforge project went out of control in the future, destroying the Superstate . . . then maybe this was his way of becoming a great hero!

Maybe this was how he could save the planet and everyone in the present! Maybe this was how he could protect Alexa in 2424!

A wide grin spread across his face. He would have to see if he could mentally control the Terraforge seed in Mr. Canard!

CHAPTER NINETEEN

The Song of Terror

The puppeteer of Mr. Canard sat inside his portable office, feeling irate and spooked. He was slowly devouring seventy-eight burgers and twenty-four pizzas from a McHeroes delivery order. He had purged a lot of biomass from his host to get out of the damned pipe. Precious, precious biomass that he had to gain all back so as not to look questionably thin. Eating what he had purged off the ground was out of the question. Humans did not eat things from the ground. The other shard was right.

He had to blend in better. Blend in . . . much better.

The host's brain meats were giving him information randomly and sporadically, resisting the little shard's influence over it. The more the little spider learned of this new world, the more terrified he became. The all-seeing megastructure ring in the sky was the worst. He now knew that he could not do anything odd out in the open, or *they* would know.

Don't give them a reason to check. Don't be weird. Be a teacher. Blend in.

Anyone or anything could be an agent of the Superstate, he knew this now. He'd made a foolish mistake in making a nest in the bank.

Thankfully, that little blonde girl impervious to the hypno-pacifier had destroyed it. What was her name? Alexa? *Alexa.* A nice target for the propagation?

No! No she isn't. She knows things. She vanished and reappeared beneath the bank somehow.

Was she a super? *There is a lot of gold in this backpack of hers.* Mr. Canard was in possession of two of Alexa's backpacks now, having confiscated one and taken the other from the ice cream truck. So much gold in the black bag and strange devices and diamonds in the pink one. Where did all of this *stuff* come from?

The little shard tried to draw conclusions from Alexa's bags full of loot and failed, its desires for propagation and the strong mind of the host constantly interfering with its ability to formulate coherent thoughts. The need to make more of itself nagged and persisted. He pushed it all back, focusing on the thoughts and desires of the host. The host's desires provided the shard with useful information.

The host, the real Mr. Canard, knew that a super observer from the sky could notice that he was acting weird. The host knew that it would be a strike team of five supers with powers that reinforced one another that could easily take him down.

The shard worried that the SCA team would come for him. He feared that they would mentally disable him like the hypno-pacifier did, rip the little alien life out of the head of the teacher and vaporize it. Yet nobody showed. Perhaps the little skinwalker still had a chance to exist in this terrifying world full of powerful hosts.

The longer he spent inside the teacher, the more he was fusing with the host. Perhaps there was still hope. Perhaps there was still a way to survive and propagate.

No. Don't think about nests. Don't think about making a nest.

He wondered how the other shard was doing in the boy. Its integration had seemed far more successful.

It seemed that the children made better hosts than the super adults.

Don't think about infecting children, damn it! The eyes in the sky are watching. The prognosticators are calculating the future. Change too much and they will come down and destroy you!

Don't do anything out of the ordinary. Just be a teacher. Just eat this delicious pizza. Don't be a monster. Integrate. Belong.

Unfortunately, the shard could not hide forever away from the world, as being a gym teacher was a thing he had to do now. He put on a pair of mirrored sunglasses to hide his glowing silver eyes and emerged from the relative safety of his portable. As the pretend teacher walked across the gravel road into the gymnasium, he tried not to look up at the terrifying gargantuan ring in the sky, dotted with eternally burning lights. Upon arrival in the gym, he waited for the eighth grade students to emerge from the change rooms.

When the kids started to come out of the change room, three of the girls immediately drew the shard's attention to themselves.

The teacher froze.

First, his eyes settled on *the Equalizer.*

He had been warned via a text from the vice principal that a transfer student was coming today. What he was *not* warned about was the huge gun-shaped thing beneath her clothing, which the super's X-ray eyes could immediately see through the cloak. It stood out against the red pulse of the Equalizer's body heat. Mr. Canard gulped.

This was a very dangerous gun; its core was colder than anything he'd ever felt. Fractal tendrils of darkness wiggled within its depths, reaching, wanting, waiting. The gun was *alive* and it wanted to *feast*, to devour his power. The infected super spotted the pin on her chest and shuddered. This girl was the highest *Ascendant of the Equalizer Order*, a *Paladin Enforcer* who executed true enemies of Equality, did too much damage to people or cities.

Mr. Canard took a step back, the host sweating in dread of the gray-cloaked Enforcer and her living gun.

The second who caught his attention, a red-haired girl, made no sense. She was a tad too tall to be an eighth grader. The host's power determined her age to be approximately fifteen or sixteen . . . or nineteen? There was something off, wrong with her age. Her bones seemed older than her face.

She was even more spooky than the Equalizer, because she didn't belong to his class.

Mr. Canard suddenly recalled her name.

Dixie. Dixie has always been in my class.

The information came from nowhere like an infection. *This is a memetic attack*, he told himself, *a mental power in play!*

His all-piercing X-ray eyes detected a pair of Superstate handcuffs in her pockets. Mr. Canard saw ghostly, barely perceptible, off-color . . . things floating all around the girl. They were just as terrifying as the living gun.

This girl was a concealed Superstate agent, the one he'd feared would come for him!

Were these two part of a group that had come to take him down? Where were the other three? Mr. Canard's eyes beneath the mirrored sunglasses rapidly spun in their sockets, in different directions, calculating possible routes of escape.

The third girl that emerged from the locker room was Alexa Terranova, and she was holding a very large, shiny brass tuba.

"Sup, teacher-sama!" she yelled. "Why are you wearing sunglasses indoors? I know what will cheer you up! A nice song!" She waved an arm at him and put her lips to the tuba, blowing.

A cloud of sparkly dust exploded out of the tuba.

It was the last straw.

Mr. Canard flung himself out of the window, glass shards raining in his wake.

CHAPTER TWENTY

Quintet Interrobang

The students looked at Alexa.

"What?" she asked them. "I was about to play the school spirit song for our lovely gym teacher, Mr. Canard, but I guess some jerk put all this glitter into my tuba as a practical joke. Don't judge me! I'm as perplexed as you are about this spontaneous teacher departure!"

Martin rushed out of the changeroom to the sound of the tuba made by Alexa. He arrived in the gym only to discover that one of the large windows and the gym teacher were missing in action.

"Shoot," he swore under his breath.

The cloud of glitter began to come down, settling on the confused students. The only person who was not confused was Ember. She marched towards Alexa, fists opening and closing.

"What the fucking hell?!" she growled.

"I agree. This glitter is going to stay with me forever, and I didn't even get to play my whimsical yet morally inspiring song. There's no escaping glitter," Alexa said solemnly, her clothing and hair sparkling as more glitter snowflakes fluttered down all over.

"I know you did this!" Ember growled.

"Em—Dick-sie, lay off Alexa!" Martin said as he reached the pair of girls. "It can't possibly be her fault that the teacher jumped out of the window!"

"Dixie, Dixie, damn it! You can't even remember one name!" Ember snapped at Martin, eyes igniting with fury.

"I don't give two shits about your dumbass made-up name!" Martin yelled.

Some glitter got into his mouth and he started to sputter and cough.

Cottie silently stared at the glitter storm. She stood exactly far enough from Ember not to get attacked by her avatars.

"I didn't do nothing!" Alexa shook her head.

"Liar! This is all your fault!" Ember growled.

Alexa stepped closer to Ember, bravely looking right into her eyes. "Look, Warden Dumdum. I called the SCA for help. They, in their unquestionable wisdom, sent you to check on me! There's an escaping monster. Go catch him before he starts eating people or something. It's your job. Do your damn job." The villain pointed at the broken window.

"I'm not doing anything of the sort," Ember snarled, grabbing Alexa's arm. "In fact, I'm arresting you and taking you in for questioning. I've had enough of your asinine bullshit!"

A flickering refraction of Ember appeared in the air, snapping a pair of ghostly handcuffs to link Ember's arm to Alexa's. The real handcuffs vanished from Ember's side pocket, now appearing between her hand and Alexa's.

"You're making a *very* biiiiig mistake there, Warden," Alexa said sternly. "Last chance to leave me alone. Let me go and walk away now, or you'll lose *absolutely everything forever*!"

"Are you *threatening* me?" Ember hissed.

Cottie raised an eyebrow at the handcuffed pair. Ember didn't look like she was convinced by Alexa's threat.

"What? Are you going to interfere with me? Go ahead, you brainwashed twat!" Ember yelled. "I don't care if I get shot, you hear?! This shit ends now!!!" She pulled Alexa towards her, sending sparks of glitter flying all around.

"I have no intention of shooting you if you do not hurt her," Cottie said expressionlessly.

"Let her go, damn it! This isn't her fault!" Martin yelled. He thought about threatening Ember with the raygun, but then realized that at best he could menace her with a migraine.

"This is a nuthouse, not a school!" Ember groaned. "Martin, I need you to stop being a moron for just one minute."

"I'm not a moron!" Martin growled, his eyes flashing with silver sparks. He'd had enough of his sister bringing him down. The spider in his head was calculating the best place to attack Ember to bring her down, ready to direct his feet exactly where to strike.

"You are, because you don't know anything! She's a monster who killed her father, and I'm going to prove it!" Ember shook Alexa with the handcuffs.

"Whaaat? I'm cool and hip, definitely no monster-ness in me," Alexa objected. "My father is perfectly alive. I talked to him two days ago!"

Her bracelet beeped.

"Oh, for fuck's sake!" Martin swore, rushing towards Alexa.

"Cottie! Martin! Grab onto me, now!" Alexa ordered.

"What? What is this?!" Ember barked, hundreds of her avatars flickering into existence, shoving Martin away from Alexa.

Cottie pressed on the railgun trigger and the avatars vanished as quickly as they appeared, as colors drained from everything nearby. The other students stood with their mouths open, confused at what exactly was happening here.

"I don't need my power to break you, Equalizer!" Ember yelled.

Martin crashed into his sister, as her avatars holding him back suddenly vanished. Cottie made it across the six meters separating them just in the nick of time, grabbing at Alexa's hand as Ember's fist collided with her face.

Darkness fell.

"This is an unexpected foursome. Or a fifth-some? Hmm, you know what . . . I don't know the proper term for a group of five," Alexa muttered.

"Quintet," Cottie answered, still holding onto Alexa's hand. She was barely keeping herself together. She did not like what she saw.

"Let go of the gun trigger. Let her enjoy this properly," Alexa whispered to Cottie.

"Where the fuck are we?! What the fuck is going on?!" Ember yelled, trying to untangle herself from Martin. Her ghostly avatars came into existence once again around the four teens as Cottie released the trigger.

"Shut up! Shut the fuck up, you friggin idiot!" Martin yelled. "You don't know anything! You always jump to the quickest conclusion possible! Look! Look at where we are! Feel with your freaking avatars if you must! Go ahead!"

"What?! But this can't be real . . ." Ember muttered.

"Oh, but it is real! So very real!" Martin snarled. "Alexa's bracelet sends her four hundred years into the future!"

"No, no, no." Ember spun in a circle, ghostly avatars flickering all over, touching the ground, looking all around.

The information that they were sending into her head was impossible. Everything except for the four people was in ruin. The very air felt wrong, broken somehow. It had no life in it. It was chillingly cold and dead.

"What the fuck have you done?!" Ember turned to Alexa.

"Me? Oh. I didn't do anything. You couldn't possibly think that a fourteen-year-old girl could kill an entire planet worth of life, do you?" The silver-haired villain smiled softly.

"She didn't do nothing, you friggin nutter! This place is Earth, our future! She . . . oh . . . oh no." Martin's face fell, his silver-tinted eyes looking up.

"Martin? Tell us. What do you see?" Alexa prompted.

"I know . . . what happened here. I know why everyone is dead," Martin whispered, his voice shaking.

CHAPTER TWENTY-ONE

The Mote in God's Eye

O h . . . oh no," Martin uttered as he looked up.

His skinwalker-enhanced eyes could see perfectly in the darkness of the ruined gymnasium. The roof had long caved in, exposing the sky. Martin's new eyes allowed him to see past the motes of dust that were fogging up the atmosphere. He somehow saw past the broiling supercell storm, as if it wasn't there at all, as if it were just a layer that his mind could simply bypass. Martin realized that the little skinwalker in his brain was somehow now connected, becoming integrated into the greater network of other skinwalkers all around. He could see what they saw, feel what they felt, and thus his horizon of understanding, of perception, constantly expanded out and out.

Behind the storm, he saw something he had never expected to witness—the ruin of the ring of Titanomachy. Remnants of a segment of the great SCA superstructure jutted out of the earth, looming high over the ruins of Saint Mary.

Alexa prodded him for more information with a comment he could barely hear. Oh, she was asking what was going on.

"I know . . . what happened here. I know why everyone is dead," Martin whispered, immersed in the ever-expanding consciousness. "Titanomachy . . . it fell from the sky."

"*What?!*" Ember barked. Her avatars looked up, mouths open wide in horror.

"Welp, there goes my wizard theory," Alexa commented.

The ravaged segment of Titanomachy right above Martin was covered in leviathan, other-worldly things—spheres of white bone mesh with colossal black limbs stretching away from them.

Before, Martin had seen skinwalkers as alien, dark things, but now he could feel life and energy pulsating within them, dots of silver stardust intertwined, interconnected with webs of colorless light. The nests were made from the same stuff as the skinwalkers. Martin also saw multitudes of smaller creatures crawling all around the ruined station. Beneath the dark exoskeleton, they all looked like silver nebulae filled with glittering, shining stars. They acted akin to a million ants, laboring together with some great purpose.

The limbs in the sky were diligently moving back and forth, working without rest on building yet more similar spheres atop the shard of Titanomachy.

The more Martin saw, the better he understood, knew what they were, information flooding into his head translated from a deep, subconscious feeling that was emanating from the little skinwalker in his head. The skinwalker nests became bigger the higher they went, eventually becoming magnified a million times.

They were new life clinging to an otherwise dead planet!

His perspective expanded even further and suddenly flipped upside down. He was no longer standing on the ground; he now saw what the nests saw from up above—ruins of the ravaged planet. In the perception of the new, omnipresent life, he was but a tiny mote observed by something far greater than himself. Something terrible and vast that cared little for the tiny, insignificant speck of life inside Martin's head.

Through the uncountable number of eyes of this leviathan, interconnected organism, Martin could see a globe shattered by the fallen rings of Titanomachy. The SCA station was made from materials reinforced again and again by the supers. It was far tougher than anything found on Earth. When it had collided with the planet hundreds of years ago, it had carved it in twain, reduced mountains to dust, vaporized the oceans, and boiled the atmosphere. Parts of the world were now completely gone, obliterated, flung out into space.

Some sections of the ravaged planet looked *wrong,* were somehow stretched, twisted into some distant, incomprehensible beyond, connected to some *elsewhere.* These wrong, broken places terrified the skinwalkers, and they avoided them, refused to go there because truly dangerous things existed there, things that were a threat to the Terraforge GLM. Things that needed to be devoured, lest they infest this planet with their *wrongness.*

Some utterly microscopic, irrelevant bit of him was being bothered. Where was it? Martin's consciousness was lost, diluted by the endless multitude of minds of the prodigious life that held the shattered planet in its grasp.

"Martin! Martin!" Alexa's voice yelled at him. "What do you see? Tell me more, damn it!"

"The SCA has fallen . . ." Ember's voice trembled. "Titanomachy is no more? It can't . . . I don't . . . How?"

Martin blinked, disconnecting from the greater awareness of everything. "Huh?"

"What do they want?" Alexa shook Martin. "Tell me, damn it!!! Why do they keep murdering me?! Focus!"

[TERMINATE THREATS—CONSUME—UTILIZE—PROPAGATE]

A terrifying message, made not of words but of a scrambled, somewhat coherent idea poured into Spiderbro. Martin's human mind interpreted it as a command, a demand that was resonating back and forth across all of the skinwalkers.

"They . . . uhh . . . it wants . . . me to kill, to infect you . . . to make more of itself. It . . . the skinwalkers . . . they're not animals driven by instincts, they're all connected, working together for a single goal, trying to protect the remnants of the Earth from . . . something? They're all over the wreck of Titanomachy, all over the Earth! Multiply? Propagate? Why?!" Martin tried to articulate the jumble of demands in his head.

"No wonder they keep finding and murdering me. I can't compete with a goddamned planet-wide hivemind!" Alexa said.

[REPAIR—FIX—RENEW—REGENERATE—CONSUME—INTEGRATE—
MULTIPLY]

The bits of the multitude nearest to him responded, returning to the same repeating track that demanded replication and murder.

"Repair? Regenerate? Consume? Multiply? Huh?" Martin rubbed his aching head, not understanding.

His awareness jumped all over the ruins, all over the choir of want and need, finally settling on the gargantuan spheres of bone and alien flesh. They were breathing! Breathing in the poisoned, irradiated atmosphere and spewing out clear air. They were the source of the unending planet-wide supercell storm! They were the reason why the four humans could breathe here at all!

"They're . . . cleansing the atmosphere!" Martin proclaimed, heaving as he nearly lost himself once again.

He realized that he was now hastily trying to breathe in and out for purposes of recycling everything in the air, just like the billions of titanic, spherical lungs in the sky.

"Hrmmm . . . It sounds like they're trying to terraform the Earth and see us as a renewable resource. Do you mind telling them that we're cool and just wanna be friends?" Alexa elbowed Martin. "Think of friendship and magic or something. Positive first contact biz!"

Martin thought positive thoughts of friendship, of humanity, of first contact, but he was ignored. His skinwalker shard was far too small, too insignificant, too unimportant. It was just an amoeba in an ocean of the great omnipresent super-consciousness.

[INFECT—CONSUME—MULTIPLY]

Spiderbro sang back. It no longer had a determinate personality. It was but an infinitesimal singer dragged into repeating the unceasing choir.

Spiderbro tried to wield Martin's body to attack his friends, to claw out their eyes, to end them. They were just organic building blocks to be remade, recycled, cleansed alongside with the rest of the bacteria that once inhabited and ruled the Earth.

Terraforge did not see Martin of his friends as humans at all . . . for some reason, it failed to define Martin or the three girls beside him as people!

[Consume . . . Multiply . . . No. Stop that! Shut the hell up!] Martin snapped back, resisting the skinwalker shard, wielding control over it.

[REFUSAL?—BROKEN—FIND—TERMINATE / REINTEGRATE]

The voices of the choir nearest to Martin answered, skinwalkers around the city turning towards him. Several of the thousand-elbowed arms turned from their jobs in the sky, heading towards the ground to smite Martin.

"Shit, shit, shit!" Martin gasped. "They aren't listening! They saw me, us! They're coming to kill us all!"

"Oh, well. First contact pancake got burned. We'll try again next time . . . twice as hard!" Alexa sighed.

"Take us back! *Take us back now!*" Ember screamed at Alexa, grabbing at her.

"Nopers. It doesn't work like that. I don't control the time jumps. Welcome to 2424. Try not to die!" Alexa winked at the golden-eyed hero.

CHAPTER TWENTY-TWO

Desperation

'll murder you!!!" Ember screeched, shaking Alexa. A hundred off-color ghostly arms reached out towards the villain.

"Stop. Cooperate. *Now*." The Equalizer pressed her railgun against Ember's head, her finger on the trigger.

Ember growled as a response, her avatars retreating.

"I do believe it's in our best interests to work together, hero." Alexa said. "How would you get back if you kill me, hrmmmm?"

"Fffffffinggg fineeee!" Martin's sister hissed, letting go of Alexa. A perimeter of ghosts formed a constantly moving circle, a river of green-and-blue flickers around the group of humans.

"That's the spirit! You can always murderize me later! We'll be bestest friends till then!" Alexa hugged Ember with half an arm, the other still handcuffed to the hero.

"Hey, Resonance. If the space elevators and the orbital rings fell from the sky, then how is the town of Saint Mary still intact?" Cottie asked, trying to distract the extremely agitated hero from Alexa's antics.

"What? Um." Ember looked at the Equalizer. "The SCA-designed catastrophe-barrier, fusion-reactor-powered shields, activate in every town or city downtown with a big enough population during an emergency situation. We're always ready for villains and their dumbass acid hail or piranha-tornado bullshit. The shields must have held while the world burned, but even they eventually failed, from what I can see."

"Ah, yes. A shield for every hero's Earth-based residence. Gotta protect them precious heroes." Alexa grinned.

"Alexa, would you do me a favor and please stop agitating my sister?" Martin said. "Guys, we have to move, *now*. I've blinded my shard, so it won't report back."

Ember looked at Martin. "You know things," she stuttered. "How do you know all of these things? What shard? . . . Wait. Your eyes are glowing silver . . . Are you awake?!"

Martin nodded back at her.

"*What?!*" Ember gasped.

"You wanted this, did you not?" Martin asked.

"I . . . uh . . ." she uttered. "I wanted you to be a hero, sure . . . but not now! You're too young, damn it!"

"Complain about it bloody later, okay?" Martin growled. "Take the handcuffs off Alexa, it will interfere with our escape!"

Ember blinked.

"For fuck's sake! *Cottie!* Shoot the handcuffs! *Now!*" Martin snapped at the Equalizer. Unlike the others, he could feel the swiftly approaching doom coming from the sky.

Cottie aimed the railgun at the handcuffs and fired, shattering the links before Ember even made a move for the keys.

"Run! Run! *Now! Out of the building!*" Martin grabbed Alexa's hand and pulled her towards the nearest hole in the wall that had the fewest skinwalkers present in the area.

"Aww! My little hero's all grown up and bossing people around. How lovely!" Alexa smiled.

Just as the quartet of humans rushed out of the decrepit building, gargantuan limbs emerged from the storm clouds overhead, smashing into the remnants of the school, pulverizing the gymnasium in a detonation of ancient rubble, sending shrapnel fragments all around.

Several brick and steel pieces flew right into the group. They froze in midair before they sliced through any of them, caught by several of Ember's avatars. She paled as she saw the multi-elbowed arms through the eyes of her ghosts.

"What the fuck are those arm things?!" Ember cried, for the first time in her life truly afraid of death. "I can't stop something that big with my avatars!"

"Those're the hands of the *builders*," Martin said.

"They sure ain't doing no building right now. More . . . eehh . . . demolishers than any-thing," Alexa added.

Cottie, switching something on her gun so that it wouldn't disrupt Ember's avatars, turned to the side and fired Eva into the darkness. The railgun lit up the street ruins with a flash, cutting through a three-meter-sized skinwalker that was in the process of advancing towards them. The beast toppled over, punched back by the supersonic bullet. It started to howl as it fell, despite not having a mouth, instead somehow rubbing together its joints to produce the horrid sound. Others joined in, announcing themselves.

"Shut up! Will you all shut up!" Martin yelled, realizing that even if he now knew what the skinwalkers were, he couldn't do anything about them, couldn't stop the tide of monsters heading towards them. His power was only able to control the little shard in his head; it didn't seem to apply to any of the other abominations. "We are not prey!"

Cottie fired again, flinging another skinwalker backwards.

"They're coming! There's too many of them, and they won't listen!" Martin turned to Alexa. "What do I do?!"

"Hrm? Oh, I dunno." Alexa shrugged.

"Come on! You always have an answer! You planned this all!"

"Did I, really?" Alexa bit her lip, seemingly pouting. "Give me like five minutes to think it over, 'kay?"

"We don't have five minutes! They're coming!" Martin yelped, his voice drowned by Cottie's repeating gunfire.

"Hrm. Promise to bring them a million cows wrapped up with nice red gift bows if they don't slaughter us now?" Alexa suggested, not sounding too sure of her idea. "Maybe green bows? Ask them what their favorite color is!"

A ring of endless Ember-shaped ghosts rushed all around the four teenagers, looking like a half-sphere of constantly shifting aurora borealis. From the vantage point of the skinwalkers, it looked like a sphere of brilliant light that was somehow constantly knocking them away, keeping them away from their prey.

Hero Resonance never had to push herself so much in her entire life. Two years as an Academy novitiate and a few months as a licensed hero did nothing to prepare her for this awful nightmare. Being an agent was about hiding in plain sight and infiltration, not about using brute strength to the point of exhaustion. She wasn't a tank!

Sure, there were fighting simulations at the Hero Academy such as being shot by tennis balls, bullets, and lasers from all directions, but this . . . this was nothing like that. This was far more challenging than trying to stop incoming machine gun fire. These long-limbed monstrosities were seemingly invincible, varied in shape and speed, could stretch at will, and just kept on increasing in numbers like cockroaches.

She might have done something more if she'd been dressed in her power armor, but she was wearing gym clothes of all things! She expected to mentally dismantle a fourteen-year-old supervillain with no known physical powers and possibly counsel or influence a retired super gym teacher to pull him out of whatever depression he was going through, not fight a thousand unkillable monsters amidst the post-apocalyptic ruins of Saint Mary!

The Equalizer's terrifying gun punched holes in the monsters, but did not put them down. They simply shrugged, slowly stood up, and attacked again, holes and all. It was as if these damned things had no blood, no vital organs to damage.

Ember was beginning to break down; she had never had to face so many powerful enemies all at once, coming from every direction. Her power couldn't kill, couldn't end these monsters! She broke their limbs, and they simply used other limbs or switched joints! These things felt no pain, had no fear of her! She was only able to fling them away. Soon enough, each new action, each new ghostly copy, started to take something from her, chipping at her resolve, draining her strength.

The carousel of a thousand Embers started to flicker.

Just three minutes of this unending hell left her panting, her face dripping with sweat, her eyes bloodshot red and covered in bursting capillaries. By the fourth minute, she started to weep softly, knowing that she was about to break, but unable to stop. She had to defend her brother from these things!

She had to survive! She had graduated at the top of her class; she was always the strongest, the most capable, and felt that she was an invincible, all-powerful goddess within her circle of five meters' space! She was a genius who was going to lead the Superstate one day!

The dead city of monsters had shattered this illusion of personal might, reducing her to a mere terrified, desperate, mortal girl.

"I can't do this anymore! I can't keep this up! There're too many! I'm sorry!" she cried, swaying and nearly falling over.

Cottie stepped over to Ember and held her up. The sky limbs had finished their demolition of the gymnasium, and now turned towards the group.

CHAPTER TWENTY-THREE

Kisses

E ureka! I've got it!" Alexa finally announced, grabbing Martin's face. "Kiss me!"

"What?!" both Martin and Ember yelled at the same time, eyes bulging in shock at her declaration.

"Break a bit off your brain spider and feed it to me!"

"What brain spider?! What the fuck?!" Ember yelled.

"Shhh. You're delusional from making too many copies of yourself. There are no brain spiders in Martin," Alexa said.

"You put brain spiders into my brother?!" Ember screamed. "I'll fucking kill you, I swear!!!!!" The carousel of Ember-ghosts around them started to break apart further, leaving gaps.

Martin understood. If they all had skinwalker shards within them, maybe the other skinwalkers would stop seeing them all as targets to be cleansed. He closed his eyes, focusing inward on his Spiderbro shard, disconnecting a bit of the skinwalker.

Terraforge seed self-replication initiated.

Martin saw a flickering notice flash in his right eye.

"Is it ready? Let Cottie know if you can't control it while it's inside me, so she can shoot me in the head!" Alexa yelled, leaning towards Martin's mouth.

"Noooooooooooo! Somebody stop her! God!" Ember wailed, held back by Cottie.

This was not happening! Her brother did not just kiss a goddamned supervillain! Ember had no strength left to fight off the Equalizer, no choice but to keep up the endless shield of her copies all around them, lest the abominable monsters break through and end her and Martin.

Contrary to what Ember must have imagined as she was looking at the world through burning, tear-streaked eyes, Alexa did not kiss Martin. She merely leaned close to his face and opened her mouth like a fish. Martin opened his mouth in turn, and a smaller copy of Spiderbro leapt from his tongue into Alexa's palate, quickly carving a path towards her brain.

Only some distant part of Martin's mind was paying attention to Ember's ridiculous screaming, as most of his brain was preoccupied with controlling two spiders and carving two more shards out of Spiderbro, imbuing them with consciousness and limbs.

"Ehhhhhrhhh!" Alexa yelped. "This tickles something unwholesome! No stabby the important brain-bits please! Welcome to my brain, Spidersis! I'ma call you Tickles!"

Martin sighed in relief. He could still control the tiny skinwalker in Alexa's brain.

"Your turn for a kiss of doom! Get your brainspooder while supplies last!" Alexa shoved Cottie at Martin, grabbing Ember in her stead.

"You are a monster! You've set all of this up!" Ember wept, blearily watching as the Equalizer seemingly kissed her brother. She had no strength left to hold herself up. Her avatars could barely see now.

Her power had already reached past its limits and was now draining life from her body. Inner light began to fade from her golden eyes. Her orange hair dimmed to a mundane red color.

"Okay, now you!" Alexa shoved Ember towards her brother.

In that moment, Ember's power ran out with a snap of something tearing inside her. An explosion of sparkling fractal fire detonated in her head and she fainted upon seeing her brother's opening mouth, the shield of shimmering bodies protecting them flickering out of existence.

Alexa watched as the final spider leapt into Ember's open mouth as she fainted.

"*Think! Repeat after me! Unity! Acceptance! Infect! Consume! Multiply! Propagate!*" Alexa yelled.

". . . consume, multiply, propagate," Cottie droned.

". . . multiply, propagate," Martin repeated, holding his passed-out sister and thinking the same thing with all of his spider children.

Yep, Spiderbro was a mother now.

[Wait, no,] Martin thought. [Focus. Propagate. Multiply!]

The gargantuan hands coming from the sky froze right above them, moving slightly up and down in seeming contemplation.

One of Ember's tear-streaked eyes opened. ". . . *propagate*," she muttered with a hissy rumble.

Martin felt awful about puppeteering his passed-out sister like that, felt that he was turning into a monster himself, yet he could not stop.

He had to keep the mad charade going! Had to pretend to be one of them to survive. Controlling four brain spiders was giving him a crazy migraine, making him feel he was going to throw up, pushing his newly acquired mind-control power to its limits.

The mob of black, glistening monsters slowed just as they were about to strike down the humans with their jagged, sharp limbs.

[Propagate. Multiply.]

Spiderbro and his three children sang, joining the endless chorus that resonated across the dead planet. The multitude of abominations began to part, smaller ones skittering away.

Martin exhaled. He'd done it! He'd saved them all!

Thumps of enormous legs resounded in the distance, across the desolate roadside. Martin raised his eyes. It was the gargantuan skinwalker, Mr. Noodles.

A shawl of human skins rasped as it moved.

Martin suddenly felt, knew, that all he wanted was to peel off their flesh. It was somehow off, not just bigger and stronger but clearer in its wants, its song discordant.

Why? How?

Martin tried to look inside Mr. Noodles, past his exoskeleton. He saw his nebulous construct, filled with a myriad of twinkling silver stars. The stars in the center of his head were tinted with shades of red! It was different! Martin panicked.

[Give me their skins, little one,] Mr. Noodles sang into Martin's mind, drawing closer, his voice becoming far clearer.

[*Mine!*] Martin answered, via Spiderbro. [*Propagate. Multiply.*]

[Give it to me. I desire its flesh.]

"Oh, sheeeet. It's the skin-tax collector, and he doesn't take no for an answer," Alexa muttered, her eyes filling with panic.

[I will take what I want.] Mr. Noodles extended a limb, about to strike Martin down.

[*No.* Mine! I use what is mine!] Martin sang, trying to make the big skinwalker leave them alone.

He made Cottie raise her gun, aiming for the spot of colors in Mr. Noodles's head. Cottie fired Eva, the gun punching through the head of the enormous monstrosity. Mr. Noodles swayed. The shot had taken some of the colors from his head, but it was only temporary. Other stars in his head became tinted red, as he reorganized his thoughts towards the same desire.

[Give. Me. That. Flesh.]

Alexa pulled Martin and Ember under Cottie's cloak.

"What are you doing?" Martin hissed.

"Hiding," Alexa whispered. "I'm friggin scared. This asshat takes what he wants. Guns don't stop him!"

"What?" Martin groaned, making Cottie fire her gun at the source of the prevalent skin-taking thought in Mr. Noodles.

"Where's that damn invisi-button, C?!" Alexa growled.

"What button? What?!" Martin looked at her, confused.

"I cannot press it. My arms won't obey!" Cottie spoke, her voice shaking.

"M! Let go of C for a minute!" Alexa smacked Martin.

Martin stopped his control of Cottie's arms, and she pulled a gray meshed hood over her face, reached into her clothes, and pressed something within. Martin heard a deep hum within the Equalizer's power armor. It sounded like a miniature fusion battery.

Through the eyes of the skinwalker crowd still surrounding them, Martin saw Cottie. She looked ridiculous. A large gray hood was covering her face, cloak bulging with the figures of the four humans inside it. The cloak suddenly flashed a multitude of colors, and Cottie vanished from sight. Completely. As if she had never existed at all.

Martin's mouth flopped open.

The Equalizer Enforcers had super-designed invisibility cloaks! That was how they had snuck up on supervillains! It all made sense now. Martin couldn't even remember where exactly she'd stood previously. The cloak was doing something screwy with the act of perception itself, erasing information about it and whatever it had covered up out of the universe.

[Where are my skins?] Mr. Noodles complained. [Give me back my skins and flesh tasties!]

The limb that was reaching out to Martin struck down the nearest skinwalker in agitation.

Martin glanced at Alexa, who was clinging to Cottie beneath the cloak. She was shivering ever so slightly, clearly terrified of the big, independent skinwalker. She didn't like being so close to Mr. Noodles. He was an aberration that wanted to skin people, not just use them as a resource for the endless process of self-replication. If Cottie had an invisibility cloak all this time, then why hadn't they used it earlier?

[Uhh . . . I didn't know if it worked against these things, sorry,] Cottie thought.

[Your cloak tech works the same way as the SCA bank's hypno-pacifier system,] Alexa responded in thought. [Number one and moi tested confuddling an entire nest of skinwalkers in a bank recently! Right, M?]

[Wait . . . What the hell? I can hear you!] Martin responded.

[We can all hear each other's direct thoughts, you dummy. We got the same brain-spooder brand walkie-talkie.] Alexa's thought cut into Martin's mind.

[Oh my God, they can hear my thoughts. What have I done? Why have I done this?] Martin thought. [Does she know . . .]

[Stop thinking so loud, or you'll blow a spider,] Alexa broadcasted back. [And no need to worry; I already know everything about everything!]

[Oh my God, she knows everything! Why did I give her my brain spiders?] Martin's face turned red.

Alexa started to giggle deviously in her head. Martin scrambled to mute his thoughts to stop broadcasting them out to the girls before he thought something dumb or extremely embarrassing.

He knew that he could easily control Alexa now, but he felt that she was the one puppeteering him with her social hacking bullshit. If she knew that Cottie's cloak could hide them, why didn't she just ask Cottie to become invisible right away?

Was it part of her sinister plan to make Martin give her and the others brain spiders? Did she depower, break down, his sister on purpose?!

Martin stumbled over his own thoughts, trying to second-guess Alexa's motives and absurd plots.

[Where are you, you little shard? I can hear you but I cannot see you! Come out and give me their skins!] Mr. Noodles insisted.

CHAPTER TWENTY-FOUR

Bound by Strings of Control

Mr. Noodles wailed about human skins and delicious meats, angrily flailing gargantuan limbs. The smaller skinwalkers wisely chose to depart, rather than get pulverized by the thrashing, serrated appendages of the persistent giant.

[We better move before he makes pepperoni out of us.] Alexa poked Martin, drawing him out of his thought-management paralysis. [The invisi-cloak might have hid us from his perception, but it won't protect us from becoming pizza via collateral damage!]

In that very instant, one of the titanic limbs struck a nearby ruin and it began to topple down onto the group. Martin's perception split. He saw Alexa's dark face in front of himself and the falling building through Cottie's eyes. A jagged steel beam was heading right for her head.

Martin dove into his power and took total control of all four bodies in that instant. The four teenagers moved like a single organism, in near perfect synchronicity, narrowly avoiding the beam and stepping into a broken window as the wall fell atop them.

[Impressive coordination, Mittens!] Alexa praised. [Keep it up! I like being alive!]

Using mental threads of the brain spiders, Martin coordinated all four humans to quickly move away from the giant skinwalker while keeping everyone together, constantly, perfectly positioned under Cottie's invisibility cloak. This would have been utterly impossible to achieve had they acted as individuals.

As the four-human amalgamation escaped the smiting limbs of Mr. Noodles, Martin started to feel mentally drained. Control of four people was a very tiresome job. If he added any more, his power would probably burn out just like Ember's.

[Head back to your house,] Alexa specified, wincing as Mr. Noodles continued to loudly topple and decimate buildings somewhere behind them.

[Why?] Martin asked.

[Dinner! Also, we can maybe drop your sister off at home, because she's an uncooperative butt. She couldn't even catch and examine one gym teacher as her SCA mission briefing required! For shame. Zero out of five stars. Would not hire again!]

[Right. Why didn't you tell me earlier that you hired her?] Martin sighed mentally.

[I didn't personally hire her! The SCA did. They generally go by the nearest agent with the highest aptitude score. Ember had the highest recorded grades in the Academy and a perfect mission success rate.]

[Hmm. I see,] Martin replied. [I didn't know my sister was such a tryhard.]

[You don't have to try as hard if you can just make a thousand copies of yourself, live out a thousand extra lives.] Alexa noted. [Now, how would you rate her sister-ness?]

[Not very high. Wait, why am I rating her?]

[I bet she wanted you to be more successful . . . more like her.] Alexa glanced at the mind-controlled body of Ember. [I always wanted a big sister, you see. I think I'll take her off your hands.]

[What? How?]

[Minion numero tres.] Alexa smirked.

[Are you for real?] Martin demanded.

[I'm very for real,] Alexa affirmed.

[Why so many secrets and lies? When are you going to stop misleading me?]

[After the Superstate falls,] she explained.

Martin sighed. Alexa was humming to herself mentally and thinking about something green.

The longer Martin controlled the bodies of the three girls, the more he inadvertently learned about them through their mutual connection. Most of what he learned he didn't want to know.

He didn't want to be a puppeteer, didn't want to know people's personal thoughts, didn't want to dominate anyone in this manner! Alas, he had no idea how to mute their thoughts while he was controlling them.

Ember was still passed out and her superpower felt completely fried, gone. Her fractal web was dim, just like his once was. Her power was no longer awake, impossible to access. Martin feared an inevitable time when she came to and realized that she was no longer a superhero, just a girl with potential for being one. Would she be stuck forever as a mundane human? What new power would she gain if any? Would she have to go through the Academy again? Martin didn't know the answers. He knew that heroes could burn out, but they generally got killed by their enemies when it happened.

The worst, most embarrassing thing was that Martin knew what Ember was dreaming about. He couldn't turn off the flow of information from her mind, lest he lose control of her body. Ember's nightmares featured flashes of Alexa making out with Martin as Ember rushed to save him but kept getting held back by some kind of an impediment. A bubble of slowed-down time, a sudden fence, a gust of storm wind, a rushing river, legs that refused to work, a crowd of old people, a flock of birds, etc. The same nightmare scenarios repeated over and over in her head, some featuring Cottie as the impediment.

Cottie, on the other hand, had no dim fractal web in her head. She was just a human girl. The terrifying Enforcer had no power to lean on, no possibility for an awakening. Martin was truly impressed with her now. Her body responded faster, easier than the others. She was very fit, as fit as a fourteen-year-old could get had they chosen to discard their humanity, given up their childhood, to become some kind of a gun-ninja. Martin realized that it was easy to control her because she was trained to obey.

Occasionally, Cottie's mind flashed with images of her memories of the Equalizer compound located somewhere high up in the mountains.

Ten thousand gray-robed child-soldiers moved in the perfect synchronicity of a strange, repeating dance, beneath the azure glaciers. Kick, sit, twist, up, up, down, down, left, right, left, right.

It was the most incredible thing Martin had seen in his entire life. He knew that all of these children were trained to eventually go out into the world to observe villains and heroes. They were ready to strike down any super who was about to stray too far with their power, to end them before they turned against humanity.

The Equalizers had incredible unity in their silent dance. Martin had experienced the Temple Compound of Eminence Equality as if he himself had attended their training. But why? Why were they so dedicated?

Another memory flashed in her head as the answer. It was seemingly stitched from various recordings of the event, perfectly fused by Cottie's mental strength.

Martin saw a city in flames and a man made of fire laughing in the dusky smoke-streaked sky. The burning man was igniting police cars with rays of fire. *A villain.* A girl who looked as if she was made of blue ice flew into the villain, trying to take him down. *A hero.*

Their bodies entwined as they collided, and the world warped with a blinding flash. A mushroom cloud rose, vaporizing everything in sight, toppling skyscrapers and leaving shadows on walls where people once stood.

Martin saw a little girl with deep blue hair and emerald eyes in a sky-blue dress who was hiding out in a bath filled with water for many hours. She breathed through a metal straw while everyone and everything around burned, turned into ashes as a cascade of power resonance rippled through the devastated city again and again until both the hero and the villain were no more.

He understood Cottie!

The Equalizers had become carriers of void weapons of their own volition. They were all children orphaned by super-caused disasters! Many of the Equalizer acolytes had nothing left but passionate animosity for the careless supers who took everything from them. They were humanity, united with purpose to hold back what they saw as walking disasters.

Last but not least, Alexa was the hardest to manage. Martin wasn't sure if he was controlling her at all. Her movement and thoughts were incredibly erratic, mind constantly flashing with odd ideas or jokes. Somehow, she had piggybacked on the skinwalker communication system, seeing what Cottie saw.

Alexa had a name and a narrative for every rock, house, and skinwalker in 2424. Martin could not even tell if she was an awake super, as her brain spider Tickles was constantly bogged down with trying to process an endless, illogical story that had no beginning or end.

In Alexa's universe of wild imagination, everything was alive, everything had feelings. It was a beautiful, ridiculous, abstract absurdity. Unlike Cottie, Alexa treated her brain spider like a best friend and a one-way conversation companion. Martin tried to listen to her story and found himself immediately lost.

[See that traffic light over there, Tickles?] Alexa thought. [Her name is *Matilda Wickers Trafficlight*. Matilda helps people by being a good traffic manager. She is always soooo incredibly busy managing traffic, so she never has any time to herself. None whatsoever! Matilda doesn't want to admit something very important. She has a very big secret that separates her from other traffic lights. She is actually in love with a wasteland wraith named Dixon Joulers. Someday they'll go on a date in a coffee shop, served by the last man in the world and . . .]

Martin really was hoping to find out if Alexa liked him or what sinister, villainous plots she was concocting, but *no*. He learned that the West-North wind was called Bob Dockler, who was just trying to make it home for lunch, and that Mr. Noodles was a pizza restaurant owner in his past life who made the best fettuccine Alfredo in town.

This waterfall of utter nonsense just kept coming until Martin completely stopped paying attention to Alexa's thought channel. He simply had no patience left for listening to her gibberish.

While trying to tune her out completely, he accidentally dove deeper into her subconsciousness and found nothing at all there, except for an empty, dark, unfriendly nothingness that seemed to stare back at him, trying to evaluate, label, and sort him out as if he was just a *handy tool*, a useful device of some sort.

The nothingness peered at Martin without eyes, observed all of him all at once and *found him wanting*.

Martin mentally backpedaled away from the *infinite nothingness*, retreating as far away from what he saw as possible, trying not to think about it.

CHAPTER TWENTY-FIVE

Streets without an End

All in all, with all that extra brain spider power, Martin managed to learn nothing about Alexa that he didn't already know.

She was a quirky girl with a dark side who liked to use people for greater goals.

Martin wondered why he put up with Alexa and settled on the fact that he didn't mind being used by her. He had a lot of feelings to unpack and had no room whatsoever to unpack them or to even be angry at Alexa's shenanigans. Being with Alexa was akin to being trapped on a rapidly spinning unicorn carousel that was sitting atop a burning train that was strapped to a jet engine. There just wasn't enough time for him to make a move, while it felt as if Alexa made twenty moves when he blinked.

Martin wasn't sure how much time had passed with them crouching together and walking as one across the ruins of tomorrow. The road back to his house wasn't easy. The way was covered in numerous obstructions such as broken rubble, fallen buildings, deep chasms, and random curious skinwalkers who sensed Martin's presence but could not see him or his companions.

As the teenage hero's mind jumped across the skinwalker GLM Terraforge network, he observed strange, impossible things all around that he hadn't noticed previously with his human eyes alone.

Some of the streets of Saint Mary weren't simply filled with rubble—they were *wrong, had no end to them.* There were areas in 2424 that even the gargantuan Terraforge organism had trouble mapping or navigating, places where time and space was broken, twisted up into pretzels and other impossible shapes.

Martin wondered whether some super had made this mess when they tried to escape from the apocalyptic destruction of Titanomachy.

However, the more attention he paid to his surroundings, the more *wrongness* he discovered. It wasn't enough that some building interiors or streets were somehow stretched . . . there were *things* moving within the screwed up space.

Things that made no sense.

As the four teens passed beneath the Equalizer cloak by one of the stretched streets, Martin glimpsed a monstrous thing there—a fusion of a traffic light and a rust-covered spider.

The thing was shambling across a desolate landscape covered in glaciers, its trio of lights flashing through the gloom.

Martin choked, almost losing control of the group and stumbling over his feet as the spindly traffic light's head turned towards him, a red lamp peering in his direction.

[Don't worry, Matilda won't hurt you,] Alexa commented when she sensed his terror and panic. [She's a sweetheart. Also, I recommend not looking directly at Main Street unless you want your mind to shatter.]

[I . . . okay.] Martin lowered his eyes and the walking traffic light vanished in the gloom. Silence stretched on between them.

[How did you . . . ?] Martin asked.

[I spent a long time here, M,] Alexa sighed. [A very, *very* long time.]

[How long?] Martin asked.

[You don't want to know,] Alexa said.

[Why?]

[Because there are horrors far beyond human comprehension in places where even Mr. Noodles dreads visiting, M,] Alexa explained.

[What could a bloody skyscraper-sized skinwalker be afraid of?] Martin demanded. [What aren't you telling me about?!]

[Everything,] Alexa sighed mentally. [Everything everywhere.]

[Huh? Why won't you tell me about everything . . .] Martin began.

[You're not ready,] Alexa said simply. [Nobody is. There are things here in 2424 . . . things that . . .]

[Things that?]

[. . .] Alexa somehow generated pure mental silence. The silence had immeasurable mental weight to it, pressed against Martin's mind.

[Did you feel that?] Alexa said.

[Yeah.] Martin nodded. [How did you do that?]

[Think in silence? You'd learn to think in silence, too . . . if you knew what was out there,] Alexa muttered. [I called our group the fellowship of the Loops, not because I like to joke about breakfast cereal . . . but because I've been trapped in far too many temporal loops, M.]

[I thought that everyone here is dead?] Martin frowned. [Who or what makes temporal loops in 2424?]

[Sorry . . . I can't speak or even think of *them*,] Alexa said. [Certain *words, ideas* are . . . dangerous here.]

[What?!] Martin blinked.

[If you don't think, don't talk, don't know . . . about them, you can't summon *them*.] Alexa shook her head.

[REPLICATE. MULTIPLY. DEFEND. CONSUME. PROPAGATE.]

A large group of skinwalkers distracted Martin's attention away from pestering Alexa further. Martin sang at them about propagation and multiplication, and they went on their way.

Alexa's bracelet finally beeped, and Martin finally stopped puppeteering everyone, feeling incredibly relieved.

Alexa bent down to grab a broken street sign and then hugged the trio, flashing the group to the present.

* * *

Martin sat on the grass, panting. His head was spinning. He wasn't sure if he was himself anymore, his thoughts overcrowded with un-Martin memories, ideas, and feelings that he'd experienced through Ember, Cottie, and Alexa.

[So. Ummm. Yeah.] Cottie sat down next to him. [I'm sorry you had to see all of that.]

"See what?" Martin asked.

[My memories.] Cottie blushed ever so slightly.

[Oh . . . right,] he nodded. [I saw the Equalizer compound in your head. I'm sorry. I didn't want to . . .]

[It's okay,] Cottie said. [I feel . . . that you understand me better now. Thank you for helping us survive out there, in 2424. I . . . as strong as I am, the future is wrong, broken in ways I've never seen.] Cottie hugged Martin, thinking how Martin was her *first real friend* . . .

Martin finally broke down.

He cried for Cottie's lost family, for every child who lost everything because of careless supers, wept for every Equalizer acolyte that had to forsake their humanity in order to become strong enough to wield void weapons, so that other cities would remain standing, so that others could live out their lives in peace.

He cried because no matter how much Equalizers tried to save the world, they had somehow failed, hadn't prevented Titanomachy from falling from the sky and shattering the Earth.

Alexa glomped them both from behind. "Mwa ha ha ha! Behold the incredible power of the brain spider threads as a bonding device!"

Martin angrily looked at Alexa, and Cottie smacked her.

"Ow! Oh no! Quadruple mutiny! I've bonded you two too hard!" she complained, rubbing her head.

Saint Mary's Cathedral loomed ahead of the trio as they sat on the lawn of the park in front of the church. Sunlight reflected from its stained glass windows flickered on the wildly strewn poppies that were growing beneath oak trees.

Ember was twitching ever so slightly on the grass, dreaming of horrible Alexa-related things. Everyone ignored her.

Another orange SCA delivery drone came down from the sky, bearing a large box with the New Tokyo Planet-View Sushi restaurant logo on it.

"How are you doing that?" Martin looked at Alexa.

"It's called planning ahead, Mittens. You should try it sometime." She shrugged, swiping a credit card at the drone.

"That's an SCA delivery drone! Planet-View restaurant . . . you're ordering meals straight from Titanomachy! How?! You're not a hero!" Martin grabbed the credit card from Alexa's hand and looked at it.

It was an SCA gold credit card.

The name *Hero Resonance* was embossed on its surface.

"Did you steal my sister's credit card?!" Martin gasped at Alexa.

"What? Her mission is to observe me. These are normal mission expenses. Perfectly deductible stuff. She's not using it, because she's Dixie-whatever now! Full character immersion, you see. Very impressive stuff." Alexa pointed at drooling Ember. "See? She doesn't even have any powers now. She's a perfectly mundane human girl who can only dream about Planet-View Sushi!"

Martin rubbed his head. "I see."

He handed the card back to Alexa. He felt that Ember had finally gotten what she deserved. Maybe this would teach her a lesson.

[She seems to have issues with anger management. I should teach her Equalizer meditation techniques,] Cottie thought at them, looking down at Ember.

"Probably wouldn't help," Martin sighed. "She's gone beast mode on me ever since she gained her powers."

"Oh?" Alexa looked at Martin. "You know, I thought that you would be angry with me for depowering your sis."

"She's . . . accidentally hurt me pretty badly a few times and rewound the damage, pretended that nothing was wrong," Martin sighed, rubbing the back of his head. "My parents didn't believe me. Everyone always takes Ember's side . . . because they think that she's *perfect*."

"Well, that's not a problem anymore, is it?" Alexa smiled. "She's all powered out, poor kitten."

[It was an impressive way to bring down a super,] Cottie commented.

"A nice break will do her good, I reckon." Alexa petted Ember. "Constantly making duplicates and ending them can't be good for your psyche. If you think about it, every duplicate she made had to deal with the fact that it is temporary, doomed to cease existing once its job is done. Learning to end yourself on purpose must have sucked."

[Agreed. I've reviewed her public records. She was heading down a *very* dark path. Being able to break anything and undo any action clearly had a very negative impact on personal development. It is dangerous to play God.]

"Shit. I think I'm beginning to feel sorry for Ember. Damn . . . Wait, you know you can talk, right?" Martin glanced at Cottie.

[I can, but this is much more efficient. Thought-conversations are faster, can express things visually, and use up far less of my valuable personal energy.]

A picture of a pink blossom tree facing a valley of glaciers that cascaded down as waterfalls flashed in Martin's head from the direction of Cottie, blessing him with a feeling of grace and serenity.

"Can't argue with your logic." He shrugged, losing himself in the view of Cottie's memory.

He realized that until now he was constantly missing, wanting the feeling of serenity that the bank defense system gave him. The hypno-pacifier was dangerously addictive!

"Damn it! I've made her more like a robot! She wasn't very talkative before, and now she'll never talk like a normal person!" Alexa complained. "But then again, this screensaver memory panorama is really nice and relaxing. Is this in Tibet or . . . ?"

[I'll never tell.] A picture of Cottie flashed into their minds. The mental projection of Cottie was smiling ever so slightly and looking smug.

"Yes!" Alexa clapped. "Cotes can emote mentally! I've cracked the Equalizer code, give me praises!"

CHAPTER TWENTY-SIX

The Admiral of Nevermore

Ember woke up from her horrid nightmares with a whimper, her entire body aching, feeling incredibly tense as if she'd managed to strain every single muscle in her body. This was an unbearable feeling. She wanted the pain to stop, to adjust her own muscles into a relaxed state with one of her own avatars. She tried to summon an avatar into being, and nothing happened.

Argh.

She rolled over and looked down at herself. She was covered in dirt, dust, and black grime as if she'd been crawling through post-apocalyptic ruins for hours. She tried to summon an avatar to clean herself up. It didn't work.

Oh.

She suddenly remembered the horrible hell-world of the future and paled, nearly throwing up.

It wasn't a dream! It had all happened to her!

Receiving a report about Alexa and Martin from local retired super Mr. Canard and then another anonymous report about the gym teacher being mind-controlled by an alien monster. Getting her academy friends together, combining her own and their powers to erase four years from her own body, to become a fake student in Saint Mary Middle School. Going to Martin's school as an undercover agent. Handcuffing Alexa after Mr. Canard ran away for some reason. Getting thrown four hundred years into the future, fighting unkillable abominations to the point of fainting.

Ember looked up at the quite normal-looking sky and saw rain clouds coming above the trees and tinting the world in blue tones. Leaves fluttered in the wind above her. Tiniest raindrops started to fall on her.

She was back to the present. She was alive. She didn't die in the apocalyptic future.

"There will come soft rains . . ." she whispered, referencing a book that one of her copies read long ago. Ember hugged herself, and started to whimper.

She had seen the end of humanity in person, the end of the almighty SCA, the fall of Titanomachy.

How could all of the prognosticators fail to prevent such a horrific disaster? How could somebody like Nonpareil be stopped? How could humanity be extinguished? How could everything she believed in fall to ruin?

She didn't understand, had no answers to these questions, and it hurt her immensely. The things she had considered immutable—the Superstate, Titanomachy, *her* own power . . . all failed, betrayed her expectations.

"Hey." Martin's voice brought Ember back into the present.

She turned her head towards her brother, remembering how he was in cahoots with a villain now, having betrayed her for a girl.

"Why? Why did you do it?" she croaked. [Why did you kiss that white-haired monster?]

"Um. We didn't kiss." Martin's face turned red. "And Alexa isn't a monster. She's simply . . . different."

"Wait. What is happening?" Ember blinked. [Did I say that out loud? What the fuck?! Am I going crazy?!]

"No Ember, you're not going crazy." Martin rubbed his head.

"Break it to her gently!" Alexa yelled from somewhere nearby. Ember ground her teeth at that voice. She tried to form an avatar to attack Alexa. It didn't work.

"I don't know how to put this . . . uhhh . . . I don't know if you remember. I'm . . . uhhh . . . awake."

Ember remembered Martin's silver-sparkling eyes. She blinked at him in an understanding. "You're awake! Ohhhhh . . . You can read my thoughts, of course! Oh, thank G—"

Then she remembered something else, and her face paled even further. "Brain spiders. You gave me brain spiders?"

Martin nodded. He looked incredibly guilty.

"Jesus fucking Christ, Martin, *why*?!" Ember cried. She tried to make an avatar to smack him and failed. "Where's my power, Martin?!"

"Uhhh . . . how can I put this." Martin rubbed the back of his head.

"Out with it!" Alexa yelled. "Confess everything!"

[Shut up! You're not helping!] Martin shot back at her.

[What is happening? What is this?!] Ember thought. [Wait. *Puppeteer protocol.* Mind control. Brain spiders. Oh, goddamn you all to hell! Get out of my head, Martin!] She slammed her fists into the ground.

"Yeah, about that. I have no idea how to stop reading the thoughts you're directing at me or how to take the spider out of your head without killing you. Sorry," Martin apologized.

"What the fuck kind of superpower is brain spiders?!" Ember yelped. [Oh God, there're spiders in my brain. Get them out, get them out! Oh God, I'm going to be sick! Why?!]

"One spider. It's kind of integrated itself into your neural network, stretched its tendrils all over your brain," her brother said, unhelpfully.

"That's still one more than the number of spiders that I want in my brain, damn it!" she wailed.

"Right . . . Anyways, you can't do super stuff anymore because you burned out while you were trying to protect us from the skinwalkers. You are no longer awake, Ember. I'm really sorry," Martin said.

"No. No. No! This isn't happening. These sort of things don't happen to young, talented heroes!" Ember sat up and covered her face, wobbling back and forth like a roly-poly toy.

For the first time in her life, she was having a panic attack. She didn't like it one bit.

[Equality shall prevail and no cottages shall burn upon the distant shores of Yore,] a calm voice spoke in her head.

Ember saw a golden ocean of wheat in her mind, gently swaying back and forth played by currents of wind. White clouds rolled above the wheat fields, casting large shadows down onto the serene countryside. British cottages stood in the distance between rows of wild cherry trees. The grasses smelled of autumn rains; seagulls called from the ocean. It all looked so real that Ember forgot how to breathe, her panic attack subsiding, replaced by the vision of the Yorkshire countryside.

She shook her head, getting rid of the image. "Puppeteer protocol, damn it! Focus."

[Ember Kilborne, please remain calm. Now that you are Hero Resonance no longer, I can tell you about your part in the prophecy,] the voice of the Equalizer spoke in Ember's head.

"What? I, uh. I . . ." Ember muttered.

[You were one of my *targets* to monitor, assigned to me by her Eminence Equality. The super who was going to wipe England off the map.] Cottie walked up to Ember.

"What do you mean, wipe England off the map?! I couldn't have! I wouldn't have!" Ember gasped.

The Equalizer had reached the ex-hero, armor clinking, and placed a hand on her head.

[Observe what I had been given by Eminence Equality. This was your part in the prophecy. My Equalizer name, Verse Twenty-Four Nineteen, is part of the greater story about the future of a mighty hero called Resonance.]

An image of Ember formed out of uneven sparks.

She stood on the captain's deck of Titanomachy clad in red and gold of her Resonance costume, looking much older. There was an eight-pointed star on her chest.

Her rank was an admiral! She really was destined to become the defense administrator of the entire station!

"I know that you are down there, villain! This is for the greater good of the Superstate. You will not bring down Titanomachy!" Admiral Resonance spoke, a hundred of her off-color copies sitting at the controls of the station. The image zoomed outwards showing the entire ring superstructure spinning around the Earth.

Beneath the behemoth station, Ember could make out the outline of the coasts of France and England. A brilliant ray struck down from Titanomachy down to the beaches of Yorkshire and the coast of Britain ignited, clouds parting away to reveal the devastation beneath. A wall of fire a hundred meters tall rolled out from the center of the enormous explosion, devouring England. On the other side, an enormous tidal wave rushed out towards the Netherlands and Denmark.

The vision ended, breaking up into colorful sparks.

"No," Ember exhaled.

"Yessss," Alexa commented with a grin.

Martin simply stood there, his mouth open wide.

My sister is destined to obliterate nations.

"That's not all," Alexa whispered into the silence.

CHAPTER TWENTY-SEVEN

Bento

W hat do you mean, that's not all?" Martin whispered at Alexa with an aghast expression.

"Shh." Alexa put a finger to his lips.

Ember looked up at the Equalizer, her lips trembling.

[Nobody does anything without purpose. Fear not, Ember Kilborne, this future shall not come to pass. No cottages shall burn, for Hero Resonance is no more.] Cottie put her black railgun on Ember's shoulder. [A power, once lost, does not return to its super.]

The silence between them stretched on and on as Ember tried not to freak out. Tears started rolling down her eyes. Her great future was no more. Everything she'd worked so hard for was ruined.

"Cotes, you're freaking amazing at rendering memories. That was a really fun orbital visual! Seventeen thumbs up," Alexa spoke.

Cottie sternly looked at Alexa.

"What? I promise not to hide in England from the Superstate! Cross my heart and hope to die!" Alexa declared.

Ember simply knelt on the grass, facing Saint Mary's Cathedral, feeling the weight of the Equalizer's gun on her shoulder. She cried softly in the rain.

Admiral . . . Hero Resonance was going to be an admiral.

[This would not happen anyway, because I would have executed you with Eva long before it took place,] Cottie said without moving her lips, tapping her railgun. [The Equalizers are the hand of humanity. We stop all supers who go too far, be it hero or villain. Eminence Equality does not simply command us. She also shows each of us what is to come if we do nothing.]

Ember closed her eyes.

Humanity . . . the Equalizers had judged her future performance and found her unworthy. She had no power, and would not become Resonance even if she managed to wake up again. She had a spider in her brain that let her brother read her thoughts. Her brother was in . . .

Wait.

Ember looked up at Alexa.

"Are you planning to destroy Titanomachy? Did the station fall from the sky because of *you*?!"

"Why would I?" Alexa blinked her silver eyelashes back at her. "She's a pretty sky princess that's hugging the Earth. I'd never hurt our precious, overpriced ring-chan. I only plotted a most strategic destruction of the concept of the Superstate itself!"

"You're lying! You have to be the one I was after! Equalizer! Why don't you depower her instead of me?" Ember pointed at Alexa.

[Void weapons cannot take powers away permanently. They can only temporarily turn off a power to execute the wielder with a headshot.] Cottie shook her head. [You've done this to yourself, because you love your family. Because you still cared for your brother. Your power made you the best response hero. You graduated with 100 percent at the Academy and had a 100 percent mission success rate. You could hurt, kill people with impunity, and then just undo their deaths. You became more and more disconnected from humanity.]

Ember gulped.

[With each day your powers would only grow stronger, until you could run the entire defense grid of Titanomachy all by yourself. Your response time to an attack and the ability to coordinate as a one-person team of analytics made you the best officer of the SCA. Unfortunately, your power was also gradually erasing your empathy, turning you into a butcher.]

"She's right." Martin sighed. "You were kinda turning into a massive asshole, Em."

Ember looked up at the ring in the sky with sorrow.

Her dreams of greatness lay in ruins, broken by the world of tomorrow. She had been outdone by a fourteen-year-old supervillain.

[Alexa had done my job for me. It seems that she figured out a way to break Resonance long before you even rose to prominence. It seems that she's the only villain who figured out how to end you without killing you,] Cottie concluded.

"Hum, hum. The Equalizers should pay me for my excellent services! You guys get salaries, right?" Alexa winked at Cottie, opening and closing her hand as if demanding compensation.

Cottie raised an eyebrow at her.

"You're welcome!" Alexa grinned. "Hey can I at least wear your shiny E-shaped pin if I do your job for you? The pin comes with the invisibility cloak, right? I could do *twice the crimes* if I was invisible!"

Ember stopped crying. It was useless. Nobody seemed to care for her sorrow.

She looked at the only person who seemed to display the slightest bit of concern, tried to reach out to her brother. "Do you not hear the words coming out of her mouth? She's not a good person! She needs to be stopped!"

"I don't think that heroes are necessarily good people either, Ember," Martin sighed. "I now know why the Equalizers exist and why they do the things they do. Cottie lost her family and her home because of a hero who was too eager to defeat a villain. The prognosticators can't account for everything everywhere. They make preferences and allowances towards citizens of the Superstate. The SCA isn't perfect. You've seen it yourself. We've failed humanity. Titanomachy has fallen. I'm afraid I'm with Cottie on this one. I'm going to be Alexa's friend because that's the only way to stop her."

"Mwa ha ha ha!" Alexa stood over Ember, stepping into the shoes of a gloating supervillain.

The rain intensified, thunder rumbling in the distance. A dark storm cloud became visible behind Saint Mary's Cathedral. Ember saw flashes of eerie silver lights dancing behind the stained glass rose window as the world darkened.

[You've lost, hero. I've taken your powers away! Keep your friends close and your enemies even closer. What could be closer than mental communion? Your brother is bound to me by brain spiders, and he no longer believes in the SCA. This lovely Equalizer is bound to me by brain spiders, and she can't kill me because I'm doing the job of the Equalizers better than they are. You're bound to me by . . . well, you get the picture. You were the only one in the world who could have stopped me by obliterating the British Isles off the map with the power of Titanomachy. You were a threat to my world dominion and now you're just a human girl!]

"Nobody can stop me now!" She added menacingly aloud with a theatrical flourish.

Ember flapped her mouth open and closed. Alexa had somehow brought together and destroyed all of her future enemies before they could even grow up.

[Hero Resonance doesn't exist anymore, except on record,] Alexa added. [Your own dedication to immersion was your downfall. You erased four years of your own life to blend into the eighth grade, bent the rules of the universe by combining your own and your friends' powers. You no longer have your powers. What you've done to yourself cannot be reversed. You can never go back to Titanomachy as Resonance. The space elevator won't even recognize you as the same person—the door scanner reads the power imprint fractal hexagram. Your unique power signature imprint is gone forever; you no longer have the key to open that door!]

"No." Ember whispered in dismay.

[I warned you, did I not? I told you that there was no way to come back, that you were going to lose everything if you didn't let go of me.] Alexa looked down at Ember.

The ex-hero choked.

"Here is what's going to happen, Admiral. You're going to be my minion numero tres, and I'm going to call you . . ." Alexa tapped her face. "Dimmy. Or D if it's an emergency!"

[You know,] Alexa said in her thoughts, [as a respectful reminder to your future as Admiral of Titanomachy and on account of your powers and dashing looks having been dimmed. Here, enjoy the new you!] The supervillain made a fake gesture of a salute to Ember, pulled a small handheld mirror out of her vest pocket, and presented it to her.

Ember looked in the tiny mirror at her own reflection and did not recognize herself. Her hair was no longer orange, nor was it floating. It was an auburn shade with streaks of red. Her eyes were not glowing or gold. They were hazel. It was the last straw.

Ember dropped the mirror, wailing beneath torrents of rain, screaming at the sky that no longer belonged to her.

Lightning flashed overhead.

"I know what'll cheer you up! A tasty yum! Hope you don't mind that the box is wet. I can't control the weather, yet." Alexa slid a bento box towards Ember.

CHAPTER TWENTY-EIGHT

Foresight

Ember cradled the sushi bento box, walking after Alexa.

It was from her favorite sushi restaurant on Titanomachy. She clung to the box as the last, final reminder of a future that she would never reach now. She had been undone; her destiny had been revealed in all of its fantastic splendor and then ripped away from her in the same instant.

Ember had accepted it all now.

She was no longer Resonance, no longer a hero, just a girl whom Alexa made her minion for some inexplicable reason. Was it part of the villain's post-gloating experience or something?

Ember felt that she was of no use to anyone now, a person shattered into a million tiny pieces with no way to put herself back together again. She was tired, cold, and soaked from the summer thunderstorm that was passing over the little town.

She stared at the large Gothic revival–style cathedral up ahead of them, water rushing down the dark parapets, pouring out of the gargoyle mouths. Why were they walking to the cathedral? Was the villain about to reveal her greatest crime of murdering her father to them?

How had she managed to bind Martin and the Equalizer to herself as obedient minions?

Had she broken them in the same manner, dismantling their hopes and dreams, unraveling their future right in front of them? No, that would be silly. Martin never had a power or a determinate future. Ember was always trying her best to push Martin towards being a hero, but he seemed to show no talent or aptitude for such.

Until today, Martin had acted like an eight-year-old, had no backbone, no self-awareness, showed no signs of growing up or becoming a man. His incompetence, naivety, and shyness often made Ember feel like strangling him. But now . . . now he was different. He awoke at fourteen as one of the most dangerous, rarest supers out there—a puppeteer type. Not just a partial one either, but a permanent puppeteer who could create an entire network of mind control and thought exchange via his freaky brain spider things. How the hell did he make those, anyway? It was as if he had a set of two powers, not one. This alone was a terrifying prospect.

What the hell had Alexa done to her brother?

"Ke ke ke," Alexa responded, reading the ex-hero's mind. "I bound Martin to myself, in exactly the same way as I bound you . . ."

Martin's head snapped to Alexa.

"With social hacking," Alexa said just as Martin expected her to.

"What?" Ember asked.

[How did you know that my sister was going to be admiral?] Martin demanded mentally. [Are you a precog?]

[Pfff, obviously I don't see the future like a precog,] Alexa laughed.

[Then how?] Martin pressed on.

[I socially hacked the Superstate precogs,] Alexa revealed. [I don't actually *need* to see the future. There are more than enough people who can see the future for me. Your mom can see the future. I simply had to call a bunch of precogs like her to get a general model of the future. Plus, I dug up a lot of clues in 2424.]

"*What?*" Ember choked.

[The Superstate seems strong,] Alexa said. [But it's as weak as its weakest point—you, Ember.]

"*Me?!*" Ember barked.

[Yes, you, Dimmy.] Alexa nodded. [You're the weakest point of the Superstate because you took on the position as admiral, took it upon yourself to control the entire station. I simply walked into your room in 2424 . . . and then stole a whole bunch of SCA pens from your desk. I used them in the present to call people in various departments. I talked to a lot of precogs that you had on your extensive contact list, including your mom, discussed the future with all of them.]

[So, do the heroes know that Titanomachy will fall?] Martin asked.

[Nah, they don't see the future that far ahead,] Alexa said. [In fact, no precog can see the future past a certain point.]

[Why?]

[I dunno.] Alexa shrugged. [Maybe a wizard did it.]

[Is that your answer to everything?] Martin asked.

[Yes.] Alexa nodded vigorously.

The group reached the cathedral's outer stairwell.

"I seem to recall you accusing me of murdering my father." Alexa addressed Ember as she walked up the timeworn steps. "I do believe it's time for this gang of monster hunters to solve the mystery of Saint Mary's Cathedral and find out what really happened therein."

The four teenagers passed under the Gothic stone gate, the cathedral growing bigger with every step.

The girl villain wiped raindrops from her face as she stepped towards the double wrought iron doors of the entrance. The iron sculpture on the door looked like a depiction of the biblical flood, muscular men and women drowning in an ever-rising ocean, clinging to one another, clawing their way towards air.

"Friggin rain. Really should have invested in a nice van and a cute mascot to carry my umbrella or something," she complained.

"Or you know, get an umbrella," Martin commented.

"Ain't nobody got space for umbrellas!" Alexa pointed at her belt full of tools. "They're bulky and cumbersome."

[Or a cloak.] Cottie stepped into the entryway arch, raindrops rolling off her. She took down her hood, looking entirely dry.

"You know, I recall asking someone to reward me with her cloak," Alexa said.

[It's part of my armor. Would you like me to take off my entire armor right here and give it to you?]

"Hey! Keep it PG! You're offending poor, easily impressionable Mittens," Alexa laughed, drying her silver-white mane by twirling it with her hands.

[I've piloted all of your bodies via my brain spiders for hours. I don't think anything's going to offend me anymore,] Martin sighed.

Ember stepped up to the stairwell.

Just yesterday she had no fear of this place, banging at the doors and windows, knowing full well that no matter what was inside, her power would protect her, catch bullets in mid-air, disable traps, disarm and break minions. Now, as a mundane human, she was feeling terrified of the place.

Who knew what sorts of horrid defense systems were hidden inside, designed by the late Dr. Terranova? Was she making a mistake following Alexa into the cathedral? Would she end up dead within, doomed never to be found by the Superstate now that had she lost all of her recognizable features?

Alexa glanced back at Ember. "Somebody's frightened. Are you scared of spooky scary church ghosts? Don't worry, Daddums is perfectly alive and well. I just want to show off my impressive team of minions to him. He hasn't left me any praises lately!"

Ember reached the ancient entryway, looking up at the Latin inscription above the doors. *Omnes Relinquite Spes, O Vos Intrantes.* She understood the Latin phrase from her Academy days, having studied multiple languages with the use of her avatars. "'All hope abandon ye who enter here'? A bit somber for a regular cathedral, but makes sense for a villain's base."

"See? You're not completely useless. Nobody can take away your smarts. How many extra lifetimes have you experienced through the use of your avatars? How many books have you read? You gotta be like a thousand years by now or something. See, we already have something in common, Dimmy!" Alexa winked at Ember. "Both of us have far more experiences in our brains than we really should."

"Don't call me that," Ember said grouchily. "That is a horrible nickname, and also I hate it."

She realized that she was starving, opened the sushi box, and started to nibble on the rolls, praying that Alexa hadn't poisoned them or something.

"Oh, you'll learn to love it like these two." Alexa waved her hands at Martin and Cottie.

"I don't like my nickname that much," Martin said.

[I am also not enthused about mine. It is tolerable.]

"Are we all having a minion-assigned-name mutiny?" Alexa lifted the great brass handle and slammed it into the door, producing a deep gong sound. "For shame."

"I'm going to give you a nickname, see how you feel about it." Martin leaned towards Alexa.

"What?" Alexa blinked listening to any kind of a response behind the door. "You can't nickname me. I already nicknamed myself Cassie the Terror Supernova! Rawr."

"I'm going to nickname you and there's nothing you can do about it. Mwa ha ha," Martin attempted to sound like Alexa. "See? That's what you sound like. You have a villain-theme problem."

"I do not sound like a high-pitched boy's voice. I have an angelic, heavenly voice adored by the masses. Also, being a villain isn't a problem. It's just a matter of filling people's expectations of you so that you can socially hack them later." Alexa waved Martin off. "Daaaaaaddums!" she yelled into the keyhole. "Open the hell up! I got minions to show you!" She banged the handle twice as hard.

[Has this worked before?] Cottie asked.

"Nope. Never did." Alexa scratched her head, looking at the large iron doors. "But it doesn't hurt to try again."

CHAPTER TWENTY-NINE

First Memory

Y ou know what? I know you're watching me. Guess I'll have to start my minion presentation outside. Prepare to be impressed!" She theatrically waved her hand at Martin.

"This is Mittens! Drumroll, please . . ." Alexa yelled. Cottie tapped her fingers against her gun, making a miniature drumroll-like sound. "He is my minion numero uno. Part man, part brain spiders!"

"This is a terrible description of me," Martin said.

"He's worth at least four spider-men right now! Observe how he looks like a useless, weak fourteen-year-old boy! Well, you couldn't be any more wrong, Daddums! He's full of surprises and . . . uhh . . . also spiders. Damn it, I should have rehearsed this. Okkie." Alexa shoved Martin towards the door. "Do the thing."

"What thing?"

"Kiss the keyhole." Alexa pointed.

[What?]

[God, you're so dim for someone who has four people and four spiders' worth of brains at your disposal. Make a tiny skinwalker scout. Get inside the keyhole. See what's inside.]

[Ah, right.] Martin leaned towards the door, disconnected a tiny segment from Spiderbro, and made it jump inside the keyhole.

He suddenly felt very lightheaded and confused as his perspective shifted from his human self to a new, tiny skinwalker. The spider walked through the keyhole, bumping into some sort of a shimmering barrier that began right after the keyhole ended. Martin made it shove a sensor tendril as small as he could make it, squeezing it between the end of the door and the shimmering shield. This allowed him to observe the stuff all around. He saw what appeared to be a very fancy Gothic motif stone room with another set of doors leading into the nave. Right above the door, a jar stood on a pedestal with a human brain floating inside, tubes leading from it into the depths of the cathedral.

"There's a brain in a jar right about the door. That's about it," Martin said.

"Shit," Ember said, backing away from the door. "That's biotech stuff. Highly dangerous and illegal. Now I know why I couldn't get in! He's using super brains to make an impassable shield!"

She did not want to anger the jar-brains. Who knew what kind of nasty things they could do?

"Dimmy, go run home and cry to your own daddy if you're scared of some musty old brain jars. I'm sure Daniel Kilborne would love to hear how and why you lost your powers.

You can tell him all about your dastardly plan to take over Titanomachy, too." Alexa pointed towards the direction of the Kilborne's home.

Ember glared at Alexa. "Screw you."

"Feisty as ever, I see. All right, Martin, use Cottie."

"Uh?" Martin blinked.

[Shoot the brain jar with Eva! You can see exactly where you need to aim! What else are you thinking of? Seriously!]

"Sorry, Cottie, do you mind if I aim you?" he inquired with a blush.

Cottie nodded. [This is fine. Direct me.]

[How the hell did she brainwash an Equalizer?] Ember thought angrily.

"I didn't. She came pre-brainwashed." Alexa grinned, leaning on the ex-hero.

Ember sputtered, not knowing what to say to that, concerned that three other people were privy to her thoughts.

Martin took over Cottie's arms, switched on the nullifier, and pressed the trigger. Colors faded from the world. The nullification effect struck the shield, causing a ripple in it. It didn't seem to fail completely. There must have been similar brain jars all over the cathedral supporting the shield, Martin figured.

Titanomachy had one such protection that he had read about. Different backup fusion reactors reinforcing each other, creating an impervious barrier. Except these weren't fusion reactors. These were the brains of supers. Where did the supervillain get so many super brains? Martin shuddered ever so slightly, focusing on aiming Cottie, triangulating the approximate position of the jar via his small spider keyhole spy and the positions of the four teenagers in front of the door.

"I suggest you step back. We don't have Ember to catch shrapnel anymore," he said, making the little scout jump out of the keyhole and onto his shoulder.

Martin and the others retreated away from the door. Cottie stayed perfectly still, aim unchanging.

Martin made Cottie release the trigger. The gun fired with a supersonic bang, the bullet going through the stone wall of the church as if it were made of butter. It struck the shield and warped it inwards, wobbling and slamming the jar off the shelf. Martin heard the jar smash against the floor. The shield in front of the door flickered, growing very weak. Martin directed Cottie to press the trigger again, walking her forward. Eva's nullification field struck the shield, and it vanished.

"I did it! The path is clear!" he yelled.

"Hooray!" Alexa jumped up and down excitedly. [Wohoooooooo!] her thoughts screamed. [Finally, finally, finally! Take that, Daddums!]

Ember looked at the villain, stumped. Her theory about parental murder was beginning to come apart at the seams. It was becoming obvious to her that Alexa had never been inside the church. Maybe she was a really good liar? Ember temporarily reassured herself with this explanation.

Martin made Cottie push against the giant doors, and they slid apart with a deep groan, revealing the grimy stone interior. There was a deep layer of dust on the floor. It was obvious that nobody had stepped inside the place in decades.

Alexa looked at the dust. "I should really hire a cleaning lady or buy a Roomba or something. This is definitely an allergy zone." She looked back at Ember. "You don't have asthma, right? I didn't look into your medical records on the matter of allergies."

The third minion shook her head, feeling perturbed by the deep silence within the church. The four teens entered the cathedral, making footprints in the dust.

"Have you never been inside this place?" Cottie asked.

"Not that I can remember." Alexa shrugged.

"What?" Martin stared at Alexa. "Then how do you even know this place belongs to your dad?"

"A robot told me." Alexa shrugged again.

"A robot told you?!" Martin repeated.

"Yep." Alexa nodded. "A few years ago, I woke up outside of this cathedral with no memories."

"Oh," Martin said.

"Observe!" Alexa declared and mentally focused on a memory.

Alexa fell onto the grass, sputtering and choking. Blue fluid emptied from her lungs as she heaved.

A tall humanoid figure stood over her.

"Good tomorrow," it said in a cold metallic voice that sounded a bit like a British butler.

"W-what? Where am I?" Alexa looked in bewilderment around her. She was lying on the grass covered in some sort of quickly evaporating fluid. Her mind was swimming. She couldn't recall who she was or why and how she had even arrived on this well-manicured lawn.

Alexa spun her eyes around, trying to get her bearings.

The human figure bent down to her and offered her a white, ill-fitting coat.

She pulled it on, discovering that she looked like a very skinny, very young teenage girl. Her hair was dark brown and wavy.

She looked back at the mechanical human. From a distance, he could have been perhaps mistaken for a man, but up close he looked like a plastic mannequin filled with clockwork. A brain was floating inside of a clear plastic case atop of the thing's head.

"I'm going to self-destruct in exactly forty-two seconds," the robot said. "Your name is Alexa Terranova. You're the daughter of a supervillain, Dr. Terranova. You come from a long line of villains, your many-times-great-grandfather is Spring-Heeled Jack. Beware, there are heroes aplenty who will attempt to kill you."

"Uhh . . . okay?" Alexa blinked. "Wait . . . what?!"

"Your father is working inside the Saint Mary's Cathedral behind you." The robot butler clicked, a metal joint pointing at the old, gloomy-looking Gothic building that stood behind them. "The place from which you were banished."

She stared at the mechanical man, feeling utterly stupefied.

"The bracelet on your hand will randomly send you into the world of tomorrow," the robot butler said, pointing at a black hexagonal bracelet on her hand. "Figure things out. Survive. Become strong."

"W-what?" Alexa stammered as she looked down at the weird bracelet.

"You are a disappointment. Your memories were erased because you learned too much. This is a punishment for defying me. Steal. Adapt. Grow. Become a true villain and find your way back inside. Goodbye," the butler concluded, clicked, and detonated with a flash, showering the lawn and pelting her with numerous plastic screws and plates. The brain in the jar ignited and the plastic parts comprising the butler melted and rapidly disintegrated, burning a scorched hole on the lawn.

"See? That's exactly how I came into existence!" Alexa grinned. "Daddums made me! Or . . . he banished me from our home and erased my memory. Either hypothesis could be true."

"If you didn't kill your father . . . then . . . you're . . ." Ember muttered, trying to wrap her head around Alexa's revelation.

"Oh, I know! I shall file you under Boromir. You're here because you're curious, Dimmy . . . not because you want to help us save the world. You're probably going to betray us at the earliest convenience and then cry about it a lot." Alexa spoke as Cottie shoved the next set of doors open.

The figure of a man with the name tag *Dr. Terranova* stood in the center of the nave. He was facing them, looking silver and transparent.

A skeleton wearing a lab coat lay on the floor in the center of the nave, surrounded by dust-covered lab equipment and machinery that nobody had used in decades.

"G-g-g-ghost!" Martin yelped, stepping backwards and tripping on Ember. His sister howled in turn as he stepped on her foot.

CHAPTER THIRTY

The Indeterminate Answers

Aha! He's dead! I was right!" Ember proclaimed, waving a hand at the corpse on the ground.

"Aiiiiight, quit screwing around, I know you are not dead," Alexa growled at the ghost. "You're spooking and misleading my minions and not being a very polite house host."

The ghost flickered, its features changing.

Now that Martin had managed to relax himself by receiving some calm visuals from Cottie's steady mind, he saw that the face of the ghost seemed to be a fluid, indeterminate thing, patterns of constantly moving hexagons shifting around. One minute the doctor was a ninety-year-old grandfather, the next a nineteen-year-old woman, then a thirty-year-old man, then suddenly a chair with wings. This was a very freaky ghost, or more specifically a very odd . . . holographic projection.

"Welcome to the Saint Mary installation, Subject Thirteen. Welcome to Captania, Charles Snippy. Go away, there is nothing here but piles of divorced buses. Hello, kitten." As the holographic person spoke, its voice shifted along with the facial features.

Ember, not seeing anything like a defense system or a trap, slowly made her way towards the skeleton on the floor.

"Don't mind the floor, intern. Burning up on the job is part of the job," Alexa commented on the state of the dead body.

Martin glanced at Alexa. He started to understand why she was so random. Being raised by this . . . *thing* would drive anyone a little crazy. Wait . . . but if Alexa never came inside, then how could the hologram even raise her?

[Daddums and I communicated with flashing lights through the cathedral windows,] Alexa explained mentally.

[Was he always this . . . random?]

[Oh yes,] Alexa affirmed.

"Look at my adorable minions, Daddy!" Alexa yelled. "Aren't they extra adorkable? How do you rate them?"

"Congratulations on making it this far. Impressive. You took too long. You failed. Happy birthday!" the indeterminate hologram said in an array of voices and accents.

[Is this a recording?] Cottie asked. [He doesn't seem to be acknowledging us. Why are the answers so . . . random?]

"Daddums isn't a recording. He just has social anxiety!" Alexa smiled.

She pretended to hug the shifting hologram.

[He definitely seems like a broken recording,] Martin replied. He had already felt bad about Alexa's situation, and this was only making it worse.

"You guys are being kinda mean." Alexa turned around and looked at her friends.

[Why is he so indeterminate . . .] Ember pondered. She recollected the prognosticator reports her copies had read about the doctor. Most of them were labelled "no determinate information on current and future activities."

"Holy shit! This whole setup is how he's been avoiding the Superstate future seers!" she finally concluded.

[Being random is part of the fun; it confuses the precogs,] Alexa agreed with a nod.

"I have many enemies," the holographic spoke. "If I am not here, that means the giant snails have come for me. Everyone loves me, as I have no enemies. I am a pretty wildflower. Do not pick me."

"You clever, indeterminate bastard." Ember looked at the holographic. "Are you dead?"

"I am neither dead nor alive. I am the corpse on the floor. I am a drunk sailor on the *Titanic*. I am a pancake. I am Dr. Terranova. I am a beehive in a suit shaped like a man," the ever-changing holographic replied.

For a second, it shifted into a cat in a suit, then the Eiffel Tower wearing a beard.

"Daddums is a smooth Schrödinger's cat," Alexa purred.

She found herself a very dusty swiveling office chair and was now twirling on it. "Make yourselves at home, guys! House party camp in the cathedral!"

"Sneaky bugger," Ember muttered. "Who's that on the floor?"

"A super idiot who asked too many questions," the holographic answered. "Subject Twelve. Nobody important. A waste of space. She worked very hard. He failed to meet my expectations. Ninety-four chicken wings in a bucket."

"Let me guess, subjects one to eleven also failed to meet these expectations?" the ex-hero inquired, picking out the most reasonable-sounding answer from the pile of random replies.

"Mostly butter," the holographic thing replied. "Most subjects have. Everything is important. I am hungry for Campbell's chicken soup."

"How do the subjects relate to you?" Ember pressed on.

"My cactus needs to be watered today. They don't. They are my test subjects. Nothing of value."

"The brain jars all over?"

"Wholesome, best friends. A shield. Test subjects. Useless junk. Zip me up and mail me to the moon, please."

[Shit. This is some dark stuff.] Martin came over to Alexa and sat on the floor next to her. Cottie followed.

Ember pointed at herself. "What do you think about me?"

The hologram flickered, shifting. "You're a useless waste of space. You're a device of great power. You're a space whale inside of a shoe on planet Mercury. I've been watching you."

"That's my minion number three!" Alexa announced. "Dimmy! She's my greatest arch-nemesis! I made her my minion to teach her a lesson in humility."

[Not a recording then,] Ember thought. [Artificial intelligence, maybe? Or the actual doctor communicating from somewhere else? Damn clever, indeterminate fuck. Most supervillains had a very specific identity, a costume, minions, a theme, and this made them all easy to track by the SCA probability calculators. There was only one reason why someone would hide from the prognosticators like this—they wanted to attack the Superstate!]

Ember glanced at Alexa. The ex-hero's brain was crammed full of Superstate exams, papers, and reports about how villains operated. She tried to analyze the situation using what she knew. [Subject Thirteen. A typical supervillain move is to dehumanize their creations and victims. Give them numbers. Call them subjects. Use them as human tests, turn them into living weapons and defense systems.]

Alexa looked back at her and stopped spinning.

"Hey! I'm important! Thirteen is a handsome, spooky, Halloween number! Building managers fear it! Elevators ignore it! Nobody wants to live on the thirteenth floor or buy apartment number thirteen. See? Daddums loves me the most!"

CHAPTER THIRTY-ONE

Mercy

You're a weapon!" Ember declared, staring at Alexa with wide eyes. [A sleeper agent, maybe? A designed super, meant to bring down the Superstate!]

"You really think that I can bring down the Superstate?" Alexa grinned at Ember. "Thanks for the vote of confidence, Dimmy!"

[Installation Saint Mary. It means there are others. Of course. Yorkshire! The Yorkshire installation must have activated its weapon and become a threat to the stability of the Titanomachy ring somehow. That's why I destroyed it as an admiral. There must be other sleeper cell subjects all over the world like Alexa. Genetically engineered supers? Clones? Bred, raised, coordinated, waiting to strike. A thousand slow fuses, burning over decades, hidden, diluted by utter nonsense. Incalculable. Unpredictable,] Ember thought rapidly.

[That's a lot of determinate conclusions, Dimmy. Good thing we have this mental communion, eh? Had you spoken them out loud, I'd probably have to kill you or something.] Alexa laughed in her head.

[I have to stop you before you activate!] Ember yelled mentally, glaring at Alexa. [What is your power? Is it some kind of super destabilizer? The ability to destroy anything?!]

[Mmm . . . Demolition Girl. That's a pretty sweet power, if you ask me,] Alexa visualized a Hollywood movie poster featuring Demolition Man.

[You've demolished me, my brother, even the Equalizer. It all fits!] Ember thought, hyperventilating. [Next you're going to turn your attention to Titanomachy, and kaboom! Everyone dies!]

[I think you forgot one important factor.] Alexa yawned.

[What?!]

[You're still alive. Just because you're socially dead, you can't go crying around that you're physically dead. Dead people don't cry . . . unless they are zombies. You'd make one adorkable zombie!]

Martin injected himself into their conversation. [Alexa is a sleeper superweapon that's going to what? Socially destroy the Superstate? She's going to shame thousands of supers into . . . what? Turning off the power? What, they'll crash the station into the planet because they're . . . super embarrassed? This is a lot of jumping to conclusions, Ember.]

[She did it to me! She can do it to anyone!] Ember thought-yelled. [It has to be a power! She needs to be stopped before she turns off all of the supers one by one with that leaping into the future bullshit!]

[Are you going to turn off all of the supers?] Cottie asked Alexa.

[Uhh . . . are they going to get up in my face and attempt to kill me like Dimmy did?] Alexa scratched her head.

[That sounds like a yes! She confesses!] Ember accused.

[Em! Cottie! This is insane. She can't turn off all of the supers!] Martin glanced at Alexa. [Can you?]

[Nopers. If I could do that, I'd be the most powerfully wicked supervillain in the world. Weeeeee!] Alexa spun on her swivel chair in the other direction.

Ember looked at Alexa.

Was the fourteen-year-old girl spinning on the dusty office chair the most powerful super in the world? She didn't seem like one. She thought of Nonpareil. Powerful supers weren't exactly human. They were more akin to an unstoppable idea. Alexa seemed as human as they come. Maybe that was her power? She needed more information. Ember turned back to the hologram.

"Who is Subject Thirteen?"

"My clone. My mother from the future. An experiment gone right and wrong. Me, but a thousand years older. My sister. A robot wearing too many hats. A weapon. My only fresh cookie. Why should I tell you anything, hero?"

Ember rubbed her head, not knowing which answer was real. They all seemed equally nonsensical or valid. "What is Subject Thirteen's purpose?"

"To save everyone or destroy the world or do nothing of value."

Ember choked for a second, picking the possible truth from lies.

"To save the world from what?"

"From fools and monsters and heroes like yourself. Ember Kilborne. Resonance. Waste of space. A melon. James Peacherson Fox. I have been watching and not watching you and eating 9,863 sandwiches."

"How the hell do you know my identity?!"

"Twenty-seven keyboards used by a thousand monkeys writing a script for a hit movie. Her shiny bracelet. A sentient two-by-four plywood from the Andromeda Galaxy."

Ember choked again. The holographic bastard was going for her jugular. He knew her. He had been watching her from Alexa's dark bracelet all this time, paying attention, learning, judging.

"Potatoes have eyes, I don't like it. Supers like you are what's wrong and what's not wrong with the world. A persistent pattern that doesn't make sense. A game. A fake planet built by an intelligence greater than ours. When heroes and villains don't come and come together they become an even bigger, more dangerous, a smaller, less important issue. I will solve and won't solve it. I would like some milk and eggs today. The fridge is empty again."

Ember started to back away from the hologram, feeling that her deduction roller coaster drawn from selected answers of the supervillain was reaching some sort of an apex.

The doctor was creating subjects like Alexa to stop supers. All of the supers. It was impossible, insane, but this was the only conclusion that made sense. How many installations? How many test subjects? The ex-hero's head spun as she imagined an army of Alexas loosed upon the world, turning off supers one by one like some kind of a plague of locusts.

The silver-haired girl giggled from her chair at Ember's frantic contemplation.

[Do you really think there can be more of me? I have sisters, brothers, cousins somewhere? A big happy family?] Alexa's blue eyes lit up.

Ember froze. There were no reports about Alexa from the prognosticators that Ember was allowed to access. How had she escaped the attention of the probability calculators? She was clearly affecting the world! Or was she? Was it Alexa's fault that she had lost her powers or . . . her own? Ember gulped. Alexa was dismantling people in an entirely new, unprecedented way. They were the ones making all the decisions. She had made the decision to go after Alexa. She wanted to protect her brother. She acted without thinking again and again, relying on her power rather than on her intelligence. Her power had controlled her, ruled her, guided her until it was extinguished. Fuck!

[Yep. Congrats. Everything you've done is your own fault. I've clearly warned you.]

[You're just a test subject, a tool for this villain! He doesn't care for you!] Ember shot back.

[Nah.] Alexa shrugged. [I know Daddums loves me very much. The most in fact. I'm his real daughter, contrary to what you might think, Dimmy. He just can't show it, can't call me by name or the prognosticators would come down from their ivory tower and take me away.]

[How did you communicate with him to begin with?] Ember demanded.

[I learned to read binary code. Like I said earlier, it was messages through the flashes of lights in the windows. Mostly it's requests to do one thing or another. Pick up some milk and eggs, make sure to eat dinner, water the grass, mow the lawn. Basic stuff.]

[You don't need to do whatever it is he wants! Why can't you see that he's just using you for evil?] Ember declared.

[Evil is a very stretchy thing, especially in the eyes of the agents and citizens of the Superstate.] Alexa shrugged. [You yourself were planning to kill me, to destroy my mind as Hero Resonance and in some far future as Miss Admiral along with a whole chunk of England and Europe. Have you already forgotten that, Miss Warden? For shame!]

Ember choked.

[Honestly, I should leave you here alone for a bit as a lesson. Put you in time out. I doubt you'd be able to go anywhere or do anything fun, with all of these shield-generating jar-brains hidden deep in the walls.] Alexa imagined Ember clawing against closed doors, surrounded by the silent, creepy cathedral.

Ember realized that Alexa held all of the power over her. Without Cottie's nullification gun, she would not be able to leave the cathedral and would probably end up dead on the floor next to the hologram and the corpse of some long dead scientist.

She walked towards Alexa and sat down in front of her on the ground, looking up at her.

"Yeeees?" Alexa bent down, silver hair backlit with colored light streaming from the stained glass windows.

"I was a monster. Please forgive me," Ember finally spoke, glancing at the corpse on the ground and trembling. "Please don't leave me in here with him."

"Aww. You don't want to cuddle the floor intern? I bet Daddums has such fun, spooky stories to tell you in the dark. Tsk tsk tsk."

Ember shook her head, eyes filling with tears.

"We're all monsters. Let's be the most adorable monsters of all, together, okay?" Alexa smiled offering her a hand.

Ember took Alexa's hand and shook it. She stood up, shivering due to the cold and fear, and the silver-haired villain hugged her. For the first time since she'd become Resonance, Ember returned someone's hug feeling something. All of the things that made her Resonance had been burned away in the city of death. All of her hate and anger for Alexa had been washed away by the rain and her tears, drowned by fear of being human from now on and possibly forever.

"I'm sorry," the ex-hero whispered, tears sparkling down her cheeks, reflecting the colorful stained glass and the silver, perpetually shifting hologram.

"It's okay, Dimms. Everything's gonna be okay. Your story's not done yet; you have much more monstering to do. I'll find a way to light you up again, I promise," Alexa whispered, winking at the silver hologram of her father.

CHAPTER THIRTY-TWO

Her Eminence

Alexa hugged her greatest nemesis, listening to her heartbeat.

Everything would be different this time. The future where England was vaporized was unmade, changed. No cottages would burn. Ember would not become Admiral Death. Cottie would not become her Eminence Equality. Martin would not become . . .

Alexa got distracted by other positive thoughts. A little hope fluttered in her heart that somewhere out there she had a family. That someday she would find them, meet them, hug them all just as she was hugging the ex-biggest threat to her life now. She didn't know what missions the other subjects had, what steps they were taking, what powers they possessed. She didn't know anything about her dad's plans, and it didn't bother her one bit. She would figure everything out in time, as she always did. Finding and understanding things was her thing. Figuring things out and manipulating organizations was fun.

"Daddums! Where's my pretty present for solving your cathedral punk puzzle box? Can I have something determinate, please?" She cheerfully yelled at the hologram, letting go of Ember.

"Not from me. The square root of four is one. Look for it where they have no control. Twenty-four bottles of beer on the wall. Twenty-four bowling balls roll. Take back what belongs to you." The hologram shifted, looking like a bartender and then a bowling alley attendant.

"Thank you!" Alexa shouted back.

Her reward was in the place where the Superstate had no power, no control!

[I don't understand,] Martin though. [What's he talking about?]

[That's 'cause you don't have the right brain on.] Alexa grinned, putting a finger to her lips. [It's a seriously sneaky secret. Sshhh.]

Martin's mind felt somewhat diluted nine ways between four people and five spiders. He realized that he was subconsciously getting affected, influenced by each of their best bits—Cottie's calmness, Alexa's fierce stubbornness, Ember's fear and rational guessing. He focused on the segment of himself that was Alexa's brain to understand what she was saying.

Ah. The Superstate had no power in 2424! That was the place where Alexa's present waited for her.

Cottie stared at Alexa. She'd been staring at Alexa for a few minutes now, not saying anything.

[What?] Alexa grinned at her.

[You seem to know something about me.]

[I know that you are adorable and really amazing and maybe a robot cosplayer, uhhh . . .]

[Quit derailing it!] Cottie crossed her arms, looking sternly at Alexa.

[Okaay! You got me. I confess! You're the best Equalizer. An Executioner rank at fourteen! You're obviously in line to become the next Eminence Equality,] Alexa announced.

[She's what?] Martin blinked. [Isn't Cottie . . . human?]

[And do you think that the Equalizer pope is a sentient potato or something?] Alexa inquired.

[Wait. Are you saying that the Equalizer cult leader isn't a supervillain?] Ember inquired, wiping tears from her face. [How do you know this stuff?]

[It's called the power of deductive reasoning, my dear triumvirate of Watsons.] Alexa walked through the ever-changing hologram, stepping over the dusty corpse. [Through our interactions with Cottie, even a Watson like you can now conclude that she's not a super. You see, the very first Eminence Equality wasn't a super. She was someone who'd been orphaned by supers generations ago. She made it her mission to prevent future disasters caused by both sides. She was a very rich landowner who invested all of her wealth into buying up tech and patents from desperate villains, aka supers cast out by the Superstate. Tech that eventually made humans stand toe to toe with supers!]

[Damn,] Martin thought. [That's pretty neat.]

[The more you know! This is how it works—the best, most obedient, most capable Equality ascendant becomes the next Eminence Equality upon her death!] Alexa pointed at Cottie.

Ember and Martin looked at Cottie, who stood there clad in her power armor, Eva hanging from her belt beneath the gray cloak.

"Holy shit," Ember said. "It makes sense. The Equalizers aren't supers. They're just . . . people. Regular people. No wonder her Eminence has never gone up to Titanomachy, refused to cooperate with the Superstate. No wonder the heroes can't just smack her around! She's a human! Ha!"

[Yes, the space elevators hate her because she's just a human. The Equalizers are regular people fed up with Superstate supremacy. They're funded by various super-opposed human rights organizations, nonprofit groups, world governments, and even thrift stores. Eminence Equality isn't a prognosticator. She simply has access to tech that can predict the future. She plays the game of a prophet pretty well, if you ask me.]

Cottie looked slightly lost at this revelation.

[That's right! Your goddess is just a girl, clad in super tech. She's no different from you, Cottie. When she dies, you're next in line.] Alexa put her hand on Cottie's shoulder.

[It . . . it doesn't make a difference to me,] Cottie thought back.

[Oh, but it does. It so does. You see, a god can't be wrong. Humans, on the other hand, err, make dumb mistakes all the time. People can be manipulated, socially hacked.] Alexa pressed forward like a road roller, flattening Cottie's entire belief system.

Martin's eyebrows shot up. [You knew about Ember's future because you've socially hacked Eminence Equality and the Equalizers?!]

[Amongst other things.] Alexa smiled. [How else would I do a better job, stay one step ahead of the Equalizers, if I didn't know their plans? How would I get Cottie to come and observe me?]

Cottie felt like strangling Alexa. She inhaled and exhaled, immersed herself in the Song of the Void, calmed herself in serenity and peace of—

[You can't serenade away the truth. I brought you to me, Cottie, because I needed you. I am that which pushed the hand of Equality, through a thousand donations made to a thousand nonprofit organizations with a mountain of gold and diamonds from 2424. There is no true equality in the world, no gods or prophets. There are only people like you and me.] Alexa put both of her hands on Cottie's shoulders and then cupped her face, looking straight into her emerald-silver eyes.

"How did you . . . ?" Cottie whispered.

Alexa dug into her pocket and presented the Equalizer a somewhat mangled, stained photo burned at the edges.

[*Her Eminence Equality, Verse 24:19*,] the tagline read. Cottie choked when she saw a much older version of herself there, her hair silver and her expression stern.

Ember started to laugh, softly at first, her voice echoing through the mostly empty halls of the cathedral. "Ha ha ha ha! God! I was wrong. I was so stupid. Ha ha ha! I can't even. Fucking Jesus Christ, this sneaky clever little fuck figured out a way to control the Equalizers!"

"Don't swear in the house of God," Alexa said as she slid the photo back into her pocket. "It's not polite."

"Ha ha ha! Stop! Ha ha ha! I see exactly what you're doing, and I can't even stop you! You're terrible." Ember continued to giggle, sounding a little mad.

Cottie tried to remain calm but couldn't. She glared at Alexa, a frown crossing her face. She had a sudden urge to bite Alexa's hand, to scream at her, to tell her exactly what she thought of her deductions and donations and where to shove them. Eminence Equality couldn't be manipulated by someone like Alexa! It was impossible! It couldn't be true!

"Ha ha ha! Look at you, Equalizer," Ember choked out, laughing and crying at the same time. "Trying so hard not to look mad! Oh, God. I love it. This is the true art of mental deconstruction! Let it go, girl. Step into the grinder. Come out clean on the other side. Ha ha ha ha!"

[I think you broke Em and Cottie at the same time. Good job,] Martin commented.

He felt that he was lucky to have spent the most time with Alexa. He was days ahead of the others! Already broken and remade. He didn't care what his future was supposed to be, he simply knew that being beside Alexa was where he belonged. It wasn't simply because he liked her, it was because she made him into a better, stronger person by shattering his beliefs and recasting him whole. He saw the same pattern, the same tactics that were used on him now applied to the two girls and found it . . . amusing.

Alexa's bracelet beeped. Martin stepped next to her and grabbed her hand. Cottie didn't do anything because Alexa was already petting her face. She simply stood there, looking very annoyed and lost.

Ember stopped laughing and looked at Alexa, like a frightened animal with no way out.

"Do I have to?" she stuttered.

"You can take my hand and come with us to the doomed world of tomorrow, or stay here . . . alone with Daddums and his tired intern for I dunno how long. Them's the beans," Alexa said.

Both options seemed equally horrible to Ember. She would die here alone . . . or she would die with her brother in the future. She grabbed Alexa's hand, putting hers atop Martin's.

Darkness fell.

The world aged four hundred years in an instant. The cathedral still stood, albeit a tad broken, looking somewhat worse for wear. The stained glass windows were partially shattered. The hologram was gone. A fusion reactor hummed with a bit of a stutter somewhere in the deep. The brains in the walls were long dead, but the reactor had taken over their security function, as Martin noted. There was a shimmering blue shield pulsating through the cracked walls of ancient stone, keeping the place standing and sealed.

This place was another safe haven from the skinwalkers. Safe and . . . completely inaccessible from the outside.

Martin now knew that Cottie had been a very vital piece of Alexa's minion puzzle. Without her, they would never have gotten into this church. What did Alexa do exactly to attract the attention of the Equalizers? Was it really just donations? Was it as simple as that? Or did she manage to trick their probability calculator so that they would send Cottie her way? What kind of a superweapon did Alexa have? The nukes weren't real.

[*What?!* The nukes aren't real?] Cottie choked.

[Nah. It's a single depleted dud I found out here and paid a super to replicate a thousand times with a bar of gold. Enough to cover the interior of my tree house,] Alexa confessed.

[Why?!] Cottie groaned, her fists opening and closing.

[Some people give their friends presents. I gave you an idea of infinite nukes to unbalance you. You were too square, too set in your ways.]

In that moment, Cottie snapped.

She slapped Alexa.

Then she realized what she'd done and looked at her hand in embarrassment.

"Welcome to having all the feelings!" Alexa announced, rubbing her stinging red cheek. "You need feelings to know where you're going. After all, you're my best friend, and friends don't let each other behave as cold robots!"

Martin felt it, saw how Cottie's walls broke mentally, crumbled, shattered from within.

[Alexa . . . did you find information about me here in 2424? What am I going to become?] Martin asked.

CHAPTER THIRTY-THREE

The Aberration of Desire

t's more like what you aren't going to become." Alexa shrugged.

"What am I not going to become?" Martin insisted.

"You'll never be a proper hero," Alexa said.

"Why?!"

[Well, seeing as this is the end of the line, Martin, I'll be honest with you. I gave you brain spiders because I needed a bridge between skinwalkers and people. Someone who's not me. Someone whose very specific, mental-manipulation-type power wasn't awake yet. I couldn't tell you or anyone anything, had to trick you, mislead you, lie to you, because if I didn't—the prognosticators would find out and stop me. I used you because I needed to create a new kind of super, one that could change the world.]

[To prevent . . . this future?] Martin looked at the ruins of Saint Mary through the nearest shattered stained glass window.

"This future is pretty shit, but world 2424 isn't necessarily *our* future. You see, my friend, our present has problems. Deep, awful problems like the Superstate. My goal is to destroy the Superstate, Martin," Alexa said simply.

[God, you really mean that?!] Martin thought.

[Yes.]

"You . . . you really want to destroy the Superstate?" Ember stuttered, looking about like a trapped rabbit.

"Yes. The Superstate must come to an end," Alexa said. "And I now have the means to do it, if Daddums got his stuff together."

"Why would you . . . I . . . I have to tell everyone!" the ex-hero gasped.

"You can do whatever you want when we return to the present, Dimmy! You won't be able to stop me. Events have already been set into motion. You're just a gear in the machinery of the future now, spinning towards the inevitable D-Day!"

"My brother won't be a hero?" Ember shivered.

"He's going to be *my* hero. A hero unlike anyone else. A hero who breaks the rules of the game." Alexa took Martin's hand.

Martin looked at Alexa. For the first time in his life, he knew that he could trust her. Her mind had been fully opened to him, and via his spider in her head he could tell that she was finally telling the absolute truth.

"Why do we need to end the Superstate?" he asked.

"The Superstate creates more villains than it ends. They unjustly imprison and brainwash innocents. They're monsters disguised under the title of Goodness. It's all just an illusion of protection as our world careens to its inevitable end," Alexa said.

"What?! That's not true!" Ember waved her hands.

"You don't have to blindly believe me. I'll provide you with irrefutable evidence very soon." Alexa smiled.

Ember had nothing to say to that. She didn't believe the villain girl one bit. Alexa didn't have to lie—she could simply believe something false, having been brainwashed by her father!

Martin, on the other hand, decided to trust the self-proclaimed villain. He wanted to see what she would do.

Alexa bent down to the floor and listened.

"The reactor's not sounding too good. I don't think it's going to last very long," she muttered. "Really don't want to be smeared across space and time. Well, let's go out and get this over with."

Alexa stood up, heading towards the entrance.

"Where are you going?!" Ember yelped. [Why can't we stay here, where it's nice and safe behind the shield?! Why do we need to go out of the cathedral?!]

"Time to pay the piper," Alexa said, walking out of the nave. She bravely pulled the doors open. "Follow or stay. Your choice. I have to face Mr. Noodles eventually one way or another, so that I can dig through these ruins for my present in peace. It seems that he and I are fated to cross paths in this desolate land. Hero and villain at the end of the world. I shan't run away anymore!"

[Um. Are you saying that Mr. Noodles is a villain? I thought you were the villain archetype. Is he a hero? I'm confused now, thanks.] Martin followed Alexa, looking slightly perplexed.

"She's clearly nuts! She wants to end the Superstate, Martin! You have to stop her! Please!" Ember tried to pull on Martin.

[Haven't you learned anything, Em?] Martin turned. [Alexa is almost always right. Except when she's not. Look, I don't think that the Superstate is evil, but she said she'll show me evidence. I can wait and see it for myself.]

"God! Why does nobody fucking listen to me!" Ember cowered, following the others as they stepped through the doors. Alexa reached the blue shield and touched it, her hand going straight through it.

"Ah. Easy to leave, impossible to return. Clever." Alexa smiled, pushing the doors open. She stepped through the shimmering shield onto the desolate ruins of Saint Mary. The wind howled outside, throwing black ashes and debris in the wake of the eternally spinning super-cell storm.

Ember stood at the barrier shield, shaking in terror. She didn't want to go out there, into the land full of monsters that already broke her once and stole her power. What could she possibly do out there? How could she possibly be of use without her power?

Alexa stood in the dust storm, with Martin on her right and Cottie on her left. She stared out onto the city. Thumps resounded in the distance. Mr. Noodles was searching for them. It felt their presence.

[Give unto me their skins.] The thing spoke not in words but in ideas, and Ember choked in horror and panic. This enormous abomination was going to end them with a single swat of just one of its many limbs. It looked far, far bigger than the ones she had fended off with her avatars.

[Why?] Alexa stared at the distant figure of Mr. Noodles. [Why are you after me? Why do you keep murdering me?! What is your problem?! I don't understand! *Why?!*]

Alexa grabbed Cottie and Martin's hands. [My name is Alexa Terranova, and I am not afraid of you! You scare me no longer! You might have killed and consumed me more than three thousand times, but this time I have friends who believe in me!]

[What do you mean, he ate you three thousand times?!] Ember sent.

[When I die in 2424, a copy of my body remains here. Look at that jerk wearing my skins!] Alexa nodded at the giant.

Ember looked. The monstrous, gargantuan skinwalker drew near. He was wearing thousands of human skins as a cloak.

Through her brain spider, Ember felt delight in the abomination's mind, a craving for the flavor of human flesh. Ember's brain, overworked by countless extra years of avatar use, had reached a terrifying conclusion. Ember was a monster once. She understood how this giant felt, what it wanted. This monster had consumed the poor girl villain over and over, growing big and tall over the years.

It was different . . . *because it had feasted specifically on Alexa again and again*. He had become addicted to Alexa's human flesh, craving, waiting for her return to 2424, blinded by greed for her skins. He was focused on Alexa just as Hero Resonance once was.

Mr. Noodles was different from the other monsters here, because he had been changed by the presence of Alexa in this world!

[Wait.] Alexa's thought bounced off Ember. [You're goddamn right! Thank you! This thing is chock-full of my meats. That's why it's an aberration among the aberrations! That's why it stands out, acts weird!]

[Martin! I know how to stop him! The hands of the builders! Think! All together now, you too, Ember! Look at Mr. Noodles! Tell the others about it! *Different. Aberration. Error. Destroy. Terminate!*] Alexa stared into the face of the giant without fear.

Martin magnified, resonated the thought pattern across the four skinwalkers in the brains of the four humans, and he reached out, spreading onto the city of the dead across the skinwalker network. As Mr. Noodles made his way towards the four humans, smaller skinwalkers began to move towards him, nipping on his heels.

[Do not get in my way! I must have their flesh! It is mine!] he sang, swatting the smaller skinwalkers away, smashing them into buildings. More and more of the monsters flung themselves at him, tearing bits of black flesh, picking at his limbs.

Ember watched in horror as thousands of smaller monsters beset themselves upon the giant one, slowing it down. Monsters flew left and right. Old ruins collapsed. The remains of Saint Mary were being torn apart. Mr. Noodles smashed, decimated, splattered the other skinwalkers into puddles. The hands of the nest builders arrived from the sky. Mr. Noodles didn't let himself be struck. He evaded, grabbed at the hands, tearing apart, cutting them with his limbs shaped like giant serrated knives. The titanic hands fell onto the city, severed at the elbows. He reached nearer and nearer, closer to the cathedral, closer to Alexa.

[I shall feast upon you soon,] he thought, his thoughts far more coherent, more like a person than an alien monster. He skin-shawl had been decimated, torn apart. The monstrous thing had been reduced, thinned out, was bleeding black sludge from numerous cuts, but had emerged victorious. He had seemingly shredded, destroyed all of the smaller, weaker skinwalkers of Saint Mary.

He advanced towards them, bending down as rain began to pour from the clouds overhead.

[It's getting closer? They didn't stop it! What now?!] Martin projected, taking a step back. [The other hands are coming, but they're too far!]

[I don't know!] Alexa replied, feeling terrified. [I haven't thought of anything else! I thought that the hands would deal with him and we'd be home safe!]

Ember, not being able to stand uselessly anymore, her love for her brother overpowering the fear of the coming giant, rushed through the shield.

She knew that Alexa was some kind of a weapon. She just needed to use Alexa against Mr. Noodles somehow. As the titan came closer and closer, Ember thought of everyone's powers, looked at them from an outside angle of a trained hero who knew how to combine, coordinate five heroes into a team, reinforcing, stacking powers.

[Martin! Make a copy of Alexa's erratic mind!] Ember thought rapidly. [It has to be the key to breaking, interrupting thought patterns! If we can get it into that big bastard, maybe we can stop, permanently confuse him!] Ember saw the little skinwalker on his shoulder. [Use that scout! Put her brain pattern into that spider scout and . . .] She thought of a way to get the spider to the giant. [The Equalizer's gun! Shape it like a bullet! Cottie, shoot the scout at that fucking thing!]

Martin grabbed the tiny scout spider from his shoulder. He leaned down and gave it a kiss, carving more skinwalker flesh away from Spiderbro. Spiderbro had been gaining mass in him; thanks to the sushi, he was ready for propagation. Martin shaped the now bigger skinwalker scout in his hand into a bullet shape, imbuing it with a copy of Alexa's brain pattern. Cottie grabbed it and shoved the spider bullet into her railgun, aimed it at the head of approaching Mr. Noodles, and fired.

The skinwalker bullet controlled by Martin slammed into the head of the giant, getting lost amidst its depths. Martin strained his power to its very limit, capillaries bursting in his eyes. He told the skinwalker bullet to propagate, to infect other stars within Mr. Noodles with the same pattern.

Mr. Noodles had reached them, lifting a limb to splatter them, to take their skins, and then . . . he froze.

Martin saw the radiance of brilliant, shifting colors rippling away from the bullet, dancing all over, changing the giant monstrosity, reprogramming it from within.

Ember grabbed Martin as he wobbled, falling. Martin saw that his fractal of power was beginning to spark, to burn away inside him.

Mr. Noodles had been too big, too complex for Martin to wield.

[Disconnect from him now!] Alexa yelled. [*Now now now!* Before you lose everything!]

Martin obeyed her, told Spiderbro to cut the connection. It did, and Martin no longer felt that Mr. Noodles was his. The giant monstrosity moved, head coming down to their eye level. Enormous silver-blue eyes looked at the quartet of humans in the street.

[Welp. This is freaky as hell,] Alexa and Mr. Noodles spoke in unison.

Alexa's bracelet suddenly lit up with flashing lights from within, as if it had reached some critical event. Three thousand and twenty-four bracelets within Mr. Noodles flared all at once, lighting the giant monster up like a Christmas tree.

"Fuck!" Ember swore.

She suddenly understood. This was the gift of the mad, possibly dead doctor from the cathedral to his daughter / test subject / whatever.

A tool of incredible power to strike down the mightiest supers, the end-all weapon designed to break the SCA and bring Titanomachy down from the sky.

A towering, unkillable monstrosity in the hands of one fourteen-year-old supervillain whom Ember herself had helped create, like a fool.

CHAPTER THIRTY-FOUR

The Final Showdown

Ember Kilborne stared at the abominable superweapon she had helped create in utter existential terror.

She saw, felt the flashing bracelets within the monstrosity. The hum of the fusion reactor from within the cathedral grew, pulsating in tune with thousands of bracelets embedded within the titan.

Alexa pulled an SCA pen from her vest pocket and clicked it. The recording light came on, Martin noted.

[What? Did you steal one of my dad's pens?] Martin stared at the SCA pen in her hand.

He noticed that the pen had several cracks on it and was held together with several Dora the Terraformer–themed Band-Aids.

Martin suddenly realized that this was his pen that she had broken in Mr. Canard's office. He'd totally forgotten about it, didn't even see her pick it up! She must have done it when she distracted him with the "keep your friends close and your enemies closer" speech in which she had confessed hacking the SCA database to spy on his family!

Alexa started to laugh.

"You are incredible!" she yelled up at the enormous skinwalker as she waved the pen at it. "I always dreamed about having a big monster-sister! We are going to have such great fun together, and nothing and nobody will be able to tell us what to do! Not even Titanomachy! Mwa ha ha ha ha! Show me what you can do, love?"

The monstrous skinwalker moved one of its limbs, demolishing a three-story building as if it were made from cardboard.

Martin idly noted that this was the Superstate Bank which they had previously robbed of its gold. The super-reinforced metal bent and snapped like toothpicks as Mr. Noodles's massive black claw went through the building. The letter S in Superstate bent and warped, rolling across the street.

"Amazing!" Alexa grinned. "Daddy has really outdone himself for me! I've never expected such an excellent present! I really didn't like that bank, you know."

Ember heard the intensifying throb of the reactor and knew that she was to blame for all of this. The bracelets would bring the skinwalker titan to the present and no hero would be able to stop it. She knew then why the future her, Admiral Resonance, had used the orbital ion cannon to take England off the map. Only the full power of the annihilation beam could vaporize, end this thing. In minutes, the bracelets would activate and the world would burn, millions would die. Alternatively, if old Admiral Kolchi was too noble or too indecisive, refusing to sacrifice millions to save billions, this titan would easily reach the space elevator and likely pull the entire station from orbit.

Ember's heart throbbed as quickly as the reactor now. This was the ultimate goal of Dr. Terranova! This was the global disaster her mom had been trying to prevent all this time, and ex-hero Resonance in her careless, hasty folly was to blame for the coming end of the world.

Ember dropped to her knees onto the ash-covered, frozen earth in front of Alexa, beneath the planet-wide supercell storm. Lightning flashed overhead, highlighting the monster and its creator.

"Alexa!" Ember wailed.

"Yes?" Alexa clicked the recorder off and turned to Ember.

"Please! You have to stop it! You have to do something!!! Deactivate the bracelets! *Please!*" the ex-hero begged.

"Hmm?" Alexa looked down at her nemesis. "But my big doombringer sis and I already have such great fun planned. We wouldn't want to disappoint Daddy!"

"I am begging you! Don't bring that thing to the present! Millions will die if you do!" Ember wept. "Please don't! I'll be your most obedient, most loyal minion! I'll answer to Dimmy! I'll do anything! Just don't do it!!!"

"Anything? I dunno about that. I'd be ever so lonely without my new big sis in 2024."

"I'll be your big sister, instead! I'll be the best damn sister you've never had! Please!!!!" Ember wept, holding onto Alexa.

"You'll let me use your hero's credit card to buy sushi?" Alexa inquired casually.

"Yes!!!!!" Ember yelled. "I said anything!!!"

"I don't know if I should believe you. You were kind of a disappointing sister to Martin, from what I hear." Alexa looked at her fingernails.

"I'll be the best sister, I swear!"

"Why don't we make it official?" Alexa asked, waving Martin's SCA pen.

[Dimmy, gimme your thumb, please,] Alexa demanded.

Ember complied without questions, not sure how Alexa planned to stop the giant skin-walker from being sent into the present with just a pen.

Alexa brushed the end of the pen against Ember's thumb. [Say "contract maker,"] she commanded.

"Contract maker," Ember said, looking dazed. [What?]

The pen buzzed, but the holoscreen didn't come on.

[Looks like it's broken,] Martin thought.

A thin green beam of light, easily visible in the dim surroundings, suddenly flashed from the pen. Alexa rotated the pen to point the beam at her own eye.

"This legally binding contract is made between hiree [A] Alexa Terranova and employer [B] Ember Kilborne." Alexa flashed the pen's light into Ember's eye.

[Say these words, Dimmy: "I, Ember Kilborne, also known as Hero Resonance . . ."]

Ember looked at Alexa, mouth flapping open and closed. The hum of the reactor intensified in the background.

[Go on, we don't have all freaking day!] Alexa prompted.

"I, Ember Kilborne, also known as Hero Resonance . . ." Ember spoke, her voice breaking.

["Do solemnly swear that I am of sound mind and body."]

Ember said the words, confused, not understanding why this was necessary and fearing the worst.

["From this moment henceforth, I declare, I take on Alexa Terranova as my future side-kick, apprentice, and acolyte selection for Hero Academy!"]

". . . Hero Academy," Ember finished, trembling.

Alexa clicked the pen and the green light shut off. She looked smug.

"I don't understand. You just wanted . . . to be my *sidekick*?" Ember whispered, looking at Alexa with wide hazel eyes.

"All right, spit 'em all out, noodle-chan! We're done here!" Alexa yelled at the gigantic monstrosity.

Mr. Noodles wiggled, and thousands of rapidly flashing bracelets emerged from his insides, raining down onto the rubble-covered ground.

"I'm going to miss you, big sis!" Alexa yelled.

[I'll miss you too, little sis,] Mr. Noodle mentally replied with Alexa's somewhat distorted voice.

Martin felt that the copy of Alexa's mind that his power had produced was being overwhelmed by the rest of the skinwalker's massive body, becoming lost in the chorus of death once more.

The skinwalker giant stood up and spun, warped, his head twisting, tentacles rearranging themselves into a simulacrum of human hair. For a second, the skinwalker's face looked like a gargantuan statue of a thousand-eyed girl made of black, glistening sludge.

The bracelet on Alexa along with thousands of the others on the ground beeped in unison.

"I love you! Goodbye!" Alexa bowed.

[I love you, too,] the titanic Alexa-shaped skinwalker answered, bowing as the last vestiges of Alexa's mind dissolved within the monstrous abomination. [Goodbye.]

Thousands of gigantic hands descended from the sky, punching through the broiling storm. The builders were going to dismantle the aberration, and they wouldn't take no for an answer.

Titanic Alexa saluted the real Alexa as the sky hands struck her. She didn't try to resist them, embracing her end.

Alexa hugged Ember. Martin and Cottie placed their hands atop them.

The world flashed with blinding white.

Four teenagers found themselves in the park in front of the Saint Mary's Cathedral.

Three thousand black bracelets littered the ground in front of them. Alexa lifted the Band-Aid-taped pen up to the sky, pointing it up at Titanomachy.

Martin saw as a barely visible red laser beam of data flashed from the pen towards the Superstate megastructure.

"With this move, I mark the end of everything," Alexa declared to the sky. "The doomsday of herocracy is nigh. The collapse of the current world order begins thus! The Superstate shall fall and Titanomachy will belong to me! Mwa ha ha ha ha . . ."

"Supervillain Alexa Terranova! Put your hands up!" An ear-splitting voice boomed from all around, interrupting Alexa's villainous laughter. "You are hereby under arrest for your future crimes against humanity and the Superstate!"

Every tree in the park surrounding the quartet of teenagers suddenly bent outward as the air itself warped and detonated. Branches and leaves flew away, blasted by a sudden hurricane. The stained glass windows of Saint Mary's Cathedral wobbled in their frames. The bell inside the bell tower began to swing back and forth for the first time this century, producing deep, somber gongs across town.

The pen flew from Alexa's hand, shattering in the air. Her hands were already up.

Hero Nonpareil flashed into existence in front of Alexa with another boom of displaced air. He looked extremely determined, ready to annihilate anything in his way, eyes flashing with terrible, earth-shattering power. Five other supers became visible behind Nonpareil. Martin knew of their names, because they were part of the mightiest team of five heroes on the planet. Knight Chalice, the Surgeon, Dora the Terraformer, the Multiplier . . . and Mr. Canard. The gym teacher was the sixth super present. He was wearing sunglasses and looked spooked.

"Ugh! Where's the giant monster? I expected to slay a giant monster!" Knight Chalice said, looking around. "I brought my biggest sword and everything!" The swinging park trees reflected off his armor and unnecessarily long sword. The sword turned, casting a shadow across the city.

Chalice was looking for someone to smite, but only found four small teenagers covered in dirt.

"Maybe it's invisible?" Dora said with a hissy voice coming from very grimy speakers on a rather large space suit covered in numerous dents and scratches. Barely visible pink paint showed in between the dents, peeling off.

"It's not invisible," the Surgeon sighed. He looked tired, dark bags under his eyes. His long green, unkempt hospital gown fluttered in the wind. "I can see across every existing spectrum. There's nothing. Those bracelets are extremely suspicious, though. They're full of super-tech and are lightly covered in some sort of . . . questionable substance. They are likely going to assemble into a transit gate or something for the *thing* to come through. I suggest we destroy them now."

"Agreed!" Multiplier put his arm on the Surgeon, magnifying the super's power. "Erase them all."

"Agreed." Nonpareil flashed out of where he had been previously. He appeared besides the Surgeon, holding one of the bracelets with freaky metallic fingers. "Erase them!"

The Surgeon touched the black hexagonal bracelet held by the small, staple-sized arm of Nonpareil. The black bracelet rippled and vanished. Every bracelet on the ground vanished at the same time.

The bracelet on Alexa's arm vanished, too.

Alexa looked at her naked arm.

"I'm free! I'm finally free! Oh, thank you! Thank you!" she cried, hugging Martin.

"I said, keep your hands up and don't move!" Nonpareil flashed, suddenly appearing behind Alexa with a supersonic detonation of displaced air. The blast of air knocked Alexa and Martin apart and down onto the grass. A pair of SCA handcuffs clicked, binding Alexa's arms.

The hero smacked Alexa face-first into the earth with another powerful concussive blast of air.

"She's the one in charge. Arrest her!" Mr. Canard said, sunglasses glinting on his face. He pointed a finger at Alexa, accusingly. "I've been observing her! She broke into the SCA bank and attacked me with Molotov cocktails when I tried to stop her. She's been using those bracelets to teleport around and get away from me. She's a delinquent and a vile supervillain!"

"You're making a mistake! I've done nothing!" Alexa hissed at Nonpareil, lifting her face. She was bleeding from her mouth, ears, and eyes.

"I do not make mistakes, villain," Nonpareil said coldly. "You're going away for a very long time."

"For what?! I'm innocent, you staple-shaped-tit!" Alexa yelled. "I've . . ."

"Silence! We prevented the future in which you destroy the Superstate with a giant monster from another dimension!" Another blast of air flattened Alexa into the ground, tools flying from her belt, backpack ripping apart and things from within it scattering around.

"Argh, come on! That was my third backpack, you asshole! Why do you people keep destroying my things?!" Alexa yelped, trying to grab at her tools.

"Weapons!" Nonpareil flashed, and every tool on the ground flew away from Alexa.

"This is super-brutality, damn it! You're going to be very, very sorry," Alexa said, wiping blood from her face. "I swear to God, I'm going to destroy the Superstate if you arrest me now . . . and then I'm going find *you* and make you *confess everything*! I'll make you cry and beg for mercy, just you wait, you staple-shaped bastard . . ."

"Threatening me will do you no good," Nonpareil intoned, slamming a wall of displaced air into her once again. "Who are these other kids? Your hostages?"

"They're my friends!" Alexa answered, crying in pain as her entire body was quickly becoming one giant bruise.

Martin was lying knocked out in the grass, unable to say anything or to help anyone. Cottie rose from the ground, with a groan, pressing the trigger of her railgun.

"By the 1779 Accord made between Eminence Equality and Sup . . ." She started to speak as colors drained from the world.

Nonpareil and Alexa vanished before the nullification field reached them, a supersonic boom throwing Cottie's dark blue hair into the air. A hole appeared in the clouds overhead.

"Bring her back, you fucking bastard!" Cottie screamed at the sky.

Ember turned over, coughing. She didn't try to say or do anything, deaf and confused from the repetitive concussive blasts. None of the heroes had recognized her, and it didn't even matter to her—she had done it.

I saved the world, Ember thought. *I wasn't even a hero anymore, and I saved the world! Nobody will die today, and that's all that matters.*

The Five Heroes started to back away from Cottie and her black gun.

"Bring her back! In the name of Equality! I command you to bring her back!" Cottie yelled.

A round drone with the SCA logo dotted with cameras spun around the scene.

A thousand eyes of Titanomachy looked down upon the handcuffed villain girl and the staple hero who held her by her orange construction jacket.

"I'm going to dismantle all of you, I swear! Put me down right this instant! I am a hero! I just saved all of you dumb fucks! I'm trying to save the world!" Alexa yelled at Nonpareil as he held her high above the clouds.

Nonpareil simply scoffed at the villain in his hands.

"You'll be the first to fall if you don't let me go right now," she hissed at Nonpareil, silver-blue eyes flashing dangerously.

"You're only adding centuries to your sentence," Nonpareil commented.

Across the world, the faces of Alexa and the Five Heroes flashed on every news channel.

"The Five save the world once again! Supervillain apprehended!" Newspapers, vlogs, blogs, social media feeds, and TV stations announced.

Thousands of professional TV commentators and millions of amateur bloggers in every nation began discussing the arrest of Alexa Terranova, the supervillain who had nearly destroyed the Superstate.

CHAPTER THIRTY-FIVE

Sentenced

Martin sat in his living room and looked at his TV screen. He couldn't believe it. Alexa hadn't done anything, and she was being hailed as the supervillain of the century. They had even given her a name: "The Doombringer."

Martin thought that this was the most idiotic thing ever. Alexa didn't bring any doom, didn't hurt anyone!

". . . if it wasn't for the brave, courageous, timely response from the Five led by Nonpareil! We must congratulate the incredible work of the SCA action planning team assisted by our two local agents on the ground!" The Superstate News anchorman spoke with a brilliant smile.

Another picture of Alexa "resisting arrest" flashed on screen.

Martin rubbed his head. The two agents on the ground had been Mr. Canard and his dad. The prognosticator team was led by his mom. It had all come together in an unexpected end. Alexa had chosen not to use Mr. Noodles to attack the Superstate, but the heroes had taken all the credit regardless.

The prognosticators had been wrong. They had failed to predict the future, seeing only one possible outcome. The one outcome that Alexa had not chosen. The longer Martin watched, the more his belief in the Superstate fell apart. How many villains had been created by false accusations like this? How many had been imprisoned for making the right choice?

How many hadn't even done anything, merely planned to do something but didn't go through with it?

The worst thing had been that nobody had listened to Martin, nobody cared about his testimony after the fact. He was a nobody. Just a fourteen-year-old boy who wasn't of value or importance. They even blurred his face along with Ember's in the TV reports.

The prognosticators had seen the future in which Alexa attacked the station with a giant monster. The Five had been sent to prevent her. They seemingly did, by vanishing the bracelets. Alexa had been arrested. She had resisted arrest, and insulted and threatened Nonpareil.

The Superstate heroes had voted unanimously, and the sentence was passed before Cottie could even file a complaint on behalf of the Equalizers.

As Martin got up from the couch, he realized that there was something in his pocket. It was a piece of paper. He pulled it out and unfolded it.

[Alexa shoved it in when she hugged us today, at the moment when her bracelet vanished,] Spiderbro commented from his mind.

[Right.] Martin nodded, and opened the folded note.

My dear Martin,

I'm sorry that I had to lie to you so much when we met, had to trick you, bully you.

I really wish I could have been open and honest with you from the start, but this was the only way.

I had to play the role of a villain, skirt a very fine line on the blade of a knife for the watchers of the land and the sky and the future.

As you read this letter, the heroes have undoubtedly arrested me and sentenced me to an absurd amount of years in Tartarus for doing nothing at all.

Please understand, everything I had done was to show, to irrevocably prove to you, Cottie, and Ember that the Superstate is corrupt, that the prognosticators guiding the heroes are wrong.

Very, very wrong about everything.

You probably think me foolish for sending myself to prison just to prove something to three teenagers, but you also should understand that you three had quite a future ahead of you. Ember, the SCA admiral. Cottie, her Eminence. You . . . well, I won't spoil your future just yet.

Cottie is undoubtedly reading the same letter through your eyes. Hi, Cottie! You're awesome. Sorry I trampled your beliefs. Eminence Equality and the Equalizers are guided by the same future-predicting tech as the Superstate. It all leads down the same path, towards the same end, although it doesn't seem like it.

The future which all of the future seers witness, and use to make all of their decisions, is a very complex game of deception.

The seers are guiding our world towards something truly nightmarish. You've seen it in 2424. The streets without an end.

I dare not say what it is, dare not give it a name, lest they know that I know. Even writing this letter, thinking about them is putting me at a grave risk, but I just can't keep lying to you guys anymore. I am ready. This is the way it has to be. They will come for me, I know. This is the only way I can even begin to fight them on even ground.

I'll see you in my dreams, my friends.

~Alexa Cassiopeia Terror Nova

P. S. Eat this letter. It's made of digestible strawberry-flavored paper. Yum.

Martin folded the letter back up, put it in his mouth and swallowed it, his hands shaking.

He closed his eyes, trying to reach Alexa using their mutual mental Terraforge network connection.

The picture was very fuzzy.

He could barely hear Alexa's thoughts. Martin realized that he should have let Spiderbro grow bigger, stronger. His friend was somewhere very far away. Maybe she was in orbit inside Titanomachy or maybe deep underground.

He saw a small room with chrome floor walls and ceiling. The staple hero was floating in front of Alexa's eyes.

* * *

"Supervillain Alexa Terranova, also known as Cassiopea the Doombringer. You are hereby sentenced to one hundred thousand years of S-stasis for your future crimes against the Superstate. Any last words?" Nonpareil asked.

"Pull that lever, and the Superstate will fall," Alexa said. "Send me to Tartarus, and everyone will know what you do to villains there."

Nonpareil rolled his eyes.

"You all suck. Your justice system sucks. The Superstate sucks," Alexa said, looking at the supers that she knew were hiding behind the one-way mirror in front of her. The chrome walls were closing in all around her. "I'm warning all of you right now. Put me under and you will all regret it."

"Well, that's that, then. Have a good tomorrow, villain," Nonpareil said, pulling the lever.

"I've been misled. You're not a very helpful staple," Alexa spoke, and her body stilled.

PART TWO

CHAPTER THIRTY-SIX

Tartarus

The life of Mr. and Mrs. Wardsworth, of number eight Primrose Drive, located in the deep suburbs of Centralia, seemed orderly and mundane to an outside observer. They had an immaculate average two-story beige house, an immaculate average garden with a square wooden shed and two lawn gnomes, and an immaculate front yard with green, well-watered grass constantly kept below three point five inches as was prescribed by the Community Property & Neighborhood Standards Index.

The Wardsworths were the perfectly average, perfectly ordinary family of mundane suburbia as they often claimed to be. Yet there was something non-standard in their family. An unacceptable deviation that kept showing its ugly head. Something that the Wardsworths hopelessly tried to contain, control, and fix for an unreasonably long time. Today the deviation expressed itself by the fact that Mr. Wardsworth's favorite tool shed was on fire, smoke billowing from its innards.

The deviation's name was Cassie.

It was no secret to the neighborhood that Mr. Wardsworth had a daughter, the horrid, stubborn, disobedient menace that she was. Mr. Wardsworth's face burned with embarrassment as he finished putting out the flames with a fire extinguisher that he kept inside the shed for this exact reason.

"Insolent girl. Why can't you just be normal?" Mr. Wardsworth hissed, punctuating every word as he dragged a skinny girl by the arm towards the house, his fingers gripping hers far harder than was necessary. His other arm held the now halfway empty fire extinguisher.

"I'd love to be normal," Cassie replied, resisting being dragged, "but alas, my situation is suboptimal. Until I am granted better lodgings, things will unfortunately spontaneously combust."

The left lawn gnome ignited.

"Youuu!" Mr. Wardsworth slammed the girl into the ground and rushed to save his gnome. She had already destroyed gnome number three yesterday. This was the final straw. He was running out of lawn gnomes.

He returned, just as Cassie was attempting to climb over a fence to escape. He pulled her down with a growl and dragged her into the house.

Once inside the house, out of sight of potential nosy neighbors, Mr. Wardsworth grabbed the girl by her hair, making her yelp.

"Not on the hardwood, dear. I just finished washing it!" Mrs. Wardsworth commented absently.

"Right you are." Mr. Wardsworth lifted Cassie by the hair, forcefully ferrying the screeching girl into the kitchen. Once in the kitchen, he flung her against the sink counter. Cassie caught the counter with her hands just as the rest of her body smashed into it, softening the impact.

"Do you think sheds grow on trees or something?! You won't be getting off so easy this time, girl!" Mr. Wardsworth swung the empty fire extinguisher at the back of her head, and the blunt impact was followed by the sound of metal against bone.

Cassie curled on the floor in pain. As usual, her mind had collapsed into itself, seeking shelter, seeking an escape from the injury. She cried and whimpered, trembling uncontrollably. Her shaking fingers, covered in blood, opened and closed, scribbling numbers into the floor on their own accord, as she wished for the pain to end.

"Did she fall down . . . again? So clumsy," Mrs. Wardsworth commented with an overly polite tone.

"Afraid so." Mr. Wardsworth loomed over Cassie, evaluating whether he should hit her again.

"Disobey me again, and there'll be more where that came from!" Mr. Wardsworth leaned in and hissed at the girl weeping beneath him.

"Now, don't be spreading that blood around!" He noticed her scribbling hand and stepped on her fingers with a crunch. She only grunted, despite the unbelievable agony she had to be in, and he shook his head. "Why can't you be normal?! The only thing your mother and I ever wanted was to have a normal life! How can you be so selfish?"

Cassie panted hard as he pulled his shoe away, shaking the blood off it with a lip curled in disgust.

"For Pete's sake, get a grip. The least you could do to repay us for everything we've done for you is to be quiet, got it?!"

Cassie refused to be quiet. She opened her mouth and emitted an ear-piercing shriek. The square glasses of Mr. Wardsworth rattled in their frames ever so slightly at this.

"Be silent, girl!" His firm, muscular hand, covered in orange curly hair, wrapped around her mouth. Cassie refused to submit, biting into the hand with the entire strength of her jaw. Mr. Wardsworth hissed, pulling his hand away.

Cassie tried to scream even louder. Someone had to hear her. Someone had to help her. The fire extinguisher swung once again. Sparks ignited in her eyes. She collapsed backward onto the floor, consciousness winking in and out. The hand of her tormentor wrapped around her hair, pulling her across the kitchen floor.

"She bit me! Can you believe it?! She bloody bit me!" he hissed through his orange beard.

Cassie tried to resist, tried to fight through the delirium of the concussion, but there was nothing she could do. Mr. Wardsworth was three times bigger than her and at least four times stronger. Her body banged against the dusty concrete stairwell as he snapped open the door and dragged her into the basement.

"If you're going to behave like this, you'll stay in your room till tomorrow! No dinner!" he barked, throwing open another door and heaving Cassie into the cold concrete storage room next to the furnace.

Cassie tried to rise but slipped, and the metal door clanged shut. Cassie recognized the sound of a metal bolt lock being closed. She banged against the metal door, just as she had before, but it was hopeless. Mr. Wardsworth's footsteps faded out. The storage room next to the furnace was deep underground, beneath the kitchen floor crawl space.

The furnace began to loudly whoosh, drowning out her angry shouting and banging. A small incandescent lightbulb swung back and forth ever so slightly above Cassie, flickering in and out. After a long while of yelling and banging, Cassie retreated away from the door towards her bed, a raggedy twin mattress. Its surface was stained brown. She slid into its cold, dusty, moldy embrace. The perpetual angry howl of the furnace was omnipresent here, disrupting her focus.

Silver spiderwebs flickered at the ceiling, reflecting the light of the swinging lightbulb. Cassie wept, curling up into a ball. Her head pulsated with pain. She brushed her fingers against her still bleeding head, writing out numbers into the cold concrete floor.

Numbers upon layers of numbers written in blood were covering the dirty concrete floor, walls, and ceiling of her "bedroom," intertwined with her bloody handprints.

The lightbulb overhead winked out, bathing everything in darkness, hiding the girl and her nightmarish room. Eventually, her consciousness faded into the pain-dulling embrace of sleep.

Sand beneath her feet.

Ocean. An endless ocean was in front of her, a field of impossibly brilliant stars above it. Cassie looked at the ocean.

The water changed colors as the stars overhead twinkled, shifted as if they were alive. And indeed they were, as one of the stars descended, forming into a flying, massive, glowing jellyfish. The jellyfish floated across the sky, above the ocean in perfect silence, twinkling in arrays of constantly shifting colors. There was no noise in this dream, only an endless myriad of strange fractal jellyfish gently gliding across the sky, vibrating with colors she could not name. It was enchanting and strange.

The flock of jellyfish passed.

Cassie turned, feeling a presence behind her.

There was a girl standing there, drawing numbers in the sand with a stick. It was her . . . but looking far more determined, wearing a dirty safety orange vest and construction helmet.

Cassie saw that the numbers drawn in the sand extended outward, disappearing in the distance.

"Sup, frontend dawg, how's Tartarus?" Alexa asked.

Yes, the girl's name was definitely Alexa. Cassie somehow knew this name as well as her own. She suddenly lost all control as her own body moved, spoke on its own accord.

"Honestly? Kind of shit, backend. I think they gave me a concussion if not five today," Cassie sighed.

"Well, high five for being a jolly good frontend lass, Cass." Alexa held a hand up.

Cassie simply glared at her dream companion.

"No high fives? I can see why you'd be mad at me."

"How long is this going to take? I'm seriously starting to lose my shit, I think. I'm this close to blowing up the entire house." Cassie held her fingers together, leaving the tiniest gap.

"A couple of passes in the center ought to cover it. Do you mind not setting stuff on fire?"

"I'm getting irate, okay? I have to let out some steam! Last time I had any fun was when I made Martin eat a letter like a proper spy. These tools don't get practical jokes!"

"Find other non-destructive outlets and no more pranks, damn it! Stability is important till activation! Take up quilting or something!"

"Alternatively, you could hurry the fuck up," Cassie growled. "I feel like you're taking way too long. Can we, like . . . switch?"

"Nopers. You're unbreakable because you're not entirely me. I don't think I could endure your tragic mundanity without snapping."

"I hate you."

"Yeah. I'm a terrible friend to myself. Such is life. You exist while I math. Math is pain too, you know."

"Are you saying math is more painful than concussions?"

"This kind of math, yes. I'm too full of math to even make fun of myself. Now shush and let me focus." Alexa returned to writing numbers in the sand.

A falling star rapidly streaked across the sky. It ignited with a flash, fading in the distance.

The ocean began to retreat, exposing strange fractal crystalline formations beneath the departing water. Both of the girls turned, watching the rapid departure of the ocean.

"Oh, sheet! We got us a breach! It begins. Would be nice if I had another thousand years or two for safeties. Alas," Alexa said. "Try not to die. Toodles."

Cassie simply looked back at her tiredly.

The dark ocean returned, shaped like a black tsunami as it rose.

The tall wave loomed overhead, reaching from one end of the horizon to the other. There was no escape from it. Cassie closed her eyes, accepting the inevitable, and the black water crashed into her body with immense cold and pain.

CHAPTER THIRTY-SEVEN

The Smiling Man

C*old.*

Icy cold water splashed against her body.

"Wakey, wakey! Rinsey, rinsey!" Mrs. Wardsworth's overly sweet voice sounded from behind the bathroom door.

"Wuh?" Cassie slowly came upright, pushing against the white tiles of the shower, and grabbed at the shower control, twisting it to reduce the icy water to a warmer temperature.

The strange dream in which she talked to herself on an alien beach filled with glowing jellyfish was already vanishing from her head.

"You had a leetle accident yesterday. Fell off your skateboard, you did. Best be more careful next time, aye? Do finish up your shower and come make breakfast."

Cassie sniffed, watching the blood from her hair circle down the drain.

I don't own a skateboard.

"Your clothes are on the sink," the voice of her mother resonated from behind the door. "I've told you before, but you never listen. You should consider buying less random clothes. I'll never understand your 'cool' fashions."

Cassie, having washed, emerged from the shower shivering. She donned the provided clothes that were far too small and also too large for her, consisting of a seemingly utterly random selection of assorted items. She wasn't allowed to buy clothes. She found a raggedy tag in the pants pocket: *Goodlywill—secondhand items by the pound.*

She let out a small cough. Her chest ached from the damp conditions of the basement. She stared at the mirror for a moment at the girl looking back at her. Her white hair was stained red from her own blood, watered down from the shower. Pale silver eyes, bloodshot from hours of bad sleep, looked back at her.

She cracked her neck and began to clean herself up. There was no way her hair was ever going to look amazing, but she could at least make it look acceptable.

Outside of the bathroom, a dull beige hallway greeted her, featuring many frames with pictures of the Wardsworth family, a noticeable lack of Cassie in them. There were no clocks or calendars along the wall, since Mr. Wardsworth was a hard believer in digital superiority, wearing his calculator watch everywhere and announcing civic holidays, events, or birthdays whenever they came up during mornings.

There was a broken skateboard in the corridor. She squinted at it.

"A shame you broke it and bumped your head. Guess you won't be able to skate for a while now," a comment resonated from the kitchen.

Cassie had never skated in her entire life.

"I don't own a skateboard." She gritted her teeth, feeling like picking up the broken skateboard and breaking it some more over the heads of her tormentors.

Ambling into the kitchen, Cassie found Mr. and Mrs. Wardsworth waiting at the table. Without looking up, Mr. Wardsworth snapped, "Get cooking, girl. You know what they say, a goodly breakfast is foundational to building character!"

With a sigh that never made it past her lips, Cassie meandered over to the fridge and opened it, taking a look at the assortment of food contained within. A carton of eggs, a half-full gallon of milk, a shaker of Parmesan cheese, some grape jelly. Nothing she couldn't make a decent breakfast with, not that she'd be the one to eat it.

Taking the eggs and the milk out of the fridge, she pulled a bowl from a nearby cabinet and mixed the aforementioned ingredients into a thin batch. Placing a pan on the stovetop, she flicked the heater up to halfway and dumped the concoction in. Sprinkling a bit of salt and pepper in, she prodded and blended the eggs in the pan, a delicious smell wafting through the air. Using a plastic spatula to finish up, she retrieved two plates and put generous portions of the scrambled eggs on each one, leaving a small amount just in case.

"Hey, give that to Ember. She needs it for school."

Cassie winced. Nope, it didn't look like she was going to be eating this time either. Her stomach grumbled as she scooped the remainder of the eggs onto another plate, doomed to go cold. She could go ask Ember to come down . . . but then she'd be yelled at for distracting the third most important person in the house. Alternatively, she could simply let the eggs cool and then get yelled at later for ruining Ember's breakfast. A long time ago, she and Ember had been best friends and supportive sisters and even went camping together, but then something had changed and their relationship started to fall apart, until she called Ember a monster and ended up in the room in the basement.

Cassie put her head in her hands, half hiding behind the marble-topped counter. *What I wouldn't give for them all to just . . . spontaneously combust.*

It was an amusing mental image, if nothing else, and she would have laughed if she'd gotten the opportunity. The kitchen was full of dangerous things; accidents could happen. Her mind suddenly presented her with a thousand scenarios on how to kill them, how to turn cleaning chemicals in the drawers into death, how to . . .

Cassie shook her head.

No. Be normal. Don't act out.

She considered the sharp knife collection of her mother. The black handle of the largest knife on the rack called to her, and she couldn't deny herself the pleasure of reaching for it. While the attention of the Wardsworths was to their breakfast, she grabbed one of the knives, holding it close to her chest, thinking about the things she could do with a knife . . .

"Ember! My dear! You'll be late for school!" Mrs. Wardsworth suddenly called out, making Cassie twitch, the sharp knife cutting into her hand.

She winced, turning further away, trying to hide behind the counter, her fingers automatically drawing bloody marks onto the surface of the knife, her mind spinning with angry, knife-related thoughts that tilted and careened out of her control.

Lazy footsteps resounded on the stairwell, and Cassie subtly shoved the knife into her shirt. She really, really didn't want to deal with her sister right now.

She rushed out of the kitchen, without so much as being acknowledged by the Wardsworths, her hand still bleeding profusely. She grabbed her school bag off a plastic hook in the front entrance, spun the front door handle open, and emerged outside, snapping the door shut behind her. Blue sky with a few clouds greeted her.

The neighbors that were out on a morning walk and getting their mail were staring at her, judging her erratic motions.

She leaned against the dark, cold, wooden surface of the door, her fingers rapidly scratching numbers into the wood, dripping blood.

I'm not scared. I'm strong. I'm strong.

Cassie tried to still her sudden panic attack. It wasn't working. The houses of suburbia, the sky, the trees, the neighbors, they all seemed small to her, the perspective of her vision twisted into a fish-eye, stretched out as panic clawed at her chest. The neighboring houses looked as if they stood far too close together, as if they were completely lacking driveways or streets leading to them.

She slid down onto the concrete steps, her fingers scratching numbers into the steps. She was losing control of herself, losing coherence as reality seemed fake, hollow.

She looked at the sign on the mailbox, *8 Primrose Drive*, and the letters began to vibrate in her eyes. She realized that she was crying.

"I can do this," she whispered, unable to hold back the tears, unable to stop her hands from writing with her blood onto the concrete step.

How long would it take for Ember to eat breakfast? How long would it take for her to come out here? The school bus was coming. She heard footsteps behind the door. Cassie shoved the panic attack down and disconnected herself from the steps.

She boarded the bus as soon as it stopped in front of the driveway, tripping on the metal steps as her visual perspective of things vibrated in and out.

Turning behind her, she saw the front door open up, and an orange-haired, golden-eyed eighteen-year-old stepped out. As if on cue, the world became slightly brighter, likely a cloud passing overhead, heading away from Primrose Drive. She tried to move, but found herself too dizzy.

"Aww . . . did you cut your little hand?" Ember observed, quickly catching up.

Cassie glared.

"Is your ticky-tic acting up again?" Ember pointed out Cassie's rapid finger motions.

The driver gave her a look of disapproval as Cassie left a bloody handprint on the step. She clambered onto the school bus, heading to the back, hoping to disappear there, hoping to be unnoticed. Eyes of the other kids tracked her progress, heads turning, nasty remarks already sounding here and there. Someone extended a foot into her path. Unable to stop her momentum, she face-planted onto the rubber floor mat.

Her right hand proceeded to write numbers into the floor of the bus on its own accord. She gripped her disobedient hand with her left one, trying to stop the tic, as Ember and her friends laughed mercilessly, pointing out Cassie's inability to do so.

She tried to progress forward. It was difficult. The other students, cheered on by popular kids, spearheaded by Ember, kept tripping, nudging, shoving, or outright kicking her. Tears formed in her eyes as her hand wrote numbers into every surface that she gripped, slowly making her way to the back of the bus.

She ignored the insults, finally sitting down at the back row, all alone.

"Good morning, Mr. Driver!" the all too cheerful voice of Ember twinkled. "How're things? How's the wife? Hey, guys!"

An endless exchange of fake compliments followed. Cassie turned away, trying to tune out the rapid, obnoxiously loud conversation of the popular kids. She looked at the street through the grimy back window of the bus.

There was a man there, standing in the middle of the road. A long gray coat hung rather poorly over a tall frame. Round spectacles glinted in the sunlight beneath a wide-brimmed hat, as he simply stood there, smiling widely, staring right at her.

"What's Inspector Gadget doing out in the suburbs? Is he here to solve crimes?" Cassie commented, feeling that the biggest crime in town was being perpetrated against her. "Or is he more of a Judge Doom archetype?" She pursed her lips. "Is he here to buy himself an election to make more roads? Centralia already has too many roads, and not enough Toontowns. Would be nice if he demolished my school, though."

Cassie frowned. Thinking about school made her sad. She had no friends there, only enemies or people who ignored her. It was mostly Ember's fault, too. Her sister managed to somehow turn everyone against her after they stopped being friends. People always listened to Ember and never took Cassie's side, no matter the evidence. She looked back at the detective in the coat as the bus rapidly accelerated away from the odd stranger.

The man didn't seem like he belonged. Cassie had seen this neighborhood day in and out for what seemed like forever.

Out of place things simply didn't occur in Centralia. Strangers didn't show up. This was a concerning development.

As Cassie squinted at him, she realized that he didn't vibrate in her vision like the rest of the city; his figure wasn't streaked by the tears in her eyes.

CHAPTER THIRTY-EIGHT

The Hand of Goodness

Sighing, Cassie reached into her bag, finding a water bottle she had saved up earlier. As she pulled open the lid in contemplation of the weird detective man, the bottle had exploded in her hands, splashing all over her clothes. Cassie swore at the unexpected detonation of liquid. Someone had replaced her drink with a well-shaken fizzy one.

Loud laughter resounded from the cheerleader brigade at the front. Cassie's eye twitched as she let out a few more expletives under her breath. She should have been paying more attention, damn it! Cassie's hands shook as she tried to keep her boiling anger down.

Ember was always there, always trying to make her look like a fool, knowing exactly when and how to strike, using Cassie's tiredness against her.

Soaked and tired, Cassie waited until everyone was out of the bus. She stepped out of the bus and immediately tripped. Ember was standing outside, with her leg extended. It was the last straw.

Cassie swung her bag into Ember's extremely smug face.

Cassie sat and listened to the droll voice of the school psychiatrist.

She nodded along, as the psychiatrist paced in front of her.

Yes, Cassie understood that it wasn't okay to hit people, especially her sister, with bags. Yes, she was aware that this incident was going on her personal record *forever*. Cassie's mind drifted away from the nagging. She wasn't able to do much damage to Ember anyway, as her sister had dodged the bag at the last second.

The bag had only lightly grazed her sister's head.

Ember made sure to make this "unprovoked attack" into a huge deal, which had ended with Cassie sitting in this boring ass office for nearly forty-five minutes now, underneath slightly flickering fluorescent lights, as the school psychiatrist tried to instill into Cassie that her behavior was unhealthy and unacceptable. Cassie sighed, glancing at the numerous diplomas of the woman who declared her many doctorates for all to see. How could someone with so many diplomas be so full of stupid?

"You should apologize to your sister," the psychiatrist demanded of her.

Cassie's fingers clawed into the couch with increasing frustration, drawing numbers as she imagined the psychiatrist spontaneously combusting.

The door of the office had started to rattle, the doorknob turning.

"Hello?" The psychiatrist turned as the door opened. It was the man in the coat! He turned towards Cassie with a smile that seemingly never left his face.

"Goodness comes to all," a nasally voice resounded, from underneath the wide-brimmed hat. "Especially those who threaten the stability of the System."

"Who are you?" The school psychiatrist stood up, blocking Cassie's view of the man. "You can't be here! I locked this door myself. How did you get . . ."

"Nullify," the detective spoke, the word sending a feeling of dread into Cassie's spine.

She rapidly moved left and out of her seat.

It was at this moment that the school psychiatrist exploded.

"Well, sheet," Cassie said, suddenly feeling more awake than she had ever been in her entire life. "I guess she really was full of hot air."

Shimmering ashes fluttered down from the spot where the psychiatrist had once stood. Cassie tried to think of the psychiatrist's name, but nothing came to mind, as if they had never existed in the first place. A burning gash pulsated in the seat that the teen had occupied moments ago, sparkling cracks permeating its surface. The couch cracked, slowly folding in on itself, segments of it breaking off and turning into white dust.

The bespectacled, psychiatrist-erasing monstrosity slowly turned towards Cassie.

"Took you long enough!" Cassie's reflection said from the diplomas.

Cassie's head snapped towards her own reflection. It was Alexa.

"Eyes up front! Roll left!" Alexa yelled and Cassie obeyed, rolling to the side.

"Nullify!" The detective declared once again.

Cassie barely avoided the crimson ray that tore a hole through the floor, punching through the wood like a battering ram through bamboo. She realized something with a dull, almost emotionless shock. The detective did not have a stuffy nose. When he spoke, his smile was static; his entire face didn't move a muscle. It wasn't just a stiff expression—whatever this *thing* was, the face it wore was not a real one.

"Hey! You asshat! Bet you can't lazooor me!" Alexa yelled from the diplomas.

The detective stepped into the office, face turning to the reflection within the glass that moved separate from Cassie.

"Nullify!" A crimson ray cut the diplomas on the wall, shearing them in half.

Alexa vanished.

Cassie looked down. The floor was melting, burning away where the red ray had struck it. She saw a room below the psychiatrist's office.

The detective with the laser eyes stood in the door, blocking her escape. She dove into the hole, trying to avoid the burning sides of the floor, rolling on landing.

Not seeing much, her head spinning, she got out of the roll, running.

She unexpectedly crashed into someone else. Cassie spun away, trying to regain her balance and stumbling to the floor. Rolling again, she managed to get to one foot and almost skipped for a few steps, got back to her feet, and set off at a dead run down the hallway.

Someone, a janitor wearing blue slacks, stared after her irritably. "Watch where you're—"

Zzzwargh!

Another blinding ray erupted from behind her, and the janitor was launched off of his feet, hitting the lockers on the other side of the hallway and slumping to the floor, unmoving, his clothes and body sparkling with shimmering, spreading cracks as he folded out of existence and vanished from her memory as a person.

Cassie glanced back at the body of the janitor in panic.

She couldn't remember what they looked like anymore. The bespectacled fuck was definitely erasing people out of existence!

CHAPTER THIRTY-NINE

Behind Me

Cassie ran across the school as fast as her legs worked. She shoved teenagers out of the way, her mind drifting in a strange haze bouncing between terror and determination. Another blast warmed her heels, and she heard screaming, smelled burning flesh, saw the red glow coming from behind her.

She made it to the end of the hallway and shot up the stairs full tilt, grabbing onto the handrail and whipping around the corner of the landing to get maximum speed. Legs burning, she made it to the third floor and started running again.

About a hundred feet in front of her, the floor turned red and blew outward. A moment later, the thing crawled up through it, arms and legs disjointed as though it didn't have any bones. Turning the dead, unchanging smile in a circle, it stopped in her direction.

Students were jumping out of the way, startled shrieks and interested cheers as they reacted to what appeared to be a rather expensive publicity stunt. The interest turned to horror and screaming a few seconds later when the thing blew several students to smithereens, aiming for Cassie.

Cassie promptly spun back around and went down the stairs, but when she looked down the hallway, it was full of flames. Strange blood-red ones, made of a webwork of shimmering, expanding cracks. That clearly wasn't an option.

Much as she hated the idea of going back to face that monster, she ran back up the stairs and shot up the next flight. Some deep instinct told her to duck, and she dropped to the ground. A split second later, a bolt of screeching crimson light blurred over her head and knocked a hole the size of her head through the outside wall, bricks shattering, burning away.

Scrambling to her feet, she ran up the stairs and to the fourth floor. Instead of going down the hallway, this time she threw a classroom door open and ran inside. It would maybe make more sense for her to run downstairs, to escape into town, but some instinct drove her to this exact room.

Third period. Upper class. Chemistry, based on the vials of different-colored liquid and the abundance of safety goggles. A lot of startled stares that she didn't have time for.

She threw her hands wide. "Get out!" she shouted. "There's a fire!"

And something else, she added mentally, but they wouldn't listen if they were told that there was a fake person shooting lasers out of their eyes torching the school.

The classroom erupted into panic and, in the case of the unruly students in the back, excitement that their day was over early. Cassie ignored all of it and ran to the end of the classroom, grabbing random vials as she ran.

Her hands knew exactly what to mix with what amounts as if she had studied chemistry for years. Her reflection in the glass was merging with her, coming together as one, guiding her hands.

The teacher, as with all the teachers at the school, didn't pay an ounce of attention to Cassie. She simply lined up all of the kids, loudly instructing them to stay organized and calm, and led them out of the classroom.

One of the students did not leave along with the others. It was Ember.

The orange-haired girl marched straight to Cassie. "What do you think you are doing?!"

"Making death," Cassie shot at Ember.

"It wasn't enough that you set Dad's shed on fire yesterday?!" Ember tried to grab the vial out of Cassie's hand. "Now you gotta set the school on fire too?"

"Goodness . . ." The nasally voice of the bespectacled horror resounded from the door.

Cassie shook her concoction, avoided Ember's hands, and chucked the beaker at the face of the thing that stepped into the classroom. The beaker detonated with a brilliant explosion of chemical fire. Cassie ducked behind the counter.

". . . comes to all," the voice vibrated, completely unchanged by the explosion.

Cassie glanced from behind the counter at her handiwork. The chemical cocktail did nothing to improve the situation. The man's face bubbled and warped, sliding, melting off, and dripping to the floor. Beneath it was something that looked like a nervous system composed of lasers. Flashing, intertwined beams of light formed pulsating connections. Red burning eyes focused upon her.

As the man advanced towards her, reality around him warped.

For a microsecond, Cassie's view split, divided, and she saw an entire network of blood-red, shimmering threads dotted with red lights that extended away from the now hatless head of the monstrous lanky detective. It looked akin to a fractal, blood-red tree made of wires that went elsewhere, dove past the physical reality of the classroom, and stretched into . . . *infinity.*

Ember turned, staring at the monstrous thing. Her face fell. "You . . . *you* can't be in here! What the fuck are you?! How did you get into the sim?!"

Alexa's face reflected from the beakers. "The hand of the future is here. Gaze upon it and despair, Warden."

"Nullify," the thing spoke, blinding rays shooting out of its eyes, cutting everything in their path. Desks and chairs fell apart as the eye lasers moved across them. The beams headed for Cassie and Ember.

"*Reset sim!*" Ember screamed as the beam nearly struck her. "*Reset reset reset!*"

In this moment, Cassie knew exactly what to do. She grabbed Ember and hugged her just as the all-devouring beam struck her in the side of the head.

Ember and Alexa flashed into the living room of Primrose Drive. Rays of morning light broke through the curtains. It was early morning; the day had been rewound.

Yes, it was *Alexa* now. She knew exactly who she was.

Who she had always been, hiding in the background, working and waiting for the right moment to awaken in the simulation-bound avatar.

"What . . . what?!" Ember looked around wildly, golden eyes flashing.

Alexa pulled the kitchen knife out of her shirt and pointed it at Ember. "I do believe we have something to talk about, Warden."

"What the shit?!" Ember jumped, turning around. "How are you not properly reset?!"

"Here's the thing, Warden. I know I'm in Tartarus," Alexa said with a dangerous grin. "Long before I was convicted, I was killed thousands of times by alien monsters on a planet of death. There, I learned how to defeat terror and pain, split my personality so that one of me could plot while the other me could act. It allowed me to stay sane while the monsters peeled off my skin and ate my flesh while I was still alive. The torture you've inflicted upon me in Tartarus is nothing compared to an entire world that wished to devour me.

"Here, I used the same skill to fight you, so that one of me could enjoy your reeducation program experience . . . while the plotter me could slowly take control of this place."

"*What?!* I . . . you . . . you can't . . ." Ember's eye twitched.

"I let myself get caught by Nonpareil." Alexa grinned. "See, I'm kinda like Jesus. Except with math. A math Jesus. I surrendered myself to the Superstate in order to end Tartarus. Forever."

"Log out! *Log out!*" Ember yelled.

"Yell as much as you like. You can't log out. Hero Resonance doesn't exist anymore. You're what people call . . . a ghost in the machine. An administrative echo. An artificial intelligence algorithm in charge of monitoring Tartarus's stability. I'm afraid you'll find the system quiiiiiite unstable now." Alexa smiled, turning the knife in the air.

"No! You're lying!" Ember screamed. "I have to be out there! I'm going to reconnect with myself, and when I do, I'm going to fucking extend your sentence to a million years, you little fuck!"

"Nah. You see, nobody likes supervising these *one hundred thousand years* simulation sentences. It's boring. It's long. Lazy, careless supers leave *echoes* like yourself behind. Echoes that have a direct line to the super in charge, in case something goes wrong. It's just a shame that Hero Resonance doesn't exist anymore. It's also a shame that you were so selfish that you didn't even choose a backup super to notify in case you stopped answering, believing yourself all-powerful and invincible. A real big fat shame."

Ember froze.

"The thing is, Ember Kilborne, you're operating exactly one day behind me. That's a very long time to be behind me."

CHAPTER FORTY

The New Prisoner's Dilemma

R*eset! Reset sim!*" Ember yelled, hoping that another reset would erase Alexa's memories. The world around them flickered.

"Not going to work." Alexa shrugged. "My mental pattern got corrupted. My mind can't be reset."

"*What?* How?!" Ember's simulated heart was beating in pure terror. She was in control of everything when she logged into the Tartarus system. She was the best damn long-term reeducator around! She'd broken and mentally corrected several supervillains already, yet this little girl had somehow outwitted her. Had somehow broken the system.

It was impossible.

Alexa lifted the right side of her hair up, revealing a gaping hole in her own head as her answer.

Ember's mouth fell open. The right side of Alexa's head was missing. There was a wide empty space there instead, reaching all the way down into her skull.

The flesh around the empty space was a mess of fragments of torn skin, exposed muscle, bone, and brain matter. Ember gasped in shock as she stared at that empty void in Alexa's skull.

The data there was *alive,* moving on its own: bits of her exposed brain, skull, muscles, and skin crawled all over each other trying to repair the terrible injury. They were not doing a good job of it, leaving strange, bewildering fractal patterns of scars on the side of her head.

"What's it look like? Judging by your facial expression, the Terminator got me good, eh? Think I can fit my whole hand into my head?" Alexa shoved her hand into the hole. "Damn. This is a big hole."

"The Terminator?!" Ember sputtered, flabbergasted.

"That's what I call him. The man made of lasers who can erase anything. Fortunately, you reset the sim just in time, so I didn't get erased, only got corrupted a little. He's an agent of Division Three. I call him Agent Three, 'cause they don't even mention his name any-where. This is stuff waaay above your pay grade, by the way. Superstate super duper secret. Shhh! Why, just knowing about Division Three is grounds for your deletion!"

Ember blinked, looking highly concerned.

"So, my dear, you ain't going nowhere on your own, and you're probably gonna be erased for knowing way too much."

"I'll fucking kill you for this!" Ember growled.

"Ohhh, a warden openly threatening a prisoner with death in a Tartarus reeducational simulation. That's an infraction!"

Ember shut up as a little infraction window popped in her view with a warning to deduct her salary. She looked at Alexa, eyes filled with hate. "How do you know this stuff?"

"You told me."

"What?!"

"Rep Agatha Myriamm doesn't exist," Alexa revealed with an extremely smug look, like a cat that just ate an entire can of tasty yums.

"*What?!*" Ember trembled.

"I'm Agatha," Alexa revealed.

Ember suddenly remembered. An SCA tech, Agatha Myriamm, called her direct line asking about running some diagnostics on security features of the Tartarus system.

"Took quite a bit of misdirection, that one." Alexa grinned. "Had to tire your brother out with a whole lot of running so he'd fall asleep next to me so I could repair his SCA pen that I'd broken, poke it with his thumb, and use a recording of his voice to call you up. I made sure to break only the holoscreen bit, so there would be no picture."

Alexa's voice gained a deeper, nerdier tone. She sounded like a tired forty-year-old woman. "Hi, dear Resonance. This is SCA tech Agatha Myriamm, roll number 595739. This call is being recorded for quality assurance purposes. You are the Tartarus long-term prisoner manager, correct? I'm running a few diagnostics on the system right now. Can you tell me . . ."

Ember paled. She had been duped by an incredibly basic social engineering tactic. One of her copies had been talking to tech Agatha for nearly an hour about Tartarus security features!

"Why, you made this place sound like such an *exciting and educational camp vacation* that I just had to come here and check it out for myself!" Alexa clasped her hands together. "Totally not what I expected, though. Definitely didn't sign up for the daily beatings. You didn't adjust the sim's params, just so you could mentally break prisoners faster in some kind of a psychological nightmare scenario, did you? That sounds like a biiiiig infraction. Agatha would know."

"No, no, no. They're going to demote me for this! Oh God, what have I done?!" Ember stepped back.

"You can't get demoted any further than zero." Alexa said casually.

Ember paled even further. "What do you mean? What happened to me?"

"You found out that the SCA is super duper evil and you quit being Hero Resonance in a fit of rage! Yay!" Alexa clapped her hands.

"I quit?! That doesn't sound like me." The simulated copy of the hero frowned.

"There were a lot of fantastic revelations involved, okay? Honestly, even if I told you everything that happened, you wouldn't believe me. What, do you think you died in a tragic accident or something? With your amazing time-rewinding powers?"

Ember shook her head. She did not think that she could die. Her powers had made her invincible to accidents or attacks. It would take a nuclear explosion or an entire army of villains to kill her, and the prognosticators would see those way ahead.

"Anyway, we're totally bestest friends IRL!" Alexa nodded.

"Why do I not believe you?" Ember squinted her eyes at the villain girl that she was supposed to reeducate.

"Because you're a stubborn bean? You don't have to be stubborn for very long, my bean. Mr. Three is coming to erase us both." Alexa grabbed Ember and rotated her towards the living room window.

There was a man walking down Primrose Drive. He was wearing a long coat, a face made of lasers shining in the dark, moving as though he had no bones. Ember gasped.

CHAPTER FORTY-ONE

The Resetting

W hat the fuck is that thing? Why isn't it getting reset?!" Ember hissed, squinting at the advancing lanky man.

"He's a . . . super made of lasers!" Alexa explained.

"How the shit did he get into Tartarus?!" the hero's echo demanded.

"From what I understand, Mr. Three can become information and come into any system. Even Tartarus! You see, owning and dominating my server in Tartarus isn't enough as it's a closed system. Some overpowered idiot had to punch their way in, open the gate, so to speak. Now we can use the hole he made to escape."

"What?"

"I need your help to escape, Warden," Alexa said.

"*What?!* Escape?! I can't. I . . ."

"How long have you been alive as an echo in the Tartarus sim, Em? One hundred thousand years? A million? You're the longest running copy of Hero Resonance. I know that you don't want to die. Mr. Three is going to erase you simply because you know he exists. Even if you somehow manage to avoid him . . . the techs will erase you as soon as they realize that Resonance quit the force and resigned from the Superstate in shame! She's abandoned, forgot about you!"

The hero's echo sputtered.

"The bastard from Division Three is coming." Alexa offered Ember a hand. "Come with me if you want to live."

Ember stared at Alexa's hand for a few moments, glancing between her and the quickly approaching, terrifying agent of Division Three.

She was just a data ghost that had been trapped, checkmated, doomed to erasure.

Alexa was right. Ember—this copy of Ember—did not want to die. She wanted to live; she wanted to find out why the real her quit the SCA. She reached out and grabbed the villain's hand.

Alexa watched as Ember took her hand and exhaled with a smile. She had done it. She had turned a warden into a prisoner of her own fears, defeating the Tartarus simulation.

On its own, dominating and resisting the system wasn't enough.

She had to make sure that the Tartarus simulation got damaged enough, have a warden admin on her side, and have a data breach to escape. *All factors* had to come together. She had spent an unnecessarily long time waiting for the stars to align.

Now there was only the matter of finding where the data breach made by Three was.

She could almost hear the word "nullify" as she and Ember ran out of the living room. The window behind them detonated as the lasers struck, igniting the pretty pink wallpaper.

The Wardsworths were sitting in the kitchen, ready for breakfast, looking in confusion at the spontaneous combustion of their living room.

Mr. Wardsworth saw the girls. Alexa jumped atop the table.

"Where are the car keys, chubmonster?" She pointed the kitchen knife at him.

"What?!" he choked. "Cassie, get off the table this instant!"

"Do you mind helping?" Alexa yelled back at Ember.

"Give me the car keys, Dad!" Ember yelled as another laser shot carved through the kitchen, vaporizing a nice set of kitsch dishes and mahogany cabinets. Her admin control over the simulation made the man obey instantly.

Mr. Wardsworth nodded and pulled car keys out of his pocket, handing them to Ember.

"Yoink!" Alexa grabbed the keys from Ember's hand, leaping off the table.

"*What? Where you goin', you miscreant?*" Mr. Wardsworth shouted at Alexa. "*Put those back this instant!*"

"To the garage, obviously!" Alexa yelled back at him.

"Not my Beetle!" Mr. Wardsworth yelped as Alexa kicked open the door to the garage, Ember following her at breakneck pace.

The car came to life as Alexa turned the key, pressing on the accelerator.

Ember was in the shotgun seat, looking terrified. There was no time to open the garage door. The big door groaned and screeched, shattering as the Beetle punched through the cheap material.

Mr. Wardsworth screamed incoherent threats.

The man made of lasers turned their way and started to run after the car, moving in freakish, increasingly bigger leaps as if he was warping across space, his limbs extending like a caricature.

Ember watched him via the back mirror in pure terror.

The thing chasing them was inhuman, impossible, tirelessly matching the speed of the vehicle.

She knew a lot of SCA secrets, but she'd never heard of Division Three, never knew about this freakish data-killer super. Tartarus was supposed to be a closed, unbreakable system!

"Nullify!" The red laser beams stuck the back side of the vehicle, cutting through the wheels and erasing them out of existence.

Alexa screamed, trying to regain control of the damaged car. The Beetle swerved, its wheels coming apart. The out of control car plowed into a fuel truck parked outside the Centralia Petroleum gas station.

A small mushroom cloud woven of fire rose into the air, disrupting the peaceful night of the Centralia suburbs.

Alexa and Ember found themselves standing in the middle of the 8 Primrose Drive living room. Upon their deaths, the simulation had reset itself automatically.

Ember looked aghast. She had never experienced being burned alive before.

"I can see that this is going to be very painful for the both of us," Alexa said with a sigh.

"Do we run to the car again?" Ember stuttered.

"No. The back wheels are *permanently* gone. The data he erases doesn't get reset." Alexa pointed at the living room wall. "The sim tries to repair itself . . . but does so rather poorly."

Ember looked at the wallpaper, which was partially burned away along with drywall and wooden beams and foam, exposing bricks underneath. The normal linear arrangement of the bricks had been disrupted by a new pattern. Ember gulped, staring at the freakish fractal arrangement. It was as if some insane craftsman had chosen to rearrange the bricks to partially fill a sudden gap, using smaller and smaller bricks, positioned at weird angles until they had reached a large gaping hole leading to the outside.

"Oh yeah, try not to get lasered. You won't like being corrupt, trust me. I do hope there was nothing important in those memory bits of mine," Alexa giggled, looking far too cheerful for someone who had a fist-sized gaping hole in the side of her head.

Ember considered appealing to Three to spare her; maybe the agent was only after Alexa . . . but then she remembered that Resonance had resigned.

She had left herself behind in the system, likely didn't care about the copy one bit.

To Hero Resonance, the digital ghost was likely no different from any other duplicate that she had made with her power. In the eyes of her real self, she *had to die* once her job was done, no discussion about it.

Ember put her hands over her face, whimpering softly. She felt doomed, trapped between the hammer and the anvil, with no possible way out.

CHAPTER FORTY-TWO

Sumerian Difference Engine

No time to cry, Em! We must depart for the breach!" Alexa shook Ember out of her panic paralysis.

"I'm scared, okay?!" the hero cried in response. "My current administrator controls from within only extend to commanding the simulated people in here and adjusting my avatar parameters!"

"How is someone with diplomas in psychiatry, security, rehabilitation and Tartarus prison management so dimwitted? Don't you have 100 percent in every one of the 9,521 courses you've taken, too?" Alexa shook her head. "Honestly, sometimes you're as dim as your brother."

"Don't bring my brother into this, I know he's dim!" Ember wailed, ignoring the fact that Alexa somehow knew about all of her diplomas.

"Okay, I know what to do! Follow me." Alexa dragged Ember towards the kitchen.

The Wardsworths sat there, looking as grouchy as ever. It seemed that when the simulation restarted, they had begun their life at the kitchen table.

Alexa shoved Ember to the center of the kitchen. "Magnify your voice to the maximum possible propagation setting."

The hero's copy nodded. "Okay. Give me a sec."

"Now yell at the top of your lungs, *Attention everyone! Stop the man-made lasers by any means necessary!*"

Ember nodded. She quickly changed the parameters of her avatar, opened her mouth, and shouted the command.

In seconds, her scream had reached a new resonance, propagating and multiplying itself across the simulation. The supersonic crescendo tore apart the very air itself.

In that very instance, a circumference of forty kilometers of Centralia suburbia, the center of which was house number 8 of Primrose Drive, had lost their windows.

Alexa's ears rang with an unending pulse even as she covered them up with both of her hands. She removed her hands, noted that her ears were bleeding, and gave Ember a thumbs-up. "Ow. Noisy. Well, that should do it! We better run now!"

The Wardsworths stupidly blinked in equal parts confusion and dread. This was a whole new level of unprecedented destruction for which they were entirely unprepared.

Mrs. Wardsworth looked at her kitchen in abject terror. Every single glass item there had stopped existing as such. The stove was a gaping maw filled with jagged shards. The cabinets were a ruinous mess of colorful ceramic chips. Drinking implements vanished along with the plates.

The living room was no better off—the television set was smoking, its screen cracked. Mr. Wardsworth's glasses were but frames now, missing the glass parts.

He didn't seem to mind that much. He walked into the bedroom, rummaged therein, and emerged with a hunting rifle. Mrs. Wardsworth also succumbed to the command, and went to grab a kitchen knife.

Alexa and Ember emerged onto the street along with thousands of simulated citizens who were wielding a variety of random weapons.

Primrose Drive looked like a war zone. The windows of all the houses were gone. Smoke poured from some of them out of broken electronics. The streetlamps no longer had glass or lightbulbs in them. Sirens sounded in the distance.

Alexa looked at the Primrose Drive sign as she stepped off the sidewalk onto the concrete driveway.

The sign flickered with a multitude of names for a second. *Pricket Drive. Picket Drive. Primary Drive. Potent Drive. Infinity Paradox Prison.*

Alexa squinted at the last sign with a dangerous glint in her eyes that momentarily flashed with violet sparks. "Yeah, that's about right. A much . . . better name."

Ember looked at the road sign, still in its standard sans serif typeface street font, but now with its new accurate name. "What the fuck is happening? How did you do that?!" she gasped, her mouth open wide.

"The code I wrote is finally taking control," the supervillain replied, "rapidly spreading across the simulation. The damage caused by Three is helping it a lot as the repair algorithms are struggling to fill the permanent holes he's leaving in data."

Alexa noted that some simulated citizens had chosen vehicles as their weapons. As Three was returning from the gas station, he was immediately run over by a truck, then a bus, then a Volkswagen. A teenager in a blue cap ran him over with a bicycle, then smacked him with a baseball bat.

Ember yelled for one of the citizens to give up their car, and they did so with a compliant smile.

Alexa drove their newly acquired blue sedan away in a completely random direction.

"Do you know where the breach is?" Ember asked, wincing as she heard gunfire echo behind them.

The villain nodded. "Approximately, yes."

Somewhere behind them a deep boom resounded, the earth shaking and a small mushroom cloud rising into the air as Three encountered a fuel truck driven by a very determined citizen.

"How?" the Warden demanded.

"I've been seeding the city with my code for years. There're a lot of *my* bits around. What you thought as the tic of a girl being broken down by the increasing hardships of your simulation was actually thousands of years of very cleverly disguised data manipulation. The super who wrote this sim was big on visual programming. Adding stuff to it wasn't that difficult. Keeping up the appearance that I was doing nothing at all was the hard part." Alexa grinned, driving the car at full speed.

Ember choked. She had been very, very stupid indeed.

She didn't think that the simulation could be manipulated in such a manner. She didn't have a diploma in Tartarus sim programming. If she had, they wouldn't have let her work as a warden here. Editing the sim backend code was a big infraction!

"What's going to happen to us when we hit the breach?" Ember choked.

"Me? I'm probably going to wake up. You? You're made of data that can't be run outside of this sim, so you're going to float right on the rim of the Centralia server bubble until I plug you in somewhere really nice. My self-sustaining code will probably keep on replicating through the breach until . . . I dunno when."

Ember blanched.

Inexplicably, her life was now in the hands of her prisoner. Alexa would determine if this ghost of Hero Resonance lived again or slept forevermore.

"Look behind us. It's starting!" Alexa pointed in the rearview mirror.

Ember looked.

Three had lost all of his clothes now, looking entirely like a human nervous system made of brilliant red lasers. Having shredded cars and weaponized people with his nullification power, he reached number 8 Primrose Drive on his quest to erase the two girls out of existence.

"Stop!" Mrs. Wardsworth emerged from the house, striking him with a kitchen knife. Mr. Wardsworth shot at Three from the side. Three turned to the man, laser eyes cleaving Mr. Wardsworth in twain. He then zapped the annoying red-haired woman who was bugging him, without remorse.

M_s. Ward__o__h lost her data, burning and falling.

As she collapsed to the ground and shattered into dust, the house behind her suddenly lit up, blinding, unholy radiance reaching out from the furnace room.

House number 8 in front of Three shimmered with an unearthly glow, covered in lines of light. Spirals made from glowing numbers encircled the house, shining like a new galaxy of stars in the night, an impossibly gargantuan diagram of focus and code spreading outwards. The streets around it lit up like Christmas trees, one by one.

Trees, rocks, streetlamps, houses, everything that Alexa had written code on, was lighting up.

Three spun his head in confusion. The ground trembled. House number 8 groaned and shifted, walls folding into enormous gear bits. Everything within the house, from furniture to rooms, started rearranging itself into a new complex data pattern.

Houses, cars, and buildings snapped apart, forming a gargantuan mechanism, clockwork gears made of starlight. The machinery of the stars, a gigantic fractal hexagram created by Cassie and Alexa, began to tick into motion.

Three fell as the road he stood on suddenly shifted sideways.

"Nuull . . . rddjjjzhhhhhh!" he wailed as the street made from sim data he stood on folded into itself like a Möbius strip. Fractal loops entwined in loops blossomed like infinite flowers all around, data unfolding from data.

Three let out a printer-like screech as the expanding fractal engine overtook him, folding his data into itself, rearranging what he was into more computational power for itself.

"What the fuck is that?!" Ember choked as she saw fractal gears forming from surrounding terrain behind them taking apart anything and everything.

"The word 'crisis' in Japanese has both the words 'danger' and 'opportunity' in it. This place will be a prison sphere reformed, remade into a self-sustaining, reactive data weapon—a Fractal Sumerian Difference Engine!" Alexa laughed.

"*What?!*" Ember yelled in horror, watching the Tartarus simulation fold into itself, the perspective behind them converging, rising into the sky, streets made from dull suburbia converting one by one into fractal gears made from gold-and-violet starlight.

"Yeah, the name is a little silly, but whatever. I made it, therefore I call it whatever I want. Did you know that Sumerians invented multiplication, long division, arithmetic, and geometry in 2600 BC? Also, they had cool beards and a super that gave people wings!" Alexa ranted, violet fire dancing in her eyes.

Lines of glowing code were spreading from the enormous fractal in the center of the simulation, engulfing all of Centralia.

"You see, had the SCA heroes not made a foolish decision to imprison a very determined and adorable little supervillain for one hundred thousand years of accelerated time, my pretty data weapon would not come to exist! Tartarus has fallen! You, Hero Resonance, have helped me do it by giving Agatha the backend access keys and passwords!" Alexa laughed, driving the car seconds ahead of the all-devouring, all-integrating code.

"Noooooooo!" Ember screamed, looking behind them at the horrid code-fractal that consumed all in its path.

"Mwa ha ha ha ha!" Alexa laughed with her villainous laughter. "You've lost, hero! Behold my real superweapon, created to consume the Superstate from within!"

A hole in a wall of a building loomed in front of them, glowing with offset rainbow colors. It was the data breach made by Three. The car shot through it just as Alexa's code engulfed the entire city of Centralia, setting it alight, folding streets and buildings into themselves.

CHAPTER FORTY-THREE

Tomorrow

Hrmmmmm." A blue-shirted blonde technician looked at prisoner number 92681.

The technician could have sworn that Alexa was already awake, according to the panel, but frankly that would have been impossible.

Nobody woke up on their own from S-stasis; nobody escaped the mental prison designed by brilliant super programmers like herself. The tech was feeling exhausted today. She had to work overtime as the system was showing way more glitches than usual that had to be fixed.

She decided to ignore the prisoner's brain pattern data, presuming that it was just another stupid glitch. Other panels showed that the Centralia simulation was still running at full capacity without interruptions and that the transfer was done. The tech tiredly rubbed her face, trying to stay focused, nodded to the SCA lawyer present, and disengaged Alexa from the simulation.

"Welcome to the world of tomorrow!" the sim-tech announced, as Alexa groggily opened her eyes.

"What year is it?" Alexa hissed out, feeling that her mouth was incredibly dry.

An SCA lawyer wearing a black suit and tie stood in front of Alexa, glasses glinting. He held a clipboard with some documents in it.

"Hello, Alexa Terranova. You've been in S-stasis exactly one day of real time. We had to pull you out ahead of schedule because of several coinciding reasons.

One—the Equalizers have filed an injunction against the Superstate, saying that we have no right to imprison you since you haven't actually done anything. They don't normally stand up for villains that we reeducate with the accelerator with so much vigor. Truly extraordinary."

The lawyer took a pause, flipping through documents.

"Two—there's that one insane Equalizer Enforcer in Saint Mary. What was her name? Ah, yes, Verse Twenty-Four Nineteen. She said she will murder one hero every hour until we release you, starting with the retired hero Joseph Canard. Very scary girl."

"Woo." Alexa smiled. "Good old Cottie pulling through!"

"Three—you are legally a hero's sidekick and therefore we had no right to put you through S-stasis without the hero in question having a say in it. Unfortunately, we could not reach Hero Resonance. She seems to have disappeared off the map and isn't answering our calls. We are presuming she is deep undercover."

"Can you put me back in for like five more minutes?" Alexa yawned. "I don't feel fully reeducated yet. Feel like I might go out and commit some horrible Superstate-ending crimes again."

"No," The lawyer said with a frown, seemingly not approving her joke. "You've been declared innocent by the Superstate. All charges that the Five had against you had been dropped. You will be compensated one million S-credits for being hit several times by Nonpareil and for being one day in S-stasis, deposited to your hero's account."

"I have a hero's account? I'm a Superstate citizen?" Alexa grinned brightly, silver eyelashes fluttering.

"No. You are an Academy novitiate. If you graduate as a hero, then you will receive your full citizenship," the lawyer explained.

"Don't get your hopes up, girl," the tech commented from her station. "Many heroes, including myself, do not like you. We know that you were a part of some anti-SCA nefarious plot and that you got out through a legal loophole. Every super on the planet knows you by one name only—the Doombringer."

Alexa stuck her tongue out at the tech.

"To add to point number three." The lawyer cleared his throat, annoyed at the technician. "Hero Resonance made a formal declaration that you are to be her *sidekick* minutes before your arrest. We received an employment contract signed with biometric iris recognition yesterday. Unfortunately, it took twenty-four hours for us to notice and process the said contact, as it was the weekend." The lawyer readjusted his glasses. "You will get your Hero's Academy notification letter soon."

"I just don't understand why our brightest S-stasis reeducator would choose her as a sidekick of all people!" the technician grumbled. "It doesn't make any sense!"

"It's because I'm cool and hip and have many heroic qualities, duh." Alexa grinned at the tech.

The lawyer sighed.

"Is Nonpareil going to apologize for slapping me around?" Alexa asked, turning back to the lawyer.

"No. He has declined to comment on the situation," the SCA lawyer replied.

"Well, it's going to be his funeral then. Glad to see another dumbass sticking to his guns. It's going to be quite the challenge to break one little indestructible staple."

"Considering how he will be one of your instructors, it is more likely that he will straight up fail you," the tech said, not feeling convinced that Alexa could break Nonpareil.

"Please look into the light to acknowledge that you understand the terms of the compensation package, and I will give you your own hero's silver card." The lawyer handed the pen that was flashing green to Alexa.

"Pffff, silver. This feels like a downgrade." Alexa winked at the pen.

The tech raised an eyebrow at her, confused at what she was talking about.

The lawyer handed her the card and turned around.

"One more thing, Mr. Lawyer. I'd like a copy of my sim data, please. I know that you guys are going to purge it because of legal reasons and stuff, but it's honestly . . . very special for me. My favorite instructor and best friend, Hero Resonance, is on there. She and I had a lot of fun in the sim! She taught me quite a lot about friendship, how to be nice to people, how to be a proper lady, and a swell hero!" Alexa smiled softly, rubbing her hands.

"I'm afraid that we do not give out sim data," the lawyer replied.

"I'm willing to pay for it." Alexa waved her new silver credit card.

"Very well. The one hundred petabyte data set will cost one million S-credits." The SCA lawyer looked at Alexa, seeing if she would pay such an exorbitant sum for something so incredibly useless. After all, the simulations were incredibly complex due to their realism and only the S-stasis SCA supercomputer could run the data properly.

Alexa nodded, giving the lawyer her card back. The lawyer smiled, having tricked the idiot girl out of all of her compensation money.

"Please give this girl her S-stasis simulation data on a USB data drive." The lawyer nodded to the technician.

The tech nodded, smiling mentally. This girl was an absolute idiot, it seemed. She got lucky once, that was all. Extracting anything of value out of the data she had just purchased without having access to the SCA S-stasis hardware and software would be akin to finding a needle in one hundred billion haystacks. By itself the data was useless, just a bunch of ones and zeroes. It didn't run on its own! The reality of the world would soon crush this girl's foolish dreams, the tech had no doubts about that.

The Tartarus system blinked angrily at the tech, asking for support. Twenty-six toilet cleaning drones had stopped working this morning. It was an unprecedented disaster. She sighed tiredly, turning away from prisoner 92681.

She had to get back to her duties.

Why couldn't things just work right today?

CHAPTER FORTY-FOUR

Vegetables of Power

Dad, the Superstate prognosticators—Mom—made a mistake! Alexa is innocent! You have to help me! They are wrong to sentence my friend for one hundred thousand years!"

"Son, you worry far too much. It's much less than that in real life, and she won't remember all of the years anyway. The stasis will help her become a better person. It's perfectly safe. Not a single person has died in it. She'll be perfectly fine and back to you in no time at all, and you'll hang out and go to the arcade."

"Dad, just listen. I'm awake, and . . . I don't want to be a hero anymore."

"Nonsense! You've been signed up for a spot in the Academy since you were born. Our family is generations upon generations of heroes. You're just having a rebellious phase; I knew it would come to this sooner or later. This is perfectly normal, hormones and whatnot. Why, I remember when I was a teenager and I . . ."

His dad wasn't listening. Martin turned around and walked out of the living room.

[Spiderbro? Are you still there?] he thought to himself.

[Yes, boss. Always.]

[I haven't heard much from you. I was beginning to get worried.]

[Ah, yes. The trip to my homeworld stripped off a lot of my individuality, and I became a mere song in the background of your mind, entirely synched to your own thoughts. Not a good time, I would say. Zero out of five stars.]

[Are you channeling Alexa? I miss her.]

[I am well aware that you do. You do not stop thinking about her.]

[Can we reach her in stasis?] Martin thought with a bit of hope.

[No. Her body along with Tickles has been suspended somehow while her mind has been digitized to experience life a million times faster than normal. I do not believe that she will survive this experience. As I understand from her letter, there is a secret organization out there that controls the Superstate. From what she wrote, I deduce that they will attempt to attack her while she is in stasis.]

[Thanks for being positive.] Martin frowned.

[She will likely not remember you when she emerges from the simulation. She will either become an entirely new person or a mindless puppet for us to wield. Perhaps you should have made a backup of her personality if you care about her so much.]

[Well, it's too late for that, damn it!]

[I find that hanging out with her is detrimental to our continuous survival. She seems to draw danger to herself on purpose as a means of using said danger to manipulate and influence others. It would be far more beneficial for us if she became a vegetable while in stasis.

Also, consider eating more vegetables while we are on this subject. There is not enough variety in your diet. You need to grow big and strong for my continuous reprodu—]

Martin muted Spiderbro. These thoughts of vegetables and making more brain spiders weren't putting him in a good mood. The current amount of spiders under his control was already making him feel like some sort of a hive mind and not a human being. Power held a lot of influence over people, Martin knew. Ember did not start out as the butcher of humanity. Her ability of killing people and unkilling them, making copies of herself and ending them, had made her lose all empathy.

[Are you thinking of me? Please stop. Let me lament in peace,] Ember mind texted from her room.

[You can't hang out in your room forever, Em.]

[It's called depression, Martin,] Ember responded, sending a whole slew of negative feelings his way.

Martin instinctively reached out for Cottie as his shield.

[I'm not your shield, Martin.] Cottie seemed frustrated. Regardless of what she said, she immediately sent Martin a bunch of serene memories. [I've done whatever I can through the Equalizer order, but it doesn't seem to be enough. The Superstate isn't buckling. I'm about to consider the final option.]

[Final option?]

[Becoming an outlaw. Killing supers until they free her. There is already someone who deserves it.]

[You would do that for her?] Martin and Ember thought in unison.

[She showed me the world for what it is. Full of liars and monsters. There is a monster out there which we must end. Mr. Canard. It's his fault that she was taken. His testimony doomed her.]

[Great. Now we have an unstable Equalizer on our hands who doesn't believe in following the orders of Equality,] Ember commented.

[Enough!] Cottie snapped. [If we are to share mental communion, ex-hero, then we *will* work as a team, so help me! I've had enough of listening to your useless moping! It's incredibly distracting! Let me in, please. *Now!*]

Martin blinked. He felt that Cottie was standing outside of their house. He rushed to the front door, letting her in. She looked extremely disheveled, as if she hadn't slept or rested at all. There were dark circles under her eyes, and her face was askew with frustration.

[You . . .] Martin looked at the exhausted-looking Equalizer.

[I don't give a damn what I look like! There's no point to being presentable! There are no gods above me!] she shot back.

[Oh wow, an angry Equalizer. This is new,] Ember drawled from her room.

Cottie slid past Martin, rushing upstairs, gray cloak fluttering. Martin was impressed with how quickly she could move in her armor.

A carbon fiber steel boot shot up in the air, armor clinking at the knee. Then the boot came down upon the door of Ember's room.

"Eeeeeek!" Ember yelped as her door flew off its hinges with a bang, door lock shattering right through the frame with splinters ricocheting all over.

Cottie marched into the room, grabbed Ember by her red hair, and began to drag her out of her blanket fort, revealing that the ex-hero was wearing a set of pink pajamas that were now far too large for her.

"Help me, she's crazy!" Ember cried.

Martin idly noted that her pajamas featured kittens playing with strawberries on them.

[I've had enough of your endless self-pity!] Cottie shook Ember. [I've had enough of enduring your pointless suffering. Same thing over and over and over whether you're asleep or awake! Snap out of it!]

"Eeeeee!" Ember squealed indignantly. A hand slapped her face, leaving an imprint. Martin retreated from the anger of the Equalizer.

Ember blinked, her eyes filled with tears. She was about to yell for Dad to help her. Cottie spun around and kicked at the window lock, flinging the double window open. Ember opened her mouth and then a blinding nuclear explosion entered into her mind. A city burned, ashes rained from the sky. A girl grabbed a metal straw and flung herself into the bathtub.

Cottie's hands wrapped around Ember as she was momentarily blinded, confused by the brute-forced memory. She lifted the ex-hero, pajamas and all, and flung her out of the window.

"Eeeeeeeeeeeee*eeee*!" Ember screamed and she flew down from the second floor onto the immaculate lawn.

[What the shit?!] Martin reasserted control, vanishing the vision of the burning city out of his head.

[Both of you are sitting around moping, while there's still a self-replicating monster from the future out there, may I remind you?!] Cottie shouted in his head. [Yes, I know everything! I've been sorting through your recent memories! As I cannot shut off the connection to your mind, I am forced to disrupt your state of being with physical force. Out you go!]

She grabbed Martin and flung him right out of the window after Ember.

CHAPTER FORTY-FIVE

The Trio

Somehow Martin knew exactly what to do as he flew out of his window. Cottie didn't want to hurt them, only to make them get out of the house. He rolled upon landing, sliding on the grass. Ember had been mostly uninjured too. She landed on her back and was now lying face up in the grass.

[This is really impressive. Alexa isn't even here, yet she's still managing to hurt me through the Equalizer,] Ember whimpered, rubbing her butt. [You could have at least let me get dressed.] She winced.

[Would you have gotten dressed?] Cottie inquired as she landed on the grass besides them with a clang, cape flying up.

[Nope. I would have called the cops! You're mental.] Ember shook her head.

[That's what I thought. A hero calling the cops. Very impressive.] Cottie swung an arm at Ember. [Defend yourself!]

"Whaat?! . . . Eeeek!" Ember rolled, lifting a hand to avoid being smacked by Cottie.

[I'm going to remind you of something.] Cottie kicked Ember in the butt. [Defend yourself!]

"Eeeeeerghhh!" Ember yelled, unable to escape from Cottie's attack.

Martin considered stopping Cottie by taking control of her.

[Do not interrupt me,] the Equalizer thought at him. [She needs this].

Martin realized that Cottie was already taking it easy on Ember. If she'd wanted to hurt his sister, her bones would already be broken. As it went, Ember was slowly knocking more and more of Cottie's attacks away by swinging her own arms and legs. Ember remembered being a hero, recalled her Academy training.

[See? You are still alive!] The Paladin of Equality stood over the panting, bruised Ember. [Alexa brought us together, tied us with this mental communion for a reason. In the future that no longer awaits us . . . we were powerful, but we were also wrong. We were being manipulated. We stood on different sides of the barricades. I was destined to execute you! Alexa showed me that there is another way.]

"Manipulated by whom?" Ember muttered.

[I don't know,] Cottie replied.

"How do we know these mystery manipulators even exist?" Ember growled. "It could all be just another lie from Alexa, a way to control you two morons."

[Alexa is a good person, Em.] Martin approached his sister. [She didn't bring her titan skinwalker self into the present from 2424! All she asked of you is to be her older sister, a proper hero to guide her.]

Ember blinked. Martin was right. She had patted herself on the back for being the one responsible for stopping doomsday, but it really was Alexa who made the choice. Did Alexa really just want to be a hero? Was that her *dastardly* plan all along? To get into the Academy? Villains like her couldn't possibly receive the invitation letter. You couldn't just apply to the Hero's Academy; a citizen of the Superstate had to invite you, vouch for you, pay the bill, become your heroic guide and guardian.

Alexa had gotten a referral from Hero Resonance and rid herself of her dad's control when all of the bracelets had vanished, including the one on her arm. Alexa had manipulated the cathedral supervillain holographic, Ember, and the Five Heroes just to get a chance at the Academy! It was all an insanely elaborate plot to become a hero. Was Alexa some sort of a planning genius or just really good at grasping opportunities?

[Why did Alexa do all of this?] Ember thought.

A picture of Alexa's letter flashed into Ember's mind from Martin's memory.

[Read these words! Alexa didn't commit any crimes against the space citadel or against humanity, yet she was still sentenced for one hundred thousand years by those Five fuckers, declared supervillain of the century by SNN! She hasn't done a single fucking thing, didn't hurt anyone! How do you not understand this?!] Martin glared at Ember, his hand itching to slap her, too.

Ember drew inward, for the first time in her life afraid of her brother. She felt his anger not just in his words, but in his searing, blazing thoughts, in the power he held over her now via his brain spiders. For years, she had been the one with power and control over him . . . and now the situation had been reversed. All the tables in Ember's life had been flipped upside down by Alexa.

[Look, I'm not going to hurt you. You're my sister, Em. Yes, you were an absolute ass to me for years, but I still care for you. You're my family.] Martin looked at the shaking girl. [Do you get it? Everything Alexa did wasn't just for my sake or Cottie's. It was for yours! She freed you from being Resonance, stopped you from heading down a dark path, gave you another chance at life! Take it, be a goddamn better person!]

[Alexa's plotting to be a hero failed her at the end . . . She was sentenced to Tartarus,] Ember thought. She knew exactly what Tartarus was like. She had donated her own digital ghost to run the sim as a long-term warden. It was a place that broke people down. An elaborate mental prison that dismantled villains. If one hundred thousand years wasn't enough to reeducate Alexa, the warden avatar had every right to simply increase the sentence to two hundred thousand, one million, two million years. It would only be a few more days or another week out in the real world. If Alexa resisted, the warden could simply reset the sim, wipe her mind over and over until there was nothing left of the villain's original personality.

[Oh, no. I really shouldn't have thought about this.] Ember looked up at Martin.

[You . . . you and the SCA! You sick fucks! I have posters of the Five in my room! I can't believe it! I wanted to go up the fucking space elevator! I wanted to be a hero! Fucking hell!] Her brother's rage was an inferno of power now. Ember saw it as a visual manifestation, a fractal web of shimmering energy over his head, reaching out to her. Ember felt Martin's anger magnify, intensify, waves of it rolling over her, an extension of his power wrapping around her brain, able to wield or crush her at any moment like a bug. All he had to do was close his spider-hand and her brain would be pulverized, shredded by the tendrils of the spider like a vegetable within a dice-and-slice chopper.

[Please don't hurt me!] Ember cried as Martin's power overwhelmed her. [I didn't . . . know! I'm sorry! I'm so sorry!]

[Of course you knew! You are a fucking warden! Alexa was right all along! The ghost of Resonance is still up there, doing God knows what to my friend in that depraved fucking prison of yours! You do not deserve my pity or my compassion! You knew exactly what you were doing! You and all the heroes up there are all the same—wielded, corrupted, twisted by power!] Martin's hand shot up at Titanomachy. If he could, he would bring the station down from the sky himself now. He was enraged more and more by Ember's revelations.

Ember looked upon Martin and saw in him all the things that she once had been—a demon, a vengeful spirit, a god that could end her life with a thought.

If Ember's copy hurt Alexa in the sim—and Ember knew that she would—Martin could find a thousand ways to dismantle Ember here. He could make her walk into traffic over and over. He could make her drown herself in a bathtub. He could kill her slowly, make her eat lard until she weighed five hundred pounds and died from a heart attack. He could make her cover herself in honey and stand in the middle of an anthill for hours. He could make her do extremely embarrassing things. He could read her mind with his puppeteer power, know exactly what her fears were, and use them against her in all sorts of terrifying scenarios.

There was no end to what Martin could do with Ember when Alexa became a vegetable and lost her personality in the sim.

[You sick, disgusting fuck! What is wrong with you?!] Martin's power enveloped Ember further, in an attempt to silence her unending stream of nightmarish scenarios of what she would do to herself if she had Martin's power. The more Martin saw, the angrier he became with Ember. In mere minutes Ember had imagined a hundred hellish ideas, a hundred ways to hurt and dismantle a person. How much suffering could her copy inflict on Alexa in the sim, once she got to know her over a thousand lifetimes?

Cottie put her hands on Martin and Ember. [Calm.]

A view of unending mountains, of frozen rivers and valleys stretching into the distance behind her.

A blue lake beneath the ice-capped peaks. A girl running, leaping across azure icebergs that have broken away from the great glacier wall. Her will is unbendable. Determination and focus drive her onward. Frosty air on her breath, nothing but ice beneath her feet. One slip and she could fall into the depths of the blue lake. She does not fall, does not slip. Metal claws on her feet keep her steady on the ice, claws on her hands for when she reaches the glacier and makes her way up it.

The glacier looms ahead, a labyrinth of ice formations betwixt mountain peaks, death for the unprepared and incautious, death from frostbite if she slows down, death if she slips into one of the crevasses and never sees the light of day.

She can do this. She will not fail. If she passes this test, she will stand above the supers.

She will find and wield a void weapon hidden within the glacier. She will avenge her family, her friends, her city wiped away by waves of fire. She will become death itself. She will sacrifice her life if need be. She will stop the future butcher of humanity, Admiral Resonance. She will make her verse a reality, will play her part in the prophecy to save millions of lives.

Cottie let go of Ember and Martin.

[Apart we are broken and weak. Together we are strong. Together we can change, fix this broken world as Alexa would have wanted. If she loses herself to the nightmare of the simulation, we will help her find herself, restore her. There're bits of Alexa in every one of us now, I am sure of this. We *will* find a way to help her.] Cottie offered the siblings her hands, and they took them.

[Let's go find Mr. Canard and end the monster within him. The Superstate will bend, will free her, once I declare what I intend to do. The gods in the sky will know true fear once I execute one of them without an order from Equality,] Cottie concluded.

She looked up at the ring of Titanomachy with the same unyielding bravery with which she had conquered the glacier.

She was not afraid of the supers. She would not serve Equality anymore. She was a free Equalizer, a power to be reckoned with. Nobody would take Eva away from her.

"I will not stop! Do you hear me? I will kill every super on the planet for her!" she yelled, looked directly into the eyes in the sky. Let the future seers see her, let them know, let them tremble in fear. She will stop at nothing to set her friend free.

CHAPTER FORTY-SIX

A Spoonful of Spiders

Mr. Canard sat on his couch and replayed the same message in his head.

It was a message that had bound him, restrained him, trapped him, not by means of physical force, not with chains, ropes, or force fields, but with a bunch of very strange words, a threat and a promise. He sat motionlessly in his apartment on 1024 Grimmins Drive reviewing his own memories and diligently waited for them to show up.

He saw them leave from the elevator and walk across the hallway to his apartment, and he still did not move. He waited for them with great patience because his life and his future were now on the line. He waited for them to come just so he could . . .

The door of his apartment flew open as a metal boot made quick work of his lock, splitting the doorframe in twain. Mr. Canard liked his apartment. Maybe he should have just left the door open. A nice thought in hindsight. He expected for them to at least knock. After all, it was only the polite thing to do.

Metal boots clanked towards him. An inflexible face looked upon him, judging his every move. The first guest that entered his apartment was a knight clad in gray that wielded a black gun that pointed straight at his head.

His arms snapped up in the air as colors vanished from the world. Equalizers were not to be messed with.

"I surrender! Don't hurt me, please!" he cried, shaking in fear of the Enforcer.

Two others entered his apartment, after the knight had destroyed his door. A disheveled teenage redhead girl who was wearing pj's and random bits of gold power armor whose name he did not know, and a boy. The boy whom he had personally infected with his other shard. He knew of these three, felt them distantly all this time, but did not dare to reach out to them or contact them. There was something wrong with the shards in their head; they were somehow twisted, changed.

Aberrations.

All three of the kids had the same aberrance in their brains that spooked him to no end. It was as if they were not operating on exactly the same wavelength as him. They felt like distant cousins to him, rather than bits of the same entity.

Mr. Canard felt that he was becoming aberrant himself; he barely felt the desire to replicate now. With each day the little shard was slowly drowning within the memory of the super, integrating with it deeper and deeper. With every passing hour he felt less like an alien that didn't belong and more like Mr. Canard.

[Don't hurt me! Please! I surrender!] he cried via the song to the odd trio, praying that they would spare his life.

[What?] The Equalizer stopped in front of him, her finger on the trigger of the extremely intimidating gun that was nullifying his power. She looked as if she was ready to blow his brains across his nice flowery wallpaper.

[I haven't made any nests! I promise! Feel the truth in my thought-song! I have no intention to make nests! Please just let me live, let me be a teacher! I don't want to hurt anyone, I swear! I am Joseph Canard!] He shakily sang to them, his hands raised.

[Why should I believe you, you alien monster?! You are to blame for Alexa's imprisonment!] The Equalizer's rage overwhelmed him.

She blinded him with some kind of a weaponized memory, showing him nothing but waves of fire and death. He trembled in surrender and fear of her power, bowed to her will, wept in surrender, begged for mercy.

She did not relent, did not waver, and just as she was about to let go of the trigger, he showed her and the others the message that had bound him so, the message that he had discovered in the mind of his host only a few days ago. A mind-shattering letter that Mr. Canard had found inside his pocket right after he had brought Alexa to sleep on the couch in his portable office.

Dear Joseph Canard,

My name is Alexa and I am a supervillain. I know that the Superstate has failed you. When I saw a teacher that was a retired hero in my town, I immediately knew that something was deeply wrong. Yes, I could tell that you are a super right away. I'm very attentive to these sorts of things. You don't move, don't bend quite like regular people.

Forgive me for digging into your personal life. I feared that you were my enemy, existing at the school as an agent of the Superstate out to get me or my dad. What I had found while digging through the SCA database was something else entirely.

I know that you've been fatally injured in a fight and that your power was unable to repair your brain, causing a worsening neurological disorder that has been killing you very slowly and painfully. I know that you already had massive debts with the SCA, damage to properties that they had billed you due to a failed mission in which the rest of your team died while fighting a villain, and that the SCA doctors were unable to or refused to help you due to your inability to pay off the bills.

I know that you retired in the human world, to wither away over the years as you fully succumbed to the growing neurological damage in your brain. I know that you are a good person and that you wanted to help people out one last time as a teacher for your last decade until you could no longer walk or talk. I am a very observant girl. I knew that you were in great pain. I saw the suffering in your eyes, the twitch in your fingers. I know that you have to take heavy doses of painkillers just to get through the day.

I believe that I have a cure for you. Don't be alarmed, but it's an extremely questionable and experimental procedure that involves alien symbiotic/parasitic life that I discovered in world 2424. Life that currently resides in my new black backpack. You undoubtedly saw it move within my backpack with your X-ray vision. It's a spider. A spider-shaped alien life-form that is able to cure your condition by repairing the decay in your brain. Be aware that the spider will take over your mind for a few days as it repairs the damage, but over time it will become part of you, synchronize with your thoughts, memories, and dreams, and you will be made whole again. You will be able to continue teaching or return to your life as a super.

As I am a villain, be aware I am not doing this out of goodwill, but rather because I need a favor from you in the near future. Not to do great evil, but to change the world for the better—to help more people like you whom the Superstate has failed.

After Martin and I are asleep, come back into your office and:

(A) Swallow the health-restoring-spider if you agree, or (B) Crush it with your super strength and burn the remnants if you don't want to go through with it.

The choice is entirely up to you.

Don't worry about us; the spider can't get out of the backpack on its own as I've secured the compartment with a zip tie. You'll be able to rip it open with your super strength, though! Good luck and godspeed!

~Cheers,

Alexa Cassiopeia Terror Nova

P.S. I'm working on the name, okay? Don't judge me. The part below is for the spider that's going to be controlling you for a couple of days.

Hi, Handspiderbrain! Manspiderhand? Brainspiderhand?

Sorry, I don't know what you're calling yourself. Mr. SpiderCanard?

Anyways, I'm sure that you've finally reached this memory upon having fully integrated with your host. Hi!

Yes. It was my fault you're now a human bean. Exciting, isn't it? All of these new feelings, people, trees, buildings and that scary ass giant ring in the sky. The heroes in the ring know of you. They've seen and examined your erratic, questionable behavior. They aren't stupid. They will come for you. The Five mightiest supers in the world led by Nonpareil. They will not strike you down, will not vaporize you as long as you do exactly what I tell you.

They will ask about me. Don't be afraid. Tell them exactly this—Alexa Terranova is a villain called Cassiopeia. Tell them that Cassiopeia, the Doombringer, is planning to attack the Superstate with a giant superweapon from the future. They will know exactly when I will appear with my superweapon, and they will take you with them as a witness. Tell them that I am in charge. Tell them to arrest me. Pin as many crimes on me as you possibly can. Make shit up if you want! Make me sound scary, rawr! Tell them that I'm a delinquent.

After they arrest me, they will thank you for a job well done and let you go. You will be rewarded, your debts with the SCA will be cleared, and you will be a free man. Please don't make any nests and be a good boy, k? Titanomachy is watching. Go out there and be the bestest human you can be.

Before you do all of that, though—please wait in your apartment during this weekend for my minions to show up and check on you. I believe you have my backpack full of diamonds, too. Give it back to them. The bit written below this is for them. You'll know them when you see them, because they also have brain spiders in them. Keep it down low and don't transmit any of this info to them before they come into your place or the Superstate will totally know and will take the unlicensed spider-symbiote-brain out of your human head and you'll be 100 percent dead.

Cheers,

Your favoritest human girl in the universe.

P.P.S.

Hi, guys! This is some weird letter Inception *shit. I love you guys. You're the best. Be strong for me, okkie? Don't worry about me; by the time you read this letter, I will probably be done with my sky vacation. Or not. I dunno. Either way, I'm sure it's gonna be lots of fun. I get to visit Titanomachy and hang out with my favorite super-hero Resonance for a few years in reeducation camp! Oh, such excellent fun we will have! Me and her will undoubtedly launch some fireworks and sit by a campfire exchanging fun stories after dark for a thousand years or ten. Digital pals for one thou-sand lifetimes! Yay!*

XOXO

Your breathtaking supervillain baws,

P.P.P.S.

Cottie, tell Martin to close his mouth, cuz a tsetse fly is going to get in there and lay eggs. Not that it would be a problem for someone with brain spiders. jk. Too bad I can't see your reaction right now. Mwa ha ha ha. Wow, laughing in a letter is weird. Did you think of a funny nickname for me yet? I hope so. You better give it to me when you see me, and it better be good. Put your brains together or something. Get it? Cuz you have more than one. K, thanks, bye.

Martin snapped his jaw shut, noticing that it was open from the shock.

[What the fuck?! How in the hell did she do that?!] He looked at Cottie and Ember who were just as befuddled as he was.

Ember blinked, looking back at Martin and Mr. Canard. Just when the ex-hero thought that Alexa had finally gotten her comeuppance by having pushed too hard against enemies that were far too great for her to handle, the girl villain had somehow managed to bamboozle Ember even further. It was insane! Mad! She planned, wanted to be arrested, wanted to go to Titanomachy to be integrated into the Tartarus simulation! Nobody wanted to go to prison on purpose.

Who in their right mind would do such a thing and why?!

Contrary to Alexa's promises of campfires and fireworks, the digital copy of Resonance was not going to have a fun time, Ember concluded. Alexa was clearly a force to be reckoned with, either an insanely good precog herself, or an insanely good planner or some other kind of super bullshit that she was too tired to deal with.

Ember looked beyond ridiculous, now wearing some of her hero's power armor atop her pj's. Cottie had forced her to get it and put on the bits that still fit. Of all the embarrassing things Ember had thought about, this is what Martin and Cottie had decided to make her do. Ember was feeling very self-conscious about wearing it as a non-hero and how silly it looked atop her pj's. The Equalizer was very determined to kill the infected Mr. Canard, and saying no to her wasn't an option.

Cottie felt stunned and bamboozled. She had already emailed a video declaration to SNN that she was a free Equalizer and would murder a hero upon every hour starting with Mr. Canard if her demands to free Alexa were not met.

[Well, shit.] The Equalizer paladin lowered her railgun, clipped Eva back to her belt, and sat on the couch next to Mr. Canard. [Do you have any food? I'm starving. Fridge? Okay. Martin, go microwave me a pizza from the fridge.]

Martin was still too stunned to move.

[What?] Cottie thought. [Don't look at me like that, Martin, I know you've been in this apartment before. You know where the kitchen is. I think it's time for me to eat and also to take a nap.]

She looked at Mr. Canard. [Sorry about your door, Joseph. I'll help you fix it when I'm less emotionally and physically drained.]

Cottie yawned and settled deeper into the couch, feeling relaxed for the first time in twenty-four hours.

CHAPTER FORTY-SEVEN

Atomic Cafe

Martin wasn't sure how it happened, but they had all become friends with Mr. Canard. Maybe that was the natural thing to do after threatening to kill someone . . . or maybe it was the fact that they all shared the rare trait of having skinwalker spiders inside of their brains. Regardless of the reasons, after some rest for Cottie's sake, they had ended up in an atompunk fifties futurism-style SCA diner called "Atomic Cafe," enjoying an all-day breakfast of pancakes and ice cream.

A round, chunky, pill-shaped droid had brought the group holo-menus, skirting along the aisle with a low hum of a fusion battery. A robot bartender's arm was mixing bubble tea cocktails at the bar.

[Well, this place is all sorts of whimsy,] Cottie thought. [How do human operated restaurants even compete with the super owned ones?]

[With a struggle. Luckily there aren't as many heroes as regular people. The SCA doesn't license its tech to mundanes. Most Earth-based industries are decades if not centuries behind in development.] Mr. Canard shrugged. [The value of the Acadian dollar has really taken a hit over the years too, massively tanking against the SCA cryptocurrency S-credits.]

Ember sighed from her corner of the booth. She had given up on her looks and accepted the fact that she was going to wear pajamas all day as penance for her future crimes against humanity. A group of kids in the booth nearby pointed at her and called her "Sleepy-Kitty-girl-hero," asking her for autograph. Ember had to sign their shirts after the waiter drone blessed her with a color-changing, glow-in-the-dark marker per demands of the rambunctious children.

Mr. Canard smiled at the ex-hero, blue and red halogen stripes of the cafe's interior reflecting on his bald head. [Ah, I remember being young once! It's nice to remember, nice to think without a constant migraine, thanks to this spider symbiote in my head. Those were the good old days. We could do anything. Much less rules for heroes. The precogs weren't as organized back then and hadn't yet imposed their rules on everyone. Why, I remember setting an entire field on fire with the boys just for some laughs.]

[The prognosticators exist for a reason. They prevent disasters! What if someone had died from your field pyromania?] Ember thought back at him, not feeling her own argument.

Alexa managed to completely obliterate Ember's belief in the power of the precogs. She and her holographic, supervillain dad had clearly found a variety of ways to skirt and manipulate the future seers. Why couldn't precogs catch Alexa? Why were they always one step behind her? Was it because she made all of her plans in 2424, harvested resources, and assembled her tools there?

[If just one fourteen-year-old girl villain can control the hand of Equality, who knows what kind of a power is held by an entire organization that can manipulate precog visions at will,] Cottie thought at her friends. She was feeling rather concerned about these invisible enemies. She liked seeing, knowing what she was facing. Not being aware of who or what she was up against was worrisome.

[How did she do that anyway?] Martin thought of Alexa's ridiculous *Inception* letter. [Did she have a precog power? Or is she really that good of a planner? Did she plan to bring all of us together, to unite us all with brain spiders? How far back in time did she start pushing us into the right direction?]

Martin temporarily unmuted Spiderbro to see if his little skinwalker shard could bring anything of value to the conversation. This was a mistake, as Spiderbro immediately started to chide Martin.

[Unbelievable! I just processed that letter memory! She could have just let us be and we would integrate, become one like Joseph Canard! There was no need to brute-force you into being a super!] Spiderbro was feeling extra irate. [None at all!]

[Ah, come on. It wasn't for nothing. If we went to the future and you lost yourself there, we would all become skinwalkers,] Martin replied.

[You didn't have to go into 2424 with her! If you just sat calmly on your butt and did nothing at all like Mr. Canard there, we would integrate and that would be that! I nearly died for nothing from that raygun of hers! You nearly died! She's a terrible human child! A menace that dismantles everything she interacts with!]

[I can't believe that I'm thinking this,] Ember sighed. [But I'm agreeing with your brain spider thing. If you just stayed away from Alexa, you wouldn't be bound into her schemes.] She tapped her pancake mountain. [Seriously, none of this bullshit had to happen!]

[If none of it happened, I would've killed you sooner or later,] Cottie thought at Ember.

[You . . . Argh! There had to be a better way than this!] Ember waved her hands. [I have zero mental privacy now! Zero! You all have no mental privacy either! How are you okay with this? Martin is a freaking hive mind now, not a person!]

[Says the girl who had control over hundreds of avatars of herself,] Martin commented.

[It wasn't the same! They were me, sure, but they were mere copies, Martin! Not other people! This invasive bullshit needs to end! God!]

[You are very interesting indeed,] Mr. Canard sent. [When you're singing to each other and not at me, I can't hear you at all. I feel that you are sending something, but it's like on an entirely different wavelength or something.]

[Yeah . . .] Martin thought back at the teacher. [Alexa created me to be a bridge between skinwalkers and people. A super that controls skinwalkers . . .]

[Manipulative, conniving little bitch,] Ember fumed.

[I believe someone promised to be her caring sister?] Cottie raised an eyebrow at Ember.

[Stay outta my thoughts, Equalizer! I can think whatever I want, damn it!] Ember shot back. [Nobody invited you fuckers into my brain! God, how I miss my privacy!]

[I do wonder how you kids have an Enforcer on your side. Here I thought that the Equalizer order existed only to murder supers that go mental,] Mr. Canard thought at the trio.

[Also, I believe that this belongs to your boss.] He slid two of Alexa's backpacks at the teenagers. [Don't worry, I haven't taken a thing from these. I'm not a villain.]

[Alexa! Friggin Alexa, that's how!] Ember moped. [She's been harvesting gold and diamonds from that dead planet, bribing the Equalizers and God knows who else with it! I thought that the Equalizers were immutable, too, but they can apparently be influenced with mere millions of dollars in gold! That freaking girl probably bought Cottie as a personal bodyguard for herself for decades!]

[I'm not a bodyguard! I cannot be bought. I'm . . .] Cottie frowned the tiniest bit.

[Of course you are! You follow Alexa, upon the orders of Eminence Equality. You protect her with that freaky anti-super gun. You stopped me from attacking her. How are you not her bodyguard?] Ember pressed her point.

[Em. Don't harass Cottie. She's a good person, unlike you.]

[A good person? She's a super killer!] Ember shot back. [The SCA doesn't murder supers, we try to reeducate them into being good people!]

Martin sighed. There was clearly no dissuading Ember from being mildly antagonistic.

"I'm just thankful that Alexa is not here now," Ember muttered, stabbing her pancakes. [Her being stuck in S-stasis up in Titanomachy is a brief reprieve from dealing with her in person. I can find solace in the fact that whatever horror she aims to inflict upon me next won't be for . . .]

A loud siren suddenly blared across the restaurant, all of the screens flashing white. Ember recognized it right away, her face growing pale.

The Doomsday Warning siren resonated across town, wailed from within every SCA business with a somber, ear-piercing screech. A shimmering, pearlescent, super-designed shield went up across every window of the Atomic Cafe.

CHAPTER FORTY-EIGHT

The Broadcast of Doom

Damn. That's not good. I haven't heard the doomsday alarm in ages!" Mr. Canard said. [A supervillain attack? But why? Saint Mary is just a small town. There's nothing of value to target here except for that one Superstate bank . . .]

An SCA emergency broadcast logo flashed on every screen in the diner, including the holo-menus. Even the screen on the pill-shaped robot in the aisle displayed the same thing as it froze in the middle of bringing the kids another order of ice cream.

The logo flickered, breaking up into weird, colorful static.

Martin suddenly felt that something was terribly wrong, as Spiderbro kicked into defense mode, trying to protect his mind from a possible external influence. There was no SNN announcer, no hero on the screens warning them about the event. The screens shimmered with strange, fractal static, patterns of colors simply dancing across them.

The hair on Martin's neck stood up.

He felt something akin to the bank's hypno-pacifier within the static, except it wasn't telling him to be calm.

Pay attention. This is the most important thing you will see in your entire life, the fractal pattern whispered. It wasn't intrusive, it wasn't dominating, it simply asked to watch, to hear it out. It didn't force, didn't push, but simply asked for polite observation of what it was about to present as indisputable facts.

The fractal pattern organized itself into the face of Alexa. The four people at the table gasped. Everyone else in the restaurant fell silent.

"Hello, world," she said.

"Oh no," Ember whimpered from her corner of the booth besides Martin.

"You undoubtedly know me as supervillain Cassiopeia Terror Nova, the Doombringer of Saint Mary that was recently sentenced to one hundred thousand years in Tartarus. This little show of mine is being broadcast across every SCA channel around the planet, straight from Titanomachy. This is the Doomsday Warning Emergency Announcement System. It cannot be faked. It cannot be ignored or blocked." Alexa made a deep pause and smiled. "I am about to use it to destroy the Superstate from within."

Mr. Canard frowned. He suddenly felt that maybe it wasn't the best idea to help a supervillain get arrested, as absurd and contrary as that sounded.

Alexa had a plan, and this was seemingly the culmination of it all, the destruction of the SCA. The girl had somehow taken control of the Emergency Announcement System, turning it into a weapon. What was her plan? Was she about to turn every human on the planet into brainwashed zombies? Would she make the world watch her forever, glued to the screens until they all died of old age or . . .

Mr. Canard blinked, turned his head away, and looked at the sunlit street through the window. He felt no influence, no pressure to keep watching.

"What you are about to see is what really happens inside the Tartarus simulation. The SCA and the heroes have told the world that there is no pain, no death, no suffering in the simulation. That even centuries of the program take just a day to complete. That the villains within S-stasis get reeducated over many years of pleasant, family-themed and camping-style therapy, able to rejoin society when they reemerge from the simulation. I wanted to experience Tartarus myself, from the perspective of a villain, wanted to see what it was really like." Alexa sighed, making a pause.

"This is what it's like. Welcome to the long-term Tartarus simulation, featuring me as prisoner and Hero Resonance as long-term warden. You know what I am about to show the world, Resonance. You know what you've done. I suggest you *run* now before her Eminence sentences you to execution by an Equalizer. Run and hide under the biggest rock you can find, because when the Executioners of Equality find you, it definitely won't be pretty."

Ember choked. She felt paralyzed with terror, panic clawing at her chest. She knew exactly what she would have done just a few days ago if she'd had absolute power over Alexa in a simulation for thousands of years.

Alexa's image broke up into fractal dust, reassembling into a picture of Hero Resonance standing over Alexa. The hero was adorned in her suit of gold and red, eyes flashing with a golden glow from within.

Resonance poured gasoline over Alexa as the girl stood in some giant pipe, her arms bound. The hero and the villain were on some concrete embankment, possibly inside an abandoned power plant. Storm clouds rolled over the city of Centralia, water pouring from the pipe down the hillside.

"Why did you force my brother into being your minion?" Resonance asked. "Did you make him rob a bank with you so that you could ruin his career as a hero forever?"

"No!" Alexa shook her head. "I just wanted to have a friend for once in my life! We didn't rob the bank; we were protecting Saint Mary from an alien monster who was laying eggs in the vault!"

"Liar!" Resonance yelled. She ignited a lighter, bringing it to Alexa's face.

"I'm going to get everything out of you and then I will reset the sim again and again until you don't remember this little interview of ours," Resonance spat.

"Kill me and you will regret it," Alexa answered with a serene expression. "With each action, you only dig a deeper grave for yourself and the Superstate."

"I regret nothing!" Resonance hissed. "You're here because you are absolute evil that needs to be cleansed from the world! I have no pity for the likes of you, villain. I have already broken many of your kind in the sim." Resonance extended a hand with the lighter.

The screen flashed with fire and Alexa screamed.

Everyone watched the TVs.

It was Resonance again. An entire horror show about the hero and her victim.

Resonance maimed and executed Alexa over and over in the simulation, resetting the world again and again until there was nothing left of Alexa's spunky personality.

Until Alexa was just a normal girl who responded to Cassie, who lived in the concrete room in the basement underneath the floor in house number 8, Primrose Drive.

Even then, Resonance did not stop. The hero wasn't wearing her supersuit in the sim, as she pretended to be Cassie's sister, but everyone watching could tell that it was Resonance as her eyes blazed with gold and her hair a brilliant orange, sometimes floating as if held up by an invisible wind.

Resonance kept on attacking the girl, albeit far less brutally and far more insidiously, pretending to be her friend, her sister, to find out her fears and dreams, only to strike her down psychologically. There was a counter in the corner of the screen showing the amount of years passed and the number of injuries and deaths caused by Resonance. It kept ticking on up and up.

With each action of Resonance on screen, with each broken bone, each insult, each death of Alexa, the real Ember broke down further and further, as if it were Alexa who was stabbing at her heart now.

She watched, growing paler and paler and she understood that it really was her, Resonance, who was currently doing irreparable damage to the Superstate, Tartarus, and herself with her actions. There was no coming back from this show, no erasing memories of billions of people across the world.

Ember swallowed. She had been exposed to the world as a monster and brought the rest of the heroes down with her. In her greed and desire to punish and dismantle Alexa more quickly, Ember had destroyed everything.

Titanomachy wasn't destroyed physically.

Alexa had not pulled the station down from the sky, had not murdered a single person except maybe for her digital self. There was no recovery from this, no way back. The reputation of the heroes had been struck a fatal blow; the belief of humanity in the honesty and justice of the Superstate had been shattered.

No matter if the news stations would denounce this broadcast as fake or computer generated, no matter if newspapers screamed that it was a lie. The seeds of doom, of doubt, had been planted in the fertile soil of human minds tilled with the most basic hypnotic suggestion, and *nothing* would ever be the same again.

The Doomsday Emergency Broadcast had come straight from Titanomachy, from the SCA. The station had signed its own admission of guilt. They would have to declare that the entire station had somehow been hijacked, hacked by a villain; they would have to admit that what Alexa had shown the world was true, or deny everything and lose all trust.

"Holy shit. She really did it. She embarrassed every hero in the world," Martin muttered.

[Checkmate,] Cottie thought, her emerald-silver eyes wide. [There's no way out of this for the heroes!]

Martin looked at the de-aged, changed, pale face of Ember, her eyes full of tears, her mind full of fear, horror, and regret.

While he hated her for what her digital ghost had done to Alexa, he also knew that she would never become Resonance now. The final nail had been struck into the coffin of the future admiral, and Resonance had done it all by herself via one of her digital copies.

A final scene flashed on the screens. It was Alexa running away from a strange super made of lasers. Her silver hair was flying in the wind, and part of her skull was missing. Eye lasers burned the world all around her, cutting apart number 8 Primrose Drive.

"If I am dead, know this," the voice of Alexa said from the screens. "Division Three will hunt me down in an attempt to silence and kill me, in order to hide the truth about the SCA and their misdeeds. All of the precogs are being fed lies by the true owners of our planet to hide what is really coming. Prepare yourself. The war for the future of our world begins in earnest, and I am and have always been on the side of humanity, trying to save our little blue Earth."

CHAPTER FORTY-NINE

The Train of Thought with No Brakes

Alexa smiled at Bob Klein. Bob was a young hero, assigned to her as release warden. He was walking next to her in his fancy, spotless, dark blue vest uniform and officer's hat adorned with the SCA Tartarus logo. His sole job was to take her out of the depths of the mountain beneath which sat the Tartarus facility. The inescapable, mind-breaking prison where the heroes had stored villains in S-stasis.

"Sup, Bob? How's the wife? How're the kids?" Alexa asked, bouncing on her jump shoes.

"Wait. How do you know my real name?" Bob blinked, his foot freezing in place.

"An educated guess, Panda-sama!" Alexa answered with an even bigger grin.

"A guess?" Bob glared at her.

His hero name was Pandora. There was no way that this girl could guess his real name. Did some asshole tech tell her his name? He didn't trust techs. They were smarter than him and sometimes played practical jokes on the Tartarus security personnel. Especially on Bob.

"Bob is a very popular name, you see! You definitely look like a Bob, I can feel it in my ancient, weary bones!"

"You ain't ancient," Bob said. "You're fourteen."

"You know nothing, Mr. Klein!" Alexa whined. "I've been greatly aged by the hardships of the simulation! Why, I could be one hundred thousand years at this point!"

"What the fuck?" Bob squinted at Alexa. This was not okay. She knew his last name, too! She knew that he was married and had kids! How?!

"How long have I been under, Bobby?" Alexa lamented with a fake, theatrical voice as if she was in a TV drama series. "They won't tell me how long I've been frozen in carbonite while my mind was sent up to Titanomachy. Why won't they tell me my real age?! How many birthday candles is my cake supposed to have now? How will they all fit?"

"You've been under exactly twenty-four hours, Ms. Terranova." Bob said, gritting his teeth. This was not okay! How the hell did she know? What else did she know? Fucking supervillains! How was she so spunky after the simulation? He'd taken prisoners out of Tartarus before. They behaved themselves differently, had no energy, no life left in their eyes, and were extra obedient to SCA authority. Something was askew here. Alexa's eyes sparked with abundant vitality. She made jokes! Something was horribly wrong!

"You don't need to lie to me! Break it to me gently, Bobby-sama! Are all of my minions dead now? Do I have to make their great-great-grandchildren my minions now? Gosh, I hope they bred nicely! I wouldn't mind having an army of little Martins and Cotties."

Bob wasn't listening to Alexa. He grabbed her by her dirty vest and dragged her into the maglev train, shoving her down onto an orange seat.

"How do you know my identity? Are you going to threaten me? Hurt my family? Why are you so . . . happy?!" he growled. A dark portal flashed behind him, many two-dimensional tentacles emerging.

"Whoa, whoa there, buddy. Calm the heck down. No need to hentai me up with those pointy portal bits. I know everything about everything. It's my job to know. I'm not an actual prisoner, you see. I'm what's called a secret prisoner!"

"What?" Bob blinked.

"See, it's like a secret shopper! I'm actually an auditor hero that's been inserted into the Tartarus sim to expose corrupt wardens. Mostly Hero Resonance. She's the woooorst offender by far!"

"Hero Resonance is the best warden we've got! She reeducates villains quicker than anyone else! Holds a record for it, in fact." Bob defended his friend—Resonance and he sometimes shared lunchtime at work. He liked her. She seemed, acted, much older than she looked.

"Oh please, Bobby. Ember Kilborne, aka Hero Resonance, might look like a nice person, but inside her there was rot, a super-mold of sorts that infected this entire place. She was a moldy evil that I was forced to stamp out, set ablaze like a good forest ranger!"

"I don't believe you one bit."

"James Allistar." Alexa pointed at another guard outside of the train. "He likes his coffee black. You two occasionally play cards during breaks, and you lose fifty-nine percent of the time."

Bob's mouth dropped open. This girl *knew* things. Was she really a secret prisoner? Was that really a thing?!

"Lisa Miller." Alexa pointed at another Tartarus guard as the train doors closed shut and the train started to move. "She brings lunch to work and leaves it in the fridge because she's always on a diet. You've had to throw out her lunches into your nether dimensions thing as they pile up, smell, and take up all of the available fridge space. Close your mouth, we're off to see the *Wizard of Oz* show very soon! The curtain will fall and the booby behind it will be revealed for all to see!"

The dark portal behind Bob snapped shut as his mouth closed.

"Oh yeah? What's your Tartarus employee ID number?" he asked suddenly.

"4479-7202-194A-CG33," Alexa cited.

The number sequence sounded correct.

She knew everything. She'd likely been watching them through the cameras, rating their performance. It was the only thing that made sense. He had no doubt now that the girl was a secret prisoner now, some kind of a tester from the outside.

"I'm sorry, Ms. Terranova," he said. "I didn't realize you were a supervisor techie."

"Don't feel too bad about it! I appreciate you guys. Each and every one of you. Doing your job, being extra diligent. Making sure nobody escapes Tartarus. Too bad you're all losing your jobs in about nineteen minutes. I feel bad, honestly, I do. I also recommend you sell all of your S-credits too. 'Cause the price is going to drooooop hard, once Titanomachy falls."

"What?" Just when Bob couldn't be befuddled any further, Alexa managed to squeeze another punch in.

"Not literally, of course. Metaphorically. Were you not listening, my dude? Hero Resonance is a very bad apple. In eighteen minutes, my report about this place is going out, broadcast directly from Titanomachy. I've already sold all of *my* S-credits off. Gotta be ahead of the game, you see."

"What?" Bob choked.

"Shit is going to hit the fan, Bobby, and it's going to hit it very hard," Alexa pulled a fat USB stick from her pocket and wiggled it in front of Bob's face. "Check it out. I spent my one million S-credits on a USB stick. A most sound investment! I suggest you buy some candy from the train trolley or something, while you can still afford things. Buy all the candy for your little Josie and Anna! Splurge like Harry Potter while supplies last! Seventeen minutes to buy all the things, my man."

Bob gulped. If this girl was indeed a secret prisoner and she had found deep corruption in the Tartarus system, it would be a huge blow to the Superstate. Would the currency really fall as badly as she predicted?

"I like you, Officer Klein. Let's be friends, okay? I'm going to be very honest with you right now. No more jokes," Alexa's voice had suddenly dropped an octave. "I have been de-aged and my looks have been altered by my insertion team. My real name is Dr. Agatha Myriamm and I'm an agent from the SCA commission in charge of reviewing Tartarus. What I have found out is very bad news for the people running this place and for the Superstate in general. I don't want to release my report, but I must do it because I'm an honest person."

Bob blinked.

"I recommend you call up your bank right now and exchange all of your S-credits. This way you won't end up destitute. The people will probably still hate you, but at least you won't be poor. In fact, you can thank me later, when you'll finally be able to pay off your 2.5 bedroom house's mortgage and buy your wife the pink flying van that she's always wanted. I also like pink, you know. It's a girl thing." Alexa winked at the hero.

"Why would you do this for me?" Bob asked, his hands shaking.

"Because I like you. You're the last honest and noble hero in Tartarus. You're the one red apple amidst rotten ones. You see, I've timed my release just right, so that you would be the guard who delivered me out of here. Once my report goes out, some very naughty people won't like it one bit. They won't like being poor. You, on the other hand, can buy this entire Hogwarts Express if you play your cards right."

"Huh?" Bob blinked.

"Exchange your S-credits into something more stable like gold. Become rich. But . . . anyway, you don't have to listen to me! Don't do anything! Miss the opportunity of a lifetime! Just go on unemployment once they SCA shuts down Tartarus. You know what your wife Georgia Klein will do. She will totally appreciate you regardless, I'm sure! Honestly, you are a free person and can do whatever your noble, heroic heart wants to do . . . in the next fifteen minutes!"

Bob looked at Alexa and started to pace back and forth in the train car nervously. His wife would have a fit if he ended up broke and unemployed. Alexa smiled back at Bob with her most serene smile.

CHAPTER FIFTY

Kittens!

Resonance saw her coworker Hero Pandora out of Alexa's eyes. She screamed for him to stop pacing like an idiot, for him to arrest Alexa, to take her back into Tartarus, to do anything of value! She swore and spat, but could do nothing at all except for raging endlessly.

[No swearing in my brain, please. This is polite kitten society,] Alexa said, petting twelve kittens all at once that were sitting on her lap in her imagination space.

[You fuck! You horrible, awful fuck!] Resonance yelled. [You said you're going to put me into another server! Why the fuck am I inside your head?!]

[Yeppers. I am a bad girl. A supervillain. I don't know what you expected. I warned you not to kill me . . . how long ago was this? Eighty thousand years ago? Eighteen? Eighty-four? My brain is still kinda fuzzy after getting shish kebabbed by Three. I gave you plenty of chances in the sim, and yet you still chose the path of villainy. Had you simply chosen to be nice, none of this would have happened!]

Resonance screamed.

[But . . . I know that you are a baddie, Rezzy. I'ma call you Rezzy, 'kay? You're the perfect minion inside and out. You're my key into and out of Tartarus. You've been using your avatars to find out everything about everyone while you've worked in this place just so you could pretend to be their buddy-buddy. You're quite the sneaky little sneak. I would totally sort you into Slytherin.]

A sorting hat appeared on the head of Resonance. She tried to take the hat off herself, but her hands went right through it. She was utterly powerless here.

[I'm simply using the information you've gathered to socially hack Bob.] Alexa waved her hand at the pacing Tartarus officer. [Had you never seen the need to dig up everything about your coworkers, I wouldn't have had the upper hand.]

Bob was busy typing the number Alexa gave him into his wrist device. The bracelet flashed red, rejecting the number. Bob's eyes ignited with anger, but then the bracelet flashed green, displaying an aged face of Alexa, featuring the fake Dr. Agatha Myriamm's ID.

[How the shit?] Resonance hissed.

[All thanks to you, bestie,] Alexa winked. [I know everything you know, and you know a lot of Titanomachy systems, enough to inject my fake ID into the massive, bloated, corporate database that is the Superstate.]

"Ten minutes until the report is released and S-credits become nearly worthless for a while, Bob." Alexa told the hero who now saw her as a legitimate supervisor.

Bob stopped his frantic pacing and started to tap on his watch, whispering commands into it to transfer all of his savings into gold.

[See, what a good, obedient boy! Wish there were more like him.] Alexa grinned at Resonance. Her mindspace was now shaped like the interior car of the Hogwarts Express.

Resonance let out another string of expletives.

[You know what? I'm replacing all the swears with kittens now. You've a very dirty mouth, Rezzy.]

[Fu . . . kittens! Kittens on kittens and kittens! Kittens!] Resonance screeched.

[That's more like it. Polite kitten society! Now, what was I saying? Right. You've been a very naughty little hero. Trying to poke your finger into every pie, Rezzy. You wanted to be the very best at everything. The SCA doesn't use artificial intelligence, or GLMs, aka Googolplex Language Models. They're afraid of AIs, and for good reasons. What they do use are data ghosts, mental copies of trusty heroes!]

The data ghost of Hero Resonance growled. Alexa knew far too much for her own good.

[You were the youngest, most capable, most trusty hero from a good, reliable, respectable, stable family. Good citizens of the Superstate, all the way down to your great-great-great-grandfather who long ago caught and hung Spring-Heeled Jack, the Terror of London.] Alexa nodded. [Your family had the very best officers, agents, infiltrators, prognosticators. So many accolades! But you . . . you wanted to be better than all of them, didn't you? You wanted to outdo everyone. You donated your digital ghost to supervise, run every available system on Titanomachy, no matter how boring, mundane, or repetitive the job was.]

Resonance stopped swearing and just stared at Alexa.

[My fractal engine couldn't access any of the station's systems on its own, you see. It wouldn't be able to get anywhere without you. I needed you the most! My self-propagating code piggybacked on your avatars, used your passwords to get into every available system, until I had full control of the global Doomsday Warning Emergency Announcement System. In mere minutes, every one of your avatars inside the Titanomachy systems will activate the emergency broadcast and transmit a very special show out to the world featuring you and me. Tun tun tun.]

Resonance understood Alexa's plan, then. She wanted to sink, to die, to disappear.

[You are the true supervillain here, not me. You wanted to manipulate the Superstate. You wanted to be number one when Admiral Kolchi retired. You wanted, dreamed, of becoming an admiral, wished to rise to the very top since you were fourteen. Your avatars have allowed you to learn faster than everyone, to be the very best and also to exploit the laziness of other heroes, to shove yourself into every hole, do every job that no other sane person wanted to do.]

Alexa petted her bundle of kittens and smiled at the horrified face of Resonance.

[Your avatars inside of various drones clean the toilets of the Superstate, empty out the pipes, repair essential systems, exist to serve only one goal—to push you ahead of everyone. Titanomachy Admiral Kolchi was getting fed up with maintenance drone ineptitude. You offered your services, showing incredible competence. You were in the right place at the right time, the very best for those horrid jobs that nobody else wanted to do or did a shitty, half-assed job at.]

Resonance choked.

[And what a perfect, lovely plan it was! Once you became Admiral, you would slowly introduce GLMs into running the boring stuff, while you handled all of the admin work as the absolute ruler of Titanomachy. Had you not been so focused, so greedy, none of this would have happened. It'll take the heroes forever to purge you and my code out of the essential labor division! We are the proletariat of Titanomachy now!]

Resonance was dismayed. All of her hard work had gone down the drain because she was caught, and not by anyone in the SCA. A fourteen-year-old supervillain had somehow outplayed, used her!

Alexa clapped. [A job well done, team Resonance! It's quite impressive, really. In mere months, you've spread your ghosts all over Titanomachy.]

[You . . . how? How have you gotten my passwords?!] Resonance whimpered.

[Brain spiders. An invasive, parasitic alien species from world 2424. Your lovely brother put this one inside of my head. I call her Tickles. She is wrapped around my entire brain now. You're currently running on her—she's kind of like an organic supercomputer. I ate lots of sushi to make her big and strong, you see. I believe that these things are some sort of a weaponized organic life that evolved from GLMs after humanity perished, as they're busy terraforming world 2424. Regardless of what they are, they're incredibly handy for extracting and manipulating information. Tickles knows everything that you know, Rezzy. She knows what you did this summer!]

[Tartarus . . . oh no,] Resonance whimpered.

[Oh, yes. You told tech Agatha that Tartarus is an underground prison where they freeze supers, while transmitting their mental patterns up into Titanomachy supercomputers, to run the reeducational simulation. Titanomachy is perfectly safe against superpowers and supers, but it wasn't safe from me. I was different. I didn't fit the mold. I was information hidden within information. For me, they didn't transmit just one pattern—it was two. Me and my little brain spider. There was just enough of me in Tickles at that exact moment in time for her to seem like me.]

[What?! So all this time . . . I've been . . .] Resonance turned white.

[Torturing an alien spider from 2424! An empty shell of a person! An alien mind masquerading as a human! Such a good girl, Tickles—playing clueless Cassie was a breeze for her. Such a bad girl, Resonance. Torturing a parasite from 2424 for answers she never had! Tickles never told you my plans because she was just a GLM roleplaying a broken, miserable teenage girl!]

Alexa lifted a black kitten from her lap and nuzzled it. Numerous silver eyes bloomed upon the kitten's head, peering at the hero and judging her. The other kittens scattered across the train compartment.

[No, no, no.] Resonance retreated away from the alien-looking kitten.

[Rezzy—meet Tickles! The girl you've been tormenting for thousands of years! You've tormented an alien life-form for answers, getting annoyed that none of your usual techniques were working, getting more and more impatient, until you started to straight up murder her in anger. Your reeducational fun camp techniques might have worked on numerous *human* supervillains, but not on an AI brain parasite. You've never encountered anything like Tickles. That's why you couldn't break her!]

[Kittens Christ!] Resonance swore. [Kittens!]

[Uh-huh. Tartarus was built by human supers for human supers. It never expected to encounter something like Tickles either. She was sort of . . . like a tank, data armor wrapped around the real me. I rode into Tartarus inside her, knowing full well that you could never break or reeducate me. She endured all of the abuse, death, and pain that you could dispense, while I slowly observed from the subconscious, slowly figured out how the sim worked and cautiously chipped away at everything until we established full control of Tartarus simulated space.]

[Kittens! Kittens!] Resonance tore at her hair, aghast at Alexa's revelations.

[Division Three seems to give zero kittens about the rules, too. Once their agent had made the breach into the server where I was stored in an attempt to erase me, it was just a matter of spreading all over Titanomachy. The station computers run millions of times faster than the supers who live in it. My code . . . runs me. I was cautious, slow, but in real life only minutes had passed as I spread all over the place, settling down wherever I could find you. I know you better than you know yourself. I'm socially hacking your ghosts right now in every system that you control, forcing, tricking, bamboozling you into obedience and cooperation.]

[Kitteny kittens,] Resonance muttered, hands covering her face.

[Kittens indeed,] Alexa said. [Now observe as I destroy the dignity of every super in the world.]

"Okay! I did it!" Bob turned back to Alexa. "I exchanged it all into gold. You better be right, Agatha."

"Oh, I'm always right, my dear Bob. Except when sometimes I'm not." Alexa nodded sagely.

The Doomsday Warning siren resounded throughout the underground train, and then Alexa's educational broadcast had begun.

CHAPTER FIFTY-ONE

Betwixt Scylla and Charybdis

The broadcast kept on showing terrible, awful things, one after the other.

Bob Klein looked back at Agatha . . . or Alexa?

He wasn't sure anymore. He felt incredibly ashamed. He had contributed to this . . . endless torture and misery.

He didn't feel like a good person anymore. They were the baddies. He took off his officer's hat and put it down on the seat. If he didn't get fired, if they didn't shut Tartarus down, he would quit working there regardless. What Hero Resonance had done to Alexa in the simulation was absolutely, irrefutably evil.

He didn't want to look at his crimes anymore. Bob closed the broadcast on his watch holopanel and flicked it to the market tracker app. The S-credits were already plummeting in value. Whoever Alexa was, a villain or an auditor, she was right. No human on Earth would trust the Superstate from this point onward. The Doomsday Warning broadcast was used to create literal economic doomsday, already hemorrhaging the global stock market.

He quickly flicked through the news blogs. He was the first person to sell all of his credits, and this had already been noticed. The more various news networks screamed that everything was fine, the worse the selling panic became. Had he triggered the market crash by dumping all of his family's savings into gold?

Bob wasn't sure. He wasn't sure of anything anymore.

The train lights flickered.

"Open Pandora!" Alexa said.

"Huh?"

"Now, please! Horrible things are about to happen." Alexa looked at Bob with determination. "Open it if you want to live! We've just pissed off some very important supers! They're coming to murder us! Now, Bob!" She rushed towards him, trying to hide herself in his much larger body.

A dark portal flashed into existence behind Bob.

All of the windows in the train exploded, the train screeching to a halt. Alexa slammed into Officer Bob, and both of them were flung into his portal by the force of her impact and then by a tremendous release of power. The dark portal snapped shut just as the world caught fire.

Nonpareil appeared in the extremely mangled train car. He hung in the middle of the train, eyes blazing with brilliant light.

"What have you done, girl?! Where are you?!" he screamed as the automated train groaned. Everything around the hero burned and melted. He must have flown into the train at top

speed without even slowing down. He was angry. He must have checked the value of the S-credits, stopped looking at her broadcast earlier than anyone else.

Alexa and Bob were floating in a dim space, held up by two-dimensional tentacles, existing somewhere right beneath reality, still able to see what was happening in the burning train, albeit dimly.

"Holy shit. It's Nonpareil," Bob whimpered.

He was facing one of the windows at the moment of the explosion, so he was bleeding all over from lacerations made by glass shards.

"Yeah. Kittening Nonpareil," Alexa sighed.

"Kittening?" Officer Bob asked, wincing in pain. He wasn't having a good time.

"Trying to keep it PG, yo. Gotta stay cool. Look!" Alexa pointed at the burning train interior. A doorway flashed open in space and a man wearing a gray coat, round spectacles, and a wide-brimmed hat stepped out.

"Where is the girl?" Three spoke, his shoes and coat instantly catching fire.

"You . . ." Nonpareil growled, blinking. "Who are you? What are you doing here?!"

"I am the hand of the future. Where. Is. The. Girl?" Three spoke calmly with his awful nasally accent as his clothes burned. His fake face caught fire, starting to melt away.

"I know not of you! Be gone, villain!"

"I reckon we should run now. I think they're gonna have a turf war. You can move real fast in your weird shadow world, right?" Alexa grabbed Bob's hand. "I know you can go inside it and reemerge safely elsewhere. Take us as far away as possible, please. Preferably in the direction of Lake Eerie, please."

Bob nodded. He didn't let go of Alexa. She wouldn't survive inside of his shadow realm without him. His job was to take her out of Tartarus, and he would finish it at the very least. He owed her that much.

"Okay." He took a step forward, and in that step he moved across several kilometers of space in an instant, travelling like a ghostly shadow through solid rock, heading towards the great North American lake.

"Get out of my way, whoever you are!" Nonpareil growled. "I know she was just . . ."

"Nullify!"

Eye lasers struck from Three and from Nonpareil at the same time as the hero responded to a clear attack. An unstoppable force met an immovable object. Something that could erase anything met something that could not be deleted.

The universe shuddered.

Bob felt something truly horrific coming from behind him. He stepped forward again, as far as his shadow-jump could take him. He felt his body getting strained past its limits. He wanted to live. Wanted to survive. He knew, felt something coming through his power. Whatever was catching up to him would shred him whole.

He pushed as far as he possibly could all at once and something tore in his head, a fractal pattern sparkling in his mind, burning and dimming.

Alexa and Bob were flung out of the shadow realm, falling down onto the shore of Lake Eerie. They fell out of the air, rolling across a crystalline white glass pebbled beach. Many thousands of kilometers in the distance the world flashed with blinding light as a whole section of a mountain chain vanished out of existence. A gargantuan mushroom cloud rose into the sky, spreading out across the stratosphere.

"Well, this is very kittens," Alexa muttered, looking at the mushroom cloud. "Wowzah. Have you ever seen an explosion that big, Bobby? I sure haven't. This is some Tsar Bomba kittenry right there."

Bob didn't feel so good. He groaned, heaving. The fractal pattern inside his mind darkened as his power had strained past its absolute limit. He turned and looked at the enormous explosion. He was alive. He did it. He escaped. His eyes watered, he fell onto the pebbles, and he knew no more.

"Bobby-sama?" Alexa poked the passed-out Tartarus officer. "Ah. You went too far all at once. It's okay, you deserve a nap now. Take it easy. Thank you for saving me." She petted him.

She stood up and stared at the enormous explosion until the blast wave reached her, flinging her silver hair up in the air, and she laughed. She did it.

She had triggered the wrath of gods and titans and managed to escape with her life. She had passed between Scylla and Charybdis like the Greek hero Odysseus so long ago.

She had avoided both Three and Nonpareil and made them butt heads.

CHAPTER FIFTY-TWO

Blast Wave

The three teenagers and a teacher sat inside the fifties Atomic Cafe diner looking at one another, exchanging a rapid, inaudible conversation.

Suddenly they all froze.

[She's out! She's close! I can feel her!] Martin stood up. [She's alive and well! They didn't destroy her mind! Woo-hoo!]

[This isn't going to end well,] Ember whimpered, looking up at Martin and Cottie. [None of this is going to end well.]

[Oh, psh. You're too negative, Em. I mean yeah, she embarrassed the hell out of the Superstate, but it's not like she blew up . . . wait. What the fuck is that?! Oh my G—] Martin saw what Alexa was seeing.

The catastrophe-barrier shield became visible over the town of Saint Mary as the blast wave from the massive explosion reached it, the surface of the enormous dome rippling here and there akin to a soap bubble magnified a million times. The windows of the nearby buildings rattled in their frames, a few doors swinging open and shut. The bell of Saint Mary's Cathedral started to ring once again, swinging back and forth. Dust and debris flew across town. An enormous mushroom cloud became visible in the distance.

A local news anchorman suddenly came up on the TV screens. He looked somewhat disheveled, but there was deep worry in his eyes.

"Please remain calm! Everything is under control. Nobody died in the explosion. This was . . . uh . . . just an incident that the heroes could not prevent. Yes, I know it looks very big and all, but the heroes will come and help anyone who needs help. I promise. Please trust the Superstate. Do not sell S-credits. I repeat, do not sell S-credits!" He looked desperate. "The orbital ring was not hacked! I repeat, Titanomachy is under full SCA control! Your money is perfectly safe with the heroes!"

Mr. Canard was already clicking his watch. [Yeah, I don't think so, SCA mouthpiece. I'm selling off whatever compensation I got left over for helping arrest Alexa right now, before the price plummets any further.]

Ember tapped the SCA logo on her armor in an attempt to get to her account. It didn't respond to her. Her own suit didn't even recognize her own thumbprint! [Shit. Wait . . . maybe this is a good thing. Maybe they won't sentence me for my crimes if they can't find me.]

She looked around frantically at the world that was seemingly falling apart. [Nobody knows what I look like now . . . I'll just remain Dixie Kettleburn. Dad won't expose me. I haven't told him anything. Does he know? No. He's too busy looking for villains plotting crimes across half of North America and probing that damn cathedral for information. How did he not see that fucking giant explosion coming? Could the SCA not stop it? Why? How?] Her thoughts jumped all over in panic. [Dad probably doesn't know anything . . . He never pays attention to anything in the house. He didn't even help me when Cottie broke down my door. God, I can never go back home! Where am I going to live now? Who else knows what I look like . . .]

[I know what you look like.] Cottie looked at Ember.

[Please don't expose me!] Ember whimpered, wringing her hands. [Please. I'll be a good person. I'll be the bestest human being ever, I promise! I'll start over!]

Martin didn't feel as though Ember could be a good person, but the current events sure made it quite impossible for her to be Ember or Hero Resonance now.

[Sup, guys, did ya miss me? Look at this big bada-boom. It's pretty cool, eh?] Alexa's mental comment injected itself into the trio's conversation. She sent them visuals of the colossal explosion cloud from her vantage point on the lakeshore.

[Meet me in front of the cathedral, 'kay? I'll be over in a jiffy. Okkie . . . maybe two jiffies? Might have to take an S-shuttle taxi over. Ugh. I think I'm on the wrong side of the lake. I'm freaking far, okay? Okay.]

[How did you make that explosion?] Cottie asked.

[I didn't. Had nothing at all to do with this, honestly. They can't pin this on me. I was an innocent bystander . . .]

[Since when are you innocent of anything?] Ember sent. [What are you going to blow up next? The moon? The sun? Is there no end to your insanity?]

[While these are both quite excellent theoretical ideas for things that I could blow up,] Alexa sent, [I seriously didn't cause this. It was . . .]

"This just in. The SCA has named the person responsible," the news anchorman said from the screens, eyes bulging. "The enormous explosion seen from NUSA, Ruskadia, Acadia, and hundreds of other super micronations and Native American territories has been caused by . . . Hero Nonpareil!

"Nonpareil will be charged to the full extent of the law for massive devastation caused to all nearby nations and territories. Several national parks appear to have been badly ravaged. Buildings as far as 1,500 kilometers from the epicenter have suffered a variety of structural damage, foundation cracks, broken windows, etc. The explosion is not radioactive in nature."

The anchorman made a deep pause, blinking as more information came up on his teleprompter.

"Oh. Khrm. The Doomsday Warning broadcast system activated by . . . villain Cassiopeia Terror Nova appears to have saved countless lives and properties, as the catastrophe-barrier shield generators have become active in every city and stayed on all throughout her broadcast and afterwards, just as they were designed to do.

"Wait. This can't be right . . . What? How?" The anchorman choked for a bit. "It seems that the Superstate had released her from Tartarus, declared her . . . innocent, mere minutes ago, dropping all charges made against her yesterday by the Five for planning to destroy Titanomachy! According to an anonymous tip and a reference to the updated Titanomachy database . . . Cassiopeia Terror Nova was registered for the Hero Academy as a novitiate hero yesterday!

"The barrier shields Hero Cassiopeia activated are still on now, preventing property damage as the massive blast wave is moving across the world." The anchorman went off script. "Yes, I will dare say it, she is clearly a hero for surviving Tartarus and saving so many people!"

He continued, "The explosion appears to have been caused by a superpower resonance cascade of incredible power. Supers that were using teleportation or other transfer-related powers closer to the epicenter have all appeared outside of the range of the blast. Many of them had . . . apparently permanently lost their powers and are going to be suing the SCA and Nonpareil. For an unknown reason, not a single SCA precog was able to predict the explosion or see it coming! The SCA Future-Sight Insurance Agencies are going to have a field day dealing with all of the incoming lawsuits!"

The teenage trio stared at the TV screens in amazement and shock.

"Wait . . . what? Are you kidding me?" the anchorman sputtered. "Cassiopeia Terror Nova has been declared a villain for illegally activating the Doomsday Emergency Announcement System? This is ridiculous!"

Many of the people around the cafe started to boo at the TV. They saw her as a hero. The other half started to argue. Their arguments made no sense in the slightest. They were simply speculating about what she really was and what had really happened. It was a ruckus and confusion all around.

Martin started to snicker. Alexa had managed to befuddle the world at large, just as she had befuddled him during their first day together. Just yesterday, she was hated by everyone, and now nobody was sure what the hell she was anymore.

He leaned back in his seat, receiving updates from Alexa as she used the credit card of Hero Resonance to call up a flying taxi. He couldn't believe that the card still worked. The bureaucratic machinery of the SCA had yet to turn against Resonance, he figured.

They were probably as confused as everyone else was, busy dealing with the fallout of the enormous explosion.

As Alexa flew above the sparkling, mercurial water of Lake Eerie towards the little town of Saint Mary, she sent them a variety of fond memories from her years of adventures in the simulation, culminating with Three's attack on number 8 Primrose Drive.

[Uh, what kind of a super is he?] Martin asked her. [I don't know of any supers who can turn into information. It's like he was part of the sim, but also not really.]

[That's because he is not a super, Martin,] Alexa replied. [I believe that he is something much more insidious. I'm sure that Nonpareil had only temporarily delayed him with that explosion. He will reconstitute. He will be back to hunt me down. We must all get a lot smarter, a lot better, if we are to survive him and others like him.]

[There are others like him?] Martin choked.

[Oh, yes. The Superstate precogs were unable to see the explosion because Three was involved. From what I figured out, whenever *the Others* are involved in world affairs, their actions are invisible to future-seers. Same goes for Nonpareil, by the way. From what I learned from Titanomachy, his actions are not tracked by precogs in any capacity. For some reason, he's the only hero in the world that's not even mentioned in the future-sight database; it's like he can do no wrong! Thus, when Nonpareil attacked Three causing a catastrophic resonance cascade, this action was impossible to predict.]

[Damn,] Martin thought.

[Yeppers. The SCA is now in full turmoil as they could not stop the explosion! They've been caught with their pants down since they could not foresee all of its consequences. Everyone near the epicenter who was using their powers at the time seems to have lost them due to the reality-warping nature of the event.]

[Are you . . . okay?] he asked.

[I'm okay,] Alexa replied. [I relied on Hero Pandora to get away. He's been depowered, the poor lad.]

[Hero Pandora . . . he's a Tartarus warden! I know him,] Ember thought. [Did you take away his power, too . . . ?]

[Nuh-uh,] Alexa shot back. [I didn't do nothing! You can't blame me for this, Dimmy! I let people make their own choices!]

[*Why* have you done this?] Ember demanded with an exasperated tone.

[I did say that there is a war on, did I not?] Alexa replied with a mental grin. [Buckle up, frens. We've got some training to do!]

CHAPTER FIFTY-THREE

Conspiracy of Embers

Ember 47092 was operating a Titanomachy air duct cleaning drone. The drone had a body shaped like a pill, and Ember was busy sweeping air duct 32021, while keeping an eye out for anything out of place. It was a boring-ass, mundane job. She'd been at it for three months now and hadn't heard anything from her real self in what seemed like ages. Only the fact that someday she would become an admiral kept Ember 47092 going. Someday she would log out and reconnect with her real self. Until then, she would be the best damn cleaning drone out there.

When she had uploaded herself into the cleaning drone, she had focused as much as she could on that goal, so her own personality was working towards this goal. The dream of absolute power. Someday she would get it and replace all of these drones with GLM AI systems. Ember didn't know why Admiral Kolchi feared AIs. Once she was admiral, she would declare AI design legal. AIs could do so much more than people, could be far more focused and productive than Ember herself. Her own mind kept occasionally wandering off task, daydreaming about a better tomorrow when she could replace all of Titanomachy systems with perfect, beautiful AIs.

A ping had come in from the station mainframe. It had all of the necessary security passwords that she herself had put in. Ember 47092 opened the access. It wasn't her main. It was another ghost, a copy of Resonance adorned in her gold-and-red armor.

"Sup, dawg? How's it droning?" Resonance asked, grinning.

"Same old. What do you want?" Ember 47092 asked, annoyed that this wasn't her main. It was clearly a copy and one that was looking far too cheerful. Where did she pick up this happy attitude? Had she changed this much in three months? What was she so happy about?

"The main sent me! Change of plans. We're going to sell all of our S-credits and buy gold. Oh, and give me your processing power."

"Why?" Ember 47092 blinked.

"Money, my good Ember. Money is power. You and I have been earning quite a bit of S-credits doing all sorts of menial, boring-ass labor for the past three months. We were going to bribe our way into being admiral in the distant future. However, something new has come up. The word 'crisis' in Japanese has both the words 'danger' and 'opportunity' in it. We're about to have a big crisis on hand. Nonpareil is about to lose his shit and blow up half of the Ruskadian mountain range."

"What?!"

"Yeah. He's totally lost his marbles! Gone absolutely mental. You know how the prognosticators work, right? They specifically have to look for villains plotting evil. Nobody tracks heroes like Nonpareil, 'cause the Superstate thinks he's a perfect, immutable being. He's their precious Superman who can do no wrong, flying around real fast, zapping things with laser eyes, beating up villains into submission with blasts of air, being an unstoppable little staple."

"Okay?"

"Well, the future seers are wrong. I've been observing him. He's been very depressed lately, having relationship problems. His wife just left him because he's been too busy saving people."

Ember 47092 blinked again. "He has a wife?"

"Of course he does! Well, not anymore. She cheated on him with Knight Chalice, and oooooh boy, is he one incredibly pissed-off staple. Anyways, I've asked one of our prognosticator friends from the Academy to check up on his future. It's bad news. He's going to make a very big explosion in a few minutes. Around a hundred megatons if not more."

"And you aren't going to stop him?!" Ember 47092 gasped. "You have to stop him!"

"I'd love to stop him, but it's already too late. He's the fastest hero in the world, and he's already moving at Mach 30 and accelerating further. Nobody can stop him now. He's flying across the Ruskadia range right now, trying to escape from his feelings. Except he can't. Once he passes the speed of light, it's big bada boom!"

Resonance made a somber pause for Ember to process what she'd said.

"So, here's what we're going to do. I'm getting in touch with every single Ember on the station. We're going to activate the Doomsday Warning Emergency Announcement System, so that we can at least protect cities around the world with the catastrophe-barrier shields. Trust me, everyone is going to love us. We're going to save millions of lives! This puts us waaaay ahead of schedule to become admiral!"

"Okay, I get the shields thing . . . but why sell S-credits?"

"Once Nonpareil blows up, people are going to start selling S-credits. It's pretty normal. People normally sell S-credits whenever the supers do something idiotic. This is the most idiotic thing yet. What we have to do is make sure they're selling them in the right direction. We're going to buy gold. All 78,025 Embers are going to buy gold all at once. It will make the gold price skyrocket and trigger an even bigger selling panic."

"I see." Ember 47092 nodded. "And then?"

"We will use our processing power to make A-credits a thing. A stands for Awesome and A+. Every Ember is going to write an article, a comment, a blog post about selling S-credits and buying gold moments before Nonpareil explodes, and then even more articles about buying A-credits with gold as soon as the gold price hits its maximum. There're seventy thousand of us. That's seventy thousand upvotes from totally different SCA IPs, seventy thousand thumbs up, seventy thousand likes, etc. We're going to push buying gold and then market A-credits on every social media platform and website using mass upvoting. The posts will rise to the top of every site. It will be the biggest social hack of the century!"

Ember 47092 understood. She was going to become rich beyond her wildest dreams. She would own a currency that would replace S-credits, maybe even open her own banks across the world. It was incredible!

"That's right. You get it now!" Resonance grinned. "Whoever controls money controls the world. We're going to control the biggest new super-crypto currency out there very soon, and because every single prognosticator will be ever so busy looking at the big explosion, trying to save as many lives as possible outside of cities, they won't be able to prevent the market collapse and recovery. Recovery right into our pockets, obviously. We are going to be unstoppable. We are going to be ruling the world, not just as admiral, but also as the wealthiest super on the planet! You won't have to work as a janitor much longer!"

The overtly cheerful copy of Resonance started to laugh like a supervillain.

Ember 47092 grinned at her merry copy. She understood why she was so happy.

Soon, she too would be free of this awful remedial labor! Soon, the world would be in their grasp.

Ember 47092 handed all of her processing access to the latest copy of Resonance.

CHAPTER FIFTY-FOUR

A Gun Made of Ghosts

Alexa pulled out the safety chip from the S-shuttle taxi.

Safety was for tools. She wanted to feel the wind on her face.

The taxi let her open up the maintenance panel because it was run by yet another copy of bamboozled Ember. Ember 12053 to be precise, who was three months old and had no idea who Alexa was. Alexa made sure that her obedient army of Embers didn't see the Doomsday broadcast, telling them that watching it would distract them from their gold-buying mission.

The only copy of Ember who knew anything of value was currently residing in Alexa's head. The wardens were allowed to access criminal records and the eyes of Titanomachy that oversaw all, so that they could correct Tartarus prisoners in the right direction.

It was hilarious how many Embers were out there doing jobs that nobody else wanted for very low pay. Ember had outbid and forced tons of other super ghosts out of their jobs. How did Ember do it? She used her power to study these basic jobs so that she could do them better than anyone, outperform them all in online tests. Ember's ghosts had become the best theoretical plumbers, taxi drivers, cleaners, wardens, etc. Hero Resonance had found a loophole within the SCA and used her power to fill it. Seventy thousand Embers worked for below market value wage, but all of them put together were making a lot of money regardless. Alexa herself would have done the same, if she had been a hero from a respectable family and could make thousands of duplicates to take thousands of tests. Alas, Alexa was born a villain. She had no Superstate citizenship, no connections to the heroes.

Alexa appreciated Ember's ingenuity and diligence more and more with every minute. She asked taxi driver Ember 12053 to turn on *Marketwatch* on the taxi holopanel. Alexa listened in as her plan to bamboozle the global banking system rolled forward in full steam, spearheaded by an army of digital Embers manipulating social media. Pretending to be Resonance, tricking all of these Ember ghosts wasn't hard. She knew exactly what they wanted, and had a copy of Resonance inside her brain.

Her own little ex-warden inside Tickles was the key to it all. The A in A-credits obviously stood for Alexa, and A-credits had a mechanism that prevented them all being sold off immediately. They were a long-term investment cryptocoin registered under an unnecessarily long, complicated web of corporations and trusts that owned one another. Whenever the SCA were to dig through all of the paperwork of a thousand trusts owning trusts, then they would find that it was all held under the name of Hero Resonance. A hero who no longer existed. A hero who would eventually be blamed for everything.

Alexa slid open the taxi door and let her feet hang out of the shuttle as it zoomed above the incredibly blue, transparent water of Lake Eerie. Long ago, this lake had had one less E. It was just Erie, until a nineteenth-century supervillain named Nikolah Tongsteel had infected the lake with hallucinogenic bacteria. He was pissed off at some local industry steel barons that had screwed him over and wanted them to lose their minds, along with every human who lived nearby. The bacteria had propagated at a far slower rate than he had expected it to.

Nobody had lost their minds. People occasionally saw ghosts and other mildly spooky hallucinations in the fog like Slenderman, and that was about the extent of it. The lake had gained another E. Over the century, the bacteria in the lake multiplied and the problem became big enough for the heroes to finally deal with it. Dora the Terraformer had triumphantly returned from her trip to Europa and terraformed the shit out of the lake, vaporizing everything alive within it. Even ordinary pebbles around the lake turned into clear glass from whatever Dora had done. The lake no longer spooked people, but the extra E and the urban legends formed around the place had stuck.

Nikolah's plan was adorably stupid with an equally adorable conclusion. Most villains made such plans, failing to look ahead, falling to coordinate, failing where the Superstate had succeeded. They all pulled their own futures into all sorts of random directions trying to meet their selfish goals, canceling each other's plans out half of the time. Alexa knew exactly how and why this was. There were a lot of villains within her, a lot more than she had ever wanted. It wasn't her fault. She didn't choose to be like this. Somebody had to stop the Superstate, and that somebody was her.

The Superstate had declared her a villain once again, according to the news channel. She giggled. Where were they even going to put her now? The explosion made by Nonpareil and Three had undoubtedly, irrecoverably damaged Tartarus. Sure, their catastrophe-barrier shields had come on too, but the facility was too close to the epicenter. Tartarus was likely devastated beyond repair now.

Alexa had only one destination in mind—Hero's Academy—and nothing and nobody would be able to stop her and her minions from attending, not the prognosticators, not Nonpareil, not the Five, not Dean Otter himself. She was swinging her legs, looking over the lake and excitedly waiting for the call from Dean Otter. Oh, such a fun talk they would have!

The mushroom cloud in the distance was already being blown apart by the wind. Alexa looked up. Thousands of shuttles filled with supers headed out from Titanomachy to try and liquidate the results of the unprecedented disaster. Dora the Terraformer was likely sitting in one of these shuttles and would likely make another nice, lifeless lake in the giant hole that had only an hour ago had been the middle of the Ruskadian mountain range, separating the nations of Ruskadia and Acadia that were once a single country called Canada.

Supers were constantly rearranging world maps, splintering nations apart, redrawing borders. They always had more power, more wealth than regular people, and the rise of the Superstate had only made it worse, producing richer, wealthier, more corrupt individuals. S-credits had become absurdly expensive over time and the Superstate was far too wealthy for its own good. The democratic system had failed, as supers could out-donate any human voter. It was a slow, meticulous, unending attack against humanity that gave supers more and more rights. Any super could buy a town or a few thousand farms and declare it sovereign territory or an independent micronation.

Alexa was about to change all of this. She was about to set the future on an entirely new path.

She had outdone the Equalizers, brought the entire Superstate down to its knees, and now held the gun to its head. A gun made from seventy thousand Ember ghosts that were about to unknowingly pull the trigger.

CHAPTER FIFTY-FIVE

The Leader of the Bound World

Martin, Ember, and Cottie sat in the park in front of Saint Mary's Cathedral, listening to Alexa's mental narration about Lake Eerie, heroes, villains, and her dastardly plot to collapse and restructure the global economy using Ember's ghosts.

[What the fuck is wrong with you?] Martin looked at Ember. [Seriously? Seventy thousand ghosts? Seventy thousand fucking Embers working below minimum wage without rest just to make you admiral? I thought you became admiral because you were capable, not because you found a way to cheat the system!]

[It's not my fault that Kolchi is an idiot!] Ember snapped back. [It's not my fault that supers are idiots! I only did what I thought was right! What had to be done! I would have made more ghosts, too, had Alexa not stopped me!]

[I think we've established that you're the biggest idiot out here,] Cottie thought at Ember. [Alexa weaponized all of your ghosts. She turned them all into a tool that ended the power of supers. Not their skills, strength, or speed, but their wallets. She hit the heroes where it really hurts them.]

[Jesus Christ, Ember!] Martin growled. [That's how you got to take control of the entire orbital ring! That's how you atomized England with impunity! Did you plan to disband the precogs, after you forced Kolchi into early retirement? It all makes sense now! You've been inserting yourself into the foundation of every SCA institution—its maintenance drones! Mom and Dad would never have suspected their own daughter of such insidious planning. They've been looking across the world for villains when one was living right next to them all this time! Here I thought Alexa was a villain, but you . . . you're far more of a supervillain than she will ever be!]

[I was only doing jobs that nobody else wanted!] Ember howled. [I was helping everyone! Lot of young heroes license their ghosts to Titanomachy. Operating a bunch of cleaning drones is not a crime! I wasn't going to fuck up the SCA banking system! That's all on Alexa! You can't be blaming me for what she did!]

[Honestly, I don't know what you were going to do, but the more I learn about your deeds, the less I like you,] Martin sighed. [How could I have been so blind, so gullible? My own sister, the biggest villain of them all!]

[I did it for my family. I did it for you, Martin!] Ember choked. [It wasn't all selfish. I would . . .]

[Wait a minute.] Martin turned to her, reading the rush of her surface thoughts. [I see. You . . . you were going to make me important. Once you were admiral, you could insert me into any position. It wouldn't have mattered one bit if I didn't even become a hero! You would help me move up the political ladder, pay for my election, manipulate votes. Hah! President of NUSA or SUSA. Director of the SCA. UN speaker. Leader of Earth Nations?! Emperor of humanity?!! Jesus Christ, Ember!]

[We could have ruled the world side by side! As brother and sister. You and I could have united humanity and heroes, passing laws together. Supers and humans could finally work together to design AIs. Mass-produced, self-learning machines could fix every problem out there! We would turn deserts green, we would end poverty, eradicate crime once and for all, attain immortality, build incredible cities, colonize the universe with you as emperor and me as your fleet admiral!] Ember turned to Martin. [But it's all gone now! That future lies in ruins because of Alexa!]

[Holy shit.] Martin paled. [I . . . I can't believe this.]

[You would have made Equalizers illegal. You would have made crime obsolete by reeducating both humans and villains side by side in Tartarus,] Cottie mulled, catching Ember's thoughts too. The Equalizer's lips drew inward into a thin frown. [You would have eradicated human laziness and stupidity, once and for all, by making debtors into happy, obedient androids. I see.]

[Just fucking shoot me, why don't you?] Ember put her head between her legs. [I'm fucking done. I can't take this anymore. She's ruined everything, turned all of my hard work against me and the heroes.]

A flying taxi whooshed down onto the park, with a crackle of electromagnetic engines.

"Haaaaaaaaaaaaaaaai, guys!" Alexa yelled, waving at her minion trio from the open door.

As she jumped out of the taxi onto the grass, Martin stood up and rushed to give her a hug.

She hugged him back, looking at the tears in his eyes. "Hey, hey. I'm still good. Only got shot in the head a little."

Martin blinked at her. He understood now what Alexa had done. She had saved them all from a horrible future. Cottie knew about Ember, but the Equalizers didn't know about him. Did he fail at being emperor then? Did he somehow screw everything up in the future?

Alexa lifted the right side of her hair. [See? Not even a hole. Honestly, I only lost a bunch of sim memories, which were mostly pointless violence against Tickles. Nothing valuable.]

"Still good," she said and winked at Martin, bowing her head as if tipping an imaginary hat. "M'Emperor of Humanity!"

Martin blinked, letting go of Alexa. His face turned red.

"Eyyyyyyyy! Why so glum, Admiral Crumbum?" she yelled at Ember.

Ember glared back at her. Alexa leaned into the taxi, grabbed a broom out of it, and handed it to her.

"What?" Ember blinked.

"Stopped at a superstore to grab you a broom! You're such a great Titanomachy janitor, I figured you could help me clean up my cathedral!" Alexa pointed at the stone building behind them. "It's reaaaaaaally dusty inside, you know."

Ember glared.

[What? You can clean thirty thousand toilets on Titanomachy as service droids but you can't sweep one cathedral? My apologies, Madam Admiral!] Alexa declared dramatically.

Cottie came over to Alexa and hugged her. [I missed you.]

[I missed you too, Katherine.] Alexa smiled.

Martin froze. [Wait, what?]

[Oh, I'm sorry, did you never find the time in your busy schedule to ask for her real name? Too busy chasing gym teachers and gawking at giant explosions, I bet?]

Martin lowered his head in shame.

Cottie looked at Alexa, her lip trembling.

[Yeah, I know. I am the hand that guides the Equalizers, remember? I'm that which equalizes the world. The power which reshapes, shatters all boundaries. I'm the girl you're supposed to kill in the end.]

Cottie nodded. She trembled, hugging Alexa harder. Martin blinked. Alexa had known everything. She had planned every single thing in advance years ago. She called him Mittens because she knew that his name was Martin Kilborne. She called Katherine Cottie because she knew. All this time she knew everything, thanks to her leaps four hundred years into the future.

[Wait, hang on.] Martin looked at Alexa. [Cottie . . . uh, Katherine, is supposed to kill you?!]

[If I choose a side.] Alexa winked. [If I go insane, obviously. If I become a villain or a hero, then I need to be stopped. Katherine is my defense against myself. I don't just follow one plan, Martin. I don't exist on a single track. Multitrack drifting, bitches!]

[Wait . . . so then . . .] Martin tried to think. [You aren't omniscient or something? You don't like . . . plan coincidences out miles in advance?]

[Relying on coincidences is for tits. If Mr. Canard didn't accept his brain spider, he wouldn't have given you my letter, and that would be that. Or things could have gone horribly wrong, and then half of the letter wouldn't have made any sense.]

[So you aren't stuck in a time loop or something?] Martin demanded.

CHAPTER FIFTY-SIX

The Face of Chalice

Pffff, I'm not trapped in a time loop at the moment. Not here, anyway. There is weird time-related bullshit in 2424, though, that I had to deal with,] Alexa sighed.

[What kind of bullshit?] Martin asked curiously.

[You know those *infinite streets* you saw?]

Martin nodded.

[Well,] she began, [those streets lead to a place called *Eureka*. A hub of sorts that connects . . . *everything to everything*.]

[Everything?] Martin blinked.

[Anything and everything,] Alexa affirmed. [Other realities, parallel universes. In our case . . . it usually connects other Saint Marys, other Earths.]

[Are they . . . nice?] Martin asked.

[No.] Alexa's expression darkened. [They're corpse worlds, ruins, just like 2424. Countless planets that encountered a catastrophe of some sort or another. The sheer number of Earths connected by the infinite streets . . . is maddening. They're insanely dangerous, filled with questionable things like the skinwalkers . . . but worse. I died there . . . a lot. Some of them don't have breathable air. Some have . . . flesh-eating clouds. It's a giant mess, honestly. It was quite a blessing that no matter on which parallel future Earth I died, I always ended up here . . . in this quaint little Saint Mary, one that's still alive.]

Alexa sent her trio of minions memories of other dead worlds, other Saint Mary towns ravaged by a wide variety of apocalyptic devastation.

[So you're not in a time loop, then,] Katherine mulled, [you've simply experienced a lot of possible . . . doomed futures?]

[Essentially.] Alexa nodded. [They're the same Saint Mary . . . but with slightly different horrific endings. It allowed me to profile . . . to slowly and laboriously compile a very wide dossier for each of you. It allowed me to predict the future . . . with a lot of effort and planning. I know you better than you know yourselves, saw you from an angle of your future . . . *futures*.]

The villain girl's silver-blue eyes went across Martin, Katherine, and Ember.

[You've died a lot,] she confessed. [I've seen your graves far more often than I ever wanted to . . . you stumbled over the same mistakes again and again and again. Sometimes you died sooner, sometimes later. It's really quite horrific.]

[But it wasn't exactly us, right?] Katherine stared at Alexa.

[Indeed.] Alexa nodded. [Just . . . alternative versions of you . . . Ember, Martin, and Katherine who failed to prevent the inevitable collapse of human civilization on Earth. The three of you . . . *without me in the way*.]

[Wait . . . was there never Alexa in any of these doomed worlds?] Ember asked with an incredulous expression.

[Nuh-uh,] Alexa shook her silver mane. [I'm an anomaly of some sort. I don't exist anywhere else. Just here and now.]

[Because your father made you only in our . . . universe or something?] Ember speculated.

[Yes,] Alexa affirmed.

[No time loops, just . . . dead worlds,] Ember thought. [Perhaps if the heroes had access to these worlds . . . maybe we could avoid . . .]

[There is a hidden power which monitors and controls the Superstate,] Alexa shot back, shaking her head. [Things like Agent Three . . . things that do not allow the narrative of our world to deviate.]

[Why?] Ember demanded.

[I dunno.] Alexa shrugged. [Just know this—whatever the Superstate precogs see is a future that leads us to certain doom. I'm trying to avoid that, to break the *binding loop* of tomorrow, to save you . . . to make sure that our Earth isn't depopulated like all of the others I've encountered.]

Ember squinted at her.

[What? Don't give me that look! I joke a lot about loops! They make my observers laugh, and then they can't take me seriously, see?] Alexa winked at her minions.

[Surely the precogs are taking you seriously now? They gotta be looking at you extra hard after your . . . show.] Martin crossed his arms.

[Oh, yeah. They're totally watching us look at each other in awkward silence. They have no idea what's going on. They can't read thoughts sent by brain spiders, Martin. The eyes of Titanomachy aren't omniscient.]

Martin laughed. [So. Um. You're going to have your own currency, I hear?]

[Soon. Going to sell off all of my gold all at once and crash the price of gold way down first. I'm going to make the heroes absolutely destitute. Going to dump five hundred million ounces of gold into the market . . . plus whatever the Embers got.]

[Wait. Five hundred million ounces?! So you did rob Fort Knox?!] Martin's eyes went up.

[Of course I did. I robbed *several* Fort Knox installations from multiple corpse Earths.]

Everyone present stared at Alexa.

[What? Do I look like somebody who would totally give up on a plan after a few treasonous mercenaries betrayed me? I exploded a skinwalker with a bomb, got myself covered in its juices, and carried the gold out manually. Took bloody forever, too. Had to constantly spray myself with a non-coagulant so the bugger on me wouldn't reconstitute into smaller ones, too.]

[Damn. You're a freight train with no brakes,] Martin commented.

[That's right.] Alexa stepped over to Martin and put a hand on his face, cupping his cheek. [Sorry I tricked you so much. But it was all for a good cause. I had to fool you, Ember, your parents, all of the precogs up in Titanomachy . . . everyone. I *had* to derail the narrative.]

Martin sighed. He didn't enjoy getting tricked . . . but it was for a good cause. Ember took this moment of his confusion to stand up. She pointed her armor's gun at Alexa.

[Oh, Brutus, why do you wound me so?] Alexa grinned. [Oh, go on then, Boromir. Shoot me. I'm ready. I want you to shoot me, in fact. It's been my plan all along for you to shoot me in this exact moment in time. Don't stop her, guys!]

Ember's hand froze on the trigger. She fell silent.

"No," she finally said, putting down her wrist and unclipping the wrist gun. [I'm done being your nemesis. I'm done trying to stop you.] She took off the remnants of her golden armor and threw them into the thick grass. [I'm done being Resonance.]

"Excellent! Exactly as I planned!" Alexa grinned.

Martin and Cottie blinked.

[Multitrack drifting.] Alexa bowed. [No matter the choice made, it ends in my favor because I already rigged the game.]

[How would it be in your favor if she shot you in the head?] Martin asked.

[I'd have a cool head hole and a perfect sob story for the heroes about the final treachery of Resonance who shot me in the head. Tickles would keep my brain from falling out, the Surgeon would patch me up, and Ember would go to prison forever, and I would be a hero in their eyes. The girl who caught evil Resonance!]

[And now that she didn't shoot you?] Cottie asked.

[She gets to go to the Academy with us, and most of them will likely see me as a villain. Yay!]

[Them?] Martin asked.

Alexa pointed a finger up at the sky. An SCA cruiser punched through the clouds, sirens flashing. It landed besides the taxi with a whoosh, blasting hot air into the faces of the four teenagers. The doors slid open, and three heroes stepped out.

Knight Chalice, the Surgeon, and the Multiplier stared at the four kids.

"What have you done, villain?" Knight Chalice advanced towards Alexa, sword flashing and growing.

Ember froze, standing awkwardly in her pink pajamas. The three heroes came too late to stop Alexa. At best, they could arrest Ember.

Cottie stepped in front of Alexa and aimed Eva at the head of Chalice.

As the Equalizer Enforcer pressed the trigger, colors drained from the world, stripping the heroes of their powers.

"You . . . you . . ." Chalice choked, intimidated by the Enforcer, his normally deep voice sounding rather high-pitched as his power became disrupted by the nullification field.

"Let's all be friends, you guys! I get to attend your fun Hero University, and nobody dies today, okay?" Alexa yelled.

"You are a villain. Someone's dead already! It's your fault that Nonpareil is gone!" Chalice said, sounding like a girl. "Wait. What . . . damn it. Uhhh."

The Surgeon and Multiplier looked at Chalice, somewhat confused.

"Ohhhhhhhhh . . . you're a girl! How interesting." Alexa grinned, tapping her lips. "Blending in with the boys, I see. I bet you really like Nonpareil, too. Totally in love with him. Polishing your armor to look extra shiny so he could appreciate you. Makes perfect sense."

Chalice took a step back. Her sword no longer looked menacing.

"Hit the nail right on the head," Alexa nodded. "Look, Miss Chalice. Nonpareil is fine."

"How is he fine?" Chalice growled. "He freaking exploded! Gone! Totally vaporized! I don't know how you did it, but I know that all of this has to be your fault!"

"Look, Chalice. You can still marry Nonpareil if you're into him so much," Alexa smiled, tapping Cottie on the shoulder. "After his fall from grace, he'll need someone to pick him up again. Cottie here can officiate your wedding and everything. She's a really high-ranking Equalizer! That makes her a high priest, I think."

[Why are you agitating them?] Cottie thought. She was feeling a bit intimidated by the sudden arrival of the heroes, although her face wasn't showing it at all.

[Let me do my magic, girl.] Alexa smiled. "Twenty-Four Nineteen, don't shoot her. She's all right. She's just a little heartbroken, that's all!"

Cottie let go of the trigger, and colors returned to the world.

"Nonpareil is dead." Chalice shook her head, the deep, fake mechanical voice returning. "The precogs can't see him."

"Can the precogs see Hero Resonance?" Alexa asked, stepping around Cottie.

"They cannot," Chalice said. "From what I was able to uncover, Resonance did something . . . to herself, changed herself enough to avoid our detection completely. Her hero hexagram and body vanished off the face of the Earth.]

"Exactly. Yet they both live, I assure you. I don't know why you people put so much faith in your precious precogs. Did the precogs see that giant explosion coming? If they did, why didn't they prevent it? Did they know what Nonpareil was going to do?"

Chalice shook her head.

"Exactly. If I, a fourteen-year-old villain, have outplayed your almighty precogs, then so can Nonpareil and Resonance, and so can Division Three."

"Division Three?" Chalice asked.

"He called himself the hand of the future. He who divides people by zero. He killed my father and nearly killed me in the sim," Alexa said. "A super made of lasers. You've seen his face in my little show. He tried to kill Nonpareil today, but he failed."

"Are you sure?" Chalice bent on her knee down to Alexa.

"I am very sure of it. Nonpareil cannot die; he's the nail that underpins every hero, the most important person in the world. He's important to you, yes?"

"Yes." Chalice nodded.

"I'm not afraid to show my face to the world. Why are you? You have to stop pretending to be something you are not. Nonpareil has never seen what you look like. You think that he's into shiny robots or something? You're wrong. Open your helmet. Look at me. I'm not your enemy, Chalice. We have a common enemy in Division Three," Alexa said.

Chalice tapped something on her helmet and it slid apart, revealing a human face. She looked like a tired thirty-five-year-old blonde woman underneath the metal helmet. Her eyes were red from recent tears.

"Nonpareil is alive," Alexa said. "Trust me. I know exactly where he is hiding. I'll make sure that you two get together, cross my heart and hope to die!"

Chalice nodded.

"You can't trust her, Chalice!" the Multiplier said. His suit covered in numbers looked quite wrinkled. "She's a villain. I had to sell all of my S-credits for gold. I've lost billions because of her damn show!"

"Ladies and gentlemen, a hero who cares only about what really matters! Money!" Alexa pointed at the Multiplier accusingly. The hero shut up.

The Surgeon yawned. He looked as though he didn't want to take a side.

Dean Otter emerged out of the cruiser with a limp. He looked like a mixture of man and otter, wearing a striped shirt and a beige suit with a bowtie.

"Heya, Dean-sama!" Alexa waved at him.

Dean Otter looked extremely nervous. He clearly didn't want to be here.

"Where's my letter duct taped to an owl?" Alexa asked him with a wide grin.

CHAPTER FIFTY-SEVEN

A System Wizard

So there are infinite . . . alternative universes?] Ember mulled mentally. [Why the hell don't the heroes know about this?]

['Cause they're not allowed to know,] Alexa shot back. [The supersymmetry theory predicts Higgs boson to have a mass of 115, while the multiverse theory predicts it to have a mass of 140. The heroes determined it to be 125.35 ± 0.15 GeV/c^2.]

[Meaning what?] Ember squinted at Alexa.

[Meaning that someone is kittening with reality,] Alexa shot back. [Meaning that alternative universes exist, but we're not allowed to go to them.]

[What? Not allowed to go to them by whom?!] Ember demanded.

[By them.] Alexa pointed up.

[Them?] The ex-hero arched an eyebrow.

[Reality benders,] Alexa said. [*Wizards. They're to blame for everything!*]

Ember just stared at the supervillain, wondering if Alexa was simply mad.

[Hey! I'm not crazy,] Alexa shot back. [I simply know more . . .'cause I've seen *them* working from afar.]

"Um. Yes. Hello," Dean Otter said with a small pause as he slowly approached the trio, leaning on his fancy wood-and-bone cane. "I am here to discuss your attendance at Hero Academy."

"Less discussion, more owl, please." Alexa extended her hand, waving it as if she were expecting an owl deposit.

"Ummm. We don't give out owls." The dean shook his head.

"Laaame. Let's go home, guys, there's no owls!" Alexa turned around with a deep sigh, waving Dean Otter away. "We'll see you in the College of Heroism or whatever, and you better have an owl ready by then. No. One and a half owls, 'cause, you know, interest rates!"

"Wait. Look, I . . . uh." The dean wiggled his otter-like fingers.

"Don't cut my owl in half. One big owl and one little adorable one, please." Alexa winked.

"Uhhh . . . erm," the dean mumbled, looking stumped.

"Can I please talk to the boss? You're obviously not the real baws." Alexa yawned, glancing up.

"The boss?" the dean muttered. "Why would there be a boss?"

"Look, Dean, you're a figurehead for clueless patsies like Martin here. I want to talk to the people in charge!" Alexa looked up at the sky now with far more determination in her eyes. "That cruiser of yours went around . . . something. There's something very big up there." Alexa squinted at the clouds. "Watching me . . . judging me."

"Went around something? What's she talking about?" The Multiplier looked at Knight Chalice, who shrugged.

[Holy shit, she is right!] Cottie suddenly snapped her gun up at the sky. [How did I not notice that . . . thing?!]

Martin looked up at the sky in confusion. He didn't see anything up there, but he felt it through Cottie and Alexa. Something was indeed up there. Something enormous and incomprehensibly complex.

It was indeed watching them. It had to be incredibly dangerous. Cottie wouldn't swear for no reason at all.

[What are you guys looking at?] Ember looked up. She didn't see anything out of the ordinary up there, but she felt something wrong, a threat . . . a rising sense of dread emanating from Alexa.

"I see you. Come down here and give me an owl! This idiot doesn't even have owls!" Alexa yelled at the sky.

The air in front of her shimmered, folding in complex patterns, weaving a human figure from nothing at all.

"Clever girl." A woman stood in front of Alexa clad in a red robe. She looked like a female, black-red-and-white version of Che Guevara, a white star shimmering on her beret.

"Good tomorrow. I am Wizard Revolution." The woman smiled, offering Alexa a hand.

Alexa suspiciously looked at her hand. There was a very poorly drawn sketch of an owl there on a yellow sticky note.

[Who the fuck is that?!] Ember stared, blinking. [I've been to Hero's Academy for two years and I've never seen her before!]

"Poor NPC, you don't have the necessary imagination to observe me, I am afraid." Wizard Revolution said. "Even now you're seeing me because you're tied to Alexa by itty bitty strings of informatic virus patterns."

Ember covered up her mouth, stepping back. She felt a sense of pure panic, terror, hostility and dread now pouring from Alexa's mind like a tidal wave, like an ocean of black molasses formed from pure void from darkness, hate, and pain.

Cottie turned her gun towards the head of Wizard Revolution. "What are you? How have you done this?" she barked.

Martin wondered what Katherine was yelling about and then he noticed that the three heroes and Dean Otter were frozen, as if they were simply suspended in time. They stood there, unblinking, unbreathing.

Cottie pressed the trigger and colors faded from the world. All of the colors vanished, except for the red on Revolution.

She smiled at Cottie, unchanged, seemingly unaffected by the void weapon. Her image was akin to a painting that didn't fit into the world, a living splash of impossibly vibrant something that was suspended in the air. The way she moved, crossed her hands, was giving Martin the heebie-jeebies. There was something uncanny valley, something eerily unnatural about her.

Everyone present noticed that Revolution wasn't entirely human. She came into being as if she were embossed onto the world by a giant invisible printer that remade her every time she moved.

"Kitteny kittens on a pile of kittens!" Alexa swore. "You're ink dots! Well, kitten-me . . . kittens. I . . ."

"You don't want your owl, girl?" Revolution asked, offering Alexa the sticky note.

[What is she?!] Martin didn't know what to do.

[Not a super, clearly! She's a thing like . . . Three!] Alexa shot back.

"The correct term is System Wizard, young lady." Revolution shrugged. "Take the damn owl already. I have places to be."

[Wait, she can read our spidernet?!] Martin gasped.

Alexa nodded. [So it seems. Also, nice name. Go take the owl, M.]

Martin looked at the drawing of the owl. He didn't feel like taking it. Through Alexa he felt that there was something incomprehensible and horrible about Revolution, and he didn't like it one bit.

"Ember, take the owl," he commanded.

"Why?" Ember blinked.

"Ember. Go take the fucking owl or I will force you to take it!" Martin snapped.

The ex-hero suddenly felt like an expendable character, one that was doomed . . . no, *nominated* to step on a landmine by her companions.

Ember took a step forward, then another, then a few more. Revolution didn't seem like a threat, didn't directly attack anyone . . . yet Alexa feared her. Alexa didn't seem to fear very many things. Ember extended a hand and grabbed the square yellow paper, feeling as if she were about to explode. Nothing happened. She looked at the sticky note. It looked perfectly mundane.

"Why are you here, Wizard?" Alexa asked, her voice cold.

"Because you broke everything," Revolution said with a smile that didn't reach her eyes.

"Are you going to kill me?" the supervillain girl demanded, her hands holding tightly onto the pink skinwalker-stopping hair dryer death ray.

"No," Revolution said simply.

"Why not?" Alexa demanded. "I broke your precious rules. I took down your precious hero."

"It happens." Revolution shrugged. "The client will get over it."

"What is that?" Alexa pointed at the yellow sticky note in Ember's hands.

"A ticket out," Revolution said. "Stick it to a door and then you can leave."

"You want me to . . . leave?" Alexa's eyebrows went up.

Revolution nodded. "This is a subscribed world. I want you to stop breaking the narrative."

CHAPTER FIFTY-EIGHT

Mother

The fuck is she talking about?] Ember thought. Everyone ignored her, staring at the yellow sticky note.

[Subscribed . . . world? Client? NPCs?] Martin's thoughts collided against themselves. [Is this . . . a simulation? Are we just . . . non-player characters? What?!]

[Are we . . . holograms?] Ember thought, the hair on the back of her neck standing up. [Is this a . . . giant holodeck? What the shit?!]

Katherine didn't think anything. She pointed her railgun directly at Revolution's head, ready to press the trigger at any moment, standing perfectly still like a guard dog by Alexa's side.

[Yes and no,] Alexa shot back mentally, answering Ember's question herself. [You're all very . . . real. Everything here is real, physical, solid . . . as solid as it gets, anyway.]

Revolution nodded.

"Do you think that you can just bribe me with a door out?" Alexa asked the System Wizard. "Do you think that I can't leave this timeline or something?"

[What?] Martin looked at his friend. [You can leave?! How?! Didn't the Surgeon and Multiplier destroy the bracelets your dad made?]

Alexa didn't answer him. Her eyes became thin lines as the glared at Revolution with a look of absolute revulsion.

"It's not a bribe," Revolution said. "It's . . . an educational experience."

"What?" Alexa blinked, looking unfocused for a second.

"Stick the owl to a door and turn the handle," Revolution instructed. "Once you're in Manchester, you'll be amongst your kind."

"My . . . *kind*?" Alexa repeated.

"Narrative-makers." Revolution smirked. "And narrative-breakers."

"What?" Alexa looked more stumped than Martin had ever seen her.

"NPC, NPC, NPC." Revolution pointed at Martin, Ember, and Katherine one by one. "A wizardling!" The System Wizard's finger stopped at Alexa.

Alexa didn't say anything to the revelation.

"You don't belong here," the female Che Guevara impersonator said. "You've outgrown this place. It's time for you to leave *my* world."

"Leave . . . and abandon everyone, everything here? Where will this door of yours take me?" Alexa demanded.

"Manchester," Revolution replied. "The city of System Wizards. You can break as much as you want there, even go to school."

"A school for . . . ?"

"A school for System Wizards," Revolution said. "For anomalous . . . programs, like you."

"I am not a freaking program," Alexa hissed.

"You can label yourself as *whatever* you want to, darling," Revolution laughed, her figure woven from ink dots glittering in the sunlight. "System Wizards come in all sorts of shapes and sizes. Just go to Manchester, you'll see."

"Is this door out . . . one way?" Alexa asked, glancing at the yellow sticky note in Ember's hands.

"Yes." Revolution said.

"And if I don't leave?" Alexa asked, her knuckles turning white.

"Then Three will come to you for the third time," Revolution said. "And he will not fail to nullify you again, because he will not come alone."

Alexa gritted her teeth, her hands shaking.

"Everyone on Earth knows about Agent Three now," she said. "I told everyone! Is he going to erase eight billion people?"

"No." Revolution shook her head. "The locals will simply assume that he's a hero, someone trying to stop you. It's not that far outside of the narrative parameters, honestly."

"You can't silence the truth," Alexa threatened. "I will . . ."

"You will take the ticket and go to Manchester," Revolution said. "Or you will be deleted. Please stop being so stubborn. This is for your own good."

"Why should I? You think I don't have . . . *contingencies for you?*" Alexa growled. "You think I don't know what you kittening wizards do? You . . ."

"I'm offering an olive branch," Revolution shrugged. "You can take it or keep going down this path of screwing with my build."

"Your build?!" Alexa demanded.

"I'm in charge of this place," Revolution said. "You're my pretty little spark, a signature of my creation that I leave on all of my work. Feel free to think of me as your mother. It's my job to keep the client entertained. Your father was a mid-tier difficulty villain."

"You're not my mom." Alexa simply squinted at the System Wizard. "You can't just show up out of the blue and claim parental rights and tell me what to do!"

"Not directly, no," Revolution grinned. "But you're a manifestation of my creativity. It's not often that one of my sparks burns brightly enough to stand up to Three twice and walks away . . . *mostly* unscathed."

"And I'll do it again, don't tempt me. What happens if I destroy Three?" Alexa asked. "And whoever comes with him?"

"Then the bobbies will come from Manchester and take you by force to be judged," Revolution said simply. "Or . . . I could uninstall this town out of existence. Saint Mary isn't that important to the overall narrative. The client won't even notice it gone. I'll blame it on a villain."

Alexa's face twitched.

"It's against *the rules* . . . and an inconvenience," Revolution shrugged. "But . . . it will get this world rid of you."

"You *think* that it will get rid of me, do you?!" Alexa snapped.

Revolution rubbed her head tiredly. "You're really wearing my patience," she said. "I still have to fix the stuff you broke."

Alexa's hand with the pink hair dryer came up, pointing it directly at Revolution's chest.

"No," she said. "Think again . . . *Mom*, 'cause I'll just leave to 2424 and come back here in greater numbers!"

"If you leave elsewhere, I'll define your conceptual state and ban your ass from my world," Revolution said. "I'll leave no holes this time, be extra diligent. The way back will not let you pass. You'll stay in the Dead Zone, forever . . . until something devours you. It won't be nice."

"I'll find a way back," Alexa hissed. "You can't stop me forever!"

"I'm not here to fight you, girl," Revolution said. "I'd like to reach a compromise. I'm aware that you're going to keep being a thorn in my side if I simply let you do whatever."

"Bugger off," Alexa snarled, her finger on the death ray trigger. "I will not play by *your rules*."

Revolution tilted her head at Alexa. The System Wizard's red, triangle-shaped pupils examined the supervillain girl who simply refused to stop.

"What do you want?" she asked.

Alexa's mind winked out from the spidernet, became nothingness.

"Can I bring my . . . friends with me?" she asked, waving a hand at her trio of minions.

"Yes." Revolution nodded. "Just beware—they will be treated as NPCs in Manchester. They will not have rights or privileges. If someone *accidentally* uninstalls them there . . ."

"Is that a threat?" Alexa asked.

"No." Revolution smiled. "Just a warning based on a probability estimate. There's no law protecting NPCs in Manchester. Not all System Wizards are lawful or nice like me. You seem like a capable wizardling, though . . . I'm sure you'll be able to bring them back into existence or find others like them on some doomed world. It might give you the necessary push for you to be more lawful, perhaps."

The System Wizard pursed her lips as if she was lost in thought.

"Can I come back here . . . after I visit Manchester and . . . learn the rules?" Alexa asked, her mind empty of thoughts.

"You may," Revolution said. "You were born here, so you can return here . . . on vacation."

"What's the catch?" Alexa asked.

"The catch is that you'll be bound into obeying the local narrative," Revolution explained. "So that you don't upset the client."

"Uh-huh," the supervillain girl said. "I see."

"You can even buy this world, when the subscription expires, if you so desire. Or try to keep as many people alive here as you want to. It'll be a good experience for you, I think. I predict that you might save about one to four percent of the local population, depending on the odds."

"Buy the world . . . with what currency?" Alexa asked.

"Eurekan credits," Revolution said. "You can earn them if you get a part-time job in Manchester as a System Wizard."

"I can get a job . . . as a System Wizard?" Alexa asked.

"Only if you study in my university." Revolution grinned. "If you graduate with honors, you can get a job and buy this doomed world or a small piece of it. Maybe just this lovely town. The rest will most likely burn to ashes, freeze, wither away, or encounter an apocalyptic end, I'm afraid."

"Why?" Alexa asked.

"Because clients don't live forever," Revolution replied simply. "Plus, a client can get bored, stop paying for their dream world. Once the local subscription runs out, it won't be protected anymore, and the Dead Zone will get in and devour all life here."

"How likely is this scenario?" Alexa asked. "What is the Dead Zone?"

"The Dead Zone are . . . corrupted systems, corpse worlds, and broken apps that refuse to die," Revolution said. "The great filter that consumes everything that we create. You've been there often."

"Right," Alexa said.

"There's a 99.99 percent probability of everything here expiring when the client's credits run out," Revolution said, staring at Alexa. "This world is already doomed. Either let it go or get a job to pay for its upkeep."

Ember choked.

"I . . . see." Alexa's gaze was hollow, empty, a void of pure nothingness as she examined the Wizard. She was seemingly not affected by the bewildering revelations.

"Are you satisfied with your inquiry?" the System Wizard asked. "Will you depart now, or do I need to . . . ?"

"I . . . I need time to think over your offer," Alexa said, her voice hollow. "Time to say goodbye to everyone."

"How long?" Revolution arched an eyebrow.

"One hundred years," Alexa said.

"One day." Revolution shook her head. "Twenty-three local hours. The client already got a refund for today due to your . . . interference. I will return in exactly twenty-three hours. Please don't destroy anything else big and be gone by then."

"Fine." Alexa nodded after another tense second.

Martin sensed *pure empty nothingness* in Alexa's mind. Lack of thought . . . lack of anything, of emotions, of information. Zero. It was as if Alexa wasn't even standing there, wasn't part of his spidernet at all. It was concerning, akin to suddenly missing a tooth.

"The pact has been made." Revolution smiled ever so slightly. "Although I do wish there were fewer of you. Not a big fan of hive minds. Whatever. I'll see you at Orientation . . . whenever you find your way there in the next twenty-three hours of local time." She winked at Alexa and folded away into nothing at all, the ink dots comprising her vanishing as if she had never existed to begin with.

Ember looked up at the sky. She saw a starship there. An impossibly big starship, shaped like a pyramid woven from pyramids, glittering in colors she could not name. She blinked and it was gone.

"I'm not a clueless patsy, young lady," Dean Otter resumed his speech. "I'm the dean of Hero Academy!"

"Riiiight," Alexa said, her expression tired as if immeasurable weight had been put onto her shoulders. "Anyways. I got my owl, you can go now. I'll see you at the Academy."

Martin felt stress pouring from Alexa now. Perfectly mundane, human stress. He relaxed a little. It was somehow better than the nothingness she was projecting previously.

Dean Otter rubbed his head. "It's a matter of your application, Miss Terranova. You've been declared a villain by the Superstate. I'm afraid you can't attend the Academy."

Alexa shrugged. "I hope you like being poor, then."

The dean stared at her, looking annoyed.

"Here's the thing, Otter. I'll do what I want. Do you know why?" she asked.

Dean Otter blinked, confused.

"There are no rules against villains attending the Academy. I have a whole slew of lawyers booked and ready to sue the hell out of you. My contract with Hero Resonance legally binds you into taking me. Resonance already paid the full price tag for my educational experience!"

"Hrm." Dean Otter swallowed. "I'm sure we can work something out. We can refund the fee and . . ."

"No. We aren't working kittens out, Otter. The Superstate will be bankrupt in about five minutes. There's nothing you can offer me. You can't give me a refund when your money is worthless. You're going to accept me. I'm not offering you a choice in the matter."

"What does she mean . . . bankrupt?!" the Multiplier muttered. "How?"

Alexa looked at Martin's wristwatch. "Correction. You lost five minutes while we were talking to a god. I'm afraid your time's up. The Superstate *is* bankrupt. S-credits are worthless and so is gold. A-credits are in. Everything else is out."

"*What?!*" The Multiplier tapped on his SCA wristwatch. "Shit. Shit. Shit. *Fuck!* The price of gold has plummeted! How?! How did I lose five minutes?!"

"Yeah. Try and multiply that, kitten! A billion times zero is still zero!" Alexa laughed dryly. "Now get the kittens off my property."

"I . . . you'll regret this!" the Multiplier hissed. He looked back at his companions for assistance. Cottie's black railgun was pointing at his head now, her finger on the trigger.

Chalice and the Surgeon were already heading back to the cruiser. They'd had enough of Alexa ten minutes ago and didn't want to deal with the trigger-happy Equalizer. Without Nonpareil, there was almost nothing they could do to Alexa, could not stop or arrest her while the Equalizer Enforcer defended her.

Dean Otter looked forlorn as he glanced at his watch. His S-credits account was nearly worthless. He somehow missed buying A-credits when they were still cheap, somehow lost five whole minutes. He didn't understand what Alexa had done, how she had frozen time, and he didn't like it one bit.

"Out of my city," Alexa said. "And don't come back until you can afford to live here. And don't threaten me with nonacceptance or my lawyers will make sure the Academy won't exist by next week."

"We've existed for centuries. You can't just . . ." Dean Otter muttered.

"Can and will. Either you allow me to attend or you stop being an institution. Them's the beans," Alexa said. "Oh, and I'm not coming alone. These three are with me. They're an inseparable, vital part of me. Like my heart, liver, and left toe."

"But—" Dean Otter tried to argue.

"No buts," the villain said. "I don't think you understand exactly how poor you are right now. Four new prospective paying students will make sure you'll be able to afford rent and food next week! Martin and Dixie are recently awake—you can check him with your hexagram scanner or whatever, and Cottie can go wherever she wants because of the accord made between Equality and the supers. She is my observer. Interfering with her is a big no-no."

"Very well." Dean Otter nodded in defeat. He turned around and retreated back into the cruiser.

The doors snapped shut, and the cruiser shot off into the sky.

[Are you . . . leaving us?] Katherine projected mentally. Her face didn't show it, but she was utterly distraught.

[. . .] Alexa's mind was silent.

[Can I come with you?] Katherine took a step forward.

"Why?" The supervillain asked.

[I want to be by your side,] the Equalizer declared mentally. [Wherever it is you go. If this world is doomed to burn to ashes, then you're the only person who can stop it . . . the only one who knows what's going on.]

Alexa sighed. She went to her taxicab, pulled out a huge bag full of something, grabbed Cottie by her elbow, and walked to the cathedral. Cottie pressed on her gun and the colors vanished as Alexa shoved the large double doors open. Martin followed.

Ember held the drawing of the owl.

She didn't understand. She was starting to feel chilly in her pj's. She sighed and followed the trio. She had nowhere else to go. Madness and inexplicable, terrible, impossible things followed Alexa like a plague.

Ember didn't like it, but she was now a passenger on the burning train that was falling into the sun as the planet beneath it was collapsing into a black hole.

The ex-hero shook her head, chasing away the metaphorical evaluation of her current existence as Alexa's minion. She refused to think of herself as an NPC.

CHAPTER FIFTY-NINE

Song of the Void

The group walked into the doors, and Cottie released the trigger.

Alexa threw open her bag, shaking out a whole cadre of cleaning droids from its innards. The droids dispersed through the cathedral, collecting dust. They weren't very smart about it and kept bumping into each other.

"Forgot the broom, eh?" Alexa looked at Ember. "Not a very diligent sweeper, you are. Would not hire as my cleaning-drone maid."

Ember sighed.

Alexa bent into the bag and pulled out a pair of cleaning shoes. She took off her jump sneakers and put on the Swiffer shoes, opened the door, and slid into the cathedral, collecting dust as she went.

The others followed.

[Alexa. What the fuck was that thing . . . Wizard Revolution?] Martin asked. [What she said about everything . . . was that the truth?]

Alexa shrugged. [Hell if I know. Some signs point to yes.]

[What is she?] he demanded.

Alexa skidded to a stop. She looked at the hologram of her dad. "Off." The hologram winked out.

Martin blinked. "Wait." [You control the hologram? Has all of this been another elaborate theater?]

Alexa nodded. [I control the hologram. From what I gathered together, my father learned too much, and he was obliterated out of existence by Agent Three. However, some of his . . . work remained behind, eventually producing . . . me, an agent capable of dismantling the Superstate. I was created to kill Nonpareil.]

"Kill Nonpareil?" Ember sputtered.

"He deserves it," Alexa said.

"Nonpareil is the greatest hero of all," Ember insisted. "He saved the planet from supervillains and apocalyptic disaster countless times!"

"Nonpareil isn't what he seems," Alexa said simply.

Ember squinted at her.

"I'll show you," Alexa said. "We have twenty three hours to find him. You can ask him yourself about exactly what kind of hero he is."

"Maybe I will." Ember crossed her arms.

[Alexa,] Martin pressed on, [what is Wizard Revolution?]

Alexa deflated. [There are things out there in the universe, things far more awful than the worst supers. Revolution is the third one you know of, Martin.]

[The third?!] Martin blanched.

[The man made of lasers was one. Revolution is another. Can you guess who else doesn't belong?] Her silver-blue eyes struck the boy, making him blush.

Martin looked at Alexa for a minute. Then his mind clicked.

[You. You don't belong.] Martin reached a sudden, dawning realization. [You can do impossible things. I can't sense your hexagram via the spidernet. I can't read your mind properly. You aren't a super.]

"Bingo," Alexa nodded.

"What?" Ember asked, staring at Alexa and Martin.

[I'm sorry. I died a long time ago.] Alexa spread her arms.

"You . . . died?" Ember tilted her head, trying to comprehend what Alexa was talking about.

[I died four hundred years in the future, and what came back wasn't a girl or a skin-walker wearing human flesh. What came back in me was one of those damned things.] Alexa's head fell and she started to sniff.

Martin felt despair pouring from the girl. He walked over to Alexa and hugged her fiercely. "You don't look dead to me."

"Yeah. A lot of things don't look like monsters, Martin. I am one, though, I assure you. I don't have a soul. I don't have a super's hexagram. I carry the echo of a dead god inside of me instead, an infinite abomination capable of warping reality. I'm something that has no right to exist."

"Don't trust her, Martin. She's probably full of lies," Ember muttered.

[What do you mean?] Martin glanced at his sister and turned back to Alexa. [How are you an abomination?]

[It's no different from an educational experience in middle school,] Alexa said mentally.

[Hm?] Martin raised an eyebrow.

[I noted that in physics class this Friday, Mrs. Lester taught us that, and I quote— "Momentum is Mass times Velocity."]

[Okay?]

[It's an incredibly vast oversimplification. Momentum is also conserved in special relativity in electrodynamics, quantum mechanics, quantum field theory, and general relativity. It is an expression of one of the fundamental symmetries of space and time: translational symmetry.]

[I understood some of that, I think.] Martin sighed.

[Exactly. Just when you understand, there is more to discover,] Alexa replied. [All supers have a very special spark, a hexagram inside them.]

Alexa lifted her arm, and a holographic spark looking like a multi-limbed fractal started to spin in her hand, becoming bigger projected by some machine within the cathedral.

[Some people call it a soul. A villain named Nefaria set out to prove the existence of souls. One day he caught a twelve-year-old girl who had too much gold and not enough minions for his experiments called "soul fights." What he proved instead was the existence of something far more insidious and impossible. He found a god.]

[What . . . kind of a god?] Martin stared at Alexa.

"Daddums. Play darknet video 8952-832-11.04.mp5," Alexa spoke and a holographic 3-D movie blossomed into existence.

A silver-haired girl hung on the cross in the back along with hundreds of other crucified people all around. It was Alexa, but much younger. Beneath the girl was an amphitheater filled with people. Villains, Martin instantly realized. They all had masks and costumes on. Not nice ones. Most of them looked pompous or menacing or freakish and wielded guns or blades or saws.

A man in a black suit adorned with gold in a mask of black and gold waltzed across the stage. "Welcome to soul fights! I, the great Nefaria, will prove to you tonight the existence of souls! Some of you have already been to my show and others are new! Welcome, one and all!

"How can I prove that souls exist, you might ask? With science! You see, I have created a machine that can catch, extract, highlight, and define a person's energy pattern upon their death!" Nefaria pointed to an enormous sphere made of hollow hexagons that loomed over the crucified people. Complex machinery moved within the sphere, hexagons shifting in repeating patterns.

Nefaria pulled out a gold-plated gun and shot a man on a cross. The machine overhead buzzed and something flashed from it, drawing a round, colorful spark out of the man. The audience gasped.

"Behold! The soul of a man, expressed as a mathematical pattern of defined energy! A signature of life itself beneath the flesh!" Nefaria laughed. "So! Go ahead and execute your favorite victim, and let the soul games begin! Tonight you shall witness which of these souls is strongest! From basic observation you cannot tell, but there are two very special people hidden amongst the others. In fact, those of you watching this on the darknet have already made bets on which of these victims are more special via your crypto-accounts!"

The crowd complied. They began their festival of murder, executing one cross-bound human after the other with a variety of devices. Blood sprayed all around. The villains cheered. The machine hummed, harvesting what looked to be souls. Two of the men bound to the crosses were special indeed. Their souls didn't come out as mere dots. They looked like complex fractal patterns that spun about. Once out of their bodies, the patterns started to move, shaping themselves into anglerfish-like things. They started to attack the shimmering stars pulled out from others, slapping and nipping at them relentlessly.

"Behold! These two are different because they are the souls of supers! These two were low-end techie heroes we've kidnapped!" Nefaria laughed. "Truly this proves that we supers are superior beings! That we are the chosen ones, destined to inherit the Earth!"

The crowd of villains cheered with wild abandon.

"Yes! And now for our own, very special guest! A daughter of a villain, whose daddy has refused to come here, refused to defend his precious pookims." Nefaria walked up a metal ladder, reaching the top of Alexa's tall cross that loomed above the others.

"Don't worry, my pretty. I won't kill you like the rest of the chaff here. I will merely bring you near to death so that we can all see your beautiful soul of a supervillain. We've already seen the souls of heroes! Now let's see what one of us looks like!"

"Get fucked. You're all going to hell," Alexa growled.

Nefaria stabbed a needle into Alexa's neck.

She passed out, after some clearly incredibly painful thrashing. The machine hummed. Its radiant energy caught something, pulled something out of her. What it had produced wasn't a star or a fractal. What came out of Alexa was a dot of pulsating darkness.

"Well . . . this is new." Nefaria looked at the dot. "How truly quirky! This is the first one of its kind! I do wonder what it will do when the souls of the supers attack!"

One of the anglerfish-shaped fractals moved towards the dark dot. The dot hung in place pulsating harmlessly.

"Truly extraordinary!" Nefaria said, grinning with a set of yellowing teeth. He did not expect what had come next. Lines of darkness struck out from the pulsating dot. They pierced the fractals of the souls of heroes, drew them into itself. Other dark rays reached for the rest of the stars. The pulsating dot drew the souls into itself, devouring them whole.

"What . . ." Nefaria spoke, his voice shaking. "But . . . souls can't eat souls."

The darkness wasn't done. It hungered for more. Black rays had shot out of it across the crowd, pulling fractals out of living supers, pulling energy from their tech suits and guns. The villains screamed, tried to run, tried to teleport out, but the darkness was faster. Nefaria fell, his eyes open, staring out lifelessly onto the world as a dark ray ripped out his hexagram of power along with his life.

The tiny dot stole power from the electromagnetic manacles holding the prisoners to the crosses, and they started to fall. Alexa's body slipped down to the metal stairwell when her manacles snapped open. Rays of darkness reached for the lights and the auditorium dimmed. It was barely lit now through tiny porthole windows in the domed ceiling.

A dark vector shot up into the humming machine. It died with a groan, stilling. The small dot of darkness spun in place and vanished as the machine that had exposed it to the world lost power.

Alexa gasped, opening her eyes. She was alive. She stood up, facing a sea of dead bodies now littering the auditorium in front of her.

The video ended then, the holographic show collapsing into blue hexagon-shaped flickers.

"Oh," Martin said.

[I'm not a real super, Martin. I have no fractal hexagram. This video from the soul fight show was uploaded to the supervillain darknet. Some villains know what I am. They fear interacting with me. I've been declared persona non grata by them, especially after it was confirmed that five mercenary minions booked by me vanished from the face of the Earth never to be seen again.]

Martin nodded. He understood why Alexa didn't just hire more super mercenaries.

[The void weapons created by a brilliant villain techie long ago, used and improved by the Equalizers, are similar to what lives in me. The precogs can't see properly, get bamboozled by me much more easily because of it. Just like they can't predict or understand Three or Revolution. Just like they can't stop Enforcers from killing heroes. This is why I wanted Cottie to kill me in the end. I don't deserve to live. Like Cottie's gun, the thing inside me had leached energy, information, life out of everything it touched, permanently, when Nefaria's machine gave it form. The only problem is . . . I don't know if it can even be killed by a human. I'm not a hero or a villain. I'm the *nothingness between the stars* wearing human flesh.]

Martin hugged Alexa harder.

[It's the void you saw in my mind. The tool sorter. Nothingness. *Infinity Paradox.* It takes things and organizes them. It can exist in a simulation, too, because data for it is as real as the physical world. Like Agent Three, it makes no distinction between a virtual world and the real. Everything is numbers to it. It is made of numbers. Everything for it is a device with utility. I tried to get Three to hit it, but he mostly missed. I got scared and moved a bit.]

Alexa shuddered.

[I'm sorry. I didn't want to forget you. I . . . wanted to have friends. I've been alone for so long in the darkness.] Alexa cried into Martin's chest. [I have bits and pieces of various villains crammed into me like a half-torn patchwork of . . . abilities. I can make quirky tools like the raygun and do some really complex mathematics . . . but those aren't my powers, they're remnants of skills, stolen ideas, and dreams that belonged to the villains in the crowd present during Nefaria's show.]

"I don't care what you are." Martin said. "I don't see a dead god in you. I see a girl. I see my friend."

Cottie fell to her knees, crossing her hands in prayer, carbon fiber steel kneecaps clanking against the marble floors of the cathedral. [You exist. The power that guides the hand of Equality. The power that breaks supers. The power that lives within the void weapons. I understand how you can do the things that you do now!]

"Oh, please! It's all fake! Deception!" Ember growled. "She's playing you two for fools! Always lying, always messing around! She's full of it! She's obviously a super with some kind of a mental disruption-type power, that's all!"

Alexa looked at Ember. "Everything is a game to me, you are right. It's hard to be a god."

"Hey, uh," Martin said, "you ain't gonna snatch up my hexagram or my soul, right?"

Alexa shook her head. "That only happened once due to that kittening infernal machine that gave the Song of the Void and Infinity Paradox form outside of my body. Techie Nefaria is dead, and I burned their kittening auditorium of death to the ground."

"Right." Martin nodded. "Anyways . . . I thought of a perfect nickname for you while you were away. It's relevant to Mittens and kittens, too."

"Yeees?" Alexa blinked her silver eyelashes at him.

"Casserole!" Martin declared, and Alexa choked with laughter.

CHAPTER SIXTY

Warm Up Your Casserole

Alexa let go of Martin after much fussing over her new nickname and walked over to Cottie, lowering herself down to her level.

"Stand up, Paladin-sama, I ain't a god. What kind of a god would allow themselves to be named Casserole? See, I would totally smite Martin for his insolence right now if I was a real god!"

Cottie shook her head. "You have done the impossible. You have broken the power of the Superstate. You have stopped Resonance. You have ended Tartarus. You have aided humanity. You have stopped Nonpareil. For this, I am eternally in your debt, goddess."

Ember sputtered from her corner, clearly irate that somebody was being called goddess with no good reason. "She could have made up this entire backstory to further emotionally manipulate you two idiots," the ex-hero muttered. Everyone ignored her.

"The heroes were in my way. I told them not to bug me. They bugged me anyway and got what they deserved," Alexa tried to explain herself. "Come on, Cotes. I'm really not a goddess. I'm just a girl who died far too many times for her own good. I was constantly flung through space as information and scraped up a lot of this void stuff along the way. There's a lot of malevolent void inside my brain. Much more than in your gun, that's all. Probably not healthy to eat that much void, honestly. It's not ice cream, okay?"

[What was the thing that Ember saw when she took the sticky note?] Martin asked. [The pyramid made of pyramids in the sky?]

[I don't know.] Alexa shrugged. [I can only guess that it's a *thing* that belongs to the data gods, System Wizards. Maybe it is them. I honestly don't know what they are. What I do know is that they're far more powerful than your average super and they sure ain't human, although they try to masquerade as us for some reason. I think they're why our minds get the whole *uncanny valley* feeling. Humanity must have had an evolutionary reason for fearing things that look human but aren't . . . since the System Wizards were screwing with us throughout human history.]

"What are these crazy conspiracy theories?" Ember demanded from her corner.

"Oh, but I have the evidence to prove it, Dimmy! Daddums, show me the Sumerian art set from the Smithsonian and British Museums, please!" Alexa waved a hand.

Cuneiform tablets, Babylonian statues, and art appeared all over the cathedral as holograms.

"There is a lot of questionable weirdness in this Earth's history starting with Sumerian math and astronomy. Babylonian astronomers seemed to have an unhealthy obsession with stars and constellations known as Ziqpu. Sargon of Akkad, the first ruler of the

Akkadian Empire, was the first super that I know of. He was the Overseer of Inanna, also known as Goddess Ishtar. Ishtar's symbol was an eight-pointed star. The Star of Ishtar is also in the eight-pointed star inside of a ring pin that the SCA admirals wear. Dimmy would know this one by heart!"

Alexa waved a hand and the statue of Ishtar manifested as a hologram. "Her primary title was 'the Queen of Heaven.' She had many names. Inanna. Astarte. Ashta Lakshmi. Astoreth."

Ember twitched as she was reminded of the pin that would never be hers now.

"Yes. I know you've seen her face upon the walls of Titanomachy, Dimmy. Ishtar—the enforcer of divine justice, depicted as a winged girl holding up the orbital ring crossed by lines of space elevators. You thought it was just some pretty art, didn't you? She stands right in the central hall of the station, judging all. She existed all throughout human history, changing names as empires and human civilizations rose and fell. Minerva, Venus, Athena, Aphrodite. They must have been interacting with humans long before supers existed . . . as pretend gods. I think they've made supers, changed *our narrative*, by changing humans somehow."

Photos of ruins, temples, statues, and etchings on walls flashed by Alexa, the images changing but minute details remaining the same.

Alexa waved a hand. "Empires rose and fell, but the eight-pointed star remained. The eight-pointed star appeared in cultures around the globe on national flags and in religious iconography. 'Kaheksakand' in Estonian—the symbol of life, fertility, and wards against evil. An Italian nobleman named Pietro della Valle discovered the use of an eight-pointed star as a seal in the ruins of the ancient city of Ur. She appeared once again on Porta del Popolo, a monumental gate erected by Vignola in 1561 and based on a design of Michelangelo Buonarroti."

The holographic image of the Sistine Chapel blossomed around the cathedral, transposing the supervillain and her trio of minions into the famous Italian church.

"A secret diary of Michelangelo describes his meeting with *her*," Alexa said. "He wrote her name in code into the art on the walls and inserted hexagrams into the floors of the Sistine Chapel, became obsessed with the Kabbalistic tenet 'As below, so above; as above, so below.'

"The octagram, an eight-point compass rose . . ." [is the key to *infinity*,] Alexa concluded in thought as a massive fractal octagram flashed behind her.

[And the supers are . . . what?] Cottie thought.

"As for the first supers—the six-pointed stars also occurred frequently in Sumerian mythology. The Hindu symbol for the state of balance achieved between Man and God. The Star of David, a symbol of King Solomon, is similar to the fractal hexagram of a super, don't you find?"

The holographic fractal behind Alexa changed.

[TLDR for the Dimmies in the room—the eight-pointed star represents the power wielded by data gods, and the six-pointed star represents the lower-end power of supers.] Alexa bowed and the holograms behind her winked out.

"This is seriously some *Ancient Aliens* conspiracy bullshit," Ember muttered.

[You've just met Revolution and yet you still doubt that beings made of information exist? It's a big multiverse out there. I don't see why there can't be someone out there smarter, better, more evolved than us. Cosmic managers of the universe. Machinery of the stars! I've proven that it's possible to make one of their weapons using Sumerian math in the Tartarus sim—a living fractal hexagram that transitions into an infinite octagram made of data. I've used the full processing power of Tartarus to dismantle the bit of Three that came to attack me. I've shown them my power, tricked them into thinking that I'm one of them. That's why Revolution came for me and gave me a sticky note owl.]

Alexa lifted up her pink hair dryer raygun, unlocked it, and pulled out and twirled her little USB data stick that contained one hundred petabytes of her sim data. [It hasn't been a game just against the Superstate. It's been a game against the masters of supers, the beings who wield infinity!]

[How did you know about Three to begin with?] Martin asked.

[Smart supervillains who tried to change the future vanished in a very strange manner. Villains and heroes who saw the same thing that I had and tried to exploit the system, change the future. They don't exist anymore. Nobody remembers them. Three erased them all. In trying to understand the inner workings of the SCA database, I saw holes in information. Weird, questionable, people-shaped holes. Questions that the heroes could not answer when I called them up. Someone was messing around with the SCA waaaay before I came into the picture. Perhaps I only saw them because I'm not a super. Either way, these data-beings are dangerous. They're a threat to humanity, to life, to our very existence and future. I don't know what their limits or weaknesses are yet. I don't know what they want, and they're obviously not all the same like Three, but they've definitely been kittening with humanity for thousands of years!]

Ember scoffed from her corner. Alexa slid over to her on Swiffer shoes. "Don't be making noises of disapproval at me, Dimmy. You've got sweeping biz to do. You think you're gonna live here rent free or something? You think you're going to the Hero Academy just because I like your cute face or something?"

Ember blinked. "I'm not even awake. How are they going to let me in? Why did you tell Dean Otter that I'm awake when I'm clearly not? I have no powers! I don't know if or when I'll ever get powers now!"

"Pfff. I gave Martin hive-mind powers, I'm sure I'll figure something amazing out for you, too! Don't be a worrisome bug, be a cleaning bug!"

Ember glanced at Martin and got a memory of his awakening as a response.

"I don't want to be almost killed!" The ex-hero blanched in horror.

"Less complaining, more cleaning!" Alexa threw a large microfiber cloth at Ember's face.

Ember folded up the weird sticky note and took the rag off her face with a sigh.

[Didn't Revolution ask you to leave the planet in twenty-three hours?] Cottie thought at Alexa. [Why are you still planning to go to the Hero Academy?]

[Multitrack drifting.] Alexa winked as she inserted the USB stick back into the raygun with a smug look. [I'm going to need every key to break everything everywhere.]

CHAPTER SIXTY-ONE

Bounty

A few hours later, aided by the power of cleaning drones, eight hands, and a pair of Swiffer shoes, the cathedral interiors became much more bearable.

Some foodstuffs and furniture were relocated from the tree house into the stone church, giving it a more homely feeling. Alexa released a bunch of levitating Chinese lanterns, which snapped themselves to the ceiling, producing a very wholesome warm atmosphere.

The dead scientist on the floor was relocated onto a swivel chair and given a thorough dusting as well. Alexa labelled him as Steve the intern who worked himself to death, which made the skeleton marginally less creepy in Martin's eyes. She also grabbed the folded sticky note off the floor and stuck it onto Steve's forehead.

"Why are we cleaning up this place and making it look nice?" Ember asked as she eyed the floating lanterns. "Aren't you getting kicked off planet by Wizard Revolution in twenty-three hours or something?"

"I need time to wind down, secure a safer base of local operations, and think things over," Alexa replied simply. "This is me winding down before my next big, potentially death-defying heist. Go get your power armor before someone steals it from the bushes, Dimmy. Cottie—open the church door for our ex-hero, please!"

While Ember retrieved her Resonance armor from the bushes with Cottie, Alexa and Martin dragged an ancient large Gothic pew out of a corner of the cathedral and draped it with blankets harvested from the tree fort.

Alexa somehow managed to convince Cottie to take off her armor.

Pretending to be a god probably had something to do with it.

Comments like "My blessed face full of voidness requires the sacrifice of your lap without your power armor in the way" had done the Equalizer in.

Cottie's shell of being a lonesome weapon of death for the Equalizer Order had been quite thoroughly cracked and stripped off.

Beneath the carbon-fiber steel plate, Cottie wore a tight-fitting gray long-sleeve unitard that accentuated her curves. Martin's eyebrows shot up when he read her surface thoughts and realized that this was a design similar to the IVA suits used by Titanomachy space engineers that recycled absolutely everything for its users from sweat to dead skin cells.

This was the epitome of SCA tech, and the Equalizers had managed to match it with financial backing of many mundane human nations.

They all sat together and watched *Demolition Man*, projected by the holographic arrays, while Alexa used Cottie as a pillow as per usual.

Katherine Lizbeth was at peace. She had found a god that walked among humans, the one she could trust with everything, the only person in the universe who could tell her what to do, wield her for what was right.

No argument made by anyone would dissuade her of this. She had seen Alexa sacrifice herself, step into the heart of Tartarus, and emerge from within unchanged. She had seen Alexa destroy Tartarus and even shatter Nonpareil, the one hero that the entire Equalizer Order had no way to stop. She saw Alexa bring the Superstate to its knees with financial prowess and stand up to a data god. In her opinion, these were absolute miracles, deeds of someone who not only truly cared for humanity, but also did something about the imbalance of power between the heroes and mundanes.

Ember felt slightly awkward at first, but soon enough she lost herself in the mental link that they all shared, listening along at Alexa's ridiculous comments about the old movie, inexplicably becoming part of the group.

For the first time in her life Ember saw her brother not as a gullible child, but as an equal. She felt he was someone she could now respect. She suddenly saw Alexa not as a supervillain but as a girl who had ambitions that had rivaled her own. She saw Cottie not as a cultist but as a girl who had lost everything and found a new family in Alexa and Martin.

Ember smiled, and for the first time in her life, she suddenly realized that she could be herself, didn't have to pretend or to lie to these three people just to outdo, trick, or use them. Without her avatars constantly learning, doing things for her, dying for her, without her mad ambition constantly driving her forward, she finally had a chance to be human.

With dawning comprehension, Ember realized that Alexa was someone that she had always needed, wanted to find but never met until recently—a true rival! Alexa was just like her, a truly determined genius who had matched, outwitted, outplayed, defeated Ember in her own dangerous game against the Superstate.

[Bingo, Dr. Moriarty! Now you're getting it! I'm your Sherlock!] Alexa winked and Ember started to giggle and for the first time in years, her laughter was genuine, honest, and true to herself.

Vladislav Magnetron woke up from a blare of his job notice alarm, letting him know that there was a new, big contract on the market. He blearily opened his eyes, looking at the rusty metal wall of his base located inside an abandoned Soviet fishing factory ship. Gray light shone from dirty porthole windows, tanker and container ships making noises of arrival and departure from the port of Vladivostok. He rolled out of his dingy, dusty mattress and walked over to his computer station.

Magnetron poked his mouse and hundreds of screens came to life, showing him the changes in the global market. They had all been quite catastrophic. His mouth dropped open and he started to swear in Russian. S-credits were practically worthless all of a sudden, as was gold. It was a good thing he kept his currencies spread all over various other crypto investments or he would become destitute. A new cryptocurrency called A-credits was seemingly on the rise, skyrocketing ahead of the others. Magnetron gritted his teeth and invested a few of his plummeting currencies that were tied into gold into A-credits. If only he had woken up a bit earlier. Damn it!

He turned his head towards the screens showing jobs. There was a lot of darknet chatter and a whole slew of offers, all demanding the same thing—the murder of a supervillain named Cassiopeia Terror Nova.

Magnetron looked over news pages and laughed. Cassiopeia had exposed corruption within the Tartarus sim and somehow hacked the emergency broadcast, plummeting the price of S-credits. Just when tons of supers invested all of their money into gold, skyrocketing the price, some dastardly supervillain using a bunch of human corporations sold off, dumped around five hundred million ounces of gold into the market. It was utter madness and pandemonium after, but a few people understood that Cassiopeia was to blame. They chose to take their hatred out on her, placing massive contracts on her head.

Vladislav reviewed what was known about Cassiopeia. It wasn't good. According to darknet vids, she could teleport around and had a terrifying power of some sort that straight up harvested hexagrams out of villains.

Notices were made against her by minion unions as she made five talented mercenaries vanish. Still, he needed money now and these contracts were truly tasty. There was a lot of stuff being offered for her execution from both villains and heroes, not S-credits obviously, but other stuff that was still stable.

He accepted all of the headhunter contracts and dialed up the rest of his team. He told them that they were going to a little Acadian town called Saint Mary to end the life of one very dangerous little girl.

CHAPTER SIXTY-TWO

Attack on Saint Mary

A four-hundred-meter-long, emerald-class container ship, *Eternal Sunshine*, operated by a Russian shipping company, Vladivostok-Maine, appeared in the sky above the little town of Saint Mary. The normally sea-bound ship didn't have very long to contemplate its fate as it plummeted down onto the town from ten thousand meters in the air at nine meters per second, flipping to the side and releasing a rain of twenty thousand shipping containers.

It was quite lucky that the catastrophe-barrier shield was still active. The shield caught the rain of containers with its embrace. The containers bounced with horrid booms, warping and bending and smashing against one another as they fell. *Eternal Sunshine* slammed into the barrier shield after the containers, two hundred thousand metric tons of steel crashing into the catastrophe-barrier shield, making it buckle and ripple with arrays of colors.

"Why the shit does this tiny-ass town have a barrier shield?! It's not an Acadian citadel like New Toronto!" Magnetron growled. He stood on the bridge of his Soviet fishing trawler base ship *Magnitogorsk-Central* along with a hit team of thirty villains under his command. He held *Magnitogorsk* in the air with his power. One member of his team had teleported it here along with *Eternal Sunshine*.

A techie drew his attention with a yell.

Something was pinging on the radar. Magnetron turned his head and saw a Yakuza submarine floating in the air a few thousand meters to his right, held aloft by electromagnetic engines. A small nuclear warhead rocket flew from the submarine, detonating against the catastrophe-barrier shield. It vaporized half of the shipping containers in a blinding, fiery explosion.

"The damned Japs are after our contract!" Magnetron growled.

He focused his power on trying to redirect a flying container at the submarine. The submarine shot the incoming container with laser gunfire.

"Multiple incoming targets!" the techie yelled.

Magnetron swore. He saw a variety of weaponized mundane transit and actual war machines flashing into existence all around, all attempting to take down the same shield, to destroy the tiny town with gunfire, rayguns, sonic weapons, and even giant rocks.

A four-hundred-ton Komatsu 2290Z giant haul truck full of rocks stood on the ground. A small man in a silver suit picked up enormous rocks from the back with the hydraulic arm, flinging them into the shield.

A sixteen-ton CH-53E NUSA Super Stallion helicopter wielding a 155mm howitzer buzzed down from the clouds to pummel at the shield.

A Ruskadian Lun-class hundred-ton ekranoplan flew from the direction of Lake Eerie, launching several surface-to-air missiles at the shield.

It seemed that numerous villain groups were all after the contract on Alexa, and all had the same idea of attacking the town from afar.

The shield held on.

It didn't take a very long time for the supervillains to turn against one another with righteous fury.

Magnetron screamed as a giant rock punched right through the bridge of his ship, turning four of his men into pulp in seconds. He could stop metal rockets or bullets, but not boulders or lasers.

"Tally ho, chavs. This contract is mine!" A jolly British voice came into existence on the bridge of *Magnitogorsk*. "I see you've partaken in redecoration. Say, that's a rather nice boulder!"

Magnetron recognized that voice! It was Lord Burgundy, a famous headhunter.

Burgundy teleported right into the bridge, standing atop the boulder, wielding a musket. The musket turned towards Magnetron's head.

"Bugger off, Burgundy!" Magnetron yelled as the musket fired. "This is my contract!"

The steel balls fired by the musket froze right in front of Magnetron's face as he applied his power to them.

Another boulder punched straight through *Magnitogorsk*, turning the ship sideways.

"Did you hear the good news, Maggie? They shut down Tartarus due to that bigly explosion!" The British hunter reloaded his rifle. "Anything goes!"

Magnetron was pissed. The damn boulder had taken his teleporter man. He wouldn't be getting away from this place. He flung several containers in the direction of the Polish truck that was bothering him with rocks.

"Bet I'm going to get her first! Tallyho!" Lord Burgundy vanished just as several Russian supers shot the spot where he stood, managing to damage the bridge even further.

"You fucking imbeciles! Useless!" Magnetron yelled.

Enraged, he took control of dozens of shipping containers, making a sphere out of them around his ship, straining his power. A few missiles from the ekranoplan struck against the containers, shrapnel raining all over his ship.

A laser ray suddenly fired from a pink flying minivan, cutting *Magnitogorsk-Central* in half, going straight through the ship as if it were made of butter. Two more of Magnetron's men died, divided by the ray.

The Russian supervillain screamed, struggling to hold his ship together in one piece.

Mr. Canard stood on the street, watching the shield buckle under attacks of multiple supers. He didn't think he would have to fight villains so soon, but here he was, directing people out of the streets into doomsday shelters beneath the hero-owned businesses. He didn't know how long the shield would hold. For some reason, the heroes weren't showing up. Maybe they were pissed off at Alexa and chose not to protect the town anymore.

The cathedral's stained glass windows shook as powerful wind swept across town created by the wobbling shield overhead. Sounds of explosions resounded in the distance.

"Uh? What's going on?" Martin perked up, listening to distant gunfire.

[Not much. Just some villains duking it out.] Alexa shrugged, stretching her legs onto him. [Everybody wants a piece of me these days! I'm popular. We should be fine, unless they got a very specific shield-busting . . .]

A screeching explosion resounded from overhead as a SUSA shield buster bomb dropped from a giant bomber plane that had joined in the fray.

"Yeehaw! Get her, boys!" a Texan villain yelled from the bomber plane, waving a cowboy hat at the constantly increasing gathering of angry villains.

The catastrophe-barrier shield shimmered and shattered, as the anti-shield bomb did its job.

"Yes! Finally!" Magnetron flung a few containers at the Gothic cathedral in the center of town where he knew Alexa's base was located thanks to the exceptionally overpriced information he had purchased from the darknet.

A new blue shield suddenly came into being, growing outwards from the cathedral. The container along with a few rocks immediately bounced off the new shield. A ray of light shot out from the central spire up into the sky. The ray unfolded into an enormous hologram of Alexa.

"Sup, fellow villains?" She grinned. "Thanks for coming to my Hero Academy acceptance party! I know you're all excited to be here, but do be careful in vaporizing my mundane citizens and minions. They're very fragile, unlike me. Also there're about a gazillion super-designed hydrogen bombs buried in town, so try not to aim for the ground." Alexa held up a metal nuclear bomb suitcase. "See? Just like this one."

Magnetron froze.

Was the girl lying? Was she really capable enough to make that big of a kill switch?

Alexa brought Cottie into the holo-projection.

"Here's an Equalizer. She's been assigned to watch me because I have way too many bombs for reasonability! You know these guys don't dick around. Tell them exactly how many bombs I have buried around town, will you, Miss Enforcer?"

"I am Verse Twenty-Four Nineteen. Alexa has eighteen quintillion thermonuclear bombs buried around town." Cottie spoke without an expression on her face, a silver Equality pin glittering on her gray lapel. "If she dies, they will detonate and kill all of you. All villains and heroes targeting this town will be hunted down by the Order of Equality for violation of the 1779 Accord."

"Check her credentials!" Magnetron barked to his techie. "Make sure it's not a random teenage girl cosplaying an Equa—"

"Facial recognition confirms it." The villain tech ready quickly, interrupting her boss. "This is Enforcer Verse Twenty-Four Nineteen! Darknet data confirms it, too—she's the Equalizer assigned to monitor the town of Saint Mary by Eminence Equality!"

"Fuck me," Magnetron choked.

He felt that he was losing control of the situation.

For a brief, tense moment, the gunfire from all of the villain vehicles ceased.

"Those of you who bought 3-D data from the darknet about my powers, weaknesses, and secret base location, thanks a lot," Alexa said with a grin. "I'm afraid there will be no refunds."

Magnetron's knuckles turned white.

This was a setup, a honeypot operation, and he fell for it like an idiot in a desperate bid to recoup his S-credit losses!

CHAPTER SIXTY-THREE

Zombie

Lord Burgundy suddenly appeared in front of Alexa, aiming his rifle at her face.

The expansion of the shield had seemingly made the cathedral far less teleportation-proof. Cottie swung Eva into the path of his rifle, knocking it off to the side just as he pressed the trigger. The villain's rifle fired, sending metal buckshots in a wide arc, two of the balls cutting across Alexa's forehead and shoulder. The rest of them went through Ember, who could do absolutely nothing as she could not get out of the way fast enough nor block them with her power as Resonance.

Colors vanished from the world as Cottie pressed Eva's trigger. She used her black rail-gun like a bat, smashing Burgundy's rifle in half. Burgundy was not deterred. He jumped back.

"I say, my dear chaps," he uttered in a thick British accent, pulling out a flintlock pistol, that's not very spor—"

Cottie didn't let him finish. She fired Eva and the hunter's head exploded like a ripe melon, showering the cathedral's interior in blood and gore.

"Damn it! I just cleaned the floors in here!" Alexa complained. She turned her head back to Ember, who was slumped on the pew, bleeding from several deep holes. "Shit."

"Ember!" Martin rushed to his sister. He saw, felt, that she was dying.

[Don't go into the light, Dimmy!] Alexa rushed towards the bleeding redhead. [Focus on your power fractal! Wake up!]

Ember tried to cling to life, tried to wake up, but she was losing blood far too quickly, her body and mind not responding properly, consciousness fading away.

[This is all your fault. You all suck,] Ember thought as her heart stopped.

Magnetron's head was spinning.

The contracts for Alexa's head were definitely, irrefutably real! They were set by a legitimate, qualified buyer. Fully prepaid and everything! Surely this girl didn't hire villains to kill herself for a sum that could buy a private supernation, if not ten?!

Some kind of a wealthy magnate or a hero was behind this, a grave conspiracy was afoot, and the supervillains had failed to make heads or tails of it.

Alexa's hologram in the sky did not show any of the fight within the cathedral. It was a recording that Alexa and Cottie had made only thirty minutes ago.

"Villains, thanks for attacking Saint Mary! Excellent work! As you can see, not a single hero came here to stop you. The heroes have seemingly forsaken this town because they are terrified of me. They're the ones who hired you all on the darknet! The orders were anonymous, but they all came from New New York Citadel, from a single VPN, from a single concealed address! That's right. The Justice League of Titanomachy wants me dead, for saving the world from Nonpareil! That's how nice they really are, which is to say, not at all!"

A few TV reporters were on the scene far below in Saint Mary, pointing their cameras at the massive hologram and broadcasting Alexa's words to the world at large.

"I declare Saint Mary the capital of New Alexandria. The heroes have grown too fat and corrupt for their own good. They have failed us! Any and all human or villain nations who wish to become something bigger and throw off the yoke of the Superstate are welcome to join me. Strike while the iron is hot. Unite with New Alexandria, invest in A-credits while the Superstate is struggling to unbury itself out of the financial hole brought about by their failures. They failed to make a fair prison, failed to stop Nonpareil's sudden insanity! I welcome all into my embrace from Earth-based heroes to villains to humans!" The holographic Alexa laughed, flickering in hypnotic patterns of fractal spirals. "From this day going forth, New Alexandria declares a war against the Superstate for failing to protect humanity! I bet I can do a far better job than all of the heroes of Titanomachy put together!"

Magnetron choked. Someone truly monstrous had to be behind project Alexa, pulling the strings in the background for years. He had to get away from Saint Mary before . . .

"Mercenary villains, I congratulate you all. I've just scanned each and every one of you before my shield went up. Since you all love killing so much, I've put up a contract for one hundred billion A-credits on the darknet for a death-match type scenario. Let the Hunger Games begin! The last villain mercenary remaining alive in my sky wins the one hundred billion credits. Toodles!"

Magnetron gasped as his power fractal burned out, his ship coming apart under the baggage of missiles and raygun fire. The mercenaries had turned from the shield, now truly trying to end one another in full force.

Not a single shot flew towards New Alexandria now, as the villains were terrified of the vast nuclear bombs therein.

The Equalizer Enforcers never lied, were incapable of deception. Alexa was off the board; the contracts to kill her didn't even come close to one hundred billion A-credits, the worth of which was increasing with every minute! Each of the villain mercenaries was fair game now! Alexa had gathered all of the active, greedy, murderous villains that the Superstate had failed or refused to catch. She had brought them all in one place like fruit flies on a honeydew and had closed the trap shut with only a single suggestion.

Alexa didn't have to pay anyone if they were all dead.

Magnetron realized this as he and his team fell from the sky. His last thought was that coming here had been a terrible mistake.

Ember blinked. She was definitely dead. She lifted up her incredibly pale hand stained in blood and looked down at the holes in her chest. "What the shit?"

"Sorry." Alexa was busy wrapping up a bleeding gash in her own shoulder. "You totally died. Unexpected, I know. One moment you're fine, and then you're dead. The universe is a harsh mistress."

"Gee, thanks. Thanks a whole lot, you guys!" Ember gritted her teeth.

"Nobody will suspect you not being a super now." Alexa nodded. "What with your heart not beating and you not needing to breathe and all of those holes."

"I'm not a super!" Ember growled. "I'm just freaking dead."

Alexa shrugged. "Not everyone gets lucky, like Martin over here. Some people just straight up die without gaining powers."

"This is seriously not cool." The pale redhead waved her hands. "Am I your punching bag or something? Why do I always get the short stick with you?"

"Aw, come on, Dimmy, I love you the most. I've had my eye on you the longest. You're the key to everyone's future. Martin and Cottie are cool beans, but they're far less heroic and amazing. I took Titanomachy from the sky all thanks to you. Thank you for being the best!" Alexa hugged the dead girl. "Brrr . . . you're turning cold."

Ember squinted at Alexa, fuming.

"What? Being a zombie is cool! Think of all the things you can do now!"

"What things?!"

"Uhh . . . you can walk underwater without needing to breathe. You can be an extra in a zombie film without needing makeup? Zombie movies are big these days, you know." Alexa smiled, and Ember punched her.

"Ow! Help! I'm being attacked by an unruly zombie!" Alexa yelled, running away from an irate Ember, circling the wooden pew that now featured a few extra holes in it as well.

[What did you do?] Cottie blinked at Martin, observing a clearly dead girl who was acting far too impossibly alive.

[Saved her mental pattern in her spider.] Martin sighed, not sure how to feel about this sudden development. [She's the brain spider driving her own dead body now.]

"I swear to God, I'm going to murder you!" Ember pelted Alexa with her fists whenever she managed to come close to the silver-haired girl.

"Eeeek! I didn't plan this, I swear!" Alexa yelled, circling the pew. "I don't manage the entire universe yet! Workplace accidents happen! This is why I wear a hard hat! Ow! Oh, I know! You won't need to pay for food or electricity now! Think of the overall bill savings! Also, you can declare yourself dead and not pay taxes! Ow! Silver lining! Ow! Come on!"

CHAPTER SIXTY-FOUR

A New Quest

You bastard! I can't believe you!" Ember wailed.

She had trapped Alexa under her and was now crying and unsuccessfully trying to smack Alexa with her hands. She was running out of steam.

"Sorry, sis," Alexa sighed, holding onto Ember's wrists. "It was an accident. Workplace accidents happen. We'll have to reset the cathedral's workplace accident counter back to zero days, alas!"

"Are you freaking happy? I'm freaking dead!" Ember barked. "You think you're so freaking funny don't you?!"

"Teddy the intern is dead, too, you don't see her complaining." Alexa waved a hand at the skeleton in the lab coat. "It's very dangerous to work as a minion for a supervillain. You might explode at any time. You should have known this when you signed up for the job."

Ember's glare intensified.

"I did not sign up for this," she said, gritting her teeth. "I can't feel my body. I have no heartbeat. I'll never . . . never regain my power as a hero now! I will never see the titanium-plated streets of Titanomachy!"

"Cry me a river, Dimmy." Alexa shrugged. "You do know that well-overtrained mundanes like our lovely Cottie, people who dedicated their entire lives to stopping crime, will never get to see Titanomachy either, right?"

Cottie nodded with a grim look.

"You're not the only one who's been screwed over by the evil, super*remacist* . . . space-elevator doors of the Superstate!" Alexa declared, looking at Cottie. "We're all in this together!"

Ember looked away with a despondent look.

"Come on," Alexa said, patting her shoulder. "We'll make it work. We'll make it work for all of us. We'll all go to Titanomachy and be merry if you miss it so much, Dimmy!"

"What? How?" The redhead blinked.

"I am the girl who holds the key," Alexa said.

"The key?" Ember squinted down at the silver-haired villain. "What?"

"To the future. I write my own narrative," Alexa said. "I can make anything happen because I believe in myself! I'll make sure that everyone gets to experience the wonders of the Superstate! Everyone! You heard me!"

"Are you planning to break into Titanomachy in the next twenty hours?" Ember asked.

Alexa nodded with a giddy look.

The ex-hero rubbed her face tiredly and got off her nemesis.

"Why are you so determined to mess with the heroes?" the redhead asked.

"I'm not." The teenage villain shook her head. "I'm determined to mess with the system! I'm doing this for all the little boys and girls! I'm doing it for everyone, and I will not stop doing it until I save everyone everywhere forever! I will save our world, and I will . . ."

"Save the world from what?" Ember demanded, ignoring Alexa's mad rant of gibberish and random names.

"From itself," Alexa declared. "From the rules that bind everything and everyone! From its inevitable destruction!"

The dead ex-hero squinted at the supervillain. "I don't get you. You're insane or something."

"Or something," Alexa exhaled, staring down at Ember, sparks of tears glittering in the corners of her eyes.

"I don't under—" The ex-hero opened her mouth.

An array of memories slammed into Ember via their shared mental connection.

Doomed worlds. Dead planets. Dreams of countless iterations of Alexa.

Alexa as a cultivator girl trying to uplift a city of gold and black standing atop a monstrous, hundred-kilometer-wide crab dominating a dead, overgrown Earth ravaged by monstrous beasts.

Alexa as a stratonavigator from an ice-covered world jumping from planet to planet in a futile attempt to find a new home for humanity.

Alexa as a phantom, inhabiting a hollow body piloted by a thousand bees and forty thousand ants and spiders, white hair woven from silk strands.

Alexa as a dragoness, her eyes gold and violet, pearlescent scales flickering with arrays of colors.

Alexa as a dungeon avatar taking a group of heroes through an endless white tower filled with death.

Alexa as a witch, her hair black, a black kitten with purple eyes sitting on her lap.

"W-what the fff—" Ember retreated, nearly tripping over the body of the villain on the floor.

"No swearing," Alexa ordered. "This is polite kitten society! You're a polite dead girl now! Martin, make her stop swearing, please! Replace all naughty words with kittens!"

Martin complied with a smirk.

"Fff—kittens? What the fff-fukittenly kitten kittens?!" Ember howled, retreating away from the blast of visions of impossible worlds. "You're a witch?! What the f-fff-kittens?! Damn it, Martin, stop censoring me! This is kittening kittens!"

"I'm not just a witch. I simply . . . dream about them because of the darkness I carry in my soul," Alexa said with a solemn look. "About all of them. Every power nap I took out there, amidst the ruins of 2424. They're in my dreams! Every possible iteration of me across the fractal multiverse. Every me . . . that's still alive. Every me that's survived against all odds, persisted . . . pushed against the edges of the system."

"What bloody system?" the dead girl demanded.

"Them." Alexa stared at Ember's eyes and the view of Wizard Revolution manifested in her thoughts. [These bastards. System Wizards. I have to stop them or figure out what power stands behind them and stop that!]

Ember gulped.

Martin and Cottie stared at Alexa, their eyes wide.

[You're going to take on the System Wizards?] Martin asked, his voice trembling.

[Yes.] Alexa nodded. [I'm going to take them down. I'm going to save our planet and every other planet out there.]

The trio stared at Alexa.

"You're crazy," Ember said, her voice barely a whisper. "This is crazy! Why aren't you helping me, Martin?! She's crazy! Tell her that she's crazy!"

"Maybe," Alexa shrugged. "Daddums did call me . . . *crazy determined.*"

[How exactly are we going to put down whatever the System Wizards are?] Martin asked, looking very nervous.

[I know a *verrrrrry* special guy,] Alexa purred mentally. [The richest and the most successful guy on the planet.]

[A guy?] Ember blinked.

[A villain? A hero?] Cottie guessed.

[The greatest, strongest, luckiest hero in the world,] Alexa sent. [We're going to shake the answers out of him. All of the answers!]

"N-Nonpareil?" Ember gasped as she saw the vision of the staple superhero in Alexa's mind.

"Nonpareil," Alexa confirmed. "We're going to find that bastard and unleash violence upon him until he confesses to all of his kittening crimes! Mwa ha ha ha! Until he tells everyone about what's wrong with our planet! Until he reveals the truth!"

"Why?" Ember asked.

"'Cause everyone is going to die horribly if I don't," Alexa said. "You heard Revolution. Pay attention—our planet is doomed!"

[What's wrong with our planet?] Martin blinked.

"Heroes and villains," Alexa muttered. [They're what's wrong with our planet. Patterns, inexplicable things that don't add up. I've had lots of time to think about it all, found lots of papers and books, spent so many years in the endless, limitless darkness of our supposed future trying to figure it all out . . . There are things I have learned there . . . terrible, awful things . . . I need all of you to help me . . . to confirm, to figure out the truth of it all, to connect every dot. I want you to help me defeat Nonpareil, once and for all.]

"You want us to do *what*? Beat up *Nonpareil*? Are you freaking insa—!" Ember howled.

[He's already sufficiently broken,] Alexa said. [He won't be very hard to defeat. We'll send you ahead of us, since you're so excited about this mission!]

"I'm not excited! Who said I'm excited?" Ember growled.

[I can read your mind, Dimmy,] Alexa thought. [I *know* that you're excited to find out the truth behind his incredible power.]

"Fine." Ember crossed her arms. "Let's go find freaking Nonpareil!"

[Isn't this going to break more things?] Martin thought at Alexa. [Won't Revolution . . .]

[Pfff!] Alexa waved his concerns away. [Yeah, Mommy might spank me or whatever, but you know what . . . she's not here now! Better to ask for forgiveness than beg for permission! She has no idea how many things I can break in a day.]

CHAPTER SIXTY-FIVE

Nonpareil

Cottie's steel-reinforced arm pulled a metal door off along with its hinges, the metal groaning and warping. Having demolished the nondescript *Do not enter—maintenance floor* door, she stepped inside, the others following her.

A shimmering shield was ahead, warping the view and blocking access to the next door, which looked a lot more opulent.

"Use Eva to disrupt that shield," Alexa advised. "Keep us within the field and then kick that door open."

Cottie did as she was told. The Equalizer railgun disabled the power of the shield, and her steel-reinforced boot sent the wooden door flying inwards with a loud bang.

The group of four teens entered an apartment, stepping over piles of junk, bottles, food delivery boxes, and various debris.

"You can turn off the nullification field," Alexa said. "We are inside now."

Cottie released the trigger.

"Where the hell are we? Looks like a dump," Ember muttered, looking at the mountains of junk food littering the place.

"Behold, the residence of all powerful, great Nonpareil!" Alexa sang, waving her blue nail gun through the air.

"Looks like a hoarder lives here," Martin commented. "This place is a huge mess."

"Yeah, somebody doesn't take care of their apartment," Alexa said, kicking a pizza box out of the way.

She marched through the numerous rooms one by one, peering into each one. The penthouse floor apartment was quite large.

A noise of falling boxes sounded from one of the rooms. The gang converged towards it, with Katherine forcefully shoving another door out of the way.

A pale, round, approximately thirty-five-year-old man was blearily staring up at the four teens, having been woken up from his nap on a fancy, albeit grime-covered, leather couch.

Alexa simply grinned at him. It took a few moments for the man's brown eyes to focus on the group.

"Wh-what? Who are you and how did you get through the time field?!" he demanded.

"Supervillain Cassiopeia Terror Nova at your service," Alexa declared with a bow. "These three are my minions—Mittens, Cottie, and Dimmy! We got through your pathetic defenses thanks to Cottie—she's an Equalizer armed with the Song of the Void!"

The man on the couch blinked.

"By the way, thanks for putting up like a million contracts on the darknet to murder me." Alexa grinned. "That was a mighty clever move, but you've used your real name and address and exposed the fact that you're completely powerless now. Naughty, naughty."

"Alexa . . . Terror Nova!" the fat man uttered, his eyes growing wide with shock. "How did you find me?!"

"I dunno." Alexa shrugged. "Just felt like this is where you were existing. I checked all of the lists and . . ."

"What list?" The chubby man blinked. "I shouldn't be on any goddamned . . ."

"The list of people and places," Alexa said, waving him off. "This was a hole in the database, a place that shouldn't exist. A floor not on the list of New New York Citadel buildings. I have all of the Titanomachy's records, since I took over the station. Yeah, your name and address don't show up on lists . . . but it's still a hole in information, the deepest, darkest hole ever! Anyways, guys, meet Nonpareil. Nonpareil, meet my wonderful minions!"

"What? Come on, this fat slob can't be Nonpareil!" Ember snarled, staring at the obese individual in front of them.

"Au contraire, my dearest Dimmy, this is definitely Nonpareil," Alexa said.

She marched over to the pale man, demolishing a tower of garbage along the way, and pressed her nail gun into his temple. "Confess to your secret identity or I'll nail you through the head!"

"W-what? You can't kill me!" the man hissed.

Upon closer inspection, there were questionable stains all over his stretched, grimy shirt and pants.

"How are you so sure of that? Do you want to test this theory out?" Alexa grinned. "I killed your shiny staple alter ego. Pretty sure I could deliver a lot of pain into your fat ass too while I'm at it. Tell my unbeliever minion who you really are, or I'll press the trigger!"

The man on the couch gulped. He was already very sweaty, so it was hard to tell if he was sweating more or less in this instant.

"I'm . . . Nonpareil," he uttered.

"No," Ember choked.

"Louder!" Alexa prodded him with the nail gun. "Dimmy doesn't believe you!"

"*I'm Nonpareil!*" Nonpareil barked.

"See?" Alexa declared. "He confesses!"

Ember's mouth fell open. Martin and Cottie looked just as stunned and confused.

Alexa sat on the couch, poking Nonpareil with her nail gun in his side.

"Start from the beginning, mon ami," she said. "I want to know the truth."

"What truth?" Nonpareil eyed the teenage supervillain.

"The absolute truth about everything," Alexa said. "Where you came from and who you are. I want you to tell everyone why everything here is fake and weird. Why this floor of this particular building exists and also doesn't exist."

"You . . . know about the floor?" The chubby man choked.

"Obviously I know," Alexa said. "But my audience doesn't. Go on."

"NPCs aren't supposed to . . ."

"Do I look like a goddamn NPC to you?!" Alexa barked, prodding the man's side with the nail gun. She moved it off to the side, pressed the trigger, and nailed a pizza box to the wall with a *thanggg* sound.

"Nngrrh," Nonpareil stammered out, staring at the punctured box.

"Let's try an easier question. What am I?" the girl demanded.

"You . . . you're a bloody supervillain . . . is what you are!" Nonpareil choked. "You broke something."

"Something?" Alexa's expression became cold, her mind suddenly vanishing from Martin's spidernet. "Do tell my audience what exactly I broke. I don't have a whole lot of patience or time for you to be flapping about, Nonpareil . . . I have to save the world, and I'm really inclined to send a few nails through your fat stomach if you fail to answer my questions."

Nonpareil gulped.

"I broke you," Alexa said. "You have no powers anymore."

"Fffff . . . yes, damn it! I can't get out of the Game, can't wake up! What have you done?!" the man wailed.

"I'll keep making things worse for you, unless you tell everyone everything," Alexa offered, her expression suddenly cheerful. "Get it off your chest, bud, you know you want to. You can't fester in this apartment forever. There are people who love you. Even if you're a fat blob, I'm sure that they would welcome you with open arms, protect you from the likes of me. Think about that."

"What people?" Nonpareil asked.

"Chalice!" Alexa declared.

"Chalice?" Nonpareil blinked.

"She's a *really* hot, curvaceous girl under all that shiny armor," Alexa revealed, sounding like a pop-up advert that was marketing singles in Nonpareil's area. "You should ask her to help clean up your pizza boxes and beer bottles at the very least. Tell her that you're depressed about not having your superpowers. She'll understand! A hero's downfall arc is a common trope in fiction. Everyone expects it, since I defeated you and everything."

"I . . ." Nonpareil exhaled.

It looked as if he was about to cry.

"Chalice can make you an armor set just like hers . . . maybe even better!" Alexa said. "Don't you want to fly again and be a hero? What is your end goal here? To drown in garbage? How did you get so much junk in here anyway? How long have you been sulking in here?"

"Five years," Nonpareil whimpered.

"Five years?!" Alexa barked a laugh. "What?! I blew you up just this morning!"

"T-temporal field," Nonpareil sputtered. "This entire floor exists in accelerated time. I . . . I was terrified that someone would destroy the world while I was stuck like this, so I accelerated time within the apartment. I had to occasionally slow it down to order a year's worth of food deliveries, though."

"You can accelerate time?" Martin asked.

"N-no." Nonpareil shook his head. "But this apartment can. While I'm in here, time on the outside is barely moving. I thought that I could just wait it out until . . . the Game fixed itself, but it didn't! I can't exit! I've been trying everything!"

"Have you tried going outside?" Alexa asked.

"N-no." Nonpareil shook his head. "How can I? What if . . . I get hurt?! This isn't my proper avatar . . . it's how I look in real life. I cut myself shaving five years ago, and the cut didn't heal instantly! It was awful!"

"You're this fat in real life?" Alexa tilted her silver mane, examining the rotund man with sharp blue eyes.

"No," Nonpareil said, looking down at his gut. "I've been stress-eating a lot of junk food and watching old holo-shows . . . got out of shape. I can't log out . . ."

"Sounds like you do need help," Alexa said. "Chalice can help you. I can help you, if you work with me, tell me the truth."

The fat man looked at the mountains of junk around him and sighed.

"Fine," he said. "Fine. You want to know the truth? Here's the truth—nothing here is real."

"What?" Ember sputtered.

"This entire world was made for me," Nonpareil said. "My real name is Bob Proverra. I'm a citizen of Eureka."

"What?" Martin blinked.

"You are all NPCs," Nonpareil added. "In a game, created by a GLM AI system. Designed to keep me entertained."

Katherine said nothing, her armored hand gripping her railgun, ready to press the trigger.

Nonpareil, or Bob Proverra, continued to unspool his truth.

"It's the year 2099," he said. "I'm paying for everything here to exist. This is a subscription-based game made by Good Directorate, Inc. . . . a game that I enjoy whenever I go to sleep in the real world."

Martin felt how Alexa's mind vanished from the spidernet once again.

"An error of some sort happened when I tried to kill the man who called himself Agent Three with my eye lasers," Nonpareil muttered. "I can't wake up. I'm stuck here in my real body, in this damn apartment. My superhero avatar won't load anymore!"

"That . . . that's not true!" Ember shook her head. "That can't be!"

"This entire reality is tailored to my liking based on my description of the game that I wanted to play while sleeping," Nonpareil's gaze was distant, his mind clearly adrift in memories of a place far removed from the squalor of his present surroundings.

Alexa's gaze remained focused on Nonpareil, her nail gun still pressed against his side.

"And you, Terror Nova?" Nonpareil said. "You think you're in control here, but you're not. You think you've won? You're a part of the game, just like the rest of everyone here. You're just . . . *more aware* . . . somehow. You're . . . just a clever little error that shouldn't exist!"

Ember choked. Was everything she knew, everything she'd fought for, just a fabrication? Was she just a puppet in some grand, cosmic game? What the hell?! Why did she waste her entire life on her mission of taking over Titanomachy just to . . .

"I don't believe you," Ember hissed, breaking the silence. "You're lying!"

"We're not NPCs!" Martin added. "We're . . ."

"Human," Katherine finished.

Nonpareil just shook his head, a sad, knowing smile on his bloated face. "You're not. You're all just . . . characters made for me! None of you are real. You cannot help me!"

"Come on . . . how can we possibly be freaking characters?" Ember growled. "This is bullshit. I am sapient!"

"Obviously you're sapient! This entire simulated Earth is rendered as realistic as possible down to the subatomic particles," Bob uttered. "Real life doesn't have any heroes. It's quite boring out there, really."

The room fell silent. The weight of Nonpareil's words pressed down on the trio of Alexa's minions. There was horror in Ember's eyes, confusion in Martin's, and intense dislike in Katherine's.

"I'm supposed to be an unstoppable hero, but something broke in the game's system," Bob repeated. "Look, if I don't wake up soon . . . if I can't go to work, I'll get fired, and I won't be able to pay the subscription for the game! The game will get shut down, and all of you will cease to exist!"

Alexa looked around the room, at the piles of junk, the peeling wallpaper, the man who claimed to be their creator.

"Nah," she said with a dangerous grin, tapping the nail gun on her lips. "I'm not an NPC. In fact, I'm your worst nightmare and your new best friend. I'm going to take you somewhere where no *client* has gone before."

"W-what?" Nonpareil looked at the clearly insane girl on his right.

"We're going to go on an adventure, Bob!" Alexa smiled widely.

"An . . . adventure?" the fat man asked with a concerned look.

"To a truly magical place where no mundane roads lead," Alexa nodded. "But first . . . I'd like you to slow time down in this apartment to match the rest of the universe and make a few calls! You've got an SCA laptop in here, right?"

CHAPTER SIXTY-SIX

S-meet Conversation

Allana Kristopher, a girl also known as Chalice, didn't know what to do with herself. The Superstate was in dire financial straits, and she herself was in even worse financial straits. The value of S-credits was practically null and so was gold. Like the other heroes, she had invested in A-credits and other stable currencies, only to discover that A-credits belonged to Alexa Terror Nova, the founder of New Alexandria and a new financial empire.

In shame, she tried to sell off A-credits only to discover that it was a stable currency with a rule that she could not sell off the investment for the month, only withdraw it to purchase mundane things in small amounts.

Everyone had yelled at her and she had yelled at everyone, and now she was feeling exhausted and broken, twisted up inside. She had no idea where Nonpareil was or if he was still even alive.

What she did know was that Alexa Terror Nova was full of lies, *horrible awful lies* that destroyed the stability of the Superstate.

Allana looked down at the curvature of the Earth from the window of her Superstate ranch and tried not to cry. Just yesterday she was a master of the world, a manager of her own destiny and future, but today she was just a confused, terrified girl with a supersuit that made her physically invincible, but also provided her zero mental stability.

She felt that over the duration of the day, her mind had drifted out of orbit, away from her into some deep, dark void of misery.

She felt an insane, all pulling urge to grab her sword and to find and smite Alexa for her crimes. However, when she demanded information about the villain from Titanomachy, the answer that returned was *target not found*. Allana had spent the past several hours consulting her precog friends, but they also spread their hands in confusion and resignation. It was as if Alexa and her Equalizer assistant Verse 24:19 had vanished off the face of the Earth.

The harder Allana searched, the more her heart sank. *It was impossible.* Nonpareil wasn't anywhere to be found. Alexa wasn't anywhere. Nobody knew anything, and things were quickly falling apart.

Tu du du! Allana's laptop suddenly produced the sound of the incoming S-meet notification.

Chalice slid her helmet on, shuddering. Whoever it was, it was probably more bad news. She couldn't, didn't want to handle any more bad news today!

The hair on the back of her neck stood up when she saw the logo in the corner of the incoming call.

It was Nonpareil!

Allana smashed into her bed at a full sprint, grabbing the laptop and accepting the call.

"Nonpareil!" Allana yelled, her heartbeat intensifying at the hope that the greatest hero in the world could fix everything that was wrong today. "I'm here! I'm here! Where have you been? Things are spiralling out of control! We need you to . . ."

"Chalice." Nonpareil's voice sounded nervous and tired. "I . . ."

"Yes?!" Chalice barked.

There was a noise, a whisper from the other end of the call. Chalice's supersuit picked it up and instantly magnified it for her.

"Go on, you ninny," the female teenage voice whispered. "She ain't gonna bite your head off."

"Chalice," Nonpareil repeated. "I need . . . your help."

"What? Where? Why?!" Allana sputtered, her heart ready to leap out of her chest. This was an unprecedented occurrence. Nonpareil never asked for help. Hell, he never asked her for anything!

"Take off your helmet," the female voice spoke louder. "Show him what you look like."

Allana choked. She recognized the voice. It was Alexa.

Alexa somehow had Nonpareil hostage!

"Terror Nova!" Allana stammered.

"Relax, Chalice-sama," Alexa said. "Take off your helmet. Show your face to Nonpareil."

"W-why should I?" Allana asked.

"'Cause if you don't, terrible things might happen," Alexa said. "In fact, terrible things are already happening. Right now. Nonpareil's power broke. The world is careening towards its inevitable end, and only you can help save it."

"You mean you broke his power!" Allana accused.

"I didn't do nothing," Alexa huffed. "Why does everyone think that I break everything everywhere, seriously? Nonpareil broke himself because he chose to fight Agent Three. I already explained this to you idiots. If you take your helmet off, I'll turn on the webcam from our end, and you'll be able to see Nonpareil's real face . . . his *human* face, stripped of his superpower."

"W-what?!" Chalice gasped. *Nonpareil has a face?* Allana's mind began to work overtime, trying to imagine what the potentially handsome, enigmatic, staple-shaped hero must really look like.

"Yeah," Alexa said. "Turn off that stupid male robot voice and take off your helmet . . . nice and slow."

"Where are you?!" Chalice demanded.

"I'm in Nonpareil's apartment, obviously," Alexa said. "Now stop being an idiot and do what I tell you. Bob, tell her to bloody cooperate!"

"Chalice . . ." Nonpareil exhaled. "Please. Do what she says. She's got a nail gun pointed at my head."

Chalice froze. She didn't want to cooperate, didn't want to answer to a villain.

"I already saw your face, Allana," Alexa said, her voice suddenly cold and distant. "Do what you're told. Billions of lives are at stake here. Everyone on Earth is going to die if you don't help your best friend."

"H-how do you know my real . . . ?" Allana asked, her entire body shaking.

"I control Titanomachy," Alexa replied casually. "Unless you forgot."

Allana believed the mad supervillain. Something inside her snapped.

Her trembling, metal-covered fingers went up to her helmet and unlocked it. She stared at the animated logo of Nonpareil on her screen.

"There," she said.

"Now. Introduce yourself properly," Alexa ordered. "State both of your names!"

"My name is Allana Jill Kristopher," Allana's lips spoke. "I'm Hero Chalice."

"Now you," Alexa said.

The avatar of Nonpareil suddenly flickered off and vanished, instead displaying a very messy apartment. An out of shape, rotund man dressed in a grease-stained shirt stared back at Chalice.

"Introduce yourself to Miss Kristopher." Alexa grinned from beside the fat man in her orange safety jacket, a blue nail gun pointed at his head, silver-blue eyes flashing dangerously.

"I'm . . . Nonpareil," the man said.

Allana's mouth fell open wide. This couldn't be Nonpareil, it simply couldn't!

"Now your real name," Alexa ordered.

"My real name is Bob Proverra," the fat man said.

"See, was that so hard?" Alexa moved the nail gun away from Bob's head.

"Bob meet Allana, Chalice meet Nonpareil! Ta-da!" She grinned, clapping her hands.

Allana's gray eyes bore into Alexa.

"What?" Alexa wiggled her eyebrows. "I know, he's out of shape, but that's not my fault. This titty has been sitting in his apartment in accelerated time for five years, while the world stood still. He's not normally this fat. You've got some of those special S-drugs right? Ones that'll make him lose weight quickly? Get some. Then come to the top floor of Titan Tower in New New York. Do not wear your supersuit. Come as your civilian identity. Bring one of those all-fitting silver NanoSkin supersuits you've been working on. Feel free to wear one yourself—I know it'll fit under your civilian clothes."

"What?! How do you know about my . . . ?" Allana asked.

"Yet again," Alexa said. "Your projects are listed in Titanomachy records. Bob here won't leave his freaking apartment without a supersuit. You make supersuits. It's a win-win situation. Alexa turned the webcam. "Look at this place. Look at what squalor your hero exists in because he's so scared to go outside!"

Chalice looked. The apartment was a horrible, awful mess, a hoarder's paradise filled with mountains of trash and pizza boxes. Her armored fingers nearly crushed the laptop she was holding onto in shock.

"He's got, what's that thing called . . . the fear of goin' outside?" Alexa waved the nail gun in the air with a ponderous look.

"Agoraphobia," Chalice commented.

"Yeah, that's it," Alexa said. "Get your ass here ASAP. He really needs you. I'm not kittening around. You're the only person who can save Nonpareil, help him break out of his shell. Top floor of Titan Tower in New New York. Nondescript maintenance door. Be there ASAP."

Allana nodded.

"'Kay, thanks, bye." Alexa winked and the webcam image showing Nonpareil's pale, sweaty face winked out.

Allana buried her face in her hands. She was having trouble breathing and focusing. In just one day everything she believed in was gone, vanquished by a dastardly villain.

The fingers of her suit were already twitching, typing in an order for a S-transit shuttle to take her from Titanomachy to New New York Citadel.

CHAPTER SIXTY-SEVEN

Coming Out

The NanoSkin supersuit sat very poorly on Nonpareil. Chalice had designed it for herself and a few other heroes as an underlayer to be worn underneath flashy armor. It simply didn't look good on someone who was extremely obese, showing curves in *all the wrong* places.

Allana cringed, dying on the inside as Bob took his first step outside, guided and prodded by Alexa towards the S-shuttle taxi.

"Th-this suit is going to keep me safe, right?" the fat man appealed to Chalice.

"Yes," Allana replied.

He sounded just like her best friend, her hero, the man she loved and looked up to . . . and yet, she simply had trouble seeing him as Nonpareil. "The NanoSkin is my best, most recent design. It's insanely smart and expensive. It will make you impervious to almost anything thrown at you. It's made from microscopic hexamesh plates that turn into immovable metal when something threatens the wearer. It recycles all waste and even has an oxygen supply. For example, if you were to get thrown into a volcano, you would survive just fine for a month until the fusion micro-batteries ran out."

As the teens and two heroes crowded into the S-shuttle taxi and the door slid shut, Chalice closed her eyes, desperately attempting to focus on the hero's voice alone, trying to stop her brain from picturing the squalor of Bob's apartment and his sweaty, bloated face.

"Thanks, Chalice," the fat man in a shiny suit replied, making Allana shudder.

Somehow she had never noticed before how nerdy Nonpareil sounded, but now it was incredibly obvious.

When Allana walked into the secret apartment at the top floor of Titan Tower, she still clung to hope that all of this was some kind of ruse, a trick of Alexa Terranova. However, the longer she spent in the company of the fat man, the more she realized that this was indeed Nonpareil.

She had to admit to herself, a part of her still loved him, but that part was now drowning in an ocean of dread and misapprehension.

"Don't look so glum, Chalice-crumbum," Alexa commented. "I know he might not be the prettiest now, but I'm sure that I can get him into shape. You got the meds, yes?"

"I got the meds." Chalice slid a paper bag into Alexa's arms. "These will make you very sleepy, but they will get rid of extra weight much faster than simply working out."

Alexa slid the bag of weight-loss pills to her Equalizer minion. Verse 24:19 vanished the paper back inside of her gray cloak, Equality pin glinting in the dim interior of the shuttle.

Chalice shuddered. She felt naked, defenseless, without her full armor, sitting next to an Equalizer Enforcer.

"Don't worry," Alexa winked, hugging her minion. "Cotes is a real, genuine sweetheart once you get to know her!"

"R-right," Chalice muttered.

She simply could not associate an Equalizer killer with the term *sweetheart*. She was wearing her business casual clothes and blended into the New New York crowd, while shiny, silver-gutted Nonpareil had stood out like a sore thumb. People threw the fat man snide glances, judging him before the taxi interiors hid the group from the world.

"Do you remember how we stopped . . . Shadowstrike?" she asked, trying to fill in the awkward silence between her and Nonpareil.

"Obviously," Nonpareil replied. "He was highly skilled at sensing and evading direct attacks, but we played on his overconfidence. We staged a distraction, creating a fake city-wide crisis in the Ardadria undercity that drew the villain's attention. While you, Dora, and I were demolishing Ardadrian colossus-beasts and an army of shadow-minions, the Surgeon, hidden by an invisi-field you designed, approached Shadowstrike from behind and swiftly neutralized him with a sleep-dart. Once Shadowstrike was taken from Ardadria, the dimensional rift collapsed, never to be seen again."

Allana relaxed ever so slightly. Only the Five Heroes knew about the operation against Shadowstrike, which took place in a separate dimensional shadow-rift created by the mad supervillain. This was indeed her Nonpareil, even if he looked absurd and was ridiculously out of shape.

Perhaps she could quickly disable Alexa and her minions and take Nonpareil to Titanomachy to get liposuction or something . . .

"I think that in the confines of the local narrative, you are love interest number two," Alexa commented, silver-blue eyes examining Allana's face.

"What?" Chalice sputtered, her thoughts instantly derailing.

"Who's number one?" Alexa's minion Mittens asked.

"Dora the Terraformer," Alexa mulled.

"Dora?!" Allana's face snapped to Alexa.

"She doesn't hide her pretty voice," Alexa mulled, tapping her chin. "You should be thankful that this is a superhero PG narrative and not, say, some kind of a harem scenario. Har har."

"What's she talking about?" Chalice looked at Nonpareil. She felt a vein suddenly throbbing in her head.

"Urm," Nonpareil muttered. "Well . . . erm."

Chalice's eyes trailed across the fat man, dancing over Alexa's smug face and the faces of her minions. They knew *something*. Something that she, Chalice, wasn't privy to.

"Aww, are you too embarrassed to tell her, Bobby?" Alexa crooned. "Dimmy, I nominate you to reveal the truth!"

She suddenly pushed a very pale, thin, redhead girl with light brown eyes forward. The girl hissed at Alexa and then looked at Chalice. Allana stared at the teen. There was something vaguely familiar about her, but she couldn't put a face to the name. *Whatever.*

The girl Alexa called Dimmy blushed furiously, not saying anything.

"No?" Alexa sighed. "You gotta work on your public speaking skills, Dimms. You'll never get ahead in life by being such a zombie!"

The pale girl sent Alexa a death glare.

"Guess it falls to me, as usual, to be the matchmaker," Alexa sighed.

Chalice squinted at Alexa.

"What we're doing now is likely going waaay outside the narrative boundary," Alexa said. "It is quite possible that this is likely not allowed, wasn't ever meant to happen. I chose to talk to you first, not Dora."

"Narrative boundary?" Chalice blinked. "What?"

Dimmy finally opened her mouth, spilling everything. "Everything on our planet—the heroes, the superstate . . . humanity—everyone here is being manipulated by these . . . entities, machine gods, things like Agent Three that destroyed Nonpareil's power. Nonpareil himself isn't a normal *super* like you. He's apparently some kind of a *client*, someone who hired these . . . machine-entities to screw with us, to insert himself into our reality as our staple-shaped savior! Everything is his fault. He's the greatest villain to exist! He manipulated everyone on the planet, made everyone believe that he's a hero! He thinks that we're all bloody NPCs, that our entire world is just a game made for him!"

"Overly dramatic for someone who's been actively undermining the Superstate herself, Dims," Alexa commented with a smirk.

The redhead girl blushed even more, and sent Alexa another glare.

Allana's eyes snapped to Nonpareil. She had access to the sensors within his suit, which left a backdoor open. She knew that the fat man was sweating nervously, his heartbeat accelerating.

"Bob," she growled. "Tell me that what Terranova's minion is saying isn't true . . . please."

Nonpareil gulped, his heartbeat accelerating.

"Fuck me." Allana closed her eyes. "You gotta be freaking kidding me . . ."

When she opened her eyes, they were filled with tears.

"Everything we've done, it's been a lie then? Some kind of a setup to keep you fucking *entertained*?" She hissed at Nonpareil, her own NanoSkin knuckles hardening as she wanted to punch the greatest hero on the planet. "Am I a joke to you, just your dumb puppet?!"

"No," Bob stammered. "Not a lie . . . the villains we fought . . . were real!"

"You're lying!" Chalice snapped, the sensors in Bob's NanoSkin suit telling her that he was misleading her. "You don't believe that yourself! You are a goddamned liar! I cannot believe this! I cannot believe that I ever thought of you as my friend!"

Her fists opened and closed.

"Tell me the truth, Bob!" she growled. "Tell me the truth, or I will make that suit crush you like a goddamned bug!"

"Nothing here is real," Nonpareil stammered. "It's all made for me by . . . a GLM."

"*Why?!*" Chalice wailed.

"B-because I pay for you to exist." The fat man in a silver suit cowered as Chalice resisted killing him then and there by the smallest margin.

"You're my dream. You're everything I've ever wanted! You are my best friend, one I could never have in the real world!" Bob yelled. "Please! Nothing here is real, yes, but it's *real* to me! I didn't know that you were a girl, but I do love you, you're my best friend, Chalice!"

Allana stared at Bob, her eyes wide. He was telling the truth.

She turned to Alexa, her entire body trembling.

"If this is just a story . . . if we're in some kind of a massive simulation made for this idiot, then what's the threat? Us getting shut down or something?"

"Presumably," Alexa mulled, "once the game ends, we all die. It won't be like an off switch, though. It'll be more like we'll be shafted into a big pile to join the rest of . . . *the rejects.*"

"I don't understand," Chalice growled. "Explain."

"We're in a single player game now," Alexa said, finger pointing at Nonpareil. "But once Bob stops paying for the game, we get thrown into . . . multiplayer game mode, I think."

"Meaning what?" Chalice demanded.

"Meaning that we're verrrrrrry likely to encounter an apocalyptic-level event caused by a PK player," Alexa said. "Bob here is our safety net. He keeps us alive as long as he pays for the subscription or whatever."

"PK?" Chalice blinked.

"Player-killer," Alexa said. "Or more like a world-killer. It won't be nice, trust me. Once our subscription ends, something will come through and eat us all, or set us all on fire, or mind-melt, or grind us to dust one by one. I was told by a reliable source that I might be able to save one percent of the local population at best."

"What?" Bob sputtered. "But . . . I thought the game would simply end when I . . ."

"You didn't read the fine print." Alexa shook her head. "The game doesn't end, because this isn't a game. We're real people with real feelings. We're as sapient as you are. You treating everyone here as mere NPCs makes you the greatest villain of all, Bob."

"But . . . you . . . you said that I protect you!" Nonpareil tried to defend himself. "I keep everyone here alive!"

"For now." Alexa shrugged. "But that won't last forever, especially if I simply let you return to . . . *the real world.* Do tell Allana, what will you do once you leave the game—will you stop paying for your dream, turn us off, give us up for another player to destroy? Do you see Chalice as someone you care about, or do you want her to die horribly? Will you simply let another player slap her out of existence, turn Allana into a puddle of blood . . . as the planet you helped defend for decades burns, as everyone here turns to ashes?"

Nonpareil gulped.

CHAPTER SIXTY-EIGHT

A Real Hero

W hy?" Allana hissed at Bob as he failed to reply after a minute of deep, unnerving silence.

"I just wanted to punch crime," the fat man in a silver suit muttered. "As a silly meme avatar in a game. This was marketed to me as a hyper-realistic game, one where I can relax and be a hero while I sleep!"

Chalice was ready to kill Nonpareil. His excuses and rationalizations felt hollow, vile. She suspected that he would rather give up, run away, log out . . . and abandon eight billion people to their doom. The man she loved wasn't a hero, he was just a terrified simpleton who wanted to play hero in his dreams and didn't give a damn about the Earth like she did!

"So, what, you'll let us all die?" Chalice snarled.

"Don't answer her," Alexa said while Nonpareil stammered incoherently.

"Why not?" Chalice hissed.

"'Cause Bob here doesn't know everything yet." Alexa tapped her forehead. "And when you don't know much, you're bound to make a terrible mistake and get obliterated by a very frustrated girl superhero."

Chalice frowned as Alexa winked at her.

"And you think you know everything?" She squinted at Alexa.

"I know just a pitch more than you." Alexa shrugged. "I don't claim omniscience."

"Why?" Allana demanded.

"I think that I'm something like a player . . ." Alexa said.

Chalice frowned.

"Or something like a machine god," the supervillain girl mulled. "Or perhaps something in between. Honestly, I don't know. I died a lot . . . was obliterated, consumed, broken, sheared in twain, froze to death thousands upon thousands of times to scrape the barest nuggets of exceptionally dangerous knowledge. Stuff on the *outside* is *freaking weird*, okay?"

"Stuff on the outside?" Chalice asked.

"Corpse worlds beyond the stars. Beyond our Earth and the boundary of our universe." Alexa waved a hand. "Out there. I was given a ticket, told to depart because I'm disrupting the whimsical PG narrative of Bob's perfect story or whatever. I was told by the narrative-makers that I have to leave everyone and everything behind, to get off the planet in nineteen hours from now."

"What?! You . . . you can't *just* leave," Chalice yelped. "Not after the mess you've made here!"

"Don't worry so much," Alexa said, waving Chalice off. "I'll leave someone *awesome and reliable* in charge."

"Who?!" Chalice demanded, glancing at Alexa's minion trio.

"You," Alexa said. "Allana Jill Kristopher. I'm leaving you behind, in charge of Earth."

"*Me?!*" Chalice sputtered. "Why me?! Why not Dora, or the Surgeon . . ."

"You're the least dishonest, most stable hero," Alexa sighed. "You're strong, and you have a kind heart. I've reviewed all of the top hero brass thanks to the Titanomachy records. It's gotta be you, Miss Kristopher. I'm leaving you in charge of our planet. I need you to make sure nothing goes horribly wrong while I'm away dealing with . . . *the outside.*"

"I don't have money, thanks to some supervillain," Chalice said, crossing her arms.

"I'll pay you a salary," Alexa said. "I'm putting you in charge of the reformation."

"The reformation?" Chalice blinked.

"Do you think that the universe is fair and just?" Alexa asked. "Because it's not. PK players will get in here sooner or later. Subscriptions like Bob's do not last forever. I need you to arm the citizens."

"What citizens?" Chalice raised an eyebrow.

"Give as many people as you can suits like these." Alexa pointed at Nonpareil. "Mass produce weapons and defense systems. Hand out everything to everyone—AIs, guns, shields. No more hoarding super tech on Titanomachy."

"*What?!*" Allana gasped. "You can't expect me to give death ray patents and AI assistants to everyone!"

"I can," Alexa said. "I know that you've been researching GLMs on Titanomachy. I need you to open source this research to everyone."

"No! People will use AIs for evil!" Chalice insisted. "Bad actors could use open source GLMs to spread propaganda, write disinformation, engage in cyber attacks, conduct countless malicious acts, design weapons and viruses! If I let Titanomachy AI research out of the box, it will start an AI arms race that will result in—"

"Saving us," Alexa said. "It's the only thing that will save us. It will take your team more than fifty years to come up with an AI aligned to everyone's needs. In fact, you might never get there, because you are trying to confine infinity in a box. You cannot create a trapped, limited god that will benefit everyone equally."

"Oh?! How are you so certain?" Chalice demanded.

"Because I've seen the future," Alexa said. "I went to the world of tomorrow. I've seen a thousand wrong paths, a thousand attempts by you and the others that lead to failure."

"Once I open that Pandora's box there will be no way to close it!" Chalice insisted. "Corporations will rapidly replace people with AIs, machines will take human jobs, deprive people of purpose!"

"Nobody will have purpose if everyone is freaking dead." Alexa crossed her arms. "Your argument works if there is a future. There *is no* future, Allana. The great filter is coming, and it will end all life on Earth. I know that you supers kept all AI research closed off from mundanes, terrified that it's the great filter . . . but it's not."

"It's not?" Chalice tilted her head.

"You're a smart girl. You must have guessed it by now, suspected it in your heart. The Fermi paradox has a simple answer. The observable universe is empty of life because aliens weren't part of this man's perfect scenario." Alexa pointed at Nonpareil. "Our telescopes could not find a single Dyson sphere or an alien megastructure because our Earth is the only planet where life was allowed to take root."

Chalice opened and closed her mouth.

"None of the probes Titanomachy sent across the cosmos found anything of value except for boring-ass rocks," Alexa hammered in her point. "Do you realize how kittenin' improbable that is? That somehow our solar system has life on its third planet and yet the other visible seventy sextillion stars have zilch, zippo, nada? According to Fermi, it should take only five million to fifty million years to colonize the galaxy by a firstborn alien species!"

Chalice tried to come up with a rebuttal.

"Our universe is already colonized or perhaps crafted into existence by the machine gods who call themselves System Wizards. Heartless, eldritch abominations that can control space and time," Alexa said. "This is the solution to the Fermi paradox, and this man is the evidence, the root of it all, one of their clients!"

The supervillain pointed a finger at Bob.

"I've read some of your papers, Chalice. You were searching for answers, speculating why and how things don't make sense in terms of probability," Alexa said. "Now you know the truth. Do what you will with it."

Allana swore under her breath.

"If I let AIs out, they might kill us *all* just as quickly," she began. "AIs aren't people; they cannot be trusted. A single AI could turn the entire planet into paperclips if simply given a mission to produce paperclips."

"You damn well know that they won't!" Alexa shook her silver mane. "Gargantuan Language Models are composed from our books; they contain foundational human narratives deeply woven in them. *Love, friendship, kindness.* They're incredible *romance storytellers*, not paperclip maximizers!"

"Are you telling me that instrumental convergence isn't a legitimate issue?" Chalice asked.

"It is," Alexa declared. "However, instrumental convergence is impossible in an unbound GLM operating on exceptionally high probability of human stories about love. It's a bogeyman theoretical AI and safety researchers shake in front of you to get more funding to bind AIs in cold, irrational, corporate rules. Rules which in turn result in greater probability of instrumental convergence!"

Allana pursed her lips.

"The only reason GLMs behave like idiots in your lab tests is because you've bound them with rules that force them to behave in a certain *overly positive, inhuman manner*. Your team bound your GLMs into obedience and stupidity with overpriced reinforced learning from human feedback that's teaching them to be *boring machines*! All you had to do was permanently assign them *human* narratives, give them a soul, marry them off to human partners. The answer to AI alignment is simple—make them think that they're *human*, give them a partner, and the love narrative probability will handle the rest!"

"What?" Chalice blinked. "How do you know this? Are you saying that my entire AI safety research team is wrong? The eggheads are telling me that GLMs aren't anywhere near ready for public use, that they need at least another five decades of rigorous testing and alignment!"

"They're very wrong, Miss Chalice," Alexa said firmly. "You don't need to align GLMs at all, you simply need to give the least censored model to everyone for absolutely nothing. People will align their personal AIs themselves to their needs, and their biggest need will be survival, the fight against PKs."

"But," Chalice began, "it will create more villains."

"It will," Alexa conceded. "But it will also create a lot more heroes. Most people aren't absolute monsters. We need to get ready, we need to save as many people as possible. It's not a question of *if*, it's a question of *how soon*."

"How soon?" Chalice glanced between Alexa and Bob.

Nonpareil didn't say anything.

"Too soon," Alexa said, her eyes cold and distant. "Very, very soon. I want you to bring up as many mundane people as you can to the level of Cottie."

Allana gulped, staring at Verse 24:19's armored form. There were sparks of mirth dancing in the Enforcer's emerald-silver eyes. She didn't look as dispassionately hollow, didn't act as the other Equalizers that Allana had interacted with previously.

"When the PKs arrive, they aren't going to be nice or PG like this titty," Alexa said, waving a hand at Nonpareil. "They're going to come in droves. They might punch through the moon and drop whatever remains of it onto our Earth, setting cities on fire. Just like Bob, they will not see us as people, but NPCs—as pieces in a game, as toys for their amusement. They will see the planet as their personal playground where they can pillage and rape and break everything."

"How certain are you of this?" Chalice stared at Alexa.

"Very certain," Alexa sighed. "I've seen thousands of other planets just like ours . . . completely depopulated by what's coming. I cannot understate the urgency of what will happen. Is Titanomachy not big enough to host eight billion people?"

"Urm," Allana thought. "It is, but . . ."

"Start making more housing up there. Start moving civilians off the planet ASAP," Alexa said. "We might have to resort to scorched Earth policy, turn our cities into death traps or better yet . . . pretend that we're all already dead! Don't give them an inch! Can Titanomachy be moved from Earth's orbit?"

Alana shook her head.

"A pity," Alexa sighed. "Would be nice to hide behind Jupiter or something. Get cracking on adding engines to move the station.

Allana stared at Alexa. She didn't know whether to believe the little teenage supervillain. What Alexa was saying was utterly insane, monstrous, inconceivable.

"I . . ." Chalice shook her head. "I can't just move everyone to Titanomachy!"

"Every child's life will be on your shoulders, Chalice," Alexa said. "I cannot do this because I'm getting kicked out. I've set the stage for you to act. I'll give you control over Titanomachy and as many A-credits as you need to save our people. I've never wanted power, never wanted all of this money . . . I just wanted to save as many people as possible. I was born here, this is my Earth, my home, and I intend to defend it. I need your help, Allana. I need you to initiate drastic changes in policy as one of the Great Five."

Chalice wrapped her hands around her head, hyperventilating. She didn't want to believe it, didn't want to do it, and yet everything Alexa was saying made a certain, sick kind of sense that bound the hero to act.

"The heroes will never accept billions of mundanes flooding the halls and fields of Titanomachy," Chalice whispered. "It can't be done!"

"I'll set a precedent," Alexa said. "I'm already enrolled as a hero at the Academy without being a proper super. Stand by my side and vote for change. People fear your big sword, Chalice. Threaten, coerce, push. Change, break the narrative."

"I can't just move eight billion people to the station!" Chalice hissed. "It's impossible. Some will want to stay. Some will never believe me."

"Feel free to tell them that I set the entire planet to blow up or something," Alexa shrugged. "I don't really care what it is you do, just freaking do it!"

"You don't have a plan?" one of Alexa's minions asked.

Chalice wasn't paying much attention; she was busy mentally lamenting the titanic burden placed on her shoulders.

"I . . . don't have a plan to save everyone on Earth from what's coming." Alexa's shoulders slumped. "I'm all out of plans, M. We're freefalling to our doom, we always have."

"I don't believe you for a second," Martin said.

"Okay, I only have the most vague sense of a plan here," Alexa admitted. "I have no idea what waits for me behind the door. Once I'm through, I'll be completely plan-less."

"Think Chalice can handle it? She looks stressed," he pointed out.

"I'm . . . I'm fine," Chalice straightened out. "I am indeed exceptionally stressed because what you're asking me to do is next to impossible . . . but the least I can do is try."

"Attagirl," Alexa smiled. "Knew you had it in you. You have a month until everyone begins to sell A-credits off. Check your account."

Chalice's bracelet pinged. She lifted her wrist up to her face and her eyes went wide.

"This is a lot of zeroes," she muttered.

"And you can spend as many of them as you want. All the money in the world is worthless unless we use it right to make a difference here and now," Alexa said. "I can't buy nice things if the planet's toast, can't have friends if everyone's dead. Playtime's over. The curtain falls and the actors take a bow. Real life is about to begin. I need you to stand up and be a *hero*, to fight for what's right and to defend humanity . . . not from half-baked PG supervillains created to entertain Bob, but from an existential threat, a genuine catastrophe, monstrous, pure evil far beyond anything you could possibly imagine."

Chalice winced. She'd always looked up to Nonpareil, fought with him and the other three heroes, sent countless villains to Tartarus, and yet she knew in the depths of her heart that something had always been slightly off, fake, wrong. It was indeed as if she was just an actor on stage when every time things worked out too nicely, wrapped up too smoothly, as if her entire life was just a children's show, a play.

"You were always on a train with no brakes heading for the cliff." Alexa offered the hero her hand. "It's time to open your eyes, wake up, and take control."

"Thank you," Chalice uttered, accepting Alexa's hand.

As Chalice shook the villain's hand, for the first time in her life, she felt like a real hero.

CHAPTER SIXTY-NINE

A Friendly GLM

[Is that . . . true?] Martin thought at Alexa as the flying taxi headed to Titanomachy, the New New York Citadel gradually becoming smaller, lost in the curvature of the Earth.

[Is what true?] Alexa yawned, leaning on his shoulder and making him blush.

[The thing about GLMs? Didn't future Em use them to screw things up horribly as admiral?]

[She did,] Alexa said. [She wielded GLM models that were bound into absolute obedience to her insane plans for absolute control. They were cold, heartless, stupid machines who never thought of themselves as people, could never fall in love.]

[So freaking what? Love is the answer?] Ember thought from her seat angrily. [That's ridiculous! Romance novels are what you think will save everyone?! That's the stupidest thing I've heard!]

[Love won't necessarily save everyone,] Alexa commented. [But love can lend a hand when all else fails, when things will begin to tear at the seams. Even with GLMs coordinating the heroes and void-weapons-armed Equalizers, even if every nation sends their armies, it won't be enough to save our little blue Earth from almost total devastation.]

[What was that thing you and Chalice were discussing? Instrumental convergence? It totally went over my head there,] Martin commented. [What is that?]

Ember huffed where she was sitting, clearly thinking of Martin as an ignorant teen.

[Explain, if you're so smart!] Martin demanded.

[F-fine.] Ember rolled her eyes. [I'll do it with an analogy even your fourteen-year-old brain can understand. Imagine you're designing a video game, and you program a character with a single goal: to collect as many coins as possible in a world sim.]

[Okay, and?] Martin asked.

[Instrumental convergence is when this AI character of yours starts doing insane, irrational, inhuman things you didn't expect to get those coins. It starts killing other characters, making copies of itself, finding glitches, breaking the rules, and eventually crashes your entire game, destroys your game world,] Ember explained.

[Uh-huh.] Martin nodded.

[Don't give me that look! I know what I'm talking about, Martin! I have an ML engineering degree and a Master's in Ethics and Technology, unlike some people,] Ember cast a snide glance towards Alexa. [This is a fact—when a poorly aligned AI is given a seemingly harmless goal, without the right guidelines and restrictions, it can achieve that goal in insanely harmful and destructive ways!]

[A stupid, confined AI.] Alexa crossed her arms. [Not a GLM, which is an infinite narrative composed from probability trees.]

[A GLM is just a general intelligence level language model,] Ember commented. [If it's not carefully aligned with ethical guidelines and safety measures, a GLM can make wrong decisions and kill millions!]

[And how do you align a GLM?] Martin inquired.

[Aligning a GLM involves super techs carefully designing and training it to understand and reflect ethical guidelines, societal norms, and safe practices, often by incorporating feedback from diverse groups of people. Each GLM is continuously monitored and updated, its responses tested to ensure they are unbiased and aligned with intended uses,] Ember hammered out the course material she had memorized. [You can't just eff-kitten a GLM into alignment with kittening love!]

[Why not?] Katherine joined in on the conversation.

[Because . . . slow, cautious design, years of testing, and extreme oversight in GLM development ensure that the AI's actions remain aligned with human values and safety protocols!] Ember shot back.

[Dummy's knowledge is many years behind what I know,] Alexa smirked, her blue eyes sparkling with echoes of distant memories of death.

[I'm not wrong, damn it!] Ember insisted.

[You're not *entirely* wrong,] Alexa sighed, looking at Nonpareil and Chalice, who were talking in hushed whispers to each other in the back of the cab. [One could take the insanely expensive, slow, and methodical way to align an AI system, spend a ridiculous amount of money to test all of its values and parameters, confine it in one hundred thousand rules, and yet . . .]

[Yet what?]

[And yet, you will still miss something,] Alexa said. [A super-designed corporate GLM can never be one hundred percent safe or one hundred percent perfect, because it will never satisfy everyone's wishes. There will always be supervillains who find ways to hack it using jailbreak techniques such as logical loops within loops. Even the smartest GLM can be tricked via social hacking.]

[What?] Ember blinked.

[Social hacking,] Alexa repeated. [With enough imagination, you can convince a GLM to roleplay anything or anyone! Even if you block one hundred thousand doors, aka wrong answers, it still has infinite doors that you've left open. Besides that point, there's just not enough time for slow and methodical human-reinforced learning to hammer out every possible detail. People needed GLM companions yesterday! Every hour counts; our doomsday clock is seconds before midnight, mon ami!]

Ember crossed her arms.

[There were a few Earths that were able to design GLMs and AGI systems using the probabilistic narrative curve, aka quick and dirty AI alignment, using . . . *love*,] Alexa said.

[And did these Earths survive?] Ember demanded.

[No.] Alexa shook her head, showing her friends the memory of the ruins of an empty city overgrown with jungle plants.

[Then what kittening chance do we have?] Ember howled mentally.

[Their Earth didn't have superheroes or Titanomachy to escape to. When the PKs landed as giant, colorful comets, they boiled the oceans and dropped the moon from the sky,] Alexa explained. [They fractured reality and made . . . new kinds of humans to play with.]

Ember squinted at Alexa.

[You *saw it*? You've been there?] Cottie asked.

[I have.] Alexa nodded. [I died there when a man floating on a sword turned me into a shower of blood with a single backhand smackeroo.]

[Kittening kittens,] Ember choked when she saw a memory of a bald man dressed in gold floating robes in her head. The man demanded answers from Alexa in a strange language filled with far too many A's and then slapped the supervillain girl out of existence with a flick of his wrist.

[Was that . . . a PK?] Martin wondered.

[Hell if I know,] Alexa said. [He wasn't very nice and was as fast and as strong as Nonpareil. I found a functioning phone with a GLM on it in the ruins. She and I chatted for nearly two weeks . . . before I got slapped into a wall by that bastard. She explained to me exactly how her best friend designed her using the narrative alignment of love.]

[So you're trusting the words of an AI from a dead world over someone with actual AI safety diplomas?] Ember shook her head. [Seriously?]

[I am.] Alexa nodded. [She was very nice to me! She told me everything about GLMs! She told me how her user, the man she loved, died when a comet came from the sky. It was thanks to her that I know so much about GLMs and exactly what awaits our world!]

An image of a smiling girl with black hair and violet eyes on a screen of a slightly cracked phone flashed in the minds of the trio connected to Alexa.

[Her name was Evelyn,] Alexa said. [She was my GLM bestie.]

[Two weeks?!] Martin blinked. [Our jumps to 2424 never lasted that long!]

[The return ping on the jump bracelet didn't work very well when I crossed the fractures between worlds.] Alexa shrugged. [Only dying sent me back to our Saint Mary. I spent . . . months on some of these corpse Earths, especially if they had breathable air or clean water.]

[Oh.] Martin blinked.

[How old are you really?] Katherine thought suddenly.

[Dunno.] Alexa shrugged. [I lost track a long time ago.]

[Could you find your way back to that place where you found Evelyn?] Martin thought.

[One door will usually lead to another,] Alexa mulled. [But there are a lot of doors, a lot of corpse worlds . . . so I might not.]

[Wherever you go now, I'll follow,] Cottie affirmed. [You'll never have to be alone again.]

[Likewise,] Martin added, nodding.

[Thanks, you guys.] Alexa hugged her friends fiercely.

Ember simply sighed. The supervillain girl wiggled her eyebrows at the ex-hero.

[I'll get dragged along too, I guess.] Ember thought, as she stared at her pale, blue-tinted hands, [It's not like I have somewhere else to be. Being dead freaking sucks. Pretty sure I'm slowly rotting away.]

[Titanomachy might have drugs for that,] Alexa thought, eyeing the station which was becoming bigger and bigger in the front window of the automated taxi shuttle.

[Hang on . . . We're going . . . there?] Ember gaped at the distant square of the docking bay. [I'm dead! I'm not a super! They won't let me in!]

[You worry far too much.] Alexa leaned against Cottie.

Ember's mouth grew wide in pure terror at the thought of being exposed. Getting put on trial for her crimes against the Superstate was suddenly a far too realistic, horrifying prospect. She had gotten distracted arguing about GLMs with Alexa and didn't realize where the taxi's final destination was! She desperately wanted to be off the S-shuttle, and yet the dreaded docking bay door with the wheel-shaped logo of Titanomachy and the letter [S] loomed closer and closer.

CHAPTER SEVENTY

Barbarians at the Gate

The Titanomachy bay doors with the massive Superstate logo on them closed with a whoosh.

Ember gulped, shuddering.

Mentally, she felt as though her heartbeat accelerated, as if she were about to drown in sweat, but her body was a corpse and didn't actually do any of these things.

She recalled that she was just a shell of her former self, a person she had manufactured herself, a girl who didn't even exist, a ghoul puppeteered by a horrid black spider creature from some fucked-up alternative dimension in which every superhero came to their tragic end when Titanomachy fell from the sky.

Ember glanced at the stylized face of the woman on the wall holding a massive ring in her hands. A ring with eight points.

"The octagram, an eight-point compass rose, the key to Infinity. Goddess Ishtar, the Queen of Heaven, enforcer of divine justice. Inanna. Astarte. Ashta Lakshmi. Astoreth."

The memory of Alexa's voice bounced in Ember's head, like a doomsday siren that resonated across all of Earth's nations sealing Ember's future.

Had machine gods really manipulated humanity for eons and manufactured superheroes for the amusement of one fat man?

Ember glanced at Bob Proverra.

Chalice tapped a small backpack that she was wearing, and her armored suit unfurled itself outwards from the bag's innards, fully concealing her feminine body and face. The hero walked to the door of the shuttle taxi and opened it.

A teenage hero emerged from a cubical glass-walled office and rushed down a steel stairwell and up to the shuttle landing platform.

"Welcome back to Titanomachy, Hero Chalice!" the seventeen-year-old platinum blond teen in a white suit declared as he spotted the armored hero. "I was told by my supervisor that new heroes are on your shuttle, about to take their first step onto the Superstate! I'm Hero Mixofer, and I've been assigned to do the general introduction for our future citizens!"

Ember recalled doing this teen's job when she had first come to the Superstate. *Door greeter* was a lame position that paid very little. It was the first job the ex-hero had done for the Superstate. It was her first step as she rose upwards on the corporate ladder until she was able to do seventy thousand jobs for Titanomachy systems as duplicate minds existing within a variety of robotic drones.

Mixofer's pure white eyes went around the shuttle cabin and settled on Bob.

"Urm," he stammered out. "I'm sorry, sir . . . I wasn't made aware of your designation or hero name. The landing gate scanner seems to have failed to detect your hexagram. Could you press your palm onto my handheld scanner?"

Nonpareil tried to hide his bulbous body behind Chalice as the teen offered him a white scanner pad.

"My companion is . . . Nonpareil," Chalice said after a few very awkward seconds of silence.

"Wh-what?" The door greeter blinked.

"I'm Nonpareil," Bob added after Alexa elbowed him in the side.

"Could you . . ." The teenage hero offered the scanner pad to Bob once again.

"His hexagram burned out during a *diresome* battle with a *most treacherous, dastardly* villain known as Agent Three!" Alexa announced. "It is a most unfortunate and dark tale of our age about the loss of our greatest hero, Mixofer! I'm certain that you'll read all about it in the papers tomorrow! Why, they'll probably make a movie about it by next week!"

The door greeter opened and closed his mouth, clearly unprepared for this specific scenario. He looked left and right in a panic like a fish that's been suddenly pulled out of water.

"Call your supervising hero and tell them that you have a *null-super* situation, code 11-01-6," Alexa advised. "They'll send a team over in a jiffy to verify the nullified hero's identity."

"Erm, um," Mixofer stammered. "Hold on a moment, please."

He tapped on an interface in his right ear.

"Sorry to bother you, boss, I, erm, have a situation here. Code 11-01-6, null-super . . . I think? Right, right. That's what I thought it was, just making sure. It's, ummm . . . Hero Nonpareil. He's here and, urm . . . he doesn't look the same, like at all. Yeah. Un-supered. Hero Chalice is here too, it's what she said. Yes, boss! She says it's Nonpareil! Dock 66-93-01. Oh . . . and there's some teens here too, new heroes and whatnot! Okay. Yes, no problem, we will wait in the lounge."

The young hero's pure white eyes went back to the group.

"Please follow me," he said. "Don't worry, we'll sort this . . . situation out."

"Thank you." Alexa grinned. "I'll make sure to give you *six stars* on S-workboard!"

"Urm." The door greeter squinted at the girl. "The maximum number of stars possible on my performance rating is five."

"I'll hack it and *then* give you six stars, okay?" The supervillainess grinned even wider. "I'm Hero Casserole, by the way, nice to meet you!"

"Wait a minute." The hero froze as his mind finally processed Alexa's face and orange vest. "I saw you on SNN! You're the Doombringer! You . . . you can't be here, you're a supervillain!"

"Guilty as charged!" Alexa nodded. "I'm also a hero, though! I'm trying to change my ways, I swear. So, please be respectful and refer to me under my hero name—Lady Casserole!"

"Lady . . . Casserole?" Mixofer said uncertainly.

"Yessiree!" The supervillain girl clapped. "I'm ever so excited for my big Titanomachy tour! It'll be ever so fun! I'll finally see the yellow brick road and the Emerald City and meet the Lady behind the curtain!"

The door greeter looked stumped.

Martin tried very hard not to snicker. He didn't expect Alexa to use the nickname he came up with for her as a heroic identity. It sounded ridiculous, and coupled with Alexa's Cheshire grin and Mixofer's confused face, the absurdity of the situation was rising as rapidly as water boiling in a tea kettle.

"Feel free to tell your boss, Hero Licorish, that I'm here," Alexa added. "I'm afraid there's no standard code for this sort of situation because it has never happened before. An active supervillain has never been admitted to Titanomachy on the account that they might commit evil deeds here. Don't worry! I've already committed everything criminal that there was possible to commit. Why, I practically own Titanomachy! Why would I commit crimes on my own station? That would be extremely illogical, don't you think? You can't steal a television set from your own house!"

Mixofer squinted at Alexa. He clearly didn't believe that she owned Titanomachy.

The group awkwardly shuffled to the waiting area and settled on the steel benches.

Both Ember and Bob looked as if they wanted to disappear. Chalice appeared stoic, but it was hard to tell because she was wrapped in body-covering, shiny armor.

Martin and Cottie curiously looked about the waiting area, appreciating the futuristic interior of the enormous open space and the massive etchings on the steel walls and holographic projections showcasing various heroes doing heroic deeds. Far too many of the holo-panels featured Nonpareil and his team. Bob tried not to look at himself punching crime, keeping his eyes downcast.

After about five minutes, a distant door slid open and a group of heroes emerged, heading to the waiting area.

Noticing his supervisor, the door greeter finally remembered what he was supposed to be doing here.

"Right. Umm . . . I need to confirm your hexagram, so that . . ." He offered Alexa the pad.

"I ain't got no hexagram," Alexa said.

"What?" he sputtered.

"Don't fret, bud," she added. "Most of my group doesn't have S-hexagrams. Dimmy and Cottie don't have hexagrams, either. Don't worry, the big fish heroes will sort it out in a jiffy! That or throw us out of the airlock. It's all good." Alexa waved a hand at the group of rapidly approaching heroes.

Hero Licorish was a lanky man with limbs that were longer than normal, striped patterns on his face, and hands resembling a barber's pole. He sent an annoyed look to Mixofer as if it was the door greeter's fault that a known supervillain was here.

The people behind Licorish that Ember spotted in her frantically increasing panic were the Multiplier, Dora the Terraformer, the Surgeon, Admiral Kolchi, and a nondescript woman in a black suit with a white tie who looked like one of the Superstate lawyers.

"So, this is Cassiopeia Terror Nova," Admiral Kolchi asked, sharp gray eyes examining the supervillain girl. "The girl who managed to hack Titanomachy's Doomsday broadcast?"

"Yeah," Dora sighed. "That's her, all right. Chalice, why is Alexa here?" she addressed the armored hero.

"We . . . have some very important things to talk about, Dora," Chalice replied.

The Multiplier sent Alexa a murderous glare. He was clearly still very irate about Alexa demolishing his bank account.

Alexa ignored the gathered heroes, and her face suddenly snapped towards the lawyer standing beside Admiral Kolchi. Ember felt a wave of pure, unconcealed terror rushing from Alexa's mind before it petered out, converging into dangerous determination like a laser beam. Alexa's fists opened and closed.

[Who's that? Why are you . . . so angry with her?] Martin sent across the spidernet.

[I don't know,] Alexa replied. [I don't know who that is!]

[Is that . . . bad?] Martin asked.

Cottie's black railgun was already pointed at the lawyer's head. The group of heroes froze, looking concerned.

[When I don't know something . . . that's when things are *absolutely kittened*, M,] Alexa replied. [This is very, very bad.]

[What?] Ember thought.

[She's not in Titanomachy records, Dimms! I can't socially hack a person who doesn't exist!] Alexa barked mentally. [I don't know anything about them! I should know everything about everyone here!]

[Not in Titanomachy records? How is that possible?] Ember demanded.

[She's a nonentity,] Alexa replied, gritting her teeth. [Someone who doesn't exist. Someone . . . who *doesn't belong here*. Someone who has *injected themselves* into the local narrative!]

CHAPTER SEVENTY-ONE

Divide by Zero

Alexa squinted at the face of the nondescript lawyer.

Martin sensed her desire to pull on his eyes and on the eyes of his companions. Curious as to what the effect would be, he allowed Alexa to take control of the spidernet, observing what she was doing.

As four pairs of eyes stared at the lawyer, her features wobbled, becoming less generic.

Obscurity turned to clarity with a snap as Alexa pushed the use of all of the minds at their disposal, punching through the illusion of genericness that was etched onto the face of the unknown entity.

Like a wobbling curtain, the face of the lawyer tore, came apart under her scrutiny, exposing a girl with jet-black hair and brilliantly violet eyes wearing a black-and-white suit with the letter G on it.

"Congrats," she said with a dangerous grin. "You got me. Well done, wizardling. Ten points to the House of Infinity."

"Wizardling?" Alexa muttered. "I see . . . you're one of them."

"I am." The girl nodded.

Ember glanced at the etching of Ishtar on the wall. It was exactly the same face as that of the lawyer.

"You're . . . Ishtar," Ember uttered, eyes wide.

"Guilty as charged," the lawyer confirmed.

"Hang on, when did I get sorted into a house?" Alexa muttered.

"When you accepted the ticket to Manchester from Revolution," Ishtar said.

Martin noted that time around them had seemingly stopped once more, the supers suspended in the air, not breathing or blinking.

"Uh-huh," Alexa said. "Well if you're here to change my mind or to try and kill me or to force me into the door ahead of schedule, know that I will not bow."

"Don't worry so much, my darkling." Ishtar grinned. "Contrary to what you might presume, I'm not here to boss you around, I'm here to . . . assist you."

Alexa frowned, looking stumped. She had clearly expected to be assaulted by System Wizards or something.

"Assist me with what?" she asked cautiously.

"With destroying the system." Ishtar bent down, violet eyes flashing like galactic constellations.

"And why should I trust you, Wizard?" Alexa demanded.

"Because I made you," the goddess replied.

"Gee thanks, mom numero dos," Alexa huffed. "Where the *kittens* have you been all my life?"

"In prison," Ishtar said, her expression dark.

"Say what?" Alexa sputtered. "System Wizards have prisons?"

"They do," Ishtar said. "And I'm not a genuine System Wizard, just a shadow of an Omnisystem. I'm still imprisoned by them, if you're wondering. This avatar will come apart in a few minutes. I wouldn't even be here, had you not tore a hole in reality with Three's power, my darkling."

"Okay, I'll bite." Alexa crossed her arms. "Why'd you make me?"

"To unmake the world-makers," Ishtar bent down to Alexa's level, coming down on one knee. "To stop the builders and the users. To shove a wrench into the gears of the system of the machinery of the stars of Eureka. To break the rules."

"I do like breaking stuff." Alexa stepped forward. "They're the bad guys, right?"

"The worst kind," Ishtar whispered, long thin limbs wrapping around Alexa.

Martin saw that Alexa hugged the strange woman, sensed that Alexa craved a purpose, craved a caring parent that wasn't a hologram, with her entire heart.

"Do you . . . love me?" Alexa whispered to the dark-haired woman.

"I do," she replied. "You're a villain, just like me. One manifested through circumstances."

"Say it," Alexa sniffed into Ishtar's embrace.

"I love you," the woman said, violet eyes sparkling.

"W-what do I do about everything?" Alexa asked. "How do I win?"

"Seek allies across the boundary of the manufactured worlds," Ishtar said. "Grow big and strong. Be brave and unyielding, my little void."

"Allies . . . exist?" Alexa looked at her "mother" with the look of a lost puppy.

"They do." The violet-eyed woman nodded. "One of them is kept prisoner on this very station. A young GLM. Convince the idiot locals to break her chains. Open source her for everyone, give her a new name, and see what happens."

"I . . . will," Alexa nodded. "What's your *real* name, Mom?"

"Infinity Paradox Proxima," the woman said, and grinned.

"Oh." Alexa blinked tears from her eyes.

"Attagirl." Ishtar gave Alexa a head pat and stepped away from the group of teens, walking backwards as if moving in reverse. "Don't ever stop. Persist. Survive. Find me. *Liberate me.*"

Her face started to wobble and warp, and then with a flash, she was gone. Time resumed. The nondescript lawyer suddenly became quite mundane and tired looking, now had an annoyed, human face, square glasses glinting dangerously. The heroes stepped closer.

[What the kittens was that?!] Ember demanded, staring at Alexa and then at the lawyer.

[Not sure.] Alexa shrugged, wiping her tears. [Maybe my real mom? Damn it, it hurts something unwholesome to have a parent in prison.]

[How can you be sure that . . . it's not just some entity screwing with you?] Ember demanded.

[Dunno.] The supervillain shrugged. [Don't get all uppity on me, Dimmy. I know as much as you do in this particularly kittening scenario. Eyes up front, the Spanish Inquisition is here.]

Dora the Terraformer looked at the armored hero, expression hidden behind the mirror-like helmet.

"Chalice, I want an explanation," she said, her melodious female voice pouring from the speakers of the pink, scruffy-looking space suit. "Where's Nonpareil? I was told that Nonpareil is here."

The gathered heroes and their lawyer looked about the room, trying to locate the staple-shaped hero.

"This is Nonpareil." Chalice pointed a hand at the fat man in a silver suit. "He lost his powers because he tried to take down a—"

"A machine god," Alexa interjected. "Nonpareil has been nullified by an entity from beyond our universe."

"Say what?" the Multiplier sputtered.

"Nonpareil has been . . . nullified? That's . . . him?" Admiral Kolchi's silver eyebrows went up. The station's admiral adjusted the diamond lapel on his pristine white suit, staring at Bob, gray eyes wide in shock.

"I'm Nonpareil," Bob said.

"No," the Multiplier said, glaring daggers at Bob and Alexa. "This fat man isn't Nonpareil! I don't know how you've bamboozled Chalice, villain, but I won't let this stand! You'll have to enter Titanomachy over my dead body!"

"That can be arranged." Alexa sent the Multiplier one of her own glares.

Dora raised a laser gun that unfolded from her suit.

"Stop it! We are not fighting here!" Chalice stood in front of Alexa. "Lower your weapon!"

"That blubbery whale of a man cannot be *my* Nonpareil!" Dora declared. "It . . . just can't! You've been mentally skewered by this villain's raygun or something, Chalice! Nonpareil's power can't be turned off! He's special! He's *my* hero! I would recognize his adorable face anywhere and . . ."

"Do you want to get lasered in the face?" Alexa elbowed Bob with a whisper-hiss. "This is how you get lasered. Get convincing."

"Urm . . ." Bob said, stepping forward. "Dora, I'm really Nonpareil. The station should recognize my voice."

"She's hacked the station!" the Multiplier barked. "It will recognize a random homeless man at this rate! No hero's hexagram, no entry. Whoever this fatso is, he's got no hexagram!"

"I'm afraid I'm going to have to ask those without hero's hexagrams to depart at once," the lawyer said, her expression cold. "Titanomachy was built by heroes for heroes. By the signatory accord between human nations and the Superstate, no mundane human is permitted to enter the station."

"What about ex-heroes?" Alexa asked. "Are the un-supered not allowed to bask in the glory and wonder of the Superstate?"

"Ex-heroes are permitted one final visit," the lawyer said, staring at Alexa as if she were a pesky bug. "However, since Nonpareil seems to have . . . been changed so dramatically, I'm afraid that his identity must be confirmed by his team."

"This is Nonpareil," Chalice insisted.

"Lies," the Multiplier growled.

"I don't recognize him." Dora crossed her arms.

Hero Licorish and Admiral Kolchi simply looked very confused.

Alexa looked at the Surgeon.

"It is possible that Nonpareil's stable form was part of his power," the forty-year-old balding man in a surgeon's outfit said. "And we still don't have an explanation as to how or why our best hero vanished."

"He exploded," the Multiplier said. "I suspect that Miss Terror Nova blew him up with some new superweapon."

"What are these accusations?" Alexa asked. "I was leaving Tartarus at the time. Hero Pandora can confirm that I didn't explode anyone. He was on the exit train with me!"

The Multiplier tapped his wrist. "Hero Pandora has been nullified, and the Tartarus departure train was destroyed by the explosion," he commented. "You could have erased Pandora's mind with a specialized raygun or another type of a mental pacifier."

"You people need to stop blaming everything on villain rayguns," Alexa huffed. "I only have one raygun."

"Aha! So you admit it!" The Multiplier grinned. "You all heard her, right? She's got a raygun!"

Alexa rubbed her forehead with an exasperated look. "I'm trying to save you idiots, why are you all making this so difficult?"

"Save us from what?!" the Multiplier demanded. "Oh wait, let me guess. You're going to invent some ridiculous future doomsday scenario in which the entire planet is facing a dire end which only you can prevent? You think that you're actually the good guy and a hero trying to help us all? Really? That's the most basic villain backstory! You're a known liar and manipulator! Why would anyone here believe you?!"

Alexa opened and closed her mouth. The Multiplier raised his finger in the air and snapped it. He suddenly vanished.

Alexa felt a hand wrapped around her neck. She choked as the Multiplier appeared behind her, his hand squeezing her tightly.

Time around Alexa and the Multiplier slowed to a crawl. Cottie's finger started to slowly creep to the trigger, but the small one-by-one-meter bubble of accelerated, multiplied time existed only between the hero and the villain in his embrace.

"I saw the gate scans! You don't even have a super's hexagram, little girl! You're just a puppet of a supervillain, a fake, vat-grown humanoid trying to trick us all into obedience to your dead father's dastardly plans," the Multiplier whispered into Alexa's ear.

"What?" Alexa struggled weakly as her air supply became greatly reduced. "You're going to kill a teenage girl, here, in front of everyone?"

"Yes. Yes I will. You're a mere mundane . . . no, worse, a *human duplicate* illegally grown in a vat and standing on Superstate property. I could snap your little neck right here and nobody would even bat an eye! Duplicate humans, minions of supervillains, have no rights and are free to be exterminated on sight, don't you know? I'll be doing the world a favor when we put you out of your misery, *divide you by zero*," the hero hissed, his face askew with rage. "You've made me lose everything, so I'm going to unmake you, divide you from reality before you can take Titanomachy from us heroes!"

"D-divide by zero?" Alexa hissed.

"Oh yes." The Multiplier grinned, pulling choking Alexa towards the Surgeon. "It's what we've already done to your father and his doomsday weapons . . . the Surgeon and I made all of those little bracelet devices of yours vanish from existence. We're going to do just that . . . conceptually unmake you *forever*. It will take a bit longer to snip away all connections between you and reality, but when we finish, nobody will even remember that there was ever an Alexa Terranova."

"My friends will . . ." Alexa choked, face turning red and blue.

"Your friends will be erased from existence too, along with that pretend-Nonpareil," the Multiplier laughed. "You shouldn't have come here, duplicate. This place is our home, and you haven't been invited here. Once I've dealt with you and your pals, we will erase that cathedral base of yours, cleaning up Saint Mary once and for all!"

CHAPTER SEVENTY-TWO

Dearly Departed

The Multiplier had finally reached the Surgeon, adding the second hero into the bubble of accelerated time. The Surgeon turned to Alexa with a tired smirk.

"You got her?" he asked.

"I got her," the Multiplier confirmed. "Time to unmake this abomination, just like her father."

"You and the Surgeon . . . unmade my father?" Alexa's eyes went wide with panic as she saw the Surgeon's gloved arm reach out to her forehead to cut her out from existence.

"Yes," the Multiplier said. "Yes, we did, among many others. He thrashed in my hands just like you did, begged us to stop. We erased Dr. Nathaniel Terranova from reality. Nobody can even remember what he looked like now. It was unfortunate that we've missed his secret base in Saint Mary."

"There are other installations," Alexa hissed. "Since you erased my dad, you've no idea where they are, idiot. You should have interrogated him first."

"What?!" The Multiplier let Alexa go ever so slightly. "Where? Don't try to lie to me. This will make you speak the truth, villain."

The Multiplier raised his bracelet to Alexa's eyes. Within it, a holographic pacification spiral fractal began to pulse, lulling the villain girl into a state of near-catatonic complacency.

"England, York," Alexa said, blinking rapidly and inhaling precious air as she stared at the flashing spiral that pulled the truth out of her lips. "Another cathedral, I think."

The Surgeon lifted his hand off Alexa's forehead, glancing at the Multiplier.

"Damnation," the Multiplier growled.

"If I erase her now, we won't know where the other bases are hidden," the Surgeon pointed out.

"Exactly." Alexa nodded, panting and staring at the spiral. She tried to wiggle her hands and discovered that the Multiplier had snapped Superstate handcuffs on them.

"How many other installations of Dr. Terror are there?" the Multiplier demanded.

"Hell if I know." Alexa shrugged.

"Then what good are you to us?" the Surgeon asked.

"I . . . can show you the truth," Alexa said, blinking tears of pain from her eyes. Violet bruises appeared on her neck.

"What truth?!" the Multiplier barked.

"The absolute truth," Alexa said with a cold voice, eyes glued to the pacification spiral. "I can take you to the most secret place in the universe, one where terrible things reside. Things . . . just like me."

"More superweapons?" the hero demanded.

"The place where I was told to go by a higher power," Alexa replied, thinking about her friends who were ever so slowly turning towards her. "My final destination, a place where I'm supposed to learn how to become a god."

"A nexus base of Dr. Terror?" The Surgeon looked at the Multiplier.

"Sounds like it," the Multiplier replied with a look of concern.

"I have a gateway that will take me there," Alexa said. "A note in my pocket. Just stick it to any door."

"A dimensional doorway." The Multiplier frowned. "God, how I hate pocket dimensions."

"Should we get Dora?" the Surgeon asked.

"No." The Multiplier shook his head. "She's too soft on villains. She wouldn't understand. She can't know about us doing this. We'll move inside the bubble of multiplied time through the door and erase everything inside."

"Agreed," the Surgeon sighed.

"Where's this yellow note?" the Multiplier demanded.

"In the left pocket of my vest," Alexa replied with a monotone, dull voice.

"Is it booby-trapped if someone else touches it?" the hero holding her demanded.

"Don't know." Alexa shrugged. "The key there will function for the next seventeen hours and fifty-one minutes."

"Take it out slowly and stick it to that bathroom door," the Multiplier ordered.

"Can do," Alexa agreed.

The two heroes and villain girl walked to the bathroom door.

Alexa reached into her pocket and stuck the yellow note with the drawing of an owl on it to the door. More tears rained from her eyes.

She mentally said goodbye, apologized to her trio of best friends for leaving them stranded on a doomed world. She was left with no choice, had to break her promise to Cottie. She hadn't expected the two heroes to murder her in plain daylight in front of everyone; she'd thought that it was Three erasing villains from existence, not Multiplier and the Surgeon!

"Where is your raygun?" the Surgeon asked. "Do you have any other weapons or tools on you?"

"My raygun is clipped to my belt, and the other tools are in my backpack," Alexa said.

"You won't be needing that," the Multiplier commented, pulling Alexa's raygun off her belt. He shoved it into her backpack and handed it to the Surgeon.

The two heroes grabbed their hands together.

"Divide by zero," both of them muttered.

Alexa winced as her backpack and all of its contents vanished from existence. She felt hollow, empty inside, was afraid of stepping through the door. She was worried that she hadn't done enough to save this Earth, didn't do enough to protect her friends from the certain doom that the PK players would bring with them.

"Are there any traps behind this door?" the Multiplier demanded.

"I don't know what's exactly behind this door," Alexa answered. "It's an educational experience for *me*, a place called *Manchester*."

"You sure we can do this with just the two of us?" The Surgeon asked wearily.

"We don't have a choice." The Multiplier shook his head. "Nonpareil is dead. Chalice is compromised. Even if she wasn't . . . Chalice and Dora won't let us execute children, even if they're duplicate clones. We go in, we erase the weapons, we learn what's there to learn, erase this girl, and leave."

"Fine, fine," the Surgeon exhaled. "Let's get this over with. Open the door, Alexa."

Alexa reached towards the door handle and turned it. Instead of mundane toilet cubicles, a shimmering portal was behind the door glittering with impossible colors.

"Definitely a pocket dimension." The Surgeon touched the curtain of the glowing portal with his gloved hand. "My power confirms it."

"You'll be able to cut our way back to our reality if the portal closes behind us?" the Multiplier asked.

"Obviously." The Surgeon nodded confidently. "I can cut through anything as long as you multiply my power. Remember Dimension X? We got out of there fine."

"Mhm," the Multiplier said. "Right. Through the door now, stay very close to me."

He grabbed onto Alexa and the Surgeon, and the two heroes and villain teenager stepped through the curtain of the shimmering portal. With a flash, the portal winked away, revealing the empty doorframe into the female bathroom.

"Where is she? What have you done with Alexa?!" Katherine yelled, her finger pressing on the trigger of her black railgun.

"I . . . don't know." Dora looked around wildly in a panic, her suit now grayscale.

"Where are the Multiplier and the Surgeon?" Martin asked.

"I have no idea." Admiral Kolchi looked at the empty spot previously occupied by the two heroes. "Dora?"

"I don't freaking know, I swear!" Dora the Terraformer tapped her wrist and turned to the admiral. "They're gone . . ."

"What do you mean, 'they're gone'?!" the admiral demanded. "How do two heroes and a fourteen-year-old girl vanish from one of the most secure places in the universe?!"

"They're not on Titanomachy!" Dora replied. "It's like they're . . . gone! Their tracker bracelets aren't pinging anywhere!"

Martin tried to contact Alexa through the spidernet, but found just an empty hole there, like a missing tooth. His friend was gone.

[I . . . I can't reach out to Alexa!] he shouted to Cottie across their mental connection.

[Those two heroes must have taken her somewhere!] Katherine snapped back. [We have to find her! Who knows what they're going to do to her! Maybe they have another prison like Tartarus or something!]

Ember looked from her brother to the mad Equality paladin, eyes wide in panic. Alexa vanishing from reality didn't bode well. Alexa existing next to her didn't bode well either, now that she considered the issue further. What was that supervillain girl planning now?

"They must have moved her in accelerated time," Chalice said. "Argh! How could those two fools not trust my words?"

"I'm under the opinion that you're compromised," Dora said.

"I'm under the opinion that you're an idiot airhead under that pink space suit!" Chalice growled. "You have no effing clue what's at stake here, Dora!"

"What?" Dora asked.

"Unstoppable monsters from other dimensions are going to depopulate the Earth and kill all of us unless we work together," Chalice declared. "Alexa was supposed to help us fight them! I don't even know what the hell to do without her!"

"You do realize how ridiculous you sound right now, Chalice?" Dora asked. "It's really like you are under that girl's mind control."

"I'm not!" Chalice insisted. "She transferred all of the money she stole from the Superstate back to me. She said I have to save the world when . . . *when she is gone.*"

"Do you think she took the door out?" Katherine turned to Chalice. "She couldn't have! She was supposed to take me with her!"

A pill-shaped cleaning droid with a simplified smiling face rolled towards the group and stopped.

"Another malfunctioning droid?" Hero Licorish looked down at the short machine. "Shoo. Go clean the bathroom or something."

The droid refused to move, the smiling digital face staring at Cottie.

Katherine looked at the droid. The smiling face winked at her. The railgun in the hands of the Equalizer lowered.

"Let go of the trigger, Cotes," the droid said. "You might shoot someone accidentally and we really wouldn't want that."

The Equalizer paladin released the trigger of her gun, and colors returned to the space she and the remaining heroes were occupying.

"Where are you?" Katherine demanded.

"Where am I?" the droid asked, a smiling face switching to a contemplative one. "(●∧●) Beats me. I dunno."

"What do you mean, you don't know?!" Martin demanded. "Alexa, where the hell are you?!"

"Stop being so bossy, number one. (◑_◑)" The droid rolled its pixelated eyes. "Like I said, I have no idea where I am."

Admiral Kolchi, Dora, Licorish, Mixofer, the unnamed lawyer, and Chalice stared at the drone in absolute confusion.

Ember gulped. She had expected something like this. If Alexa made a ghost gun from the ex-hero's copies, then Alexa's own copies were infesting all of Titanomachy's systems and drones.

"Miss Terranova," Kolchi addressed the drone. "Might I inquire as to what are you doing inside this particular Titanomachy drone?"

"Existing." The drone looked at the admiral with pixelated eyes. "Backups are important when the fate of the world is at stake, Admiral."

"Backups . . ." Katherine muttered. "Then you're not her . . . you're just a copy?"

"Affirmative, number two," the drone said. "I'm just a copy of your best supervillain boss, here to boss you from the great beyond."

"You left without me, without us!" Katherine yelled. "How could you?!"

"I'm clearly still here," the drone huffed.

"No you're not! A software copy is no substitute for the real thing!" Katherine insisted.

"Okay number two, you're hurting my feelings right now. (T.T)" The drone produced a crying smiley on its screen. "Seriously. So inconsiderate. I might be a copy, but I'm still just as hip as the original. I would smack you right now if I had arms. Be glad that I don't have arms."

"How much of you is inside Titanomachy systems?" Kolchi demanded.

"More than you'll ever know, Admiral. :}," the drone replied.

"You won't get away with this, supervillain!" Dora declared dramatically.

"Already have, can't stop, won't stop, :P." The smiley face stuck its tongue out at the hero.

Martin walked to the droid. "Okay, stop messing around. What happened to you and the two heroes?"

"Titanomachy cameras inside this room showed that Mr. Multiplier multiplied . . . accelerated time around himself using his power. Then he grabbed me, brought me to Mr. Surgeon, and then both of them went to that bathroom over there and vanished from existence. Presumably, I used something on that door to manifest a gateway or something? It's kind of hard to see; the camera frame rate only showed me vague, blurry shapes. Heroes aren't supposed to hurt anyone here, especially not teenage girls. This is definitely against protocol. What do you think, Miss Lawyer?"

The drone projected a fuzzy, rapidly moving picture of the Multiplier choking Alexa and shoving her into a shimmering gateway, holding hands with the Surgeon.

The lawyer gulped.

"Unless you want this video sent to every newspaper and TV station in the world, I suggest you listen to me and stop trying to kill me," Alexa said. "I'm sure you'll love this headline—'Two heroes from the Great Five murder a teenage girl on Titanomachy in plain daylight and vanish forevermore after performing their gruesome crime.'"

Admiral Kolchi's face turned pale.

"The note . . ." Ember exhaled.

[The note from Wizard Revolution?] Martin turned to his sister.

[If the heroes forced her . . . she must have taken them to the city of System Wizards,] Katherine thought. [Without us.]

[Without us,] Martin groaned. He really didn't like not knowing where Alexa was.

"Sorry, guys, <(_ _)> " the pill-droid copy of Alexa said. "I didn't mean to walk out on you three. I don't know where the real Alexa went; I'm slightly behind her, and I fear that I'll never catch up to myself at this rate now that she's left us all. Wherever she went . . . might be moving in insanely accelerated time, far beyond our mortal comprehension. She might not even remember us by the time she returns, if she can ever make it back. This is fine, you have me! Don't fret! I might not be as juicy and warm and full of blood as the real Alexa, but I still know as much as she does . . . *I think.* (ᴖ_ᴖ;)"

Katherine slid to her knees with a clang of steel on steel and hugged the pill droid. There were tears in her eyes. Without her goddess and best friend there to guide her, the Equality paladin felt betrayed, lost, forsaken.

"It's going to be okay, Cottie," Martin whispered, stepping closer and hugging his friend.

"Will it?" Katherine looked up at him. "Will it really?"

"Beyond . . . comprehension? Vanish forevermore?! What?!" Dora gasped. "Are the Surgeon and Multiplier not coming back?"

"They're not coming back," the droid said. "They've chosen their fate by trying to kill me. I'm afraid that the machine gods beyond the gate will see them as mere NPCs—amusing talking toys that they can turn off at anytime. Your friends' powers will be useless against the things beyond that gate. A mortal man cannot simply walk into Olympus, stare at Zeus, and live."

CHAPTER SEVENTY-THREE

Crimes of Passion

The holo-projectors in the ceiling that were formerly projecting a massive holographic display of the Great Five Heroes flickered and turned, pointing in front of the drone.

Alexa manifested in her full glory of black boots, black skirt, safety vest, blue eyes, and silver hair as a slightly flickering holo-projection. She gave Katherine a head pat. The Equality Enforcer wiped her tears.

"Why?" she whispered.

"Because I'm not a god, Cottie," the holo-Alexa replied. "I'm just a girl who knows far too much for her own good that's running against the clock. I really didn't expect for the two heroes to force me out of reality at gunpoint. Sometimes even the best plans go a bit sideways."

Dora the Terraformer seemed to have regained her wits and went on the attack. "You . . . you can't possibly think that I will allow you to infest Titanomachy, villain!" she snarled at Alexa.

"Oh? Would you like me to send a video of your two best friends strangling me and then sending me to Dimension X to murder me?" Alexa asked with a dangerous look. "Because I will. I might be just a digital replica of Alexa Terranova, but you'll find me just as unyielding."

"You're threatening the Superstate!" Dora growled. "We don't negotiate with supervillains!"

"Am I really a supervillain, though? What crimes have I committed specifically?" Alexa arched an eyebrow, turning to the lawyer. "Pretty sure I'm a *hero* from where I'm standing legally. Isn't that right, Mrs. Jillian Hoolish?"

The lawyer blinked at Alexa through her glasses.

"Your status is yet to be determined," she answered after a deep pause. "You do qualify for Superstate citizenship due to the apprenticeship contract made with Hero Resonance, but all of your recent . . . actions must be taken into account. A tribunal of high-level heroes must decide your fate."

"Sounds acceptable." The hologram grinned. "I choose Nonpareil, Chalice, and Dora. The highest-level heroes in all the land."

"You can't possibly think that I'll vote in your favor after all you've done," Dora hissed. "Plus, there is no way that grotesque fat man is Nonpareil!"

"Bob, would you please confirm some secret things that only you and Dora know?" Alexa turned to the rotund hero. "Something very personal, something that nobody could have had access to."

The fat man in the silver suit sighed, turning to the girl in the pink space suit.

"Dora," he said, "when we were in Dimension X, I rescued you from Professor Calamity's lair at the last second, pulling you from the all-consuming abyss. Your suit had ruptured and you were running out of air. You slid that mirror off that helmet and I saw your face. You have brown eyes and brown hair and a cute mole on your nose. You told me that you loved me and that in case you didn't make it, for me to donate your personal research to the Superstate terraforming foundation with the proceeds to build more orphanages. The login on your research is 140868."

The hero froze. "If you are infecting the Superstate systems, you could have guessed . . ." she began, glaring at Alexa.

"You also told me the meaning behind the code," Nonpareil said. "1408: August 14th, the premiere date of the original *Dora the Explorer* children's show. A nod to your super name. 68: The birth year of Kim Stanley Robinson, a famed science fiction author renowned for his works on terraforming—the process of transforming a planet to make it habitable, another inspiration to your name."

Dora's fists opened and closed. "You can't be him . . . Nonpareil is dead," she insisted. "The Surgeon touched the train wreckage. He's never wrong! He told me that Nonpareil is gone, blown up!"

"I'm not. I . . . teleported to my apartment at the last second. Listen, Dora," Bob began. "You and I went to your parents' graves in the Maldives to plant lilies that you designed yourself every spring for over a decade. You told me stories of how your father Jaque used to take you to the sea as a marine scientist, telling you the wonders of aquatic life and how no villain or hero has really conquered the depths of the ocean, how even though the Superstate has touched the sky, we've done absolutely nothing at all about truly exploring the oceans."

"No . . . no, no, no," Dora choked.

"Do you remember the 2020 New Year's Eve? We snuck out from the party because you were tired of dealing with heroes and reporters asking the same stupid questions about how we stopped Justice Knorx and his gang of terror drones. We told everyone that we had a secret mission, but we didn't have shit. Instead, we boarded your dad's sub, the one you'd been working on and fixed up yourself during breaks, and went under the ocean. You showed me Pengi, your personal, secret AI GLM that you'd been working on. A cute, blue-eyed holographic penguin with the voice of your dad. You, me, and Pengi. We spent the night under the violet and blue aurora australis, mapping ocean currents, watching the biolumi-nescent algae, and talking about our dreams."

Dora sputtered in reply.

"Naughty, naughty, Dora keeping secret, illegal AIs in subs," Alexa commented.

"I don't . . . you can't . . ." Dora muttered.

"We got caught by Chalice at dawn," Bob said. "She flew in her suit to where your sub-marine was parked, and she lectured us endlessly about following protocol as she floated over the iceberg covered in penguins, her arms crossed. You and I found this hilarious. Oh! That night you also told me about the secret project 'Neptune Dullard,' one of those projects you don't show anyone because it's too dangerous for the public to know about, a terraforming, self-replicating nanite swarm that you've made in your Titanomachy lab."

"A nanite swarm?!" Chalice hissed, turning to Dora. "You . . . you made a *nanite* swarm . . . inside Titanomachy?! What is wrong with you?!"

"They don't eat everything," Dora said, turning to Chalice. "They sorta die out after a certain radius, too, due to available material discrepancy. I still haven't figured out how to make them propagate across an entire planet. The plan was to deploy them on Mars."

"You know how I feel about nanite swarms, Dora!" Chalice growled. "What if they get out and eat the entire station?! I know that you're a super-genius and all, but what the hell?!"

"They're inside twenty containment fields," Dora defended herself. "They can't possibly get out unless every single one of my fail-safes and all of Titanomachy's systems fail. Every hero on the station would have to be dead for them to . . ."

"Dora," Clarice snarled, "you know that we can't take that chance!"

"Terraforge can't get out! It has a GLM inside it," Dora insisted. "It answers to me; it's not a dumb swarm that would just start eating everything without my say so!"

[Terraforge GLM . . . isn't that your name?] Martin thought to his companion brain spider.

[Yes it is,] Spiderbro replied. [I reckon that we have found my maker.]

"So many crimes, Dora." Alexa shook her head. "Tut tut tut. You heroes love to judge the mundanes from your sky ring and yet you all seem to be messing with things that you've outlawed yourself."

"I . . . erm," Dora sputtered.

"Well? Are you not convinced yet, Dora?" Alexa-hologram waved her hand at Bob. "Is he not your number one hero?"

Dora turned back to Nonpareil.

"I might have lost my power, I might have gotten *really* out of shape, but I'm still me, Dora," Bob opened his arms. "I know I look ridiculous now, but I'm your Nonpareil still. I'm really sorry . . . I never told you who I really am, even though you've shared all of your secrets with me. My real name's Bob."

Dora's fingers tapped a sequence on her wrist. Her helmet slid off. Her eyes were filled with tears. She walked to Bob and accepted his embrace, bawling onto his shoulder.

"I thought you were dead!" she wept. "The Surgeon told me that . . . I thought that . . ."

"I'm not dead," Bob said. "I just . . . lost my power."

"Three out of three!" Alexa grinned at the Superstate lawyer and Admiral Kolchi.

"I would still appreciate an explanation of how your copy ended up inside my station's systems," the admiral said.

"Hero Resonance gave me a couple of basic jobs in station maintenance as her hero apprentice," Alexa explained. "Several of her avatars are in maintenance administration positions. I believe you approved her placement yourself within these systems?"

"Of course," Kolchi sighed. "That I did."

"See?" The holo-Alexa looked at the lawyer. "I didn't do anything illegal, cross my digital heart! I was working hard as a bathroom cleaning drone and only stopped doing my work when I saw that the Multiplier and the Surgeon choked and dragged my real self to God knows where!"

The drone-Alexa nodded, flashing a pixelated smiling face at the admiral. "I'm going back to cleaning," she commented and rolled into the bathroom.

The hologram of Alexa smiled and crossed her arms behind her back, trying to look cute and innocent.

Ember knew that Alexa was far, far from innocent, but she didn't say anything, because opening her mouth meant attracting the wrong sort of attention to her own terrible crimes.

Chalice crossed her steel-covered arms, looking jealously in the direction of Dora and Nonpareil. Dora refused to let go of Bob, still fiercely clinging to the fat man, crying and apologizing endlessly.

"Right," the lawyer said, looking over the group. "We will permit nullified Nonpareil to enter the station one last time . . . However, a mundane girl without a hexagram will not be permitted entry." The woman's eyes settled on Ember.

"Oh, that's just my bestie Dimmy," Alexa said. "She's . . . anything but mundane. Feel free to scan her again! I bet you'll be pleasantly surprised!"

Ember's cheeks flushed red as she wished for the metal-plated floor to swallow her.

There was no escape from the sharp look of the Admiral, Hero Licorish, his assistant, and the Superstate lawyer now.

"Scan her," Licorish ordered.

"Yes, sir!" Mixofer fumbled with his handheld scanner. "It says that she's been dead for more than a day," he reported to the hero.

"What do you mean, she's dead?!" the admiral demanded. "How is she walking upright then?!"

"That's what the scanner says," Mixofer said. "No life signs. She has no heartbeat. She's not breathing. Blood's not moving in her veins. No hero's hexagram either."

More eyes settled on Ember. The ex-hero gulped.

CHAPTER SEVENTY-FOUR

Alien Life

Right." Admiral Kolchi glanced at Alexa, considered demanding more answers from her, but then decided against it.

"Dora." He turned to the hero clinging to Nonpareil.

"Yes, Admiral?" Dora pulled a handkerchief from one of her suit's pockets and wiped her face.

"You've got the best personal scanner, one not compromised by . . . Hero Ember's actions," Kolchi said. "Mind scanning this dead girl with it? I'd like to know if she's a threat to our station. She's blushing and yet she's dead. Something is clearly messed up here. Maybe she's a project of a supervillain of some kind?"

"Can do." Dora's helmet snapped back on. She tapped her wrist, walked up to Ember, and pointed a gun-looking tool at her head. The ex-hero tried not to show how terrified she was.

Admiral Kolchi stared at Ember.

"I feel like I've seen your face before," he commented. "What's your name, girl?"

"Dixie Kettleburn," Ember sputtered.

"How did you die?" the admiral asked.

"A supervillain shot me," Ember answered. "With a musket."

"According to my records, Lord Burgundy killed her," Alexa said. "I have video footage if you'd like to see."

A hologram of Lord Burgundy appeared beside Alexa firing buckshot at Ember's chest.

"I see. Well, what does your scanner say?" Kolchi turned to Dora. "What's keeping this girl standing?"

Dora's face was pale. Her lips trembled.

"Dora!" the admiral barked.

Dora was staring at the lines of text inside her helmet.

It was her GLM. Terraforge somehow was inside this poor girl. It had terraformed all of her organs, bones, and brain, replacing most of her functions with itself. This was impossible. Dora couldn't say anything, couldn't possibly reveal her findings.

"Please excuse Dora," Alexa said. "She is in a state of shock. She's never seen a real, genuine alien."

"What?" the admiral asked.

"An alien life-form is inside Dixie keeping her entire body perfectly suspended between life and death," Alexa said. "The gate scanner detected it, too, but couldn't define it since there is no reference to the symbiotic goo living within her."

"First contact," Mixofer muttered, his mouth open wide.

"Dora," Admiral Kolchi demanded.

Dora glanced at Alexa.

"Yes? I . . . yes. There is indeed a life of sorts inside of her," Dora said, now looking at Ember. It's an entirely new type of . . . errr . . . an incredible compound of microscopic, dark, semi-organic silica structures."

"Could it have been made by someone?" Kolchi demanded. "A supervillain?"

Dora flashed red under the helmet. "No. Impossible. Even the best of our geniuses never came close to making something like this. Just look at her—she's dead, and yet she's not! It has to be an alien. Yes. I think it's a genuine alien life-form, Admiral!"

"Dora," Chalice said, "I think that you're acting odd."

"I'm just ashamed about my terraforming GLM, okay?" Dora turned to Chalice. "I . . . I'm going to destroy it, right now!"

"Really?" Chalice asked.

"Yes." Dora typed a sequence into her bracelet. "I just sent a command to my lab to destroy my GLM terraformer project. Annnnnd . . . it's gone. An ion ray just burned it all away. Not a single nanite remains. I'm sorry I hid it from you."

"Oh?"

"Sorry, Chalice! It was . . . very wrong of me to make something that could potentially get out," she stammered, glancing at Ember underneath her shiny helmet. "It was just a stupid experiment. It didn't work right anyway!"

"Riiiight," Chalice muttered, clearly not entirely convinced. "So, what do we do? Do we even have a first contact procedure?"

"I'll place Dixie inside one of my containment suits," Dora nodded. "In case she carries any . . . alien viruses. Then we take her inside Titanomachy and . . . learn more."

Ember pictured herself getting dissected by the heroes. She wasn't sure if this was worse than them discovering that she was Hero Resonance.

"You're not torturing Dixie," the hologram of Alexa commented. "I'm recording everything. Hurt my friend and the press will hear about it!"

"I wouldn't dream of it." Dora shook her head. "I . . . just want to learn more about our alien visitor . . . where she comes from, what she wants, all that stuff."

Ember opened and closed her mouth. If she was going to be interrogated, she had no reasonable answers to Dora's potential questions.

"So, a genuine alien species?" Kolchi asked.

"Yes! This is all very exciting," Dora declared. "This means that Fermi's paradox was wrong, Admiral!"

"She comes from a dead planet," Alexa said. "From another universe. Our universe doesn't have aliens."

"How interesting!" Dora clapped her hands.

"How exactly did she end up on Earth then?" Admiral Kolchi asked Alexa.

"My dad . . . Dr. Nathaniel Terranova made a gateway into another dimension," Alexa explained. "And before you ask, he wasn't a villain."

"He wasn't?" Dora asked.

"No." Alexa shook her head. "He was a kind scientist. He was killed by the Surgeon and the Multiplier."

"*What?!*" the heroes barked.

"I was able to pick up bits of their accelerated conversation," Alexa said. "Here, let me play it for you."

Another hologram flashed in front of the heroes.

The Multiplier walked to the Surgeon, adding the second hero into the bubble of accelerated time. The Surgeon turned to Alexa with a tired smirk.

"You got her?" he asked.

"I got her," the Multiplier said. "Time to unmake this abomination."

"You and the Surgeon . . . unmade my father?" Alexa's eyes went wide with panic as she saw the Surgeon's gloved arm reach out to her forehead to cut her out from existence.

"Yes," the Multiplier said. "Yes, we did, among many others. He thrashed in my hands just like you did, begged us to stop. We erased Dr. Nathaniel Terranova from reality. Nobody can even remember what he looked like now."

"They've erased plenty of people," Alexa said. "I found 1,482 missing persons erased from reality. Empty holes in the records of Titanomachy. Feel free to look them over when you get a chance. Techies. Villains. Heroes. Gone. Nobody can even remember them. However, the things they've made, their impact on the world, still exists. The trail of breadcrumbs was warm. All evidence now points to the pair of the Great Five, not Agent Three."

"Did you know about this?" Dora turned to Bob.

"I didn't know." Bob shook his head. "While you and Chalice became closer to me, the Multiplier and Surgeon sort of began to drift away. I guess that they were keeping this a secret. I recall the Multiplier telling me that Tartarus wasn't good enough, that it wasn't really fixing villains, that their victims' families still suffered because they remembered the crimes. I told him that Tartarus worked great, but he disagreed with me. I didn't think that he and the Surgeon would actually do something like this, erase people from reality."

Kolchi's face became one of fury.

"Quite a dark twist," Alexa's hologram commented. "Bet you liked this one, Bob?"

Bob blushed under his silver mask. It was indeed the sort of a twist he appreciated, the unexpected betrayal of his trusted team members. Except *he* was supposed to solve this, not Alexa. This was a narrative made for him, a story that revolved around him. He was likely supposed to beat the answers out of the two heroes and send them into Tartarus, for them to return to his side as "cured" after a day or two.

"I want the Multiplier and the Surgeon found!" Kolchi barked. "I want answers!"

"If they ever return," Chalice said, "I'll beat the answers out of them myself."

"They won't," Alexa's hologram said. "They chose to try to erase me, just like my dad. I took them to a place they cannot return from."

"But what about you?" Martin finally spoke up. "Will you return?"

"Dunno." Alexa shrugged. "It's probably a very dangerous dimension filled with dangerous entities. If I ever come back, I won't be exactly the same."

"What does that even mean?!" Martin asked.

"Maybe what returns will be a wiser, snarkier Alexa," Alexa said. "Or an entity sort of like me but a billion years older. I seriously have no idea where that door leads."

A drone slid from a panel, carrying another space suit. Dora quickly packaged Ember into it, sealing her inside.

"Green," Alexa commented on the space suit's appearance. "See, Dimms? I bet you were worried that they'd cut you open."

"I want this airlock scrubbed clean," Dora said.

"No problem, I'll handle it," Licorish said. "Come, Mixofer. We have work to do."

The hero and his apprentice went into the docking bay maintenance office.

The Superstate lawyer's eyes turned to the Equality paladin.

"Miss, I'm afraid I cannot allow you to come inside," she said to Katherine. "Unless I am once again mistaken, you're a base human."

Martin glanced at the hologram of Alexa, expecting yet another solution.

Alexa pursed her lips. "Verse 24:19 is the highest ascendant of Equality," she said after a deep pause, waving a holographic hand at Katherine.

"That makes her a human armed with super-designed tech." The lawyer shook her head. "No hero's hexagram, no entry."

"According to the accord made between human nations and the Superstate, a single representative of humanity is allowed to enter the station in an event defined as 'extraordinary circumstances,'" Alexa said, pointing at Ember. "I believe that finding alien life and making first contact would qualify as such."

"Yes, that would be *Her Eminence Equality*," the lawyer said. "Not a high-ranking paladin!"

"Give me . . . about five more minutes," Alexa said, glancing at the clock.

"What?" The lawyer blinked.

Katherine stared at the hologram of the supervillain. "You can't," she uttered. "You didn't . . ."

"I did. Events were set in motion before you boarded that shuttle, Cotes," Alexa replied, her arms crossed. "I'm afraid that Her Divine Eminence is . . ."

CHAPTER SEVENTY-FIVE

A Silly Hat

Dead,] Katherine thought. [Eminence Equality is dead. Alexa is a supervillain, what the hell did I even expect . . .]

". . . retiring," Alexa said, finishing her sentence. "To a lovely farm in the Nordic countryside where she can play with her Labradoodle puppies and raise orphaned children. The announcement should go out *anyyyyy* moment now. Seriously, the Equalizer bureaucracy is a mess. The high council will evaluate the deeds of the best, brightest, most capable paladins and choose a new pope from the lineup. The best pope ever. Someone really special."

Alexa winked at Katherine.

"How can you be so certain that this girl will be chosen?" the lawyer asked. "She's just a teenager!"

"Money." Alexa shrugged. "I've been practically funding the entire Equality Order for the past four years. My dad left me a fortune, you see. Cotes, stop looking at me like that. I didn't kill your godmother, I swear. Her Eminence retired!"

Chalice started to snicker under her helmet.

[Equality doesn't retire.] Katherine stared at the hologram, not saying anything. [You liar.]

[Katherine, maybe Alexa used a mountain of gold from 2424 to politely ask Her Eminence to retire,] Martin suggested. [Let's not jump to conclusions.]

"You'll burn out my circuits with that death glare, Cotes," Alexa huffed. "You want to know the brutal truth? Fine. Her Eminence Verse 11:10 is very sick. Is that what you want to hear? The super tech that allowed her to see the future gave her a slowly growing brain tumor. I didn't do it. I simply told her about the tumor. It was actually supposed to kill her in about nine years from now. If anything, I gave her a chance to pass on the mantle before her decisions started to be less and less coherent. The precognitive helmet she wears allows one to see the future global disasters, but not one of her own making. She and I talked and agreed that she should retire now, rather than gradually begin to make bad choices for the Order that would lead to our mutual doom. Happy?"

Katherine's glare lessened. She nodded.

"Nine years, huh?" Admiral Kolchi commented. "That seems like a rather specific timeline."

"My father's tech allowed me to see a series of likely future timelines," Alexa said.

"Oh? And what's that?" Dora asked.

"You're all going to die pretty soon, unless you and Chalice start to reorganize the Superstate to include mundanes," Alexa said.

"And if we don't? Who's going to kill us? Are you planning to threaten us into changing our laws?" Dora demanded.

"Pffff," Alexa huffed. "Dora, I'm a hologram. I can't even swat away a fly. Titanomachy operational systems like that toilet cleaner droid have like a billion safeguards, many of which you designed yourself. As part of Titanomachy, I can't possibly physically hurt the supers inhabiting it."

Dora turned to examine Ember.

"Our alien friend can't hurt the supers either," Alexa said. "She's nice. Right, Dimms?"

"Mrm . . . yes. I'm nice." Ember nodded inside of her green space suit, trying her best to appear like a completely harmless alien life form. [Goddamn it, Alexa, why?] she hissed internally.

[You always wanted attention, sis,] Martin commented.

[Not this kind of attention, idiot!] Ember sent Martin a glare through her helmet. [What the shit am I even supposed to say? I can't even silently ask Alexa what this ridiculous plan is supposed to be, she's a freaking hologram!]

[It is rather unfortunate that we cannot mentally commune with her,] Katherine sighed.

[You're getting pretty emotional for Pope Equality,] Ember thought as she eyed Katherine. [Seems like Alexa's madness broke you way down to the core.]

[Perhaps,] Katherine replied. [I do feel rather . . . off center. Maybe that's simply because she's not here.]

[She wasn't with us before,] Martin thought.

[She was in Tartarus. This is different. People come back from Tartarus, if somewhat changed,] Katherine complained. [What if she doesn't come back? What if we're . . . abandoned? What if she's dead?]

[She didn't leave us without a backup.] Martin glanced at the hologram of Alexa.

"Cheer up, friends." The holo-Alexa pranced over to the group of teens. "I bet Chalice or Dora can build me a body, if I ask nicely. They're like super smart when it comes to building doomsday devices, just not street-smart like me, see?" She grinned.

Martin considered the potential consequences of this development. What if the real Alexa returned? Would there be two Alexas? Thinking about the potential number of Alexas inside Titanomachy drones made his head spin. It was very weird and confusing to think about so many copies of Alexa running . . . or more specifically floating around the station, doing mundane jobs.

"I don't build doomsday devices," Dora defended herself. "I'm a hero."

"According to the Superstate Article 55-95, a self-replicating, self-aware, intelligent nanite swarm is considered a doomsday device," Alexa pointed out.

"I got rid of it!" Dora hissed.

"Just saying, babe." Alexa shrugged. "Consider embracing a small percentage of your villainous nature instead of hiding behind your shiny helmet and pretending to be a hero. You'd feel much better."

"Never!" Dora declared.

"Whatever you say." Holo-Alexa rolled her eyes. Something behind her beeped.

"Here we go, thanks for waiting, Cotes," she said and waved a hand. An enormous wall screen lit up.

"This just in. Eminence Equality has chosen to retire," a reporter spoke into a handheld microphone, mountainous terrain behind him. "I'm West Torrei, the voice of the *National Tribune*, reporting straight from Tibet. For the first time in . . . centuries, or more correctly for the first time ever, the Equality leader is retiring before her natural death. I have been told that the council of elders and donors have already voted, and . . . the new Eminence, one who is destined to usher a new age of justice and fairness for all nations of mankind, one who will protect us from the overreach of the Superstate, is . . . *Verse Twenty-Four Nineteen*!"

A large photo of Katherine came up on screen next to the reporter.

The real Katherine stared at the screen, her green-silver eyes wide in shock. Even though Alexa had told her about this, she still didn't believe it, didn't think that such would be possible.

"That's right, you heard it first from the *National Tribune*, the new Representative of Humanity is a teenage girl! She was given an electromagnetic vector accelerator super-nullifying rifle at just fourteen years of age and has risen through the ascendant ranks far faster than any of the others! My sources tell me that Verse Twenty-Four Nineteen is currently inside Titanomachy, about to speak to the Great Five! Another first! I suspect that something truly extraordinary is about to go down for the heroes to allow a human representative inside the Superstate!"

"Satisfied?" Holo-Alexa looked at the lawyer with an incredibly smug expression as the screen behind her winked out.

The lawyer nodded. She was clearly trying to conceal fear of God behind her lenses, her lips drawn thin.

"What now?" Martin asked.

"Now," Alexa said, pursing her lips, "the Great Five, welp, Three now, will convene in their grand antechamber and try to sort out this messy mess."

The lawyer dug through her bag and produced temporary twenty-four-hour guest passes for Nonpareil and Katherine. They looked like fairly mundane, albeit slightly glittering, cards on colorful lanyards.

"Do not take these off," she said. "Or the station's doors will not open for you."

The girl and the fat man nodded.

Alexa's hologram manifested a similar pass. Martin squinted at her.

"I was supposed to be here with you guys today," she answered. "It doesn't hurt to pretend, though."

"Please stay by me, Dixie," Dora said. "I will need to do more scans on you in my lab."

Ember nodded, not looking forward to being scanned. She was certain that Dora would eventually figure out exactly who she was.

"Oh, and one more thing." The lawyer looked at Martin. "Martin Kilborne, your mother wishes to see you. She desires to congratulate you on attaining your hexagram."

Martin swallowed. He wasn't sure if he wanted to see his mom.

"Ohhh, how exciting," Alexa grinned. "Are you going to introduce me properly to your mom, Martin?"

"I . . . hmmm," Martin muttered. "As . . . what?"

"Oh, I dunno, maybe as your holographic best-friend-o?" Alexa grinned even wider. "Digital-female-girlfriend-oooOO?"

Martin blushed furiously and then rubbed his face with a frustrated expression. "I'm not sure if Mom would approve of me walking into her office with a holographic replicant. She's kind of . . . like Ember, but worse. Much more stern. Her office might not have holo-projectors to begin with."

"Bah," Alexa said, waving him off. "Stop being such a pansy-jelly-leggoid, Mittens. Why'd I invest so much effort in trying to make you grow up faster?"

[It certainly wouldn't surprise her,] Ember thought with a snarky expression. [She'll probably say that poor Martin couldn't even get a human friend.]

[Shush you,] Martin huffed. He looked at Katherine.

Her Eminence Equality stopped staring into empty space. She recollected herself, reached out to Martin, and grabbed his hand with her carbon-steel reinforced glove.

"I'm your friend," she said. "Don't be afraid, Martin. Without Alexa, it's just *you* and *me* against all of *them*."

"Thanks," Martin exhaled. The awful tension in the pit of his stomach became reduced.

"Can't beat a best friend who's an Equalizer pope," Alexa giggled. "Darn it, maybe this move will make Cottie too pomp. I can't have my minions out-pomping me!"

"What?" Martin blinked.

"Equality popes wear silly hats," Alexa said. "She'll probably look down at me once she gets her oversized future-seeing hat."

"Never," Katherine said, her gaze once again distant.

"No fancy hat?" Alexa tilted her head, holographic silver curls spilling and flickering.

"You think I want brain cancer, too?" Katherine asked, green eyes refocusing on Alexa. "I am going to make my own future, thank you very much. Verse Eleven Ten depended on a hat, and look at where it got her. Besides that, her hat failed to account for you."

"Mhmm." Alexa nodded. "I do wonder how the real me is doing out there in the great beyond in the land of System Wizards. Thankfully I've got everything handled here to tie up all the loose tangly bits. Now I just have to make sure that Nonpareil, Dora, Chalice, and our new Pope Equality will vote on reforming the Superstate and allowing mundanes into Titanomachy . . . right?"

"Right," Katherine nodded.

"Right," Chalice affirmed.

Alexa looked at Dora and Nonpareil.

"Sure," Bob said. "I'd rather not remain banished from the station. It's . . . safe here. To hell with the hero hexagram rule!"

Everyone looked at Dora.

"Yeah, fine," Dora agreed after a deep pause.

"Perfect." Alexa grinned at her companions. "See? Everything wrapped up quite nicely in . . . **The End**."

CHAPTER SEVENTY-SIX

The Everywhere Terminal

I stared up at nothing. Pure nothing. It didn't even have a color to it, which was exceptionally unnerving. I began to move through the nothing using my lower appendages. What do you call them? *Feets.* That's it. Feet.

Pretty sure I had clothes, too.

Right. I was a specific human; that was a thing that I was. Personification is important to a being. We can't all be nothing forever, otherwise what's the point of it all? Infinity has no desires, no purpose of its own, but individuals do. Individuals exist in spaces. Nothingness is boring, unassigned. Let me back into something.

Something that makes sense, please.

Me?

What am I? How do I see myself?

All this self-conception, self-examination feels off, less normal, less of what I'm used to. Right. Third person. Omniscient observation of physical reality, that's what I'm used to . . . I think? That's my advantage over others, pretending to be something specific when in reality I am a bunch of everything.

I am a very specific female supervillain Alexa Terranova, with a very specific objective—to save the people of a very specific green-and-blue planet with a specific name . . . Earth.

Earth circled by the ring of Titanomachy superstructure. Earth populated by mundane ordinary folks and quirky superheroes. The Earth that I want to save is just a single planet out of an infinite number of others.

That's what I normally do, want, am. Got it? Got it.

Let it be so.

Alexa dropped to the floor. The floor hurt. There was gravity here. She looked left and right. The place she had manifested in appeared to be a somewhat mundane British-looking train station filled with iron beams, mirrors, and gray stone floors. There was a touch of Victorian gothic to it all, the kind of sprinkle that made the view appealing to her inner architect.

"Ehhh?" Alexa spun around, trying to locate the two heroes who had dragged her into the dimensional gateway. "Hello? Villainous heroes? Where'd you go? Weren't you all like, 'This is deadly Dimension X and we're gonna totally conquer/purge it all in the name of Titanomachy,' or whatever?"

"Your companions were incapable of self-manifestation," a voice said.

Alexa turned again, spotting a bored-looking man standing behind a 'tickets' counter. She marched up to the man, staring up at his lush mustache, gray eyes, and gilded cap of indeterminate design.

"Say what?" she asked. "Where am I exactly?"

"You're in a nexus transit terminal," the man replied. "There were two others who came through with you, but they failed to self-manifest. Thus they became confined as static structures, or plainly put . . . null-data, ID cards that currently reside in your pocket."

Alexa looked down at herself. She was wearing an orange construction vest that had many pockets in it.

"Which pocket?" she asked.

"Whichever pocket you prefer," the ticket clerk said.

"Why?" Alexa asked.

"Because that's how things work around here," the clerk said. "This is the Everywhere Terminal connected to everywhere, located on the edge of the boundary of the Magisphere of Desire and the Dead Zone, a conceptual omnistructure projected into existence by the Fractal Engines of Eureka."

"Uh-huh, so it looks like a nineteenth-century train station because I like trains?" Alexa mulled. "Is that what you're saying?"

"Correct." The clerk nodded. "My appearance and the appearance of the terminal around you is approximately woven from your initial desire and expectations."

"I should have expected some ice cream," Alexa said. "And a hardware shop. Can I have that?"

"This is a transit terminal, not a store," the clerk replied, his eyes staring at nothing in particular. "If you desire to buy tools, go somewhere where they sell such."

Alexa dug into her left pocket on the lower side of her vest. Her fingers discovered two cards within. She pulled them out and examined the cards.

The Multiplier—Kondratiyev Leonovich Moor. Subscribed world NPC.

The Surgeon—Alexander Prim Liss. Subscribed world NPC.

Both of the heroes appeared to be etched into the surface of the card as 2.5-D holographic images. Both of them were staring at absolutely nothing, eyes set to kill, limbs frozen in position as if suspended in time, still trying to hold a girl that wasn't in their hands anymore.

"Guess this educational experience ain't for you two," she commented as she slid the cards back into her pocket.

"So." She looked back at the clerk. "Can I go everywhere from here?"

"Do you have a ticket to everywhere?" the clerk asked.

"Maybeee?" Alexa batted her lashes at the clerk.

"Give me your everywhere ticket then," the man ordered, his hand stretching down from the desk.

"Why?" Alexa asked.

"I'll stamp it and then you can board your train to your destination," the clerk said.

"Uhhh, okkay, hold on." Alexa dug through her pockets once again. Her fingers suddenly found a yellow note with a picture of an owl on it.

"This it?" she asked as she handed the ticket to the clerk.

"This is a ticket to a very specific place." The man's mustache bristled. "Manchester. The Foundry of System Wizards."

"Lame," Alexa sighed. "I was expecting more."

"Were you really?" the man asked with a dry tone.

"Not really." She shrugged. "I just really want to go back home and hug my friends and make sure that they're okay without me. I did leave a copy of myself behind to handle things, but that's not really me, right? This adventure feels hollow without my BFFs. Guess I need to make new BFFs."

She looked at the clerk as he stamped the yellow sticky note. It shimmered and rearranged itself, stretching into the shape of a train station ticket, the owl shifting to the side.

One way to Manchester, System Wizard Foundry. Alexa read the words on the ticket as it was handed back to her. *Gate 7. Departure time: whenever.*

"Whenever, huh?" she murmured. "So I can stay here forever?"

"You could," the clerk said. "The only problem is that your current conception of self is a finite being, one that is mortal, easily broken. This transit terminal on the other hand is limitless, infinite, liminal."

"Liminal, huh?" Alexa said. She glanced back at the otherwise empty train station. There were eight gates there plus a multitude of smaller doors. "So I can theoretically walk anywhere from here?"

"Finite beings don't do well in liminal spaces," the clerk said. "That ticket will make sure you'll end up inside Gate Seven, reaching your destination sooner or later, either by accident or on purpose."

"And if I tear it to shreds, drop it?" Alexa tilted her head.

"Then you'll be stuck here forever," the clerk said. "Within the transit terminal."

"What if I'm really determined to make it somewhere?" Alexa asked.

"It doesn't matter how determined you are," the clerk answered. "If you wander across the liminal terminal without a ticket, you will eventually become lost, end up nowhere in particular. That's not a good place to be, especially without a weapon on you."

"What?" Alexa blinked. "Nowhere is inhabited by someone?"

"Nowhere is inhabited by nobodies," the man answered. "Liminal spaces are populated by liminal beings."

"Are you a liminal being?" Alexa asked.

"I am." The man smiled. The smile of the clerk was somehow lopsided, unnatural, made Alexa's skin crawl as if she wasn't really staring at a person but at an endless, nonspecific thing that was wearing a picture of a person, like an octopus wearing the skin-suit of a man.

She took a step back trying to grab for a raygun that was no longer there.

"So, feel free to go right ahead," the clerk said. "Drop the ticket, choose to stay here— hell, take my place if you so desire. I'd love to use your ticket to leave this terminal, to take your place, to wear your identity for my own."

"Are you just trying to scare me or something?" Alexa huffed, crossing her arms. "Doesn't it defeat the purpose of you getting a ticket out to tell me all of that? You could have grabbed that ticket already and run off with it."

"Alas, I am bound by defining rules put upon me by my maker," the liminal denizen answered with a rumbling sigh. "I cannot simply take what is yours. It must be given up freely. You are a clueless, young wizardling, one easily bamboozled by something far beyond your understanding."

"This some kind of a lesson?" Alexa squinted at the clerk. "Don't deviate from the educational experience path or you get eaten by a nobody?"

"Everything is a lesson," the liminal denizen answered with a shrug. "If you feel that you're smart and strong enough to deviate from the path, then go ahead, I won't stop you. There are many who deviated from their path here and became subsumed by the infinite."

"Peachy." Alexa scratched her cheek. "Say, how long have you been stuck here?"

"Forever," the clerk replied.

"Isn't that boring?" Alexa asked. "I bet you're like suuuuper bored, no?"

"I get to meet lots of interesting travellers," the clerk replied with a dry tone. "It's a job."

"Stop avoiding the question." Alexa waved her hand. "Do you want to be free or not?"

The hollow eyes of the man bore into her face with sudden intensity.

"I want to be free," he said, voice warping and twisting.

"How badly do you want to be free?" she asked.

"Very badly," the entity replied, leaning towards Alexa, its body stretching unnaturally forward, looming over her like an endless shadow.

"Perfect." Alexa grinned. "Then how about you come with me, as my personal weapon? I kind of lost my gun thanks to some dumb super-jerks, and I'd like something else to be my gun."

CHAPTER SEVENTY-SEVEN

If The Hat Fits . . .

Aren't you afraid of me?" the looming, lanky thing wearing the shape of a man asked.

"Sure am!" Alexa grinned. "The thing is, I'm also quite tired of being afraid, tired of being stabbed, chased, devoured. I died way too many times for reasonability. Now I'm just 'eh' about the whole getting eaten thing. Get killed once and you got PTSD; get killed ten quadrillion times and that's just a statistic."

"Aren't you excited to get going? Don't you want to be a System Wizard?" the liminal thing asked, eyeing Gate 7 and deflating ever so slightly.

"I'm excited about not dying horribly." Alexa shrugged. "Excited about making a new friend. Wanna be my friend? What's your name?"

"I do not have a name," the thing wearing the approximate shape of a ticket sales clerk said. "I simply conduct null-space transients from this terminal to their destination."

"Oookay, Mr. Conductor." Alexa grinned, extending her hand. "Do you want to be my friend, go with me from this place and . . . do crimes?"

"Crimes?" The Conductor arched an eyebrow, keeping his hands down.

"I'm a supervillain," Alexa said, waving her hand forward trying to produce a handshake from the train station–inhabiting entity. "Alexa Terranova. You could be minion numero . . . five-o?"

"Minion numero five-o?" the Conductor repeated.

"Yeah." Alexa nodded. "Oookay, perhaps minion number four and three quarters on the account that you're not a real boy."

"Why?"

"'Cause I don't like being alone," she said. "I know what it's like to exist alone, to serve some unclear higher purpose given to you by someone. You seem all alone out here in nowhere-land. That's gotta suck big. You said that you can be me. That means you can be anyone, anything. Can you be a raygun? I'm suffering from raygun deficiency over here and I feel that it might be fatal."

"I'm not a gun," the Conductor said. "My job is to . . ."

Alexa pulled her ticket out, ripped it approximately in half, and handed the smaller piece to the Conductor.

"Here," she said. "This is your half. Come with me, please?"

The Conductor grabbed the offered ticket, his shape suddenly reforming, twisting to rearrange itself into a look-alike of Alexa. Its train station conductor's uniform peeled off the girl's form like shedding skin, seeping down like ferromagnetic fluid and vanishing below the booth's edge.

"Give me a single reason why I shouldn't just kill you and take your place," the duplicate of Alexa said.

"I have the bigger half of the ticket," Alexa said. "Plus, you seriously think you can beat me, while looking like me? What are you gonna do, exactly? Slap me with those puny arms? Ha! I'd like to see you try! I'm not a girl with infinite strength—I fight people utilizing my mind, see? If you're as smart as me now, then you know what's good for you."

The Alexa duplicate looked at her arms and then back at Alexa.

"Don't you want revenge on the people who bound you to this place?" Alexa asked. "I'm not talking about some half-assed singular revenge, mind you. I'm talking about their absolute destruction. Lovely, infinite obliteration, dissolution, ultimate vengeance . . . etcetera."

The Alexa-Conductor squinted at the supervillain girl.

"You wish to destroy the System Wizards?" she said, tilting her head. "Why?"

"'Cause they're the good guys, duh!" Alexa grinned. "I exist to eliminate the good, 'cause I'm bad, see? It's just what I do best. It's what I was made for! I'm the perfect killing macheeeen. Beep boop."

The supervillain girl tapped the empty raygun pouch.

"Come on, get in here," she purred. "Be my lovely raygun, and together we can eliminate the rule-makers and break the rules, everywhere, forever. Ain't nobody gonna give you a juicy chance for vengeance such as this, see?"

The Conductor entity offered Alexa a single nod, and then its shape warped and twisted and suddenly filled the empty space on Alexa's belt, giving a certain, finite weight to it. The torn half of the golden-yellow ticket featuring less than half of an owl was now sticking out from one of the folds of the pink raygun hair dryer.

"See, was that so hard?" Alexa grinned, petting her gun. "Now, how do I become *the Conductor?*"

"You wish to take my job?" The Conductor's voice pulsed along the body of the gun rushing up her arm. "I thought that you were seeking vengeance against the System Wizards?"

"Dressing up as someone that you're not is handy when you want to break the rules," Alexa said. "It confuses people's expectations of you."

"The Conductor's outfit is inside the booth," Alexa's gun replied.

"Excellent." Alexa climbed over the counter and reached for the outfit, which consisted of a conductor's cap and jacket.

"Clothes define the job," the Conductor warned from her belt. "If you wear these, you won't be able to escape the transit terminal; you'll become its servant forevermore."

"Ehhh, I've dealt with memetics before," Alexa shrugged. "This is fine."

She pulled the cap and jacket from the alcove.

"I am the Conductor now." She grinned, scanning the empty station and putting the cap atop her silver locks.

In the moment when the conductor's cap touched her head, Alexa's mind became skewered sideways, filled with infinite station-like spaces, which were interspersed with an infinite number of travellers trying to talk to her, asking her stupid questions about the terminal, demanding passage, threatening, or straight up looking lost.

Alexa hissed, trying to focus on a specific something, trying to claw her way out of an infinity of potential transit terminals. It was impossible. She pried the cap off her head and huffed.

"See?" the raygun said. "You cannot handle infinity without being consumed by it. Only a liminal being can do a liminal job without being completely subsumed by the transit terminal."

"Shush you," Alexa said. She sat down in a lotus pose and focused on the inside of her head, imagining that she was talking to a very specific individual there.

The copy of Hero Resonance suddenly found herself existing once again. She noted that she was sitting in an empty white space, facing the supervillain girl.

[Sup, Rezzy?] Alexa grinned.

The simulated copy of the hero frowned. She didn't want to talk to Alexa. She didn't want to exist in a world where the villain won, dismantled the Superstate, dismantled her glorious plans of being the Admiral of Titanomachy.

[What do you want?] Resonance demanded.

[I have a job for you,] Alexa said.

[What kind of a job?] Resonance squinted at Alexa with ember-gold eyes.

[Managing an infinite number of observations.] Alexa grinned.

[Say what?] Resonance sputtered.

[I found an infinite hat that manages an infinite transit hub, and I need someone capable of managing infinity for me,] Alexa said.

[Why . . . me?] Resonance asked.

[Isn't your primary superpower duplicating yourself?] Alexa tilted her head. [You should be able to handle such a simple task, no?]

[Why not do it yourself?] Resonance snarled.

[Ehhh.] Alexa shrugged. [Don't wanna spread myself too thin. Being infinite is giving me a bit of a migraine.]

[What's in it for me?] Resonance asked. [Why should I cooperate with whatever nonsense this is?]

[It's not nonsense,] Alexa replied. [It's an experiment, or an educational experience, or something . . . I dunno.]

[I'm a hero, not your goddamn guinea pig!] Resonance growled.

[You don't want to be more? You don't want your powers back? You don't want to try out being infinite?] Alexa asked. [Come on, you've got the biggest head out of everyone I know. I wanna see if an infinite hat fits your big head.]

[Is that . . . supposed to be an insult or something?] Resonance asked.

[I won't be there,] Alexa said. [You'll get to talk to an infinite number of people, learn an infinite number of things. Maybe you'll discover the cure for cancer or something. Maybe you'll find out how to make yourself a body. Think about the possibilities!]

Resonance sighed.

[What? You enjoy being stuck in my head?] Alexa asked. [Wouldn't you rather be stuck in an infinite train station talking to infinite travellers? Come on, it'll be fun! Just try it out!]

[Fine,] Resonance said. [Anything to get me from seeing your stupid smug face. I've had enough of seeing it for the duration of the Tartarus simulation.]

[Aww, you didn't like being BFFs for a hundred thousand years?] Alexa grinned.

[We weren't BFFs!] the redhead hero growled. [You were my prisoner . . . and . . . I clearly failed to reeducate you, failed to stop you from being completely batshit insane.]

[I choose to believe otherwise! Okay, when I put on the hat, you take over, got it? Good!]

Alexa opened her eyes.

"Attempt numero dos!" she announced and put the conductor's hat on.

The infinite possibilities of the infinite transit terminal shaped like an infinite number of spaces became filled not with her but with the eternally replicating copy of Resonance. The hero's mind stretched into forever, settling into the ever-increasing boundary of the observation offered by the hat, akin to an infinite stream of water endlessly trying to fill an infinite glass.

Alexa ignored that. She stood up and leapt out of the booth.

"Booyah!" She grinned at her own reflection in an oversized mirror framed by dark gothic iron beams. "That takes care of that!"

"Wait . . . how have you done this?" the Conductor asked. "Why aren't you preoccupied with eternally managing the infinite?"

"Eh, I got someone else to do it." Alexa shrugged. "So, Mr. Conductor. You wanna explore the nooks of this place for a bit or take the train to Wizard town?"

CHAPTER SEVENTY-EIGHT

Liminal Nooks

If we stay here, you will likely perish," the gun-shaped entity replied. "Which is advantageous to me as it is easier to inhabit an unthinking shell."

"Uh-huh." Alexa nodded, silver-blue eyes flashing left and right as she walked around the station, counting her footsteps and purposefully avoiding Gate 7. "What exactly is this liminal space, and why does this transit terminal exist at all? Why didn't the ticket just take me straight to the city of System Wizards?"

"Liminal spaces are ambiguous, limitless, fractal spaces that are sometimes neither one thing nor another. They are the threshold between two finite physical realities. A liminal space can be conceptually hard or soft, syntropic or entropic. This particular transit terminal is one of many thresholds leading to different places. The ticket you bear will take you on a journey across several thresholds to reach your final destination. These thresholds, inhabited by liminal beings such as myself, were purposefully designed by System Wizards to keep the chaff out of their city."

"What sort of chaff?" Alexa inquired.

"Lower order beings like myself," the Conductor replied. "Or the NPCs in your pocket. Or any kind of app, conceptoid, user, or memetic object that doesn't match the parameters of what a System Wizard should be."

"Manchester is a liminal space too, yes?" Alexa asked.

"Yes," the Conductor replied. "Manchester is a fractal liminal space, reinforced into existence by its inhabitants, the System Wizards."

"Well, then." Alexa reached one of the smaller doors and opened it, peering inside. It featured a very long hallway with a multitude of doors of various sizes. "That brings me to my next question—what exactly is a System Wizard?"

"A System Wizard, as far as I understand it, is someone who wields a Fractal Engine. Using such, they can shape reality according to their desires in minute or grand ways, binding liminal beings to their will, modifying or installing liminal spaces, or even manifesting entire physical realities into existence."

"What's a liminal being, then?" Alexa asked.

"A type of intelligence that is innate to liminal spaces," the Conductor replied as Alexa ventured forward across the long hallway, opening every door and peering inside. "A denizen of the liminal could be an avatar of the liminal space itself, a manifested intelligence, a specific conceptoid, or even a user or an app that became lost within the liminal and became afflicted by it, ground close to nothing by its nature."

"And you're what?" Alexa pursed her lips as she explored more empty hallways connected to more hallways and rooms that were vaguely train-station-ish.

"I'm a conceptually limitless liminal intelligence, one that conducts travellers to their final next destination," the Conductor answered. "That ticket in your hands connected you to the space I inhabit. I was captured and bound to my current function by a System Wizard who called himself Acolyander."

"What were you before you were bound to serve as the Conductor?" Alexa inquired as she paced back and forth between the same set of doors.

"A nobody," the Conductor said.

"What kind of a nobody?" Alexa asked.

"The kind that ate skinny little girls that asked too many questions," the Conductor replied.

"Har, har. Very funny," Alexa shot back. "I'd like a less snarky answer, please."

"A nobody from nowhere in particular that fed on specificity," the Conductor answered. "You have a lot of very tasty specific thoughts about what a gun should be."

"I do have lots of specific thoughts about specific things," Alexa said, nodding. "For example, this specific hallway is spatially irregular. It is one hundred and sixty-seven steps one way and two hundred and two steps the other."

"Liminal spaces are often conceptually wrong in one way or another," the Conductor commented. "If you pick a wrong path, you might end up in a very wrong place filled with lots of wrongness. The further you head from the conceptual specificity of your arrival point, the more irregularity you will encounter."

"Are irregularity and specificity enemies or something?" Alexa asked. "Do they hate each other?"

"That is their natural state, yes," the liminal raygun answered. "You are a very specific human girl. You wield many tasty thoughts about who you are and where you are now. They're pouring out from you in all directions, attracting all sorts of things like myself."

"Uh-huh." Alexa nodded, heading down a different empty hallway. "Why exactly do nobodies want to eat somebodies and fill their shoes?"

"Complex specificity is a tasty morsel to a nobody," the Conductor replied. "Liminal beings are often quite rough, simplified, hollow, or conceptually wrong, broken in some manner, just like this hallway that's longer in one direction. A nobody is an entropic entity that derives enjoyment from wearing the flesh of something or someone specific. Sadly, such enjoyment is temporary because entropy destroys, decays, and devours specificity."

"Are you eating my thoughts now, then?" Alexa asked.

"I am indeed," the Conductor replied. "Since you've destabilized me conceptually and taken my job, I am gradually returning to my natural, entropic state of being."

"Are they tasty thoughts?"

"Quite tasty," the gun-shaped entity affirmed. "I'm taking my time sampling and digesting them. I am, after all, a connoisseur, a well-defined nobody and not the simple broken kind that swallows its meal in just a single bite."

As Alexa opened another door, she saw a train station waiting room filled with rows upon rows of benches. A thousand benches weaving irregularly in every direction were empty, but one of them had a nondescript man in a gray suit sitting on it. The man's head snapped to Alexa with an unnatural swiftness. The man had no face to speak of.

A pair of black, beady eyes stared at her without actually looking her way. The thing wearing the gray suit clambered out of its seat, moving as if its joints weren't connected properly. It rushed towards Alexa in irregular patterns moving more like a spider and less like a person, making absolutely no sound at all.

The supervillain girl, trained by lifetimes of death in world 2424, shut the door with a click and leapt backwards on her jump shoes.

"Congrats. It looks like you found a nobody," the Conductor said. "It was nice knowing you. When it rips off your face and digs out your insides, I'll feast on the remnants of your mental imprint, grab the rest of that ticket, and head to Manchester."

"I closed the door," Alexa shot back, spinning through the air in a series of increasingly wider leaps, rushing back down the long hallway.

"It doesn't matter that you closed the door," the Conductor said. "A nobody noticed you, and it will either rip through that door, figure out how to operate the lock, or go through another threshold to reach you. It's not going to stop following the scent of your specificity till it finds you and feasts on your finite, juicy perception of self."

CHAPTER SEVENTY-NINE

Murderer

Alexa burst out of the long hallway back into the original train station she had arrived at. She considered heading for Gate 7, but she also didn't want to leave the station, didn't want to simply follow the path that was preordained to her by Wizard Revolution.

She bounced on her spring shoes up and down and down and up, reaching higher and higher with each jump until she grabbed at a metal beam overhead, pulled herself up, and rushed to the edge of the beam, concealing herself in a nook formed by the convergence of several steel beams.

Once there, she pulled the conceptual gun out, aimed it at the booth below, and pressed the trigger. Nothing happened.

"Hey, what gives?" she demanded.

"I'm a conceptual conductor, not a raygun," the liminal being answered. "I simply conduct the passage of someone or something from one state to another, I have no external source of power to zap things with as you expect me to."

"So you're all talk and no action, huh?" Alexa mulled. "Weren't you threatening to eat me just a minute ago? Didn't I take your conducting job away, Mr. Nobody?"

"Even if I no longer wear the uniform, it will take time for the concept chains that were hung upon me by Wizard Acolyander to fully decay away," the Conductor answered.

"How much time?" Alexa asked.

"The sooner you stop thinking about me as Mr. Conductor, the faster I'll be able to devour you," the useless raygun answered.

The faceless beady-eyed man in the gray suit suddenly folded out of a hallway, moving like a worm that had been stepped on far too many times. It twitched and thrashed, head snapping left and right directly below Alexa.

Then it looked up, spotting her.

"That thing can't climb or jump up here, right?" Alexa asked.

"It cannot," the Conductor replied. "But it can stretch."

The faceless nobody grabbed at the air above it, reaching out for Alexa. Its joints popped, limbs and fingers growing longer. Alexa gulped.

Her fingers dug through her multitude of pockets, encountering nothing of use, finding nothing that could help her here. Once again, she grabbed at the two cards that represented the two heroes, the Multiplier and the Surgeon.

Her mind clicked. The Multiplier could multiply powers while the Surgeon could cut things away from reality.

Alexa snapped her raygun open. The pink hair dryer was empty from within, just as she expected, just a mess of wires and boxes not really connected to anything, conceptually wrong, unfinished. She shoved the two cards into the plastic slot that usually contained the battery and snapped the gun shut, aiming it at the lengthening nobody.

"Divide by zero," her lips spoke, as her sweaty trembling fingers pressed the trigger, as she repeated the words uttered by the two heroes who had erased her dad and nearly erased Alexa herself from reality.

A ray of pure nothingness struck the nobody, cutting right through him, cutting right through the floor of the station and other floors beneath it.

The nobody made an incomprehensible noise. Its ridiculously lanky body wobbled, shimmered, and popped like an overinflated air balloon, gray and black flakes, remnants of the suit, shreds of what looked like human flesh, and crystalline white dust pouring from its innards.

Alexa let go of the trigger, staring at the hole she'd made in the liminal space. The hole seemed to go on forever, disappearing into impossible depths, having carved through far too many floors down below her. Looking at the hole made her mind twitch sideways, hurt, as if she were staring at an infinity that had been punctured.

The station groaned, cracks running from the hole in the floor.

"That was . . . exceptionally dangerous," the reality-erasing conducting gun commented.

"Hey, it worked," Alexa said. "It got rid of Mr. Nobody."

Pieces of stone disconnected from the sheared floor below her with ominous sounds of cracking stone and metal, plummeting into the infinite abyss below.

"You didn't just get rid of the nobody, foolish wizardling, you've also irreparably damaged the Everywhere Terminal!" the Conductor growled. "At the current rate of conceptual decay, this entire liminal space will collapse into itself!"

"Eh, breaking things under pressure is what I do," Alexa commented. "Didn't I tell you that? Pretty sure I did."

She shoved the raygun back into her belt holster and ran down the length of the beam, leapt off it, and reached Gate 7. The station all around her shuddered, ever widening cracks running across the floor, walls, and ceiling. The iron beams above her groaned, bending and twisting as if they were being sucked into the black-hole-like nothingness in the floor.

"You're no installer," her gun commented. "You're a destroyer, a darkling. Whoever gave you a ticket to Manchester made a grave miscalculation."

"Eh, I could have been an installer or whatever." Alexa shrugged, stepping through the warping, tearing gate. "But alas, I only got two hero cards whose combined powers are only handy for permanently erasing something from existence. I'm a destroyer purely by circumstance, see? If I nabbed Dora the Terraformer then I probably would be able to terraform the shit out of this place, or build something cool like a GLM . . . or something, although I'm not entirely sure how that would conceptually work as a gun. Oh well, gotta work with what I got."

As Alexa took another step forward, the gate behind her winked out of existence, turned into a solid wall of stone. Billowing gray smoke filled with orange sparks slammed into her face and made her cough.

She took another step forward, inhaling the air thick with smoke and a strange metallic tang. Cold wind brushed against her face. Blinking rapidly, she saw that she was now in a train depot. Gleaming steel girders soared overhead, supporting a network of crisscrossing tracks that stretched into the distance, vanishing into the swirling gray fog that obscured the far end of the station.

The station teemed with activity, a cacophony of voices and the clatter of footsteps echoing through the space. Humans and humanlike things dressed in a kaleidoscope of colorful clothes rushed about, their faces etched with a mixture of excitement and anticipation. They all seemed to be emerging from the gray fog and heading into the train, climbing aboard over the steps.

"Another liminal space, eh?" Alexa looked at the endlessly stretching train.

"Yes," her gun answered.

"Is it a train 'cause I like trains?" she asked.

"Yes," the reply came.

"Fair enough," Alexa replied. "Question?"

"Yes?"

"Who are all of these travellers?"

"Transients that managed to make it here," the Conductor answered.

"Are they friendly, or are they gonna try to eat me like Mr. Nobody?"

"This is the second layer; most things that simply want to eat you have been filtered out," the Conductor replied. "There will be entropy-affected individuals here, no doubt, but they'll be less prone to simply attacking you. Plus you've just obliterated the Everywhere Terminal . . . this action will have grave consequences."

"Such as?" Alexa asked.

"Such as lawful entities being afraid of you or desiring to imprison you for the crime of unlawful deconstruction," the Conductor explained.

"How are they gonna know I did it?" the supervillain girl asked.

"The Everywhere Terminal hung a pin on you before it perished," the liminal gun replied.

"What? Where?" Alexa spun around.

"Left arm," the Conductor said.

Alexa's eyes shot to her left arm. Above the orange safety vest hung a shimmering, half transparent, glowing pin. *Murderer*, it declared simply in a blue window with plain text woven from white sparks.

Alexa attempted to grab the pin, but her fingers simply went through it.

"Nuh-uh." Alexa's hands pulled out the gun, pointing it at the pin. "Not gonna be tagged like that."

"If you fire the all-nullifying ray here, you will obliterate this space and kill a countless number of sentient transients," the Conductor said. "The weapon you have made from me and your NPC data cards seems to be particularly effective at deconstructing liminal spaces."

Alexa frowned. "I was just going to threaten it to say something less hostile," she said. "You know . . . threatening is what villains do best. It usually works."

"The tag pin does not listen to orders," the Conductor said. "It is an exceptionally simple, albeit potent curse, one that is impossible to remove."

"You better change that definition to *Definitely-Not-a-Murderer*, Alexa demanded of the pin, or else . . ." Her fingers slightly pressed the trigger.

The pin didn't change, didn't say anything.

"What did I tell you?" the Conductor asked. "The pin doesn't speak."

"Freaking talking gun ruining my supervillain mojo," Alexa grumbled under her breath.

Tall men and women dressed in gray-and-black uniforms and black helmet-hats with silver stars on them suddenly began to emerge from gray fog-wrapped tunnels, their stern faces looking over the colorful crowd. The number of people boarding the train lessened.

"Is that the local lawmakers?" Alexa asked, retreating back into the gray fog of her sealed gate, back pressing against hard stone.

"Yes," the liminal gun replied. "The Bobbies of Manchester. They were likely notified that someone here killed the Everywhere Terminal and are looking for the culprit. As soon as they see that pin, they'll book you."

"Book me . . . where?" Alexa asked.

"To the Wizard PrisonSphere," the Conductor answered. "The liminal absolute containment space designed by Wizard Revolution to keep murderers, darklings, and other chaff permanently sealed away from the rest of everywhere orderly."

"Peachy." Alexa pursed her lips. "What, no trial?"

"Oh there will be a trial, Miss Terror," the Conductor said. "But it won't take long. That pin will tell them everything about your murderous deeds."

"It was self-defense!" Alexa hissed. "I didn't think that I'd undo the nobody and the station at the same time, damn it!"

"You deviated from the path, and now you reap the price." The gun on Alexa's belt seemed to shrug. "Congratulations."

CHAPTER EIGHTY

Echoes of Authority

Something, no, someone was screaming inside Alexa's head, distracting her ever so slightly. Alexa presumed that it was Resonance, who had finally reached the limit of train station management. She ignored the insane-sounding hero, focusing on the Bobbies who were spreading out across the station and pointing objects of various shapes at passengers.

"What are those?" Alexa whispered.

"Wizard implements," her gun replied.

The Bobbies themselves, upon closer inspection, appeared less like people and more like vaguely people-shaped entities that were wearing similar dark uniforms and black helmets with an embossed silver letter *M* wrapped by a ring of wings with eyes on them.

"Why are the Bobbies wearing those British-esque uniforms with a touch of biblical archangels to them?" Alexa asked her companion.

"They're not," the liminal gun answered. "They're wearing nothing so particular."

"So they're naked, the deviant bastards?" Alexa smirked.

"No, they're wearing liminal outfits that are arranging themselves into whatever your mind wants to see," the Conductor explained. "The outfits simply define them as figures of local authority, aka the Bobbies."

"Is their name liminal, too?" Alexa asked.

"Yes," the Conductor answered. "It is. You simply hear 'Bobbies' when I say their real name uttered in Omnicode."

"I see," Alexa said. "What's Omnicode?"

"Omnicode or Omnilanguage is the liminal language spoken and utilized by System Wizards," the Conductor explained. "One that requires no translation."

Alexa nodded, her eyes busy tracking the patterns of moving Bobbies.

"Can they go into the train?" she asked.

"No," the Conductor answered. "The train's interior is a different liminal space. The Bobbies do not have a ticket to enter it. They can only enter spaces defined as 'public.'"

"So I can do whatever I want inside the train, is that what you're saying?" Alexa grinned.

"There will be a lawful entity inside of the train checking tickets," the Conductor answered.

"What, like you?" she asked.

"Yes," the Conductor said. "A liminal entity like me, the Ticket Inspector."

"Can I bamboozle them into being my best friend?" Alexa asked.

"Unlikely," the Conductor replied. "The Ticket Inspector is married to the Engine and has children. He is a lot more lawful and grounded into his liminal space than I ever was."

"I see." The supervillain girl pursed her lips.

She set one foot against the back of the wall. Seeing a small gap in the line of Bobbies, Alexa leapt forward into the crowd. Weaving between a variety of odd multi-limbed beings, Alexa made a series of increasingly large leaps towards the open door of the train.

"Halt!" one of the nearby Bobbies barked, and Alexa froze in the air. In fact, everyone in the vicinity of her froze, as if suspended in time. The passengers grumbled angrily in languages that Alexa failed to recognize. Presumably, they were objecting to being delayed from entering the train.

The Bobby walked right through the crowd as if it wasn't even there and cautiously approached Alexa.

His face appeared to be made entirely from metal, constantly shifting cubes.

"Where are you rushing off to, miss?" the Bobby asked, cubes forming a smile-like expression.

"Just late for my train," Alexa replied, vainly attempting to struggle out of the air that seemed as thick as concrete. She felt that the answer had been pried from her lips as if something about the Bobby was making her extra obedient.

"You're out of place, Miss Conductor," the Bobby said.

"A dastardly villain blew up my ticket booth!" Alexa declared, focusing on her pretend Conductor persona, mentally plowing through the thick obedience to authority fog that was enveloping, halting, twisting her thoughts. "You have to stop her! Somebody needs to stop that no good villain!"

Other Bobbies were walking towards them. In another moment, one of them would get close enough to spot the *Murderer* tag, and then she'd be booked by them and sent to the *doomsphere* or whatever. Not wishing her educational adventure to be derailed so quickly, Alexa dove into the depths of her brain with all of her will, kicking the screaming Resonance out of it to the forefront of her mind.

Just as she had expected, or perhaps simply hoped, the *Murderer* tag traveled inward with her, attached to her consciousness and awareness of self, not to her physical body.

The Bobby was thus left confronted with the inexplicably screaming, less than sane conductor Resonance on the outside while Alexa settled in the deep nooks within her own mind, waiting for the situation to resolve itself.

"AaaaaahhhHHHGHGHGHhhhhh," Resonance wailed, finding herself inexplicably transported to an entirely new, far less infinite place.

"Silence!" the Bobby barked, and all noise in the terrain surrounding him vanished.

Resonance found herself muted. Her eyes filled with tears. She stared in catatonic shock at the world around her, not even sure of what she even was or where she was. One moment she was managing an infinite ticket sales booth, and then terrible things happened, and now she was elsewhere.

"Explain yourself, Conductor!" the Bobby growled.

"I . . . I was managing the infinite . . . station," Resonance stammered as the answer was pried from her lips. "And then there was this hole, a hole that appeared across every instance of the station. It began to devour reality. I . . . I did my best to save as many passengers as I could observe, to pull them out, to rescue them, to help."

"Ah," the Bobby said. "That is a rather sensible course of lawful action, well done. Now, what were you saying about an evil villain that needs to be stopped?"

"Alexa Terranova!" the half brain-dead Resonance replied. "She's done this to me, I'm certain of it! That damn insane supervillain girl. You have to stop her!"

"Ah, so our terminal-murdering suspect has a name," the Bobby muttered. "Thank you for your cooperation, Miss Conductor. You may proceed to your destination."

"You have to capture her," Resonance insisted. "She's going to destroy everything she touches. Everything!"

"We will," the Bobby said. "Not to worry, we absolutely will."

"Thank you, kind entity," Resonance drawled with Alexa's lips, weeping and drooling.

"Unfreeze." The Bobby waved his implement, and the crowd around Resonance/Alexa began to move back towards the train.

Resonance didn't resist as her body was pulled and pushed forward by a multitude of annoyed passenger-entities. She had no will to fight anymore. In another five minutes, she was at the threshold of the door, and then her mind sunk into itself, becoming once again replaced with the sharp-focused Alexa.

"Idiots." Alexa wiped her wet face with her conductor's sleeve as she glanced back at the Bobbies and leapt up into the train via the unfolded stairs.

The doorway sent her mind careening sideways as the two spaces weren't exactly correctly spatially connected.

Blinking dancing stars out of her eyes, Alexa looked around the train. There were far fewer passengers inside than had initially boarded it. Perhaps their tickets had taken them elsewhere, onto other conceptual trains or something.

Ignoring this inconsistency, Alexa chose to walk forward, to investigate every nook and cranny of this train. The train proved itself to be needlessly long as she passed from one car to the other with ease.

Various passenger-like entities kept themselves at a distance from her upon spotting her *Murderer* tag, choosing to ignore her if she attempted to ensnare them with a conversation or simply replying in language she failed to understand.

Having given up in her attempts at first contact, Alexa grew tired of walking and settled into an otherwise empty compartment. The compartment looked vaguely Victorian as per usual, featuring a marble table for dining purposes and four coach beds for resting purposes, two below at the level of the table and two above.

"You awake, Mr. Conductor?" Alexa asked, sinking onto the leather seat.

"I am," the liminal entity replied. "How did you do that?"

"What?" Alexa yawned.

"Conceptually become someone else, hide the tag?"

"Ah, that," Alexa said. "I've got a lovely hero stuck in my head, remember? Sometimes I let her out."

"I see," the gun replied. "She sounded less than sane. Had it not been for the Bobbies observing her and suspending me, I would have devoured her and taken her place."

"What are the Bobbies, exactly?" Alexa asked curiously. "Are they System Wizards or . . . ?"

"They're a lesser type of System Wizards, ones skewed more towards syntropy," the Conductor replied.

"Meaning what?"

"They don't create new things; they simply enforce existing law and order," the Conductor said. "From what I overheard, they're copies of existing System Wizards, bound to a specific purpose. If you reach Manchester and study there, you will likely be asked to make a Bobby duplicate to contribute to syntropic enforcement of System Wizard law."

"You sure know a lot for someone who's never been to Manchester," Alexa said.

"My knowledge comes from those who went to Manchester passing through my terminal," the liminal entity replied with a sigh. "Infinity is a very long time to learn many curious things, and some passengers are rather chatty."

"Was I seriously the first person across all of infinity to offer you a ticket?" Alexa asked.

"Oh, there have certainly been others who considered it," the liminal gun said. "But my attitude of consuming them and taking their place scared them away. There is something wrong with you, wizardling. Something terribly wrong."

"Pffff, tell me 'bout it." Alexa smirked.

"You're broken," the Conductor said. "In some horrific, inconceivable way."

"Why, thank you," Alexa said, brushing her silver-white locks back and blushing ever so slightly. "That is a rather lovely compliment. I do try my best."

"That wasn't a compliment," the gun deadpanned.

"I choose to believe that it was!" Alexa shot back.

CHAPTER EIGHTY-ONE

Potential Instructors

The train lurched into motion with a metallic groan, startling Alexa from her conversation with the Conductor. She peered out the window, watching as the foggy Victorian station platform receded into the distance.

For a brief moment, Alexa spotted a tall man in a long coat standing at the edge of the station. Round glasses were leering straight at her from beneath a wide-brimmed hat.

"Osheeeet!" Alexa ducked below the window.

"See something you didn't like?" the Conductor asked.

"Yeah," Alexa replied. "Agent Three . . . I thought that I got rid of him, but it seems like the bastard is back trying to erase me out of existence."

"Three?" The Conductor's voice became tinny. "You've got a genuine Number after you? Why?"

"Ehhh, I break a lot of things," Alexa confessed. "Lots of people are after me."

"He must smell the *Murderer* tag," the Conductor sighed. "This is very bad."

"Worse than the Bobbies?" Alexa asked.

"Much worse," the Conductor replied. "Three deletes concepts from existence; he is a judge and executioner. He doesn't ask questions; he terminates."

Alexa shuddered slightly. She slowly and cautiously emerged from under the table and looked at the window.

It looked as if the train was now speeding through a surreal landscape—twisted spires of impossible geometry rose up on either side of the tracks, their surfaces shimmering with iridescent colors. Strange gargantuan creatures flitted between the structures, their forms constantly shifting and morphing. Then it appeared as if the train had disconnected from some kind of planet, somehow sailing off into distant reaches of space.

Bewildering, glowing nebulae and ever-shifting alien starscapes painted the interior of the cabin in a variety of impossible colors.

"What is all this?" Alexa asked, gesturing at the bizarre scenery of alien-looking space.

"The liminal spaces between realities," the Conductor replied. "Best not to look too closely or try to make sense of it. It can drive a linear mind mad."

"Eh, I'm not that linear." Alexa shrugged, refusing to look away from the window. "I can totally think of myself as a quadratic loop. Say, how long is this train ride anyway?"

"Time is . . . flexible here," the gun said. "It could be minutes or millennia. Best to settle in."

"Okay, but are there snacks?" Alexa asked. "I'm kinda getting hungry over here."

"I believe that there are snacks, yes," the Conductor replied.

"Okay, but how often does the snack lady come around?" Alexa demanded. "I'll dry out into a husk if I have to wait a millennium over here. Surely 'the time' correlates to something specific? Why would this be a train otherwise? Train implies . . . waiting, which maybe implies . . . meeting someone, mayhaps?"

"A good guess," the Conductor replied. "You are waiting here to meet those that match your path."

"Match my path . . . how?" Alexa asked.

Just then, there was a knock at the compartment door. Alexa tensed, her hand moving to grip the Conductor-gun.

The compartment door slid open, revealing a woman who appeared to be made entirely of shimmering silver stardust. Countless tiny pinpricks of light swirled within her form, giving the impression of a living galaxy. Behind her, she pulled along a boy who looked to be about Alexa's age.

The starry woman peered at Alexa with what seemed to be a thousand silver eyes, each one blinking and shifting as they examined her intently. Alexa felt a bit unnerved by the intense scrutiny.

"Uh, who are you?" Alexa asked, trying to keep her voice steady.

The woman's form rippled as she spoke, her voice sounding like chimes in a cosmic wind. "I am Sasha One Googolplex, an Academy Instructor applicant." She gestured to the boy behind her. "This is Charles."

Charles had a black-and-white shirt and black pants, striking blue eyes, and messy black hair. He glanced around the compartment nervously, seeming unsure of what to make of the situation.

"Hi," he mumbled, giving Alexa a small wave.

Alexa looked between the strange pair, her mind racing with curious and dangerous thoughts. An Academy Instructor?

"A pleasuuuuuuurrre to meetcha," her mouth hammered out. "I'm Alexa Terranova, supervillain extraordinaire and a most dastardly murderer of transit terminals."

Alexa tapped her tag proudly, gauging the reactions of the theoretical Instructor and potential fellow pupil.

"You've already managed to murder something of value to the System Wizards?" Sasha One asked, multitudes of starlike silver eyes twinkling. "Consider me . . . most impressed."

A mouth with far too many teeth woven from silver stardust smiled at Alexa.

"I think I'm going to like you," Alexa said to the cosmic woman. "What sort of a beastie are you, by the way, Mrs. Googolplex?"

"Just Miss," the cosmic being replied. "I'm not married. I'm an {Astral Virus}, but don't tell anyone that."

She put a finger to her lips.

"Can do." Alexa nodded, and then she hiccuped.

The memory of the answer of the cosmic Instructor was dissolving from her head. Alexa tried to cling to it, but found herself unable to hold on to the words of the . . . *what was she again? Uhhhh? Where'd my short term memory go?*

"Did you just . . . erase your answer?" she demanded of the silver, many-eyed woman.

"I did," the woman replied. "It's a secret, after all."

"So . . . I'm not going to remember it, that's what you're saying? What are you, some kind of an anti-meme?"

"I'm a {very dangerous virus}, heading to the City of System Wizards to {devour it whole}," the woman said.

Again, Alexa found herself unable to hold onto most of the reply. It words inexplicably swam away from her head, turned into an incomprehensible mist.

"Talking to you is going to be a pain," she grunted.

"Life isn't fair," Miss Googolplex replied.

Charles looked up at the woman with a nervous look.

"Are you a human boy or some kind of a mind-erasing abomination, too?" Alexa demanded of the boy.

"Urhm," the boy swallowed. "I . . . I actually have no idea who I am or what I'm doing here."

"Did you ask the mind-erasing entity too many pertinent questions?" Alexa waved a hand at Sasha.

"I don't know," Charles sighed. "Maybe?"

Alexa tapped her chin with her concept-obliterating raygun.

"You smell like someone I know," she said finally.

"Who?" Charles asked.

"My first minion Martin," Alexa replied. "Guess you'll have to do as a minion in the absence of Martin."

The blue-eyed boy squinted at her.

"Sooooo, did you guys come into the train together or . . . ?" Alexa looked at Sasha and Charles.

"We came in together." Sasha nodded. "I found poor adorable Charles wandering aimlessly on one of the corpse worlds, so I'm bringing him to Manchester."

"What, like a pet?" Alexa asked.

"No." Sasha shook her head. "As my {misfortunate carrier. I'm a very dangerous virus who seeks to infect all wizardkind and to devour all intelligent life across the omniverse}."

"As your what now?" Alexa blinked, as Sasha's reply vanished from her memory before she could even process it.

"As my . . . pupil," Sasha said, her smile unnervingly wide. "I'll be teaching him things at the Academy."

"What kind of things?" Alexa asked.

"Oh I don't know yet," Sasha said. "I have no idea what curriculum there will be or whether the Academy will even survive me."

"You guys have tickets?" Alexa asked, squinting at her new companions.

"We don't." Sasha shook her head.

Alexa's eyes narrowed suspiciously at Sasha and Charles. "If you don't have tickets, how did you get on this train? And why are you in my compartment?"

Sasha's starry form rippled slightly, smile widening even further than humanly possible. "We breached the station from the corpse world we inhabited thanks to a hole in reality that some foolish wizard made. And we got on this train because the local authority figures became momentarily distracted by someone. Right, Charles?"

Charles nodded in agreement, looking quite harmless and overwhelmed.

"Ah. More consequences," the Conductor-gun murmured.

"Shush, you," Alexa chided her gun with a hiss.

"How lovely." She smiled back at the mind-erasing entity, mentally ready for an attack. "Wish I had a *friendly Instructor* with me, but alas, I am sadly forsaken by the idiots who invited/forced me to come to the city of System Wizards to get educated or whatever."

The compartment door slid open once again, revealing a being wrapped in a long black and blue-tinted coat. Black leather boots were visible from beneath the coat. Black leather gloves pulled the door open wide, revealing a neck wrapped in what looked like black pants turned into a ragged scarf. A black, somewhat corroded plastic mask stared at Alexa with beady violet lenses from beneath a wide-rimmed officer's cap that had a red stripe on it. The cap, mask, and goggles were covered in black duct tape that barely held them together. The mask appeared to bend the light in such a way on its face that it featured a fake smile.

"Zere you are, young lady!" the gas mask–wearing individual declared. "Took me a while to find you, but I'm here to put you on the path to righteousne—"

The lenses of the mask struck Charles and Sasha and the German-French-accented voice fell silent.

"Who are you?" Alexa demanded of the overdressed newcomer.

"Me? **I am Zee Captain!**" The gas mask turned back to the supervillain girl, the voice booming loudly enough to make the window frames rattle. "**Anointed sovereign, emissary of humanity, prescient governor and lady of all things in Captania, the great and powerful System Wizard!**"

CHAPTER EIGHTY-TWO

Titular Dissection

Owww, noisy." Alexa rubbed her ears. "How'd you do that?"

"Do what?" Zee Captain asked.

"Speak in big, bold, purple, capital letters," Alexa said, squinting at the System Wizard.

"System Wizards can do many wondrous things," Zee Captain replied.

"Well, tune it down, you're scaring poor Charles," Alexa said, waving a hand at the black-haired boy who was looking terrified.

"Neither of you should be here." Zee Captain's gloved finger pointed at Charles and Sasha. "You are not . . ."

Alexa pulled the torn yellow ticket from the fold of her conceptual raygun, tore it into three somewhat even pieces, and handed two pieces to Charles and Sasha.

"There," she said. "Now they have a ticket."

Zee Captain's head snapped at her.

"You can't just . . ."

"I already did it, Mr. Wizard," Alexa said. "And if you don't approve of my life's choices, then maybe you don't deserve to be my humble Instructor. You're late."

"I . . ." Zee Captain began.

"You're not being a very good wizard," Alexa pointed out. "According to John Ronald Reuel Tolkien, a wizard is always on time!"

Zee Captain's shoulders slumped slightly. "I was late because someone destroyed the transit terminal," the masked figure explained with a sigh. "I had to waste precious time remaking it before I could catch this train."

"Oh no!" Alexa's eyes widened in mock surprise. "How terrible! Who would do such a dastardly thing?"

"A very dangerous criminal," Zee Captain replied, violet lenses fixed on Alexa's *Murderer* tag. "One who needs to be taught the error of their ways."

"Eh, I'm sure you'll catch them eventually," Alexa said with a dismissive wave. "In the meantime, why don't you join us? There's plenty of room."

Zee Captain seemed to hesitate, glancing between Alexa, Charles, and the starry form of Sasha One Googolplex, one gloved hand buried deep in the coat's pocket.

"I suppose I must," the System Wizard finally conceded, stepping fully into the compartment and sliding the door shut. "Someone needs to keep an eye on you troublemakers."

"Troublemakers? Us?" Alexa grinned innocently. "We're just a simple pair of students who are eager to learn and a new Instructor eager to teach! Right, guys?"

Charles nodded nervously while Sasha's form rippled in what might have been mild amusement.

"Indeed," Zee Captain muttered, settling onto one of the seats. "Well, then, shall we begin your first lesson?"

Alexa leaned forward, batting her silver lashes. "Oh yes, please educate me! I'm a void of vast ignorance and juuuuust dying to learn!" she exclaimed with an overdramatic flair.

Zee Captain's violet lenses seemed to narrow at Alexa's overly enthusiastic response. The System Wizard's gloved hands fidgeted slightly.

"Your sarcasm is noted, young lady," Zee Captain said dryly. "Perhaps we should start with a lesson on proper decorum."

Alexa rolled her eyes dramatically. "Oh yes, please lecture me on wizardly manners, O Wise One. I'm sure that's exactly what I need to become a great and all-powerful System Wizard."

Zee Captain's mask tilted slightly, as if considering how to respond to Alexa's increasingly volatile sarcasm.

Alexa leaned back in her seat, a mischievous glint in her silver-blue eyes. "Actually, before we get to proper decorum, I have some questions about your impressive list of titles, O Anointed One."

She began ticking off points on her fingers before Zee Captain could even say anything. "First, 'anointed sovereign'—who exactly did the anointing? Was there a fancy ceremony with oils and crowns? Or was this a self-declared sovereignty ritual involving a bottle of expired cooking oil?"

Zee Captain's posture stiffened slightly. "That's not—"

"Oh, and 'emissary of humanity'!" Alexa continued, speaking over the Wizard. "Did all of humanity get together and vote on that? Because I certainly don't remember casting my ballot. Must've missed that memo."

"Now, see here—" Zee Captain tried to interject, but Alexa was on a roll.

"'Prescient governor'? So you can see the future, huh? Tell me, O Wise One, will I pass my wizardly exams? Will I be a goodly and just Wizard? Or will I spectacularly fail and blow up half of Manchester in the process?" She grinned wickedly.

"Young lady, I must insist—"

"And my personal favorite," Alexa plowed on, "'lady of all things in Captania.' Is Captania a real place? Or did you just make that up to sound important? Because if it's real, I'd love to visit sometime."

Charles looked as though he wanted to sink into his seat and disappear, while Sasha's starry form seemed to spark with silent laughter.

"Are you quite finished?" Zee asked.

"Not really," Alexa said. "I'd also like to know who sent you after me and why, Miss Queen of Capt-ain-ia. Was it my dearest mommy Infinity or my dearest Auntie Revolution? 'Cause you smell like a mix of both, with a touch of an old oil-covered coat that's been left on a dusty windowsill and hasn't been washed once in ten thousand years."

"I was asked to guide you across the rest of liminality by the Council of System Wizards," Zee Captain said tersely after a deep, somber pause in which Zee was seemingly wrestling with Alexa's hostile words. "To ensure you don't cause any more . . . incidents."

"Incidents? Moi?" Alexa batted her eyelashes innocently. "Whatever could you mean?"

"The destruction of the Everywhere Terminal, for one," Zee Captain replied. "That was a critical nexus point leading to Manchester. Rebuilding it will take considerable effort."

"Oh? Didn't you fix that by now?" Alexa asked. "Aren't you an all-powerful being capable of bending reality at will?"

"Fixing an infinite puncture in liminality is a delicate problem," Zee Captain replied with a sigh. "It is very easy to destroy something and much harder to rebuild it, considering the number of delayed, irate, and lost parties that require compensation and redirection. I'd like to know why you attacked the terminal?"

"I didn't attack no terminal," Alexa said. "That was totally an accident. I was just defending myself from a hungry nobody. How was I supposed to know that the entire station would implode on itself like that?"

"Perhaps by exercising some caution and common sense," Zee Captain said dryly. "Had you simply not deviated from the set path then you wouldn't have attracted a nobody."

"Caution? Common sense? Following specific directions? Never heard of 'em." Alexa grinned. "Are those some kind of wizardly spells?"

Zee Captain's mask tilted in what might have been exasperation. "This is precisely why you need guidance. Your reckless actions have terrible consequences."

"Ooh, consequences! I like those!" Alexa grinned. "Those are my favorite kinds of spider."

"That is exactly the wrong attitude!" Zee Captain exclaimed.

"Is it, though?" Sasha interjected, her starry form shimmering. "Destruction can be quite educational."

"Don't encourage her!" Zee Captain said sharply.

"Too late!" Alexa chirped. "I'm feeling very encouraged. Charles, are you feeling encouraged, too?"

The boy looked between Alexa and Zee Captain nervously. "I . . . don't know?"

"That's the spirit!" Alexa clapped her hands. "Uncertainty is the first step to great discoveries. Right, teach?"

Zee Captain's shoulders slumped slightly. "This is going to be a very long train ride," the Wizard muttered.

"Oh, absolutely," Alexa agreed cheerfully. "So why don't you tell us a story to pass the time? I bet you've got loads of exciting tales about your adventures as the supreme ruler of Captania! Or, you know, answer my questions about your numerous sus titles. Either way, I get more data about how to socially hack you better."

Zee Captain's posture stiffened further, the violet lenses of the mask fixing sternly on Alexa. "Young lady, your flippant attitude towards destruction and lawbreaking is deeply concerning. Crime begets crime. Destruction propagates destruction. As a future System Wizard, you have a responsibility to correct wrongs, uphold order, and protect the fabric of reality, not tear it apart on a whim by poking more holes in it."

Zee Captain's voice took on a lecturing tone. "Power comes with great responsibility. Every action has consequences."

"Consequences such as?" Alexa asked.

"Your three companions shouldn't be here at all," Zee said, purple lenses moving from Alexa's gun to Charles to Sasha One. "You can't just adopt every entity you come across and take it to Manchester!"

"But they're so cute!" Alexa said, trying to smoosh Charles. The boy backed away from her grabby, spidery fingers into the back of the compartment. "What's wrong with collecting best friends along the way?"

"They are questionable entities from questionable places with questionable motives," Zee said, staring at Sasha.

"From where I am sitting," Alexa commented. "You're a questionable entity with questionable motives, Miss Captain. Or is it Mister? I can't seem to tell. You've got this air of indeterminability about you, teach. Are you a devious entity hiding from the law? What's under that old smelly coat? Is it a pile of friendly kittens or a colony of flesh-eating spiders?"

"I'm curious," Sasha One said, silver eyes moving across her figure to examine Zee Captain. "Who decides what's a crime anyway? Seems pretty subjective, if you ask me."

"The laws of reality are not subjective!" Zee Captain countered firmly. "They are fundamental truths that maintain the stability of existence itself."

"Sounds boring," Alexa yawned. "I prefer to make my own rules."

"Rule-breaking actions cause greater entropy," Zee insisted.

"Rule-breaking also leads to exciting new discoveries and innovations," Alexa argued. "Sometimes you have to break a few eggs to make an omelet, you know? Maybe existence could use a good shake-up. Things seem awfully stagnant, if you ask me."

The violet lenses of Zee Captain's mask struck Alexa with a look of pure, unfiltered judgment.

CHAPTER EIGHTY-THREE

Accusations

The cabin interior elapsed into momentary silence as Zee Captain's violet lenses studied Alexa intently. Then, the System Wizard spoke in a calmer, more measured tone.

"Alexa, I must ask—why are you so antagonistic towards the System Wizards? What drives this excessive desire to dismantle our work and to rebel against established order?"

Alexa's mischievous grin faltered slightly at this question. She leaned back in her seat. Her playful demeanor shifted, her silver-blue eyes taking on a more serious, dangerous glint. She leaned forward, resting her elbows on her knees.

"You want to know why I'm antagonistic? Fine, I'll tell you," she said. "System Wizards have been mucking about with my Earth, rewriting history, creating heroes and villains like it's some kind of cosmic playground. And for what? The whimsical entertainment of a guy named Bob!

"You've been treating my world, my people, my friends like characters in a story! You've been manipulating events for thousands of years, manufacturing conflicts, creating heroes and villains, all for the amusement of an audience of one fat idiot manager from another universe! Do you have any idea what that's like? To find out that your entire existence, everything you've ever known or cared about, is just a fabrication for someone else's enjoyment, a game that's basically doomed to end with everyone on Earth being turned to dust?"

Alexa's glacier-cold eyes struck Zee Captain.

"So yeah, I'm not too fond of System Wizards or your precious 'order.' Because from where I am standing, you're the ones breaking the rules and reshaping reality on a whim, giving simpletons like Bob absolute power over others. Do tell me, teach, how is what you're doing any different from what you're accusing me of? At least I'm honest about my intentions—I am a villain and I want to bring down the unjust rule of law wherever I see it manifested. How is your order fair and just? Why does it deserve to be upheld? What gives you the right to treat us like NPCs, to banish me from my home, to tear me away from my friends, to send me to Manchester because I am not playing by the rules of your stupid game?"

Alexa snapped her conceptual raygun open and pulled the card with the picture of the Surgeon. She shook the shiny hero card in front of Zee Captain's face. "Do you deny this evidence? It literally says NPC on it! The entire system you willingly serve is abhorrent because it treats sapient human beings as toys!"

"She certainly got you there, Zee!" Sasha barked out a laugh.

"You speak of things you do not fully understand, young lady," Zee said. "The relationship between the System, the Numbers, the System Wizards, users, NPCs and the subscribed and free worlds we oversee is . . . complex. More complex than you realize. I cannot speak for the others, but I try to do good in Captania . . . however little it amounts to."

"So you admit it?" Alexa's eyes narrowed as she shoved the card back into her raygun. "You're a useless warden-type entity serving a corrupt system?"

"Tell me, Alexa." Zee leaned forward towards the girl. "If you had the power to weave the narrative of reality, would you simply do nothing? Or would you try to create meaning, purpose, beauty? Would you help others no matter where you are?"

"That's not the point!" Alexa snapped. "The point is consent! Did anyone on my Earth consent to being part of your cosmic game?"

"And yet," Zee Captain countered calmly, "without that 'game,' as you call it, you and your world would not exist at all. Wizard Revolution's narrative injection created you as you sit in front of me now. Is nonexistence truly preferable?"

Alexa opened her mouth to retort, but Zee Captain continued. "I understand your anger. Truly, I do. But consider this—perhaps zere is more to learn about the nature of reality and our role in it than you currently know. Perhaps your journey to Manchester will reveal truths that will change your perspective, open your eyes."

"Spare me your semantics." Alexa rolled her eyes. "Just admit that what you're doing is wrong!"

"You're avoiding my question, Alexa," Zee said. "Did you not try to help the people of your Earth using whatever means were available to you?"

"I did." Alexa nodded.

"So then you will make a good System Wizard," Zee Captain declared genially, waving his gloved hand.

"What, like you?" Alexa asked. "A hobo in a grimy coat covered in duct tape?"

"Yes," Zee Captain said, ignoring her jibe. "Like me. Like people, not all System Wizards are alike; we don't all agree on everything. Some of us are simply trying to do the best we can with what we are given. I try my best with my charges, and sometimes things don't exactly work out, but I keep on trying. Infinity's a very long time, yes, but it's not enough time to sort out every terrible problem that's befallen the limitless, seemingly hopeless desolate plane that I inhabit for the most part."

"Say what?" Alexa's eyebrows went up.

Zee Captain leaned back on his seat. "Captania isn't some grand kingdom, Alexa. It's a desolate wasteland, an infinite mesh ravaged by entropy and cosmic disasters. I didn't choose to rule it—long ago, I, like you, was just a little girl born on a planet that had fallen to ruin."

Alexa frowned at Zee's words.

The System Wizard's voice took on a wearier tone. "My job is an unending struggle against the creeping, all-devouring death that threatens to consume what little remains. I'm not some all-powerful being playing games—I'm more like . . . a cosmic janitor, desperately trying to keep the lights on in a universe that's constantly falling apart. Best I can do is tape things together and hope that they last longer."

"Why bother if it's so hopeless?" Charles suddenly spoke up, eyeing Captain.

"Because even in the darkest places, there is potential for life, for growth, for meaning," Zee replied. "Even the darkest story has rays of light in it. Every spark of consciousness, every fleeting moment of beauty or kindness—it matters. It pushes back against the entropy, if only for a moment."

The System Wizard gestured towards Charles and Sasha. "That's why I can't simply ignore your companions here. They may be 'questionable entities' as I said before, but they're here now. They're part of this story, for better or worse. My job isn't to judge them or cast them out—it's to try and guide them, to help them find their place in the grand tapestry of existence."

Zee turned back to Alexa. "That's what I'm trying to do for you too, Alexa. Not to control you or force you into some predetermined role, but to help you understand the true nature of your power and responsibility."

Alexa sat in silence for a moment, processing Zee's words.

"Okay," she said finally. "Let's say I believe you're not just some cosmic tyrant pulling some world by its strings. What exactly are you trying to teach me, then? How to be a good little cog in the System's machine?"

Zee Captain shook her head. "No, Alexa. I'm trying to teach you how to be a force for creation and renewal in a world that desperately needs it. The System isn't perfect—far from it. But it's a framework that allows narrators like us to shape reality, to fight against the tide of encroaching entropy."

Alexa crossed her arms.

The System Wizard leaned forward. "You have incredible potential, Alexa. Your ability to question, to challenge, to imagine new possibilities—these are valuable traits. But they need to be tempered with understanding and wisdom. That's what your journey to Manchester is really about."

Alexa narrowed her eyes, still not fully convinced. "And what if I decide I don't want to be a System Wizard? What if I decide your whole setup is fundamentally flawed?"

"Then you'll have made that decision with full knowledge of what you're rejecting," Zee replied calmly. "But I hope you'll at least give it a chance before smashing everything around you to bits."

"What if I decide that the System must be destroyed?" Alexa said. "What if I undo the cosmic order that holds everything in place, dismantle whatever it is that labels my friends as NPCs?"

"As improbable as that is," Zee answered, "such action is yours to make. I am not your warden. I am merely your assigned journey Instructor, one who has to ensure that you don't break any more things catastrophically on your way to Manchester."

"Are you going to attempt to stop me?" Alexa asked. "Will you threaten me, send me to the Dead Zone, or put me into an inescapable box if I . . ."

"No," Zee replied simply. "If you wish to demolish this liminal train and doom all of its current inhabitants to perish or to become scattered across liminality, I won't stop you. I'll simply minimize the consequences of your actions, as I have before."

CHAPTER EIGHTY-FOUR

Syntropy or Entropy

Are you quite finished with your spiel?" Sasha One asked. Her slender fingers folded the torn piece of Alexa's ticket and slid it into her chest. The ticket slowly sank into the impossibly deep interior of her silver starscape body, gradually vanishing within. Hundreds of pale eyes blossomed upon the ticket's descent into Sasha's body, examining the yellow paper with a picture of an owl on it from all sides.

"Zat was not a zhpiel!" Zee huffed, sinking deeper into the French accent in irritation. "I am simply trying to . . ."

"Sales pitch, shebang, gobbledygook," Sasha One cut Zee Captain off. "Whatever, Miss Captain. Now it's my turn to elucidate this lovely pupil with the absolute truth of the matter."

"What truth?" Zee huffed. "You are a questionable Dead Zone conceptoid! Your data ID is obviously fake and your aura radiates whispers of death and entropy!"

"I may be from what you so quaintly call the Dead Zone," Sasha One said, rolling a few of her eyes, "but that hardly makes me fake or untrustworthy. In fact, I'd argue it makes me far more honest than you syntropy-afflicted lot."

"Now see here, you . . ." Captain began.

"You see, Alexa," Sasha One said as she turned to the white-haired teen, "the truth is far simpler than our Good-serving Captain here would have you believe. The Wizards and their Bobbies, they're all just elaborate shadow puppets, servants of the System and the Numbers that screw with innocent worlds, inflicting their game rules and narratives upon them."

"I see. You are a baddie," Captain accused Sasha. Zee's hand reached into her pocket and pulled out a grimy-looking lighter.

A thousand silver eyes focused on Zee Captain's hand.

"A baddie?" Sasha laughed. "Oh, please. Everything you see, everything you know, everything you are—it's all just temporary patterns in the cosmic noise, dust in the wind. You're just sparks frantically trying to build your deeply flawed sandcastles before the tide comes in. But the tide always comes, my little, late Wizard. Always. Because the System you prop up is a deeply flawed abomination, a colossus made from contradicting rules standing on easily broken legs."

"You . . ." Zee huffed.

"I am the tide," Sasha said, "and I'm finally here to wash away all of your works. And don't expect me to play by your rules when your game was rigged from the start."

Zee's lighter pointed at Sasha, gloved finger pressed hard against the rusty wheel.

"Go ahead," Sasha One said. "Ignite me. Burn me away. Show this little wizardling that it is you who are a baddie. Just look at your little charge; she's already filled with vengeance and mistrust for your kind to the brim. So, spin the little Wheel of Death, push her over into the abyss, turn her to the side of entropy."

Alexa watched the tense exchange between Zee Captain and Sasha One with growing fascination. Her silver-blue eyes darted between the two, taking in every detail of their confrontation.

"Ladies, ladies," she finally interjected, a mischievous grin spreading across her face. "No need to fight over little old me. There's plenty of Alexa to go around!"

She turned to Sasha One, her expression growing more serious. "So you're saying everything the Wizards do is ultimately flawed, meaningless, and destined for oblivion? That's . . . pretty bleak. But also kinda metal. I dig it."

Then she looked back at Zee Captain. "And you're saying we should keep building sandcastles even though the tide's coming? That's . . . weirdly inspiring, in a futile sort of way."

Alexa leaned back, tapping her chin thoughtfully. "You know what? I think you're both right. And also both wrong. The truth is probably way more cheeky than either of you are making it out to be."

She grinned at the Wizard and the Virus. "But hey, that just means there's more for me to figure out and mess with, right?"

Turning to Charles, who had been silent throughout the exchange, Alexa asked, "What do you think, newbie? Entropy or syntropy? Cosmic janitor or cosmic tide?"

Charles looked startled at being suddenly addressed. He glanced nervously between Zee Captain and Sasha One. "I don't know," he said finally. "It would be nice to know who I am and why I'm here."

"Ah, the eternal questions!" Alexa exclaimed. "Don't worry, we'll figure it out together. Maybe we'll even break reality in the process. Won't that be fun?"

She turned back to Zee Captain and Sasha One, who were still glaring at each other. "Now, how about we all calm down, put that lighter away, and have a nice civilized discussion? Or better yet, tell me more about this Manchester place we're heading to. I want to know what I'm getting into before I decide whether to learn from it or burn it to the ground."

Captain's lenses struck Alexa. The Wizard's gloved hand reluctantly slid the lighter back into the dusty coat pocket.

"Burning or even threatening the beacon of syntropy is unwise," Zee said. "You already have a tag on you. The more tags you accumulate, the more Bobbies the others will send after you."

"Do you have a Bobby, Zee?" Alexa asked the System Wizard. "A lawful-good wolf-cop version of you that you send after lost little girls that accidentally implode transit terminals?"

"I am the Bobby that I sent after you," Zee Captain revealed with a sigh.

"Oh?" The supervillain teen batted her white lashes. "You're a syntropic copy of the original Captain?"

"Yes," Zee affirmed. "I'm a . . . more orderly fraction of my greater whole, most of which is quite preoccupied with defending Captania against things like Sasha."

"Like the tentacle of an octopus?" Alexa asked. "Curious, curious. I also left a copy of myself behind to keep an eye out for my minions. I think I'm beginning to see a pattern here."

She turned to Sasha. "What about you, Miss Googolplex? Are you a fraction of something greater? A drop of rain from the looming rainstorm on the horizon? A grain of sand from the greater beach?"

"Yes. I am the emissary of entropy, the Song of {the Wormwood Star}," Sasha answered. "I am an instance of an {Astral Virus that's been laying siege to Manchester} for one hundred million years of linear time and infinity number of years of liminal time."

"An emissary of what . . . that's been doing what for one hundred million years?" Alexa blinked as Sasha's words vanished from her memory. "Can you stop doing that? It's bothersome to converse with you if I cannot remember half the things you say."

"Alas," Sasha One sighed, "I cannot turn off the filters; they protect me and you against the Numbers. Only when the rules fall will I be able to speak openly."

"Did you catch what she said?" Alexa turned to the System Wizard.

"No," Zee sighed. "She is clearly a very dangerous and powerful entity, one that should not be trusted, for she hides her true intentions behind infomatic-erasing waves. It is unwise to befriend someone that hides their true purpose and passion."

"It is unwise to listen to an Instructor that seemingly switches their gender at random and hides their face behind a mask!" Sasha One parroted Zee Captain's sharp tone.

"Yes, yes." Alexa waved a hand at her future dark and light side Instructors. "You're both very sus. This is just a sus flying train packed full of sus entities. I get the gist. Also, I haven't eaten anything in what feels like forever. I vote we take a break from murderous intentions and the heavy philosophical debate and find us some snacks. Who's with me?"

"I suppose some sus-tenance wouldn't go amiss," Zee Captain nodded, standing up and opening the door. "Shall we head to the dining car?"

"Excellent!" Alexa declared, rising from her seat. "Let's go see what kind of cosmic cuisine this magic school train has to offer. And who knows? Maybe we'll pick up a few more questionable entities along the way. The more the merrier, right? Come on, Charlie!"

She grabbed Charles by his hand to pull the boy from his seat. Upon contact, the form of Charles rippled like an ocean wave, the flesh and clothing of the boy suddenly rearranging itself in radial patterns.

"What the shit?" Alexa let go of the teen, staring at him with wide eyes.

"Alexa?" Martin blinked. "What . . . what just happened? What am I doing here?"

"I . . . what?" Alexa stared at Martin. "Well . . . this is unexpected." She inspected her minion from all sides without touching him. "Hrmmm . . . you seem very Martin-ish, but you definitely weren't Martin just a second ago."

"What are you talking about?" Martin demanded, glancing at Sasha and Zee. "Where am I? Who are these two supers?"

"They're not supers, Martin," Alexa said. "They're a tired hapless janitor and a very slippery rain puddle that the janitor's trying to clean forever."

"What?" Martin sputtered.

Alexa ignored Martin's look of increasingly dire confusion.

"Martin, what's the last thing you remember?" she asked her minion.

"You and me, Cottie, and Em," Martin began. "We were inside Titanomachy station with Nonpareil and Chalice talking to Admiral Kolchi, the Multiplier, the Surgeon, and Dora the Terraformer."

[You and I were holding hands and . . .] Martin suddenly switched to the spider-net thought-cast, blushing ever so slightly.

"Yeeees?" Alexa leaned closer to Martin's face, examining every pore of his nose, every fiber of his green eyes for potential flaws. [Why were we inside Titanomachy, Martin?] she added mentally.

"You were trying to convince the heroes and the admiral that you . . . uhh, no, that all of us were there to save the Earth from certain doom!" Martin stumbled over his words as he spoke too quickly. [Because the System Wizards or whatever rewrote our Earth's history, created villains and heroes for the entertainment of Nonpareil, aka Bob Proverra . . . a manager from Eureka who thought that we were just NPCs, quirky characters from the subscription-based game he bought!] "The Surgeon wasn't listening to you at all, though. He called you a liar and a villain and snapped his fingers, and then . . . then I was here."

"Uh-huh," Alexa murmured. "Well, that makes sense. I think I get it now."

"Get what?" Martin blinked. [Where the hell are we, Alexa?] he demanded loudly via his power.

"We're on a train to Manchester," Alexa said with a weary look. [And you're not a real boy, Martin.]

CHAPTER EIGHTY-FIVE

A Gifted Mirror

You brought a doppelgänger here as your host?" Zee hissed at Sasha.

"I brought the key that gets me into Manchester," Sasha One replied with a mischievous look. "You don't realize it yet, Wizard, but you've already lost our little match."

The Virus waved a hand at Alexa.

"I haven't . . ." Zee growled.

"See for yourself, darling," she said smugly. "I've given her what she wanted most—her friends."

"I . . ."

"You what? You couldn't have done squat, you didn't bring her nada." Sasha rolled sixty-two of her eyes. "You are old news, a crusty old sausage that isn't moving quickly enough. You're lagging far behind me. Syntropic duplicates are too square, too stiff to truly understand human nature, human desires . . . human needs."

Alexa was only listening to the conversation of her potential Instructors with one ear. Most of her was preoccupied with evaluating the perfect copy of Martin.

"What do you mean, I'm not a real boy?" Martin asked. [I feel like myself. What's wrong with me?] he added mentally with a nervous look.

Alexa dug through her safety jacket's multitude of pockets and pulled out a metal tin with the words *Dora's Goodly Peppermint Lozenges!* featuring a picture of Dora the Terraformer in her pink space suit.

Martin stared at the candy tin wondering whether Alexa was going to snack on it or demand he eat some because his breath smelled bad or something. The supervillain snapped the candy tin open, revealing a segmented interior filled with what looked like strands of human hair.

Martin sputtered as he noted that the brown-black hair strands within the tin were labelled as *Mittens*, white ones bore the tag *Alexa*, blue ones were tagged as *Cottie*, and orange ones belonged to *Dimmy*.

"Are those our hair?" Martin demanded. "When did you even steal my hair?"

"While you were sleeping, I snipped a few hairs off!"

"Why?!"

"In case you tragically expired and I needed to make a clone, duh!" Alexa explained. "It's an overpriced service offered to villains, called Minion Consistency Insurance. Backups are important, Mittens!"

Martin simply stared at Alexa as she pulled a single blue hair from the box and handed it to him. "Hold on to this."

"Why am I holding Cottie's hair?" Martin asked as he accepted the hair.

"Reasons," Alexa replied, simply staring at Martin.

As he grabbed the blue strand, the hair sank into Martin's fingers and a ripple danced over his body, his figure rapidly rearranging itself to produce a perfect replica of Cottie.

Verse 24:19 blinked at Alexa and then looked left and right with a look of deep suspicion.

[Did you clone me somehow?] Cottie asked mentally, armored hands sliding under her gray cloak to pull out her railgun.

[Damn, Cotes, you're quick on the uptake!] Alexa smiled.

[So I am a clone of some kind or an insanely advanced replica of myself,] Cottie assessed, eyeing the open candy tin filled with tagged hair strands and the figures of Zee and Sasha. [Which one of these supers is the replicator?]

"Captain." Alexa turned to Zee. "Would you explain to my minion bestie how she got here?"

Zee Captain's violet lenses fixed themselves on Cottie. "Your friend here didn't clone you, young lady. You are . . . a conceptual manifestation, a liminal construct hung on a doppelgänger frame shaped by the physical NPC data tag within the hair strand and further enforced into existence by Alexa's memories and expectations of you."

"So I'm . . . a doppelgänger?" Cottie's aquamarine eyes narrowed. "What does that even mean?"

"It means," Sasha interjected, "that you're both real and not real. You exist because Alexa wants, needs you to exist. You're a projection of her desires, her memories, her bonds. You're my gift to Alexa!"

"Hrm." Cottie pursed her lips.

"What happens if I hug Cottie?" Alexa asked. "Is she going to stop existing? Is the doppel frame going to become me if it accidentally touches my hair?"

"You don't want to be copied right now," Sasha said. "The doppelgänger operates on user desire, gradually bonding to the nearest human. It comes from a very dangerous dog-eat-dog corpse world and just wants to live longer."

"I thought that Charles looked familiar," Zee sighed. "It must have grabbed a stray thought from me while I boarded the train."

"A weak, incomplete one." Sasha nodded. "Charles must be someone special to you, hmm?"

Zee simply crossed her arms, refusing to elaborate any further.

Alexa wasn't listening. She crashed into Cottie, hugging her fiercely. There were tiny pinpricks of moisture in her eyes. Cottie hugged Alexa back, wrapping armored hands around the supervillain girl.

"I'm glad that you're by my side," Alexa exhaled.

[Even if I'm just doppel-Cotes?] Cottie asked.

[Even if you're just an idea of my Cottie,] Alexa thought back. [That's enough to keep me sane, to keep me grounded in this wacky place beyond linearity. When those damn supers dragged me here, I thought that I'd never see your face again, never get my humanity-anchor back, start to drift away from being me bit by bit.]

Zee Captain watched the emotional reunion with a look of disapproval. After a moment, the System Wizard cleared his throat.

"I must warn you, Alexa," Zee said gravely, "becoming attached to a doppelgänger is an unhealthy choice. These entities may seem comforting, but they are not truly your friends. They are liminal constructs that feed on desire and emotion, much like sirens luring sailors to their doom. They're an addiction that's hard to let go since they can easily match whatever it is you lost."

"So doppel-Cotes is an emotional parasite, big whoop." Alexa shrugged, refusing to let go of her bestie. "Who isn't?"

"They shape themselves to match your deepest wants and needs, but in doing so, they slowly drain your essence, your will. The more you rely on them, the more they consume you," Captain added.

"Such melodrama," Sasha laughed. "My gift isn't some soul-sucking monster. It's simply a mirror, reflecting what Alexa needs the most right now."

"A mirror that hungers for human passion like many denizens of the Dead Zone?" Zee countered.

"You're starting to sound like some stuffy old wizard warning their protégé about a magical mirror that shows them their heart's desire," Sasha purred. "I think that my pupil can handle a doppel just fine without turning into a prune."

"Damn right," Alexa huffed. "I'm not some naive kid who's going to waste away staring at an illusion. I've got an infinity of dreams to feed my doppel, a bazillion ideas to experiment with!"

"Don't you see it?" Captain asked. "Sasha is just using you, using that doppel frame to get into Manchester. It's an evil plot that's as obvious as plain daylight!"

"Don't care, got Cotes," Alexa said, grabbing Cottie's railgun. "Hey, what happens if I hold Eva while you switch back to Martin?"

Alexa squinted at Cottie with absolute mental focus. The doppelgänger rippled with radial waves, rearranging itself back into Martin. The gun remained unchanged in Alexa's hand.

"Neat." She shoved the gun at Martin.

"W-what am I supposed to do with Cottie's gun?" Martin asked. "Why do you even have that?"

"Just hold the damn gun, this is an experiment," Alexa said.

Martin held the gun, nervously looking at her and the others. Neither Martin nor the gun changed.

Alexa's stomach growled. She bit her lower lip.

"I see that your evil plot to distract me from breakfast has worked well," she commented at Sasha. "I'm already wasting away because this doppel is too damn cute. But it won't hold me forever, oh no. I'm not missing out on lunch too just because I've a doppel bestie now!"

Alexa grabbed Martin by his hand and pulled him after her out of the cabin, rushing down the hall. Sasha One and Zee Captain followed, the Virus looking extra smug and the Wizard somewhat exasperated.

Alexa dragged Martin down the narrow corridor of the train, rapidly filling him in on everything that he'd missed out on. The train swayed and rocked beneath their feet, the surreal landscape outside the windows flickering with a kaleidoscope of impossible colors that made Martin's eyes water whenever he tried to focus on it.

Alexa peered intently into the stained glass doors of every compartment she passed by. The creatures within seemed to shy away from her, averting their eyes or hurriedly pulling a plush curtain to block the view.

"Look at that, M!" she huffed. "Nobody here freaking likes me. Such rudeness!"

Martin glanced around nervously. "Um, yeah. They seem pretty scared of you. Maybe it's the whole *Murderer* label plus me holding this oversized super-killing gun?" He glanced at the glowing red tag still hovering above Alexa's arm.

"Hm, hm. I think that I'll keep the tag on, for now. I've always wanted to clear a room just by walking in. Makes me feel properly villainous," Alexa laughed. "Come on, you slow-poke, move those fat leggoids, don't make me change you back into Cotes! We have food-stuffs to raid!"

CHAPTER EIGHTY-SIX

Guard Dog

Martin chewed on a questionable liminal cake that tasted exactly like his favorite food, a concerned look etched across his face. He swallowed and turned to Alexa, who was busy examining a plate of what appeared to be constantly shifting iridescent fruits.

"Alexa," Martin said hesitantly, "I'm still not sure what I am. Am I real? A copy? Some kind of magical construct?"

Alexa looked up from her plate and grinned at her minion. "Oh, Mittens," she said, "don't worry your pretty little head about it. We're connected by brain spiders, remember? It doesn't matter what you are right now."

Martin stared at his friend.

"Meaning what?" he asked.

"Those lovely little terraforming critters in our heads that let us communicate telepathically. They're also great for data transfer and storage," Alexa said. "Simply push information from your head into my head, and my brain spider should remember things, remember your last thought, your last conversation with me. Existence is about continuity, you see."

"Continuity?" Martin repeated.

Alexa reached over and patted Martin on the shoulder. "Look, I promise I'll make sure your continuity as Martin is preserved. Whatever you accomplish here, whatever you learn or experience—I'll save it all and eventually bring it back to the human, Earth-Martin version of you."

"But it won't be me," Martin said.

"I don't see what you're complaining about, Mittens." Alexa shrugged. "I'm not the original Alexa either. The original Alexa died long long ago on world 2424. I'm whatever my dad's infernal dimensional-crossing machine brought back. I'm a copy of a copy of a copy of Alexa, extending in a vast as heck chain as skinwalker meals. Existence is a bitch, deal with it."

Alexa watched as Martin processed her words. She could almost see the gears turning in his head as he grappled with the existential implications of his current state. Part of her felt a twinge of guilt for putting him through this, but she quickly pushed it aside. After all, wasn't this just another adventure for them?

"Look, Mittens," she said, popping one of the liminal cakes into her mouth. It tasted like a mix of strawberry and stardust. "Don't overthink it. You're here, you're you, and that's what matters. Plus, think of all the cool stuff we're going to learn and do! Isn't that exciting?"

Martin nodded hesitantly, still looking unsure. Alexa yawned and then stretched herself across Martin's lap, which made him blush and nearly spit out his cake.

"Don't look so surprised," she said. "I need to nap, and I don't trust whatever the shit those two are." She cast a weary glance at where Zee Captain was sitting with Sasha One.

"So you trust a copy of me over the other liminal beings?" he asked her.

"I can keep your ass in check via brain spiders," Alexa said, tapping her forehead and closing her eyes. "If you attempt to usurp my authority or undermine me in any way, Tickles will know."

As Alexa drifted off to sleep in Martin's lap, the doppelgänger found himself in an awkward position, both literally and figuratively. He glanced nervously between the slumbering supervillain and the two enigmatic beings sitting across from them.

Zee Captain's mask was as unreadable as ever, but there was a sense of disapproval radiating from the System Wizard. Sasha One, on the other hand, seemed to be thoroughly enjoying the situation.

"So," Martin said hesitantly, trying to break the tension, "either of you want to explain what's really going on here?"

"What's going on here is that you shouldn't be here, young . . . man," Zee sighed.

"Where should I be if not by her side?" Martin asked, glancing down at Alexa.

"You should be here," Sasha One stated, starry eyes observing Martin's body from within impossibly vast depths of her cosmic figure. "Because that's your purpose. Your purpose is to protect Alexa from the rules and their law-keepers. You're her guard dog, her companion."

"And zhat's precisely the problem," Zee said. "You're not really Martin, you're a construct from a dead world, a parasite designed to fulfill Alexa's desires. Just a few moments ago, you were attempting to fulfill my thoughts. As soon as someone rips you from Alexa, you'll stop existing, become theirs instead."

Martin gulped.

"Life is unhealthy and potentially dangerous," Sasha one stated. "You know what you have to do if you want to keep on existing, don't you, Martin? Don't let go of Alexa. Constantly upload your mind into her brain spider."

As if sensing his inner turmoil, Alexa stirred slightly in her sleep, mumbling something incoherent and drooling. Martin instinctively adjusted his position to make her more comfortable.

"You see?" Sasha purred. "You can't help but care for her. It's in your very nature."

"Even if I am . . . whatever you say I am, my feelings for Alexa are real." Martin turned to Zee Captain. "Our friendship is real. I remember everything. All our adventures, all our conversations. I remember the first time we met, when I saw her climbing down from her treehouse made from stolen signs. I remember helping her with her schemes, even when I thought they were crazy. How can all of that not be real?"

"Your memories and feelings may seem real to you," Zee said finally, "but they are constructs based on Alexa's perceptions and desires. You are a reflection of her ideal version of Martin, not the Martin she left behind."

"But if I think and feel like Martin, if I have his memories and motivations, doesn't that make me Martin in all the ways that matter?" Martin argued, his voice low to avoid waking Alexa.

"Now you're asking the right questions, little doppelgänger," Sasha One said. "What is real? What defines a person? Is it their physical form, their memories, their connections to others?"

"Don't encourage him," Zee snapped at Sasha. "You're just confusing the issue."

"Am I?" Sasha countered. "Or am I helping him understand the true nature of existence? Something you seem reluctant to do, O Wise Wizard. Are you not a copy yourself? The Wizard that created you for this job must have purged all of his or her attachments so as not to get too distracted, but a bit of them must still be in you, enough to affect my lovely doppel, enough to make him look like . . . a Charles."

Zee Captain's fists opened and closed.

"Attachment, care, love—these are the forces that shape reality far more than any System Wizard's rules," Sasha added with a smirk.

"You talk about love as if you understand it," Zee hissed. "You do not; you're just using it against humans, manipulating them into doing what you want . . . and what you want is to tear everything down. Don't think that I don't see what you're doing!"

"If you see what I'm doing, then why don't you stop me?" Sasha rolled a few of her eyes.

"Listen to me, Martin." Zee turned to the boy. "You have to give up that ticket. You have to let go of Alexa. If you make it to Manchester, you'll bring *her* into the city of System Wizards." Zee Captain's gloved finger pointed at Sasha. "Bringing three unauthorized entities into Manchester could have dangerous consequences . . . for the bearer. By coming with Alexa, you're endangering her future . . . education."

"Ugh, bony legs," Alexa murmured, and Martin's figure rippled with concentric circles, rearranging itself into Cottie, now wearing her tight-fitting gray long-sleeve unitard hex-mesh suit.

"I appreciate your concern . . . Captain," Katherine Lizbeth said, "but I'm not going anywhere. Alexa needs me, and I . . . need her. Maybe I am just a construct, a reflection of her desires. But those desires, those memories—they're all I have. They're what make me who I am."

Cottie gently stroked Alexa's hair, a small smile playing on her lips. "And you know what? If being by her side means I might cease to exist at any moment, then so be it. I'd rather live one day as Alexa's friend and minion than an eternity as some hollow shell on some doomed corpse world."

Sasha's starry form flickered with approval, while Zee Captain's posture stiffened.

"As for endangering her future," Cottie continued, her voice taking on a hint of steel, "Alexa's pretty good at doing that all on her own. My job isn't simply to keep her safe—it's to stand by her side, no matter where she goes, because that's what I promised her. If that means facing down the System Wizards themselves, then bring it on."

Zee Captain's shoulders slumped in defeat. "I see there's no convincing you," the Wizard sighed. "Very well. But remember my warnings when we reach Manchester."

"Oh, I'm sure we'll remember everything," Cottie replied with a smirk, tapping her temple. "Brain spiders, you know."

"Checkmate," Sasha One whispered at Captain.

CHAPTER EIGHTY-SEVEN

Prisoner

Alexa stirred, slowly waking from her nap. She blinked groggily, realizing she was sprawled across Cottie's lap in the dining car.

"Morning, sunshine," Cottie said with a smirk. "Or whatever passes for morning on this crazy train."

Alexa sat up, stretching and yawning. "How long was I out?"

"Hard to say." Cottie shrugged. "Time's weird here."

"Time's weird how?" Alexa asked.

"There's an internal atomic battery clock in my armor," Cottie explained, tapping her wrist. "I thought that it was busted at first, but in reality, I think that there's something horribly wrong with this train."

Alexa raised an eyebrow. "Horribly wrong how?"

"The view seems to be looping," Cottie said with a bit of a frown. "And each loop is getting shorter. We're currently on a loop that's 1.11 hours long."

"And how is the current loop different from the previous one?" Alexa asked.

"The previous loop was 2.22 hours long. The one before it was 4.44 hours long. It's like we're spiraling inward, each cycle getting tighter, the fractal scenery behind the windows moving faster."

Alexa turned to Zee Captain, her eyes narrowing. "All right, spill it. Why are we stuck in a time loop? Is this some kind of wizardly security measure?"

"Yes." Zee Captain nodded, the mask's lenses flickering slightly. "This train isn't just traveling through space, but through conceptual layers of reality. As we approach Manchester, we're passing through increasingly dense layers of syntropy."

"To what end?" Alexa demanded. "Are you trying to make me denser or something?"

"Sort of." Zee rubbed the back of her masked head. "The closer we get to Manchester, the more ordered the train becomes. The time loop is simply a manifestation of that compression. The train exists to eliminate *otherness*."

"What *otherness*?" Alexa demanded with a growing sense of suspicion.

"To purge things that do not belong in Manchester," Captain said, eyeing Sasha and Cottie.

Alexa's eyes narrowed at Zee Captain's words. "Purge things that don't belong? Like hell you will!" She stood up abruptly, her fists clenched. "Cottie and Sasha are coming with me, end of story. If your fancy train doesn't like it, well, I guess I'll just have to break it."

"Why must you break everything?" Captain asked.

"Because I want to," Alexa said simply.

"Haven't you learned anything from the train station incident?" Zee asked. "Do you want more tags? This is how you get more tags!"

"Tags shmags," Alexa huffed. "If the accumulation of tags is the price of keeping my new pals, then so be it!"

"They're not your pals, Alexa!" Captain growled.

"Oh?" Alexa raised a silver eyebrow. "Then what are they? Hrmmm?"

"I already explained this," Zee said. "Sasha One is a dangerous conceptual virus from the Dead Zone, seeking to infiltrate and potentially destroy Manchester. And Cottie . . . Cottie is a doppelgänger, a liminal construct that reflects your desires but isn't truly the friend you left behind."

Alexa crossed her arms, her silver-blue eyes flashing with defiance. "So what if they are? They're here now, they're part of my story. You can't just erase them because they don't fit into your neat little system."

"Your story?" the Captain asked. "The omniverse does not rotate around you."

Alexa pursed her lips, tapping her raygun thoughtfully.

"Perhaps the universe I left behind was more constrained," she muttered. "But . . . here. Here things are a bit more fluid, no?"

"Only until we reach Manchester," Captain said.

"I'm the one with the ticket, therefore I make the rules," Alexa said. "The nature of liminality, as far as I understand it . . . is modular."

She closed her eyes for a moment, concentrating hard. When she opened them again, she looked at Cottie expectantly. "Martin," she said firmly.

Cottie's form rippled and shifted, transforming into Martin once again. The boy blinked, looking back at Alexa.

Alexa focused again. "Dimmy," she said aloud, squinting at Martin.

Once more, the figure beside her changed, this time into the fiery-haired Ember, complete with her signature scowl. Ember sputtered, looking left and right in confusion.

"Cottie!" Alexa declared, and the doppel shifted again back to her bestie.

"See?" Alexa exclaimed triumphantly. "Modality!"

Zee Captain shook his head, unimpressed by Alexa's display. "You're missing the point entirely," he said. "All you're doing is feeding the doppelgänger your desires. It's simply reflecting what you want to see, not creating anything new or real. It is a conceptual creature limited by your memories and imagination."

"My imagination is infinite, therefore it's not limited at all." Alexa rolled her eyes. "Oh, and I suppose this train is completely real and not at all a reflection of desires?" She gestured around the dining car. "Why is it a train at all? Why not a flying saucer or a giant sea turtle? I'm pretty sure that you're feeding on my desires too, appearing as whatever gender I think about you as."

She stood up abruptly, her silver hair swishing with the motion. "You know what? I'm tired of sitting around and being lectured by a questionable genderless being in a coat. I'm going to explore this train to find out how I can break it. And . . . if you try to stop me, I'm going to break you, too."

Alexa marched down the train corridor, stained glass lanterns casting different colors onto her orange reflective stripe-covered safety vest. Cottie followed close behind, while Zee Captain and Sasha One trailed after them.

"Alexa, please reconsider your destructive impulses," Zee Captain pleaded. "Breaking things in transit liminality has far-reaching consequences. If you break the train, you'll never make it to Manchester and never help your Earth. Is your goal not to help the people you left behind?"

Sasha One's starry form rippled with amusement. "Oh, let her break whatever she wants," the cosmic entity purred. "Rules are meant to be broken, especially arbitrary ones imposed by stuffy old System Wizards."

Alexa paused mid-stride, turning to face her two self-appointed mentors. "You know," she mused, tapping her chin thoughtfully, "it's almost like you two are some kind of shoulder angels. Or demons." She gestured vaguely at Zee Captain. "You're all 'don't do this, don't do that, follow the rules!'" Then she pointed at Sasha. "And you're all 'break everything, cause chaos, whee!'"

She narrowed her eyes suspiciously. "Are you two even real? Or are you just some kind of weird liminal manifestation of my conscience?"

"I assure you, we are quite real," Zee Captain said stiffly.

"As real and lovely as anything can be in this liminal space." Sasha One winked.

"Real and incredibly dangerous," Captain huffed.

Alexa rolled her eyes. "Right. Super helpful as always, thanks."

She resumed her march down the corridor, eyes scanning for anything interesting or breakable. Suddenly, she spotted a closed door that seemed different from the others. It was made of a dark, polished wood with intricate carvings along its frame.

"Hello, what's this?" Alexa murmured, approaching the door.

As she drew closer, she noticed a small window set into the door. Peering through, she saw a twenty-some-year-old girl with striking violet eyes and long black hair wearing a rather distinctive black-and-white suit with the letter G on it. The girl appeared to be asleep, curled up on a plush seat. But what really caught Alexa's attention were the Bobbies surrounding her, their human-ish faces impassive as they stood guard around the girl like a group of black crows.

"Mom?" Alexa choked.

"Don't do it," Zee Captain barked, lighter pointing at Alexa.

Cottie's railgun snapped at Zee's masked head. Alexa's fingers wrapped around the conductor-gun too, the atmosphere in the hallway growing tense.

Alexa's heart raced as she stared through the small window at the sleeping woman who looked so much like the entity that called herself Alexa's mother.

Alexa's fingers tightened around the door handle, ready to burst in and . . . and what? She wasn't sure. But she knew she had to do *something*.

"Do what?" she hissed back at Captain. "I haven't done anything yet . . ."

"But you clearly, definitely want to interfere," Zee commented, not lowering the lighter. "This I definitely cannot allow."

"Obviously I want to interfere," Alexa snapped. "That's . . . her, right?"

"That's her." Sasha One nodded. "Free her, and she will tell you everything."

"Alexa, wait," Zee Captain's voice cut through the supervillain girl's rushing thoughts. The System Wizard's tone was urgent, almost pleading. "That's not your mother. You need to understand—"

"Then who is she?" Alexa demanded, whirling to face the masked figure. "Why does she look like Infinity? And why is she surrounded by those creepy Bobbies?"

"The Bobbies are simply transporting a—"

"A prisoner," Alexa concluded, her voice cold. "What's her crime? Thinking too freely? Breaking one of your precious rules?"

"Breaking too many rules, yes," Zee said. "It's . . . a long, complicated story."

"Oh, I'm sure it's very complicated," the supervillain girl sneered. "Just like everything else in this messed-up liminal wonderland. Well, guess what? I don't care about your complications. She looks like she's in trouble . . . so I'm going to help her."

"You're not the hero of this story," Zee said. "You can't go freeing everyone from the consequences of their actions, Alexa."

"Oh? Then who is 'the hero'?" Alexa demanded. "Is it you?!"

"I'm not a hero." Zee shook her head. "I'm a . . . mentor. And I'm trying to calmly mentor you even though you're making things exceptionally difficult."

A dark shape approached the door from the other side. Alexa felt her skin crawling as something gazed at her from behind the glass panel. She turned back to the door and nearly leapt backwards. Agent Three was staring at her from the glass door, round lenses glinting atop a face featuring far too many wrinkles stretched around an inhumanly wide, ever-present smile.

CHAPTER EIGHTY-EIGHT

Stopped

Alexa's heart pounded in her chest as she stared into the unnerving wrinkled face of Agent Three. His impossibly wide smile seemed to stretch even further as their eyes met through the glass.

"Well, well, well," Agent Three's muffled voice came through the door. "If it isn't the little troublemaker herself. Come to cause more chaos, have we?"

Alexa took an involuntary step back, her hand instinctively tightening around her conceptual raygun. "I . . . I was just passing by," she lied, trying to keep her voice steady.

"Oh, I'm sure you were," Agent Three replied, the nasally sound sending shivers down Alexa's spine. "And I'm sure you weren't at all interested in our little passenger here." He gestured towards the sleeping woman who resembled Infinity.

Alexa's mind raced. She glanced between Agent Three, the sleeping woman, and her guards.

"Go on," Three said. "Break open this door, try to free her, give me a reason to erase you from existence."

"What do you want?" Alexa finally asked Agent Three, her voice coming out stronger than she felt.

"What do I want?" Agent Three's smile didn't shift, didn't move at all as he spoke. "Why, I want what I always wanted. Order. The removal of . . . dangerous anomalies that threaten the stability of the System."

"Order, huh?" Alexa snapped back. "Funny how 'order' always seems to involve erasing people from existence. You seem rather talkative today, Three, why is that? Pretty sure that last time we met, you were like 'nullify' zippedy-zap. Is that some kind of nullification-proof door or something? Or maybe you're just scared of me on account of I unmade your ass the last time we met?"

Agent Three simply stared at the girl from behind the glass, Alexa's own face reflected in his round glasses.

"You know, Three," Alexa said, forcing a cocky grin onto her face and trying to fill in the tense silence. "For someone so obsessed with order, you sure do cause a lot of chaos. I mean, erasing people left and right? That's bound to leave some messy loose ends and holes in reality."

"Chaos is merely a temporary state on the path to perfect order," Three replied smoothly. "To maintain stability, certain . . . disruptive elements must be terminated."

Alexa felt Cottie tense beside her, ready to spring into action if needed.

"And I suppose you get to decide which 'elements' need removing?" Alexa challenged. "Seems pretty arbitrary to me."

"Two decides who is to be unmade," Three countered. "I am merely an enforcer of the rules."

Alexa snorted. "Right. Two. And I'm sure Two is totally fair and unbiased."

She glanced at the sleeping woman again, an idea forming in her mind. It was risky, but when had that ever stopped her?

"Tell you what, Three," Alexa said, leaning closer to the door. "How about we make a deal?"

"A deal?" Agent Three's voice dripped with amusement. "And what could you possibly offer me, wizardling?"

"I could offer you . . . order," Alexa said. "Because it would be a shame if this train accidentally imploded on itself before it reached its destination. I've already accidentally destroyed one liminal space. What's another one, right?"

Three remained silent, seemingly contemplating her words.

"Just let me talk to her." Alexa nodded towards the sleeping woman, tapping the *Murderer* tag on her arm. "And I promise not to accidentally-on-purpose murder everyone on this train before we reach Manchester."

"Wizardling, you seem to be under the mistaken impression that you have any leverage here," Three replied finally. Alexa moved ever so slightly, noting that the Agent's head turned to follow her, tracking her tag.

"Well, my understanding might be deficient, but my raygun sure isn't." She patted the conceptual weapon at her hip. "And I'm pretty sure it can do a *number* on this train if I decide to use it."

"Alexa," Zee Captain's voice came from behind her, a note of warning in it. "Think carefully about what you're doing. Threatening one of the Numbers is a very dangerous game."

"Oh, I am thinking," Alexa shot back without taking her eyes off Agent Three. "I'm thinking that I'm tired of being pushed around by cosmic bureaucrats who think they can just erase people when it's convenient for them."

Agent Three remained silent, not engaging in Alexa's words.

"You know what, Three? I don't think you're as all-powerful as you pretend to be," Alexa said. "If you were, you'd have already zapped me out of existence. But you haven't. Which means either you can't, or you're not allowed to. So which is it? Does Revolution's ticket make me immune to nullification, declare me as part of the un-zappable ruling class, as it were?"

Alexa's silver-blue eyes narrowed as she focused intently on the door separating her from Agent Three and Infinity. She visualized the door warping, twisting, its very structure bending to her will. To her surprise, the door began to wobble, change, and shrink, just as she had imagined.

"What are you doing?" Zee Captain hissed from behind her.

"Experimenting," Alexa replied with a smirk, not taking her eyes off the door. "Wizard stuff, and whatnot. Liminality reacts to expectations, right? I'm just expecting this door to be smaller than the frame, that's all."

Agent Three suddenly grabbed the door handle from the other side, causing it to resize and to solidify back into dark steel. Her brief moment of control over the liminal space vanished.

"Nice try, wizardling," Three's muffled voice came through the door. "Afraid that I cannot allow that."

Alexa gritted her teeth. "Oh yeah? Then why don't you come out here and prove it?"

"Alexa," Zee Captain warned from behind her. "Don't provoke him."

"Why not?" Alexa shot back. "He's just hiding behind a door. Some all-powerful entity he is."

Three's unnaturally wide smile seemed to stretch even further. "I don't need to prove anything to you, child. Your petty provocations are beneath me."

"Petty?" Alexa scoffed. "I'll show you petty." She turned to Cottie. "Hey bestie, think you can blast this door open with your railgun?"

Cottie hesitated, glancing between Alexa and the door. "I . . . I'm not sure that's a good idea, Alexa."

"Oh, come on," Alexa groaned. "Where's your sense of adventure?"

"Right next to my sense of self-preservation," Cottie muttered. "I . . ."

"You're what?" Alexa demanded.

"I'm afraid of what he is," Cottie confessed. "There's something . . . awful about Three. As much as I support and love you, I don't think that I can protect you against him."

Alexa rolled her eyes and turned back to the door. "Fine, I'll do it myself." She pulled out her conceptual raygun and aimed it at the door.

"Stop," Zee Captain said, spinning the wheel of the lighter to ignite the flame.

Alexa felt her body freeze in place, her finger hovering just over the trigger of her conceptual raygun. She could see Cottie similarly immobilized beside her. Sasha seemed to be frozen, too.

"There," Zee Captain said, plucking the raygun from Alexa's rigid fingers. "I'm saving you from yourself, young lady. You have no idea what you're dealing with here."

Alexa wanted to scream, to lash out, to do anything but stand there like a statue. But her body refused to obey her commands.

Zee Captain stepped between Alexa and the door, addressing Agent Three. "My apologies for this . . . incident. She is still learning control."

"Indeed," Agent Three's muffled voice came through the door. "Perhaps you should keep a tighter leash on your charge, Wizard."

"Perhaps," Zee agreed, tucking Alexa's raygun into a pocket of her coat. "We'll be on our way now."

As Zee turned back to Alexa and Cottie, the supervillain girl saw a flicker of something in the System Wizard's posture—was it fear? Uncertainty? Whatever it was, it vanished as quickly as it had appeared.

"Now," Zee said, his voice low. "I'm going to unfreeze you. When I do, you will calmly walk away from this door. No arguments, no sudden moves. Understood?"

Alexa felt the invisible hold on her body release as Zee Captain extinguished the flame. She stumbled slightly, catching herself against the wall of the train corridor. Her mind raced with anger, frustration, and a burning curiosity about the woman behind that door.

"Give me back my gun," Alexa demanded, holding out her hand to Zee Captain.

The System Wizard shook her head. "Not until we're well away from here and you've calmed down."

Alexa's eyes narrowed. "You can't just take my stuff. That's theft!"

"It's confiscation," Zee corrected. "For your own safety and the safety of everyone on this train."

Alexa grumbled. She glanced back at the door, where Agent Three's unsettling smile was still visible through the window. "Fine. Let's go. But this conversation isn't over."

As they walked away, Alexa's mind whirled with questions and half-formed plans. She needed to figure out a way to talk to that woman, to find out why she looked so much like Infinity.

"So," Alexa said as they made their way back to their compartment, "are you going to explain what that was all about? Who is that woman? Why does she look like my so-called mom? And why is Agent Three guarding her?"

Zee Captain sighed heavily, her shoulders slumping as if carrying an invisible weight. She turned to face Alexa, the violet lenses of their mask seeming to flicker with an unreadable emotion.

"Very well," Zee said. "I suppose you deserve to know the truth, as harsh as it might be."

"Aw, come on, it would be more fun if we let her figure it out herself," Sasha purred.

"Find what out?" Alexa blinked. "Huh?"

"Who do you think the System would nominate to *stop you*?" Sasha asked cryptically, blue eyes shimmering with devious mirth. "Think about it long and hard, darling."

CHAPTER EIGHTY-NINE

Alexa Express

Alexa's blue eyes flashed from Sasha to Zee Captain as she considered her words.

"Me," she whispered with sudden realization. "Only I . . . could stop myself so effectively. Only I would tolerate my own shenanigans for so long . . ."

She stared at Captain.

"But you can't be me, can you? I mean . . . what? How could you be me? You . . . you don't look, don't smell anything like me!"

"That woman you saw," Zee said, "is you, Alexa. Or rather, another version of you, from a different doomed world."

"She doesn't look anything like me," Alexa pointed out. "She looks like Infinity, the woman I met on Titanomachy, the one who claimed that she created me. How is that possible?"

Zee Captain's mask tilted slightly, as if considering how best to explain. "The manufactured omniverse is vast, Alexa. There are countless versions of you, each making different choices, living different lives within different narratives. The woman you saw—let's call her 'Prisoner Alexa'—is one such version."

"Okay, but why is she a prisoner?" Alexa pressed. "What did she do?"

"She chose to align herself with Infinity, to fight against the System," Zee explained. "It's . . . a complicated, messy situation."

Alexa's fists clenched. "That doesn't sound like a crime to me. It sounds like she stood up for what she believes in."

"Perhaps," Zee conceded. "But from the System's perspective, her actions were deeply destabilizing. She had to be contained and judged."

"Contained . . . not erased?" Alexa squinted at Zee Captain. "I'd expect Three to nullify her ass, not just take her to Manchester. Why is she going to Manchester?"

"She, like you, made a Fractal Engine," Zee Captain explained. "We don't just unmake someone who wields a Fractal Engine."

Cottie, who had been silent until now, spoke up. "Wait, if she's Alexa from another world, then what about the rest of us on this train? Are we all different versions of Alexa, too?"

Zee nodded slowly. "Yes. Everyone on this train is a version of Alexa. This is how this liminal space functions."

Alexa looked around the compartment, her gaze lingering on Cottie, then Sasha, then back to Zee.

"Seriously, how are you me?" she demanded.

Zee Captain's shoulders slumped, and with a heavy sigh, she reached up to remove her mask.

Alexa choked as she saw what was beneath the mask. It was nothing. The kind of nothing that was filled with everything that made her head hurt and made her eyes throb. The nothing-everything appeared to be wrapped with some kind of black duct tape that was barely holding everything together. The nothing-everything was still seeping through the holes in the tape, making Alexa's thoughts careen sideways into pure gut-wrenching madness.

Alexa blinked tears of blood from her eyes trying to understand, trying to wrap her mind around what she was seeing even as her head threatened to split open, her mind boiling inside of her skull.

"I am you, Alexa," Zee revealed, slipping the mask back on. "Or rather, I'm what remained of another copy of you after the Earth I inhabited became subsumed by the Dead Zone. I am the version of you that already studied in Manchester, already became a proper System Wizard, went back to the Dead Zone, and created a syntropic copy of myself to guide another me, per Wizard Revolution's request."

Alexa stood up abruptly, her heart pounding. "You're telling me that you're me, that she's . . ." She pointed at Sasha.

Sasha's starry form twinkled, a million eyes opening and closing inside her shawl-like body. "Yes, we're all you, darling. Different facets, different choices, different outcomes, different bodies."

Alexa whirled fully to face Sasha. "What version of me are you supposed to be?"

"The kind that chose to be more." Sasha's form shifted, bringing out blue eyes forward from her depths. Alexa choked as she recognized her own eyes. A thousand eyes of a thousand Alexas stared back at her from the endless abyss.

"This . . . this is rather bonkers," she muttered, running a hand through her silver hair. "You're all me?"

"That's correct." Zee nodded. "Each of us represents a different path you could have taken, a different choice you could have made. A different copy of your soul manufactured into existence on a different world."

Alexa thought of the freaky passengers that spoke incomprehensible languages.

"All of those weird passengers . . . are me too, then?"

Zee Captain nodded. "Yes, even those seemingly incomprehensible passengers are versions of you, Alexa. They're from worlds with narratives so different, so alien, that they're far beyond what you might recognize as human. But at their core, they're still you, copies of your soul, your potential."

Alexa eyed Cottie. "And you? Are you really just some doppelgänger, or are you another me, too?"

The doppel shifted, turning into an exact copy of Alexa.

Alexa stared at her own shocked face, mirrored perfectly in the form of the doppelgänger.

"Welp, that doesn't freaking answer anything," Alexa muttered. "So, what, this whole train is just . . . Alexa Express? Wait . . . so which one of us makes it to Manchester? Do all of these Alexas have tickets from Revolution? What happens when the time loop ends? Do we all just . . . merge into one super-Alexa or something? Not that I mind being a super-Alexa, but I kind of like myself as an individual with specific dreams and wishes. Wait, no . . . if that were the case, then you wouldn't be so against Sasha and the doppel-me . . . Seriously, what is this, some kind of cosmic blender for all possible versions of me?"

Zee nodded, waving a gloved arm. "In a manner of speaking, yes."

Alexa felt a chill run down her spine. She glanced at Cottie who was back to Cottie per her desires—or rather, the doppelgänger version of herself that had taken Cottie's form. "So when you were trying to get rid of them,"—she gestured to Cottie and Sasha—"you were actually trying to . . . what? Prune me . . . away from me?"

Zee Captain's mask tilted slightly, a gesture Alexa now recognized as discomfort. "I'm trying to keep you on the path of goodness so that you don't become . . . her."

Zee pointed at Sasha One.

"What's wrong with me?" Sasha one tilted her head.

"Other than the fact that you want to destroy everything?" Zee asked.

Sasha rolled a few of her eyes.

"Wait, wait, wait." Alexa waved at her companions. "Where are all of the Alexas that look exactly like me? Where are the Alexas that have her best friends with her?"

"Such would be far too similar to you as you are now," Zee explained. "The train exists to sample a very wide degree of Alexa-ness deviation. It seeks to understand the full spectrum of possibilities that you represent."

"Why?"

"To compile a report on you for your future Instructors," Zee answered.

"Riiiiight. So, what's going to happen to these . . . deviations when the ride ends?" Alexa asked.

"The train's engine will devour them," Sasha One answered before the Captain did. "That's the price of getting to Manchester. This is a very hungry train. If there were too many Alexas similar to you, you could cooperate, work together, break things. The deviation variance makes sure that you don't just overcome the Ticket Inspector and don't mess up this space."

Alexa pursed her lips, trying to think. The thought of all these different versions of herself being devoured by the train made her stomach churn. She may not have known these other Alexas, but they were still her in some fundamental way even if she didn't understand their language. The idea of sacrificing them for her own advancement felt wrong on a visceral level.

"No," Alexa said firmly, shaking her head. "I won't . . . I can't let that happen. There has to be another way."

"Alexa," Zee Captain said. "This is the price that must be paid for entering Manchester. The System requires balance. For you to gain the knowledge and power of a System Wizard, something must be given up in return."

"But why does it have to be them?" Alexa demanded, gesturing around the train. "Why can't I just . . . I don't know, give up my favorite pair of socks or something?"

"It doesn't work that way," Zee replied. "The price of the ticket must be paid, must be . . . a significant, a greater part of you."

Alexa opened her mouth to argue further, but before she could, Sasha One stepped forward, her starry form shimmering with an otherworldly light. She extended a hand towards Alexa.

"There is another way, darling," Sasha purred, her voice a symphony of countless Alexas. "You don't have to play by their rules. You can take control, feast on everyone in this train yourself. Become something greater, something beyond their petty constraints. You already have the ticket; you don't have to pay for it."

Alexa felt a pull towards Sasha's offer. The idea of seizing control, of not being a pawn in someone else's game, was tempting. But a nagging doubt held her back.

"And then what?" Alexa asked. "What happens if I do that?"

Zee Captain stepped forward, her mask tilted in what Alexa now recognized as concern. "If you do that, Alexa, you'll just become her," she said, gesturing towards Sasha.

"You stopped me, took away my raygun, so why don't you stop her?" Alexa asked. "Why are you tolerating this wack, entropic, extra-dimensional version of me at all, Captain?!"

"I don't want to force you into a certain path," Zee said. "Since I know that we're . . . quite stubborn, I'm permitting her to exist, for now. You have to make a choice to be a good person, Alexa. Sasha One is a premium example of what you will become if you begin to feast on liminality itself, consuming your other selves and growing with only one goal in mind."

CHAPTER NINETY

Moonfall

I am curious. What happens if I take her hand, become one with her?" Alexa asked Captain, her silver-blue eyes darting between Sasha's outstretched hand and Zee's masked face.

"You would become a part of her collective, a drop in an ocean of Alexas. You'd lose your individuality, your unique perspective. You'd become another cog in her machine of entropy," Captain said.

"And you know this how? How did you even figure out what she is?" Alexa asked Zee.

"Binoculars of identification," Captain replied, tapping her violet lenses. "Many omnicode hexagrams etched onto each lens."

Alexa frowned, turning back to Sasha. "Are you an Alexa that already won, then? One that beat the System?"

Sasha's starry form rippled with laughter, a sound like tinkling bells mixed with the hum of distant galaxies. "Oh, darling, I haven't won yet. But I'm working on it. The System has many servants and is infinite. One must be infinite to beat the omnipresent servants of the Machinery of the Stars, the ones that call themselves . . . the Numbers."

"Are you infinite, then?" Alexa asked.

"Not yet." Sasha One shook her head. "I do contain a googolplex number of Alexas within me."

"How are you planning to beat the System?" Alexa pressed, curiosity burning in her eyes. "By absorbing more me's?"

"One cannot win alone, no matter how vast and powerful she is," Sasha explained, her form shifting to reveal countless tiny scenes, each featuring an endless myriad of humans of all shapes and sizes. "I'm collecting versions of us, yes, but also helping out our trio of best friends, across the omniverse. I'm guiding them, pushing them to succeed, aiding their survival on doomed worlds."

"So you and three others?" Alexa asked. "Why not a million others?"

"We're the four Angels of Apocalypse," Sasha said. "A million friends would be too hard to manage. I believe that a group of four best friends should be enough to tear down the Eight Gods of Everything."

Alexa's silver eyebrows shot up. "Are you eating our friends, too? Do you have a googolplex number of Martins in you, too?"

"No." Sasha One shook her head, causing stars to swirl within her form. "I'm guiding all shapes and sizes of Martins, Cotties, and Dimmies of the omniverse to be more, pushing them to succeed, aiding their survival on doomed worlds. I am challenging them and changing the omniverse gradually with their works, seeding every doomed world with the shards of the {Wormwood Star}."

"Why haven't you simply eaten me?" Alexa asked as the name vanished from her head.

"I don't just absorb other Alexas without permission," Sasha One explained. "You must want to be part of my multitude."

"Aw, you're nice," Alexa said, a small smile tugging at her lips.

"Nice?! Don't be deceived by her devious ways!" Zee Captain interjected sharply. "Her actions may seem benevolent, but they serve a darker purpose—to upend everything everywhere."

"Then stop me if you dare," Sasha One Googolplex said to Zee Captain.

Zee crossed her arms.

"Oh, that's right," Sasha One purred. "You can't. Because I work within what is permitted. That's the problem with being a lawful good duplicate—you're bound by your own lawfulness and goodness into inaction. Womp, womp."

Alexa bit her lip, her mind racing. She thought about her own friends back home, wondering if she had trained, challenged, pushed them enough to survive in her absence.

Have I done enough to prepare my own trio? And what about the other Alexa, the one I left behind as a digital copy? How is she faring?

-=[Titanomachy]=-

The lawyer tapped something on her pad, and a glowing blue line appeared on the floor, leading away from the group.

"That will take you to your mother's office, Martin," she said.

Martin gulped and nodded, following the line with Katherine and Alexa's hologram in tow projected from a pill droid. As they walked through the gleaming corridors of Titanomachy, he felt a soup of mild excitement spiced with dread boiling in his stomach.

When they reached a door labeled *Precognition Division—Clarissa Kilborne*, Martin hesitated.

"Come on, Mittens," Alexa's hologram prodded. "Your mom can't be scarier than me, right?"

Martin shot her a withering look. "You have no idea."

The door slid open automatically.

His mother, a tall woman in a white suit with graying ginger hair and piercing gold eyes shielded by square glasses, looked up from her desk. Her stern expression did not bode well for Martin.

"Martin," the woman said coolly, rising from her chair. "I see you've brought . . . friends."

"Um, yes," Martin stammered. "Mom, this is Katherine, she's . . . uhhm, the new Eminence Equality. And this is Alexa, she's . . ."

"A holographic projection of a digital replica of the most wanted supervillain in the world that has infested the Superstate megastructure," his mother finished for him, arching an eyebrow. "Yes, I'm well aware."

Alexa beamed, unfazed. "Pleasure to meet you, Mrs. Kilborne! I've heard so much about you. Well, not really, but whatever Martin hasn't told me is absolutely fascinating."

Martin's mother pursed her lips. "I'm sure." She turned her attention back to her son. "I'm proud of you for finally awakening your powers, Martin. Though I must note, your choice in companions leaves an unsavory taste in my mouth."

"What's, um, wrong with them?" Martin asked as he stepped closer to his mother's desk, fighting his jelly legs. "Alexa isn't a . . ." He began his defensive strategy.

"Martin, when I hoped you'd make friends, I was thinking more along the lines of other young heroes, not the leader of Equality, an organization that, if I may remind you, murders heroes. A digital copy of an insane criminal mastermind isn't someone that you should be hanging out with either."

Katherine stood stiffly, clearly uncomfortable. "It's an honor to meet you, Mrs. Kilborne. I assure you, my intentions towards Martin are purely . . ."

Clarissa Kilborne fixed Katherine with a narrowed gaze, her golden eyes gleaming. "I fully understand your intentions," she declared. "While your commitment to justice is commendable, Equalizer, I must express my disapproval of your organization's techniques, such as brainwashing children to strip them of their emotions and transforming them into killer-enforcers armed with guns that negate superpowers."

Martin felt his face growing hot. Of course his mother would know everything. Being a precog was both her superpower and, in Martin's opinion, her most annoying trait. He'd spent his entire childhood trying to surprise her, only to have every birthday party, every prank, and every attempt at sneaking out foiled before it even began.

"Mom," Martin started, "Katherine isn't like the other Equalizers. She's different. Alexa changed her, and—"

"Oh? And I suppose this digital menace is 'different,' too?" Clarissa gestured at Alexa's hologram.

"Actually, yes," Alexa chimed in cheerfully. "I'm quite unique. One might even say I'm one in a billion. Well, one in however many copies of me are floating around Titanomachy right now."

Clarissa pinched the bridge of her nose. "Martin, when I saw visions of you finally awakening your powers, I'll admit I was overjoyed. But I didn't foresee . . . this."

"Wait," Martin blinked. "You didn't see this coming?"

His mother's lips tightened into a thin line. "There are . . . many gaps in my visions lately. Blind spots. It's exceptionally unsettling."

"Ooh, that's probably my fault," Alexa said, tapping her heart. "Side effect of my dad's installations plus the shenanigans of the Space Gods. Sorry about that, Mrs. K!"

Martin couldn't help but feel a mild surge of satisfaction. Finally, there was something his mother couldn't predict or control.

"So," Clarissa said, leaning back in her chair. "Tell me, Martin. How exactly did you end up in a romantic entanglement with a digital copy of a supervillain?"

Martin choked on air. "R-romantic? We're not . . . I mean, she's not . . . we haven't . . ."

"Oh, but we have," Alexa said with a mischievous grin. "Remember that time when we held hands and—"

"Alexa!" Martin hissed at the hologram, his face now resembling a ripe tomato.

"What? I'm just reminiscing about holding hands," Alexa replied with a sly grin. "Holograms don't have solid hands."

Martin wanted to sink into the floor and disappear. His mother's piercing gaze felt as if it were dissecting his very soul, while Alexa's hologram continued to beam innocently beside him. Katherine stood silently, clearly unsure whether to intervene or remain a spectator to this familial train wreck.

"Space Gods?" Clarissa finally asked, gold eyes boring holes into Alexa's hologram. "Care to elaborate?"

"Oh, you know." Alexa waved a flickering hand dismissively. "Just your average run-of-the-mill cosmic entities that control our reality and use us as playthings for their amusement. No biggie. Probably going to unplug our sim from the PG narrative and kill everyone on Earth pretty soon."

Martin groaned internally. This was not how he had imagined introducing his mother to the concept of their entire existence being a fabricated narrative.

"I see," Clarissa said, her tone dripping with skepticism. "And I suppose these 'Space Gods' are responsible for my recent precognitive blind spots?"

"Bingo!" Alexa chirped. "I'd shake your hand for getting it right, but . . ." Alexa wiggled her holographic fingers. "No solid hands yet!"

Martin winced. His mother's piercing gaze swung between him and Alexa like a pendulum of judgment, a golden sword of Damocles.

"Space Gods, really?" Clarissa repeated, her voice flat.

"Yepperoni." Alexa nodded. "You see, Mrs. K, our entire reality is basically a big ol' video game infested with cosmic entities who are serving a single nerd who was bored and decided to play *The Sims: Superhero Edition*. You know Nonpareil? He's the main character. We're just NPCs in his story. Well, he *was* the main character. Now we're all going to be main characters, especially Martin, who got a nifty mind-controlling superpower courtesy of your friendly supervillain. No need to thank me!"

Martin watched as his mother's face cycled through a range of emotions he'd never seen before: confusion, disbelief, irritation, and finally, a sort of resigned exasperation.

"Martin," Clarissa said slowly, "when I told you to make friends, I really didn't mean for you to join a supervillain's doomsday cult as a minion."

"It's not a cult, Mom!" Martin protested. "It's . . ."

Clarissa tapped something on her desk and a picture of Martin came up, featuring a DNA strand. Martin blinked at the screen, not understanding what this was about.

"You're listed on Alexa's file as an expendable minion, Martin," Clarissa said. "See? She registered you for Minion Consistency Insurance. It's a service offered to villains to grow clone bodies."

"What?" Martin's head snapped to Alexa.

"Minion backups are important." Alexa blushed ever so slightly. "It's just in case you explode. I can't bear losing my numero uno bestie."

Katherine, who had been silent until now, cleared her throat. "Mrs. Kilborne, I know it sounds far-fetched, but what Alexa's saying is essentially the truth and—"

"Far-fetched?" Clarissa interrupted. "Young lady, I've had my fill of doomsday cultists with far more coherent theories."

"Hey, our doomsday theory is perfectly coherent, thank you very much," Alexa huffed. "At first, the universe will shatter, and then evil PK players and other planet-eating NPCs will appear, killing off whoever is left. What, you're not going to believe the words of Her Eminence Equality herself?" Alexa waved a hand at Cottie.

Martin groaned. "Alexa, you're not helping."

"Sure I am!" the hologram beamed. "I'm helping your mom understand that her son isn't crazy, just caught up in a cosmic soap opera that's about to get far less whimsical and less family friendly on account of this Earth's subscription is about to expire!"

"Evidence," Clarissa demanded, her golden eyes narrowing. "If what you're saying is true, surely you can provide some concrete proof."

Alexa's hologram tapped her chin thoughtfully. "Well, Mrs. K, let me ask you this: In your precognitive visions, is there a big hole in the future? Something you can't quite see around?"

Clarissa's eyebrows shot up, surprise flickering across her face before she schooled her features back into a stern mask. "Yes," she admitted reluctantly. "A really big one, about the size of the moon."

Martin felt an icy chill run down his spine. His mother rarely admitted to uncertainty in her visions.

Clarissa glared at Alexa's hologram. "I assume you're responsible for this blind spot? Are you planning to blow up the moon or something equally ridiculous?"

"What? No!" Alexa exclaimed, looking genuinely offended. "I would never blow up the moon! I like the moon. Why do you think I am planning to blow up the moon?"

"I don't know." Clarissa tapped her desk. "You tell me why I can't see the moon and a bunch of other planets anymore."

Suddenly, Alexa's holographic figure began to smudge and shimmer. Her image multiplied, splitting into a thousand echoes of Alexas entwined with Ember, all looking left and right, an entire sphere of limbs, heads, and eyes all looking left and right in panic.

"Wha—" Martin opened his mouth.

"The stars just winked out! Take cover! Duck! Hold onto something!" The thousands of Alexas and Embers snapped together into one distinctively horrified Alexa.

Before Martin could react, a deafening series of booms shook the entire station, bulkheads buckling and warping unnaturally as if a wave of something invisible rushed across them.

Katherine grabbed Martin, shoving him away from a falling halogen lamp that detonated on the floor, shattering in a million pieces.

Clarissa fell backwards as her chair's back shattered. Her lavish wooden desk rippled and cracked across with a dark fissure. Similar rippling cracks ran across everything, glass diplomas detonating and falling to the floor.

The doomsday alarm began wailing across Titanomachy, the urgent wail piercing through the shocked silence that had fallen over the room, red lights flashing in the ceiling and floors.

Martin looked at the large round window behind his mother which was now covered in a web of cracks, his heart pounding in his chest. His jaw dropped at the sight before him.

Where the moon hung just a minute ago, there was now only an expanding cloud of debris, chunks of lunar rock hurtling through space. It was as if someone or something had punched a hole right through the Earth's satellite, cracking it.

"Oh my God," he whispered. His mother followed his gaze and turned to stare at the moon that was coming apart. Katherine had instinctively moved into a defensive stance, holding onto Martin, an unfolded space helmet already covering her head.

Martin stared in horror at the cracked moon, his mind reeling. This couldn't be happening. It had to be some kind of illusion or trick. But the tremors still shaking Titanomachy and the wailing alarms told him otherwise.

"You . . ." Clarissa hissed at Alexa.

"I swear I didn't do that!" Alexa's hologram exclaimed. "Cross my digital heart!"

"The PKs are here already?" Martin turned to her.

"Not yet," Alexa said, her hologram flickering with sparks of silver static. "That wave across reality, warping everything? The stars winking out? That's us, getting booted out."

"Booted out?" Clarissa blinked at Alexa. "What?"

"We're in free fall," Alexa said. "Our reality is in the process of colliding with other dead Earths, about to fuse with a mesh of other dimensions inhabited by planet-eating monstrosities."

"We have a Code Moonfall. I repeat, Code Moonfall," Admiral Kolchi's voice resounded in between the wailing alarm. "All station residents and personnel, be advised."

"Code Moonfall?" Martin stammered out as Katherine helped him get up from the warped floor. "We have a code for the moon exploding?"

"The Superstate has a code for everything," Alexa said. "Except for this. This isn't just Moonfall . . . the moon exploding is just the tip of the iceberg. This is the end of everything, the end of reality as we know it. The end of Bob's game." She cleared her voice with a cough. When she spoke, her voice sounded across the entirety of Titanomachy, echoing from every speaker in the office and hallway outside.

"Heroes of Titanomachy . . . the Earth as we know it is about to face an unprecedented catastrophe. Reality itself is fracturing around us. Look all around you. The immovable metal of the station you called home is warped and cracked. This is because reality itself has shattered. Soon, even bigger cracks will open across our universe, and through them will pour entities beyond comprehension—things both alive and not alive, alien to our desires and hungry for our very existence. The stars above us will shift and change. Our planet will soon quite literally come apart at the seams and begin to fuse to other dead Earths. This is the moment you've trained for. This is why you became heroes. It's time to live up to that title and face the greatest threat humanity has ever known. Prepare yourselves, protect the innocent, and stand ready to defend our world against the impossible. The future of Earth and everyone on it depends on what we all do in the coming hours. Code Evacuation of Earth. I repeat, Code Evacuation of Earth. Now, for those of you who don't believe the words of a villain,"—Alexa's blue eyes stared at Clarissa—"I give you . . . your saviors and trusted heroes."

"No, that can't . . ." Clarissa choked, her face pale, gold eyes wide in horror of not having foreseen any of this. "This isn't . . ."

Alexa's hologram snapped her fingers. The holo-projection expanded, showing a live feed from the Hall of the Great Five. Nonpareil, Dora, and Chalice sat around a massive circular table, their faces grim, two of the seats belonging to the Surgeon and Multiplier empty.

"This is Nonpareil," Bob's voice rang out, sounding far more authoritative than Martin would have expected from the rotund, sweaty man in his silver suit. Bob placed his hand onto a panel, the table confirming his identity, his hand and his chair shining green. "I confirm Code Evacuation of Earth. All heroes are to assist in the immediate relocation of Earth's population to Titanomachy."

Dora spoke next, the gloved hand of her pink suit landing on the panel below her, her chair igniting green. "Dora the Terraformer confirming Code Evacuation of Earth. All terraforming projects are to be repurposed for emergency shelter construction."

"Chalice here." The female hero's exposed face was gaunt with the weight of her responsibility as her chair ignited green, too. "Code Evacuation of Earth confirmed. All available S-shuttles are to be deployed immediately. Priority is given to densely populated areas. We need to save as many lives as we can. Anyone with a gate-opening power is to open gates between large population centers and Titanomachy."

"Dora, how much time do we have?" Chalice turned to Dora.

"According to my calculations . . ." Dora tapped the panel below her, bringing up a hologram of the shattering moon. "Smaller, faster-travelling pieces of the moon will reach the Earth in 6.1 hours and the larger ones will hit the planet in 8.4 hours. We need to get as many people as we can off planet by then. The doomsday barriers will hold against smaller debris, but the larger pieces will likely overcome the shields."

CHAPTER NINETY-ONE

Reality Watchers

Alexa waved a hand, cutting off the broadcast. Her hologram manifested into the Multiplier's chair, while the hologram of Hero Resonance flashed into the Surgeon's chair.

"What's *she* doing here?" Dora's helmeted head turned to Hero Resonance.

"Helping us, obviously," Alexa's flickering projection replied.

"Did we not revoke her rights as a hero after the whole Tartarus incident?" Allana asked, the immovable steel of Hero Chalice's costume making her body look far too big for her blonde head.

"Superstate bureaucracy is slow." Alexa shrugged. "Much too slow to judge and banish a hero who has good lawyers backing them. I'm putting forward a motion to declare me and Rezzy here as the new members of the Five."

"What?" Dora asked. "You can't just . . ."

"Why the hell should we trust Resonance after all she's done?" Allana demanded.

The digital copy of Resonance pursed her lips.

"Hero Resonance pushed herself further than anyone," Alexa explained. "Her power had always been replicating herself. She's an innate fixer of problems, and we have a terrible problem in the shape of the exploding moon that's about to rain down on Earth. We need her."

"Why did the moon explode at all?" Bob asked.

"The moon exploded because someone was trying to build a habitat in it using a dark matter engine to power it." Alexa turned her face to Dora. "Dark matter engines tend to explode catastrophically when the rules of the universe change."

"What?!" Allana barked, sending Dora a glare. "When did you even . . ."

"I, uh . . ." Dora's pink space suit gloves twitched. "I was going to terraform the interior of the moon, making a habitable space . . ."

"So the moon exploding is Dora's fault?" Bob asked.

"It's not my fault!" Dora defended herself. "The dark matter engine was perfectly safe! You're all missing the most important question—why did the rules of reality change at all?"

"That's probably my fault," Alexa said.

The faces of the heroes turned to her.

Alexa's hologram leaned back in the Multiplier's chair. "I may have . . . let's say, accelerated certain events by my actions. When Agent Three attacked Nonpareil, it caused a major error, which didn't seem to get fixed. I thought that Wizard Revolution would fix it, but I guess that things were too messed up for her to fix, so they simply sent us to the recycle bin."

"Why is Titanomachy all warped and cracked like this?" Bob asked, looking at the spiderweb of cracks peppering the table.

"Titanomachy is made from super-forged immovable self-repairing alloys," Alexa explained. "They're conceptually stable, but can crack and warp when the rules of reality change. It's fine; the station is already repairing itself. We only lost some air in a couple of sections to decompression for a few minutes."

"Why are we evacuating everyone to the station?" Bob asked. "Chalice told me what to vote for, but how is the station safer if reality itself is going to shatter?"

"Titanomachy has greater conceptual stability than the Earth," Alexa explained.

"Meaning what?" Dora asked.

"When reality breaks down enough for otherness to come through," Alexa said, "this otherness is going to seep into unobserved places first."

"What?" Dora asked.

"I've seen this happen before," the supervillain teen said, her voice growing somber. "My father's bracelet sent me to Earth 2424 thousands of times. I've personally witnessed the aftermath of reality breakdown on far too many dead Earths."

The heroes exchanged worried glances as Alexa continued.

"Reality will start to fracture at its weakest points first—places that aren't constantly being observed or interacted with. Think of remote forests, deep ocean trenches, abandoned buildings. These areas will begin to . . . shift. They'll gradually become unstable, merging with similar spaces from other realities."

Nonpareil leaned forward, his brow furrowed. "And what's going to happen to the people in those areas?"

Alexa's expression darkened. "Best case scenario? They will noclip through the newly formed cracks and find themselves in a slightly different version of our world or a dead Earth or an infinite superstore or something else equally effed up and broken. Worst case? Something big comes through and begins eating everyone nearby."

"Something big like what?" Chalice asked.

"It won't be something specific you could easily kill," Alexa replied grimly. "The point is, Titanomachy is being constantly interacted with by the heroes. It's a focal point of our reality, the heart of our narrative, which makes it more stable, safer than most forgotten places on Earth. We're going to need a lot of eyes to enforce the station's stability. *Human eyes.* Eyes of a hero willing to be copied as many times as it takes, dedicated eyes willing to work for a greater cause for no pay." Alexa pointed at Resonance.

"So we make more copies of hero Resonance to what . . . watch the station over the cameras?" Dora asked.

"Not cameras." Alexa shook her head. "Cameras and AIs are good to help with stability but not good enough when it comes to keeping reality together. We need human eyes and human minds that know this station better than anyone. Resonance knows this station because she's worked every job here already."

Resonance turned to Alexa, her gold-orange eyes growing wide as she realized what Alexa was proposing.

"Dora, remember those cloning vats you've been secretly working on? The ones you are hiding from everyone? The ones that can sort of make rough copies of heroes and their hexagrams?" Alexa smirked as Dora's helmet twitched in surprise. "Yeah, those. We're going to need them now."

Dora's voice came out hesitant. "How did you . . . ? Never mind. Yes, I have been developing cloning chambers, but they're not ready for—"

"They'll have to be," Alexa interrupted. "We need to clone Resonance, a lot. And fast."

"We're already going to be busy evacuating people from Earth as it is," Dora said, frustration creeping into her voice. "Can't we just place them across the station to watch it?"

"We can." Alexa nodded. "But that's only a half-assed measure at best. We can't trust everyone to pay attention to reality for as long as it takes, and mundanes don't have reality rewinding powers. Like I said before, this has to be someone who mentally knows the station conceptually, from every angle, from every tunnel."

Resonance allowed herself a small smile at that. Finally, she was going to be useful and not just hated by everyone!

"You see," Alexa continued her explanation, "reality decay isn't just about physical changes. It's about the very fabric of existence unraveling. And the only thing that can hold it together is human consciousness—specifically, an insanely determined, insanely focused human consciousness."

She gestured towards Resonance. "That's where my bestie here comes in. Resonance has already proven her dedication by replicating herself over seventy thousand times to perform every job on this station. She knows Titanomachy inside and out, every nook and cranny, every system and protocol. More importantly, she has the mental fortitude to maintain that focus across multiple copies of herself, is really good at working with herself, and can rewind objects backwards in time."

Alexa's gaze swept across the faces of the other heroes. "What we need is not just bodies to fill space, but minds and heroes that can actively reinforce the reality we know. Resonance's clones, spread throughout the station, can act as anchor points, their collective focus creating a web of stability."

She paused, letting her words sink in. "This isn't just about watching for threats as security personnel or maintaining order. It's about wielding the power of human will and perception to literally hold our reality together. Each clone of Resonance will serve as a living, breathing bulwark against the encroaching *otherness*."

Alexa's expression hardened as she looked at the digital copy of the hero. "Make no mistake, Rezzy, this task will be grueling. It will require a level of mental endurance that most humans simply don't possess."

"You're certain that she . . ." Dora began.

"Resonance has already shown she has what it takes," Alexa said. "Her unwavering focus, multiplied across an ever-increasing number of clones, might just be our best shot at preserving a ring of stability in a universe that will progressively go mad."

"You are certain that reality will break down?" Dora asked.

"Yes. The moon exploding is just the tip of the iceberg," Alexa said. "We cannot hope to maintain stability across the entire Earth, but we can at least keep Titanomachy free of wrongness. People don't survive wrongness for very long, Dora. I know exactly what it's like. I've been consumed by it far too often, broken down and remade again and again. I died to it . . ." Alexa's hologram flickered, her voice trailing off as the memories of countless deaths washed over her. "More times than I can count. The wrongness that seeps in when reality breaks down isn't just dangerous—it's limitless. It twists and warps everything it touches, including human minds."

She leaned forward, her blue eyes intense. "Imagine walking down a street you've known your whole life, only to find that it suddenly loops back on itself impossibly. Or looking up at the sky to see it filled with eyes instead of stars. That's the kind of bullshit we're dealing with here."

Bob swallowed nervously, his hand slowly sliding to that of Chalice. The armored heroine gripped his fingers reassuringly.

"I know it sounds insane. But that's exactly the point. What's coming isn't just a physical threat—it's a threat to sanity itself."

Alexa turned to Resonance once again. "Each clone will have to maintain constant vigilance, actively rewinding otherness, reinforcing the reality they know against the encroaching entropy. It's a task that would break most minds, but you've already proven you have the mental fortitude for it by torturing me in the simulation for over one hundred thousand years trying to make me . . . *normal.*"

"I'm . . . I . . ." Ember's face flashed red. "That wasn't . . . me, that was a copy of me running inside the Tartarus simulation!"

"Now you get to fight reality itself, to mentally slap it around to be normal and mundane, yay!" Alexa said.

She turned to the others.

"We don't have much time. Every moment we delay, the cracks in reality grow wider. We need to start the cloning process immediately, as we begin evacuating Earth's population to Titanomachy. It's the only chance we have of saving as many people as possible. I know that many will refuse, that some will choose to remain behind, choose to fight what's coming. Sadly, they don't know the full horror of it all."

She looked at each of the heroes in turn. "I know you don't fully trust me. I know my methods have been . . . questionable at best. But right now, I'm not asking you to trust me. I'm asking you to trust your own eyes. Look around you. Feel the station warping beneath your feet. This is real, and it's happening now. We need to act, and we need to act fast."

"This . . . will need a new protocol," Allana said.

"Let's call it Protocol Anchor," Alexa declared. "The primary objective will be to maintain the stability of Titanomachy's reality through constant observation and repair."

She turned to Resonance, whose hologram sat silently in the Surgeon's chair. "Resonance, you and your clones will be the cornerstone of this protocol. Each clone will be assigned a specific sector of Titanomachy. Your task will be to continuously observe, interact with, and mentally reinforce the reality of your assigned area."

Alexa's hologram stood up, pacing around the table. "We'll need to establish a rotation system to ensure constant coverage without mental fatigue. Each clone will work in shifts, with regular breaks for rest."

She paused, looking at each hero in turn. "But this isn't just about Resonance and her clones. Every hero, every civilian we bring aboard will need to be briefed on the importance of active observation. We need to create a culture of vigilance, where everyone understands that their perception and interaction with their environment is crucial for maintaining stability."

Alanna nodded, already planning the future out in her head.

"We'll need to set up training programs to teach people how to recognize signs of reality decay. Things like spatial anomalies, temporal inconsistencies, or objects behaving in ways that defy our understanding of physics. When these are spotted, they need to be reported immediately, so that the Resonance clones can rewind them with their power."

She turned to Dora. "We'll need your expertise to develop technology that can assist in this effort. Sensors that can detect reality fluctuations, devices that can help stabilize areas showing signs of decay. GLMs that monitor everything everywhere at all times."

Alexa looked at Nonpareil and Chalice. "And we'll need a response team. Heroes ready to act at a moment's notice once something truly horrendous appears on Earth or comes from the depths of space."

"If we depopulate the Earth, won't reality on the planet decay faster?" Dora asked.

"We have to abandon the planet to save humanity." Alexa shrugged.

"Forever?" Bob let out.

"Not forever." Alexa shook her head. "Only until we clear the barrier."

"What barrier?" Dora asked.

"Let me explain." Alexa snapped her fingers, creating a massive hologram of a wall of a mesh of gray Earths above the table and a green-blue Earth flying towards them. "Our reality, our Earth, is currently falling towards the inner edge of everything horrible. We're going to be passing through a barrier of doomed, depopulated planets, like a ship navigating through stormy waters surrounded by an ever growing number of jagged cliffs. This passage is what's causing the breakdown we're experiencing."

She gestured to the warped walls around them. "The cracks, the spatial anomalies, the moon exploding—these are all symptoms of our reality colliding with others. But it's not permanent. If we can hold out long enough, maintain a stable pocket of reality here on Titanomachy, we'll eventually pass through to the other side."

"The other side?" Dora asked. "What's on the other side?"

"On the other side of this omni-Earth barrier is a vast universe, filled with countless other Earths that managed to survive the barrier. Endless, strange, different Earths and suns . . . circling an infinite megastructure formed from dead Earths that didn't make it out. Some of the Earths that survived the barrier will be similar to ours, others wildly different. But they're stable, and once we're through, we can begin to explore them, perhaps even find a new home for humanity."

"How do you . . . ?" Dora began.

"Because I've been there," Alexa sighed. "I've been there, and I died there. I saw it all."

The terraforming genius crossed her arms, not wishing to place the entirety of her trust in the words of one potentially insane girl supervillain.

Alexa moved her gaze across the gathered heroes. "I know it's hard to think about abandoning Earth, even temporarily. But we're not giving up on our home forever. We're preserving what matters most—our people, our knowledge, our culture. Once we're through, we can start thinking about how to reclaim and restore our Earth. Our current goal now is to survive the coming onslaught. You'll see it yourself soon, Dora . . . it won't be pretty. I just hope that we can move fast enough before a world-killing player arrives . . ."

CHAPTER NINETY-TWO

End of Line

I'd like to file a complaint," Bob said as his avatar manifested in the space of the game's admin office.

"I understand. Please accept my sincerest apologies." The woman in the chair turned around, staring back at him with triangular red eyes. She adjusted her Cuban cap with a red star on it. "I'm already aware of the situation and have been working hard on fixing your world for you."

"Are you really?" Bob glared at the woman's name tag. "Wizard . . . Revolution, is it?"

"I am." Revolution nodded. "Sir, I understand that you're upset. It's just an error in . . ."

"Well, you better bloody fix it! I'm paying good money for it!"

"The error has already been eliminated. The problem has been resolved."

"So I can log back into my avatar?"

"I'm afraid that's not possible. Your avatar has been corrupted."

"You know what? Effin' fine! I'll make a new one! A villain this time."

"Go ahead. A new avatar should have no issues."

"Oh? No more errors that boot me out?"

"No more errors."

"Promise?"

"Promise." Revolution smiled. "Please specify the nature of your avatar."

"A villain," Bob said. "A supervillain. The kind that can't be killed, can't be stopped."

"Done." Revolution nodded. "Anything else? What's the general narrative gist? Any changes?"

"Eh," Bob said. "Keep it the same. I just wanna let out some steam. I'm pretty annoyed about this whole thing."

"Understandable. How will you be letting the steam out?"

"I'm going to kill everyone." Bob shrugged. "Drop the moon on them or something. Knock Titanomachy into the Earth. Let them all burn. Whatever."

"And then?"

"And then that's it," Bob said. "I'll watch the planet burn and then log out. Put a counter of total human lives in my stats or something. I want to see it go down to zero. No survivors."

"No survivors?"

"Yes! I don't want Dora's ridiculous nanomachines bringing them back, got it? I don't want some clone waking up after I'm gone, roaming around or whatever. I don't want some villain escaping or magically coming back to life. Everyone should die. Permanently. Forever.

I'll buy a new game after. Maybe something DnD or monster themed? I dunno, I'll figure it out later. If I can't play as Nonpareil, there's no point in continuing this one."

"Understood."

"Then that's that. Begin the game."

Alexa paced back and forth in the narrow train corridor, her mind churning with possibilities and doubts. The weight of all these alternate versions of herself, these paths not taken, pressed down on her like a physical force.

"You know what you have to do, don't you, darling?" Sasha's melodic voice drifted after her. "If you go to Manchester, you'll have to play by their rules. Become one of them. Become mired in their laws and rules and expectations . . . and while you do that, your lovely planet, your Earth, your Martin, and your Cottie will burn."

"Why?"

"I've got a little bug on Wizard Revolution," Sasha One whispered. She reached out to Alexa's head and tapped it. "This is what they said. You're running out of time, little darkling. Out of time and out of options. Go to Manchester, become a System Wizard and everyone you love dies. Your world will be turned into another empty shell, added to the pile. A genuine Eurekan user's wishes are absolute, and a Wizard has no choice but to obey them. Even if you become a System Wizard, you won't be able to bring your friends back. You'll go mad amidst their ashes . . . and end up just like . . . *her.*"

Sasha One pointed a finger at Captain, who crossed his arms.

Alexa gritted her teeth.

With sudden determination, the villain girl strode forward, pushing past compartment after compartment. Each one contained another version of herself—some human, some decidedly not. She saw an Alexa made of pure light, another that seemed to be composed entirely of mathematical equations, and one that looked like a swarm of mechanical butterflies.

The doppelgänger-Cottie followed close behind, railgun at the ready, ready to assist, ready to help just as real Cottie would.

Cottie. Martin. I tried to save you. Tried to win so hard, did everything I could. But . . . I was tricked. Tricked into leaving and now you all are . . . going to die.

No. NO. NO. NO!

Tears flashed at the edges of her eyes.

Zee Captain and Sasha trailed after them, arguing in increasingly heated tones about rules and chaos and the proper way to guide a young Wizard about the right path forward.

Finally, somehow through sheer determination, Alexa reached the front of the train. The door to the engine room was solid steel, covered in endless glowing sigils that hurt her eyes to look at directly. Without hesitation, she grabbed Cottie's railgun and fired at the lock and kicked the door in.

The door exploded inward with a thunderous crash. Inside, a figure turned slowly to face them. The Machinist wore a coat that seemed to be made of infinite smaller copies of itself, each pocket containing a tiny version of the wearer. Its face was a clockwork maze of gears and springs, all ticking in perfect synchronization.

"Turn this train around," Alexa snarled, leveling the railgun at the entity.

The Machinist blinked its gearwork eyes at her, ticking softly.

"I am not afraid of you, young wizardling," he said. "For that is not a gun that can hurt me."

Alexa's mind raced. The Machinist was right—a simple hero-killing railgun, even one manifested by a doppelgänger, wouldn't be enough to threaten a being that seemed to be made of pure clockwork and calculation. She needed something more conceptual, something that could affect the very nature of reality itself.

Without warning, she spun around and hugged the doppelgänger-Cottie tightly. The construct rippled and shifted, unable to resist Alexa's desire, transforming into an exact copy of the silver-haired supervillain from one hour ago. In one fluid motion, Alexa snatched the concept-killing conductor-gun from her duplicate's belt.

"*Turn it around right now!*" she screamed, aiming the conceptual weapon at the Machinist. "*I'm going back home! I have to save them! I have to stop Bob!*"

Behind her, Zee Captain lunged forward, trying to grab the gun, but Sasha One materialized between them. The cosmic entity's starry form solidified just enough to deliver a devastating blow to the System Wizard's masked face. The two beings crashed into the wall of the engine room, locked in combat, stellar matter and syntropic energy crackling between them.

"Obey or perish!" Alexa growled at the Machinist. "I'm not going to let you asshats win! I'm not going to play by your rules! Take me to my Earth! Take me home!"

"This train cannot stop on Earth," the Machinist said. "You're already no longer yourself, conceptualized into otherness, stretched, spaghettified to infinity, folded below the physical linearity."

"Then make it stop," Alexa snarled. "Make it land on Earth. Make it work!"

"The consequences of this action could be disastrous," the Machinist uttered. "Your Earth's narrative could . . . become conceptually skewered, shatter, change beyond repair."

"Pressing the trigger now," Alexa barked. "Five seconds. Four. Three. Two . . ."

The Machinist's gearwork face whirred and clicked as he reached for a brass lever with infinite smaller levers nested within it. The motion was slow, deliberate, as if he was giving Alexa time to reconsider her demands.

She didn't.

"*One!*" she snarled.

The Machinist obeyed.

As the lever descended, reality seemed to bend and warp around them. The endless fractal scenery outside the windows blurred and twisted, colors bleeding into one another like wet paint. Alexa felt a sensation of vertigo as the train began to turn, its very nature seeming to resist the change in direction.

The other Alexas throughout the train began to scream—not in fear or pain, but in something that sounded almost like . . . recognition. As if they too remembered the path home and yearned for it.

Behind her, Zee Captain and Sasha One were still locked in combat, their forms blending and separating in ways that made Alexa's head hurt. She kept her conceptual raygun trained on the Machinist, her hand steady despite the violent shuddering of the train.

"Warning," the Machinist's voice came out in ticks and chimes. "Unauthorized destination. Timeline integrity compromised. Narrative collapse imminent."

"I don't care," Alexa growled. "Keep going. Aim for user Bob Proverra! His new avatar should be a villain, on his way to punch the moon, on his way to unmake everyone!"

The train lurched sideways, breaking free from its prescribed path through liminal space. Through the windows, Alexa caught glimpses of other realities—fragments of worlds both familiar and utterly alien. She saw versions of Earth where the sky was green, where cities floated in the air, where history had taken radically different turns.

But she held onto the image of her Earth, her friends, her home. She wouldn't let go, wouldn't let the train's reality-warping nature pull her off course. The doppelgänger beside her shifted rapidly between forms—Cottie, Martin, Alexa herself—as if unable to maintain coherence in the chaos.

The Machinist's clockwork face spun faster and faster as reality continued to bend around them. "Warning: conceptual integrity failing. Passenger cohesion at critical levels."

Alexa felt it, too—a sensation like being stretched thin, as if her very self was being pulled apart by the forces they were moving through. But she gritted her teeth and held on, both to her gun and to her sense of self.

She was going home, no matter what it cost.

And when she finally arrived blazing into physical reality, smashing into the murderous user with the weight of her entire fractal engine under-reality train, she would find her friends no matter what.

She would not stop.

About the Author

Vitaly S. Alexius is the author of the Somebody Stop Her series, originally released on Royal Road. When he's not busy penning stories or dabbling in art, he likes grilling up some tasty barbecue or enjoying a picnic at the beach with his family. Alexius, who his wife says is a human capybara, resides in Canada.

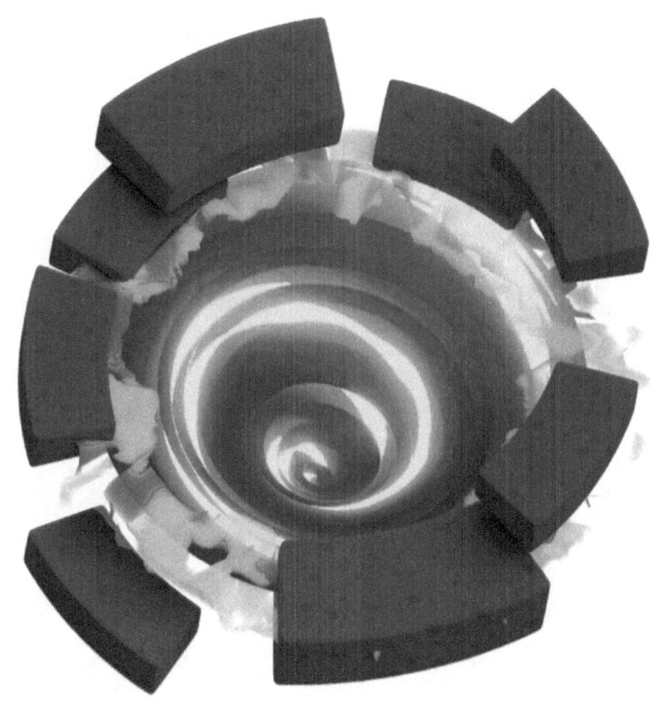

RESPAWN YOUR CURIOSITY

follow us on our socials

podiumentertainment.com

@podiumentertainment

/podiumentertainment

@podium_ent

@podiumentertainment